THE DEATH AND LIFE OF
ZEBULON FINCH

VOLUME TWO

EMPIRE DECAYED

Also by Daniel Kraus

The Death and Life of Zebulon Finch,
Volume One: At the Edge of Empire

The Monster Variations

Rotters

Scowler

Trollhunters (with Guillermo del Toro)

THE DEATH AND LIFE OF

ZEBULON FINCH

VOLUME TWO

EMPIRE DECAYED

AS PREPARED BY THE ESTEEMED FICTIONIST,

MR. DANIEL KRAUS

WITHDRAWN

SIMON & SCHUSTER BFYR

New York | London | Toronto | Sydney | New Delhi

SIMON & SCHUSTER BFYR

An imprint of Simon & Schuster Children's Publishing Division
1230 Avenue of the Americas, New York, New York 10020

For information about special discounts for bulk purchases, please contact Simon & Schuster Special Sales at 1-866-506-1949 or business@simonandschuster.com.
The Simon & Schuster Speakers Bureau can bring authors to your live event. For more information or to book an event, contact the Simon & Schuster Speakers Bureau at 1-866-248-3049 or visit our website at www.simonspeakers.com.
Jacket design by Lizzy Bromley
Interior design by Hilary Zarycky
The text for this book was set in Adobe Jenson Pro.
Manufactured in the United States of America
First Edition
2 4 6 8 10 9 7 5 3 1
Library of Congress Cataloging-in-Publication Data
Names: Kraus, Daniel, author.
Title: The death and life of Zebulon Finch. Volume two, Empire decayed /
as prepared by the esteemed fictionist, Mr. Daniel Kraus.
Other titles: Empire decayed
Description: First edition. | New York : Simon & Schuster BFYR, [2016] |
Summary: "The conclusion to Daniel Kraus's saga about a murdered teen who is resurrected to walk the earth for decades to come"—Provided by publisher.
Identifiers: LCCN 2016020171| ISBN 9781481411424 (hardback) |
ISBN 9781481411448 (eBook)
Subjects: | CYAC: Murder—Fiction. | Dead—Fiction. | BISAC: JUVENILE FICTION /
Historical / United States / General. | JUVENILE FICTION / Mysteries & Detective Stories.
Classification: LCC PZ7.K8672 Df 2016 | DDC [Fic]—dc23
LC record available at https://lccn.loc.gov/2016020171

TO
G.W.R.
(AS BEFORE)

THE DEATH AND LIFE OF
ZEBULON FINCH

VOLUME TWO
EMPIRE DECAYED

APOLOGIA

POOR ZEBULON FINCH! ✦ A man named Héctor cements him into a hidden space beneath one of the World Trade Center skyscrapers, where Zebulon begins to write his confession. ✦ Born in 1879 to the well-heeled dynamitier Bartholomew Finch and the dour Abigail Finch, but raised by stifling tutors, he runs away at age fourteen. ✦ Eager for adventure, he joins Chicago's Black Hand gang and falls in love with Wilma Sue, a prostitute at Patterson's Inn. ✦ He mistreats her, she vanishes, and he steals an Excelsior pocket watch—Wilma Sue's heart, he comes to think. ✦ Heartbroken, he dedicates himself to extortion, terrorizing those he calls the "Triangulinos," proud Italian immigrants with triangle tattoos. ✦ On May 7, 1896, he is assassinated by the Black Hand's Luca Testa (or so he believes!), who'd warned him, *You gotta have fear in your heart.*

Zebulon's mysteriously resurrected body is dredged from Lake Michigan and sold to Dr. Whistler's Pageant of Health, helmed by the Barker. ✦ Renamed the Astonishing Mr. Stick, Zebulon is used as a human pincushion to sell miracle tonic. ✦ He befriends Little Johnny Grandpa, a prematurely aged boy. ✦ Johnny helps Zebulon relearn how to speak, first with a futile trinket called the Little Miracle Electric Mexican Stuttering Ring, and second with the word "indefatigable." ✦ While defending Johnny from the Barker, Zebulon discovers *la silenziosità*, an ability to force others to glimpse their future

1

demise, but that also forces Zebulon to endure the Uterus of Time, a tantalizing look at a death he cannot have. ✦ Medicine-show skeptics jail Zebulon in Xenion, Georgia, where he uses *la silenziosità* to help the unhinged General Hazard. ✦ Released, Zebulon is visited by the wealthy Dr. Cornelius Leather, who pleads for Zebulon to decamp to Boston for medical study. ✦ Instead, Luca Testa hunts down Zebulon and delivers unnerving news: He wasn't Zebulon's killer! ✦ The Barker, tired of Mr. Stick, contrives a lucrative way to do away with Zebulon—a duel. ✦ In the chaos, however, Johnny is killed, the Barker is maimed, and Zebulon absconds to Boston.

Dr. Leather houses Zebulon and uses a Revelation Almanac to track "meat etiquette"—experiments intended to unveil Zebulon's mystical secrets. ✦ He shows Zebulon the People Garden, where he studies corpses in assorted states of decay. ✦ Zebulon finds comfort with Leather's kindly wife, Mary, who is dedicated to her daughter, Gladys. ✦ A scolding teenager named Merle arrives with shocking news: She is the daughter of Zebulon and the deceased Wilma Sue! ✦Leather's obsession grows and drives the family, now including Merle, toward financial ruin. ✦ Leather begins wearing an oxygen-delivery helmet called the Isolator, which emits a haunting rasp: *Hweeeeee . . . fweeeeee. . . .* ✦ A dinner with the influential Dr. Cockshut is a fiasco. Leather, desperate to prove himself, cuts open Zebulon's stomach at the table. ✦ Merle persuades Zebulon to flee under cover of night; there is no time to fetch the Little Miracle Electric Mexican Stuttering Ring. ✦ Mary and Gladys are left to uncertain fates.

Zebulon and Merle take refuge in Salem, Massachusetts, until the ireful Merle flees. ✦ Unmoored, Zebulon seeks out General Hazard, who has died, but his daughters, the Hazard sisters, welcome Zebulon to Sweetgum Plantation. ✦ WWI begins, and Zebulon chooses battlefield annihilation; he uses the sisters' connections to enlist in the Marine Corps. ✦ In France, he befriends Burt "Church" Churchwell, meets would-be poet Jason Stavros, and learns to accept the shell-shocked J.T. "Piano" O'Hannigan. ✦ Church's Theory of 17 hypothesizes that Zebulon must rescue as many people as he has killed. ✦ Zebulon, though, is forced to renounce the theory to save the life of Church, who is badly disfigured but survives.

Post-war Prohibition finds Zebulon running hooch in a Tin Lizzie auto for bootleggers John Quincy and Mother Mash—until the KKK hangs both of them. ✦ Zebulon nonetheless delivers their last shipment to New York City, where he moves into a squalid apartment with the jobless Church, who now wears a prosthetic cheek. ✦ A man known as the Bird Hunter begins murdering flappers, and Detective Roseborough suspects Zebulon. ✦ Zebulon pursues the Bird Hunter, only to discover that he is Dr. Leather. ✦ Just as Leather is about to divulge the secret behind Zebulon's extended death, Roseborough arrives and kills Leather.

The notoriety of the Bird Hunter case leads to a Metrotone newsreel produced about Zebulon. ✦ Enticed by fame, Zebulon abandons Church for Hollywood, where he catches the fancy of movie star Bridey Valentine; they become lovers. ✦ Bridey's passion is to produce an epic script she's written called *In Our Image*. ✦ After Bridey begins having cosmetic surgery, Zebulon, too, seeks out physical repairs, from director (and avid taxidermist) Maximilian Chernoff. ✦ The treatments fail. ✦ Seeking peace, Zebulon brings Church to Hollywood, only to watch Bridey try to seduce him. ✦ Zebulon tosses Church into a cab and finally has sex with Bridey, which robs him of his procreative organ.

Out of the blue, Merle calls Zebulon. She is nearby, held for ransom by the morphine dealer Sandy. • Zebulon kills Sandy and rescues Merle, though she rejects him for the Barker, who has reinvented himself as a burlesque promoter. • Despite being pursued by police, Zebulon escorts Bridey's melancholy daughter, Margeaux, to a school dance. • Margeaux's humiliation results, and Margeaux steers her mother's Yankee Doodle roadster into the ocean. • Margeaux drowns; Zebulon cannot. • A young man drags Zebulon to the beach and tells him that Pearl Harbor has been bombed. • Will he enlist? • Zebulon thinks another war might be just the ticket. •How much longer, after all, can his Excelsior-watch heart keep ticking?

PART SEVEN

1941–1945

—⊷◉⊷—

*In Which Your Hero Is Indoctrinated Into Matters
Of Blood And Soil And His Breadcrumbs Are Lost
In The Blackest Forest.*

I.

ADOLF HITLER WAS A HANDSOME devil. It is a fact obscured by a half century of reckless caricature: his tenacious ball-peen chin lathed into a pusillanimous nub, his modest nose protracted to a frankfurter proboscis, his imperial cranium inflated with hot air. Distortions like these muddle objective autopsies. Hitler—take my word for it—was not lumpish. The brash asymmetry of his jaw suggested a brawler's grit. His eyes were the passionate azure of a revolutionary. His ears were elfin, the one tell of his artist's disposition. Had der Führer's passions been channeled into pursuits more, shall we say, romantic, his scowl would have been one destined for T-shirts.

My Dearest, Dutiful, Patient Reader might be reading this one hundred, one thousand, one million years into the future, yet still I feel you cringe at the possibility that your Zebby has gone anti-Semite. Oh, darling worrier! You paint my disdain with too meager a brush. You should know by now that I am anti-*Human*, certain to my corroded core that our species, Jew to Gentile, true-blue to hateful, and black to tan, deserves extinction. I, our worst specimen, would volunteer to go first, if only Gød, that waggish hangman, would let me hang.

Let me try to resist aggrandizement. I admit to being oblivious to Hitler's magnetism when a mousy member of a clandestine arm of the U.S. Government removed the dictator's photo from a dossier marked *J-1121* and asked me if I could identify him.

If you have tracked my insipid saga this many pages, Reader, you will be unruffled to learn that by January 1942, I found myself in the cold custody of Uncle Sam. After having flopped from the ocean grave of sweet, bitter—bittersweet—Margeaux, I'd taken the gee-whiz counsel of the young buck who'd rescued me and, after slapping down sand-crusted dollars for a set of clean clothes, had slunk, paranoid and fearful, to the Army recruiting center in Malibu. Not two days had passed since I'd killed a drug dealer named Sandy (plus an inexact number of his goons) while rescuing my morphine-addled daughter, Merle; the quicker I could be shipped off to foreign shores, the better.

But the lax white flesh that usually provoked the living to ignore me drew scrutiny when I queued among healthy young men with dazzling Southern California tans. I avoided their glares by studying the cheery banners (SMACK THE JAPS! GIVE THE HUNS HELL!) until I was called to sit opposite a recruiter. Rotten luck. His suspicion stunk like sewage. Sadness and regret over Margeaux's death rendered me a careless stammerer, and, without thinking, I supplied my real name. He promptly excused himself and whistled for assistance, and before I could skedaddle, a posse of MPs had pinched me, and off to the local jail I was lugged.

They were not my first cell doors, and yet they made me afraid, both of a long (centuries long?) incarceration and of the guinea-pig procedures to which I might be subject by hot-to-trot medicos. Concurrently, I knew that embracing fright was the only option. *You gotta have fear in your heart* had been Luca Testa's reverberant reminder that fear—for myself, yes, but more powerfully for select others— was the single taut rope to humanity from which I dangled.

In that holding cell I feared, and fiercely, my friend, fiercely!

Shock, however, became the emotion du jour when I was brought before interrogators, government clowns in tailored suits, and saw that they had a file on me, and goodness, was it a brick. With horror I watched them pass around such artifacts as a blurry group photo of my beloved Seventh Marine Regiment in a French trench and magazine pages detailing my parasitic fastening to the arm of Bridey Valentine—grotesque grandstanding I ought never have done. Each flash of image was a pounded nail.

"Please," was all I could say. Say? No, beg. "Please put it away."

Their questions, however, were more cagey than accusatory. Who else knew the truth about me? Why had I been enlisting? What were my political affiliations? Easy queries to satisfy, but for once I kept my cold lips sewed shut. As reward, I was stripped, photographed from every angle (including ones emphasizing my peckerless groin), showered, deloused, decked in prison stripes, and robbed of my every possession, right down to the Excelsior pocket watch, surrogate heart of my dearest departed Wilma Sue: *tick, tick, tick.*

"It is no weapon," beseeched I. "Let me keep it? Show me mercy?"

The Excelsior was dropped inside an envelope that was licked, sealed, and bagged.

My carcass, bereft enough to feel filleted, was tossed into the empty stomach of a paddy wagon. I let the hum of pavement lull me into a stupor. Hours became days; hundreds of miles we drove, if not thousands. The vehicle's stale asceticism drew contrast with the fireworks spectacle of war, the neon jitterbug of Harlem, the floodlit marquees of Hollywood, and afforded me time to bid farewell to what had been, on balance, a colorful death. I guessed that where I was headed would be more achromatic. It was red lights and stop signs and gas-station breaks I cursed, for at every pause I swore I heard the clack of women's heels—Wilma Sue, Merle, Bridey, or Margeaux?— approaching to demand recompense for how I'd maligned them.

Years later, it seemed, the paddy wagon parked and the back doors opened. I was cold and numb and befuddled. The whimsical green fronds of palm trees had been replaced by alien veils of brilliant white snow, and the distant obelisk of the Washington Monument was a rocket ship built to fire my troublesome corpse to Mars.

That just might work, thought I.

My closed-mouthed captors marched me through a nondescript doorway, between saluting soldiers, past bolt-locked checkpoints, down sentried stairwells, and into a long, low-ceilinged basement of cafeteria tables and benches, a room concrete gray and cigarette-smoke brown, yet pulsing violet from overhead tubes soon to be marketed as "fluorescents." The only daubs of color were orange ceiling stains from plumbing leakage.

It was a vault built to survive a bombing, and, at the same time, it sucked away all will to live. I was told to sit. I sat. My escorts exited. I looked at the other tables, where a dozen men dressed in identical outfits of loosened black tie and rolled white shirtsleeves wolfed cigarettes and grimaced into paper cups of coffee. Fluorescents made their skin yellow; nicotine made their teeth yellow; they gestured with yellow pencils at yellow file folders containing yellow paper. All the while, perspiring men in civilian clothing sat opposite, gobbling their fingernails and nickering in fright.

Presently I received my own shirt-sleeved chaperon of wearying mediocrity—late thirties, muscle-less, balding, wire eyeglasses, black tie, sweat-stained collar. So interchangeable was he with his associates that the bloom of red ink inside his breast pocket seemed

10

a dazzling rose boutonnière. He padded his tedious way across the tedious room, sat, and slid aside the tedious ashtray to make room for his tedious briefcase. He dialed the combination locks, withdrew the bulging J-1121 dossier, showed me the aforementioned photo of Hitler, and then, satisfied that I was not a vegetable, introduced himself.

His name was Allen Rigby, and he undertook my case with all the emotion of someone taking out the trash. Like everyone else in the 1940s, Rigby smoked, but he did so as if the fate of the free world depended on it. The functionary lit a second cig off the first's smolder, and gestured with it at the room. He spoke as if a puppeteer's hand were operating from up his ass, giving so little inflection to his words that I had to demand that he repeat them.

"You're at OSS," said he.

"Oh-what-what?"

"Office of Strategic Services. An intelligence agency."

I was jumpy and at a disadvantage. My defense, as ever, was rudeness.

"Intelligence, eh? Someone should inform those goons in L.A. who manhandled me."

Nicotine had withered the lobes of Rigby's brain designed to detect sarcasm.

"They had to make sure you weren't a double-agent SS operative."

"An *excess operative*? What is that, a triple agent? A quadruple agent?"

"SS." He exhaled smoke. "You do know what the SS is?"

On top of all other indignities, I had to feel stupid? I shrugged my disinterest.

He regarded me, blank as a sheet, then took up a clipboard.

11

"Define these terms: 'Deutschland.'"

"'Deutschland.'" I rubbed my chin. "Deutschland, Deutschland. By Jove, I know! It was where Dorothy Gale met her Wizard."

Rigby made a check mark. How about that? I'd aced it!

"'Aryan,'" said he.

"'Aryan.' . . . That, I believe, is a species of bird. No—a brand of tobacco. No, no—definitely a bird."

Another check mark. Why, I was faring splendidly!

"'Rudolf Hess,'" said he.

"The full name of Santa's red-nosed reindeer. This is enjoyable, Rigby. Ask me another!"

To the contrary, Rigby set the clipboard several feet away, as if it were infected. Had my answers been insufficient? I could, at least, depend on the man's comatose civility: He lit a third, perhaps fourth, cigarette and began to lecture with such remedial slowness that I identified the weight on my head as a dunce cap.

"The men who arraigned you in California were X-2, OSS counter-intelligence. Their counterpart here in Washington is SI, Secret Intelligence. There's also R&A, Research and Analysis; they've got a man who can estimate bomb damage to European railways by tracking the price of oranges in Paris. MO is Morale Ops, anti-propaganda. Recently they air-dropped German songbooks over Nazi soldiers and hid in the lyrics advice for deserting. Finally there's SO, where I work—Secret Ops. That one we can't talk about so freely."

Now our disquisition was skipping off into worrisome woods. Some sort of plot was afoot, and my death, as you know, was already overplotted. Deportation and destruction, that was all I wanted as punishment for my evil deeds! Rigby paused to ash his cig, and I slapped my thighs (the right thigh, blown apart in 1918 but taxidermied in 1939, made a *thunk*) and stood into the violet vapor.

"'Tis a pity we must part, for as a conversationalist, sir, you scintillate. But as it is clear that my aptitudes and proclivities do not align to government standards, I shall monopolize no more of your time. Before I take leave, your colleagues cadged from me a golden pocket watch of sentimental value. Might you know where I can collect it?"

From the briefcase Rigby removed a stapled packet, and, in his deadpan, he read, "Alexander Griffith. Aka 'Sandy.' Forty-four. Dead on the scene, December 6, Los Angeles County, California. Cause of death, gunshot to the chest. Firearm recovered reported to be Griffith's own. Multiple witnesses identify the gunman as a suspect approximately seventeen years of age calling himself 'Zebulon Finch.'"

Rigby indicated the packet.

"There are more pages," said he.

I dropped back onto the bench.

"Say what you want," growled I. "Your X-2 chums took plenty of photographs. My corpse is a bag and the cat is out of it. Why do you hold me here?"

"OSS doesn't hold anyone. The choice is yours."

"Choice? I think the word you mean is 'blackmail.' Tell me what it is you want."

Rigby squared the paper edges. He was a crackerjack edge-squarer.

"I am not at liberty to say."

"So I am to wait, is that it? In this dungeon?"

Rigby's face was a blank chalkboard across which I wished to squeal my fingernails. I gnashed my teeth and, to my surprise, a single comma of sympathy contracted upon Rigby's forehead. He lowered his already low voice.

"My superiors will notify me when I can speak frankly. But might I suggest that you see this as an opportunity? Not everyone is so specifically called upon to serve his country."

The apocryphal compliment portended far more than the destruction I sought. I shuddered and searched for an escape route as I was led to a concrete-block bedchamber identified by a card reading J-1121. The compartment was doorless, but what good did that do me? My fellow cellar dwellers had their own open doors, their own case numbers, their own blackmails.

After I spent a productive afternoon flushing the toilet for kicks and a rewarding night counting the cracks in the wall, Rigby returned to room J-1121—new white shirt, same red-ink splotch—and waded us back into the fluorescents.

My toilet-flushing and crack-counting had induced reflection. I'd come to realize that every OSS agent who entered the compound deliberately removed himself of identifying traits: clothing choices that divulged any personality, accents that indicated regional affiliations, car keys that disclosed propensities toward style or speed, and so on. To know one of these men was to be able to manipulate him, and before my butt hit the bench, I'd eagle-eyed Rigby's telling detail.

His left ring finger had a tan line from a removed ring.

Reviving fighting spirits is difficult when you can still feel the sand of a Californian beach in your deepest wounds. Yet my only hope was to get this man talking, root out his weaknesses, and connive a way out of the government spotlight.

"I worry we embarked upon a false foot," said I. "Do go on about yourself. Your wife, for instance. Does she enjoy the perks that surely come with government work?"

Though it could have been the fluorescents, I believe Rigby's eyes flashed with alarm. He busied himself with hefting a file that dwarfed the dossier. It was a good thousand-pages thick, and he winced around his breakfast cigarette as he dropped it upon the table. The bang drew pre-coffee snarls from area sad sacks, but instead of recoiling, I grinned, the portrait of conviviality.

"It is unsporting that you possess these reams of information about me and yet I know nothing about you. If we are to work together, let us take this morn to break bread as brothers. You must have children. What are the names of the adorable little crumbsnatchers?"

My impolitic tongue could not sell such saccharine sap. Rigby sank back into default drabness and nodded at the column of paper.

"You have to read this."

I eyeballed the impossible tome.

"I did not think you capable of wisecrackery, old sport."

"You'll find it divided into daily allotments."

"Homework, is it? Cover yourself—my heart might burst with joy."

"My superiors wish you to establish a knowledge base before proceeding."

"Proceeding with what?"

"I'm not at liberty to—"

"Yes, of course. Here in the land of liberty, there is precious little of it to share."

Rigby, of course, did not react. How I loathed this bland bureaucrat! I pulled back the cardstock cover and found dozens of brown envelopes, each stamped with what appeared to be a due date. I untwirled the string latch of the first day's assignment, extracted a medley of documents, and absorbed the title page as one might a left hook:

NATIONALSOZIALISTISCHE DEUTSCHE ARBEITERPARTEI:
A Conspectus

My instinct for scholarship hadn't changed. I crumpled the page in a fist and zinged it at Rigby. It bopped off his temple.

"You and your so-called superiors are a pack of driveling dogs if you think I shall waste good hours attempting to penetrate phrases of such poison construction! Nay, they do not even qualify as words! They are a typewriter's vomitus, a dictionary's entrails!"

Rigby picked the balled paper from the floor and with maddening lack of temper smoothed it flat upon the table before placing it back before me. His orders, it seemed to me, were to unwad what I wadded, tape anything I shredded, replace with mimeographed copies anything I irreparably rent. Subtle sieges, Reader, are the most insidious sort.

"'The German language is agglutinative," said he. "That means the words are long but exceedingly logical. Consult the included guides. Everything is navigable."

He folded his hands to show that he was ready to receive my next tantrum. The act robbed me of catharsis; I cheeked my cud of cussing. After a minute, he nodded, stood, remarked that he'd return on the morrow, and left me to my cellarworld of furtive murmurers. I writhed in my seat and pretended that it was because of the paper meal I was being force-fed. The truth was more compromising: I *did* want to know about Rigby beyond how it might help my escape. Terse ten-minute briefings were insufficient in sating a social need I still hadn't bled from my nature.

Bored to capitulation, I learned that evening that "*Nationalso-*

zialistische Deutsche Arbeiterpartei" was too much for anyone to handle; the world had truncated it to "Nazis." I'd heard of them: snappy dressers, proficient marchers, makers of mischief. The implication that I was being groomed for a role at OSS, however, confused me. Perhaps they believed that my extended death had won me some depth of wisdom? Had they not noticed that I was still seventeen?

Regardless, I trudged into the narrative, which traced the founding, floundering, and flowering of the Nazi Party. The tome was interminable, yes, but I bulled through twenty pages of it before reappropriating the latter ten toward the nobler purpose of nifty paper airplanes.

Rigby sucked down three cups of coffee and three cigarettes during the next morning's quiz. I failed—and how, but then showed off my fleet of folded aircraft. He did not seem impressed.

"This won't please my superiors," remarked he.

"Agreed. They will observe that my planes need coloring, and they will be right."

Rigby unfolded each aircraft, which pissed me off, and filed each one into his folder as official documentation of my immaturity. Once finished, he pushed his blankness against me like suffocative pillows.

"What will it take to get you to focus?"

"You have a wife," cried I, "though you refuse to tell me her name. You have children, though you pretend they do not exist. Perhaps you also have a family pet? Well, what is it, I ask you, that a pet desires? Relax, Rigby; I do not expect you to answer, for I understand how potential pet ownership is a matter of maximal national security. I shall answer the question myself—a pet desires treats."

A curlicue of concern again dimpled his forehead.

"I was not aware that you liked . . ."

"*Things?* Oh, indeed. Of things I am quite fond. I am dead, sir, not retarded."

Rigby's jaw worked in small circles. Forced off script, he was intrigued enough that his eyes squinted one one-millionth of a degree. He took up his clipboard.

"Tell me what you'd like. I'll see what I can do."

So it happened that my research into Adolf Hitler's Third Reich became entwined with obtaining every fanciful fandangle a young man could want. First, I mastered Rigby's vocabulary words—"Deutschland" meant "Germany," "Aryan" was the Nazi idea of a master race, blah-de-blah—and in exchange my dismal walls leapt to lusty life with pinup tootsies: Rita Hayworth bursting from a black nightie; Betty Grable swimsuited with gams that could crack a coconut; and Jane Russell prickling atop a bed of straw, her gauzy top losing its brave battle against an unbeatable bosom.

Subsequent rewards included civvies a guy could feel good about (a single-breasted sporting jacket, teardrop-patterned scarf, trilby hat) and, best of all, a 16mm projector. I had to get along with a government archive of classroom crap like "Let's Learn about Good Posture," auto-safety screamers like "Danger Is Your Companion," and didactic dramas like "Sex Hygiene in the Army," but each piece of celluloid distraction helped build a wall between myself and my fresh regrets. With Rigby, there was always more to learn and recite, brick after brick after brick.

Presently I was an internationally recognized expert in Germanic studies! Ah, Reader, I hear you sniggering; you know too well my scholarly follies. Facts zipped away from me like dandelion fluff, with one exception. Elaborate wordsmithing on Black Hand ransom notes had been the literal death of me in 1896, but still nothing tickled me like big words, of which German had an inexhaustible supply. While Rigby struggled, and failed, to feed me fortifying biscuits of basic language, I instead salivated over unwieldy delectables like *Ortsgruppenfachberater*, *Bandenkampfabzeichen*, and *Ermächtigungsgesetz*. Such morphemes tasted to me like rich platters of food.

Months into my miseducation, Rigby presented me with a box of three-ring binders containing a translated work by Adolf Hitler himself. I dug into the manuscript with high hopes. Any dictator's prose, thought I, could only improve upon the artless composites of OSS typists. Entitled *Mein Kampf*, it led with a biographical sketch with which I could not help but identify: young Adolf's wayward moonings in Austria, his teenage vagrancy in Vienna, his every attempt at social advance rebuffed by doubters.

From there, it bogged terribly into fathomless polemics on the failures of Marxism and the innate evils of Jews. I allowed that the Jews' holidays were oblique and their hairstyles inadvisable, but der Führer's beef with this "world pestilence" left me perplexed. I begged Rigby to torch the damn thing. After he refused, I purloined some paste and plastered pages from *Mein Kampf* to the wall for use as a projector screen. It always felt as though a particularly obnoxious audience member kept lecturing during my movies, but one does try to make the best of one's situation.

Rigby did not approve. The poker-faced fellow almost mustered a genuine frown. He stated that he would read the book aloud to me, page by page if required. Now, that was a credible threat, and it revived my drive to find a way out. Rigby, though, had yet to divulge a single exploitable detail. I renewed the pressure. What new motion pictures had he recently seen? Had his nameless wife and indeterminate number of children gone with? Did the lot of them travel in an auto, and if so, what color was it? To all queries he gonged his tuneless refrain—*I'm not at liberty to say*—though, unknown to either of us, those reins of liberty were about to be flung aside.

II.

I N CLOSING, THE COMMITTEE DEEMS client J-1121 unsatis-factory. He is unambitious, uncooperative, indecent, and excitable. He rates high only in the category of confidence, so high that he is a hazard to all affiliated parties, and represents a significant risk of rebellion and/or desertion.'"

"Disappointing," said I. "Not a word about my velvety singing voice."

Rigby turned the page.

"'However, the committee remains conscious of the rare oppor-tunity that J-1121 represents, and therefore approves the agent's recommendation that Operation Weeping Willow be put into immediate effect.'"

Rigby, being a robot, was incapable of displaying pride through human signifiers, though I sensed a shallowing of his forehead divot. He slipped the appraisal into an envelope, licked the adhesive gum, pounded it flat, and tucked it inside a briefcase pocket. The caution seemed inordinate; we met, for once, not in the commissary but in a private room featuring the modern marvel of a door. Through the walls I could hear the muffled reactions of others in my position. One squabbled, another sobbed, yet another rattled a locked doorknob.

Such noises do not soothe the nerves of the new draftee.

"Operation Weeping Willow, eh?" I forced a grin. "I am curious as to what a recipient of such poor grades is qualified to do."

Rigby spun the locks on the briefcase and cleared his throat.

"In three weeks you will be air-dropped outside Berlin with the mission of assassinating Adolf Hitler."

A laugh darted from my throat. It cracked about the concrete like a trapped sparrow. I laughed some more, expelling a whole flapping flock.

"Oh," sputtered I. "Is that all?"

It was no joke, and I should have known it. "Joke" was as foreign to Rigby as "*Nationalsozialistische*" had been to me.

"Penetration into the Reich is SO's top priority. Within that priority are what we call Targets of Precedence. More traditional methods of approach have been considered. Blowing up the rails under Hitler's train. Poisoning his water supply. Dropping snipers onto his property in the Alps. All of them have proven too difficult."

"But punting me off a plane, that's easy? Am I intended to land upon his head?"

"Intelligence tells us that Hitler is consumed with the occult. He has built an entire unit that advances behind the battle front, emptying Europe of relics alleged to have mystical powers. There are rumors that he's acquired the Holy Grail."

"Rigby! Are we little children? These are campfire tales."

"We have every confidence that Hitler, upon hearing about your arrival, will come to see you in person. That is when you, using a planted weapon, will implement your objective."

"Let us pretend, just for laughs, that you are of sound mind. How in Gød's contemptible name could you plant a weapon I could reliably access? The Nazis would have me in chains, behind bars, at the end of a hundred muzzles."

22

"I'm not at liberty to say."

"The instant I made a move, his wolves would chew me to gristle."

"You may be harmed, that's true. But that's what makes you valuable. You can withstand a certain amount of harm and still achieve your mission."

"That's assuming I don't break my arms, legs, and neck in the drop!"

"We drop men on Germany all the time. Once in Berlin, you'll have a contact. This contact will make himself known to you. When you fulfill Operation Weeping Willow, this contact will coordinate coups at several key sites, setting off a chain of events that will hobble the Reich. You have no idea how many Germans, even officers and generals, believe Hitler is bringing their country to collapse. If we lead, they will follow."

Rigby sat back, lit his eighty-fifth cigarette of the day, and waited for me to, I suppose, produce Old Glory from my pocket and begin waving it. In the adjacent room, the sobbing man had begun to scream. Wasn't that its own answer? I crossed my arms over a heart that, had it still functioned, would have been blasting away with anxious disbelief. Wartime destruction was what I craved, but I wanted it done quickly and anonymously, and without the government I loathed doing the captaining. Rigby emitted smoke like an oil-based engine.

"The committee said you weren't ready," said he. "I stood up for you."

"That ought to teach you."

"I did it because I know the best agent is one who doesn't follow his heart."

I pictured the Excelsior, its whiskey gleam chilled inside an evidence locker.

23

"I'll grant you that mine beats no more," said I.

"And one who does not hold to ideals."

"Well, I have none of those. That's no secret."

"And one who savors deception."

I smashed both fists to the table—once, twice, thrice.

"Yes! Yes! Yes! So I fancy a falsehood now and again! What of it? You, Looney Bird, ask me, Dead Body, to self-invade Nazi Germany at her very apogee? When, according to billions of pages of your own research, she has expanded five hundred miles east and another thousand miles west? Where she controls Western Europe's industrial might and Eastern Europe's agricultural centers, not to mention the whole continent's natural resources and the free labor of millions of conquered peoples? And then you puff your cig and lament my want of excitement?"

Rigby, in a powerful display of passion, raised his eyebrows a half inch.

"So you *have* been paying attention."

I swiped the only thing available for swiping, a ceramic ashtray, and hurled it in the direction of the next-door screamer. It exploded against the wall; the screamer paused, then recommenced screaming. Rigby, having no better option, ashed upon the table.

"Sandy," recounted I. "Age forty-four. Dead on the scene. Go on, bring back your police reports, send me up the river. It cannot be worse than this preposterous sentencing."

Rigby, same as ever, folded his hands. His voice, though, was softer.

"I don't want to do that. I'd rather ask you a question. What is it you're afraid of losing that you haven't already lost?"

Four-eyed, edge-squaring, monotone automaton though Rigby was, the U.S. Government had been shrewd in entrusting him with the hellion Zebulon Finch. This man knew my heart—or what it might have looked like had it not been drained and dried. How could I clamber through day after desolate day, knowing how I'd devastated Bridey, miscarried Merle, and forsaken Church? Were I to sport penitentiary fatigues, the grave rat of guilt would gnaw at me all the same. Furthermore, though it felt indecorous to acknowledge it, a legacy of great infamy awaited the person who pulled the trigger on Adolf Hitler.

"You wangling wretch," hissed I. "When do I leave?"

Five days, that was it, before I was to join a Britain-bound battleship, and not one minute of it could be wasted. I was desperate to know how I would contact the Berlin spy, but Rigby was not at liberty to say, for nothing was more important than protecting a field agent. He yielded only that the signal word was "*Geschenk*"—in English, "gift." Be vigilant, said he, and ready for that signal to come.

Rigby's first exercise was flash-carding Nazi principals so that I might identify them should we cross paths. I was anxious, and that anxiety birthed adolescent ripostes. Martin Bormann, Party Chancellery Chief: "Egads! Which elephant stepped on his nose?" Hermann Göring, *Reichsmarschall*: "Why, look, Rigby—a two-hundred-pound baby!" Joseph Goebbels, Minister of Propaganda: "An old crone in a cabinet position? How progressive!" Heinrich Himmler, Reichsführer-SS: "No wonder the Nazis are formidable. They've taught rats to wear glasses!" Often the conditioning went past midnight; Rigby massaged his throbbing eyes and kept flipping.

Initially I was too frightened to request parachuting practice. But when five days shaved to two, I became frightened not to. Rigby, however, pshawed my petition. Falling from a plane, insisted he, was simplicity itself. His concerns were granular. OSS was paying good money to purchase wardrobes from European refugees and had amassed a warehouse from which to costume infiltrators in authentic fabrics, underwear, watches, and wallets. This was important, as I needed to make it into Berlin proper before giving myself up for arrest. Were I apprehended in the sticks, rural police might have their fun with me and never say a word to anyone.

The clothing was genuine, all right: It reeked of desperate sweat.

Travel by moon, drilled Rigby. Stick to forests. If you take something from a farmer, pay for it. If a confrontation becomes unavoidable, fight. Eyeballs are best gouged with fingers in tiger-claw formation. Knife strokes are most effective testicle-to-chin. No knife? Fold a piece of paper six inches by two, diagonally to a point, and drive it under the jaw. Firearm prep was saved for last. We threaded through tunnels to arrive at the underground range, where Rigby indicated paper targets hung fifteen yards away, and then he numerated the best areas for kill-shots. From his multifaceted briefcase he produced a snub-nosed, nickel-plated Smith & Wesson revolver that he introduced as the "Victory" model. Cradling it in his palms as though it were a kitten, he began, in his dullest drone, to define each part, from sight to cylinder to grip.

I rolled my eyes, nabbed it, pulled the pin, checked the chamber, flung the chamber shut, and fired six bullets into the target: three to the head, three to the chest. My cherished old Peacemaker the Victory model was not, but it felt fine to fire; the release of pent-up violence was the real *Geschenk*. I handed the revolver back to Rigby. His reaction was typical.

"Good. We can skip this lesson."

"We cannot," said I, "for I have yet to hear how I will obtain a gun in Germany."

Was it my imagination, or did the wooden-faced Rigby wince?

"It's next on the schedule." He gestured toward the tunnels.

Back behind closed doors, he sat me down, did his usual hand-folding, and adopted the blank visage of one accustomed to enduring forceful objections. It was probable that every OSS agent at Rigby's pay grade possessed this skill. It did not escape my notice that the neighborhood screamer had gone silent.

"Tonight you go into surgery."

"Surgery? I thought you knew my eccentricities."

"There's a rectangular flap cut into your abdomen."

If he'd hoped to shut me up, that did the trick. Multitudes of disfigurements had I, but none disquieted me so much. Dr. Leather had carved it into me atop a dining room table in 1913 to prove to a colleague that I couldn't digest food. Weeks later, Merle had sewn it shut, and throughout subsequent decades I'd forced myself to make required repairs. It had been, I realized, wasted effort; I knew before Rigby spoke another word what he was planning.

"We'll use that flap to gain access to your chest cavity. Beneath the left half of your rib cage, we'll embed the revolver you fired today. We have surgeons preparing right now to make the insertion and remodel your outer abdomen so that the flap will be undetectable if you're searched. When the time comes, you'll have to . . ."

Even Rigby blanched at this.

"Extract it?" prompted I.

He offered a minuscule shrug.

"Cut with a knife if you can. But anything will work. A piece of glass, a sharp stone. The remade skin won't be thick. You'll need ten, twenty seconds. The gun won't be loaded; we can't risk it going off inside you if you fall down a flight of stairs. The bullets will be taped to the handle. Insert them, fire, and keep firing. It's that simple."

Was it? Death had lurked within me for some time, but now I'd evolved into a dischargeable weapon. I nodded assent, but my head felt heavy, my neck weak, my body hollow. The surgeons, at least, could save their anesthesia for men who needed it.

For my last night in America, Rigby procured for me a legitimate Hollywood picture, thankfully one not headlining Bridey Valentine. It was called *The Lady Eve*, and across the curled pages of *Mein Kampf* cavorted scheming Barbara Stanwyck and gullible Henry Fonda. Everything ended in love; I rewound the reels and watched it again, then again, all night. It was a comedy, but I did not have time to laugh. Harder than I'd ever worked at one of Rigby's lessons, I labored to memorize every detail of this clean, happy, flirtatious world. Chances were, thought I, I'd never see its like again. Would anyone?

III.

I N THE NIGHT SKY OVER Amsterdam I was handed a brass snap-case small enough to tuck into a palm. Inside were three colored capsules. Rigby shouted straight into my ear over the dual-engine roar. The white one, said he, would knock out a grown man for five hours. The blue one, benzedrine sulfate, was used to combat fatigue. The third one was an L-pill—a suicide pill—encased in white rubber so that it could be swallowed without effect. Biting on it, however, would release a lethal dose of cyanide.

Psychological boons to the average grunt, but to me, worthless. Rigby, though, was a stickler for protocol, and I buckled the case inside one of my roughly one thousand pockets. This took time, so encumbered was I with twenty pounds of parachute and fifty pounds of associated gear: a zippered jumpsuit baggy enough to fit over civilian clothes, chin-strapped helmet, goggles, leather gloves, rubber-cushioned boots, life jacket, raincoat, compass, flashlight, wire cutters, trowel, and knife, should my chute need to be cut down from a tree.

Unlike most paratroopers, I forwent rations and guns, instead filling their spaces with five hundred reichsmarks of cash as well as the currency that could truly buy favors in Germany: chocolate, canned meat, liquor, cigarettes, and nylons.

The thundering fuselage of the C-53 Skytrooper was big enough

29

to fit twenty jumpers, but that night only Rigby and I rattled about. The ride was too rocky for drinking, yet Rigby glugged coffee from a thermos. Smoking was forbidden, yet he hadn't quit puffing. I'd been heartened that OSS had furloughed the bespectacled flyweight from his natural habitat of fluorescents, before realizing they'd done it only to limit my interactions to a single agent: under torture, there would be minimal data I could spill.

We'd embarked from a darkened air field outside London. Rigby explained that MI6, British Intelligence, was leery of American cowboys like us undoing years of their judicious maneuvering. But the plane that transported us was itself RAF, Royal Air Force, the result of a U.S. Joint Chiefs of Staff arrangement known by fewer than ten people on earth. Why use RAF? Because their pilots were, said Rigby, "nuts," a description he applied admiringly.

Hour after hour, a soccer ball with Hitler's face drawn on it rolled up and down the cabin. I booted it when it came close—practice, you might say, for the real thing. Polish crackled from the cockpit radio until we entered airspace rich in *Flugzeugabwehrkanone* (that's "anti-aircraft flak" to you, Civilian) and the Nazi stealth fighters known as "bogeys." Our Skytrooper made abrupt banks and shifts in altitude. We were slung about; the Hitler-ball bounced wall to wall, floor to ceiling; the Smith & Wesson sewn inside my chest rattled against my ribs, and I was grateful that it was unloaded.

Rigby noticed my disquiet, scooted close, and shouted into my ear.

"*We did a drop once. Can't say where or when. Three men. Top secret. Months of prep. It's night. We make the drop. Wind picks up. Men drift into a* Wehrmacht *unit watching a film outdoors. Our men come down right in front of the screen. Germans laughed so hard, one of our guys got away.*"

I gave him a dry stare.

"You think this makes me feel better?"

Rigby shrugged.

"It's January. Too cold for outdoor movies."

A whistle from the cockpit indicated T-minus five minutes. My stomach plummeted. Seconds later, an actual plummet—the Sky-trooper dropping to jumping altitude. I tried to unbuckle myself from the seat, but my hands shook. Rigby reached over, did the job. With the help of fuselage bars, I lifted myself, affixed my goggles, and tested my parachute straps, then again, then again. My knees waffled. I was numb with terror. Eleven years ago, I'd white-knuckled a flight from New York to Los Angeles, and here I was, only my second time in a plane, and I was about to jump out of it?

A green bulb above the jump hole lit up. My disciplined, profes-sional instinct was to take my fist and shatter the smug piece of shit before Rigby saw it, but he was already giving the pilot a thumbs-up. He unlatched the door; the moan of wind became a scream. Dark-ness, horsewhips of fog, moonlight daggering from unspecified waters. No geography to be seen, no bearings to be had—no, no, no!

I turned to Rigby, frantic to plead prudence, but the man who until that instant had betrayed only what emotion a forehead dimple could divest, was—Reader, about this I would not jest—*smiling*. A river system of wrinkles had grown from the corners of his eyes, and in their winding loops I read histories of laughter and romance; bar-becues and picnics; sports fandom and pet care; the million other fishing holes in which the American male, myself not included, cast his rod.

He held out his cigarette.

I grabbed it, inhaled, and then watched smoke waft from a dozen open wounds. I dropped the butt, saw it blink away into the night, and then glanced back to Rigby to find him extending a hand. I regarded it like a grenade before accepting it; thus was my first physical contact with the agent a crushing handshake. In hindsight, I should not have been surprised. Rigby, too, wore a suit of one thousand pockets, each packed with more fortitude than I'd ever know.

"My wife's name is Janet and we have six children. Roy, Sandra, Walter, Patty, Stanley, and Florence."

Allen Rigby was, finally, at liberty to say.

I smiled back; I could not help it.

"How do you know that I won't do what your bosses warned, and run away?"

Rigby winked and gave my hand a final, firm pump.

"I don't."

I shook my head at the beaming fool, and then, taking a full-body influx of cold atmosphere, faced the roiling black universe. The time to step into the abyss was now! Wait, wait—now. Hold on. Hold on. And—now. No! Wait. Wait. Now! Now! Go, go, go! No, not just yet. Now? The green light was blinking—yes, now, you twit, now!

In the end, it was Adolf Hitler, or at least a soccer ball resembling him, that provoked the plunge. A buffet of wind caused the Skytrooper to tip its wings; I stumbled for balance, and my foot landed atop the ball. So it was entirely without grace that I went somersaulting out of humanity's steel-and-screw placenta and into nature's amniotic oblivion.

Indeed, the plunge was twin to *la silenziosità*, though even shorter-lived. Like many a novice jumper before me, I yanked the ripcord the moment my primal brain recalled its existence. The breathless slapping of the wind's millions of palms ceased as I was jerked upward. Rightside-up again, I throttled the harness, fumbled for the steering line, and ogled upward to make sure the suspensions hadn't tangled.

It was several overwrought seconds before I accepted the nighttime shushing. I quit my infant thrashing and let myself be cradled—by Gød's own hand, I'd say, if I didn't know the bastard better. A sleeping world unsheeted itself: Lilliputian landscapes of teensy trees, bitty barns, and pygmy paths. I permitted a breeze to sweep me parallel to the earth so that I might catalogue each wonder. There in the ether I was neither *of* nor *other*; I floated on silvered currents in which I had no history, no regrets, no grief.

I wished it never to end.

So, yes, Reader, I drifted a bit off-course from the intended drop zone of a sugar-beet field. Instead I touched down in a frost-crusted stretch of wild grass, where the chute dragged me ten yards before dropping atop me like an avalanche of snow. From on high, the environs had seemed agrarian enough, but I dared not dally. I slashed my way free, stripped myself of jumpsuit and related paraphernalia, and then bunched them inside the chute and used my trowel to dig a hole beneath an overhang of trees. There, as trained, I buried all evidence of my arrival and checked my compass bearings.

Rigby had gone to lengths to show me aerial maps in case I needed to self-navigate. The maps, though, had been confusing, and I recalled only the overarching directive: *go southeast*. It was night; there was nothing to stop me. I crept through forests, copses, and vineyards, and when I had to dart across roads, I did so unobserved. It was by dawn's slate shading that I stumbled upon dangers—a pastoralist and son digging fence-post holes, two women crossing a field with baskets of eggs, a rabble of children with lunch pails beginning a trek to school. Each German looked skeptical, and to each I mumbled the talismanic *"Heil Hitler"* before scurrying.

Dabergotz? Stöffin? Buskow? Were these, or were they not, villages about which Rigby had briefed me? Blast all those nights I'd spent watching movies instead of studying! On the periphery of a farm in Wustrau, I found an abandoned, slanting barn and squatted to wait out the daylight.

That night near Kremmen, I found, to my relief, road signs to Berlin. I had a fifty-kilometer walk ahead of me (and no clear concept of what a "kilometer" entailed), so I doubled my pace, even as travel became more taxing. At night, cars, trucks, and even tanks ran the roads, and swastika-banded sentinels operated roadblocks; my woodland trajectories, meanwhile, were stymied by barbed-wire barricades. I could not make it into Berlin, not that night, and wiled away the following day among the feathers and pellets of an outmoded chicken coop.

On the third night, I buried inside hedges my money and any tools that might be construed as weapons and used my wire cutters to pioneer a path into the northwestern perimeter of Berlin. I perceived only silence and cobblestone; like the London I'd glimpsed, the city went dark at night to complicate air raids, and I felt like the lone survivor of absolute annihilation. Not quite; I heard a whistle blowing to my right, then German shouts, none of them friendly. I stopped in the middle of a street and steadied myself for impact before turning around.

The footfalls came softly but as quickly as wolves'—four men in white-piped olive-brown tunics spiffed by rank insignia, flattop caps, and knee-high jackboots. Red swastikas banded their biceps, and their black-gloved hands were at their sidearms. They encircled

34

me, hot breath congealing the cold, barking wolf-calls I couldn't understand. I kept my arms over my head and tried not to show fear, for wolves could smell it. Reader, it was a challenge, for not all of my studies under Rigby had been in vain. I knew these uniforms on sight.

Geheime Staatspolizei—the Gestapo.

IV.

T HE GESTAPO FORAGED MY POCKETS for detritus
emblematic of Berliners: house keys cut from regional tem-
plates, matchbooks of local branding, ticket stubs to district
entertainments. Unsatisfied, one of the police took my hand to check
for nicotine stains (Germany suffered widespread tobacco shortages)
and gasped at its deadness. He dropped the hand, hissed a word, and
that, Dearest Reader, was that.

I was handcuffed, hooded, and shoved into a backseat. *Panic not,*
I told myself. *This is all according to plan.* The auto hugged a hundred
hairpin turns before it jolted to a halt and I was heaved back to my
feet. A baton prodded my vertebrae, and I blundered blindly across
a threshold and into what sounded like an aviary, chirping as it was
with German jeers, and into a chamber degrees darker and colder.
There the blindfold was removed and I found myself in a jail cell
resembling the one in California, except that this one was too clean,
as if recently hosed.

Three Gestapo gorillas, fresh and hairy, stood stretching their
muscles. A doctorly sort instructed me to remove my clothing.
I detested this routine but did what he asked. He applied rubber
gloves and conducted a physical that, let us just say, was scrupulous.
Rigby's surgeons, thankfully, had been talented. The physician
detected neither my patched stomach nor the weapon beneath my

ribs. The gorillas, though, turned away, appalled by my purplish pallor, arid open wounds, and eunuch groin. The instant the examination concluded, the Gestapo hurled prison-issue shirt and trousers at my face—silly, really, considering what had to come next.

Rigby, that straightest of shooters, had described the typical scenario. Gestapo custom was to disorient new captives with a nice-to-meet-you drubbing. The Reich's security office, the *Reichssicherheitshauptamt* (what a word!), limited its agents to twenty-five strikes with a stick per prisoner. But the Gestapo was more imaginative than sticks! Their unofficial tool set included soldering irons, skull rings, testicle vises, anal electrodes, and other items too tawdry to enumerate in the refined company of my Dearest Reader.

As I dressed, my mantra grinded like teeth: *all according to plan, all according to plan, all according to plan.* My insusceptibility to pain would bring me to the attention of a senior officer, then an officer senior to that, and so on, until word reached Hitler. The path of travail was corporeal and therefore nothing for a corpse to fear.

Why, then, did I tremble like a boy of twitching nerves and pumping blood?

Before the trio of silverbacks could land a single punch, a Babel of arrival erupted. Through the wall boomed a sonorous voice, first merry, then damnatory. One of the Gestapo muttered an odd, short word—Lüth—and his mates cursed. Thrown locks cracked through the jail like gunshots, and the dark walkway was blasted by a big, bright beam of sun or, as I came to discern, a person, huger even than the gorillas.

He was both colossus and child: seven feet tall but pudgy and pink-cheeked, his gemstone eyes sparkling from above corpulent cheeks while a curled imperial mustache sprung with every long stride. Though it was but midday, he wore the evening attire of a country squire: shirt, bowtie, and waistcoat—all snow-white—beneath a powder-blue suit draped in silver aiguillettes. The ensemble was tailored to fit, but still the man's pot belly protruded, creating the impression not of an idle overeater but rather of a white whale breaching the surface. Strapped to his belt, quite insanely, was a beveled mjölnir, the kind of square-headed hammer the Norse mythological god Thor used to obliterate mountains.

The Gestapo clearly resented this impediment to bloodletting, but nonetheless stood at attention and saluted. The giant returned a *sieg heil*, but one of distraction. Quickly I shuffled through Rigby's flashcards. Could this be cross-eyed Joachim von Ribbentrop, Foreign Minister? Or dapper Albert Speer, Minister of Armaments and War Production? No; I was quite sure I'd never before seen this gussied-up grizzly.

He galloped past the Gestapo, skidded to a halt two feet away, and bent from stratospheric height to gain better perspective on my face. He mashed his lips to suppress gales of giddiness, pushed aside the mjölnir, and unclipped from his belt a leather satchel. In Dr. Leather's lab I'd met my share of worrisome implements but none so bizarre as the gadget this man extracted.

It was a slide rule, a tool capable of kindling panic in any young student, except that this one was crossbarred with needle-nosed calipers and hinged with a pair of arachnid arms. He came straight at my face with it; I, of course, juked and prepared a punch. He chuckled, his mustache points tightening, and showed me his palms—see how pink and innocent? Gingerly he placed the top caliper against my eyebrow, drew down its partner until it was snug beneath my chin, and then recorded the measurements upon a pad of paper. He used the same procedure to measure my nose, length and width, and the diameter of my skull.

The man giggled approval.

More surprises crawled from the satchel. Next came a svelte cigarette case, except that instead of smokes it contained twelve glass eyeballs, the irises ranging from sky to chestnut. He held each false eye alongside my own to make a match. Finally he brought forth a short rod from which dangled thirty tiny ponytails of human hair. He draped them gently over my forehead until he had matched my hair tone as well. He returned to his pad of paper, noted the findings, and turned the page.

"Your name, if you please."

Beneath his German accent, my melodious mother tongue!

"Zebulon Finch," exclaimed I. "Oh, thank you, thank you."

His cheeks chubbed into a grin.

"From 'Fink'—German surname."

"Is that right? How wonderful."

"Location of birth?"

"America. That is, Chicago."

"Chicago! One-sixth German population. One-sixth!"

"Marvelous," said I.

He lowered his voice to a volume better suited for scurrility.

"Are there Slavs in your hereditary line?"

"Slavs?" What were Slavs? "Heavens, no."

"And Jews? Forgive the question, but we must know."

I shrugged. "I don't think so."

He grimaced an apology. "Again, Mr. Finch, I beg forgiveness. But your ancestry must be free of Jewry through 1800. Is this something you can credibly verify?"

His hesitation made good sense, for a typical seventeen-year-old would have been born in 1926, multiple generations displaced from his forefathers. To the contrary, Abigail Finch had brought me into this wretched world in 1879, thus was it easy for me to confirm heritage.

"There is no question," said I. "No Jews."

The men I'd known who sported clipboards—Leather, Roseborough, Rigby—liked to keep them close, but this stranger let his drop. It clattered to the cell floor; I jumped; he clapped his gigantic hands once; I jumped again. He raised his conjoined fists in celebration and expelled an elated exclamation.

"*Mein Bruder!*"

His gargantuan paw gobbled mine and shook it as a dog does a rabbit.

My bafflement in that moment is, I think, forgivable, though in reflection there is no misconstruing the reason for his euphoria. Is it possible, Dearest Reader, that we have journeyed so far into my somber saga without a description of my basic physical features? 'Tis an oversight due for rectification.

Zebulon Finch is blond-haired, blue-eyed, pale-faced, strong-shouldered.

In short, the Aryan ideal.

"This glorious winter morning I was instructing a unit of *Stapostellen* regarding the relevance of the Futharkh Runes, a task I undertake on behalf of our beloved SS, when one of my students described to me the curious physical state of an apprehended American. I closed the lesson at once, for I knew that it was you! Years, Herr Finch, have I dreamt of this moment!"

"I am sorry," said I. "You know me?"

"*Ja, ja!* In Europe there exist academicians of the obscure, and in such circles you are spoken of, most often in disbelief. But have I doubted? *Nein!* I knew you must be real."

"Well, you speak English. That's enough for me."

"*Ja, Ich spreche Englisch!* Also do I *parle français* and *Latine loqui*, if you have a preferred lingua franca."

"English," said I. "Please."

He rubbed his hands with elation enough that the mjölnir whirled.

"Come, come! Let me deliver my distinguished guest from this uncivilized lodging. There is so much I wish to learn from you. So many concepts I wish to deliberate!"

From scared scraps I built a smile.

"That sounds very agreeable. Only—my effusive apologies—I am an ignorant boy. To whom do I speak?"

"*Ach!*" He gripped the head of the mjölnir, snapped his heels, and drew himself to full girth and height. "Udo Christof von Lüth, head of the *Deutsche Volksforschung und Volkskunde, Schrift und Sinnbild-kunde* of the *Forschüngs und Lehregemeinschaft des Ahnenerbe*, facilitator of the *Wahrheitsgesellschaft*, dedicated *völkisch* scholar, and very soon, I hope, der Führer's modest, deferential Minister of the Occult. I exist only to serve you!"

Even for an aficionado of Nazi nouns like myself, this was gibberish, save a scintilla of the spectacular. Future Minister of the Occult? If this von Lüth fellow was about to be inducted into Hitler's inner circle, this chance meeting would gobsmack even the unsmackable Rigby! I'd bungle it if I didn't keep my head. Oh, it was a grim struggle for a loose-lipper like myself to weigh words prior to their utterances, but I'd been coached to give a statement, and once I began

41

its recitation, I felt closer to Rigby. Despite the war-torn miles, the lie bonded us.

"If, as you say, you wish to know my heart's desire, I will disclose it. Your great führer, I would do anything to meet him. It is why I have defected. In America, I am not appreciated. They prize progress, which is well and good, but in doing so neglect the mysteries of the old world of which I am a part—of which we *all* are a part. Adolf Hitler, though—there is a man who appreciates humanity's past."

Von Lüth's eyes wobbled within cataracts of tears. He clasped his hands at his sternum as if a curtain were falling and he were impatient to applaud.

"You are a faun, Herr Finch, and your words are a pan flute played from our most enchanted of forests. Der Führer has the most curious mind; he will adore you! He and I are great friends, and it shall be my honor to ensure that your dream is realized. But first, these Gestapo who have mistreated you, forgive them. They are true-hearted but not so good at visualizing the future of the Reich. Though quite good, if I may say so, at the tactics required to make that future happen. *Ja?*"

V.

ON LÜTH SIGNED PAPERS RELEASING me into his custody, and, dressed again in my civilian wear, I followed him into the leather backseat of a silver-fendered, diesel-engined Mercedes 260D sedan, capped by a hood-ornament swastika over the grinning grill. We pulled from Gestapo Headquarters, and I craned my neck to read the infamous address: 8 Prinz Albrechtstrasse, Berlin, SW 11. OSS training be damned. Here was a shortcut to pulling off Operation Weeping Willow! Though von Lüth's lavish ensemble denoted no specific Reich faction, a black uniform with lightning-bolt patches identified his driver, whom he called Kuppisch, as SS, the *Schutzstaffel*, the most feared military division of all. Kuppisch had a bulldog underbite and mistreated our elegant auto as if it were an obstinate mule.

Berlin was a city of insignia. Uniforms, caps, and visors of black and beige, navy and gray, and green and olive painted stripes of order onto streets otherwise lacking. While I had stagnated in a D.C. dungeon, Allied air raids had churned half of Berlin to rubble. Von Lüth's bulldog rocketed the Mercedes around gnarled craters, between foothills of scorched brick, and beneath the shadows of brave walls that had withstood shellings. Even there, crisp Nazi flags flapped from existing windows, a field of blood-bright poppies.

This is why they shall lose the war, thought I. *Their budget is wasted on flags.*

43

We parked against a curb twenty minutes away from the nearest bomb site. I frowned through the window. Seeing how my escort was the grand marshal of a parade of honorifics, I had expected a sprawling estate, not a proletariat three-story, six-unit apartment building. Kuppisch opened the car door (for von Lüth; to me, he shook slobbery jowls) and took a guard dog's position, rifle held like a prized bone. Von Lüth marched into the building, and I followed.

He glided past a snoring lobby attendant and with startling grace bounded up two flights of stairs before unlocking a thoroughly unremarkable top-floor unit. *But of course!* thought I. *Those wily Germans hid their top officers in plain sight!* Alas, the interior offered further disappointment. No butler bowed; no maid demurred; no domestic hovered. The three-room abode was barren and dust-bunnied, but von Lüth showed no shame. He strode into the kitchenette and plucked an apple from one of a dozen baskets. Each contained, amid its cargo of fruit or bread or dessert, an envelope.

"Presents! They are the burden of being a confidant of der Führer." He raised his pitch through a full mouth. "'Herr von Lüth, here is *Sauerbraten* for you, here is *Spätzele*, here is cake.' I cannot refuse such generosities during days of rationing. To the proletariat class, it means so much."

I felt as if hooked to Leather's Isolator oxygen tank; the needle of my skepticism leapt. It seemed absurd that a highborn crony of Hitler's would live in a pauperism comparable to what Church and I had endured in the 1920s. I toed forth.

"Your favor cheers them. A man of your stature, sampling their wares."

Von Lüth simpered his pleasure and pointed at the ceiling.

"No more gloomy walls. Let us ascend to the sun!"

You might take this as metaphor, as did I, but it was literal. Von Lüth took a dangling piece of rope and pulled down a hatch. From it unfolded a wooden ladder. He scampered up the steps, looking in his powder-blue suit like a gigantic boy straight from Sunday School. He unlatched a metallic overhead door, and sunlight dumped down like grave dirt. Not an attic but the roof—ah, now there was the place to hold a clandestine congress of Party bigwigs!

For a third time, expectations were obviated. The flat roof was not of brick, nor tar, nor shingle, but rather of lush German forest. Herculean effort had been spent sodding the roof with two feet of soil. Grass grew to spite the cold, as did shrubs, evergreens, and—the sincerest sign of life—tangles of weeds.

Von Lüth dandled a leaf twixt finger and thumb and flattened his nose against tree bark as if snuffling for sap. I followed him across the grass until he arrived at a small facsimile of a Neolithic stone circle. There he reclined against a three-foot boulder (who had lugged *that* up there?), unmindful of his clean suit; indeed, he appeared to relish dirtying it. He crossed his ankles near a miniature creek filled with rainwater, and clouded the January air with a contented exhale.

Books were scattered about with the nonchalance of pebbles, each one dog-eared, antlered with inserted notes, foxed from the elements, and clad in jackets of damp leaves. It was here, not the apartment, where von Lüth logged research hours.

He pounded the mjölnir against transplanted earth.

"Sit, sit. You and I, we are like Hitler and Stalin before the nastiness: We have a nonaggression pact!"

My unease deepened. Here I was, a loaded weapon keen to be fired, and this oversized claimant upon the title of Minister of Occult wished to lounge about cold grass? I kicked aside a rain-stained file folder, plucked a few pencils from the dirt, and sat. Von Lüth, oblivious of my mounting disquietude, sighed.

"Modern life! It demands a city address. Whether that city is my Berlin or your Chicago, it is the same. *Eins*, it is loud. *Zwei*, it is dirty. *Drei*, it clouds brain and soul with industrial anxieties. In my heart, I am a simple burgher, and the work I do at the Ahnenerbe, our institute of historical research, is toward one goal: to bring my countrymen back to their *völkisch* roots, which so long ago anointed us as the chosen people."

"'*Völkisch*,'" ventured I. "Related to our word 'folklore,' perhaps?"

Von Lüth's face lit up.

"Young, virgin minds are the most receptive to the tenets of *Volkstum*!*"

Young? Virgin? I ignored both hilarities.

"I am sure that you are right," said I. "Say, shouldn't we be making arrangements?"

"Before we work in tandem, it is useful that you understand how everything begins with this." He indicated his wrist: naked, pudgy, vulnerable. "Blood—*Blut*." Next, he pinched a bit of soil, placed it onto his tongue. "Soil—*Boden*. Blood and soil, *Blut und Boden*: the primeval urgency of the Germanic peoples to reclaim the land of their inheritance. It is why there is war."

"Blood and soil. Both elements of which I possess too little."

"Why, then, you are like Germany! We call it *Lebensraum*, the moral right of the robust races to displace the sickly ones that poison defenseless lands. Your United States are proficient in these matters. Surely you have witnessed one race wrest property from another?"

Four years I'd spent cracking skulls in Chicago's Little Italy;

46

six years I'd toiled in poverty in Manhattan's Chinatown. You could not pace either metropolis without seeing the waving banners of this or that clan of immigrants. Block after block, pride versus pride; of course blood was spent onto soil—or, as it was, concrete.

The gun in my chest felt as ineffectual as a penny; it galled me.

"This is the rationale for conquering the whole of Europe? It is convenient if you are German."

Von Lüth rolled tight the tips of his mustache.

"Herr Finch possesses a Socratic spirit! *Nein*, my intelligent new friend, *nein*. The notion that der Führer intends to turn our continent into a killing floor is laughable. We Germans are linked to our Nordic roots through the balance of the farm, the renewing rituals of sun and moon. These principles, not violence, will water the fields of the *Tausendjähriges* Reich—the Thousand-Year Reich."

There was a rustle amid the brush. We both turned to see fronds undulate and a swath of grass shiver. Von Lüth yawped in joy.

"Look! A diligent little squirrel! Or perhaps a friendly badger! You see? Even in this capital of brick and steel, Earth's creatures find a way to commune with the soil. Industrialization is a carousel, ever turning, and only a revolutionary like Hitler has the power to properly manage it. You said yourself, Herr Finch, America marches to the drumbeat of progress. The entire world moves so quickly, never considering what is lost along the way."

Quickly? Oh, indeed! Almost five bombastic decades had passed so far in my seventeenth year. Against better judgment, I was intrigued. Nazi though he was, von Lüth had guided me from a pulverized Berlin to this flourishing oasis. Was it possible that I, like Germany, suffered so that one day I, too, might clear away the smoke

47

of battle and find within it rebirth? Might there be further ladders yet to climb? Von Lüth had been right in calling me young. I felt like a confused child before a lecturing adult. I cradled my weary face in my hands.

When next I peeked, von Lüth was prowling about, the seat of his pants smirched with grass. He checked behind the boulder and then hopped across the creek to investigate a shrub. Finally, in the perfectly illogical storage spot of a tree limb, he located a small chalkboard. He wiped from existence dozens of symbols with his sleeve and produced a kernel of yellow chalk. To my great surprise, he kneeled in the soft soil at my side and gripped my shoulder with a huge, heavy paw.

Any thoughts of casting the hand aside were erased by the mildness of his whisper.

"It hurts me to see you so burdened. This alienation and melancholy you feel? The cause is obvious. Year after year you live, and yet no one has given you reason to rejoice. Will you allow me to try? For fifteen years after the travesty of the Versailles Treaty, we Germans looked at nothing but our muddy, unworthy feet, until a man rose up so high that we, too, began to lift our heads. Now we look toward the fire of a rising dawn. So should you."

Dirty Nazi. Hateful Hun. Vulgar German. None of the slurs stirred in me the expected satisfaction. Stranger only than the spot on earth where I found myself was the compassion being offered. Not once, after all, had Rigby tried to ease my pain. I gestured, rather rudely, for von Lüth to go ahead, chalk what he needed to chalk, anything so that I might be relieved from being the focus of kindness.

Mercifully, he did so. Upon the board he drew the simplest shape.

"Let us begin with the circle, the symbol of creation, destruction, and regeneration, revolving around what we call the solar year, the time it takes to align the planets with the next house of the zodiac—in terrestrial terms, 25,868 years. A scholar of distinction named Madame Blavatsky once studied a text called the *Stanzas of Dzyan*, kept hidden for centuries in a Himalayan monastery, and from it learned that within each solar cycle evolves the 'root-races.'"

"A secret text that no one else has seen? Why, it must be true."

Von Lüth laughed, his baby-cheeks shining.

"Your doubt is invigorating! Madame Blavatsky, I assure you, was welcomed to many mysterious places: the subterranean Babylonian city of Agadi, the Shamballah oasis in the Gobi Desert—ancient, forgotten archives of esoteric insight. Blavatsky left behind directions; of course, to protect them, they were left in code. At the Ahnenerbe, we work to unlock the codes, rediscover these wells of wisdom, and with them prove the German right of dominion."

"Is that all? No harnessing of black-magic hocus-pocus?"

He chuckled and raised his hands as if admitting guilt.

"The mystagogue you speak of was the clairvoyant Guido Karl Anton List, the bearded old godfather of *völkisch* mysticism. When List was but a child, his family visited the catacombs of Saint Stephen's Cathedral, and there the lad was compelled to kneel before an altar and swear to build a temple to the Norse gods. This he did, though that temple came in the shape of a book, his 1914 classic of symbology, a response to the long occupation of our fatherland by Roman Catholics."

At the word "Catholics," von Lüth drew a cross within the circle.

"List's reading of ancient runes traced the origins of the Germanic people to a cult called Armanen, the very flesh of the god Wōden, whom you might know as Wôdan or Uuôden or Odin. This is not to be taken lightly, Herr Finch. What sort of people do you think are birthed from gods?"

"A lucky people," said I. "Too lucky, I think."

"I might agree, except for the irrefutability of List's predictions! He reported that the Armanen cult would return—and today we have our National Socialist Party. He reported that there would be a 'Strong One from Above' who would mend our divided people—and today we have der Führer. He reported that 1932 would be the year during which our unconscious desire to reunify would coalesce— and, if we can forgive List one year in error, Hitler became Chancellor in 1933. So again we see the pattern of life's cycles. And when those patterns break, they break in places not at all random."

Von Lüth thumbed away four bits of the chalk circle.

"If I follow," said I, "what you suggest is that Hitler is no mere man. He is the embodiment of the German will."

"What a pleasure to hear such insight spoken in the American accent! Now, pay close attention. In the 1890s, Jörg Lanz began collecting the beliefs of List and others into an arena of study known as Ariosophy, the proper, and long overdue, study of the Aryan race. I will bother you not with the process, only the findings: that Germans are embodied with what, in English, I can only call 'goodness.'"

I rolled my eyes within dry sockets.

"I can think of a country or two that might disagree."

"The term is insufficient," confessed he, "for the quality of goodness does not bring Aryans much good. Instead, it burdens us with a most dreadful responsibility. It becomes our duty to become dentists and extract from our land the rot of the *Untermensch*—the subhuman."

"Subhumans—I take it that these are the Jews?"

"Lanz's monograph on the subject is quite convincing. It is titled *Theozoologie oder die Kunde von den Sodoms-Äfflingen und dem Götter-Elektron*. Ah, but to translate? Let us just say that "*Sodoms-Äfflingen*" means "sodomite apelings." That conveys the essence, *ja*? I shall read you a passage! I have a copy right here. Where is it now?"

But this seminal masterwork was not to be found in weeds, grass, brook, or tree. Kicking mud from his shoes, von Lüth shrugged.

"I cannot find it," said he.

"Perhaps this is symbolic?"

"You have such wonderful oomph! To condense: Our shared racial memory recalls the historic evils of the Jew. Jörg Lanz wrote that every German is anti-Semite by blood, and I, Udo Christof von Lüth, say that all a German wants is for that blood to be stirred! This is der Führer's purpose, to bring mankind back into harmony with nature. Which circles us back to here, to this roof, among this beautiful greenery. You too, Herr Finch, are Germanic, and thus you too have a purpose on this Earth, a reason to keep existing. What was confusion is hereby straightened into order."

51

At "straightened," von Lüth did just that to the four arms of his symbol.

He cracked the chalk against the board.

"The swastika—the National Socialist Party did not invent it out of air! I curate at the Ahnenerbe a collection of relics engraved with this potent symbol. Macedonian battle helmets over two thousand years old. Chinese paintings from the Han Dynasty. A mammoth tusk that we date at 10,000 BC. The swastika, according to Madame Blavatsky, is the sign of Agnine, god of sun, of fire, of creation itself, as well as the sign of the Aryan. The mind spins, does it not? How deep go mankind's ancient rivalries, all of which must end with the same circular—and, yes, bloody—results?"

My chin bobbed above the choppy waters of von Lüth's obsession.

"I don't know. I am lost."

"To the contrary, you are found! *You* are the swastika, Herr Finch! Like it, you exist out of time. What makes you certain that you were born when you say? Is it not possible that, in some manner, you have always existed? That you are a guide, as was Blavatsky, List, and Lanz, here to lead us through the valleys of death and into the hills of glory?"

His sumptuous words handled my misbegotten ego with satin gloves. I sank into fantasy, picturing myself as a series of characters careening across history. I was Judas Iscariot, jingling my purse after giving old Jesus a killer's kiss. I was Caligula, limp from sensational whoring, bloody to the elbows from the maidens I'd tossed to the lions. I was Vlad the Impaler, leering at tens of thousands of men on spits. I was John Wesley Hardin, stabbing school chums, shooting loud snorers, staining the desert dust red.

I ripped free from the trance.

"Do you mean to bring me to Hitler or not?"

"Of course." He shrugged. "It is my duty as a German."

"We need not wait, then, until you are named Minister of the Occult?"

Von Lüth flapped a hand.

"It is, how do you say in English—a semantic matter? Der Führer opens new offices like ordinary men open canned meats. My title, I promise you, is imminent. Next week, next month? There is a rush?"

"I am impatient. It is a flaw."

He paused, hefted the mjölnir into both hands, and considered its weight, which was, I assure you, lethal.

"Eagerness of this sort might make a German doubt the authenticity of your defection," said he. "You do not, after all, seem to have a defector's political leanings."

The revolver in my chest woke as if from nightmare, thrashing and feverish and wanting out of bed. Had this rooftop discourse been a test I'd failed? I cut glances at the stones at my feet. Were any sharp enough to cut through my abdomen so that I might have a chance against this hammer-swinging hulk?

Von Lüth relaxed against his boulder like a beached beluga.

"Your purpose in coming to Berlin may be what you say it is. It may not. In truth, it is immaterial. You have a new purpose now, alongside me, and I know that you will appreciate it." He aimed the mjölnir eastward. "Right now our Führer is in Eastern Prussia,

53

presiding over victory. This will mean a period of waiting. But do not show me your long face, my eager Aryan! I will make a personal request to Himmler, who will, I am certain, arrange our meeting with Hitler. This is acceptable, *ja?*"

Himmler? Heinrich Luitpold Himmler? Second-most-powerful figure in the Third Reich? Rigby's hair, what was left of it, would erupt into flame at such a proposition. I tightened my dead muscles into marionette tensity and pulled the string that made me nod, as if this were merely the next page in an OSS script that I'd practiced for months.

I, the living swastika, would wait for the next turn of the circle.

THE ENSUING WEEKS IN NAZI Germany were oddly pleasant. When not at the Ahnenerbe, von Lüth held court upon the roof, interspersing occult orations with animated meditations upon the enigma of Zebulon Finch. He begged to hear of my every stumble and clamber, and never desisted with inquiries. I capitulated, though at a controlled pace, for Hitler dawdled at the Eastern Front and—I shall admit the truth—I enjoyed our exchanges. Von Lüth was no probing Leather; there were no experiments, no notes. He was no dispassionate Rigby, either; he would listen, spellbound like a child, and when my words moved him beyond response, he would pounce like a bear and embrace me harder than I'd ever been embraced, and I would let him, and, Dearest Reader, I would like it.

Von Lüth came to know more about Zebulon Finch than anyone else alive, and the knowledge only magnified his interest. Perhaps, then, I should not have been surprised the day he returned from the post office waving an opened envelope. He pushed aside a gift basket of candy and pressed the letter upon the counter so that I might share in his joy. I could not read it, but it was typed, signed, and stamped upon Party letterhead, and within the garble I found my full name.

"Have you made me a Nazi?" asked I.

Von Lüth's slap upon my back drove me into the counter.

"Were only my powers so great! *Nein*, but this document will afford you some of the benefits. This is an *Ahnenpass*. It attests to your racial heritage. Keep it with you. Do not lose it. Should there be trouble, should you be bothered by the Gestapo, these papers indicate that you are under the supervision of Udo Christof von Lüth and should be returned unharmed to this address."

"Returned? Am I being sent away?"

I winced at my pitch of panic. Von Lüth clucked his tongue as if I were a nestling anxious about kindergarten.

"Tomorrow I deliver a lecture in Kassel. It is part of my work for the Ahnenerbe. This will be soon followed by a lecture tour of Cologne, Ansbach, and Munich."

"All right. So long as we do not miss Hitler's return."

"Herr Finch, my unwavering faithful! You misconstrue. I have decided that you will remain in Berlin while I am gone. What brought me to this decision were the words of the great poet-astrologer Giordano Bruno: 'O Jove, let the Germans realize their own strength, and they shall not be men, but gods.' If you are to understand your belonging in our race of man-gods, you must understand Berlin."

"You want me to . . . wander about? Is that wise?"

"It is wisdom itself! You must see for yourself how our peasant class personifies the principle of *Führerprinzip*—one nation working for one leader for one purpose. You must feel it in your German blood. *Ach*, you have no blood. Then in your German bones! Do not worry; your *Ahnenpass* makes you quite safe. As additional precaution, I have asked Kuppisch to act as escort. He will not intrude. You, like every other Aryan, must work alone to resolve your *Drang nach Osten*—your Eastward Urge."

His theory was supported by evidence. Was not my trajectory eastward: L.A. to D.C., D.C. to London, London to Berlin? I shook off the notion like a light rain; I'd come to appreciate von Lüth's attentions, yes, but I was no Nazi. I was an assassin, I had to remember that, and my weeks sequestered indoors had made it impossible for Rigby's field agent to contact me. If I could give the slip to the bulldog Kuppisch, surely the spy would sidle next to me and give me my *Geschenk*, and we could get on with it.

It was, of course, 1943. My flesh had marbled and my carriage had become undeniably atrophied; the days when I could have passed as ordinary were behind me. I displayed my long-suffering right hand: Mr. Avery's fish hook, the dent from the Little Miracle Electric Mexican Stuttering Ring, Chernoff's blistered taxidermy, the bump from Sandy's embedded tooth. Von Lüth was not fazed; his gentle, understanding smile soothed me.

"We will find you gloves. A high-collared coat. A billed cap. Do not worry, Herr Finch. Few of we Berliners look as good as we once did."

Von Lüth's train to Kassel left early, so 'twas daybreak when he midwived my overdue birth from the building's belly. Though I was well costumed, von Lüth did not miss that I walked on coltish legs. He took me by both shoulders and squeezed. Despite his fervor for the rustic lifestyle, he sported another dazzling ensemble, a peach suit complimented by a greatcoat with black fur lapels and a gold swastika brooch.

"It is with proud anticipation that I await your report upon your German brethren." He winked. "Just promise to avoid the whore-houses. *Sicherheitsdienst* has all the rooms bugged!"

He fired off a *sieg heil* gutsy enough to, despite the warmongering overtone, instill me with confidence. He volte-faced, put two pinkies into his mouth, and whistled. Half a block away, Kuppisch smacked doggie lips and saluted. Without further farewell, the peach-colored titan tramped down a hedgerow path, whirling his mjölnir.

I do not think that five minutes was too much time to let settle the reality of being alone in Nazi Germany. But pots and silverware clattered from windows; Berlin was awakening and I could not hold a single block of sidewalk indefinitely. Before me was a street. To hell with it—I took it. I heard the bulldog follow from a half block back, though the crack of his jackboots made it seem as if he bit at my heels.

People exited homes holding lunch pails or pulling carts of sellable goods. I scrutinized each passing pair of lips for *Geschenk*, so it was by accident that I began to concur with von Lüth's valuation: Germans were remarkable beings. The humble folk among whom I roved exchanged *guten Morgens* as if it were a fine day in a fine year, and when they glanced at the sky, it was not for fear of seeing a swarm of RAF fighters but rather to judge the potential for rain.

This attitude of quiet resolve persisted when I entered bomb zones. Destruction there was surgical. To the left, a gabled three-family home of red clay roofing and green shutters. To the right, a whitewashed plaster colonial with brickwork chimneys. Between them, a scraggled spire of demolished brick rising from twenty feet of kibbled concrete. Such ruin had, however, sprouted a cottage industry for von Lüth's adulated poor. Men pushed wheelbarrows of brick, and lines of women passed buckets of water while their children tunneled through exciting new playgrounds of rubble.

Berlin's grid would have been perplexing during peacetime. Now, debris made nonsense of navigation, and as I threaded about in hopes of losing Kuppisch, I became lost. I passed one S-Bahn train station after another, but lacked the courage to confront ticket-takers. Around midday I came upon a band of fifty men clearing a thirty-foot blast crater. Its former life as a train depot was evidenced by the thick iron rail that twisted into the air like a middle finger to Allied bombers. Buildings on either side had sloughed their streetside layers of brick in the same way that Bridey, wizardess of wardrobe, used to let her nightgown slide down her shoulders.

This delectable, if misplaced, image brought me to a standstill alongside a lamp post sweatered in homemade flyers searching for loved ones lost since the last bombing, or the bombing before that. The lack of replies was obvious by the condition of the leaflets: charred, discolored, and so whipped by wind that they soon would be but faint recollections. I leaned against the post; it was like touching the eyelids of the dead and shutting them.

Kuppisch, always Kuppisch, pawed the pavement, hounding me forward. I was drained of any belief that I'd find my *Geschenk* when I entered the neighborhood of Mitte. Despite shop signs proclaiming, in German and English, JEWS AND DOGS NOT ALLOWED, the district teemed with both. No, Reader, I have no sixth sense for detecting religious penchant; Jews were evident by the star-shaped patches sewn to their coats. Distantly I recalled Rigby jabbering about the Star Decree of 1941, part of the Nürnberg Laws, about which he'd also jabbered. Decrees? Laws? Such tedium! I'd paid them little mind.

I cannot say I regret the inattention.

Ignorance wears so much more lightly upon the soul.

Some Jews obscured their patches with shrewd foldings of arms or totings of groceries. The indignant did the opposite, though at their own peril—the stars might as well have been targets. Old men who doddered got bopped by Gestapo batons, and women who lingered before non-Jewish establishments fielded lewd commentary.

Even toddlers were hurried along with rifle butts, the same treatment extended to tomcats.

The worst bullies were adolescent lads dressed, despite the chill, in flapless caps, black shorts, high gray socks, brown shirts, black neckerchiefs, and ornamental daggers. They were a band of *Hitlerjugend*, or Hitler Youth—quite literally a band, their slight backs strapped with snare drums, their wiry arms supporting woodwinds and brass, while a pipsqueak major with a cowlick and buckteeth swung about a tasseled baton. On the major's shoulder, as it happened, lounged a monkey wearing a red vest and fez. At this point, nothing surprised me.

The shoe heels of this ornery orchestra crunched through the broken window glass of a Jewish delicatessen as they nabbed cakes and shoved them into chortling mouths. In the meantime, the monkey executed splendid Russian squat-kicks. Passersby laughed at the monkey but did not admonish the children, not when the boys lifted the skirts of passing Jewesses with trombone slides and drum sticks, not when they dropped cake on the curb and spat at a bearded old Jew to pick it up.

Von Lüth's hypothesis that I belonged in Deutschland made sense. Elders here encouraged the young in enterprises of vandalism, theft, and debasement, and I'd performed comparable acts under the Black Hand, and in the 1920s South had witnessed, and had done nothing to stop, the ritual abuse of Negroes, up to and including the lynching of John Quincy and Mother Mash. I reached into my pocket and pet my *Ahnenpass*. I was grateful, so grateful, for my Aryan features.

The tension in Mitte had a suffocating odor—sharp blood and hot urine—but I dawdled there, loath to ask Kuppisch to lead me back. The Hitler Youth, however, satiated with Jew-cake, began to march, farting and thwacking their instruments with renewed gusto. Their path appeared deliberate, so I did what weakling lemmings have done since time untold and followed.

More boys joined the cavalcade as dusk fell, and soon it was an inharmonious philharmonic that I trailed toward a city center suffused with orange light. It was, I came to find, a towering bonfire. One block away, close enough to feel the fire's heat, our parade of high-stepping *Hitlerjugend* intersected with another, the luckiest members of which toted seven-foot standards—Nazi banners adorned with silver swastikas and golden eagles. At night, by fire, the symbology took on a slithering animation, the eagles mincing forth as if appraising carrion, the swastikas turning, one into the other, like the gears of a grinder.

Our crowd wove with others, became one people, one Party, one Germany.

One had to wonder if von Lüth had planned it.

I wove through the mob toward the fountaining sparks. From the air, it would have been a sight to behold: ten-foot-long shelves had been arranged in swastika formation, doused with gasoline, and kindled with hundreds of books. Diligent Rigby had described prewar book burnings used to galvanize Nazis against overlarded Jewish intellectualism, but this frenzy was beyond righteous nostalgia; it felt like a pagan rite, missing only its wicker man.

Orderly echelons of Hitler Youth cycled forth with armloads of books scooped from handy piles. For fifteen minutes, the steady pitching of literature into the blaze was disciplined. But these were children; it devolved into squealing anarchy, hundreds of boys sprinting close enough to be licked by flames, to shiver and spasm and eject

61

their armloads. Somewhere amid the hysteria, a monkey screamed, screamed, screamed.

Kuppisch, forgotten. *Geschenk*, forgotten. The blaze gobbled chapters, paragraphs, and sentences, and from its roaring phantasmagoria swirled fireflies of individual letters. I searched myself for satisfaction. My binge at Sweetgum notwithstanding, books had been foes since cubhood. But this was no victory. This was cremation. If nothing else, books are conversations from beyond the grave. Am I anything at all, Reader, besides this manuscript you hold?

Singed pages chased me, the last words of the damned, as I burrowed through the *Hitlerjugend* horde toward what looked to be the only area not clogged with spectators. I resolved that, should von Lüth demand his report, it would be overloaded with oxymoron. Germans were stouthearted and hangdog, hardboiled and shamefaced, dyspeptic and compliant, meek and malicious. The fact that they repeated their workaday routines in the face of rampant hatred did not, in fact, make them noble. It made them ghosts.

I reached the cleared street corner only to discover the reason that it was emptied. Upon it paced a once-handsome fellow turned street lunatic: a full carpet of curly gray hair gone flyaway, a cleft chin belittled by muttering lips, broad shoulders tapering into pendent arms. He wore a simple black suit, weak armament against the cold, but his most striking accessory was an eye patch, which lent his existing orb a doubled avidity.

Well, I'd ignored plenty of urban cranks. I continued forward. The man heard my footsteps and fixed me with his single eye. His suit, I saw, was banded at the neck by a white clerical collar. This was unexpected; Rigby had expounded on the acrimonious relations between Nazi and Christian leaders. I hesitated just long enough for the preacher to raise his battered Bible and begin babbling.

"Sorry, chap, I don't speak it," said I. "Good-bye, *auf wiedersehen,* all that."

An unwitting mistake! The preacher switched to a staccato English.

"Who is Führer?" demanded he. "Not he in sheep's clothing. It is Gød. It is Gød who is Führer. What thus say Gød? Gød thus say, 'Do not violence the stranger, the fatherless, the widow, nor shed innocent blood.'"

"Gød," sighed I. "You are barking up the wrong tree."

I stepped to the left, but the preacher shifted his footballer's body in concert.

"Where is prophets? True prophet is called traitors. True prophet is muzzled. True prophet is took away like animal. It is the Führer-beasts who is traitor."

I could hear the clack of Kuppisch's boots.

"Do you see the man with the red armband approaching?" asked I. "He would take great satisfaction in arresting you for these things you say."

But even as I offered this warning, I noticed the reichsmarks scattered about the preacher's feet, spots of reflected fire, evidence he'd soapboxed here unharmed for some time. As I puzzled over his durability, he knocked raw knuckles against his Bible and leaned close enough for me to smell his foul breath.

"You close your heart to Gød, you fall into hole. It is why we, *Volk* of Gød, suffer if we not speak the sins of Deutschland." He extended his Bible. "Pray with me. Lord, give we ears for hear your word, brains for respect your law." He shook the Bible at me. "Pray! Forgive Führer-beasts who evil against you, Lord." The preacher jabbed me in the chest with the Bible. "Pray!"

His clerical collar had popped and, like the gnarled train rail, middle-fingered the heavens. What was up there, wondered I, that deserved repeated taunts? I decided not to chuck the Bible into the gutter, for I had a grudging respect for this Gød-botherer. Life, after robbing him of an eye, had so badly jolted his brain that even the Gestapo tossed him coins of charity instead of tossing his ass into a cell.

I dug a mark from my pocket and flipped it, a fiery red comet in an ashen universe. It landed upon the Bible, then clanged to the sidewalk, eagle-and-swastika-side up. I leaned in and whispered so that Kuppisch, closing in behind me, would not hear.

"Here is a prayer. Gather the coins at your feet and buy a ticket. For a train, or a plane, or a boat. Get out of this country as fast as you can." I shrugged. "Amen."

VII.

ONE DAY, DISCOVERED RIGHT IN front of my imbecilic face, was the *Geschenk*. For hours I compiled a screed of insults with which to excoriate myself, for this *Geschenk* was neither symbolic abstraction nor metaphorical conceit, but rather a literal gift—one of the countless offerings of food that arrived unbidden at von Lüth's door. The basket was worn wicker, bedded with a white towel, and contained a crumb cake and a note:

EIN GESCHENK
Aus Meixelsperger Bäckerei

There had been hardly a day since my arrival when von Lüth's quarters and arboretum had not been redolent with the sweet steam of fresh baked goods, from *Erdbeertorten* (strawberry tarts) and *Pfeffernüsse* (pepper nut cookies) to *Apfelmaultaschen* (apple-filled ravioli) and *Laugenbrötchen* (pretzel rolls). How many of these delicacies had come from Meixelsperger Bakery with this same impatient postcard? Curse my seventeen-year-old's brain! A trip to this bakery was horribly overdue.

Finch luck, being what it was, dictated that I would have to wait whole months—while war raged, Reader, and millions died!—before von Lüth's next out-of-town trip, a four-day lecture tour of northern

65

cities. But wait I did until the departure's dawn, at which point it was all I could do not to shove the large man out the door as he dithered between suits—tangerine with mint pocket square or mint with tangerine? Von Lüth had been enthralled by my observations on daily German life, and as he bid his adieu, he again encouraged me to peregrinate Berlin during his absence so that I might greet his return with rousing tales of metropolitan "adventure."

He used the word in hyperbole, but it ended up being apt.

Meixelsperger Bakery was but ten minutes from von Lüth's building, a demure little business I recognized from countless passes. Ever was its counter queue choked and its six tables wedged with dour doughnut dunkers paging through *Signal* magazine propaganda as if forced by Luger pistol. These nondescript diners were suddenly packed with covert potential; one of them, I was certain, was Rigby's undercover dynamo, growing fatter each day as he waited upon my late, so very late, arrival.

Eternal, though, were the clicks of Kuppisch's claws behind me. Were I to shake the bulldog, I'd need to double my derring-do, triple my trickiness, multiply my Machiavellianism. On Day One of von Lüth's furlough, I foxed down abrupt and illogical side streets, but any dog could sniff out a dead body. On Day Two, I took care to never pause, counting on a dog's need to piss, but Kuppisch, it seemed, owned a bladder the size of Asia. On Day Three, I took us right past the eye-patched street preacher, certain that my bloodhounder would stop to arrest the man for vocalized treason, but the preacher's improbable luck held and Kuppisch, like so many Gestapo before him, turned a deaf doggie ear.

By the eve of von Lüth's return I'd wasted time enough on rank cowardice. At dusk on that fateful May day, I said to hell with subterfuge and concluded that day's citywide amble by crossing the street on what I hoped looked to Kuppisch like impulse and entering Meixelsperger Bakery.

Therein waited a queue of four people. I shall not forget them. Before me, a butcher, stooped from cutting-board duty and clutching a bag of wartime sausage that needed bread. Before him, a stoic mother, hands raisined from the scrubbing of clothing and children. Before her—ah, perfect!—a *Wehrmacht* tank corporal, helmet lodged beneath arm, his uniform black enough to conceal its oil burns. At the front of the line, a tram conductress lashed to a shoulder-belted coin dispenser, reciting an order to the most intimidating German I'd ever seen, Frau Meixelsperger herself, a scowling razorback with thick oven-burns crisscrossing her brawny forearms.

The five fixed me with stares. This was typical. Next, also typical, they judged my skin a sign of sickness and, in proper German fashion, looked away. I took my place in the queue and with overblown nonchalance peeked out the window. Across the street waited Kuppisch and his rifle, though I had no doubt that he would come in after me if I dawdled.

The brusque baker rammed a box of buns into the tram operator's breasts. The line shuffled forward; I was fourth. No time to waste. I inspected the bald grandfather at the farthest of the tables. Surely this geriatric wasn't the double agent? The tank corporal's loaf of bread was free; he paused at my elbow to buckle his helmet. I panicked, looked outside. Kuppisch had smelled a rat and was crossing the street. I grimaced at the closer tables. *Which of you useless Huns knows Allen Rigby?* I wanted to shout. The baker snapped at the harried mother; the queue caterpillared. Desperate, I coughed to gain the attention of the closest coffee-swiller, only to have him growl. A clatter of change. The butcher, my antecedent, was paying. I checked outside. Kuppisch's dewlaps were pressed against the door glass as he squinted to see inside. There was no time left, none at all.

"*Herkommen*," scolded Frau Meixelsperger. "*Beeil dich.*"

Customers wanted home before the streetlights extinguished. They nudged; my abdomen struck the counter, and the revolver chuckled against its ribcage holster. It would raise suspicion if I did not order food. But had I brought any money? I stared at the baker, paralyzed. Her brow thickened like dough. She cursed and gestured at the falling night, the restless queue behind me, my general idiocy. Everyone in the bakery was watching. Behind me, the door creaked open—the bulldog, slobbering to bite.

His fangs, though, never sunk into my rotten flesh.

From concrete, wood, sewer, and steel rose a groan.

If one roamed Berlin long enough, one noticed its warts: cheap metal speakers jerry-rigged atop road signs, telephone poles, and rain spouts. I'd heard plenty of air-raid sirens before, distant as banshees, but this one was on top of us and overlaid by a second, then a dozen, until the city's every other noise was stamped. For thirty seconds, the patrons of Meixelsperger Bakery swayed as if within a body of water, before the surf of truth broke upon us.

Like breakers upon rock, the queue scattered. People collided, muttered civilities, collided again, and graduated to shoving and swearing. Baked goods were dropped and flattened underfoot. The edge of my vision caught Kuppisch recoiling from the violent exodus. I looked up, even though all I could see was ceiling.

The upside to having my cadaver spattered across broken brick was outweighed by my desire to carry out Rigby's mission—he, and so many others, had placed all their chips upon me. I broke from the counter, only to have my body slingshotted back. My white wrist had been snatched by a hand even whiter, though its color came from a thick coat of flour.

"*Mein Gøtt*," said Frau Meixelsperger. "How many *Geschenke* I need send your pig-master before you come?"

I admit, Dearest Reader, that I'd relied upon my secret-agent contact being Errol Flynn: barrel of chest, lithe of limb, sly of mustache, cocksure of grin. To say the least, this she-hulk had no place in my fantasy. While I collected my idiot jaw, Meixelsperger, with considerable muscle, dragged me along the counter, around the register, and back through a kitchen humid with exhalations of fresh bread. She bashed open a rear door, and we entered an alley carrot-colored by the sunset.

Our view was narrowed by apartment buildings in which window after window darkened as lights were snuffed. Against gray clouds, searchlights began hunting after the reflective bellies of enemy aircraft. Their vertiginous loops transfixed me; Meixelsperger pulled my bony arm so that it popped against its socket. It was clear that she'd noticed my personal guard dog and did not wish to know the length of his leash.

The alley adjoined an eastward stampede of humanity. Agitation was rampant, but not so hysteria. This I attributed to the amicable stewardship of the Hitler Youth. Those sharp-toothed little cretins savored any chance to carry out orders, and already they were stationed on every corner as crisis crossing guards, swinging swastika-banded arms toward the neighborhood bomb shelter, an ugly concrete box built atop, or so I'd gleaned, extensive underground chambers.

I was less than elated to find that the neophyte Nazi closest to us was the same undersized, bucktoothed band major I'd seen raising hell in Mitte—red-cheeked, neckerchiefed, lederhosened, and shouldering a fez-capped monkey. Though the half-pint primate trembled at the cacophony, the boy was having a ball. The proof was in the strident song belching from his red lips. I know, Reader, that I am prone to embellishment, but his atonal atrocity made the air-raid siren sound like Brahms's Lullaby. I almost dug the revolver from my ribs right there.

Despite his duties and ditties, the wee pisser missed nothing. He spotted Meixelsperger and me struggling opposite the crowd and, being a helpful lad, shouted for us to correct our mistake.

"*Falscher Weg! Falscher Weg!*"

Meixelsperger's glare reduced me to plum pudding, but the upbeat chipmunk kept insisting that we were headed the wrong way, and it was starting to attract attention. Kuppisch had to be nearby; he would notice the hubbub and pounce. Without thinking better of it (perhaps by now that goes without saying?), I hissed at the infernal urchin as we passed.

"Quiet! Let us be!"

He gasped, not from dismay but excitement.

"English! I learn from teacher! I sing my song for you! *Ja, ja!*"

I came to a halt.

"What? No."

"In English, it will not rhyme. But I sing!"

"No! *Nein!* Please, *nein!*"

The boy's sour voice squealed through the sirens like a rusted scalpel. Flowers wilted. Birds dropped dead from the sky. Several RAF planes malfunctioned and crashed into the Alps. Still the monkey, that scraggly slave, hauled itself up to do the requisite hotfooting in time to the lyrics.

Jews are sinners
They slaughter Christian children
They cut their throats
The damned Jewish filth.

Meixelsperger's tugging advised that I ignore the brat. Yet I hesitated. Had this pealing pubescent any idea of what he sung? The spitty shine of his prominent front teeth suggested not. He completed his cheeping couplets and took a breath for another round. My sense of self-worth, what was left of it, could not let this pass as it had in Mitte; I held up a hand.

"No," said I. "That is enough."

He did not listen. Over siren screeches and the thunderclaps of rubble-worn shoes, he crooned the stanza over and over, mixing English and German with glee, swinging arms bent as if cradling rifle butts like a proper *Stoßtruppe*. My guts twisted. It was not in defense of Jews specifically; do not credit me that much. It was, rather, disgust at the unacknowledged privilege with which this slimy tadpole spouted his vileness, his indifference that those about which he sung—*the damned Jewish filth*—were right there in earshot.

I ripped myself from Meixelsperger's grip, fantasizing of strangling first boy, then monkey, and with considerable strength slapped down both of his dancing elbows. People hurrying by paused to gasp at my unacceptable behavior.

"*Enough*," hissed I. "You will not sing this song again."

The chubbed, pink mounds of his cheeks slackened and drained to white. I swooned with triumph and waited for the rewards owed me—his dancing eyes blurred out by tears and his giddy squawk drowned by blubbering.

Instead of oozing tears, his eyelids slitted. Instead of bawling, his loose mouth sealed shut in mature circumspection. His tiny hand, upon dropping to the handle of his ceremonial dagger, did not seem all that tiny. His shifted his eyes from me to Meixelsperger; from Meixelsperger to me. He repeated this routine for several seconds before I realized what was happening.

We were being memorized.

"*Mein Gøtt,*" said Meixelsperger. "*Mein Gøtt.*"

Her iron fingers sunk into my arm, and this time I let the secret-agent baker drag me from further disaster. If our encounter with the boy hadn't made us a spectacle, our direction did, but Meixelsperger pushed through the crowd with all the might of the German army. Masses filled our wake instantly, though still I caught glimpses of the livid lad staring after us, his total stillness accentuated by the jerking jig of the scrawny black monkey.

VIII.

N THE TIME THAT IT took to reach a vacant side street, night descended and I swore that I could see against a black sky the blacker triangles of the RAF. Frau Meixelsperger charged down an alley, through a wooden gate, and into the fenced backyard of a modest bungalow. There she squatted before a flowered hillock, parted a curtain of leafed tendrils, and knuckled a signal upon a steel door embedded in the dirt. The reply was the clang of a thrown lock; the door swung outward. Without a word, she dropped her legs into the hole and disappeared inside.

Another dark, downward path in a dark, downward death. I followed.

Meixelsperger bolted the hatch above while I surveyed the grim scene. Family bomb shelters were not rare, though I doubted that they usually crammed ten people into a ten-foot-long, five-foot-wide, four-foot-tall warren. Corrosion had worn mournful mouths through the corrugated steel walls, which supported, just barely, crooked shelves of dusty canned foods. Damp blankets had been draped to ward off poison gas, and the moldy stink mingled with that of the diesel fumes wafting from the engine powering a triad of flickering bulbs. A pile of World War I gas masks trapped the light in their lenses and turned it into gold. Fool's gold, I was certain.

I turned to the baker.

"Is there time to return to the big shelter?"

"*Dummkopf!*" she spat. "First you strike child in public. Second you complain of shelter. Is this not *gemütlichkeit* enough for Mr. America?"

"I only suggest that we might have hidden just as well in a crowd."

"It is your luck these people do not *sprechen* English. We would be out in ditch. *Mein Gøtt!*" She tossed up her arms. "Direct hit, we die anyway. This make you stop complain?"

The woman interrupted her shaming screed to arrange sandbags as a seat upon the cold dirt floor. I refused to follow suit; I crossed my arms and challenged each inhabitant's gaze. With menfolk out manning anti-aircraft flak, it was an estrogenated lot. A matron recommenced work on a half-finished knitted scarf. A young wife gathered her three children and opened a storybook to a marked page. Squatting at the far end, two adolescent girls picked up their game of chess. Only the elderly woman huddled upon a throw rug addressed me, and with spirit; she sent me the sign of the evil eye, or some such juju, before turning away.

Meixelsperger snorted.

"She no more goes home. She stay down here always. You believe this makes her coward?"

The question brought me discomfort. I shrugged.

"You females appear to judge me just as harshly."

"They should! Shelters, they are already full with disease. The measles? How do you say it? The weeping cough? They are old and with children. They are nervous because you are ill."

Oddly, her assessment left me in high dudgeon.

"I am *not* ill. I am pale."

"I need hero, and America sends me sick child."

"I am no child, madam. I can do everything asked of me. More, even."

She arched her eyebrows. Let us be factual: it was all one eyebrow.

"You look covered with brick dust, like you crawl from rubble. What do you think this make them think? Husbands, sons. Maybe they crawl from rubble as well? A very sad thing to think."

"I make them sad, do I? What do I care? Are these your friends?"

She smirked.

"Down here, Herr Finch, we keep to our own business."

Brief though my London stopover had been, I'd been regaled with tales of English camaraderie, how each Luftwaffe blitz had further stiffened inflexible Brit lips. This shelter brokered no such esprit de corps. Deep in my gut, Johnny's golden aggie, that symbol of rebellion, burned with certainty. Though this wasn't the gadget-rigged spy HQ of which I'd dreamed, each one of these females had something to hide from the Third Reich.

The first bomb fell. Distance reduced the sound to crinkling, but flakes of rust slalomed down the steel siding, and dirt dropped onto our heads. The children cheered this novel precipitation. I, as ever, loathed blemished clothing, and after brushing myself clean, crawled, with inflated reluctance, from the room's center to beside the brusque baker. As if to mock my preening, she refused to acknowledge the dirt clods caught in her hair.

"Begin talk. How do you help us with progress?"

I goggled at her demanding expression.

"Help you? I believed you were to help me! What is this *Geschenk* I heard so much about?"

"*Mein Gøtt!* The world is upside down. You hide away with Pig

Pigtof von Pig so long that all strategy I gathered for you is useful no more. If you get close to der Führer, a thing I now very much doubt, you tell me at the bakery and then, *ja,* our resistance will not disappoint, I promise you. So many little overthrows they will equal one of giant size. You tell me, Mr. American Hero, what you need, and then I rate the difficulty. How about we get rid of your beloved von Pig?"

I bit back a retort in von Lüth's defense. The giant had treated me more than squarely. His chief fault, as far as I could see, was being lost in the hedge maze of academe. I'd suffered similar disorientation as an overeducated youth, and sympathized. Forced to choose between von Lüth and this irritable operative, the decision was simple. Drop all the bombs you'd like—I'd take an open, green rooftop over this crumbling ossuary.

"Leave him be," said I. "Though, he has an SS agent I could live without."

"This is very easy. We will kill this agent for you. All it will do is reveal us, destroy all we have worked for. As long as Mr. America is happy."

"I am doing," bristled I, "what I can."

"This is not what the Americans say. They tell me you achieve nothing."

So swiftly were the winds of indignation stolen from my sails! Had Rigby, who'd pushed for my deployment, been given the lash by superiors for having believed in a lazy malcontent, if not outright turncoat, like Zebulon Finch? Rigby would have been fired; he'd be jobless in a wartime economy; by now, his whole clan would be living on stale bread and powdered milk—Janet, Roy, Sandra, Walter, Patty, Stanley, and Florence. Why did I have to remember every single damned name?

I'd planned to shut up Meixelsperger by crowing about von Lüth's promised confab with Heinrich Himmler, but the boast died in my throat; it would out me as the gullible patsy that I was. Meixelsperger, on the other hand, was a tidal power.

"America," muttered I, "is fortunate to have you."

She made a fist of kitchen-scuffed knuckles, but resisted cuffing me.

"America does not 'have' me. I am not interested in America. I have interest in Deutschland not losing all. Your Americans, they give me transmitter called Joan-Eleanor. I do not know why this name. Code, decode, all night until fingers bleed. Some of what they ask is simple. Ration reports, curfew hours. Is this building bombed? Is that? But revolution is not so small. If you, Mr. America, do your job, all will change. In *one day* it will change. Much danger for me, for everyone, but much rejoicing when—"

Detonations: one, two, four, six, a dozen, guttural throat-clearings from a subterrestrial demon that snatched our ball of soil and rattled it about like a die. We grabbed for the walls, but the steel siding vibrated like mechanical saws. Terror, terror! Meixelsperger, the bravest, cried out. The bulbs winked off, then on, and everyone was on all fours as plates of dirt chunked from the ceiling cracked across our backs. A hole opened above us—through it, a tapestry of stars—and pretty flowers dangled into the shelter like garroted bodies.

The tremors subsided. Blocks away, flak fire boomed.

The mother resumed storytime, but from a page that had been torn.

The girls pushed dual pawns, pieces that now slid through tears.

The knitter traded scarf for Russian phrasebook, practice for the aftermath.

The old lady grinned at the sky, her teeth blacked out with mud.

Meixelsperger was the sort of immovable object to which one huddled for comfort. Unlike the others, she did not participate in masquerade. She remained stomached to the floor, a half-inch forehead slash painting a tidy black stripe of blood down her cheek. She bore it as she did the dirt in her hair, proud evidence of suffering. Her country had been gelded and blinkered, and still she cantered about as she wished and took in treachery with wide-open eyes.

"How do you do it?" begged I. "For I cannot."

Meixelsperger blinked past blood.

"How do I be brave? A stupid question. You are born woman here, brave is only choice. You are 'future mother.' You are 'breeder of the master race.' Poor men—the National Socialists take their minds. But it is worse, I think, how they take a woman's body and soul."

From her deep bosom she fished a silver chain that ended in a golden starburst centered by a blue cross and black-enamel swastika.

"Look! This is greatest honor for a woman in the Reich. It is the *Mutterehrenkreuz*, the Mother's Cross. But it is not so difficult to obtain. Birth eight children, that is all."

Eight children? Though I was confident that this bruiser could cannon out one hundred sucklings without breaking for lunch, I detected no facility for petting and cooing, nor did her eyes sparkle with motherly mist at the mention of her prodigious brood. I knew why. It was all but guaranteed that most of her children were Party faithful and that some of them had already died for their love of der Führer.

A few streets over, a building exploded. It must have been of wooden construction. The splintering made the rather pleasant crackle of a fireplace, and the ensuing drop of lumber had a glockenspiel quality. But we were not fooled. The children sobbed, the girls shrieked, the old woman howled, and I pressed my face to the dirt. Meixelsperger, though, as if perversely inspired, sang through the clamor, the sleet of soil. Just four notes, a radio call sign I recognized.

"*Pom, pom, pom, pom.*" She had to shout; planes were bearing down, buzzing like a stinging swarm. "You know this BBC? Many Germans have what we call 'detector,' an item of wires for our radios. BBC broadcasts in German, for Germans, and now my brothers and sisters, they too know what I know, know of truth, know how the *Wehrmacht* loses Stalingrad. Germans begin to taste the bitters of defeat, and it is stale taste—no *Geschenk*, that is certain. When Hitler speak, what they hear now is lies. When they read newspaper, they think, is this false news? How strange, all these stories of Jews being resettled. Resettled where?"

The skies above popped with gunfire. Orange light strobed through the ceiling fissure. Wind whipped; detritus levitated; pieces of debris darted about our cave like wasps. When struck, Meixelsperger did not flinch. She looked alive, grinning like the mouse who'd outsmarted the lion. The noise was deafening now, and she shouted like a general ordering her troops on a suicide charge.

"*Something is rotten but now we smell it! Resisters grow like weeds, like the White Rose group in Munich—school children beheaded for celebrating free thought! But what happens, Mr. America, when you cut the weeds and do not pull the roots? Weeds grow back stronger! These are the children I mother! These are the daughters of dissent!*"

Meixelsperger raised her Mother's Cross, but it was yanked away when our humble hill was walloped by a wind that slung all ten of us to the eastern wall. The lightbulbs swung and shattered. The western wall caved with a sigh. We were pressed together, a black tangle of

79

flesh, mud, flesh, mud. For a moment, sound was the only sense: down the block, a hailstorm of brick cracking against the street, the muffle of the old woman caught beneath the dirt, the frantic rabbit-scratch of the two girls digging to free her. Was I still whole? I shifted my legs and stirred a lethal soup of broken glass, knitting needles, chess pieces, a set of false teeth.

The gods of war, all of them—Anhur, Ares, Mars, Mixcoatl, Pele, even von Lüth's Wōden—linked arms rugby-style and came straight at us. We curled like snails, some squealing, some praying, and one of us damning Brit and Yankee alike. It was not Frau Meixelsperger, Reader, but Mr. America himself, for I knew that there were good people in Germany, innocents and fighters for right, but after they were tilled into the soil, who would ever know it? Blood and soil, *Blut und Boden*. Here were both elements, expanding not across Europe but into the caverns of hell.

Fingers were pulling my hair. I resisted but was wrenched nose-to-nose with the half-buried Meixelsperger. In the fiery flicker, the oven scars of her forearms were revealed as war tattoos as true as Church's, as true as my own. The Mother's Cross was pooled between us, so close that I could see how all eight corners had been whetted to points. Meixelsperger had turned the unwanted honor into a weapon. Yes, it might prick her breasts from time to time, but wouldn't such stabs only sharpen the fantasy of sinking the cross into the jugular of Hitler himself?

There came a purple flash and the sound of the sky being ripped in half. Meixelsperger's arms wrapped around me and mine around her—instinct, not affection, but oh, how grateful it made me. I thought of Mary Leather, the last truly good woman I'd known, and wondered if she, with her bold buds of feminism killed off by an early-century frost, might have evolved into someone like this mad baker, able to take her life into her own calloused hands rather than let it be manipulated by man's mania.

Dry lips pressed to my ear to croak over the firestorm howl, the same as had Rigby's in the moments before I'd tripped and fallen into a foreign land, and she used my real name, a gesture that, even amid apocalypse, did not go unnoticed.

"*Down here is where myths are born, Herr Finch. The underground shapes the overground, never the other direction. We are counting on you.*"

IX.

WARTIME FACILITATES FARCICAL FLIPS OF fortune. Bomb-shelter soil was still powdering from my wounds when three weeks later I found myself reclining in a luxury train compartment. Von Lüth and I, dressed as if for a midnight ball, were choo-chooing across the country's broad chest. Germany, should you need reminding, is shaped like a torso having suffered at the hands of a sadist—both arms and legs have been dismembered. Berlin, as is fitting, is located where the heart would be, while our destination, the village of Wewelsburg, lay just beneath the liver—the gallbladder, if you will.

Reader, do you know which substance the gallbladder warehouses?

Bile.

It was evident that the train's manifest had underlined von Lüth's presence. Serving wenches paid him special mind throughout the six-hour trip, and Gestapo agents at every checkpoint saluted rather than demand identification. I did my damnedest to melt into my seat, but von Lüth basked in the fuss; his mustache wiggled like a cat's whiskers. Such treatment lent him confidence regarding our mission, which, as I shall describe, he badly needed.

After the bombing, I'd wrestled through rubble and staggered back to von Lüth's building, the relentless Kuppisch materializing from nowhere to trail me, while Meixelsperger's declaration zinged about in my skull like a trapped bullet. *The underground shapes the overground.* Von Lüth's promises to me, once as bounteous as his fruit baskets, had developed worms, and I felt toward him as I had my first friend, Giuseppe Fratelli, after he'd hijacked my Black Hand spoils in 1893. Was von Lüth's operation to bring me before Hitler a blitz-krieg or a sitzkrieg?

Before I could ambush and accost him, he paraded inside at ten that night with a piece of mail held before him as if it were a flapping falcon. His shock was such that he didn't notice my leopard spots of filth and zebra stripes of rust, and his voice, when he dared use it, was the affectless monotone of my shelter mates when they'd crawled from our blasted hole.

"This came while I was away," said he. "From Reichsführer-SS Himmler."

There went my best derisions. He'd reached into my lungs and thieved them.

Von Lüth shuffled forward, clutched the corner of the comforting counter, and contemplated the missive he'd stuffed wrongwise into its envelope.

"He . . . Oh, Herr Finch! He will grant my request! And he will do so during a visit to Schloss Wewelsburg!"

My regret at having misjudged von Lüth's intentions was quickly replaced by a cold thrill. Stand down, Mr. Rigby and Frau Meixelsperger. At last, it was happening.

"'*Schloss*.'" I thought I knew the word. "You're meeting him at a farm?"

Von Lüth brayed laughter—too loudly and too much of it.

"Herr Finch, you are a jewel! '*Schloss*' is 'castle'! Schloss Wewelsburg—

83

the brain, heart, and soul of the SS, a shrine to our Aryan past, and the foundry where we will forge the future. Schloss Wewelsburg? The honor, it is indescribable! And it is not *I* who will travel there. It is *we*, Herr Finch, in partnership. As the Americans say, you will be my trump card, the proof that I am Europe's leading intimate of the occult. An audience with der Führer will follow, I guarantee it!"

Quickened though I was by the news, von Lüth's stunned reaction to his own success troubled me, and the intervening weeks found him distracted, snappish, and unable to eat the smoked meats and candies brought by the postman. Instead he nibbled on the blandest of breads before enduring long sessions in the commode. My mission notwithstanding, I cared; I brought him glasses of warmed milk and laid out books that, by their folded pages, I judged to be past sources of comfort. He saw what I was doing, forced smiles, and did his best to partake.

The stomach upset had not quit, and the swaying of our train did little to correct it. Von Lüth's one defense was to redirect his excreta through his lips, a forceful stream of minutiae regarding the history of Schloss Wewelsburg, former stronghold of the soldier-bishops of Paderborn (whoever they were), who fought the Battle of Teutoburger-wald (whatever that was) under the great German warrior Arminius (whoever that was), thereby halting the Roman invasion into the Fatherland.

The houses in the village bowed before the castle, which lorded from a hill of neon verdancy. It was only at the foot of the hill that von Lüth paused his chatter, kneeling and bringing to his nose a handful of dirt. He inhaled, smacked at the mud it made in his sinuses, and sighed.

"May all of Europe soon smell so sweet."

Cavaliers like von Lüth knew how to broker an automobile, but as a *völkisch* scholar he would not hear of it. Listen to the trilling of the birds, the rattle of underbrush scuttlers! Here was the woodland his rooftop only mimicked. The grade was steep, but again the genial giant impressed with his starch and sinew, never wheezing as he praised Himmler's humble origins as a chicken farmer, as well as his not-as-humble belief that he was the reincarnation of King Heinrich I. Von Lüth howled at my unfamiliarity with this German patriarch, and punished me with a lecture on how Heinrich's battle against the Slavs and Franks had set historical precedent for Hitler's two-front war.

Schloss Wewelsburg was more imposing when seen from its outer gates. The castle was triangular to match the hilltop wedge upon which it sat. The northmost of the three towers jutted over the Westphalian plain and River Alme like the bowsprit of a battleship, and slotted into the white-bricked hull were a hundred black windows. It was a fortress in the middle of nowhere—anything at all could be happening inside, and that, I think you will agree, was worrisome.

Up ahead was the obligatory checkpoint. Von Lüth took an emboldening breath and marched. Four black-helmeted sentries noticed us and began heading our way. No ceremonial sabers here; each soldier double-fisted a rifle five feet in length if you counted the filed bayonet—and I, for one, was inclined to count every inch. Von Lüth halted fifty feet away, turned to me, pulled sharp the wide lapels of my double-breasted overcoat, and tightened my wool tie. I was a mannequin for his own insecurities, and did not mind.

"Himmler speaks limited English." Von Lüth's voice was soft but firm. "You are here as my guest, a foreign delegate. There should be no reason for you to speak. Only when appropriate will I reveal what you are. Do you understand?"

An old voice whispered through the grass.

Indicate that you understand.

But this goliath touched me gently, adjusting my trilby to a more deferential angle and giving heartening pats to both of my shoulders. His eyes gleamed with more than trust; it was, I knew, true fondness. Johnny, Church, and John Quincy notwithstanding, fellowship still astonished me. It was all I could do not to bury my cold face in his warm layers of fancified clothing.

I nodded assent.

Von Lüth charged off to meet the guards, and with effusive cordiality confirmed his appointment. We were saluted and directed inside the outer wall toward an entryway, before which waited another sentry. But before we halved the distance, from beneath the curved archway a figure sauntered, clad in black leather and knee-high jackboots that winked in the direct sun. Von Lüth inhaled sharply.

"Wewelsburg will one day be the Reich's Vatican," whispered he. "Here comes its future pope."

X.

IKE A HORSE GIVEN THE crop, von Lüth shifted from trot to gallop. His arm was already outstretched in a *sieg heil,* and from the distance at which I'd been left, I saw the Reichsführer-SS acknowledge the jouncing salute with the hand-to-ear gesture of Nazi elite. One second later, von Lüth was pumping the man's hand as if it might spew well water. Sunlight blazing from the superior's lenses prevented me from reading his physiognomy, but nevertheless I cringed. *Dignity, von Lüth, dignity.*

It was surreal to see one of Rigby's nettlesome photo flashcards transmogrified into living flesh. Even when I fired off the Hitler Hand, Heinrich Himmler did not deign to look at me. Instead he nurtured a squiggly inchworm smile through von Lüth's adoring assailment. I was grateful, for I required time to reconcile Himmler's fearsome notoriety with this small, sapless sniveler.

The thick leather coat was further heavied with armbands, sleevebands, cuff titles, chevrons, collar tabs, and shoulderboards, and the triangle gap above the double-buttoned collar betrayed the further weights of braided silver epaulettes, bronze medals, and a red swastika pinned upon a black tie. These garlands emphasized the slightness of the man tucked inside. He wore not spectacles but a pince-nez. His chin melted into his neck, and his brow into a peaked cap. He had a clerk's doughiness—you could see the channels left behind by a helmet strap as well as the ingrown, infected stubble.

If this man was the rebirth of King Heinrich, I was George Washington.

When emptied of adulation, von Lüth said the words "Zebulon Finch," and Himmler spilled his beetle eyes all over my body: cold shells, tickling feelers. His mustache, thinner and longer than Hitler's barber's whisk, twitched as he extended a limp hand for me to shake. I took it, thrilled to be within claiming distance of Hitler, of Rigby's pride, of self-destruction, of infamy.

Himmler smiled at von Lüth, a spurious little pout, and gestured for us to follow his duck-waddle into a torch-licked antechamber. Von Lüth mopped his face with a handkerchief the instant he was unobserved, and I could not help but make a derogatory analogy: von Lüth was to Himmler what the squat-kicking monkey was to the band-major Hitler Youth.

We arrived at a round foyer aglow from a high encirclement of windows. I'd entered grander arenas in my day—Dr. Leather's great hall, the Hazard sisters' Sweetgum Plantation, Harlem's Cotton Club, San Simeon's Hearst Castle, even Bridey Valentine's mansion. I adored extravagance—I was an American—and yet Schloss Wewelsburg had an undeniable force despite the Spartanism of its painting, sculpture, and banner.

It is my understanding, Reader, that the Reichsführer permitted no photography of the castle interior, and so I doubly regret that I can't much enrich the historical record with details. But I was distracted by von Lüth—perhaps, like a dog, I'd been trained to mirror my master's moods. He was distraught at what he saw, and though he adapted a complaisant smile, his eyes pursued the truths hidden in the stonework's runes, glyphs, and sigils.

Himmler did not detect, or did not care, about his guests' discomfort. He became animated. In a high-pitched, exuberant tone that echoed about and stung the eardrum, he narrated the room's highlights and sighed at golden, floating dust motes as if they were the spirits of forefathers. The modesty of the foyer extended throughout what areas of the castle inside which we were allowed, including more than a dozen "reading rooms," oaken chambers so fulgent with wax that they seemed like stomachs still wet from evisceration. I lingered before each. They had a sedate, timeless quality, and I found that I could picture myself recumbent and smug upon their divans. Wasn't I timeless too?

Even the castle's centerpiece, a 14,500-square-foot dining hall where SS aristocracy convened, constrained its extravagance to a signature piece: a long table chiseled about the perimeter with runes. This was mated with twelve chairs cushioned with red pig-leather and fastened with twelve silver crests, each engraved with the seat-holder's name. Twelve, said von Lüth, was the magical number—twelve zodiac signs, twelve apostles, twelve knights of the Round Table.

Here, too, I could picture myself. Oh, Reader, that undersells it! The longing was visceral. I grieved how I'd yet to earn a single monogrammed chair or piece of castle-specific flatware. Von Lüth translated such nectarous words as "trances" and "séances" and I was winged away by the Arthurian spirit of Crusade, the zest of delinquent learning, the fun drunkenness of overblown ceremony. A yearning for blood, developed over a many-course meal that had included Black Hand drubbings, Leather's meat etiquette, and the U.S. military's sanctioned killing, thickened to a salt mire in my throat. Can't you imagine a ritualistic severed head being passed from one SS officer to the next? Taste the blood dribbling from the neck? Hear the splutter of affirmation between mouthfuls?

I took a facsimile of a deep breath and tried to recall Rigby and Meixelsperger.

Himmler concluded polite preliminaries and gestured toward a winding staircase. Von Lüth, though, cowered before them, sensing disaster at the top. He delayed, asking if we might be escorted below to see something called the *Obergruppenführersaal*, a sacred crypt of sorts, I gathered, built around a pit called the Norbertus Hole. The flatteries with which von Lüth padded the request made it clear that beneath our feet was the unholiest temple of all, a center of unfathomable ritual.

But Himmler was a man experienced at ignoring pleas.

"Nein." He checked his wristwatch and indicated the stairs.

Backs as broad as von Lüth's create a spectacle when slumped. Like a child without supper, he was sent up the stairs, and I caught Himmler smirking at his guest's mjölnir, the pathetic prop, as he saw it, of a presumptuous poseur. Himmler, realized I, had dragged his overeager inferior halfway across Germany for no better reason than to mock him. Von Lüth, true-blue to the last, had no idea, and in his place, I felt the heat of shame.

That heat was scalding by the time we entered the Reichsführer's office, a space so symptomatic of neurosis that it begged for a wildebeest rout. Stacks of state documents were tidied to points, fountain pens were parallel to memoranda edges, and framed photographs were hung with precision. Himmler placed his leather jacket upon a hanger and his cap onto a rack, revealing a saucer of brown hair attached to the back half of his head. He took a seat upon a hand-carved, honey-colored chair graven with runes centered around his own initials. He gestured, and we visitors took less impressive seats.

"May we speak in English for the benefit of Herr Finch?" asked von Lüth.

Himmler shrugged, as if being asked if one might pet his cat.

Von Lüth, the poor dupe, winked at me as if this were progress.

"As you know from my letter, I have completed translations of four ancient texts on the Aryan race that I believe will be of fantastic interest to der Führer. If you might consider—"

"Der Führer," said Himmler, "is most interested now in practicalities. *Mein* Lebensborn program, for example."

His English was far better than I'd been led to expect.

"Of course." Von Lüth swallowed the rest of his plea. To cover the ensuing silence, he offered a translation. "In Old German, '*Lebensborn*' means . . . how might you say it? 'Fountain of Youth'?"

In a grave across the Atlantic, Dr. Leather's corpse rolled over.

"Lebensborn," said Himmler, "enrolls thousands of women of the finest racial heritage and prepares their insemination by SS elite. These, our proud brood mothers, will enjoy twelve maternity centers staffed by the greatest minds in medicine. You see, Herr von Lüth? Here is Aryan theory with real results for our people."

If Meixelsperger had been there, her Mother's Cross would have been at Himmler's pimpled throat.

"Remarkable," said von Lüth. "Still, if I may, wouldn't a truer understanding of our pagan progenitors only enrich such enterprises? My studies into the Irminen—the earliest Aryans, Herr Finch— have led me to solicit authorization for a new dig at the Externsteine rock formations, which I believe will confirm evidence that—"

"*Ja, ja*, the Externsteine. Last May, I traveled there with Wiligut. It did our hearts good. But Wiligut assures me, Herr von Lüth, that no further relics will be uncovered there."

Von Lüth had gone white.

"Wiligut? But . . . he has retired, has he not?"

Himmler's inchworm smile came creeping.

"A man of Wiligut's wisdom never really retires. He is more confident than ever that the Irminsul at Externsteine could be the Yggdrasil."

"*Nein!* Wiligut is mistaken!"

Von Lüth's vehemence was shocking.

Not, however, as shocking as my interjection.

"Yggdrasil," said I. "What is that?"

Von Lüth goggled at me in horror, and Himmler squinted through his pince-nez as if trying to identify a stain. A weight of dread dropped like a hanged man. What in Gød's bad name had made me break my vow of silence? Perhaps I'd heard the word in a lecture from the Barker or in a smidgen of mystical falderal from Leather? Von Lüth grimaced; his difficult job now was to fill the thunderous quiet I'd created.

"Yggdrasil, Herr Finch, is the Tree of Life. Its branches extend to heaven, its roots to every plane of existence. To climb it would be to exist in all worlds at once. It is what you might call a birth canal, but one with infinite openings."

Perhaps the visions I'd had of myself in the Wewelsburg reading rooms, or at the twelve-seat table, or in the cabalistic crypt, had been prophetic. I was here for a reason. The definition of "*Lebensborn*" as "the Fountain of Youth" I'd disregarded as a coincidental link to Leather's endeavors to find such a fountain inside me. But that the Yggdrasil was, in essence, the Uterus of Time, that swirling channel of life and death through which *la silenziosità* led me, was too much to ignore. I'd discounted similarly wild ideas from von Lüth, but the tangibility of Wewelsburg—a place that, by every right, ought to be mythical—made me believe, suddenly and surprisingly, in the equally mythical Yggdrasil. What if the secret to my existence was not a mystery to be unlocked but rather a location to which I might pilgrimage? The idea was thrillingly physical. I could climb the tree. Find the branch, the in-between world, that felt like home. Reenter the uterus, wedge open the cervix, and claw my way back into an egg.

Von Lüth, dismayed at my rapture, turned to Himmler.

"Forgive me, Herr Reichsführer, but Yggdrasil is a fable. Wiligut is mistaken if he—"

"*Mein Lieber* Herr von Lüth." Himmler's inchworm swelled to snake size. "You argue with the same vigor as your fair Otto, don't you? It is darling to observe."

If my protector had been pale before, he now went blue. Rigby had prepared me for neither a "Wiligut" nor an "Otto," but the mention of the latter set von Lüth's lips quivering. Caught as I was in Yggdrasil's branches, the disgrace I might have felt on his behalf a minute earlier did not enflame. Von Lüth's voice slipped back into German and broke into stammers of denial. Himmler, though, was finished. He suppressed a yawn, stood, penguined around the desk, and extended his hand.

Von Lüth considered the palm as if it were cradling one of Rigby's cyanide L-pills. In fact, it was suicide *not* to shake it, and so he did. When Himmler began to retract his flipper, however, von Lüth held it tight and began to yammer while gesturing to me. Ah, here came the disgrace. What von Lüth had intended to be a point-by-point presentation of my fantastic truths tumbled out like a child's discreditable whoppers.

Nazis, though, were unerring in manners. Himmler, having

salvaged his hand, offered it to me. A Death's-Head Ring, an SS honorific of skull and crossbones, rested upon one finger like a swollen knuckle. It was exquisite; I took his hand as if it were made of diamond. He gave my palm a feeble squeeze, the black dots of his eyes magnifying behind pince-nez as they toured points of interest, from the grappling-hook slot not quite concealed by my collar, to the general mottling of my flesh. His eyes traced distances brow to chin, temple to temple, and nostril to nose tip, the same measurements von Lüth had made upon first meeting me.

"Herr von Lüth is right. Your features are excellent. Are they matched, I wonder, by the Nine Virtues of the SS? The first is loyalty. Do you have it?"

If it might bring me to the Yggdrasil, thought I, *oh yes, I could be loyal.*

"I believe so. Yes."

Himmler's smile daggered through pulpous flesh. I sensed a betrayed bristling from von Lüth, but I was transfixed, unreachable.

"Very good. Obedience?"

"Yes."

That word again, when all my life and death, I'd proudly chanted its opposite. What was happening?

"Bravery?"

"Yes."

"Truthfulness?"

"Yes."

"Honesty?"

"Yes."

"Comradeship?"

"Yes."

"Readiness?"

"Yes."

"Diligence?"

"Yes."

"Avoidance of alcohol?"

"Yes."

He abnegated our handshake, his fingertips caressing my palm so that he might luxuriate in the chill.

"Right now, the most racially gifted of Dutchmen and Belgians are being Germanized. Perhaps der Führer, if caught in a good mood, might permit me to Germanize an American. What do you think?"

The Norbertus Hole. Flames slinking across SS leather. A cold corpse warmed.

"*Yes*," breathed I—a bad word used one more time.

Himmler's final question, voiced over von Lüth's asthmatic gasp, moved me the most.

"Your name again?"

I told him with gusto.

"Zebulon Finch," repeated he. He gnashed the words between jaws. "Whether one succeeds or fails, choosing to petition the *Schutz-staffel* has consequences. You will think about it? You will let me know what you decide?"

A cobalt fire engulfed my brain, and the smoke reeked of Rigby's cigarette-smog cellar and Meixelsperger's diesel-exhaust bunker. Operation Weeping Willow was all that tied me to America and, by extension, Merle, Church, and everyone else I'd wronged. My gut, however—that truss of flesh crocheted by cosmetic surgeons—remained my gut, and when a gut senses glistening foods spread upon a table at which waits a name-plated seat, that gut, every time, will growl.

XI.

ON THE NIGHT TRAIN BACK to Berlin, the play-act of sleep provided good pretext for sulking. We disembarked at dawn and trudged through mouse-colored rain to von Lüth's building. Once inside, he did not change into dry clothes or pull from a gift basket a piece of breakfast, but rather unfolded the ceiling door and continued to the roof. Hateful of precipitation as ever, I scrounged about the disheveled apartment for the umbrella before making the ascent.

The first things I saw were the jellyfish carcasses of clothing discarded in the mud. It followed, then, that the second thing I saw was von Lüth naked but for his underpants, 250 pounds balanced upon a single leg atop a gentle hill, his opposite calf bent perpendicular behind, both arms held forth at a forty-five-degree angle, and his eyes shut. He held this peculiar pose as raindrops exploded across his putty skin.

The rain tasted of Berlin; that is to say, it tasted of ash.

Von Lüth spoke a single word—*Mannaz*—and shifted to a second pose, standing tall with elbows high and wrists crossed behind his head. By the third pose—*Jera*—I recognized the names of runes; the postures appeared to be a sort of runic yoga. I huddled beneath a tree to wait out the absurd routine. When I leaned against the tree, however, it began to yaw. I hopped back to watch its thick brown roots rip from two feet of black soil. Far too shallow, realized I, to sustain any living thing for long.

In fact, the entire rooftop thicket I'd once considered a wellspring of life was revealed by the gutting rain to be closer to Leather's putrefying People Garden. Every tree pitched at an irregular angle. Bushes, gusted free, flaunted their mud-clotted roots at Gød. The creek, ersatz to begin with, had flooded and eroded to betray its plastic lining. The bloated remains of books and notes were being dragged away by water-beaded vermin—not the "diligent little squirrels" or "friendly badgers" of von Lüth's fancy but rather long, sleek rats.

It was, in sum, a shitty place to be, and a fitting metaphor for von Lüth himself—the fertile soil of scholarship rinsed away to reveal a cracked foundation. Von Lüth completed his yoga with an impressive *Uruz*, indulged in several minutes of uniform breathing, and then, as if by magic, plucked from the mud a boggy book by his idol Jörg Lanz. He opened it to a random page, wrung it of dirty water, and in a pellucid tone read aloud over the pounding rain.

"'Our bodies are scurfy despite all soaps, and are udumized, pagatized, and baziatized. The life of man has never been so miserable as today in spite of all technical achievements. Demonic man-beasts oppress us from above, slaughtering without conscience millions of people in murderous wars waged for their own personal gain. Wild beast-men shake the pillars of culture from below. Why do you seek a hell in the next world? Is not the hell in which we live and which burns inside us sufficiently dreadful?'"

Lanz, that old baffler, was lucid at last. The man-beasts from above, the beast-men from below? Why, Allied air and ground forces, of course. But also Germany's own Luftwaffe and *Wehrmacht*, for they too set firestorms to the natural world so cherished by *völkisch* ideologues.

Von Lüth flung aside the Lanz; it macheted into the loam. He stumbled from the hill, ankle-deep in mud and rid of yogic balance. He considered the discarded clothing at his feet, picked from it the mjölnir, and examined it. With a strangled cry, he swung the hammer at a defenseless sapling. A branch cracked open, revealing fresh white wood. Another cry, another blow, and the branch ripped free. The tree was young and resilient, but von Lüth kept bashing, buttocks jiggling from effort. Soon his victim was an atrocity, all shoulders, no arms, like the shape of Germany itself.

Von Lüth swiveled toward me. Rain drained from his pale lips.

"In June 1942, Himmler sends a surgeon saboteur to murder his rival, Reinhard Heydrich, on the operating table. Is this proper German behavior? It is not. Bormann, Hitler's secretary, forces his wife into a ménage à trois with an unclean mistress. This, too, is not German behavior! Göring and Goebbels, National Socialists of highest rank, each day steal millions from the Reich to buy bigger homes and prettier paintings, while the common burgher starves on the street. Not German behavior! *Not German behavior!*"

He hurled the mjölnir across the roof. Weeds swallowed it. His ragged cry made me cringe.

"Wrong, wrong, all is wrong! Himmler, professed connoisseur of the occult, does not even know the name 'Zebulon Finch'? And this Wiligut he adores? This Karl Maria Wiligut? A senile who twists the texts of List and Lanz in order to present himself as a mystic! He claims that his royal crown awaits him in the palace in Goslar, his sword in a grave at Steinamanger. Ravings! He should be expelled from Wewelsburg! But will Himmler listen to me? Will he read the documents I gathered regarding Wiligut's years in a Salzburg asylum, diagnosed with megalomaniacal delusions? One begins to wonder, Herr Finch, who exactly is in control of the Party and in what direction they are taking it."

Von Lüth's cloudburst of truths were every bit as sad and sodden as his rooftop library. Operation Weeping Willow—what a suitable name! It was as weak as a willow branch, and all involved in it ought to weep. Von Lüth had told me that *der Führer opens new offices like ordinary men open canned meats*, but if a Minister of the Occult office was being prepared, clearly the name on the door would be "Wiligut." Von Lüth had overemphasized, if not outright lied about, his influence in the Reich. Five long months, Dearest Reader, of timid wayfaring about an oppugnant country, and I was no closer to Hitler than when I'd dropped from a plane into unspecified farmland.

I javelined the umbrella, hoping it might spear a rat, and dropped my ass into the ooze. The pulsing hiss of rain covered the squish of footsteps until a pair of naked, muddied kneecaps met me at eye level. Von Lüth lowered his underweared bottom to sit alongside me. The wet ground quaked and the tree above us listed closer to collapse. He noticed neither; his back was hunched like that of an inconsolable boy, and his voice squeaked in kind.

"Year after year I devote myself to SS research, and has membership ever been extended to me, as it has been to you? Even once? Why, Herr Finch, why does no one in the Party like me?"

By now, Futuristic Reader, you have witnessed enough of my world to know the answer to that. Every clique abides one rube whose longing to belong wins him only ridicule—recall, if you will, how I'd willingly stabbed myself at dinner parties for the cheap thrills of Hollywood gadabouts.

Von Lüth sighed at my silence. Water ran down his big white back.

"Have I disappointed you that much?"

My every wound, filled with water, began to boil. Though I'd been moved time and again by his brotherhood, he'd embarrassed himself before Himmler, and by extension embarrassed me, and the flames of that humiliation caught, sucked oxygen, and burned brightly.

"*Ja! Ja! Ja!*" cried I. "Do I say this in a language you understand? My nature rebels at tiptoeing about, meek as a doe, waiting for an acorn of fortune to drop before me! How tired am I of being silent— it scrapes at me like sandpaper! At first I thought, *Zebulon, old boy, what good luck that this von Lüth chap has found you!* Now I know the opposite is true. When I am quite finished shouting, I shall leave this ridiculous roof once and forever more, rip up the *Ahnenpass* that has become my damned leash, exit this fleabag flophouse, sock your puppy Kuppisch in the muzzle, get arrested, and finagle my own way to Hitler—as was the plan before you charged into my death and ruined it!"

Von Lüth gazed wistfully across adjacent rooftops, from which silver fairies of rain did their jetés.

"You wish to shout? Then shout, Herr Finch. Shout loudly—for I have misled you. My excuse is a poor one. I was certain that with you by my side this time would be different."

"Different from what? Some previous episode of groveling?"

Von Lüth shrugged miserably. A thin coat of water slid down his face, as slow as icing from one of Meixelsperger's cakes.

"Men of power do not respond to begging," said he. "It disgusts them. It has taken me too long to learn this. But der Führer and I are one in spirit; about this I have not misled. Some ten years ago, I attended a dinner at the Berghof, a chalet Hitler keeps in the Bavarian Alps. It is true, I was there as a guest of Eva Braun; more specifically, a cousin of Fräulein Braun's with a superficial interest in pagan studies. *Ach*, it does not matter. What matters is that my presence there was no accident, just as it was no accident that I found you."

"My death is an overlong accident. Sound and fury, sound and fury."

"Once you accept the concept of fate, Herr Finch, accidents are impossible. Can I confess to you a secret? I was uncertain about Hitler at first. He spent that afternoon engaged in long dialogues with Blondi, a German shepherd dog he adored beyond seemliness. After dinner, the Great Hall was remade into a theater and Hitler oversaw further foolishness: Hollywood pictures. Forbidden in Germany, but Hitler is nevertheless fond of them. He was visibly moved by a picture directed by a Russian émigré named Chernoff and starring the American actress Bridey Valentine."

I laughed once into the sky, filling my mouth with rain. If anyone could pull a drool of desire from the wolf of Europe, it was Bridey. Perhaps von Lüth was right. There were no accidents.

"Guests began retiring to bed after the picture, but Hitler held court deep into the night. Music, architecture, automobiles. The malignities of smoking, the perks of vegetarianism. Subject matter so trivial that I began to see them as barbed wire strung before a trench. To know Hitler, you had to outlast Hitler, and so I made that my objective. At four in the morning, when I became his final congregant, he stopped speaking and requested that I—Udo Christof von Lüth, a man of trifling consequence—say what I had been waiting to say. You see? I had passed the test."

Von Lüth's cheeks rounded into glad, glistening bulbs.

"I know Hitler is dreadfully serious in newsreels. If only you could see him after a long night of relaxation! He can be quite silly, hanging his legs over his chair like an orangutan. For three hours, Herr Finch, the future world leader was spellbound by what I said. With kaleidoscopic color I painted a vision of a Germanic future shaped by a Germanic past. And Hitler! *Mein Führer!* His enthusiasm, the initiatives of architecture and culture he promised to me, were breathtaking! Early risers woke to find that he and I were locked in concord, in amity, in affinity. Word spread, and from the bedrock of that single conversation have I built my career. This is why the gift baskets all these years later, the salutes, the deference."

"He promised you something, did he? And did not deliver? Now we both know how that feels."

"'The Party needs you.' He said that; I will never forget it. 'Speak to Himmler. Himmler will set the appointment.' Was I wrong to take heart? Even now, I know that Hitler waits for me. But Himmler? Himmler is jealous. I am forced to wait for him to change his mind, which, I see now, will never happen. Why would he? He is the one with the castle. The armored train. The millions in stolen currency. And I? I have this, as you say, fleabag flophouse. Instead of the Externsteine, I possess these pebbles. What good has adherence to *völkisch* thought done me? Oh, Otto, *mein* Otto, Himmler was right—I follow your footsteps always!"

He planted his face into his muddy hands and sobbed. His back quaked, and the leaves and sticks slicked to his skin skittered. I would not feel empathy for this equivocating fabulist; I convinced myself that his demonstration was deplorable.

"This Otto is an irritant," snapped I. "Define him, or delete him from further mention."

Von Lüth's moan was muffled behind palms.

"It is an unjust, underhand world where Otto Rahn's name goes unknown. He was an archeologist, Herr Finch, the most brilliant in the history of Germany, if not the world, and the finest years of my life, the finest by far, were spent as his assistant. I took both his notes and photographs as he traveled the globe, under Party sponsorship, to seek out mankind's greatest treasures. The Golden Fleece, the Ark of the Covenant, the Holy Grail itself. If you have not heard of Otto Rahn, surely you have heard of these!"

"Even creatures like I am read fairy tales. The Grail, some stupid cup."

Von Lüth had shed his clothing like a snake sheds its skin, and now his spine hiccupped like a snake swallowing an egg.

"Romans and Jews shaped that misinterpretation. The Grail is no cup. It held no drink for apostles; it caught no blood from the crucified Jesus. Why do Americans insist on connecting everything to Jesus?"

"I am no stooge of Gød, much less his deadbeat son."

"To the contrary, Herr Finch, you are hostile to Gød! I understand; I, too, was once young and angry. But Otto showed me a better way. He was patient with believers. It was in Montségur, I believe, where Otto removed from the wall of our sleeping chamber— tenderly, tenderly!—a tawdry illustration of a bleeding Jesus and in its place hung a card upon which he'd calligraphed a beautiful verse by Wolfram von Eschenbach. It extolled not a mortal man's gruesome death but the illuminative life revealed to all men by Lucifer."

"Here we sit, sinking in mud. Fitting we stumble across Satan."

"Lucifer and Satan are not the same! Again, blame papists and Jews for the jumbling—you, Herr Finch, know what it is like to be made a scapegoat, do you not? Lucifer is the Light Bringer, the keeper of highest spiritual ideals. The Grail, or as Otto called it, more properly, the Grâl, is a stone, a Claugestiân stone, a *lapis exillis*. What Otto knew was that it had fallen from Lucifer's crown. What he tried to discover, with me at his side, was where it had fallen. Is the Grâl at Mount Etna, the fabled Doorway to Hell? Or at the bottom of an anonymous mountain gorge, being worshipped by a tribe of primitives?"

I watched a bank of soil slop into the ruined creek.

"Did your chum Otto find his Grâl? Of course he didn't. Because it is fiction. Your whole life has been wasted chasing fiction. Now we both are mired in place because of it."

"Do not you, of all people, know that searching is of far greater import than finding? The questions one asks define him. Otto and I traveled as humble yeomen but strived every day to be the Grâl knights of lore. They were magical years. We could not move a rock or dig a hole without finding bygone Albigensian symbols or cryptic Manichaean texts. Paris, Pamiers, Iceland—we shared cheese in monastery ruins and laughed in castle courtyards. Many was the night that Otto became exhausted and I, the younger, bore him home upon my breast and arranged him for sleep."

The cozy scene begged for spoof, but I could not muster it. Once upon a time, I'd had Church as that sort of friend, and for years that bond had given me reason to persist. The way von Lüth fawned over Otto Rahn was a step beyond; it brought to mind how I nuzzled the memory of Wilma Sue, an uncomfortable thought I couldn't jettison before von Lüth all but confirmed it.

"There were rumors. That Otto was a homosexual. That our relationship was improper. People say what they will. What is demonstrable is that Otto did not mention my name once in his published diaries. This he did out of love, to protect my reputation from his own. But I was young and stupid. I became upset over the omission. Our discussion grew heated. We parted ways, and eleven months later, *mein* Otto was dead, and I would do anything, Herr Finch, anything at all, to return to those days of wonder, when life's map was held by a man who always knew how to read it."

Church, disfigured, scarred, and limping about a whorehouse in 1929, had made a similar lament, longing for the grueling existence of trench warfare, where a man at least knew his objectives.

Raindrops caught in von Lüth's mustache. Tears, much oilier, razored through.

"State documents called it suicide. Who, I ask you, kills himself by sitting atop a hill in winter until he freezes? Had the Party supported Otto rather than persecute, he would have found every one of those relics you doubt exist, and his status in the Reich would be second only to Hitler. But suicide? It tars a name, and Himmler believes I have yet to scrape that tar from my boots. He is right. The tar glues me, as tar does, to a single spot—right here."

He spread his bare arms as if to pull toward him the whole festering, fulminating forest until he became buried in its piteous two-foot grave. He slid forward, slipping from our muddy mound onto his knees, where, to my dismay, he pivoted to face me. Erased were all memories of the man's dapper suits and straight back. Cascades of water made his naked flesh wobble as if behind screens of flickering heat; it was as if his whole body were crying. His arms remained open and his apologetic whispers, perhaps to his dead friend, or lover, Otto Rahn, broke into a soft plea.

"Help me, Herr Finch. Help me."

How could I resist those arms? The poor man, who'd handled me as kindly as he might a brother of blood, only wished to be handled in kind. As his slick, soiled body slipped toward nadir in the muck, I heard the mutter of Meixelsperger, the closest thing I had left to a moral compass.

The underground shapes the overground.

Von Lüth, fringe scholar, lonesome giant, possible sexual deviant, was the latter. I, flopsy puppet, harmless eunuch, hollow scarecrow, was the former. It would not be the public face of the occult and *völkisch* thought that would instigate the tête-à-tête with Hitler. It had been me, after all, to whom Himmler had posed his direct questions: *You will think about it? You will let me know what you decide?* If I wanted to provoke a follow-up invitation from the Reichsführer-SS, what I had to do was respond. To do that, von Lüth and I would need to repair our fractured friendship—for friendship was indeed what we had built together, if timidly. And so I leaned into those arms, cold with rain, heavy with mud, and was dirtied.

XII.

ORMULATING A RESPONSE TO HIMMLER was the easy part. The next morn, as von Lüth lay in bed clad in pajamas and dried mud, I wrote down details regarding my every supernatural scrape: Dr. Leather's probe into texts of magick and daemonologica and his consultation with psychics; Church's half-cocked yet bewitching Theory of 17; the blunt, bleak insights of la *silenziosità*; the naked fact of my resurrection. In short, everything that von Lüth hadn't said at Wewelsburg, I would say to Himmler, and it would deliver twice the impact for not being filtered through the broken bullhorn of von Lüth.

Von Lüth grimaced upon reading, struggling to accept that he'd become a hindrance. But ridicule and underestimation breeds its own pungent spores of resolve—this I know firsthand. He stood to his full seven-foot height and pulled tight the cuffs of his pajama sleeves. Even a corpse could not rid its gelatin blood of Marine Corps discipline. His posture demanded respect, and I found myself not only standing at attention but also swelling with pride at his rebound. Beneath his pillow-flattened mustache, von Lüth's lips thinned with cunning.

"Himmler will depart Schloss Wewelsburg soon. We cannot rely on *Reichspost* deliverymen. Our message must be sent immediately. And for that job, Herr Finch, you happen to be speaking to the right Nazi."

There was, after all, one place in Berlin where von Lüth commanded real, not imagined, authority. Thirty minutes later we raced through the ravaged city as only drivers like Kuppisch knew how and into the affluent Dahlem neighborhood, where a sumptuous mansion housed the archeological and cultural-history institute for whom von Lüth worked. For this unscheduled trip to the Ahnenerbe, he'd donned yet another magnificent suit, though his cluster of faux-medals was, for once, absent.

His mjölnir, however, he'd freed from rooftop weeds, and it swung from his hand as he charged through the door. Secretaries bid *guten Morgen*, and assistants scurried near with pressing business, but von Lüth dispelled each comer with a single shake of his hammer. I fear you will fault me, Dearest Reader, but I nearly cheered! One day ago a broken man, von Lüth had become a Panzer tank chewing the earth en route to its objective, and I had the pleasure of hanging on to the turret.

Up three flights, down four halls, and through five doors—the last a hidden one popped from a paneled wall—our quest terminated in a cube in which a shirt-sleeved quartet pressed headphones to their ears, tapped at telegraph machines, and labored over charts. They startled at their superior's raucous entry and began to stand in salutation, but it never got that far. Von Lüth brought down the mjölnir upon a plate of pastries. The plate shattered, and custard shot out in a dozen directions, staining several of the workers, but not von Lüth, for he was, in that moment, untouchable.

"Aussteigen! Aussteigen, aussteigen!"

Eyes a-bug, the team scuffled off, though von Lüth held the mjölnir out to halt the last of them. He gestured this man toward a table in the corner. The operator stole a jittery look at the hammer, and took a seat. Von Lüth grinned at the obedience and favored me with a playful look.

"You know of the Enigma machine?"

I shook my head.

"Is this so? Very good. Deutschland keeps a few secrets, even now."

Mephistopheles, it appeared, had designed a typewriter. Enclosed within a wooden box were twenty-six letters on spindles—simple enough, except that these same twenty-six letters were also printed upon small lamps above, while below was a miniature switchboard featuring those twenty-six letters yet again, each one patched into another via black cables. At the head of the device was a series of sharp-toothed interlocked metal dials.

Von Lüth presented the instrument with the same pride with which Leather had once presented his Victor VI Deluxe Model Victrola.

"In the field, the Enigma has been replaced by the Lorenz SZ40, but, alas, in wartime one makes do. The Enigma's hundreds of millions of levels of security will just have to suffice. Stations like this one exist throughout the Reich, each dedicated to coding and decoding dispatches. Messages sent in such a way are never ignored, and I am quite certain Schloss Wewelsburg has one of every model."

The operator did not appear to know English, but his shock at the sharing of secrets was blatant. Von Lüth shrugged.

"I suppose now that you have seen this, Herr Finch," deadpanned he, "we will have to kill you."

The jolly jumbo was bucking a dangerous system and, from what I could tell, having a grand old time doing it. He winked, then set to delivering catechisms to the operator. Outranked, the minion mopped his brow, consulted a key containing the settings for July, and began turning wheels and patching cables. Von Lüth relaxed in a chair and beamed at the two photographs hanging above the Enigma. One was of Adolf Hitler, but the other was of a narrow-faced man with swept-back hair and large, perceptive eyes. I consulted the name plate. It was Otto Rahn, and his equal billing to der Führer was a spit of insurrection—and I'd always admired a good spit.

This was no place for Black Hand poetics. Even after severe truncating, my message took well over an hour to transmit. We were, though, quite lucky. Three days later, RAF firebombing obligated the SS to issue an evacuation order for Ahnenerbe headquarters. Its archive of rare artifacts and texts was packaged and transported to a castle near Ulm, and the staff relocated to a remote Bavarian village. The turmoil of the move likely spared von Lüth from comeuppance for unauthorized Enigma use, though the fact that he made no preparations for Bavaria signaled the end of his affiliation with the Ahnenerbe, which had so long been his major source of pride.

In a mere fortnight—quick for a world whanging away at war—I discovered, tucked into the day's usual brick of correspondence, an envelope addressed to me in care of von Lüth. Quickly I bore it to the roof, where von Lüth had spent the past two weeks occupied not with cerebral labor but rather the physical labor of dismantling his forest. Every tree had been toppled and bush unsocketed so that the landscape of rolling green had been replaced by one of frazzled black roots. Boulders had been corralled like cows along the southern brink, and that is where I found von Lüth sweating and grunting. He grinned at me through a mud-speckled mustache, though that grin faded when I presented to him the letter.

He slit its belly and yanked its guts. The letter was on Wewelsburg letterhead and composed upon a typewriter hubristic enough to include a dedicated key for "SS." He leaned on a shovel and read it aloud. Predicting that von Lüth would be the translator, Himmler had worked into his epistle several sly denigrations. To von Lüth's credit, which, by my count, was growing by the day, he took each shot like a boxer and pushed on to the meat of the matter. Himmler would, in fact, enjoy discussing my future with the SS, should I do him the great favor of meeting him in Linz, Austria, in six days' time.

The stimulation of success was soon snuffed by concern. I was no cartographer (to Rigby's chagrin I habitually transposed Yugoslavia and Romania, Switzerland with Sweden, and don't get me started on Prussia and Russia), but Austria certainly sounded far away. I asked von Lüth how we would get there, but he was lost in thought, gazing into the rolled layers of skimmed turf.

"Linz." He said it with soft awe.

"A city of significance? I'm unfamiliar."

He met my eyes with a gentle blink of affection.

"Linz is the hometown of Hitler."

Von Lüth's smile was patient. He waited for me to understand, which, at length, I did.

"Do you think . . . ?" asked I.

"I do."

"That he's taking me to see . . . ?"

The word "Hitler" was a feather teased between two breezes.

"Linz is a full day's journey," said he.

"Then we should prepare."

The corners of his eyes crinkled.

"Just you, Herr Finch. My dear Herr Finch. This time I cannot join."

I reached for a tree against which to support myself, but they were all gone.

"Alone? With Himmler? I can't possibly—"

The soft tranquility of his voice stopped me.

"I can only damage you with Himmler. We both know this. This is the leg of your journey that you must make unattended."

"But you asked me to help you. I *want* to help you. But how can I if you don't—"

He held up a hand. The creases of his palm were black. There was nothing von Lüth liked better than German soil.

"You have already helped me, Herr Finch, more than you will ever know. Should you gain Hitler's trust and be so moved to endorse me, we will see what happens. For now, it does not matter. I am proud to know you, Zebulon Finch. Proud to have been a part of your quest to prove your allegiance to Hitler. And when der Führer makes you famous, I will buy the newspapers and attend the parades and be prouder still. This, my friend—*this* is German behavior."

How I would have liked to clamber over the boulders so that I might hurl myself from roof's edge! This man, having already quit the job he loved, was willing to throw away his dream to facilitate my goal, which I'd lied about from the start. My mission was not to become a loyal subject to his Führer, but to extract a Smith & Wesson from my chest and fire it into Hitler's own, over and over. Von Lüth's association with me was well documented; should Operation Weeping Willow work, he'd not survive the repercussions.

"I don't know what to say." It was the truth.

"Then say you will be a Grâl knight and will fight for what is worth the fight." He gestured at my dirty clothes. "Somewhere in the rubble of this old town there must remain a tailor with talent. Come, let us find him and offer him some money."

XIII.

UPPISCH DROVE. WE'D HAD OUR difficulties, the bone-breathed slobberer and I, but it was a long ride begun in the lilac of dawn and interrupted by the constant rolling down of windows to *sieg heil* at checkpoints before circumnavigating inevitable Autobahn damage, and I developed a grudging respect for his dogged stoicism. Not once did he growl about the assignment, sigh at bottlenecks, or even tap his claws to the wheel in boredom.

If this was the fortitude of the SS, I needed it. I was anvilled to the backseat with fear; the revolver beneath my ribs had turned into one of von Lüth's rooftop boulders. My distress was justified. Before leaving, I'd swiped one of von Lüth's shaving blades and sunk it into the flesh of my left forearm, where Leather, thirty years ago almost to the day, had punctured me with a serving fork at a most unpalatable dinner party. The plan, hasty though it was, was to use this blade to cut open my stomach when the moment came.

We arrived mid-afternoon at Ottensheim, a village on the Danube five miles north of Linz, a less public spot, perhaps, for a conclave of Nazi elite. The meeting place was another castle, a good deal smaller than Wewelsburg and perched upon a smaller hill. Kuppisch parked the auto and accompanied me into a courtyard where three men in identical SS garb waited. I turned to Kuppisch in alarm, hoping that our outing had indeed made us bosom pals, but the bulldog was already gone; his adieu was the crunch of gravel beneath the tires of von Lüth's Mercedes.

What was it, Dearest Reader, with Nazis and nudity? Again I was ordered to strip. It was evident these soldiers had received forewarning, for they were aloof to my leathery lacerations and degenerative bloat as they ran their weapons search. Still, they did not relish it. Their hands but skimmed over the planted razor and the diaphanous skin of my stomach.

When I was again presentable, they shepherded me through an egress and into a gravel lot, where menaced three long, black automobiles. I had no time to cultivate confusion; an SS man opened the rear door of the center vehicle and shoved me inside. My fingers skidded across soft seat leather and my nose was steeped in the odor of bleach solution, and then the three cars ignitioned, and turned, knocking my skull against the window. It gave me a good rattle, and I squinted to make out my fellow passenger, acres away, it seemed, a very slight person in a very large car.

Heinrich Himmler's abrupt presence was a shock, but seven months in Germany had disciplined me. My arm shot up in a salute, only for it to punch the ceiling. I winced. Was there a modified salute for inside a vehicle? His tittering expression hadn't changed since Wewelsburg. He unlaced his smooth white fingers and waived off my attempts at salute. His Death's-Head Ring streaked like a falling star across the night sky of his coat.

"Forgive the delay, Herr Finch. Always there are protocols. It is enjoyable to see you again."

"Thank you. You as well. Herr Himmler. Reichsführer. Sir."

He overlooked the bumbling.

"How happy I was to receive your message. Coded, even. Herr von Lüth assisted you, *ja?*"

I saw no reason to lie. "Yes."

"Good. Then he has been of use to the Reich. That should bring him peace."

The remark had the cold finality of Otto Rahn freezing upon a hill.

"There was much in your message to titillate," continued he. "Above all I am curious about this 'Theory of 17.' You will tell me about it."

Of all the mystic mumbo-jumbo I'd run through the Enigma, Church's 1918 theorem, improvised behind the Belleau Wood battle line, was the most easily debunked.

"There is little to say. The idea, I suppose, was that I was here on Earth to save as many lives as I'd taken. At the time, the number was seventeen."

"In order for what to occur?"

"I'm not sure. For my debt to be paid?"

"Debt to whom?"

The answer was gullibility itself. Embarrassed, I stared at the driver's head.

"Gød," murmured I.

"Very good. And how many people have you killed now?"

Rare was the human who could be so offhand with the question. Our caravan had gained speed enough now to indicate that we weren't stopping soon. The question, therefore, could not be dodged. I stared harder at the driver's curled nape of blond hair and operated the abhorrent abacus. How many of Himmler's countrymen had I taken by bullet and bayonet to rescue Church on Armistice Eve?

I'd never wished to count, but it had to have been at least ten—if I was being honest, fifteen. Should I count the flappers who had fallen to the Bird Hunter's vivisections? Were their murders not mine to shoulder? And what percentage of responsibility had I in the death of Leather himself? Or that of wife Mary and daughter Gladys? More quantifiable was the slaughter I'd brought to the drug den of Watts, California, in order to disentangle Merle. Last, of course, there was Margeaux in the Yankee Doodle roadster; that death, the worst one, could be attributed to none other.

"Do not be sheepish," spurred Himmler. "An estimate."

I rushed it out: "Fifty."

"That is your closest guess? Estimate high."

"Fifty-one." My, how that last one stung.

Himmler nodded as if a long-held prediction had come about. I felt lightheaded; how was it that I'd been so swiftly destabilized? I gripped the automobile door, wondering if I might yet throw it open and take my chances spilling across the racing road.

"So." Himmler adopted the flavorless tone of a regaling host. "Do you intend to vacation with us a while longer?"

His smile was the joke. There was no path out of Deutschland.

"Forever," said I.

This was, as determined by Rigby, the right response, though a harrowing one when uttered by a fellow of my deathless plight. I told myself that *forever* might not be so long after all. The hour of the blade, the minute of the gun, and the second of the bullet were close. I looked out the window. Our caravan had left Ottensheim behind. Classic misdirection, surmised I. Hitler awaited us in Linz.

"The notion of forever is interesting," mused Himmler. "What else is my breeding program but an attempt, a very modest one, to allow the

Germans of yesterday to live forever inside the Germans of tomorrow? I have done research on you, Herr Finch. You are bounds ahead of the *Lebensborn*. You lived a generation before; you live now; in future generations, you will live still. It is as if you perch upon the axis of the Yggdrasil, feet on the lower limbs but hands upon the crown."

I looked at Heinrich Himmler then, Reader; you bet I did. His coy expression suggested that he was well aware of the seed he'd planted in his office, and he wished to see if it had flowered. It had; ne'er a night had passed since Wewelsburg that I hadn't tossed about his conviction that, given time, the Nazis might find the Tree of Life. Now, his tantalizing implication was that there was no first climber more qualified than I.

Was it worth swearing allegiance to an enemy if it meant at last solving my own mysteries? We were at the outskirts of Linz; mere minutes remained to consider futures other than that of assassin. I pictured myself as leading *Hitlerjugend* in a smart cap, silver belt buckle, and baggy-thighed jodhpurs, ordering eager yearlings to polish my boots. I saw my name winking from a dining-hall name-plate at Schloss Wewelsburg and heard my own Death's-Head Ring tapping against the glossy armrests of an SS reading room. A single crumb of this fantasy was richer than a lifetime of grubbings from Rigby and Meixelsperger.

Forever did not have to be a prison sentence. It could be a reign.

From the peak of a hill we coasted into the charming hamlet of Linz. I looked across the blue Danube and bluer Oberösterreich mountains and imagined that I felt the same as lederhosened Adolf had when growing up in the environs, that there were great, wide worlds beyond those imagined by simple villagers. Himmler sighed at the grandeur.

117

"I am certain Herr von Lüth has told you how he chased his Otto all over the world. I am also certain he gave you his favorite precept about how the search for the Grâl is more important than finding it. Only a great failure would believe such a thing. Only a man who politely asks for power when he should be wresting it. Did Herr von Lüth describe the purported power of the Grâl?"

We shot through Linz without stopping, and I did not care.

"No," said I.

Leather creaked as Himmler gestured at the golden countryside.

"The right of rule. Irreducible sovereignty. It would be a more powerful birthright than even those we already possess. The point I wish to make, Herr Finch, is that you yourself are a birthright, lost for ages, but after much travel and tribulation, delivered home, where you began and where you belong."

His smile elongated ever so slightly.

"We don't need the Grâl," said he, "because you *are* a Grâl."

The scythes of sun slicing through treetops would have blinded the ordinary man. I, however, was Zebulon Finch, and had no cause to shield my eyes from even the brightest of beacons.

"This number you give me—this fifty-one? It indicates you have the aspiration demanded from the SS. The question to be answered is if you are fully prepared to assume the responsibilities of the Third Reich. Or the Fourth Reich, if it comes to that, or the Fifth, or the Sixth. You will forgive me, I hope, if I use our meeting today to institute a test, a small one, to evaluate your acceptance of your Aryan destiny."

Gravity slung me forward. Our auto was slowing. I leaned aside, peered through the windshield, and saw, looming above the lead car, a twenty-foot brickwork archway topped with an iron eagle of

118

fifteen-foot wingspan clutching a wreathed swastika. The structure to which the eagle was connected had the dusty, hewn-edged feel of a factory site. This was not the sort of place one would find Hitler. The razor blade in my forearm turned to an icicle. Von Lüth and I had misjudged the purpose of this meeting.

"We are here." Himmler rubbed together his ladylike hands. The skull upon the Death's-Head Ring rolled to the side and leered. "I think you will find this interesting, Herr Finch. This is what we call a *Konzentrationslager*—a concentration camp."

XIV.

TO BE SPECIFIC, AND I think that we should be, the camp was called Mauthausen. We parked outside of a nondescript wall, and our three vehicles spat their sputum: twelve SS officers and bodyguards, Himmler, and me. A roiling nucleus of discombobulated camp bureaucrats assembled before us, elbows twitching in eagerness to volley salutes over the Reichsführer's head.

Introductions bandied for ten minutes. I shook hands chapped, clammy, smooth, and calloused, each of them ringed. I caught the names of the two primary figures, a shifty-eyed camp commandant called Ziereis and a cruel-lipped brute called Bachmayer, the latter of whom held at bay two gleeful, galumphing German shepherds. I'd always disliked dogs, but I had to hand it to the beasts—they were the only ones who didn't offer the Reichsführer their pink bellies.

Our party was guided through a series of locked gates. It was slow going; I examined the top levels of fencing. Medieval spikes long enough to stick a man groin-to-gullet rose from among needles so fine the Defier of Death the Astonishing Mr. Stick shuddered. Machine guns lurked like dragons inside watchtowers, implying a history of escape attempts. I could not make sense of it. A camp, even one inside which inhabitants were concentrated, was surely a school of sorts, and though I agreed that school was no fun at all, it was hardly worth hurling oneself against razored, electrified fences.

Before leading us into the courtyard, Ziereis offered a few private words to Himmler. His apologetic tone indicated that it was an especially hectic day for a surprise inspection—though still, of course, the greatest of honors and rarest of pleasures!

Perhaps because the sight was so difficult to believe, I tried instead to believe the noises. This was a lumberyard, and the clacking was blocks of wood against opposite blocks. It was, however, bone to bone: knobby elbows knocking against other elbows; ball-and-socket shoulders rattling against those of brother huddlers; swollen knees cracking like billiard balls, one to the next, a skittering chain reaction across a pocketless table. There were cries as well, sobs, shouts, and arguments, but they were as listless as smoke.

The courtyard was thronged with naked men, hundreds of them, even in their indecent multitudes too weak to defy their captors. Narrow-waisted and flared-hipped, the men resembled lithe women in winter vests, except that the vests were their own ribcages, large and overhanging concave abdomens. Their nipples were apple seeds, their genitals stems, their buttocks a T-bone chewed of meat. The fortunate ones leaned against a wall painted with the slogan *Arbeit Macht Frei*, while the unluckier plodded about on flat feet, twig-arms outstretched against crowd currents that might take their rickety skeletons to the dirt.

I was pale; they were paleness.

I was bony; they were bones.

I was deadish; they were dead.

I made the first motion of a lunge toward the wall, but Himmler had me by the arm and guided me, firmly but gently, so that I might keep apace as our group parted the charnel horde. Guards maintained a ten-foot lee between us and the rabble; it was our casual ambling, I saw, that generated the tidal ebbs that sent bone against bone. Ziereis pointed at underfoot excrement and described the process of *Desinfektion*, a bit overdue, or so I gathered, due to the recent high influx of prisoners.

Oh, Reader, my callow credulity! Why, wondered I, were these men so skinny? Had the Reich hidden from its public a consumptive plague? If so, why were Nazi officers allowed to share the malignant air? Himmler, though, was untroubled. He posed polite questions and nodded at the replies. Because the words resembled English, I understood Ziereis as he proudly listed upon fingers the diverse origins of his inmates: Holland, Hungary, Italy, Poland, Russia.

We took his word for it. Skeletons all look the same.

The liced and typhous masses discharged a sour stench that had several of our party pressing handkerchiefs to their faces. Ziereis conceded the odor and gestured toward an archway. As we moved, a horse-drawn cart filled with potatoes began to creak through the courtyard. The starved fell upon it, eyeballs popping, fingers clawing, jaws gnashing. I hurried through the arch, was dipped into shadow, and was glad to have my screaming eyes rinsed clean of this vision of a scrabbling, gibbering hell, worse than any nightmared by Bosch or Goya.

Shimmering sunlight, goofball in its gaiety, paved our passage into a quieter industrial villa: roadways, sidewalks, brick outbuildings, chugging smoke stacks, and rows of barracks painted a mild green and accented with flower beds. Prisoners were visible down the road marching in lines but were, to my great relief, draped in striped livery that concealed any physical unnaturalities.

Bachmayer, or more accurately his German shepherds, took the lead. We strolled down the lane, and then, to indulge the straining canines, cut across a field of blowing grass. It was a long walk but a gem of an afternoon, and these Nazi officials were, after all, good Aryans, and delighted in the *völkisch* pleasures of watching a rabbit dart through the heather and a hawk circle overhead.

The chatter became carefree. Himmler showed Ziereis a photograph of a pigtailed little girl, and Ziereis, at Himmler's encouragement, displayed the germinal fruits of English lessons.

"Will I watch you in Berlin, Reichsführer . . . at *zwei*—at two mornings—"

"Will I *see* you *in* two mornings," corrected Himmler. "Very, very good."

". . . when der Führer will initiate the new zeppelin?"

"*Inaugurate*," corrected Himmler. "Your English is coming along splendidly. But *nein*. I have other plans that must take precedence."

Several more sentences were swapped before they switched back into German, Ziereis perspiring in relief, but I'd heard enough to send my ego a-spinning. Did Himmler's "other plans" revolve around me? Forget that swarm of filthy scroungers; these high-rankers could be my colleagues. I observed the swagger of a stupendous cypress and wondered if it might be the Yggdrasil, right there, planted before me for my Aryan convenience.

At length we reached the crest of what I would identify, years after the fact, as Wienergraben Quarry, a tiered canyon dug 150 feet into the hillside. Trunk-sized blocks of granite cut from the stratiform terrain were lowered with rope and pulley, and then, to my disbelief, strapped to prisoner backs. That their brittled spines did not snap was one marvel; another was the two hundred stone steps they had to climb to reach the hill upon which we stood. Some collapsed to their knees beneath their loads, causing the next in line to fall, then the next, and the next.

More rabbits, thought I, darting from predator hawks.

Bachmayer chuckled at the slapstick. His dogs woofed froth as survivors of the climb began shuffling past us. Beneath loads of granite, their shirts had purpled with blood. In some cases, the blood had soaked the identifying icons sewn upon their shirts: yellow stars, brown triangles, red circles, and tragic combinations. Just frequent enough to be noticed were the pink triangles indicating alleged homosexuals. I thought of Otto Rahn—no, to hell with Rahn. I thought of von Lüth. He, no friend of Himmler, might one day find his sensational suits swapped for soiled stripes, his grizzly size winning him the heaviest cuts of rock.

If I chose hawk, would that make von Lüth the rabbit?

The remainder of the inspection I recall only through objects. Tedious ledgers filled with names, half of them struck. Wooden beams gnawed by rope burns. Examination tables grooved with drains. When the sun began to impale itself with treetops, Himmler and his posse were offered water, and they paused outside of a garbage depot to drink it. It took my distraught brain five minutes to notice the homogeneity of the refuse. Dunes of shoes. Mesas of clothing. Crags of spectacles. A promontory of gold teeth.

"Herr Finch." His voice at my shoulder. "Are you ready?"

It took ten or twenty years, nothing to Zebulon Finch, to turn toward the Reichsführer-SS. Beside him, Ziereis was gesturing at a brick building that was flat, long, and pale of paint, with mold streaking from iron-barred windows like acid tears. It was as still as a crocodile. I could lie about anything, anything in the world, thought I, except this.

"I am not ready. No, I am not."

Himmler smiled with parental patience.

"Would you turn away? Like Solomon from Gød?" He indicated the sidewalk. "The guards call this the Road to Heaven. Does that not inspire you? Remind you of Christ, suffering the whips of Pilate, carrying the cross that was both his death and life?"

My eyes traced the Road to Heaven to the building. Quiet as a church, thick as a hymnal. If I prayed to Him, would He appear?

"Gød?" My voice broke; I was a child, back in a pew with Abigail Finch. "Jesus?"

Himmler, close enough to embrace, whispered.

"There is a bunker in Nürnberg. You do not know of it because Udo von Lüth does not know of it. It is insulated, waterproof. Reinforced against firebombing. Inside are the reclaimed treasures of the First Reich, including the Holy Lance, the spear of the blind Roman Longinus, who stabbed Jesus on his cross to ensure that he was dead. Jesus's blood flowed and cured Longinus's vision; thus Longinus, an Aryan, became the first Christian. The apostles, too, were not Jews but Gentiles; the story that Aryan tribes were exiled from Israelite settlements is false. Mary and Joseph, themselves descendants of King Herod's Aryan cavalrymen, beget a son, he too an Aryan, named Jesus."

Now Himmler did touch me, a gentle hand to my shoulder.

"So please, call to Jesus if you'd like, for he is your brother. If you prefer, call to his torturers, for they are your aunts and your uncles. Your family is all around you. Perhaps this is difficult to believe for one who has been alone for so long. But who, I ask you, feels the most alone? Kings, Herr Finch. Do you wish to be a king? It is said that whoever holds the Holy Lance holds the destiny of mankind. Constantine held it; Charlemagne held it; Hitler holds it. Count Ferdinand used to dip the lance in wine so that he could drink the blood of Christ."

Jesus, Gød, Aryan, Jew—I had no use for any of them. But to feel blood in my body again, any blood at all?

My back hitched, though I had no tears to cry.

Down the Road to Heaven we glided. We entered the building, shooed from a door window two ogling SS, and peered through the glass. Inside was a mob of perhaps 150 naked prisoners even less capable than the quarrymen. They were old. Or young. Or crippled. Or lesioned. Some blinked at the nozzles attached to pipe traceries as if expecting a cold shower blast, while others crouched as if expecting a punch, urine spattering to cement and streaking to meet other furious streams.

We'd seen two soldiers on the roof. They wore gas masks and carried canisters of what Ziereis had called Zyklon B. Once dropped into compartments, the chemical would fill the room with cyanide. There was a Henry Ford precision to how each Nazi fulfilled his role, and I waited for the punctual drop, the expedient cloud, the prompt panic.

But then, a curious thing. Himmler beckoned a guard, who produced a key ring and undid the lock. I braced for the hinges to shriek, but the door rolled aside like vapor. Neither was the shower room loud; a shush of prayers rustled at us like autumn leaves. As in the courtyard and quarry, the bodies inside were but rough-hewn marionettes. The heads, in comparison, were inflated caricatures, each white eye the gleaming ore of the infinite, each face so taut with starvation that it appeared to grin at its own mined riches.

"Fifty-one," said Himmler. "That was your number."

I detected the smoke I'd seen issuing from Mauthausen chimneys, and at last noticed that it had a peculiar smell, one not altogether different than the *Hitlerjugend* book burning. We were all burned books in the end, realized I, skin of paper, flesh of flame, ideas of ash.

"Choose fifty-one of them," said Himmler, "and I will see that they are deported without harm. We will test your friend's theory. We will see what happens when we even the score."

Dear Gød, thought I, but now I was certain—Gød wasn't here, he'd been afraid to come. There was a revolver in my chest and a razor in my forearm. The former I would never reach in time, but the latter I could. Even so, what would I slice? The throat of this villain? The throats of as many prisoners as possible? Or my own eyes? Yes, that was best. I shut my lids so that I might preview blindness—unlike Longinus, unhealed by Jesus's blood—but even in the dark I saw these Jews, these Communists, these men too strong of principal or too lame of leg.

"Herr von Lüth was right about one thing," Himmler continued. "You will go far in the Reich. But first you must open your eyes. Here is the test I promised. To be Aryan is to be a king of men. A king's job is difficult. Every day, choices. You must begin making them. Hurry, now. Night is upon us."

Fifty-one of 150 was over one third of these people. That was worth something, wasn't it? If I wanted a go at Hitler—and oh, Reader, I did; my wrath roared, for the camps represented an end to humanity that even I, an inhuman, could not stomach—I would need to pick my fifty-one, right now, and without emotion. Who, then, to choose? The eldest, so as to archive their libraries of experience? Or the youngest, hoping for future avengers? Neither plan was any good; I was proof that age had no correlation to goodness. Life rampaged as it would, creating saviors or genocidists with a roll of the dice.

I became neither hawk nor rabbit, but the grass over which they raced.

That did not mean I had grit enough to look Death in the face. I pointed without seeing, said "That one," and when they dragged forth a man like luggage, limbs flopping like stockings caught outside the buckles, and asked for confirmation, I roared, "Yes, yes, that one!" I kept going—*that one, that one, that one*—until Himmler pulled my sleeve to tell me we'd exceeded the number. Still I kept pointing at others who, though not present, needed saving as well: Rigby and the OSS, who had no inkling of what they were up against; von Lüth, who did not fully comprehend the Reich which he served; and myself, whose enfeebled mind had nearly succumbed to the worst of ambitions.

I did as Himmler said and opened my eyes, and the world I found was as von Lüth had described, minus the mysticism: Blood and Soil, no alchemy betwixt them. Evil was not a Norbertus Hole. It was, rather, a chain of dull paperwork, a taskmaster's accounting, a grunt's drowsy acquiescence. Nazis were far worse than evil. They were *ordinary*, men who groused about supervisors and stomached the irks and ires of daily life until, presented with a stick, they picked it up with a child's sense of banal cruelty.

Perhaps I'd been the same. Well, Dearest Reader, no longer. Even if Mauthausen was a branch upon the Yggdrasil—the only ladder I'd ever be offered with which to climb out of this world—I would refuse it. Indeed, if given the chance, I'd chop it down and burn it, my dead flesh impervious to slashing wood chips, my dry eyes invulnerable to jetting sawdust. I could feel the cold, approving, but cautious stare of the Fifty-One. Who can say if Himmler kept his word and deported them? All that is certain is that *they* saved *me*, gave me a fighting chance for my soul, and thus they would always be there, judging me, waiting for me to prove that I'd been worth it.

Before the shower room door was closed and locked, before the rooftop soldiers could drop their blue-green crystals, I disenthralled the razor blade from my arm and dropped it inside the shower. Maybe a prisoner, in this group or the next, would find it and use it. It was, at least, a tool; if one were lucky, a weapon. My lips, too, pulled back into an emaciated grin. Weapons, I was coming to believe, were the prayer books of the powerless.

Eventually I translated those words painted upon the courtyard wall.

Arbeit Macht Frei.

Work shall make you free.

It might. I had so much of it to do—nothing less than kill that bastard Adolf Hitler—and only two mornings left to do it.

XV.

BERLINERS SNIFFED THE ELECTRICAL STORM of war rolling over the Rhine, the Carpathians, the Black Forest, the English Channel. The German serfs that had for months amazed me with fortitude now humped about beneath an invisible lash. The Gestapo were on tenterhooks, and though I needed to run, I dared not. Thrice I was asked to show my *Ahnenpass*, and thrice the document's particulars were copied down for later investigation. I did not care. In twenty-four hours, one way or the other, I'd be gone.

Himmler had sent me back to Berlin the next morning with Kuppisch to gather my belongings (I'd upheld Himmler's belief that I owned a case full of oracular orbs, moon-cycle tchotchkes, and various spiritual bric-a-brac), after which I could continue to Schloss Wewelsburg, where I would become a resident, or, if you were feeling less charitable, a permanent exhibit. I had no intention of honoring the agreement. Meixelsperger needed to know that the time had come to mobilize her troops and prepare the coups, so I begged the bulldog to go fast, then faster. But road damage, worse even than it had been one day earlier, nearly cost me the sun. The bakery, fretted I, might close before I could get there. Funny how the act of bagging up unsold *Gugelhupfen* and *Rustikales brot* might change the course of world history.

My life had been too full of wrong turns, my death even more so. This time I would head in a straight line. I entered von Lüth's building, bolted for the back exit so as to foil Kuppisch, climbed a fence, and headed straight for the book-burning plaza, only to louse it up by turning my head to scan for Kuppisch, thereby colliding with a man. Beneath his damp, dirty clothes was a strong build; he only swayed, but I ended up on all fours. When I stood, I found swastikas pressed into my palms like stigmata—coins, which had been tossed all about the pavement.

It was the same street preacher I'd caught spewing anti-Nazi venom at the *Hitlerjugend* rally! My shoulders dropped, and with them, the coins from my palms. He, the luckiest turncoat alive, had not heeded my advice to desert Berlin. The eyeball not tucked beneath his pirate patch widened, and his cleft chin fell to allow a grin of recognition. He shook his rain-bloated Bible.

"Pray with me!"

Had it been six seconds since last we'd spoken, or six months?

I attempted to sidestep, but he, as always, shuffled in tandem.

"You run, but not from Gød. Sun of His goodness lights your path. But do not forget they who move in shadow."

"Let me pass," snarled I.

"When the führer-beasts come, faith will come alive."

I'd have espoused Himmler's theory of the Aryan Jesus if I thought it might jar the preacher from his doomed path. Instead, I shoved him. His gray mop tussled, his backbone rang against a lamp post.

"Quiet!" hissed I. "Do you have any idea what awaits you?"

"They, the lions," said he. "We, the Daniels."

The drip, drip, drip of fury I'd withstood since Mauthausen had softened my inhibitions to mush. I took the man's shoulders with both hands and drove his head against the post.

"You are the one who walks in the sun, who is blinded by it! You think Gød will save you when they ship you to the camps? You think Jesus will be in the showers to scrub away your pain? Let me tell you, you great fool, what the Reichsführer told me. That the healthy young, when burned in ovens, produce large, lovely, black scuds of smoke, while the elderly and infirm make but sad yellow puffs. What do you think, padre? What color of smoke will you make?"

His witless response was immaterial. I pushed hard, his legs hooked about the post, and he fell. Reichsmarks rolled about, winking in the golden dusk.

"Run." It was the shortest, truest gospel. "Run, you dumb fuck. *Run!*"

He moaned more dangerous prayer; I kicked him. He sang to his Lord, each note a step down the Road to Heaven. It was not the road he thought it was! He had to shut up.

"Get out!"

I kicked him again.

"*Get out!*"

Again.

"*GET OUT!*"

Again, again, again.

The empty square echoed back my cries; I was telling myself to get out. From some embattled bower of my brain eked self-defensive excuses. I was not, I told myself, like the SS guards prodding their prey at the Wienergraben Quarry. I was, to the contrary, hurting this man so that I might save him, just as I'd saved the Fifty-One. Surely a preacher knew that salvation was a painful enterprise.

I tumbled over his body, my heel dragging the eye patch away from a hollow brown socket, and reeled down the street. I smelled burn. Not my soul but the bakery, it had to be the bakery, just two blocks away. As I approached, the scent did not fatten into the aromas of sugary delicacies, but rather shriveled into a toxic tang.

Meixelsperger Bakery had been excised as if by science-fiction laser beam. Its quadrant of city lot had become a charred rectangle pyred with scorched wood. So tidy had been its destruction that the buildings to either side were barely singed from heat. Hungry children kicked through the warm ashes for canned goods, drooling strings of gray spit from smoke inhalation. Milling about were Gestapo agents, more than the area's usual allotment, perhaps monitoring the site for returning conspirators.

My gait, already shaken by the beating I'd given the preacher, further faltered, and that was the only misstep I could afford. Despite rickety knees, I changed my trajectory so that I might pass alongside the bakery. I was delirious, Reader; I was desperate. Surely, I told myself, this was the consequence of a stovetop left unattended? I could almost believe it until I saw what two little girls were joyfully poking with a stick.

It was a dead monkey scorched to the pavement, having either danced too close to the fire or been pitched into it by his temperamental owner. You could, in the ashen remains, still make out the ruby tint of its fez and vest.

This arson was mine. It'd been I who'd bristled at *the damned Jewish filth* singsong of the bucktoothed Hitler Youth, I who'd slapped the lad's dancing elbows, I who'd kindled his junior-detective suspicion that Meixelsperger and I were fishy characters.

Whether the cowlicked cretin and his marching-band brutes had lit the torches themselves or led a charge of proper SS, it did not matter. Meixelsperger was gone. There would be no *Geschenk* of

133

coordinated coups. There would be no Berlin uprising. I grew light-headed and wished for someone to whom I could reach for balance, but I was, more than ever, alone. Oh, if not for my hoggish pursuit of the power offered by Himmler, I could have saved weeks of time, Meixelsperger's life, and the lives of untold others who'd been counting on her.

I could not help but scan the debris for human remains. Here was a prayer I could have asked the street preacher to second: *Please, Meixelsperger, be dead.* If the Gestapo had taken her alive, I could only hope they'd not noticed the points of her Mother's Cross. The tenacious bitch would take one or two of them out, I predicted, before she took herself.

The *Hitlerjugend* had led them to one spy; their discovery of me would not be far behind. I began to trace a maddeningly gradual circle back to von Lüth's building, outside of which I lurked to ensure it was not yet being cased. After von Lüth entered with groceries, I thundered through the lobby, raced up three flights, and burst through the door. Von Lüth stared at me from the kitchen. I fell upon him, a rabid deer against a much larger bear, antlering him across the arms. The groceries fell with the splat of broken eggs, and I stood on my toes so that I could look him in the eye.

"I have only minutes," hissed I. "Listen carefully."

"Only minutes? But, Herr Finch, I need to hear of your day with the Reichsführer!"

How I longed to flood the room with the black regurgitate of truth, another mess to clean up alongside the eggs, but who knew how von Lüth would react upon learning the true purpose of what he believed were rehabilitation camps? I pictured him climbing to the roof and jumping over the edge so as to meet Otto at some mythic locale—the Jabal al-Alsinah, perhaps, the Mountain of Tongues, not the origin of the master race they'd long sought, but a private place nonetheless for two people to live, and love, as they saw fit.

If Meixelsperger's underground had any hope of realizing success, von Lüth had to remain among the ignorant overground. I fixed him with my most unwavering look.

"The Party is looking for me. Do not ask why; there is no time. I must run before they come here. If they do, tell them the truth. Tell them you do not know where I have gone. The single favor that I ask is that you occupy Kuppisch with some other business so that I might move unencumbered. Will you?"

"But, Herr Finch—what is this? Please, tell me how I can—"

I cut him off with an abridgment of the English exchange between Himmler and Ziereis.

"Tomorrow morning at seven o'clock, a zeppelin is being christened at the Tempelhof airfield. Hitler will be in attendance. I will meet you there. Tonight you must call upon every friend you have left in the Reich, demand recompense for every past favor. We must be on the guest list to tour the aircraft, do you understand? It is our last chance for you and me, together as one, to show der Führer that Udo Christof von Lüth is, and has always been, the only choice for Minister of the Occult."

That von Lüth had matured past egotism made the appeal all the more difficult to voice, but the Fifty-One were waiting, listening. Von Lüth blinked his eyes through the stinging smoke of my soliloquy and looked down at his smudged smock, the trousers with ragged holes worn through the knees, the scuffed shoes with heels chewed thin by city cement. Even his mustache, once flaunting the wingspan of the iron eagle over Mauthausen's gate, had become a limp patch of pelt. Despite his mjölnir, he was a scholar, not a warrior, and I wasn't sure that he had any fight left in him.

Von Lüth's spine popped as he straightened it.

My, how tall he was. I'd forgotten.

His arm rose, ever so slowly, into a *sieg heil*, and despite my antipathy for what the salute represented, the strength with which he used it filled me with a bittersweet pride. His haggard heels snapped together with jackboot crispness.

"Tomorrow is Lammas Day." His voice trembled with awe. "The third cross-quarter day of the Gregorian calendar. One of the eight Pagan sabbats. The first of the harvest days, before the equinox, before Samhain. And this is the day Hitler chooses for a christening? Even now, at this critical hour, he is mindful of mysticism. This is why I trust in der Führer. This is why I trust in destiny. This is why I trust in Zebulon Finch."

His tribute was a Holy Lance jabbed into my side, but I was no Gentle Jew. What poured from me were not the curative powers of belief but the injurious energies of betrayal. I fled the building and into city shadow, knowing that I would have to live with what I did—if "live" is the word we wish to use—for a long, long, long, long time.

XVI.

TEMPELHOF AIRPORT HAD BEEN CONVERTED into an assembly line for Stuka dive bombers and was thus accustomed to blanket security. The lone entry point was clouded that morning by fog and clogged by chariots of Auto Union, BMW, Porsche, and Volkswagen insignia, and through the standstill traffic I advanced on foot like a man of faith toward his firing squad, holding my *Ahnenpass* like the Bible, prepared to receive either bullet or miracle. Even among such chrome ostentation, von Lüth's Mercedes stood out. I found it idling, rapped on the window, and ducked inside.

Kuppisch was not the driver; at long last, von Lüth had leashed the canine. I had no time to gush gratefulness; I was, to be frank, a calamity. Though my trousers were passable, my shirt was a chiaroscuro of soot, mud, and rust from an overnight expedition through industrial jungles. Von Lüth, not to be beaten, looked worse. The promise of meeting Hitler again had robbed him of sleep, of breakfast, of demeanor. The shocking white suit he'd chosen strangled him—a tire of perspiring flab gathered above the collar—and he used a sopping handkerchief to push sweat to and fro across his face. He formed a fashionista's frown of horror when I asked for his jacket to conceal my smudges, but it was fleeting. It was our only hope.

Without the shrewd drape of tailored cloth, the shapes of his body rose as if through volcanic quag. His buttons crested down his chest and belly like skiers in a double-layout of doom, while suspenders carved through his back fat like roadways through Alpine peaks. I, meanwhile, was an infant drowning inside white tides. My hands did not reach past von Lüth's cuffs. I began to roll them, wondering if two circus clowns like us would be welcomed.

There were hundreds of people, though, more than enough to conceal us. After parking, we moved in a human torrent toward a hangar. It was octagonal, three football fields in length, two hundred feet tall, and of unscuffed construction at a time when all else in Berlin was bent and beaten. The mood was troublous and brooding. Hamburg, reported von Lüth, just three hundred kilometers northwest, was being bombed as we spoke, thousands dead or dying, the great medieval city gobbled by flame due to the summer drought. The fog might as well have been Hamburg's smoke; each haunted face reflected disbelief that der Führer hadn't cancelled the event.

Wonderment eroded grief. We heard the gasps before we rounded the hangar and saw the marvel for ourselves: the *Deutsches Luftschiff Fliegende Hitler*, the greatest floating airship ever constructed, though the war's coming end would ensure that it would be gone before many could corroborate it. It was August 1943; the zeppelin was a dinosaur. But what magnificent bones it would leave behind! Twenty stories of ridged and contoured silver as smooth and eyeless as a shark, both dorsal and pectoral fins painted with swastikas the size of von Lüth's building. Dozens of engineers kept the dirigible in check with cables cinched to winches, but even Germans knew how King Kong ended.

A stage draped with banners looked teensy but important beside the *Fliegende Hitler*. People huddled close while a large band fed them patriotism, patriotism, patriotism, until that, not the whis-

138

pered invocation of "Hamburg," was all that could be retched. I was sickened upon realizing the band was no professional auxiliary but rather a stockade of Hitler Youth, cheeks puffed and red-pink from atonal exhalation. Among them were the Mitte marauders, one of them monkeyless but likely sporting new medals to commend the snaring of a spy.

So it was with strange relief that I heard the crowd burst into vigorous applause as the day's speaker ascended to the stage.

Reader, are you quite prepared?

Adolf Hitler took the pulpit centered in the bull's-eye of a swastika. I was yanked, as if by paratrooper chute, back to the OSS basement: the trapped cigarette smoke, the thick J-1121 folder, the upsetting sex hygiene films, the dog-eared flashcards. *I'm not at liberty to say*, Rigby's catchphrase, had become my reality in Berlin. *I'm not at liberty to act.* Now, though, I could smell cold gun metal, taste Nazi blood. The chorus of the Fifty-One hymned approval. Could I make the shot from here?

An overrash, impatient thought! So obstructed was my view of Hitler that I couldn't see his face. I saw his hands, flailing like birch branches and crashing down like gavels; I even saw his hair, whisking in ecstatic strips; and of course I heard his voice, those piercing emphases gunned through amplifiers. Von Lüth, much taller, watched with pearled, worshipful eyes and, out of habit, murmured choice decipherings.

The 1937 *Hindenburg* explosion over New Jersey, screamed Hitler, had been an act of Fate. It was regrettable that the country's previous airship, the mighty *Graf Zeppelin II*, had been disemboweled in 1939 so that the army could harvest its duralumin metal. But today was a brighter day. With victory imminent in all theaters of war, now was the moment to show the world how Germany looked toward a postwar rule where transoceanic travel was again the apotheosis of relaxation and comfort. If the *Hindenburg* had been the "Queen of the Skies," the *Fliegende Hitler* would be the King.

Germany was winning the war? How could people swallow such lies while peppered with Hamburg ash? It was stagecraft worthy of Christ, the parceling of two fish into kibble enough to satisfy a starving multitude. Hitler's arm, all of him that I could see, gestured proudly to the *Hitlerjugend* band, while von Lüth translated the booming final proclamation.

"'When the older ones among us falter, the youth will stiffen and remain until their bodies decay.'"

It sounds, does it not, like a last-minute appeal designed just for me?

Hitler christened the zeppelin with a bottle of liquid air, and the ship's captain called upon the luckiest of guests to move forward. The crowd surged like tainted food up a gullet. Von Lüth exhaled and gave me a tight nod, and we progressed across the airfield. The fog had thickened such that the far end of the silver leviathan had vanished, though we could still read the flapping banner beneath which our column marched:

EIN VOLK—EIN REICH—EIN FÜHRER

Our names were checked against a typed list of dignitaries, and our reward was two programs printed upon finer stock than any I'd seen since Cornelius Leather had handed me his business card forty-two years prior. Sucker though I was for sturdy stationery, it did not distract me from a covey of SS blocking the zeppelin entrance. How could they resist detaining a perspiry colossus in suspenders and his cadaverous comrade?

Thankfully, the press of the crowd had the SS guards harried, and they fulfilled the minimum requirement of confiscating photo-camera contraband. Weapons of rank and ceremony, of course, from Luftwaffe daggers and Army dress bayonets to von Lüth's own mjölnir, were permitted, and with compliments.

The hammer had weight beyond the physical; von Lüth gripped it as we scaled the thrumming gangplank. We transitioned from B-Deck promenade to a bar at the top of the stairs, a space handsomely wainscotted and generously ferned but stuffed with a hundred bodies. It smelled of breath and skin, the finest of both. Men wore full regalia, and women the sort of gowns only the likes of Bridey Valentine could scrounge during wartime. Acrobatic waitstaff threaded through the bustle to deliver diversions of champagne, while nationalistic leitmotifs piped through speakers.

Von Lüth and I were corralled with dozens of others along the port side, from smoking room to officers' mess, until we were, one at a time, permitted a peek into the airship's gargantuan belly, a dizzying web of bombinating wire lashed along metal cruciforms. From there we climbed to A-Deck and its village of heated passenger cabins populated by cordial *Luftschiffbau* personnel in blue jackets, white vests, bow ties, and doeskin caps. They smiled and answered technical questions. Von Lüth's translations were balderdash: *echolot, stratoscopoe, inclinometer*.

I consulted the program. This gist, though in German, was clear. A stem-to-stern tour. Breakfast. Then, at last, a chance to shake the hands of attending luminaries two hundred meters up in the sky.

This last detail caught me off-guard. Surely my poor translation was to blame. I whispered to von Lüth.

"Flying? I thought we were only touring."

In response, the thuds and tremors of the closing gangplanks.

"To Elysium we rise." Von Lüth, white and trembling with anticipation, filled his chest with buttressing air. "Like the Grâl rejoining Lucifer's crown."

The sealing of my coffin lid was a gentle one. It was a comfort, in a way, not to have to hatch an escape plan, dwell upon a future OSS interrogation, or speculate upon a future outside Reich borders. Once the deed was done, I would be trapped, and that would be that. My heart thudded—no, it was the revolver banging against my ribs as I stumbled past a towering portrait of Hitler to the windows of the passenger lounge. I was dead, but warm air still comforted cold flesh.

The windows were cranked open and built at a forty-five-degree angle that allowed passengers to gaze down at the silly little world below. I was in prime position to hear the captain crow orders to the ground crew via bullhorn. The prop lines wriggled from the craft like snakes. Gravity leapt, and we began to rise. Everyone in the lounge staggered, then gasped, then giggled; our altitude tickled noses the same as the champagne bubbles. Only von Lüth looked sickly. I wondered if he might upchuck and ruin the whole damn thing.

Then, smoke.

With the abruptness of a pulled windowshade, a filthy black cloud enveloped the ship. Ten seconds passed like a slowly drawn inhale, and then a woman screamed: "*Feuer! Feuer!*"

Instead of further cries there was a mass crouching, as if each passenger braced for Gestapo nightsticks. I felt an unexpected head rush of gratitude to the Gød who had until then forged a nice, long career out of bedeviling me. It was an unbelievable gift. The Nazis had learned nothing from *Hindenburg*; the zeppelin was hydrogen, not helium; Adolf Hitler would incinerate to unverifiable black bones; von Lüth would never know how I'd planned to betray him; and I would be furnaced into dust, coagulated in the clouds, and transformed to heavier fog.

The martial music cut out, and in its place eased the bourbon tones of the captain's voice. One to the other, Germans blinked, then smiled, then laughed. A hand snatched my wrist, and there was von Lüth, teeth as big as fence posts. He cradled my cold cheek in his clammy palm, a gesture that only at this instant of giddiness was publicly permissible.

"Dust," said he. "Blowing off the cover. We are all right, Herr Finch. We are all right!"

Outside, the black cloud was paling. To the assembled aristocracy the dissipating dust was the smoke of not only Hamburg but the entire world war alighting from their minds, if only for the next few hours. They'd forgotten what it felt like to relax. Why, it felt fine! The zeppelin achieved altitude, the twenty-foot propellers growled into action, and the *Fliegende Hitler* began to cruise. From the window I watched the world I knew disappear into fog. Passengers cheered, and when those cheers died out, engine drones emerged to shush us children into complacency.

Behind us, a steward built a pyramid of champagne flutes to prove the steadiness of the ship. The rich produced folds of cash and bet against it for sport. Von Lüth sighed at the good German gaiety of it all and, in a spurt of camaraderie, elbowed me hard in the ribs.

The Smith & Wesson rattled audibly like a belch, slid an inch, and lodged laterally between anterior and posterior ribs. It pinched my left lung and felt thick, like phlegm in the throat. I drove a fist against my chest, three times, a human enough behavior, but the block of metal would not budge. I stared at von Lüth, wondering what twist in the plot he'd just forced, but his expression made me speechless. Look how the giant grinned, even though his nerves had been gnashed to gristle. Could he not yet feel, in the region of his back, the knife I'd planted?

I lowered my fist, hoped for the best, and tried to return his laugh.

It got lost in the drone.

XVII.

REAKFAST SERVERS ARRIVED IN CONGA-LINE configuration, coloring each table with bright cubes of cheese, sliced liverwurst and salami, batches of jams and honeys, bowls of cut melon, tomatoes on the stem, and hundreds of boiled eggs in individual pewter cups. Pastries were notably absent, proof of the Reich's new distrust of bakeries.

The ship's cargo of swanked Germans swarmed from sundry corridors. The zeppelin banked slightly with the weight, the champagne-flute pyramid collapsed, and the mess was erased in sixty seconds. No one could make evidence vanish like the Nazis could. As with many a Hollywood cocktail party I'd attended, this was an eat-and-mingle shindig, and soon everyone had a plate and glass in hand, as well as a healthy bolus of food behind which they gabbed. Von Lüth, too, snarfed smoked salmon as if it were nature's cure for nerves. If that were true, I needed it too, on the double, down in my stomach, where its spoilage might blister the gold off Johnny's aggie.

Von Lüth's plate of fish was knocked into his chest, another stain, but he gave it no mind, for the crowd was joggling for the best of reasons. Bleats of *Heil Hitler!*, though muffled through mouthfuls, and hearty *sieg heil*s, though topped by fruit-speared forks, compensated for my hindered view. The cockamamie climax dreamed up by Allen Rigby had, against all logic, come to pass.

The hand I placed over my heart gave me the look of a young Kraut overwhelmed by proximity to his Führer, but you, Dearest Reader, know better. Beneath my palm, under layers of torpid flesh and inside a cradle of ribs, was the snub-nosed revolver. After von Lüth's elbow strike, was it still removable? Now was the time to find out.

I hove sternward toward the closest lavatory, but von Lüth shot out his arm with an archer's speed, snatching me with a salmon-greased hand.

"*Nein*, Herr Finch! He is here! We must take our place in line!"

Being of pureblood pedigree, the SS were tall; it was easy to see them begin to herd the mass of restless nobles into the rough shape of a queue. Somewhere nearby stood Adolf Hitler, shaking hands and trading pleasantries.

I pulled against von Lüth.

"Please," said I. "I need only a moment."

His eyes, liquid and pink, popped wide.

"You cannot leave me! You must be there so that I can—"

I ripped free my arm. He gasped and recoiled as if struck. Oh, Reader! Gentle Reader! How I wished to whisper into his ear the urgent truths, that he must exit the lounge at once, that he could not be nearby when I attacked, not if he were to have a chance of avoiding execution. But my ears, too, fielded whispers, warnings from the Fifty-One. To risk von Lüth's reaction was to risk the lives of thousands more soldiers, Allied and Axis both, who would be ground to attritional dust, and thousands more prisoners, who would suffer and die in camps, more smoked salmon to be gnashed by implacable elder gods.

"Just some water," said I. "To splash upon my face."

Von Lüth's jowls jiggered in trepidation.

I gestured at the queue. My hand was trembling.

"Reserve our place in line. I will rejoin you in one minute."

The queue was shuffling forward. There was no time to argue. He sighed in defeat and nodded. The wax-twirled tips of his mustache were too heartbreaking to consider.

I dodged between prattling packs of Nazis, upsetting plates and sloshing iced teas, only to find the winding queue itself thwarting my route to the restroom. To red-rover its blockade would be to draw SS attention. *Think quickly, Herr Finch, quickly!*

A breakfast island was to my left. I grabbed a plate, tossed onto it food enough for a family of four, and charged starboard, where two tall, potted ferns leaned against each another like fellow lushes. I feigned a stumble and threw my plate between them. The zeppelin roared and the crowd pealed; the shatter was no louder than a spoon in a teacup. I knelt so that the green fronds draped over my back; spent five seconds gathering spilled food; and then, praying to Gød or Satan or their undecided offspring Lucifer, ran my right hand up under my shirt.

If only I'd thought to add a knife or fork to my plate before hurling it! Without a utensil, nor a dubious honor like Meixelsperger's Mother's Cross, I had no tools besides my hands. Tearing open one's body went against every human instinct, but Zebulon Finch, I reminded myself, was not especially human. I closed my eyes, thought of the Japanese we fought in the Pacific and their honorable ritual suicide of seppuku, and did my best imitation.

Having been cut open by Dr. Leather, sewn shut by Merle, taxidermied by Chernoff, and remodeled by the OSS, my gut had papier-mâché consistency. One good shove, and my hand was

147

swallowed. My fingers met large intestine, dank and reptilian; I grimaced, made a fin of my hand, and minnowed past intestines. My invader hand was one of the Barker's mondo tapeworms; it was the World War I shrapnel that had scooped from me a ball of flesh; it was a dozen other ugly splatters upon an overlong timeline. My fingertips sunk into ropy diaphragm, redirected past spongy spleen, slid up a lobe of lung, and punched my heart so hard that the old organ contracted, just once, a single thump of shocking life.

A man cleared his throat behind me. He was a chance player in history, a humble waiter, who wished for me to stand so that he might clean my spill. He tapped my back with a single finger, but with my right arm crammed up my thorax, his gesture was nearly enough to knock me over. I swayed and shouted, my German, always feeble, whittled to a single repeated word—*"Nein, nein, nein"*—while I swiveled my buried fist with an audible squish. Behind the third and fourth rib, an OSS surgeon had promised me, but fingers, it turns out, are as blind as moles.

At last, an organ colder than most—a nickel-plated revolver.

I pulled. Metal thudded. Ribs squealed. The gun was, indeed, stuck.

The waiter took my shoulder, just doing his job, urging me upward.

I yanked with all of my might. There was a gruesome double-crack of fracturing ribs, and the Smith & Wesson shot out of me, the Devil's newborn, black and coated with sour-smelling slime. Gray bits of viscera spattered the floor. A swastika-patterned cloth napkin was in reach, but I couldn't get it—the waiter was trying to lift me.

I tore free the damp tape securing six bullets to the revolver's handle, but my fingers fumbled. The bullets hit the floor. The zeppelin was slanted, and the bullets rolled out of reach; I saw three carom against polished leather shoes and high heels. If the wearers looked down—no, there was no time to entertain ruin! I palmed the last three bullets and managed to randomly chamber them before the waiter hefted me to standing position. There was an ill sensation—ribs, thought I, poking through skin. I tented my chest with von Lüth's oversize jacket, dropped the gun into a pocket, and turned to the waiter with a wretched grin.

His face was folded in concern. He patted my clothes clean, and his helpful knuckles struck the pocket with the revolver. That side of the jacket spun into the crowd, heavy and lethal. I jammed my hand into that pocket, reined it in. Inside I felt coins, and quickly transferred them into the waiter's hand to buy freedom. I stumbled from the ferned hutch and into a crashing tide of Germans. It was the front of the queue, fattening at a corner, and by the time the stream had straightened, I'd been incorporated. Suddenly I was a mere six people from Hitler.

To the front, back, and sides of me were soldiers, colonels, and generals locked together in happy banter. I felt a nudge; it was a Marine Officer behind me, rolling back on his jackboots, clacking his ceremonial dagger against his jodhpurs and gesturing that I needed to get moving. Another inadvertent historical player. This impatient young man might be the one to tackle me after I fired. His eyes flicked downward, and he frowned. Had he seen my jutting rib? I whirled away, faced front.

The line had indeed progressed; I advanced. Four people away now, so close! Hitler was flanked by two other guests of honor, but I could not be bothered to identify them. Minister of Blimps? Secretary of Breakfast? Who cared! There was Hitler's pumping hand, pink and ringless and chafed of knuckle.

What was this? I couldn't recall the pattern in which I'd loaded the three bullets! Would three empty chambers precede the live ones? Would the wasted seconds make the difference? The line lurched. Right in front of me was a woman in a blue, back-bustled dress. She teased the blond hair looping from beneath her pink hat and veil. She adjusted swastika earrings, too; their high-pitched jingle vibrated my exposed rib. Three people away now, and I could see Hitler's isosceles nose, the gray-mottled black of his toothbrush mustache.

"Herr Finch! Herr Finch!"

Dear Gød! Von Lüth had spotted me. A fuss erupted from the other side of the room, followed by the tingling of multiple medals from decorated breasts. Though I dared not look, I knew that the big bear was trying to paddle though the queue so as to join me up front. *No, idiot!* thought I. *Stay back, stay back!*

"Herr Finch! Wait for me!"

I shifted so as to conceal myself beside the woman, as if we were a couple. She had extended a gloved hand to the Minister of Blimps, and the gent was having a good time shaking it. My eyes, of course, skipped to the next man in line. Now it was I, not the *Fliegende Hitler*, who floated on air.

Adolf Hitler was no longer the virile bruiser from OSS photographs. Given the scorch of his dawn oratory, he looked strikingly old. His back, once ramrod, had stooped; his shoulders, once brash, hunched forward; his blue eyes remained avid but shimmered past purple pouches; his hair, heavied by brilliantine, crinkled his forehead with its weight. Despite all of this, he evidenced the same hunger to absorb everything that von Lüth had witnessed during his night at the Berghof. Perhaps Hitler's mind was fixated upon smoldering Hamburg, though when he spotted the woman, a swan among bovine, his distraction melted and he reached eagerly for her slender hand. His smile, noticed I, was as wee and toothless as an infant's.

I became cognizant of an impatient harrumphing. It was the Minister of Blimps, chest puffed, waiting for acknowledgment. My right hand, though, the one required to meet his handshake, was deep inside the jacket pocket, wrapped around the Smith & Wesson. Like a fool, I hesitated, uncertain whether I should expose the weapon that second or wait until I could bury it in Hitler's gut. The Minister of Blimps narrowed his eyes in suspicion.

Von Lüth made my decision for me. I saw him as a panicked blur, perhaps ten people back, flailing behind the arms of SS guards who did not like when someone rushed der Führer. Still he cried my name, but what did these words mean to the assembled? What, in fact, did they mean to me? I released the revolver and stuck out my hand, and the Minister of Blimps shook it. His tight smile curdled upon feeling cold abdominal slime. He extricated his hand and examined it in open disgust.

Disgust always made for opportunity. I shifted into the space vacated by the woman, a sidestep that felt like a paratrooper plunge. Hitler, four inches shorter than me. An exhale like the shuffling of state documents. A permeating odor of eggs. The disinterested black marbles of his pupils cracking against my own. Perhaps because my freshly shaken hand was outside the jacket pocket, it was *la silenziosità*, not the Smith & Wesson, that I felt rising in defense. Yes, and why not? It would immobilize Hitler as it had countless others, and then it would not matter if I needed to pull the trigger three times, or six, or ten, or fifty.

I hadn't summoned the deplorable ability since upsetting the diners at Hearst Castle in 1933. Though that dredging had, as ever, tortured me with fantasies of a delayed death, it had nonetheless stunned thirty revelers into silence. I had every reason to expect the same result with Adolf Hitler. He would be collared by the Grim Reaper's scythe and forced to gaze upon the pulled fish-guts of his soul.

Hitler's eyes, though, were not black pools but black mirrors.

He was only a man, a higher grade of pencil pusher than his subordinates, but some vital part of him had gone missing. What I saw, for the first time, was *la silenziosità* reflected straight back. Jarring, yes; frightening, of course; but also, I realized instantly, a chance to confirm Dr. Leather's conclusion that, though I decomposed at zero-point-eight-three percent the regular rate, I walked the same Road to Heaven as everyone else. The road's vanishing point, if not its end, should have been visible.

Why, then, did I see evidence of the opposite? It was as though I'd fallen through a fontanel of flooring and plummeted to the ship's interior, its infinite spiral of wire so much like the Uterus of Time reflected in Hitler's eyes, where there was no light of birth at the end. Did this mean I would live on, and on and on, even as a pile of bone, even as a puddle of sludge?

Inconceivable! Horrible! Unbelievable! Unfair!

I felt the revolting pressure of physical contact. No living human should touch my accursed flesh, no one! I gazed down in horror and saw my hand being pumped twice by Hitler. His palm, too, came away coated with anatomical glop, but he seemed not to notice. He looked to the Marine Officer to my left, eager to move onward.

Von Lüth shouted, almost sobbed. Men coughed unhappily at

how I'd jammed the line. The third and final dignitary beckoned me forth. All I could discern of him were pins and patches, fifty swastika refractions of the larger versions all around us. Each was a simple four-pronged gear that, when interlocked, could power a mighty engine.

But hadn't von Lüth called me the living swastika? If I turned, each cog of the Nazi machine might turn with me. Turn: I pushed my hand into my jacket pocket. Turn: I gripped the handle. Turn: I put a finger to the trigger. Turn: I slipped it from my pocket. Turn: I began to raise it.

I, Zebulon Finch, was alive and dead; the beast and the ghost; the swastika and the Grâl; above all, I was the Light Bringer. Like Lucifer, Gød had shunned me for my peculiar light, cast me to Earth rather than let me board a heavenward zeppelin. And like Lucifer, I would use my suffering as a torch to illuminate what *la silenziosità* told me was a waiting eternity of darkness.

Turn, turn.

I pressed the revolver into Hitler's stomach and pulled the trigger.

It was only in retrospect that I recognized the third dignitary. Though I'd belittled him as the Secretary of Breakfast, he was, in fact, a Nazi deserving of fête, so convincing had been his long under-cover tenure as a rambling street preacher. He'd exchanged his cleric's collar for a black tie, but that broad chest, gray curls, cloven chin, and, most of all, that eyepatch, were unmistakable. It is why the Gestapo had never detained him. By baiting traitorous agitprop on street corners, he'd surely outed countless Berliners disloyal to the Reich.

What was one more?

His hands and forehead were bruised from the brutal kicks I'd delivered to him hours earlier, but this man was a hero. He recognized me and swiped at my arm before I fired. The first chamber had, in fact, been loaded, but the bullet did nothing more than pock the floor ten inches to Hitler's left. Der Führer's body jerked once in surprise, and that became the single, short scrap of film I'd run through my brain-projector for the rest of my death: Adolf Hitler's little dance step of confusion.

Forward momentum brought the erstwhile preacher to a kneel. The pretty woman shrieked. I raised the gun for a second shot, but a company of stooges had thrown their bodies in front of their illustrious leader. I scuttled back for room, and on schedule the young Marine Officer lunged, but I brought around the Smith & Wesson hard enough to clock his temple. He went down, clutching at a gout of blood, and I ran, for when the shit comes down, the fleeing instinct is the toughest one to eschew.

The *Fliegende Hitler*'s wireless systems were first-class. The pilots knew of a disturbance in seconds. The ship banked, and everyone tumbled portside. This being my set direction, I careened as if from a cliff, crashing through one screen of would-be captors after another. Had I breath, it would have been pounded away when my opened stomach slammed into the waist-high windowsill.

Dignitaries unsheathed clumsy ceremonial weapons and teetered in my direction. They waffled when I pointed the revolver, and, Dearest Reader, forever shall I regret doing so. The hesitation bought me a good ten seconds, and with them I sought out von Lüth and found him, thereby tossing one more fresh body into my crematorium of memories.

Six different men had taken hold of his clothing. He towered above all of them, a *Hindenburg* amid toy kites, and like that bedeviled zeppelin, he was ablaze and diving. What should have been the zenith of his life and career had imploded in a loud, confusing minute. He was in his final moments of disassembling, his face as bleached as my own, lips loose, eyeballs wabbling. He comprehended the depth to which I'd deceived him, and that was bad. Worse, though, was a new understanding of his lifetime of being a sucker and how it had encouraged every condescending insult by Himmler and a hundred others like him.

He gave me a look of neither damnation nor forgiveness, only regret.

Von Lüth's mjölnir still dangled from his belt. He drew himself erect enough to rip free of his captors, clicked together his heels with inviolable hardihood, unhooked the weapon, and executed the last, best *sieg heil* of his life, thrusting upward the mjölnir in honor of his Führer, before taking the hammer with both hands and with breathtaking gusto driving it into the center of his face.

The impact was not too bad to witness; all is relative in these matters. It was, at least, fast, a pearlescent blur, a scrunch of bone, two black blurts of blood. Had only it stopped there. Von Lüth, blind but alive, dislodged the mjölnir from his dented face and fissured sinuses. It made a slurping sound; broken teeth and shards of bone shot out. It is his second blow, executed with the same mindful deliberation as the first, that haunts me. I cannot say if he died quickly from it, though once he'd fallen, the skittering of his heels continued. It was a genuine suicide, cancelling the counterfeit one of his Otto. Perhaps that was the reason for his big, bloody, broken smile.

The Fifty-One adjudged it good payment, but was it, Reader? How could it be? I turned away—to flee, ever to flee—but there was nowhere left to scramble but to the sky, so I hoisted my body onto the sill and coiled. Men's shadows threatened, so I pointed the gun at the ceiling and fired: blank, blank, *bullet*, blank, *bullet*. The shadows retracted. My nose was flattened against cold glass. I gasped at the pure silver of total fog.

I cannot say that I recall squeezing my body through the open window, but I do recall the screams and shouts for how they drowned out the phantom excoriations of Rigby and Meixelsperger. Still, how pleasant it was, in a death long choked with uncertainty, to know exactly which aperture through which to wiggle, which handholds to relinquish, which world to leave behind.

XVIII.

THE GOGGLES DID NOT FIT, and it annoyed me. Because it had been twenty-four months since I'd felt any emotion at all, I mollycoddled my annoyance as one does a campfire. One, the elastic band had been set to dwarf diameter. Two, the goggles were made of metal and were too damn heavy; I thought they might rip the flesh from my temples. Three, the round orange-tinted lenses reminded me of Dr. Leather's Isolator. Lying there amid strange red grass, I imagined that I could hear, rustling about the bamboo, my former tormentor still mocking my pitiful attempts at humanity:

Hweeeeee . . . fweeeeee . . . hweeeeee . . . fweeeeee . . .

Isolator or not, I was most assuredly isolated. Though U.S. Army Special Forces would not be officialized for another seven years, what else could I call my covert company of escorts? We'd skimmed the black waters of the bay before making our clandestine nighttime landfall, creeping for an hour past pumpkin fields and drowsy, tall-roofed temples, before they'd left me in the woodland with a bicycle, reiterating via hand signals our impending rendezvous.

Bamboo is an earthly magic. With it you can fashion a knife sharp enough to kill a beast, a bridge over which to lug the carcass, a house inside which to drag it, a plate upon which to cut it, a table upon which to eat it, and implements with which to dine upon it. I had hours to wait, too long to resist the plant's patient petition, and

157

so gave in, reliving the past two years, most of it spent in a London jail. The Limeys didn't call it that, but that's what it was. Hour to hour, day to day, month to month, MI6 Intelligence, unfamiliar with my mission, put to me thousands of questions regarding who I was, where I'd been, and how I'd made it out of Berlin. Whatever allegiance to America I'd held had expired; I gave them their answers.

After performing my meteorite act from the *Fliegende Hitler* and landing in the deep, dark waters of the Schwielowsee southwest of Berlin, I'd floated for a time beneath swirling fog, before, on canine instinct, paddling through narrower straits until coming upon the Elbe River. I followed it north, all the way to Hamburg.

The crowd at Tempelhof had been right to brood about the city's destruction. The Allies' aptly named Operation Gomorrah had peeled eight square miles of the city from the planet. Much of Hamburg still burned, and the river water inside my body cavities heated, evaporated, and generated about me a rainbow aura. I pretended that it protected me. I would not be stirred by the tarantula twists of fried corpses being chipped from cement with shovels. I walked, walked some more, and by the by came upon a band of Brits.

MI6 was frustrated by how few details of strategic worth I could supply. I hung my worthless noggin, agreed, and only lifted it weeks later when a trio of American OSS agents arrived. I nearly sobbed Rigby's name—my kind, tolerant teacher would console and advise me—but he wasn't among them. I refused to answer questions until they divulged his whereabouts, and, to their credit, they were forthright: Allen Rigby was no longer with OSS. They paused for follow-up questions, pointedly ignoring my jutting rib, but I did not bother. Rigby had bet his career on Operation Weeping Willow, and J-1121 had botched it.

Americans traveled light. When they left, they did not take me.

It was from my holding pen that I followed the terminating saga of what the Germans called *Götterdämmerung,* or the Twilight of the Gods. On June 6, the same cursed date of that first assault at Belleau Wood, the Allies invaded Normandy, setting into motion the endgame. In July 1944, men better than I—Nazis, in fact; the traitorous sort Meixelsperger had loved—succeeded in exploding a suitcase bomb beneath a table at which Hitler sat. The suitcase had been nudged a few critical feet by ignorant shoes, Hitler had survived the blast, and the conspirators were herded and executed.

Meanwhile, I, useless corpse, took six-hundred-foot dives from zeppelins and kept living.

Von Lüth's suicide proved to be a bellwether. In April 1945, after months spent roving about an underground bunker while Russians penetrated Berlin, Adolf Hitler shot himself, prideful of his slaughter of the subhumans until the end. Weeks later, Heinrich Himmler was caught trying to skip Germany, and while undergoing a British Army medical exam he chomped into the same kind of L-pill Rigby had given me in the C-53 Skytrooper. He died of cyanide poisoning, the same as millions of concentration-camp inmates, though let us not be dazzled by irony. Himmler died with a smile on his face. Why the smile? I wondered if it had to do with the rumor that, after giving the panicked order for Schloss Wewelsburg to be burned, he'd buried a chest of nine thousand Death's-Head Rings in the forest near the castle.

Some lonely nights I'd dare the darkness and ask myself if I still wanted one. The answers deserved the pillow-smotherings I gave them. The rings were out there, I knew, the same as were Nazi ideals, waiting for someone to dig them up and start the whole thing over.

For now, at least, the Thousand-Year Reich dreamed of by von Lüth had been stunted at twelve. Try as I did to sneer at the memory of the hulking bumbler, the picturing of his eager, appled cheeks reliably turned me catatonic. Go on, Allies, toss my corpse wherever you like.

Where they'd tossed me was in the red grass of Sakai, Japan, across the Bungo Channel at the southern edge of Honshū. One final mission, decreed the Americans, to make up for the one I'd bollixed, and then I'd be allowed to return home. Home? That gave me a rare laugh. I had no home, no people, no history, no future.

Allied advertising had made the case that Japs, those kamikaze dog-eaters, were as alien as Martians. But so far I'd appreciated what I'd seen and heard: the green, vascular pillars of clacking bamboo; birds of exceptional trumpet; and across the valley, wooden cart wheels clucking beneath the pops and purrs of Japanese conversation. While I'd been dunked in doldrums, a brilliant blue morning had risen.

From the city I heard a siren, different from those in Berlin but used for the same purpose. How long had I been lying there? I sat up, checked my pocket watch. Oh, yes—did I neglect to mention it? As begrudging recompense for a difficult job maladministered, the Americans had presented me an envelope containing not another *Ahnenpass* but rather the artifacts that truly identified me: the crumpled photo of Merle, Piano's faded map of the Meuse-Argonne, the Barker's Atlanta Constitution advertisement, and, of course, the Excelsior. But had some jokester agent winded it before handing it over?

The watch, you see, was still ticking.

The siren subsided, a false alarm. Army orders meant shit-all to me, but the Excelsior was Wilma Sue herself, tsking my sloth. For her sake, perhaps, I could try to reach my position in time. I stood, affixed my goggles, freed the bicycle from bamboo, and crept from the forest. My features were Aryan, not Japanese, and movement, even in the countryside, was risky. I pedaled quietly down a dirt path toward the city three kilometers north. On outlying trails I spotted other bicyclists, but no honking autos, no crashing tanks, no saber-rattling lines of men whose insignias were all that differentiated their methods of cruelty.

War in Japan, thought I, had been overrated.

Then a ship called the *Enola Gay* dropped an atomic bomb called Little Boy upon a city called Hiroshima. No class of goggles can shade one from such an event. Earth was gobbled up by the sun, a thousand-foot fireball of pure magnesium white. As the one person the U.S.A. knew to be invulnerable to gamma-ray radiation, I'd been ordered to be at Hiroshima city limits to observe up close the detonation of the so-called gadget, and I'd screwed it up. Apologies, Wilma Sue.

So I wasn't there to witness the tens of thousands vaporized into carbon dust, nor the one hundred thousand more splattered about in undifferentiated globs. I did get to see, however, the seismic wave that undulated outward from the bomb site at the speed of sound, a rolling, ink-black cloud that blew brick buildings to shrapnel and shaved grass from the ground. Bartholomew Finch, that feisty old dynamitier, would have been much impressed.

No two-wheeler, no matter how well piloted, could survive the force. I was thrown twenty feet from the bike. When next I became aware, the blue sky above had gone the color of mud. I sat up, my flesh refracting heat in glistening waves, and witnessed the uppermost contortions of the sixty-thousand-foot mushroom cloud.

Reference a history text, Reader. It was less a mushroom than it was a tree of orange bark, red branches, and leaves sizzling down like— how about that?—a weeping willow.

Here, at last, was the Yggdrasil.

It made bleak sense. Wasn't the blight of utter annihilation the truest of all possible enlightenments? For a long while, I was still, again the obedient student before one of Abigail's tutors, and through tinted goggles I studied the tree's branches for buds of wisdom before they burned away. Like its gardener, Gød Almighty, Yggdrasil was a tease, using its own vines to smother itself into an inconclusivity. What it left behind was what Gød always left behind—Old Testament fire. Hiroshima was an inferno.

It was a lesson comprised of lifetimes worth of shrieking and sobbing coming from all directions. The brown sky brightened to copper, and this noxious radiance allowed me to see the monster's approach. It was at the bottom of the hill on which I sat, weaving its slow way up the trail. I stood, knees shaking but emboldened by longing. After all, I too was a monster, and at this low, lonely point near the end of the world, I was eager to meet a second of my wretched kind.

The monster was charred black. That was all I could tell. I began to walk toward it so that I might shorten its arduous progress. I passed a cemetery of dislodged grave stones and climbed over an industrial smokestack that had blown onto the path. As I progressed, a strange rain began to fall, blotches of thick, obsidian fluid. Much later, the world would learn that, well, shucks—it was a radioactive precipitate of soot that would rot the innards of the thousands of thirsty survivors who drank it. We're awful sorry about that.

To the eyes, though, the rain had an odd beauty, as if the ink of traditional *Sumi-e* paintings had poured from an overhead bowl. Grass was black. Trees were black. Rooftops were black. The monster, black already, soaked it up and shone blacker. Closer now. It moved on hind legs like a human, and though it had a round thing like a head, there was no face. Even closer, a revision: it had a face, but its eye sockets were swollen shut, its nose was gone, and its lower jaw was missing, turning the bottom half of its head into a rapacious hole. The monster had no skin, no fingers, and no toes, but it did have a porcupine exoskeleton, unless those were shards of embedded glass, which they were.

The monster, once upon a time a man, had no senses left and yet sensed me.

It swayed in the apocalyptic rain.

A wheeze fluted from its cauterized chest.

Forget our winners and losers. Forget Hitler, Stalin, Churchill, Truman. If the lil' gadget had cracked open the Atomic Age, then this was the only offspring that counted, one fertilized by Yggdrasil cinder, a New Man nothing like the Übermensch the Germans had promised. He was not white, but black. He was not blond, but hairless. He was not tall, but shriveled. He was not strong, but diseased. Yet it was he, the Millennialist, who'd been birthed from total war, who would forevermore point humankind's way with his fingerless nubs and symbolize, for me, America's soul, incinerated in a mad dash for Progress.

Far across the Pacific, snug in beds it believed unassailable, America had that morning contracted the Millennialist's disease as well, and though it would take decades to notice the symptoms, each man, woman, and child had become my sibling in degeneration. Splitting atoms atop living subjects had been an experiment, hadn't

163

it? Not so different from the experiments upon the Mauthausen dissection tables? The results, as I read them, were conclusive to those
looking through the right kind of goggles.

America was sick.

Our empire had begun to decay.

PART EIGHT

1946–1957

—⸺◦⟨⟪◉⟫⟩◦⸺—

It Happens That Your Hero Finds Better Living, Good Hygiene, And Mutual Annihilation In A Paint-By-Numbers Landscape.

I.

AMERICA WAS AN INDUSTRIAL TARN of gluey asphalt, and upward was the only feasible direction, were I to extract myself from its eternal black slurp. Just as with my Marine Corps unit twenty-seven years prior, I'd been shipped to Virginia, the site of a military base where they handed over—carefully, so that they did not have to touch me—four years of back wages and discharged me, dishonorably it seemed, though there was no red stamp to prove it. I bought a compass and set off northward, alternating between hitchhiking and plain old hiking.

It was 1946, but it felt as though I were back with Dr. Whistler's Pageant of Health along a medicine-show circuit. I traveled through Maryland orchards, sniffing for the funk of Lake Erie, though what I smelled instead was cooked flesh. Legions of apple trees concealed a twiglike lurker—the Millennialist, that reminder of humankind's futility, his bottomless jester jaw japing. Loud though were the demands of the Fifty-One that I right more wrongs—fifty-two of them, fifty-three, up, up, up—the Millennialist's desert gasp boomed louder. I hooked west to the scrapyards of Pennsylvania; the Millennialist shuffled there, too, his wide-open arms shimmering like steel. Every Ohio valley: he slunk, a garter snake through grass. Indiana's ochre plains: he was a road sign driven into Earth's heart. Illinois's cropland grids: he advanced between stripes of soy, ashing poison.

I kept well south of Chicago, that blinking lighthouse of regret, but Iowa's ocean of corn, crackling like wind through the Millennialist's crust, brought to mind Church, a regret almost as strong. I fixed my compass and hitched into the northwest sands of Wisconsin. That wasn't north enough, so I jagged around the Duluth point of Lake Superior and into Minnesota's iron range and northern bogs until I hit the Canadian border. Despite the soft footfalls scrunching from behind, I could not stomach another expatriatism. I'd died in America; I'd live here too.

Up, up, up, this time not latitudinal but altitudinal, across the Dakota badlands and into Montana, where the Barker used to tell our audience he'd found me, living *with bland parents in a small clay hut*. Could I pretend he'd been right, that this was my second home? Miles before the logging truck I'd hitched reached the Rockies, I could see the mountains, a gray stripe like an incoming storm, and after being dropped off in Great Falls and surmounting my first foothill, I gazed past a mint valley, cerulean stream, and black firs to the snow-shouldered behemoths whose arched backs scraped the clouds. I thought of Otto Rahn as I began to climb.

Those without breath go unaffected by altitude. I ascended through white hills of beargrass, acres of loose purple rock, and into peaks so burnt by cold that all flora had been flayed away. I shimmied rock steeples until there was nowhere left to climb, then stared into the blister-white sun for signs of Gød's back, or backside, anything at which I might launch boulders.

High atop Mount Cleveland I carved myself a cave and spent months attuned for the Millennialist's cinder crunch—the sound of my conscience, you might say. Instead I found myself lulled by the clop-clop of elk, the cry of the falcon, the scritch of the stealthing mountain lion. They were straightforward, nonduplicitous sounds. I settled in, developed a crude stone chisel, and spent days sawing off the rib tip that jutted from my chest.

Winter built a blizzard megalopolis of snow castles, and I froze, then unfroze digging myself out, then froze again under the next silver storm, and the next, and the next. Spring came, snow ceding half its claim to pink rock, and little green aliens extended their weed necks from crevices. Then came the comet flash of summer, the orange-and-red skirmish of autumn, and the first entombment of a second winter. I should have welcomed the return, and yet, there among the rock, I grew ever lonelier. Even though I did not voice it, I nonetheless heard it echo all about the top of the world. After I could take it no longer, I dug a tunnel from my grotto and began pushing through waist-high snow to lower altitudes.

For several seasons, I adopted the nomadic ways of wildlife, trading territories with moose and mule deer, bobcat and badger, pronghorn and pika, emulating the way each kept an ear perked for danger. There was none, not for me. For the first time in my death, not to mention life, I was neither predator nor prey. Though loneliness clung to me like dried mud, I attempted a philosopher's ethos and searched for meaning in the dendrochronology of tree rings, the fractal spirals of raindrops in spiderwebs, the constellations of wildflowers efflorescing from a previous season's decay. Life beget death beget life beget death—only I, as always, resisted natural cycles.

I believe it was the spring of 1950 when my cliffside contemplation of a herd of buffalo was interrupted by an unexpected guest in the valley below. It moved too casually for a wolf; the buffalo, when they saw it, did not flee. It was, realized I, a human being who passed between the eight-foot, one-ton mammoths as easily as a jay. Though

I'd seen, and even heard, evidence of hikers on occasion, I hadn't laid eyes on a biped in three years. Disused parts of my brain, and heart, twitched.

Days I spent girdling the valley, but it was weeks before I spotted him again, this time at a closer perspective. He was lean and wore a cowboy hat, tinted snow goggles, a brown coat insulated with animal fur, and a cowhide rucksack, upon which was strapped an ice ax. I found him watching two grizzlies from an unsafe distance, though the bears did not appear to mind. He stood there for hours; even I, who'd mastered the art of inaction, grew impatient.

When he at last walked, he did so on boots affixed with metal cleats.

I should have let him be. But I was not full beast, not quite.

He slept in a canvas tent, and after a week he hiked for thirty-six hours to a log cabin. Nothing like the extravagant Swiss chalets I'd seen on the subalpine piedmont, this was a one-room, chimneyed affair that smelled of good, clean blood. The fellow was intimidatingly capable. He emerged periodically to parcel game and clean trout. The resultant bag of offal, he dangled from a tree out of the reach of bears until he had time to burn or bury it.

Over the full year I spent stalking the man, not once did he break from the mountain, welcome a visitor, or evidence any particular scheme against land or animal. His exile, like mine, seemed self-inflicted. Still, it came as a shock that clear, blue day he called out to me, for I'd grown certain that I'd become as faint as the Millennialist.

"You, boy." He sat upon a stump chair that, months earlier, he'd fashioned by reducing its tree to firewood. "Closer."

My instinct was to caper off like a white-tailed deer. But a mammal's eyes are what imparts its malice, and this man had hidden his by looking lapward, where he quartered an apple. The Excelsior in my breast pocket thump-thumped as I advanced with a lynx's caution. The man spat a bad hunk and gestured me in with the knife. I exited the forest canopy, felt exposed in the grass.

"These apples fixing to rot," said he. "Might as well share."

At close range he looked rather like an apple himself, one left in the sun to wrinkle and brown. Two watery eyes strained past wads of sunburnt wrinkle and through the shadow cast by his hat brim. He was at least sixty, but retained a square-jawed cattle-wrangler essence. He cut another slice, thumbed it between strong white teeth.

"Been watching you a spell. Wasn't sure you knew words."

Zebulon Finch, the boy once ashamed of his fussy diction, presumed to be a feral mute? There was a dark justice to the presumption. I cleared my throat, and to my horror it sounded clotted with years of soil, leaves, and rock, and I worried that my long-neglected voice might indeed be a savage, unmodulated thing. Echoes of old language lessons crashed about my skull (*indefatigable!*) but I was afraid to attempt them. Silence had, after all, served me well as talisman against the pain of companionship.

He scooped an apple from the pile at his feet and lobbed it. I caught it against my chest.

"You want more?" asked he.

I regarded the apple's wine gleam and shook my head.

"You cold? I got a blanket. Half burnt, but half not."

The kindness weakened me, but again I shook my head.

He pointed his knife at my feet.

"Soles worn through. I got a bad old pair of boots."

He raised his billowy white eyebrows. I looked down, wiggled my toes through the holes in the leather. He chewed, apple juice

171

dribbling down his whiskery chin, until I nodded so delicately that I was uncertain that I'd done it.

He woodchucked his apple to the core before lumbering into the cabin. My brain, long divorced from domestication, shouted at me to run, but I reminded myself that I was no hare. I was a human being—wasn't I? Before I could be sure, the man returned, tossed through the air a pair of boots, and reclaimed his stump. The boots landed at my feet. The shafts were mangled, but they would be a great improvement over civilian wear. I picked them up.

"Need anything else?" asked he.

Did I? It had been so long since I'd been asked.

He shrugged.

"All right. Get on, then."

I did what he said, the animal part of me relieved to scamper, but I did not stray far. The boot heels lifted me two inches that might as well have been two miles. I felt tall, vertical, humanlike. After a week, I laxed my lurking so that the man would spot me again. He had a deer strung up by its hindquarters and was skinning it. He was busy, but favored me with a nod, and before I left, tossed me an old coat that had been slashed by horn and thistle. I transferred my Excelsior, envelopes of government cash, and other valuables into the new coat and put it on. It set squarely upon my shoulders and brought to mind forgotten things: drinks, parlors, civilized discourse.

My dead body ached.

It did not escape my notice over the eighteen months of our odd acquaintance that my role was that of stray dog, his of scrap-offering master. By then I knew a mutt's mind. There was nothing wrong with accepting charity if it meant propagation in a harsh world. Gradually we came to spend a portion of every day together, with me, by custom, staying silent; and him, by character, speaking only when he had something to say—roughly two or three times per week.

His name? It never came up.

We were, learned I, deep inside Glacier National Park. Yes, Reader, in my race to reach untrammeled worlds, I'd stumbled into a property that President Taft had institutionalized forty years before. The man in the cowboy hat shared my disappointment. The land, growled he, belonged to the Blackfoot nation, who'd given this continental divide the more satisfying moniker of "the Backbone of the World." Despite feuds lasting well into the 1890s (during which time I'd been knocking heads in Chicago), the Great Northern Railway had effectively ended Blackfoot dominance.

Musing was all I had left to do, so I mused upon the generations of vision quests taken by Blackfoot adolescents. I liked to think, naïve though it was, that these spiritual journeys had influenced my own wanderings, and that I, like them, had drawn from solitude insight into how fragile, temporal bodies could find infinity within nature's renewals. By becoming less than human—by becoming animal— might one indeed become *more* than human?

After all, the man in the cowboy hat's objective, if not obsession, was to walk among animals without trace of fear, to feel the moist heat of buffalo exhalations, to smell the private stinks of mountain goat fur, to hear the indulgent clucks of a black bear as it watched its cubs nuzzle his legs.

Under his quiet tutelage, I too did these impossible things. The feats frightened me at first, the flickering eyes of beasts, the yellow teeth, the flexing claws. What pushed to the forefront of my mind was a battle charge near Champagne, France, where my beloved Seventh Marine Regiment gyrenes had wrestled the Blanc Mont Ridge from

173

the Germans. Both armies had leveled armaments for close combat, when a deer, still spotted with fawnhood, bolted between the forces. The soldiers, Yank and Hun alike, pulled up weapons so that this creature of grace could live without a taste of our fabled "humanity."

Glacier became the attic study where my hatted tutor drilled this lesson: animal violence bore no resemblance to that of humans. A weasel pounced upon a snake, only to become prey to a diving hawk. Animals protected their flesh and blood, not the constructs of ideology. Thirteen years after reading Bridey's unproduced opus, that filmic fable called *In Our Image*, I understood this to be its central theme.

Humans had been wretched to me; in turn, I'd been wretched to humans. Yet from my first days in the Pageant of Health, who alone had offered me respect? Insects, Dearest Reader. Vermin, Dearest Reader. Every animal, Dearest Reader, aside from the Barker's wicked Silly Sally. Rather than gobble at my corpse, as critters were born to do, they'd recognized my inhumanity and offered me the Animalia accord.

I admired the Blackfoot people, but cursed them.

You knew about all this, thought I, *and kept it secret.*

I expect that you crave anecdotes elucidating the crusty good nature of the man in the cowboy hat, our shared moments of collegiality, the reciprocating tenderness underlying our masculine exchanges. You are, I am afraid, out of luck. It took until the first thaw of our second year together before I even learned why he was in Glacier. He'd been a successful land developer, receiver of certificate and plaque for his knack for predicting new areas of growth. Years back he'd told employers that he was headed to Montana to reconnoiter for mountainside lodges, when in truth he'd grown sick about his role in the rape of land.

Therefore it smelled fishy when he began making jaunts to nearby ranger stations, returning with bags of victuals, with which I had no quibble, and bound blocks of newspaper, from which I recoiled. He began using his graveled voice regularly to recount the major world events I had missed.

It was feculent news, all of it. In 1949, despite the paired apocalypses of Hiroshima and Nagasaki, the Soviets had made a show of testing their own A-bomb. As if engaged in a hand of cribbage, the U.S. took its turn, hatching a thermonuclear hydrogen bomb thousands of times worse. The USSR answered, of course, with their own H-bomb. Pegs were breaking off in the cribbage board, making it impossible for anyone to win.

Hear that hissing across leaves?

The prankster Millennialist resurfaces.

As an animal, I could but sit there and take the updates like kicks. In 1950, America had joined a conflict in a place called Korea, where warring factions acted as proxies for big brothers America and Russia. (The Millennialist thumped his fingerless palms against the cabin walls.) The Korean War came to armistice in 1953, but on the homefront a senator named McCarthy revived Detective Roseborough's Red Scare and began witch-hunting purported Commies from every arena of life. (The Millennialist, made of ash, began to seep through gaps in the cabin walls.) In 1954, racial segregation began its path toward illegality, to raucous uproar, a mere three decades too late to save John Quincy's brood. (The Millennialist spread through the cabin air; upon him all of America would choke.)

"Stop," said I. "Stop. Stop."

They were the first and last words the man in the cowboy hat needed to hear from me. I cared about these human problems, after

175

all this time I still goddamn cared, and it was impossible for me to hide it. He folded the most current newspaper, threw it into the fire, and squatted to jab it to brighter life.

"This here's a place for wild things," said he. "Even I'll go home one day."

I pressed a cold face into colder hands. For months he'd been acclimating me to lower altitudes, yet it was hard to envision how I would survive without him, all the way back down on Earth. He'd saved me from a desolation as broad and long as the Rockies.

"Sorry, son. But you got to go back. If we wait much longer, I won't be able to help you like I'm able to help you now. They won't remember me forever."

My shoulders shuddered with dry sobs.

That night he produced correspondence he'd been trading, via ranger stations, with colleagues in residential development. There was a brand-new kind of neighborhood, he told me, that aimed to combine the best of rural life with the best of urban—ideal, or so promised his real-estate associates, for easing a recluse back into society. They called these places "the suburbs," and to encourage growth, the Veterans Administration, under the GI Bill, was offering initiatives and incentives.

Should I want a home, the VA would find me one.

The man in the cowboy hat shrugged. He didn't know shit about the suburbs, but he'd gone against his own ecological principles to ensure I could try them for myself.

"There's two kinds of courage," said he. "Shoot, out here you've seen plenty of both. There's the courage to die. And there's the courage to live."

I thought of the hawk eating the weasel eating the snake, and

176

wondered which segment of the chain was the hardest to bear.

My trip down the slushy springtime mountain was a bright, frightening one. I had taken the man's old boots and coat, but it was his cowboy hat I wanted, to shield myself from the unnatural brilliance of tin roofs and stop signs. Everything was arranged and waiting for me, including a rented car—a 1945 Pontiac Streamliner gnawed away by road salt and trembling with age—several road maps, and the name and address of a man in a faraway town who would help get me settled. The man in the cowboy hat's good-bye was as offhand as his hello: a nod, a spit, and then a turn on his heel before heading up, up, up.

I did not watch him go. I got into the Streamliner and busied myself with a dashboard full of strange buttons and levers. My prized Tin Lizzie had taught me the basics, however, and I'd spent many an hour watching Kuppisch operate a Mercedes. I got the engine running and hit a country road, which soon melted into a paved thoroughfare. The Federal-Aid Highway Act of 1956 and its 41,000 miles of new roadways was two years off, but groundwork was being laid. Cars zoomed by at impossible speeds, and gray-pink roadkill blemished the pavement—my friends the animals, having been swatted by a Gød unhappy about my earthward return.

Giant billboards, meanwhile, began to shout. The first one I saw featured a rough-hewn wrangler in a kerchief and cowboy hat, squinting past a halo of flavorful tobacco smoke. He was "the Marlboro Man," and it comforted me to see him each time he appeared along my southward journey. At last I had a name for the bronzed, grizzled angel who'd escorted me back up the Road to Heaven.

II.

HILLSBOROUGH ESTATES, HILL PARK, PARK Hills, Park Village, Village Garden, Garden Greens, Green Forests, Forest Lake, Lakewood Homes, Homes at Fairview, Fairwood Ranchos, Ranch at Elmwood, Dutch Elm Valley, Sunrise Valley, Sunset Hills. Coming Soon! Buy Today! Turn Left Here! *Exit Right Now!*

Suburbs sucked like ticks to the belly of every city, off the nearest highway and tucked just out of view, though I could hear their screams of tranquility and feel their beating fists of welcome. My rental car returned, I was in the back of a taxi, which tootled along at a speed so slow, it would incite riots in New York City. We were, of course, a long way from that city, in Wichita, Kansas. Well, outside of Wichita, the whole point of the suburbs, after all, being the distance between.

The Marlboro Man in Glacier hadn't been blind; he'd known my hitchhiking days were behind me. I'd had fifteen-hundred miles and the first reflective surface I'd seen in years—the rearview mirror—to reach the same conclusion. The arctic clime of the Rockies had, at least, preserved me somewhat. My skin was light brown, not florid purple, and instead of molting in sheets it had a claylike consistency—if you poked it, it held the impress. Luckiest of all, the cold had stunted what should have been a rancid stench; instead of stinking like a pile

178

of carrion, I smelled as if a small splotch of it was pasted to the bottom of my boot.

So I was prepared for the wince of the Marlboro Man's contact, an ex-Army lieutenant in the municipal housing department who sent me packing to Heavenly Hills, Wichita's largest suburban development. After the toothed crags of Glacier, the wending drive through the suburb was a funhouse ride of jarring geometrics: mown yards, stone-shingled sidewalks, cropped hedgerows.

Like flowers from soil popped rows of prefabricated clapboard houses, each snapped together in budget forgeries of Colonial styles. Each abode came standard with a sentinel mailbox, hugging shrubbery, detached garage, pitched roof, and picture window, through which were glimpsed scenes of such domiciliary bliss that the dormant criminal in me ticked with an urge to smash. It was only each house's bright enamel finish that suggested individuality—sandstone orange, sage green, turquoise blue, lemon yellow.

The taxi crested the gentlest rise, and I saw, beyond uncountable mazy cul-de-sacs, a cavalry of construction vehicles mauling farmland to prepare for future development waves. The American family had become the crop, and the black blood and iron ash of Hiroshima served as fertilizer. But no matter! The cloudless April day squashed all shadow. I felt a pinch in my cheeks. Was it a smile? Indeed, indeed! And I knew whence it came, for in this sun-drenched land of wobbling lawn sprinklers, each one painting a rainbow across pollen-speckled air, there was nowhere at all for the Millennialist to skulk.

The sprinklers, I am obligated to mention, hissed like snakes.

On Mulberry Terrace, we stopped before a rectilinear domicile like any other, except painted a sinister cherry pink. I clung to the seat. Was any color more threatening? After a solid minute of paralysis the driver cleared his throat, and I handed over the cash. He was careful not to touch my hand when he took it.

He drove away, going twice as fast now, stranding me on the curb. In his wake, birds chirped. Radio soap operas blabbered. Somewhere, a baby laughed. This neighborhood was no Nazi Germany, but I felt almost as lost inside it. I steeled myself, gripped my bulky suitcase (a prop, containing almost nothing), and headed up the driveway, sidewalk, and front steps. The pinkness disoriented me, but there was a railing to grip. I prepared my knuckles for knocking, before spying beside the door a big silver button. It looked as if it ought to be pushed, so I, never one to resist temptation, pushed it, half expecting a retaliatory spray of pink paint. Instead, four chimes rang inside the house—the Westminster Quarters, familiar from my youthful churchgoings. Hold on—were the suburbs theistic enclaves? I took a step back, scanned for the taxi, and considered running.

The door flew wide.

Mrs. Shirley White was younger than anticipated. She was twenty-six, pretty but stern-chinned, with natural orange hair set in a permanent-wave pin-curl cut that nuzzled into her shoulders. It was in moderate disarray; a lock had caught in the string of pearls tight around her neck. She wore a periwinkle polka-dot dress, though I could not say if it flattered her figure, because of a shin-length yellow apron. She wiped her hands on it, streaking flour. Her eyes bounced away from me after only a second.

She'd been warned about my appearance.

"Mr. Gray, is it?"

Was that the name I'd chosen? With all this color, I couldn't think. Yes, that's right, Mr. Joe Gray, for I'd been afraid that my hostess might recall the name "Zebulon Finch" from the photo spreads with Bridey Valentine in the 1940s. Alas, Mrs. White wasn't old enough to have been a *Photoplay* subscriber, and now I was stuck with the unbecoming alias.

"Joe Gray," confirmed I. "How do you do."

She did not extend her hand for shaking. Her eyes skittered down the lane, as if concerned we might be spotted.

"Come in, sit down. Can I get you a cup of Nescafé?"

My response of *What, exactly, the hell is Nescafé?* was lost, as was the sound of the door closing behind me, for the room I'd entered was not a room at all but an electric pink womb. I shielded my eyes, staggered, found a chair and collapsed into it. This was . . . a kitchen? But constructed in what kind of delirium? The checkerboard floors were pink. The curtains were pink. The refrigerator was pink. Dearest Reader, are you hearing me? *The refrigerator was pink.* And larger than von Lüth, a hulking, huffing turbine that, when Mrs. White opened it to retrieve a carafe of milk, revealed a robin egg–colored musculature of shelving, wild entanglements of golden bars and trays, hinged doors, and sliding drawers. Soda bottles jingled and plastic-wrapped jellies quivered.

Mrs. White placed the milk on the pink countertop and filled a pink percolator from the stainless steel sink. A half-eaten piece of cake was on the counter; she took it, dumped it into the sink, and flipped a switch. The sink roared to hellish life with the snicking whirlwind of a thousand sharp teeth. I jumped—a Communist booby-trap here in Midwestern suburbia!—but Mrs. White thought nothing of it, retrieving two mugs from a pink cabinet, leaning an aproned hip against the stove, and lighting a cigarette.

I detected a scent. A strange one, pleasant even, but after the

181

loamy bouquets of the mountains and the oil-stink of the Stream-liner, it was too exotic to identify.

Mrs. White's cig winked red.

"I don't know how much they told you," said she.

"Only that you have an available room."

"A room for *rent*. Nothing personal, but this isn't a charity situation."

"Of course." I indicated the suitcase. "I am able to pay."

"That's fine. But I want to be up-front with you, Mr. Gray. I have some—well, hesitations. My Charles was a soldier too, and when I heard about this program, helping injured soldiers rejoin communities and all that, I knew that's what Charles would have wanted. And I do need the extra money. But you're a single man. I can't have any trouble here. I have two children, you know. They barely understand what happened to their father. It's been less than a year."

Through a merlon of expelled smoke, she dared a longer look. By the time the percolator gurgled and its red light mirrored the tip of the cigarette, Mrs. White had moderated the grind of her jaw. I believed that she felt relief. I was, to be blunt, disfigured, and therefore my presence was unlikely to be construed by neighbors as untoward. She prepared the Nescafé, centered our cups upon pink saucers, and joined me at the pink breakfast-nook table. I lifted my cup and considered the anemic beige bilge.

"What *did* happen to Mr. White, if I may ask?"

She snugged her cig between her knuckles and with the same hand brought her cup to red-painted lips. Smoke and steam braided.

"Korea."

It was apparent that no further details were in the offing, and for that I was grateful. Mrs. White had been told that my own war had

182

been Korea, not World War I, and the fewer specifics offered about either conflict, the better off I'd be.

"So what it is you do, Mr. Gray?"

I'd had fifteen hundred miles to concoct clever cover.

"I am a writer," proclaimed I.

She ashed.

"Are you one of those men who writes about war? What it means and all that?"

I'd studied the book racks each time I'd stopped for a twenty-cent tank of gasoline. Men called Hemingway, Jones, Mailer, Salinger, Uris, and Vidal had made combat experience a prerequisite for crafting the Great American Novel; it was reasonable to believe that Korea vets like myself would follow their lead. Of course I'd read not a single published line from these literary lions. My familiarity with modern lit began and ended with Jason Stavros, the poet-soldier who'd survived trench warfare in hopes of doing exactly what Mrs. White had cavalierly dismissed.

"You have it exactly right," said I. "War. What it means. All that."

I set down the coffee cup with finality.

"Careful," snapped she. "You'll dent the Formica."

"The what?"

Her green eyes, bolder now, searched for evidence that I was putting her on. Oh, how I loathed being ugly, and yet I returned my bravest face. At last she shrugged, wedged her cigarette into the crenellation of an ash tray, and slid across the table an aerodynamic chrome cube outfitted with dual ammunition slots and a spring-loaded trigger. I tensed for action. It was a shrapnel bomb, and this woman was some kind of kitchen kamikaze.

"This toaster," sighed she. "It's made by Western Brass. They made torpedoes, you know? I figured they could make a pop-up toaster. But I'd kill to have my Toastmaster back. This thing's a hunk of junk. You can't adjust it worth a hoot. It burns one piece, then hardly heats the next."

I traced the gadget's electrical cord to the wall outlet. There, upon a platter, were piled some ten pieces of cold toast, the color of one char-black, the next virgin-white, proof of Mrs. White's unflagging siege against the alleged time-saver.

An egg-timer buzzed. The woman sprung from her chair, yanked on an oven mitt, and opened the oven. The pleasant aroma I'd detected earlier poured forth in a visible cloud, damp and sweet like a summer's morning mist.

"So, the toaster," said she. "Do you think you can fix it?"

Perhaps a fib was a dicey way to begin a relationship, but the scent was so intoxicating that suddenly I could not imagine a life without it. Survive cruel winters in the Rocky Mountains I could do; stroke the antler velvet of feeding elk I could do; but how to fix a toaster, I hadn't the first cockamamie clue.

"I can fix it," said I.

"Good. Like I said, it's nothing personal, but that's what I put in for. A man who could help around the house. I know you have an illness, or an ailment, and I'm sorry about that, but without Charles, this place is falling apart and I can't keep pestering the neighbors every time a light goes on the fritz. I know they say the suburbs are full of young couples, but that's not true, not in Heavenly Hills. Half the people here are older than sin. And they avoid me, I swear they do. It's like Charles's death was polio and they're afraid they'll catch it."

The proclamation was punctuated by the clatter of cooking pan,

184

scrape of spatula, and clang of plate being set upon more Formica. With a whirl of apron hem, she spun on a high heel and planted before me a plate of chocolate-chip cookies. I was seventeen, or seventy-five, either way too old to be hypnotized by confections. Yet something about the golden dough and gooey chocolate squeezed my dead heart.

"Toll House," said she.

I nodded, gathered my suitcase, and began to unbuckle it.

"And how much is this toll?"

She sat down, crossed her legs, then arms.

"Toll House. It's a cookie mix. You've really been away from it all, haven't you?"

Good and humiliated, and constitutionally incapable of partaking in either Nescafé or Toll House, I tried to save face by busying myself with the toaster. I peered into its twin abysses and shaped what I hoped were wise, scrutable frowns. It worked. Mrs. White stamped her cig and exhaled.

"All right. If you're willing to do some handiwork, like I said, I can lower the rent to sixty dollars a month. Including meals."

Even in pink plastic palaces crafty minxes crept. The housing honcho in Wichita had told me that Mrs. White of Heavenly Hills had advertised her spare room at fifty dollars. My hesitation at this price hike was minute, but, perhaps feeling guilty, she tightened her crossed arms and scowled.

"Charles was a wonderful man, but his financial planning . . . He didn't do as much with war bonds as he might have. The house alone cost six thousand. It was too much. I told him so, but you couldn't talk Charles out of anything once he had his mind set. Now he's gone and there's a mortgage. I have to pay it, don't I?"

The insolent tilt of Mrs. White's chin recalled Merle's, though it was plain to the eye that she hadn't my daughter's steel skeleton.

"A perfectly sensible price," said I.

"First month in advance, of course."

"Of course."

"And you'll have to keep one eye on the children on Monday nights. I have my bowling league in the city. The Lane Ladies. I can't miss my bowling league."

"No, that would be regrettable."

"And I have canasta after dinner on Wednesdays at Mrs. Shoemaker's."

"Canasta Wednesdays. Very good."

"And Junior League meetings every third Sunday. I believe volunteerism is vital for a vibrant community, don't you?"

"And how, and how."

After she exhausted herself of blather, the only sound was the scritch of her red-painted nails across the rim of the cookie plate. Two extrusive canines bungled her otherwise straight teeth, and these fangs chewed at her bottom lip as if hoping for another cigarette to facilitate a final confession.

"And I work."

Her fair skin went the same pink as the walls.

"Only while the children are at school. But from time to time my supervisor has me stay late and the children get home before I do. It's just—well, you need to know about that. I work at the library, and only part-time, but I know that's not something everyone considers proper. Neighbors come to the library with their children. I have eyes, I see how they look at me. But what the Army gave me for Charles's death wasn't enough, not even close. There's nothing wrong with a woman who works, even a woman with children. Nothing at all."

'Twas not me that she hoped to convince.

"I am a writer," reassured I. "I shall be here. Writing."

She nodded, her face draining back toward white.

"I'll show you your room then, Mr. Gray."

"You may call me Joe."

Her smile was piano-wire taut.

"Mr. Gray will be fine," said she. "And you may call me Mrs. White."

III.

THOUGH SHE WAS THE PHYSICAL opposite of the Marine Corps's Major Horstmeier, Mrs. White delivered orders at the same clip, assigning my first project within thirty seconds: a hole in the wall outside my room, punched by the negligent elbow of her son. The hole had been there for two years, sighed she. Could I plaster it and paint it? As easy as pie, I lied. I was prepared to agree to anything if it meant I could get inside that room and, hoped I, never emerge again.

The room was a former storage area, long and narrow and just wide enough for a single bed, a chipped wardrobe, and a desk-and-chair set tailor-made for an enterprising author. Though partitioned from the basement, this was no Berlin bomb shelter. Sunlight shone from three lawn-level windows that, if I jumped, allowed dandelion-obstructed views of the side and back yards. I resolved to block them out.

The egg timer again cried like an infant, and Mrs. White swished away, leaving me to unpack my sparse cargo. My single sad change of clothing I hung in the wardrobe. My envelopes of cash I stashed beneath the mattress. The last and heaviest item in the suitcase was my one prop, a sea-foam blue Royal Quiet de Luxe portable typewriter I'd picked up in Cheyenne, Wyoming—a much kindlier device than von Lüth's Enigma. I centered it upon the desk, stacked next to it a pile of "twin-pak" ink ribbons, and contemplated the forty-nine teeth of its goofy grin.

Quickly I saw the flaw in my pseudonymous ploy. If Mrs. White did not hear typing, she would become suspicious. I rifled through my belongings until I found a single sheet of paper—the receipt for the rented Streamliner, blank on the reverse. Then I—Mr. Joe Gray, Author!—sat at my writer's desk, knobbed the paper through the guide, snapped the release level, returned the carriage, and adjusted the Magic Margin stop. I limbered my stiff fingers above the sleek plastic keys.

It was at that inconvenient instant that I discovered that, given the decades of strife it had caused me, the notion of writing was abhorrent. I fished the murky waters of memory for a phrase I could type without thinking, and for my sins landed upon Luca Testa's immortal warning, later echoed by the Barker and reignited when Church almost died. It was easier to yield than resist; I made pointers of my fingers and began to type.

You gotta have fear in your heart.

Carriage return.

You gotta have fear in your heart.

Carriage return.

You gotta have fear in your heart.

Carriage return.

Not quite Pulitzer-level, but the musical *clickety-clackety-zing!* did help thwart flashbacks of each deleterious time I'd ignored the advice, as did the overhead clop of Mrs. White's heels and the metallic chokes of the toaster dishonoring another slice of bread. My fingers eased into secretarial position and soon had coated the page in Testa's augury. Upon finishing, I rolled the page back to its top, discovered the shift key, and added another patina of type atop the first, this time in capitals. Enjoyable? Hardly. But there was a gratification in watching something pure white stain black.

The sensation did not survive the afternoon. So accustomed was I to mountain vistas that the low plasterboard ceiling and faux-wood-panel walls contracted upon me; the frayed Navajo rug beneath my feet, meanwhile, made a shameful replacement for the Blackfoot wilds. How I scratched and fidgeted! When I heard from outdoors a mechanized cry not unlike the hydra inside Mrs. White's kitchen sink, I welcomed the distraction. I scooted my chair alongside the wall, stepped atop it, and peered into the backyard.

My grub's-eye view looked between the slats of a white picket fence, behind which a man in a chambray shirt pushed along a gargan-tuan tomato-red lawn mower powered by what looked like a race-car engine. It spat bright green grass like Maxim machine guns did lead. It was a hell of a thing, and I admired the impressive low-hanging cloud it emitted. At one point, the man idled to accept a glass of lemonade from a woman in an apron embroidered with pastel hearts. I pressed my forehead to the glass, eager for a gander at her goods. Even eunuchs, Dearest Reader, can appreciate a pair of gams.

A monster smashed its beslobbered face against my window. I yelped and pinwheeled for balance as thick jaws cranked wide and a pink tongue darted past sharp white teeth. Blasts of hot breath clouded the glass before a wet black nose wiped enough of it away that I could see a single crazed, idiot eye goggling at me.

It was a dog. A filthy dog.

The Whites had a goddamned filthy dog.

The hellhound snuffled and galloped off. Seconds later came shrieks of glee as four dimple-kneed legs gave chase. Here was

Mrs. White's aforementioned litter, louder than the canine's bark, louder than the grass-gobbling mower, louder than their mother's upstairs pacing. I retreated from my post and, to my disrepute, went fetal upon the bed. So much light! So much life! So much noise! This was not a suitable crypt within which a corpse could putresce in peace.

It got worse. When dinnertime arrived at the indecent hour of five thirty, Mrs. White came downstairs and cleared her throat. This fabricated world had customs, and by dint of anchoring at its port, it seemed, those customs became my own. I tugged jacket cuffs and tautened tie, and then, feeling quite sorry for myself, slumped up the stairs as if to meet the hangman.

By the time I found the dining room, the family was seated and expectant. I took the open chair, trying not to think of its bygone claimant. Mrs. White offered me a cordial smile, but her eyes ricocheted between her children, a young boy and an even younger girl. I sympathized with her concern. One look at my discolored flesh, and either child might break out bawling.

Instead the youngsters gawped.

"Children," said Mrs. White. "This is Mr. Gray, who I told you about. Why don't you introduce yourselves?"

Their open mouths could have accommodated softballs.

My dislike of ragamuffins was nothing new. Besides Little Johnny Grandpa—hardly an ordinary child—I'd shared space with but one, Gladys Leather, who as an infant had revolted me with superfluities of mucus and mewlings, and then, as she'd grown, frazzled my nerves with mood swings, asphyxiating with giggles one minute, only to asphyxiate with sorrow the next. Nevertheless, I would juggle kittens if it meant skirting turbulence.

"Salutations, juveniles," said I. "It is satisfactory to make your acquaintance."

The girl blinked huge eyes. She was a soft sprite, uncreased by life, white-blond hair partitioned into ribboned pigtails.

"You talk funny," whispered she.

"Mr. Gray, this is Franny. Franny, tell Mr. Gray how old you are."

"Five," whispered Franny.

"No," said Mrs. White. "You're six. You just had a birthday, didn't you?"

"Can I go to my room?" whispered Franny.

"And this is Charles Junior. He's nine. Junior, say hello to Mr. Gray."

Unlike that of his catatonic sister, the boy's brain was functional. He was orange-haired like his mother, though his mop was largely hidden beneath a coonskin cap that, from its crunchy condition, looked to be the unwashed mainstay of his getup. Like a raccoon, his eyes were small, bright, and nocturnal.

"Gee whiz, Mr. Gray, you don't look so good."

Mrs. White touched her pearls. Junior perceived his gaucherie.

"Oh, goobers. Sorry, Mother. Sorry, Mr. Gray. I didn't mean anything, honest."

I lifted a papal hand. "I am, in fact, not entirely well. My particular affliction does not, for example, permit me to eat the same food as the rest of you."

Mrs. White, conservator of the consummate kitchen, frowned.

"Then what do you eat?"

Toast, I wished to reply. *Piles and piles of poorly made toast.*

"I have my own stock of consumables. Vitamins, nutriments. It's all very scientific."

"Well, I—I suppose you know best. All the same, I can't have a lodger and not invite him to dinner. Even if you don't eat. Why, it wouldn't be Christian."

Her sculpted orange eyebrows rose in expectation of resistance. Damn it to hell. I could find no grounds. I nodded and hoped that my expression conveyed thankfulness rather than dread. Mrs. White shaped another joyless smile and then, without prelude, clasped her hands and bowed her head. Junior and Franny followed suit. My spirits plunged. A prayer to that welsher Gød? I'd debased myself a hundred ways in only a few hours, but there were depths to which I would not sink.

"Thank you, Lord, for the blessing of this bountiful meal. Thank you for helping me find the courage to ask for a raise at the library, which I did not get, but it was a good learning experience anyway. Thank you, Lord, for watching over Junior and Franny at school. And thank you for protecting Mr. Gray in Korea. He will need help and guidance to get healthy and become a successful writer. In Jesus's name we pray—"

"Amen," the troika of fools chorused.

While the children sparred over serving spoons, Mrs. White took pointed note of my heathen hands, which still lay flat and naked.

"What *is* your condition, Mr. Gray, if you don't mind me asking?"

The woman knew not the profundity of her query.

Rapidly I cycled through my violent genesis with the Black Hand.

"Black Hand," blurted I. "Blackhand. Blackhand's Disease."

"Oh, my," gasped she. "That *does* sound bad."

Mrs. White returned her focus to the meal, which looked, in a word, revolting. She dubbed the entrée "the Twenty-Minute Roast," though, in my opinion, if said roast is wedges of Spam spackled with orange marmalade, you ought to have spent more than twenty minutes contriving it. Side items confirmed the culinary vogue of accomplishing outré ingenuity at breakneck speeds. The "Red Crest Salad" was an ordeal of chopped tomatoes and sliced pickles suspended inside strawberry Jell-O, shirked by Junior and Franny in favor of meat pies slathered with a so-called Pink Meringue of ketchup and egg whites.

If Korea hadn't killed Mr. White, dinner might have.

So began the tinkling of forks, the glugging of milk, the sniveling spates of diplomacy regarding plate cleanings. At first, the children were too shy to speak, but Mrs. White demanded inconsequential chitchat, and after some effort, she got it. Junior updated us on his progress as third-grade "ink monitor." During Monday's rounds of filling each student's jar, he'd dumped ink on arch-rival Herbie Hinkle, resulting in a scrap, about which Mrs. White was still sermoning. Franny, meanwhile, recited a memorized list of birds throughout the meal: blackbird, bluebird, hummingbird, meadowlark, sparrow, woodpecker, wren. I looked out the picture window, hoping for evidence of aviary plague, anything to end the deadening roll-call.

Around the time the children were making Jackson Pollocks of their plates, there came a clicking of claws upon the back door. Junior leapt from his seat and yanked open the door, and a barking dragon careened into the room at such velocity that her giant paws slipped on the linoleum and she went down with a meaty *thwack*, only to scrabble back up, jowls flouncing, and shark around the table while Franny and Junior chanted the butt-licker's name as if she were some kind of national hero.

"CLOWN! CLOWN! CLOWN! CLOWN!"

Mrs. White rubbed her temples until the jubilee petered out. Once the dog stopped circling the table, she revealed herself to be a three-foot, two-hundred-pound Saint Bernard of brindled brown-and-black fur. Clown, as she was called, shoved her deadly muzzle into the crotches of both children, trailing ropes of slobber. At last my presence penetrated her dullard skull and she cocked her head, bloodshot eyes struggling to see past her avalanche of forehead flab.

The bitch did not growl in aggression, nor did she pant with happiness. Instead, an irresolute whine emitted from somewhere beneath the saliva-hardened neck scruff. Suffice it to say I did not rise from my seat until after the children had finished scraping their rubbish into the gobbling gullet of the garbage disposal and Junior had hauled off Clown for private wrestling. I sighed, almost nostalgic for the intellectual trials of Udo von Lüth's Germany. I'd survived my first suburban dinner, but the little pink house on Mulberry Terrace seemed to become more hazardous by the hour.

IV.

M Y JOLTING FIRST DAY WITH the Whites molded the template for the following eight months of Heavenly Hills living, every twenty-four-hour period composed of twenty-three underground (even during promised babysitting episodes) and one above. Highlights included stilted exchanges with Mrs. White, who reminded Mr. Gray about the broken toaster and that hole in the wall, while Mr. Gray thrust out his only defense, early rent; Mr. Gray typing gibberish upon his single page of paper, day and night, until it grew gummy with ink; and dinners at which Mr. Gray shielded himself from the children's inspection and Clown's lunatic romping by blinding himself in the gleam of his shining, empty plate.

The basement had no lavatory, so twice a day, just to avoid suspicion, I forced myself upstairs, where I entered the bathroom, locked the door, and flushed the toilet. During these turns of pretense I collected dozens of glimpses of Mrs. White lost in reverie gazing at a picture. Her melted posture of longing made it evident that it was a photo of Mr. White, probably in square-shouldered Army dress. The pink house offered no other evidence of this husband so recently deceased, no slippers waiting for feet, no cold pipe waiting to be puffed, just this single photo that Mrs. White kept to herself, her own private ritual of pain.

Now and then she caught me spying.

"Are you here to fix the toaster?" she'd threaten.

Mrs. White knew how to send me high-tailing! Avoiding her became trickier in early 1955, when she began making regular trips to the basement. Upon hearing her heels click down the stairs, I'd crack my door and peek, keeping one hand on the Royal Quiet de Luxe to propagate authorly artifice. What I'd find was Mrs. White in casual ensembles—say, a belted denim jumper behind the ubiquitous pocketed apron—from which she would remove not ladle nor whisk nor lemon zester, but rather a retractable steel tape measure.

She'd run the tape across horizontal stretches of unfinished wall and then, balanced upon a chair, across the vertical axis. She'd gnaw her nails in consternation and take notes on a slip of paper, then compare these notes to a rubber-banded pack of pamphlets also kept in the apron pocket. The kitchen forever needed attention, though, and as was inevitable, one day Mrs. White left those pamphlets behind. Feeling like the mischievous Junior, I stole across the basement. In muted daylight I read, and was, to be sure, startled by the content.

"This Is Civil Defense" was the name of the first booklet. It was a manual reimagining the suburbs not as refuge against the metropolitan grind but rather against the bugbear of Soviet attack. *If the bombs from enemy planes ever fell on your city,* read this whimsical primer, *they would not fall on a plant, or an organization, or a system of government. They would fall on you and your family and friends.* The next publication, "Home Protection Exercises," was every ounce as jolly, with illustrations of "atomic dust" preceding a list of chores for each family member after Armageddon had come calling like the Avon Lady. "What You Should Know About Radioactive Fallout" supplied fun survival tips (vacuum up nuclear dust with your handy new Hoover!), while "The Family Fallout Shelter" made the purpose of Mrs. White's measuring tape crystal clear.

Reader, it perturbed me. The petrifying hours spent cowering with Frau Meixelsperger in a tin box had convinced me I'd rather take a direct hit from an H-bomb than try that again. And one needed only to have seen the aftereffects of Hiroshima to know how preposterously inadequate do-it-yourself hints would be in the face of U.S.-USSR counterblows, which those in the pamphlet biz called "mutual annihilation."

My concerns were more pressing and practical. Should our nervous widow prevail in converting her cellar into a shelter, my corpse would be dropkicked back to the curb. If I wished to preserve my place on Mulberry Terrace, I'd need to make myself useful, and be quick about it.

"Useful"—my least favorite word!

Dinnertimes made it plain that the White children, too, had contracted atomic mania from teachers. When menaced by an especially foul dish (Fonduloha, a hollowed-out pineapple stuffed with turkey, peanuts, mayonnaise, curry, coconut, canned mandarins, and the defamed pineapple itself), Junior's tactic was to screech like a bomb siren, at which point he and Franny would dive beneath their chairs to show off their duck-and-cover technique. From my basement windows I'd even observed the brats teaching this routine to Clown. At the word "duck," the slabbery mammoth would lie flat, her barrel body planted in the snow. At the word "cover," she'd shield her snout with both front paws.

An amusing display, perhaps, were the dog in question less fearsome. Nevertheless I grew jealous of the frolicking Whites, who took for granted that their mastiff wouldn't rip their smiling faces off. I'd experienced no such fidelity since abandoning Church in Manhattan's Chinatown twenty-three years earlier, and this forlorn fact contributed to my plan. Humans had proven jeopardous to befriend—you need look no further back than von Lüth—but perhaps I could ingratiate myself to the Whites via their non-human affiliate.

In defiance of the hygienic habits of suburban living, the dog lived indoors. For hours each weekday, Mrs. White was at the library and the children at school, meaning that all I had to do was go upstairs, rouse the beast, and make my petition. Easy to say, but you try it! Listen to the switchblade clicks of the creature's pacing claws, her shell-blast sneezes, the squeal of floorboards beneath her extraordinary weight. It took me a week (or two, or three; let us not get bogged down in the extent of my cowardice) to select from a cellar lumber pile a defensive two-by-four and tiptoe upstairs on a quiet February morning.

I found Clown snailed at the foot of Junior's bed. She brought herself to four legs, dropped herself to the floor, and stared, a white stalactite of drool elongating from a jowl. A Saint Bernard's eyes are monklike, teardropped by hoods of skin, and yet I could tell by the flattening of her broad neck that she was not overjoyed to see me.

"Easy, there, dog," warned I.

The velour drapery of her lips rose to reveal jagged canines.

Oh, hell. I hoisted the two-by-four.

The drool thickened but did not snap.

I smiled placatingly and edged closer. The dog side-eyed me like my wartime nemesis Piano O'Hannigan, and from deep inside her throat began a growl. On instinct I shook the two-by-four, and the dog's lips made room for bonus teeth—incisors now, premolars. Her claws began to knead the carpet. Disaster, Zebulon, disaster! I choked up on my weapon and cursed the whole boneheaded affair. Should the Whites return home to find their precious pet clubbed to death, they would not exactly hold a parade in my honor.

"Listen here, dog. You are guardian of this home. I do not wish to replace you. I wish only to reach a jointly beneficial accord so that your tallest human doesn't turn my room into a damn bunker. Here is my proposal. I shall pat you upon your head, or scratch your withers or loin, and deliver to you meaty morsels, as many as I can smuggle. In turn, you shall wag your tail upon my approach for all to see. Is this agreeable?"

Jaws jolted forward with a splattering bark. I stumbled over a misplaced plaything and slammed back against the wall. Model war planes spun from the ceiling, and rifle-firing cowboys charged from patterned wallpaper. I cleared my vision, and there was Clown, heaving and baying, large sectors of hide seizing with an undergrid of muscle, her muzzle aimed at my crotch, my trousers already spattered with suds.

The aggression rocketed me out of Heavenly Hills, out of Wichita, out of Kansas, all the way back to the Rocky Mountains. What the Marlboro Man had taught me poured back like blood into pinched flesh. Wild though this animal was, I'd faced wilder and had avoided all stompings, gorings, and gnashings, not because I'd dominated them but because I *was* them, existing outside of the violent, noisy, plane-flying, rifle-toting human plane.

Gently I placed the two-by-four upon the floor, kneeled, and unspooled the transcendental yarn of *la silenziosità*.

The ability had betrayed me aboard the *Fliegende Hitler*, but the dog slowed her growl to a putter and brought her muzzle within inches of my face. Blasts of hot, reeking breath made my cold skin clammy, but I could not turn away, for she was the realest thing I'd yet observed in this Formica fantasy.

The dog was the first being since General Joseph Thomas Hazard in 1901 who did not fear the death she saw coming. And why? It is simple, Reader. As Animal, she was incapable of sin. She angled her head and blinked slowly at the boundless fields of grass waiting to be peed upon, the billions of bounding bunnies waiting to accept pursuit, and whatever else Gød had in store for dead dogs.

"Hello, Clown," whispered I. "My name is Zebulon Finch."

I bowed my head and allowed *la silenziosità* to slip away, and then waited to feel matching sets of fangs sink into my neck. Instead, a warm muzzle pressed against my crown. Clown sneezed moisture into my hair, sniffed my ears with gale-blast loudness, and nosed into the old gash in my neck, in each spot smelling whole histories unreachable to human noses. Only when she seemed finished did I meet her eyes.

For one long second she was impassive and lethal.

Then out plopped her tongue.

My reaction was curious: I smiled. It manifested as abruptly as a burp. The dog reacted with a huge, rippling expression of such benevolence that it scorched my arctic flesh. I picked up the two-by-four and withdrew to the basement, confused by the onrush of good feeling. Dinner, of course, required reemergence, and when Clown did her post-poop victory laps around the table, she paused alongside my chair the same as she did Junior's and Franny's, head high as if eager to accept a pat. I dared not, not yet, but the Excelsior in my breast pocket ticked harder than it had in years.

The care I felt for the dumb animal consumed me with harrowing speed. Every day I visited her upstairs, and every day—every single day without fail—she was overjoyed. She seemed to sense my physical fragility and did not leap, instead frolicking in a figure-eight pattern before sitting still for me to scratch her ears while her bushy tail *whap-whap-whapped* the floor. Wilma Sue, believed I, had once looked upon me with love, and Church's brusque handshakes had once signaled devotion, but here was something different. This was adoration. Clown assumed that I was a good person—no, the *best* person—and because there was no telling her any different, I could but stroke her fur to calm the grateful trembling of my hands.

Clown was keen to prove her loyalty. I said "duck" and she ducked. I said "cover" and she covered. I decided that this was fabulous and over the next months taught the animal a full program of tricks. In hindsight, I admit that they were consistent with my criminal pro-clivities. "Steal." I pointed at an object, and she bolted to snatch it, and if I tried to yank it away, she was not allowed to relent. "Blitz." No matter where I hid, she had to find me, even if it meant butting through presidios I'd built from chairs and sofa cushions. And, of course, "Slay"—the vicious throttling of an object, usually an egg car-ton or coffee can fetched from the trash. So gentle was Clown that it fascinated me to watch these emergences of natural force.

When I wasn't teaching her bad habits, we found satisfaction in simple proximity, me in an upholstered chair that still smelled of Charles White's Burma-Shave, Clown sighing at my feet. One day I failed to don footwear or sock, and Clown showed shy interest in my bare feet, which, due to gravity, were dark purple from blood coagu-late and therefore stank worse than the rest of me.

Clown asked for so little that I made haste in asking her to partake in the littlest toe of my right foot. Her chin dropped miserably, positive that she was being tested for bad-dog behavior, and it took me an afternoon of encouragement before she gave in to her curiosity. She licked it, then chewed it, both with remarkable tenderness. The toe, a tuber of skin of trivial import, became "The Toe," a symbol of amity shared between me and my furred friend. The crunch of her teeth against The Toe's tiny bones, the squish of the masticated flesh, and the sight of its ever more mangled exterior filled me with happiness.

I would have liked our tenderness to remain a private thing, but Mrs. White's continued infatuation with civil defense impelled me to showcase the bond I'd nurtured. It was on a repulsively gorgeous day in May that I waited for Mrs. White to go shopping, got dressed in the better of my two outfits, tucked The Toe inside a shoe, and extracted from a mudroom drawer Clown's leash. The dog went bonkers and began lobbing its two hundred pounds against the front door. Here it was, then: my true migration back to America. The question was whether I could resist my own urges to Steal, Blitz, and Slay.

V.

SUBURBIA'S SAFENESS WAS FIGMENTAL. A bicycling paperboy launched a newsprint missile at me two doors down, and I might have challenged the shrimpy sniper to a duel had I not been forced to skitter from the path of a two-toned Ford backing from a driveway. It offered me a comical honk that belied its elephantine breadth. Inside the auto and others like it, I spied the wedding bands, filtered cigarettes, and flannel suits of exurban-ite breadwinners, while waving good-bye from doorsteps were their doting housewives, torpedo-breasted from conical brassieres, and brandishing kitchen knives.

Because I wished to casually catch Mrs. White's eye upon her return (and because, frankly, the Kansan vastness of Heavenly Hills unnerved me), I cordoned myself to the immediate block, which Clown and I circled until I'd memorized every name upon every red-flagged mailbox: Falzone, Cunningham, Caruso, Schaefer, Mitchell, Romano, Dodd, Gurrieri, Brandt, Shoemaker, Schmitt, Marino, DeWitt.

But this was no Times Square, where one could stroll Broadway eating a giraffe head and go unnoticed. Pink-skinned, starch-collared, and of forward-leaning middle-class comportment, the habitants perked up at aberration. Women pinning laundry to clotheslines peeked from behind snapping sheets; men parted kitchen curtains to peer over coffee cups; a white-gloved crossing guard lowered his sunglasses, and his smile, to level at me his dubiosity.

Mrs. White's estimation had been that *half the people here are older than sin.* Pretty close—every third person I saw was aged, men so frail they could but glower at their piles of thaw-sodden leaves, and women clinging to porch swings as if convinced their seats might rocket away, just like everything else that century. Both genders muttered at me in mother tongues. One sniff was all they needed, to know I was a herald of their encroaching deaths.

Only the occasional Negro workman gave me a candid look as he pushed about his wheelbarrow of brick or evulsed three seasons of gunk from a rain gutter. These overalled chaps stared at me as if expecting a greeting. To borrow a phrase of Junior's, they could go soak their heads! I followed the exemplum of my fellow Heavenly Hillers and pretended these laborers were invisible. Until, that is, the meat hook of a horrible hunch sunk into my spine.

My darkened skin—why, the people of Heavenly Hills thought that I was a Negro! Failing that, a partial Negro; failing that, some other recipe that, whatever its ingredients, came at a lesser price than whole-grained whiteness. Freshly panicked, I beseeched the Negroes with an expression of despair, hoping they might publicly exculpate me of their brand. All they returned were frowns that seemed to ask, *What the hell are you up to, strolling around a white neighborhood like this?*

The directives I whispered to Clown got her to growl, the Negroes shrunk back accordingly, and then, jostling the leash as if it were connected to a coach-and-four, I strode past the workers as if they'd never existed. Suburban America crystallized social classes, and I was confident about the category to which I belonged.

Shortly after Clown issued the last of her three fecal deposits (there was no tabulating the gallons of urine discharged), our placid neighborhood, without so much as an alarm bell, was invaded. Giant yellow dirigibles howled down each street, hissed to abrupt stops, and launched millions of shrieking, grass-stained little Vikings, each of whom swung metal lunch boxes like medieval maces. Clown barked in delight, while I stood inert. Great Caesar's ghost, the hordes! Were the suburbs laboratories of bourgeoisie baby-making and nothing else?

Unlike their elders, the children were colorblind. They flowed past me like vomit, hot and sour and sticky. Clown, though, was a canine seer, and tented her ears at a specific call slicing through the commotion.

"Mr. Gray! Mr. Gray!"

I banked astern to catch the incursion of two miniature marauders. It was Junior and Franny, he in collared cotton and pleated shorts, she in a skirt-and-shirt combo printed with sailboat insignia—spiffy outfits that the school day had brutalized. The duo skidded to a halt, red-cheeked and gasping.

"Jumping jeepers!" cried Junior. "You're walking Clown!"

"Clown! Clown! Clown!" chorused Franny.

The siblings locked hands and skipped a circle around the dog and me, tickled to near-hysteria by this unforeseen development. While Clown responded with a four-footed fandango of her own, I mulled the curious turn. I'd hoped to impress Mrs. White, not her grubby-faced progeny, but might this tack work just as well?

"It is true," bugled I. "I have led your animal on an impressive trail of elimination."

"Elim-in-ation?" asked Franny.

"He means 'poop'!" Junior nearly fainted from mirth.

Franny changed her chant.

"Poop! Poop! Poop!"

With monkey hands they pulled me by sleeve and trouser toward the pink house, desperate to show me off as a cat does its slain mouse. As it happened, Mrs. White had just arrived, arms full of groceries and using her hip to shut the door of her olive-green Buick Roadmaster. She knew the rhythm of her children's feet and extended her neck to see past the bags. She was a woman easily embarrassed when caught unawares—her cat's-eye sunglasses were as aslant as her velvet pillbox—but Junior and Franny permitted her no time. They seizured about the lawn in their haste to recount how they'd gotten off the bus, and had then seen Clown, and had then seen Mr. Gray, and then had run up to us, and then, and then, and then, and—

"Mr. Gray," interrupted Mrs. White. "Does Blackhand's Disease allow you to be in the sun?"

"Ma'am?"

"I only assumed, because I've never seen you go outside . . ."

"Oh, right. No, I've only been busy. With . . ."

"Writing," she offered helpfully.

I twirled a finger at my noggin. "So many ideas needing expression."

Grocery weight forced her inside, but not before she nodded slowly enough to suggest that, first, she was unconvinced by my lie, and second, despite my promises of incommunicability, the daylight contrast of my brownish hue with the blush color of her offspring upset her. Even if our mingling carried no health risks, just as deadly were the risks of the neighborhood grapevine and its chief vigneron, Mrs. Shoemaker. From what I'd gathered, the tyrannical queen of

207

Mulberry Terrace plied telephone lines like garrotes.

When it came to Junior and Franny, however, the ice had been irreparably broken. They used that night's dinner as an opportunity to pelt me with the sort of blunt-object questions only ever asked by children.

"Where'd ya come from?" asked Junior.

"Where did *you* come from," corrected Mrs. White.

"Chicago." Unless, of course, von Lüth had been correct and I'd always existed in Judas's Gethsemane, Caligula's Rome, Vlad the Impaler's Romania, John Wesley Hardin's Old West.

"Whatcha like doing?" asked Franny.

"What *do* you like *to do*," corrected Mrs. White.

"Nothing much." Were that only the historical fact! What I'd liked to do was destroy the lives of my fellow man. Wasn't that the leading theory of why I'd been sentenced to stick around?

"You gone anywhere neat?" asked Junior.

"*Have* you *been* anywhere neat," corrected Mrs. White.

"Not really." But that was the problem, wasn't it? I'd been everywhere, but nowhere had I found a home, certainly not one more fitting than a six-foot hole in the dirt.

"Don't you know no tricks?" asked Franny.

"Heavens," sighed Mrs. White. "Children, your grammar."

"None, I'm afraid." The biggest trick I'd ever pulled was convincing myself that I had a purpose here on Mulberry Terrace, that the Marlboro Man had sent me here for a reason.

Mrs. White insisted upon tableside decorum and got it, instructing the children to eat their Cherry Pineapple Bologna (instant mashed potatoes stirred with bologna, glazed with maraschino cherry and crushed pineapple, and then drowned in red food coloring) and initiate school-day reportage. They sighed and complied; only I noticed their mother's preoccupation. Mrs. White knew as well as I that this was the first time in a year—since, perhaps, the death of their father?—that Junior and Franny had made it through dinner without squabble or sob.

This one fact, or so I suspect, kept Mrs. White from dictating that I leave her children alone. Thus did the routine solidify: mornings spent enjoying Clown's tussling with The Toe; afternoon dog walks timed to coincide with the arrival of the school bus; and a retreat to the basement save a final cameo at dinner, where my stinginess with personal data only further incensed the siblings' competition for my attention.

Junior, a critical three years older, held the edge. He took to bringing to the table his most favored toys and presenting them for approval. They were asinine gewgaws. A plastic Davy Crockett rifle, which swept back memories of the gun-shaped stick my mother had robbed from me at age eight. A Slinky, a colossal spring with no apparent purpose beyond becoming entangled in his sister's hair. Silly Putty, a glob of goo good for nothing except reminding me of the human melt I'd seen at Hiroshima. I was roundly appalled. Never in history had so much money been frittered on objects of such triviality.

Yet I did not fracture the rifle over a knee, hammer flat the Slinky, or feed the Silly Putty to the nearest Saint Bernard. Mrs. White toiled thanklessly for her children, but without a Mr. White to serve as traffic cop, the two ran amok, breaking things left and right that Mrs. White (delusional woman) kept adding to my repair list. Buying toys was her attempt to satiate the mania of youth.

It was the era of fatuous fads, and the White pups had to have every one—Franny's hula hoop, killer of a half-dozen vases; Junior's yo-yo, breaker of windows fore and aft; Franny's pet rock, plonked inside the Roadmaster's gas tank; Junior's famous run of Stuntarang-brand boomerangs, all five nabbed by the cottonwoods lining Mulberry. Much safer were the Picture Craft paint-by-number sets that Mrs. White shuffled to her children like poker hands. By pairing numbered land-scapes with dozens of capsules of correspondingly numbered paints, these products strangled all creativity from the oldest art and guaran-teed that any slob with a couple bucks could be a Monet. Well, except for Junior, who could not resist using up all the #47 Burnt Sienna on impromptu dinosaurs, which, of course, he unveiled at the dinner table for my critique.

"Not bad," said I. "That farmhouse deserved a trampling."

Mrs. White gave me a dirty look and tsked the anachronistic pre-historics.

"Charles White Junior, this is the exact problem with your schoolwork. If you are to get anywhere in life, you must learn to fol-low the rules."

My instinct was to huzzah the lad's insubordination, but I was kept mum by Mrs. White's look of pride as she snapped on her dish-washing gloves and gazed over her number-coloring, hula-hooping, yo-yo-ing tribe. Each night I'd dawdle before heading down the base-ment stairs, weighing the Whites' general well-being against my own family tragedy: Abigail and Bartholomew, the contemptible parents; Church, the betrayed brother; Wilma Sue, the could-have-been wife; Merle, the alienated daughter.

If Slinkys and Silly Putty were the keys to contentment, who was I to scoff?

VI.

MRS. WHITE CAME A TAPPING, gently rapping at my chamber door on the last Saturday of August, the climax of a clangorous summer vacation season, while I keyed away at my Royal Quiet de Luxe. My lucky piece of paper having long disintegrated, I'd taken to typing Testa's sentiment about fear and hearts onto a sweat sock. I rushed to the door and warily allowed the smallest opening.

Mrs. White waited in the cellar dark, hands fidgeting before her apron. Her smile was labored enough that it did not qualify as such. I squinted, hunted about for other ambushers, and opened the door another inch.

"May I have a word, Mr. Gray?"

I cursed myself and my futile ploy. My displays with Clown had failed and my room was to become a bomb shelter. I needed time to prepare a convincing rejoinder.

"Very sorry, Mrs. White. But you catch me grappling with a pivotal scene."

"Oh?"

She lifted to her toes to catch a glimpse of my masterpiece. Since said opus was, in fact, an inky sock, I shifted to block her view. Were she to see it, no doubt she would ring the Wichita author's guild to have me stripped of my writer's license before sundown. She lowered herself

211

to her high heels. I smiled, cleared my throat, and began to withdraw.

Mrs. White wrung her apron and words ran like dirty dishwater.

"Mr. Gray, it's like this. You know it's Junior's first week of fifth grade, and I promised him last night that if he finished his schoolwork, he could go to the movies today, and he did, he did finish, and even though it wasn't perfect, it's so difficult to get him to apply himself to schoolwork at all. I feel like I must make good—Charles always said it's important, as a parent, to be consistent. But I'm at sixes and sevens. I have to bake three cakes for Franny's bake sale tomorrow. And I have twenty pages of recipes to hand-copy for our Women's Bible Study recipe book—Mrs. Eldridge won't type from anything but neat handwriting, although it's not my fault half the ladies waited until yesterday to hand theirs in. That's what I get for being secretary, I suppose. If the car was working, I'd drive Junior myself, I'd make time, but it's in the shop again. Did I tell you it's in the shop again? It's doing that thumping thing. Oh, I wish you knew about cars. Mechanics cheat me all the time, I know they do, because I don't have a husband, so how would I know any better? Well, I guess that's my predicament."

I might have laughed at this information overkill hadn't the sun nudged from cloud and illuminated trenchant detail. Her bright orange hair, typically plastered into helmet contour, was corkscrewed. Her purple dress was whited with spilled flour, her white apron purpled with spilled fruit. There were stains at her armpits—a woman's shame—and even a full cosmetic mask couldn't conceal the under-eye pouches.

"I'll walk him there," said I.

She placed a hand upon her pearls and exhaled.

"Thank you, Mr. Gray. I'm so sorry for needing to ask. Your book—I know how important that scene must be—"

"What time?"

"Shall we say a half hour?"

"Fine."

I began to close the door, but before I could, she bounced back to her toes.

"Mr. Gray! One other thing."

"Yes, Mrs. White."

Again her poor apron was getting the business.

"It's only . . . well, do you think, when you are walking with Junior . . . It's not a long walk by any means, but it's long enough for two people to . . . well, do you think you might have a talk with him?"

"A talk? I'm sure I don't understand."

Her fingers, pale from pressure, made her gold wedding ring appear to glow.

"Charles was brilliant at it. Talking to the children, I mean. That was more or less our arrangement. I'd manage the children day to day, but if there were problems, little rebellions, he stepped in. Junior's at an age now where a woman doesn't always know what to say. Last night he got into a little tiff. Just like boys do, nothing awful, but still, the other child's mother was very cross, and I know how everyone watches me to see if I can handle my children."

I'd take the Oriental Pin Therapy of the Astonishing Mr. Stick over the awkward "talk" being foisted upon me! Raised without a pop, turned hoodlum as a result, and further disillusioned post-death by men inferior to the fatherly task, what broth could I pour down a lad's throat that contained a soupçon of wisdom? A slammed door, that was what Mrs. White deserved, but I saw her lips purse toward another self-defensive speech.

"Yes," said I. "Fine. All right. A talk."

213

What an inhale! Mrs. White's bosom achieved, for one second, Brideyian dimension. And what a sigh! Mrs. White's visage achieved, for one second, Wilma Sue–like contentment. This stimulating double-vision of womanhood was shattered by the demonic cry of the egg timer and the metallic crunch of another misfired piece of toast. Mrs. White cringed, nodded, and scooted.

Thirty minutes later, I was outside in a jacket and hat suitable for a summer wilting toward fall. Mulberry Terrace was a foreboding orchestra of radio chanteuses, lawn mowers, water hoses, and shrieking youth, and I shivered, thinking of the unfamiliar blocks through which I was about to trespass. What would new suburbanites looking from new windows think about a dark-skinned fellow on a constitutional with a white child?

My distress was preempted by the debut of our puny pugilist. Junior slouched outside, fists in pockets, plastic rifle wedged beneath elbow, and coonskin cap banked so I could not evaluate the damage until he was close. Mrs. White had underplayed the "little tiff." The lad sported a jim-dandy of a black eye that, I knew from experience, would blossom into sensational colors. My first instinct was to acclaim the boy's pugnacity. My second was to turn away in hot envy. I remembered Mrs. White and buried both.

"Look what a mess you've made of your face," said I.

"It's a beaut of a mouse," blurted Junior. "And if that goon Herbie Hinkle talks garbage about Korea again, I'll whip him a second time. I don't care how many shiners I get!"

His defiance so flustered me that I started off in the direction Mrs. White had explained. Junior followed, and for five uncomfortable minutes I deliberated over strategy. Perhaps I might spur myself toward sternness by imagining Junior as the *Hitlerjugend* imp with the dancing monkey. Both boys, after all, were chatty, intelligent, and rambunctious, different only due to a chance roll of the dice.

"Look here, youngster. You have your mother in a state."

"Aw, bunk." He kicked a pile of dead leaves. "Dad said wrasslin' puts hair on your chest."

Hair on one's chest was a fine thing, I had to admit.

"It's not the fighting," pressed I. "It's the disobedience. It's the poor grades."

"Golly, Mr. Gray. Didn't you ever get lousy grades? Didn't you ever get in fights?"

I ducked that line of questioning.

"The point is the burden you place on your poor mother."

"Mom's always blowing a gasket about this junk. Who cares? After the Commies bomb us, she'll be glad I know how to fight!"

"And if the Commies do not? I do not believe you possess the musculature to be the next Sugar Ray Robinson."

For a time he brooded, and I worried that I'd pushed the child, one of two living humans to hold me in favorable regard, to turn against me. Then Junior stopped short, quick-drew his rifle, and clacked out a dozen shots across Spruce Boulevard. The invisible rain of bullets was a violent expression of frustration with which I sympathized.

"Why don't you go back and tell Mom I ran away? I won't blame you if I get caught, honest. And I won't get caught. I'll go right past the movie theater until I get to the road, and then I'll hitchhike. I'll hitchhike all the way to Disneyland. And I'll get on the *Mickey Mouse Club*. And then when Mom turns the show on for Franny, she'll see how much fun I'm having with the Mouseketeers, and then she'll be sorry!"

August was not cool enough for his cheeks to be that flushed, nor windy enough for his eyes to produce that weight of tears. As he stomped down the block, I followed at a distance, turning over my own history of hopeless fantasies: taking charge of Luca Testa's blackmailing operation, joining Lucky Luciano in New York City's underworld, parlaying newsreel celebrity into Hollywood fame. If only I'd had an older and wiser architect to indicate the shoddy draftsmanship of my blueprints.

I caught up with Junior at the corner of Hemlock and Pine, plucked two bills from my pocket, and held them out.

"Here is twenty dollars," said I. "Good luck and happy trails."

He frowned at the cash, his smooth forehead knotting.

"Gee, Mr. Gray."

"This won't get you all of the way to Disneyland, but a week or two of fasting will not kill you. After all, you have all that Mickey Mouse money waiting for you."

Junior squinched his bruised eye.

"You don't care if I run away?"

"It is your mother who cares. I find your plan rather compelling."

Junior considered this. "But what if I get hurt on the way?"

"A wrassler like yourself? Inconceivable."

Junior bit his lower lip, perhaps to dam the saliva generated by the sight of such fantastic wealth. But then he did what I'd guessed he might. He gave the cash the cold shoulder and with a lope that was indubitably contrite, resumed our walk down Pine.

I stuffed the bills back into my pocket, dizzy with triumph. Why, I'd done it! With neither fist nor fury, I'd nudged a youth down a truer path! My thoughts glided to Merle, the daughter I'd driven away with round after round of fatherly fumble. My body and brain

216

remained stubbornly seventeen, but my parenting skills had, at long last, squirmed forward.

When a theater called the Orpheum landed before us, a boxy building surely more impressive when wearing a tiara of nighttime neon, I was sorry to see it. Not only had I probed beyond the protective earthworks of Mulberry Terrace, I'd done so without raising collar or lowering hat against the thrown stones of censuring eyeballs. How exquisite it was to taste a daub of my jaunty old indestructible self!

The Orpheum's signboard related the weekend menu:

DOUBLE FEATURE
IT CAME FROM OUTER SPACE
CREATURE FROM THE BLACK LAGOON
IN EXCITING STEREOVISION 3-DIMENSION

Movies and their bottomless bag of gimmicks always beguiled me. By George, thought I, maybe I'd accompany Junior into the theater itself, where I, not from outer space but indeed a creature of blackness, could perpetuate my alternate reality in a popcorn-funked dark.

While I deliberated this bold move, my eyes, traitors to happiness, strayed to a bulletin board of advertisements for upcoming films. My mood, already high, soared higher at the sight of two features headlined by Bridey Valentine—only to precipitously fall. Neither one was *In Our Image*. One was titled *Cult of the Tarantula*, the other *Granny Atom's Terror Machine*. Bridey, it seemed, had escaped Communist blacklisting (a feat, given her eccentric enthusiasms), but no number of cosmetic surgeries could prevent her from taking the inevitable tumble every aging actress took down Hollywood's steps, which fed directly into a dungeon of reprobate cults and rogue atoms. She was, after all, by then (Gød, how could it be?) fifty-seven.

The plastic prattle of the Davy Crockett rifle woke me from my stupor. Junior, his movie ticket bit between his teeth like a buckaroo's cigarette, was peppering me with friendly fire before entering the Orpheum.

"See you later, alligator!" cried he.

My mind was aggrieved and slow.

"What? I do not understand."

Junior drowned in exasperation. "You're supposed to say, 'In a while, crocodile!'"

I nodded, feeling quite old. Junior waved—I would not be joining him after all—and vamoosed into a lobby crammed with children stumbling about in red-and-blue 3-D glasses and giggling in anticipation of cinematic fright. I turned away from the box office and attuned myself to the pink house's basement beacon. My preferred role in this science-fiction/fantasy/horror hybrid was that of a harmless lodger in the quiet Wichita outskirts, but Bridey Valentine's slow spoil was a reminder that I was, in truth, just as Junior had suggested, an alligator: scaly, cold-blooded, low-lying, ageless, and in the habit of snapping in half anyone who came too close.

VII.

NO, I HADN'T FIXED THE confounded toaster or spent an iota of effort on that hole in the wall, but my safe squiring of Junior to his double-feature impressed my value upon Mrs. White as inexorably as my brutal beating of Giuseppe Fratelli had upon Luca Testa. The children, little radar dishes, picked up on the tweaked signal and began encircling me after dinner to delay my decampment. Trapped upstairs, I learned more about Heavenly Hills in a week than in the totality of the preceding year. Ever was Mrs. White rushing home from the Lane Ladies or canasta to propagate hearsay with fellow housewives, twirling her finger in the telephone cord like a teenager.

Consider the melodrama of Mr. Mitchell, who washed his steel-blue Chevrolet Nomad every Sunday morning, right across the street from us, the sudsy runoff pooling in the gutter like beer I'd seen axed from barrels by Prohibition police. The problem was that Mr. Mitchell's routine showcased that he didn't attend Sunday services—a cardinal offense, especially to Mrs. Shoemaker. Stubborn secularist though he might have been, Mr. Mitchell hadn't the heretic grit to withstand his wife's begging, and thus the ceremonial soaping of the Chevy switched to perfectly decent Saturdays.

Far more tragicomic was the story of the Cunninghams. In September their septic tank backed up, and their lawn, so attentively sodded back in spring, ballooned with a goiter of sewage. Mr. Cunningham, proprietor of a shoe-shine parlor, was caught during a lean season, and it was two weeks before he could get the blister lanced and drained. Clown adored the stench and beelined there during our walks, and for a fortnight I watched the Cunningham clan fade to ghosts—the neighbors, led by Mrs. Shoemaker, looked right through them.

You cannot blame me for worrying that my involvement with the Whites might lead to similar blackballing. Junior worried me the most. He would sit beside me every chance he got, plant his pudgy cheeks into his palms, and with disconcerting intensity search my eyes. If the boy looked hard enough, might he strike a wellspring of *la silenziosità?* He was too young to glimpse his own demise; I looked away. Yet he was like Clown when given the order to Slay. Once he'd jawed into something pungent, he wouldn't let go. One Sunday while Mrs. White paid homage to a coven called the Parent-Teacher Association, Junior cornered me after one of my fake bathroom trips, his plastic rifle at ease upon a shoulder.

"Is it a superpower?" whispered he. "I won't tell no one, honest."

I tried to angle past the runt, but he backpedaled.

"Is Mr. Gray your human name? Is it cuz you're a superhero?"

A far-flung arrow from Little Johnny Grandpa hit home.

Beg y'pardon, Mr. Stick, but I have me a question. Are y'really dead like some of them say? Are ya? And if y'are, does that mean you're an angel?

"A superhero. You know, like Superman?" Junior gasped. "You don't know Superman?!"

The name triggered a recollection of a program I'd often glimpsed while passing the family television, one which began with a broadcaster boasting how Superman was faster than a speeding bullet, more powerful than a locomotive, and able to leap tall buildings in a single bound. I'd assumed the hero in question to be an exhibitionist pervert—he cavorted about, after all, in underwear—but then I recalled the next line from the opening spiel: "Yes, it's Superman! Strange visitor from another planet who came to earth with powers and abilities far beyond those of mortal men!"

The characterization touched a nerve of mine that was not altogether dead. I, too, belonged to this world only by degrees; I, too, had physical capacities that, were you feeling altruistic, you might describe as "powers" or "abilities." So lonely was my rare condition that these barely shared traits were enough to pique a begrudging interest.

"I capitulate," said I. "Tell me about your Superman."

The pink house had a secret space, a gabled, unfinished attic redolent of mothballs and unlit but for two fly-corpsed bulbs. While I consulted my Excelsior—the PTA black mass would not last all night—Junior knelt before four cardboard boxes and, in an orange plashet of light, made introductions.

Superman, learned I, had traveled to Earth as an infant escapee of the exploded planet of Krypton. This story was certified not by gold-edged vellum-bound tomes but from stacks of comic books Junior had inherited from his father. The bulk of this ripped, wrinkled, and stained archive had been published during World War II, when Charles Senior had been a teenager. Turning each delicate page, I felt a jab of sadness with regard to this man I'd never meet. How viciously quick it was that boys became men and men became dust.

As best I could tell, Supe, as Junior called him, spent his days bashing through brick walls, tossing around trucks, and striking macho poses against a staff of incompetent baddies. According to the yellowest issues, his Krypton craft had grounded in a small, possibly Kansan town, where he was found by the benevolent Kents and brought to an orphanage. Straightaway, I felt the sting of kinship. My second youth had withstood the shocks of many a foster family. In Superman's case, the Kents returned to adopt him, name him Clark, and teach him that he must use his powers for good.

This gave me pause while Junior blabbered.

"Look, here's where Supe saves Lois from the Archer's arrow!"

Church's Theory of 17, though disproved, had given rise to the Fifty-One's badgering nags. The idea planted by Superman's creators, a pair of Jewish geniuses called Siegel and Shuster, was even simpler and more profound. Moments before we'd plunged into the ocean, Margeaux had begged to know what I wanted from life, and I'd said, *I want to fix things. To make things right.* Tossing commuter buses at arch-villains was beyond my ability, but I could start smaller, right there in that cramped attic, and do what I could to fix this one broken family. Might my failure with the Watsons—Wilma Sue and Merle—be absolved by success with the Whites?

"Look, Mr. Gray," begged Junior. "Here's where Supe busts Funny-face's shrinking ray."

I couldn't commit to the Man of Steel's generosity of spirit before contending with his name. Superman was, of course, muscle-bound. But should you, in your ultramodern space-age, have access to the original issues, select a random panel and examine it. Closer now. Closer still. See how the four-color printing process unfastens Supe's chiseled pink face into blue, red, yellow, and black dots? This I submit as a metaphor for having one's atoms scattered across time, the agony of permanent impermanence. Superman was no free, flying thing. He was a man shackled by destiny, bled dot by dot onto pulpy paper not of his choosing. Normal life was *right there in front of him*—substitute alliteration, and Mary Magdalene becomes Lois Lane—but Superman could have none of it.

Reader, I do hope this sounds familiar.

Thenceforth I resolved to think of Superman by his Krypton name, Kal-El, the survivor of a lost world. If I could convince myself that I was at least of Kal-El's breed, just some run-of-the-mill Kryptonian, I might become the white light that could burn away, at least for a time, the black tendrils of the Millennialist that had clenched Mulberry Terrace's pinkest house.

I allowed Junior to lead me by the hand toward the home's heart, the lemon-peel-yellow living room through which I'd never more than hurried. I catalogued the hooded fireplace, womanish Murano lamps, and svelte rotary phone. The shapes and colors might have bewildered the old Zebulon, but not the new one. I used Kal-El's microscopic vision (Action Comics #24) to see past the zippy paint jobs and stylish showpieces to the humble brick and aluminum beneath.

When Mrs. White returned, surly with bad blood from Junior's educators, she might have lashed out at the sight of me, the weird boarder, snugged on the sofa betwixt Junior and Franny, but I used Kal-El's face-changing ability (Superman #5) to shine upon her a saintly smile. When she, discombobulated, wobbled toward the kitchen to set down the school reports, I used Kal-El's super-speed (Action Comics #1) to dash past her and make room by pushing aside burial mounds of deficient toast. And when she started back toward the living room, confused, I bade her to relax beside her children, and I credit Kal-El's X-ray vision (Action Comics #11) for thawing her chilliness enough that she did just that.

Mrs. White looked at Junior, the target of her intended scolding, but his convulsive glee at the group gathering melted her heart. She did not appear to know what to say. She crossed her ankles. She tidied her lipstick with a pinkie. She forced a smile at the wall.

"Well, here we all are," said she. "I suppose we should watch a program?"

Junior shot from his cushion, snatched the cart upon which rested the Zenith TV—a wooden cube embedded with a glass screen no larger than a textbook—and dragged it close, the rubber wheels gnashing through carpet. He turned on the set with a loud click and plunked back down, and the four of us waited while the unit warmed up and a wan image began to surface like a corpse rising through murky waters.

Bridey Valentine had owned the first TV set I'd seen, but it had been a glorified picture frame. The Zenith contained a whole universe, lasered from Gød knew where to our rabbit-ear antenna. I do not recall which program we watched that evening, so occupied was I with monitoring Mrs. White's mood. I am willing to bet that she, too, was aware of little beyond my presence. While Junior cackled, Franny sniggered, and Clown yawned, Mrs. White and I contemplated four or five flickering worlds, hoping a clue might emerge as to how we might navigate our own.

Just as Neanderthals and Cro-Magnons gathered in radial formations before mystical fires, we four began to gather each night before our electric deity. The programming itself was nonsensical. You might not have pegged Junior as a connoisseur of experimental art, but how else to explain his engrossment in the irrational flapdoodle of *The Howdy Doody Show*, a show set in "Doodyville" and starring a deranged puppet, menacing jester, and ringmaster who forced a riser full of captured children to sing on demand. Franny, meanwhile, had an unaccountable affection for Lawrence Welk, a mumbling German who welcomed onto his stage a perplexing roster of classical, crooner, and vaudeville acts, all behind a hallucinogenic screen of bubbles. My own favorite was *The $64,000 Question*, a press-your-luck quiz show in which contestants were crammed into an "isolation booth."

"Isolation booth" was exactly how I'd begun thinking of my basement berth. I felt better upstairs, snuggled in warm blankets of static and, I admit, between warm bodies. It was significant that *Father Knows Best* was the one program in which Mrs. White, too, lost herself; the Whites, of course, longed for a father/husband of their own. This alleged comedy chronicled a quintet of simps known as the Andersons, and was set in an exact mirror of Heavenly Hills. My reaction was different from Mrs. White's. I wished to strangle each and every Anderson, except perhaps Mrs. Anderson, who reacted to her husband's every gaffe with the same morphinic smile. In my imagination I produced a midnight program centering upon Mrs. Anderson's private hours, during which she released stress by dismembering cats and self-flogging her sweaty, naked back.

It was the curious pre-recorded laughter of *Father Knows Best* that most affected my days and nights. The America into which the Marlboro Man had strong-armed me was a paradox. To be an individualist (to wash your Chevy Nomad on Sunday, let's say) was to be presumed unwholesome, if not an outright Red. Instead each person strived to be a carbon copy of her or his neighbor— and what was more Communist than that? The Andersons' laugh track mocked the trap in which families like the Whites had caught themselves. *Wa-ha-ha-ha!* It affected pity for their winless predicament. *Awwwww!* It chuckled in superiority as they strained at the leashes they held in their very own fists. *Hur-hur-hur-hur!*

It did not escape my notice that Mrs. White took child-raising prompts directly from Mrs. Anderson, including "family outings" to local pools, county parks, and Wichita-area children's theater. Mrs. White showed no relish in leading these excursions, and Junior and Franny no joy in being railroaded. Of course I was never invited— Kal-El could touch normal life, but never grasp it—and when I did optimistically edge close to their party, she'd fend me off with a seven-word $64,000 question so that I'd retreat to my isolation booth, where, like Clark Kent, I could impersonate a writer.

"The hole in the wall? The toaster?"

Cue laugh track, though nothing about it was funny.

VIII.

I CHOSE THE KITCHEN AS THE bright pink workbench upon which I'd hammer the dents, tighten the screws, and sandpaper the rough edges of this damaged family. From our first interview forth, Mrs. White had remained a mystery of cashmere, tweed, and rayon veiled by Chesterfield smoke and a magician's misdirection of Corningware. My daily advance was scored by the musique concrète of modern conveniences—the whir of the Roto-Broil, the whine of the Juicerator, the grind of the Harper Food Mincer, the scream of the Sunbeam Mixmaster.

Discordant noises indeed, but I followed Clown's example and insinuated myself underfoot until Mrs. White could not help but solicit my occasional aid. *Mr. Gray, could you fetch that lemonade pitcher from the top of the cabinet?* But of course! *Mr. Gray, could you hold the door so I can get these groceries inside?* See, I am already doing it! *Mr. Gray, could you remove your hand from that red-hot burner?* Oh dear, I do apologize, and do not mind the smoke—the burn looks worse than it feels!

My conservative estimate was that Mrs. White logged one hundred hours of work per week between the library and home, and yet projecting an aura of surplus leisure time was the dictate of all of her favorite magazines—*Woman's Home Companion, House & Garden, The American Home*—each one packed with illustrations of stay-at-home mothers of Aryan pedigree blithely awaiting the evening returns of their genetically splendid mates. All Mrs. White had was that photograph of her husband in her apron pocket. Since his death, she'd barricaded (or, to quote the ads in *House & Garden*, "hermetically sealed") herself inside the products, activities, and scruples of her decade. To be a fulfilled woman in the mid-1950s, learned I, was to complete a checklist, and insofar as Mrs. White was busy making those checks, there would be no time to process pain.

Women as discrepant as Abigail Finch, Mary Leather, and Bridey Valentine had tried, and failed, to tick all the right boxes; I could have warned Mrs. White that the checklist was infinite, mutating, and expensive, hence the terror that candled her green eyes after every Tupperware Home Party, hosted, of course, by Mrs. Shoemaker, who never quit spending the profit from her husband's booming Chevrolet dealership. Even bulwarked by my rent, Mrs. White couldn't afford such luxuries, but had discovered a wonderful invention called "Buy-Now-Pay-Later credit." So Mrs. White purchased; Mrs. Mitchell purchased; Mrs. Cunningham purchased. From my Peeping Tom's perspective, it was an orgy of consumer cupidity climaxing with gift-bag tissue paper that floated about like post-coital cigarette smoke.

What cynicism I might have managed was neutralized by Mrs. White's hopeful reading aloud of each piece of packaging, as if through prayerful repetition they might become psalms:

Our Father, which art in Maytag, / hallowed be thy Kelvinator Foodarama. / Thy Brillo Soap Pads come, / thy Crest with Fluoristan be done, / with General Mills, as it is with General Electric. / Give us this day our Cal-Dak TV trays, / and forgive us our Speedy Alka-Seltzer, / as we have forgiven our Vicks VapoRub. / And lead us not into Owens

Corning Fiberglas, / but deliver us from Armco stainless steel. / For thine is the Hotpoint, / the Frigidaire, / and the Westinghouse, / for ever and ever. / Amen.

It was after a long April day of declaring war on germs, leading the charge against bad nutrition, and being locked in hand-to-hand combat with freezer odor, all with my bumbling assistance, that Mrs. White allowed herself a moment of reprieve upon the sofa. It had been a trying afternoon, one that had crescendoed with her tearful cry:

"Oh, why is my custard so *watery?*"

The children yearned to suckle upon the television teat; it was time for *The Jack Benny Program*, sponsored by the Lucky Strike cigs they dreamed to one day smoke. But I shepherded the litter into the hall. Unlike I, they hadn't seen, propped on the kitchen counter, a leaflet for the 1956 Pillsbury Bake-Off, a contest offering fifty thousand dollars to the housewife who proved herself the most resourceful cook. Any poor soul who'd survived Mrs. White's Atomic Crab de Luxe (crabmeat, frozen spinach, cream of mushroom soup, Cheez Whiz) knew that it was a contest she couldn't win. Her attempt, though, told me she was well aware of her dwindling savings.

We heard Mrs. White's snore beneath the Lucky Strike jingle:

Light up a Lucky—
It's light-up time!
Be happy, go lucky—
It's light-up time!

I put a finger to my lips and shooed the children to their rooms. Clown, unshooable thing, followed me on quiet paws as I crept around the sofa, as I had around so many weeded thickets in Montana, hoping to catch that rare glimpse of an exotic animal at rest.

For the taste that you like,
Light up a Lucky Strike!
Relax—it's light-up time. . . .

Mrs. Shirley White was beautiful in repose, her jaw unclenched, her lips unlocked, her apron lending natural curves to her breasts' Maidenform bullets. Her dishpan hands had slackened upon her lap, releasing her pocket-weathered photograph. So snug did she appear in the Zenith's stroboscopic light that I could not withstand the urge to lay eyes upon Mr. Charles White and draw comfort from the serviceman's able-bodied strength.

I slid the photo carefully from her fingers and brought it close.

It was not a picture of Mr. White.

It was a cardstock promotional photograph obtained from some furniture vendor, labeled THE KITCHEN OF TOMORROW. The staged photograph depicted a spacious, high-ceilinged room dominated by a cinematic window through which sunlight gleamed. Backlit glass cabinets made every can of food easy to pinpoint, and below stretched a long, curvaceous counter that had every conceivable apparatus built right into the thermoplastic: a waffle iron that opened like a mouth, chilled circular holes in which jarred goods could be inserted for easy access, a sink revealed by lifting its cover of stained cedar. It was the kitchen of Krypton, but missing Kal-El—only a sedate housewife and her polite daughter were featured. The mister, it seemed, was at the office.

Except that he wasn't. The mister, in fact, was dead, bled out, maybe torturously, on foreign soil. It was an objectionable thing to dream about if you ever wished to get a good sleep, so instead of Korea, Mrs. White dreamed of the Kitchen of Tomorrow, where there might just be a switch, button, or lever that would make everything upside-down turn rightside-up once more.

I replaced the photograph and retreated, suddenly, wretchedly sad for this woman whose mania for modernity now looked like a slow suicide, a mjölnir impact at one-millionth speed, the piecemeal bartering off of her emotions in exchange for self-starting, self-cleaning, self-flushing gizmos. Take it from someone who was dead: this was no way to live.

Clown, smelling my resolve, pressed her muzzle into my palm.

IX.

AS METICULOUSLY AS THE PINK house interior had been maintained, the garage on the other side of the yard had been willfully ignored. After I shouldered open the warped door and cast away the dust clouds, I saw why. It was the undisturbed tomb of Charles White. A push lawn mower stood where he'd left it in the center of the floor, and do-it-yourself projects moldered in perpetual states of metamorphosis.

Clown paced beyond the doorway, troubled by her old master's smell.

I threw open all four windows, superficially because of the stifling heat but realistically because such spaces of manly ingenuity made citified lads like myself feel inadequate. Mrs. White's magazines made demands of men, too; I'd read a dozen times how the modern husband's value was tied to his "know-how." It was precisely what the toaster and hole in the wall needed—but what was "know-how" and how did one obtain, purchase, or steal it?

I focused upon simpler tasks. I uncovered a hedge clipper and a corroded can labeled GALVANIZED GASOLINE and emptied the fuel into the mower tank. It was a blinding afternoon, and I did not relish subjecting my putrid flesh to extended sun, so I folded back quilts of spiderweb and jimmied open a metal locker, where I found Charles himself, dangling from a rod, not killed in Korea but trapped inside a box where no one had heard his screams.

Or so went my lurid first thought. It was Charles's assemblage of work duds: painter's overalls, a denim jacket, neoprene rain gear, and roughshod Army twills. I exchanged my leisure wear for the last outfit and then—anything, Reader, to delay work—added gloves, boots, and a straw panama hat.

The backyard, until then spied only through windows, was no realer to me than the Springfield of *Father Knows Best*. It was larger than expected, of tennis-court dimension, but impinged by neglected trees, shrubbery, and flowerbeds. It did not take know-how to see that the yard didn't compare to the stringent husbandry of the four abutting properties. Though not as indecent as the Cunninghams' septic bubble, no doubt it had brought Mrs. White disrepute.

Clown found a shady spot and slept. I screwed on the panama, tugged the gloves, gave the clippers a practice chomp, and advanced upon the underbrush as if it were the Kaiser's frontline forces. The spoils of this victory, should I win it, were superficialities—Mary Leather's beautiful lawn, you might recall, had existed only to hide her husband's People Garden. Then again, what was I but a monster recently crawled down from the mountains? Mrs. White wanted this, and if I were to repair her family, the repair had best be to her specifications.

Decades had passed since I'd worked up an honest sweat. (I no longer perspire, but you get the idea.) After months spent typing humbug onto a sock, there was a palpable satisfaction in laboring toward visible results. The idée fixe of quality I'd once applied to Black Hand extortion notes returned to me. I chopped; I pruned; I nicked; I pared. I did not rest until Medusan greenery yielded geometric shapes.

It took Junior and Franny storming the yard after school to disrupt my absorption. Three of the four adjacent yards now had people in them, flogging dirty rugs and filling rubbish bins as they peeped over fences at the oddly colored boarder who'd graduated past pooping the White's dog. While Junior and Franny whoopeed my unpredicted groundskeeping, I found Mrs. White watching from behind the screen door. I could not tell if she was moved by my largesse, relieved that I'd lived up to my repairman billing, or appalled that I was parading about in her dead husband's clothes.

It was only after that's night dinner dishes were cleared that Mrs. White, at the running sink with her back to me, made a brief, but greatly unburdening, comment.

"You might have a look, Mr. Gray, at those low-hanging branches."

"Indeed?" I was as eager as Clown.

"Well." Narrow shoulders shrugged beneath taut apron strings. "Mrs. Shoemaker said a little girl on Cypress Drive was running around her yard and a twig from a branch went straight through her tongue."

It was so like Mrs. White—like all Heavenly Hillers—to masquerade personal vanity as public service. But if the remote risk of tongue-impalement brought her anxiety, I wished to deplete it! In the morning I was back at it, amputating offending branches with Charles's hatchet. The next day, I got down on knees still gravel-scarred from being dragged to the Xenion jail in 1901, and commenced weeding. The following week, I disentangled the creeper vines that throttled, well, everything. The week after, I stumbled across old bags of cement mix and set to patching the back patio and walkway. Finally I proceeded to plant flowers I had Mrs. White retrieve from the store: asters, daylilies, chrysanthemums, irises, lilacs, and petunias. And every day, my icy flesh felt the heat of voyeur eyes—the neighbors watching me, Mrs. White watching the neighbors, and all of us wondering what would happen next.

It happened, all right, on the first of July. It was a cloudless Sunday, and backyards were abuzz with children, home improvement, and radios jousting for supremacy, the dusky doo-wop of the Platters'"The Great Pretender" entangling with the drooping bass line of "Heartbreak Hotel," sung by a chronic hiccupper named Elvis. I stood on the patio, contemplating a brick-and-pebble mosaic suggested in the new issue of *Better Homes and Gardens*, when a face popped like a squirrel over the northern fence.

"Ahoy, there, son!"

I'd glimpsed this fellow before through fence slats. He was fortyish, heavyset, fuchsia-faced, and forever strangled by one of the business world's ubiquitous gray suits. That day, his thick neck had been furloughed by a polo shirt, from which poofed puffs of brown hair. I blinked at the intrusion while he settled his hamhock forearms atop the posts.

"Say," said he, "you've really gone to town back here, haven't you?"

No one on Mulberry Terrace had ever initiated dialogue with me.

"I suppose," said I.

"Now where have my manners run off to? I'm Chet."

"Chet Schmitt." As mentioned, I knew my mailboxes.

"That's right. What do you go by, son?"

"Zebulon. I mean, Joe."

"Joe Zebulon! Ain't that a corker!"

He guffawed. The fence leaned, and I winced. It was an expense we could not afford.

"You're the hardest worker I've ever seen," observed Chet Schmitt. "Every morning I leave for work, you're out here. I get home, you're still out here. Don't you ever get tired, son?"

I shrugged. I hadn't been tired since 1896.

"You know, Myrtle—that's my little lady—she's been trying to get her petunias to bloom for, heck, it's got to be three years now, and every year they wither up. She says it's the prairie dirt. But tarnation! You've gone and pulled it off. How'd you do it?"

Fourteen hours a day without food, water, or bathroom breaks, that's how I did it.

"It is complicated, Mr. Schmitt."

His grin grew crafty, and he wagged a finger.

"Trade secrets, eh? Tell you what, you explain the whole thing to Myrtle, and she'll bake you the best red velvet cake you've ever had, guaranteed. Now, when should we do it? Hey, how about dinner? A barbecue—that's the ticket! How does that sound?"

Mayday! Mayday! Mayday!

"Very fine, Mr. Schmitt, but I really shouldn't be—"

"Heck, Charles—Mr. White, I mean—he had the best cookouts this side of Wichita. He had this grill, this big old metal grill? Out of this world, I tell ya. He's missed around here, and I mean it. Hey, Wednesday is Independence Day. What say we do it up right? I'll round up the neighbors and get a potluck going, and you can show off the garden here. It's a shame only a few of us get to see it."

"That is too kind, and while I thank you, I—"

"Best to start early if anyone's going to make it to the lake for fireworks. Let's say three o'clock? You let Mrs. White know. Myrtle was just saying how it's been too long since we've seen her. She must be real happy about your work, son. I think everyone will be real impressed. All right, I know you like to work, so I won't keep drag-ging you clear around Casey's barn. Mighty fine talking to you, Joe Zebulon. Ha! That name's a real corker."

Chet winked and, for a man his size, vanished quickly.

Sunday shift at the library meant heightened public visibility for Mrs. White; the ignominy always brought her home sullen. We didn't exchange a word until we were halfway through a dinner of Tangy Tomato Aspic (a mire of sour cream and mayonnaise cupped by a gelatinized ring of tomato sauce which hid a *coeur caché* tube of aspar-agus and artichoke hearts). Though I was petrified at the prospect of confronting judgmental neighbors, silence, I told myself, was for seventeen-year-olds. I cleared my throat and affected nonchalance.

"By the by, the Schmitts will be dropping by for a July Fourth cookout."

Mrs. White's fork caught in her mouth like a twig through a tongue.

"A few other neighbors as well," added I.

Mrs. White had gone her namesake color.

I cleared my throat and indicated the food.

"My, doesn't this gelatin look palatable!"

Mrs. White pouched her venom until said dinner was finished, upon which she ordered both children to their rooms with sharp glances. I remained at the table, girding for comeuppance. Mrs. White stood and crossed her arms, staring down at the ignoble worm.

"What were you thinking?"

Thinking? Woman, I am trying, in your husband's stead, to over-haul your defective family!

"It was Mr. Schmitt's doing," said I. "His motives did not seem duplicitous."

237

She grabbed a pack of Chesterfields. Her nervous hands rattled cellophane.

"Of course they aren't. He's just a stupid man. Myrtle Schmitt, though? All the wives around here? They've been *waiting* for this." She barked laughter, billowed smoke. "To see how I'm holding up. To tally up all my mistakes."

"I fail to see any mistakes."

"Well, what did I just say? You're a man, too, aren't you? Just Wednesday I was telling Mrs. Shoemaker about the twist I've added to my Nescafé, how I've been putting a dollop of peach jam in it, and how honestly delicious it is, and she gave me such a look— Mr. Gray, you would not have *believed* this look. She said Nescafé was bitter and bad for the stomach and if I wasn't buying Maxwell House drip-ground coffee, then, well, I don't know—I might as well be drinking arsenic, I guess. And you know what I did? I drove home, marched inside, and threw out two full jars of Nescafé like it was radioactive."

She leaned her shoulders against the wall, closed her reddened eyes, and rubbed her head with the same hand that held the cigarette. The smoke appeared to rise from her skull.

"Maybe you can't see it. Maybe you're too young. But there are problems here. Problems. One of them, frankly, is you. I've told the Lane Ladies you're a paying tenant and you're ill. I've told my canasta group you're a writer and you keep to yourself. None of it does a bit of good. You're new here, and they're furious, simply furious, that they haven't been allowed to judge you for themselves."

I opened my mouth but had nothing of value to add; I was only a man, just as she'd said. Nevertheless I could smell, behind the blistering waves of outrage, her clammy fear that the collective was right and that part-time mothers like her could never achieve the benchmarks of their full-time counterparts.

Mrs. White's eyes remained shut, making it easy to overlay the face of Bridey Valentine. Now, there was a woman who'd worked! Verily, she'd outworked every man in Hollywood. Come to think of it, how about the flappers I'd met in New York? They'd been teachers, stenographers, even librarians, and I'd basked in their intoxicating moxie. Further back now: Mother Mash, tireless moonshiner; Mary Leather, general of a squadron of servants. I saw where my brain was headed and could not stop it—my cherished Wilma Sue, a "working girl" in the most colloquial of senses, slaving away at the oldest profession of all.

I had, to my surprise, a long history of loving hard-working women.

Could such madness be true? Zebulon Finch—feminist?

The nub of Mrs. White's Chesterfield sizzled. Her eyes, when opened, were steelier than expected, her voice more guttural.

"All right. We'll give them their cookout. We'll need decorations, good ones. And food, lots of food. And a grill—shit—pardon my French—but you'll have to dig out Charles's grill from the garage. Can you operate a grill? Well, you'll have to learn. Because we're going to put on a display. An entirely *normal* display. The whole block can rubberneck till they're sore, see for themselves that I'm normal, that my children are normal—that *you* are normal. All right? Mr. Gray? Do you think you can manage? We only have three days."

X.

AMERICAN IMPROVISERS REGULARLY birthed technological monsters, from Leather's Voltaic Bed to the C-53 Skytrooper that had launched me over Germany, but none of them scared me as much as Charles White's grill. It was the size of an upright piano, a hooded double-decker of iron and aluminum stippled with cockeyed knobs and illogical gauges, centered by a grate crusted with barbecues past and strewn with cobwebbed tongs, rusty pinchers, and dank bags of bygone charcoal.

My terror at manning the grill was so great, in fact, that I'd had little time to voice my dismay over Charles's barbecue garb. Mrs. White's insistence that I wear it indicated that she thought it would standardize me, but what kind of sick "standard" was a towering chef's hat labeled SUPER CHEF and a shin-length smock printed with a bumblebee cook and his idiot slogan WHAT'S COOKING, HONEY? I felt like a fool, but this whole affair was my own damned fault. I glared at the marbled sirloins and flaccid wieners awaiting my dilettante torching.

Decoration had carried on nonstop since Tuesday. Forget common crepe (though we had pounds of it) and party hats (those, too). Dangling spangles on strings had transformed the yard into a humongous American flag. One entered into the blue sector, twirling with oversized stars, before progressing to the white sector, where one could find both grill and potluck spread, and finally the red sector, where we'd built a bar complete with the folksy accent of a wheelbarrow filled with ice, Budweiser, and Blatz.

Our prep work recalled the Leathers' dinner with the Cockshuts. I felt the train-track rumble of barreling doom.

Liberty-colored pinwheels clacked. A billion sequins snagged the sun. The radio cooed a doubleheader, Saint Louis Cardinals at Milwaukee Braves. Junior and Franny stood at starched-clothing attention like trembling greyhounds awaiting the race. In the center of it all was Mrs. White in satin-piped taffeta, bosom pounding, fingertips fluttering about the radical new hairdo she'd had done that very morning, a startling departure from her conservative pin-curl. It was called, she said breathlessly, the Eska Protein Wave, the sort of Italian cut popularized by actress Elizabeth Taylor. The boyish crop piled upon her head a carefree mess of curls while leaving her swan neck unprotected, thereby emphasizing her earrings, pearls, and surprisingly shapely shoulders.

Mrs. White was out to show them all.

The Cunninghams arrived first, as Mrs. White had predicted; their ongoing penance for their septic sins required wild overenthusiasm for neighborhood events. They were a pudgy blond foursome who oohed over our stack of mosquito-encircled meat, and when Mr. Cunningham accepted Mrs. White's introduction of me and hesitantly shook my cold hand, I could see brown shoeshine polish beneath his fingernails. The man was working overtime to buy back his reputation.

The Schmitts charged the yard next. Myrtle Schmitt gasped at Mrs. White's hair, and they cheek-kissed as if it had been a Klondike expedition, not a four-foot fence, that had separated them for so long.

Chet, overcompensating as you might to someone given a terminal diagnosis, gave me a back-slap nearly hard enough to shoot Johnny's golden aggie from my stomach.

"He cooks too!" exclaimed Chet.

I asked Gød, my long-held adversary, if he wouldn't mind helping me out just this once, and with a prayer slapped a sirloin onto the grill. I'd devoured plenty in my day but had cooked none; I frowned, wondering what I was supposed to do next while it hissed at me in disgust. Chet, thankfully, was the sort unable to resist usurping masculine tasks. He grabbed three shakers of spices and began applying them with abandon.

From there it was impossible to keep track. The DeWitts, the Brandts, the Dodds, and the Shaefers might as well have been a single fifteen-person tribe, so interchangeable were their bouffants and buzzcuts, bow-shouldered dresses and Bermuda shorts. While the wives clung to Mrs. White and their dungareed kids dove through streamers after Junior, Franny, and Clown, the husbands gathered around the grill like druids. Following Chet's lead, they addressed me with a jocularity almost too pronounced to be believed.

Joe, is it? Glad to make your acquaintance! That's a dilly of a steak there! And gosh, this garden! Gigi's going to give me the dickens if I can't whip ours into shape! I think it's real swell how you're helping Mrs. White with the place! I wish my boy was more like you: quiet, respectful, no darn duck's-ass haircut! You know, Joe, my little Susie had herself some skin problems, too—how about I fix you up with the family doc? Hey, you a baseball fan, Joe? Then you need yourself a high-fidelity unit! Mosey on down to Dodd Electronics; we'll fix you up!

Having done their civic duty, they loosened their collars and decided to become hungry. Like wild dogs they attacked Mrs. White's plates of cracker-ready pimento spread, limeberry gelatin molds, prune whip, and canapés ranging from devilled ham to cheese puffs, and then pushed on to what had become a citadel of competitive cakes: Mystery Mocha Cake, Ambrosia Cake, and Black Midnight Devil's Cake, just for starters.

This last dessert came from none other than the notorious Mrs. Shoemaker, who timed her entrance with the Braves' seventh inning stretch. "Everyone, it's the Shoemakers!" cried Mrs. White, and the congregated, especially the bootlicking Cunninghams, hoorahed as if their future happiness depended on it. I didn't need the introduction. Mrs. Shoemaker, a beanstalk woman approaching fifty, announced herself with an unfrivolous sheath dress, nurse's heels, white gloves, and a look of imperial skepticism. Beside her, Mr. Shoemaker, Wichita's Chevrolet King, barely registered.

Mrs. Shoemaker allowed Mrs. White to pay first tribute, during which the elder raised her eyebrows at the showy hairstyle and naked shoulders. I flipped steaks and rolled wieners with jittery quickness, flip-roll, flip-roll, as the grand dame made a thirty-minute parade across the lawn of fawners. At last she reached the grill. I'd faced foes as cunning as the Barker, Dr. Leather, Detective Roseborough, and Heinrich Himmler, and yet a housewife pacing so confidently about her domain was a new kind of threat. I jostled the coals to create smoke cover, but her small black eyes pierced it like wasps.

"You there. You must be Mr. Gray."

Mrs. White had behaved impeccably for two hours. Surely I could last two minutes?

"Very pleased to meet you, Mrs. Shoemaker."

"You've caused quite a stir around here, young man."

"Have I? I did not mean to."

"Didn't you?"

I flubbed a wiener. It dropped onto the coals. Mrs. Shoemaker smirked. There was a coldness to her appraisal that recalled, in the worst of ways, the judgmental Abigail Finch.

"I'm just trying to finish my book," said I.

Mrs. Shoemaker had no interest in obvious lies.

"Mrs. White tells me that you are stricken with Blackhand's Disease. How perfectly awful for you."

"Yes, ma'am. Thank you, ma'am."

"In fact, I called Dr. Proctor on Sycamore Lane so that I might learn more about it. I thought I might bake a cake that fit with your dietary restrictions."

I darted my eyes rightward, hoping for Mrs. White, but she was off in the blue sector, too far away to help.

"You shouldn't have," said I.

Mrs. Shoemaker smiled, if that's what you want to call it.

"Posh. I was being neighborly, that's all. But Dr. Proctor had never heard of Blackhand's. Isn't that curious?"

Leftward I looked, hoping for Clown. I'd hiss "steal," and she'd clamp her jaws over Mrs. Shoemaker's purse, the perfect distraction, except the dumb dog was off snuffling up a yard's worth of dropped nubbins.

"Well, Mrs. Shoemaker." My idiot mind whirled. "It's, you know, a Korean disease. I contracted it in Korea. The word for it doesn't translate here. It's Korean."

"Of course, Korea. On behalf of the Heavenly Hills Welcome Wagon, I thank you so very much for your service, and in a country of such natural savagery. Tell me, which division were you in? I've studied them extensively in *Reader's Digest*."

244

Dearest Reader, I do hope that the good times we've had together will motivate you to forgive what I did next, as I cannot quite forgive myself. The degrading parlor trick with which I'd paid my way into dozens of Hollywood shindigs popped into my mind as my only salvation. I plucked a kabob skewer from a tray of grilling implements, took false aim at a wiener, and instead drove the skewer into my right arm below the wrist.

It stuck vertical like a flag pole, one more patriotic party favor. One of Junior's pet phrases, just the thing to garner sympathy: "Gee whiz, I've pulled a real lulu this time!"

Mrs. Shoemaker gawped while I unstuck the skewer, pressed my opposite hand against the bloodless wound, and babbled an excuse about fetching a bandage. I took off, weaving around minglers for the safe harbor of the garage. Once inside, I wiped a porthole through a dust-encrusted window and peeked out. Though far across the yard and thronged by kowtowers, Mrs. Shoemaker hadn't dropped her eagle eyes—she was staring right at me.

I might have harbored there till morn had not the tabernacle of Charles's dynamism (drill press, circular saw, extension ladder, soldering iron) begun to shame me anew for my cowardice. Had I really said *gee whiz*? Had I really called my stabbing a *lulu*? I had no right to help Junior achieve manhood if I insisted upon acting like a little boy. I wrapped my new wound in a cloth and slipped back outside the garage, creeping beneath the overhanging eaves.

From shadow I observed the party's final arrivals—eight cane-wielding geriatrics who hobbled into the yard bunched like white grapes. They glowered while gathering potato salad, chafed while cutting cake, and muttered old-country curses each time someone tried breaking the ice.

"Say hey, Mr. Falzone!"

"What do you know, Mrs. Romano?"

Despite alabaster cataracts and jungly eyebrow hair, the elderlies spotted me within five minutes and glared even harder than Mrs. Shoemaker. They'd lived too long and seen too much to be suckered by a coat of paint, whether it be the literal polyester lacquer that turned a sad home bright pink or the figurative veneer of normality draped over an unnatural incubus.

I peeled off hat and apron, a Super Chef no longer. The more I stewed beneath their hot glowers, the more convinced I became that the crusty immigrants had it right. Just look at them, the denizens of Heavenly Hills, getting fat and tipsy while yakking about pension plans, making the country club's par-five, and building that backyard pool. The proud empire these old folks had known had teetered, and I heard the ash-whisper of the Millennialist, urging me to look more closely.

It was as if I'd donned Junior's 3-D glasses. See Mr. Shoemaker showing off his Diners Club card? His docility was cover for a career of unrepentant backstabbing. See how Mr. Schaefer couldn't keep his eyes off little Franny? He fought against the blackest of desires. See how Mrs. Brandt looked at Mr. DeWitt and how Mr. DeWitt looked at Mrs. Mitchell? Spouses would swap, and in the end it would matter not, for each of them rolled along rails into a furnace.

These were the petty pinheads withholding approval of Mrs. White until she leapt through their series of flaming hoops? I'd tried playing it her way, landscaping her yard as I'd landscaped her family, but no longer could I stomach such shallowness. I pushed from the side of the garage and shouldered aside perspiring bodies. I was distinctly more alive, thought I, than any of them, their dull quips

246

deserving nothing better than the *Father Knows Best* laugh track.

"Timer-controlled cooking? Why, pretty soon we won't need wives at all!"

Wa-ha-ha-ha!

"George says this power steering has got all us lady drivers power-mad."

Hur-hur-hur-hur!

"I'm not sure, Shirley, that your home is right for a Tupperware party."

Awwwww!

This last cold crack, delivered by Mrs. Shoemaker, was received by a smiling but inwardly crestfallen Mrs. White. How peddling flexible polyethylene containers equated to higher social status was beyond me, but that, Dearest Reader, was not the goddamned point.

"And why not?" challenged I.

"Oh, good," purred Mrs. Shoemaker. "Our young gardener's injuries are not mortal."

Junior's comic books were jammed with Charles Atlas body-building ads, in which ninety-seven-pound "runts" were transformed, through Atlas's Dynamic Tension exercises, into "he-men" raring to take revenge on beachside bullies. I felt similarly transformed; Mrs. White's warning looks deflected off my rippling muscles.

"Mrs. White shall host the next Tupperware party," declared I. "It is only fair."

"I agree," said Mrs. Shoemaker. "It's only that, well, Mrs. White does not own a dishwasher and can't demonstrate Tupperware's washability, one of its best features."

"Your excuse is weak tea, madam. Weak tea!"

Mrs. Shoemaker swirled her mai tai in a white-gloved hand.

"You have so much oomph for one so infirm."

"'Tis only the tip of my oomph, I assure you."

"Mrs. Shoemaker is right." Mrs. White forced the words through clenched jaws. "I should've thought about the dishwasher. That's my mistake."

"There is one mistake here," said I, "and it belongs to Mrs. Shoemaker."

"Mr. Gray," hissed Mrs. White.

"Do go on," said Mrs. Shoemaker.

Not that the villainess could have stopped me!

"The belief that Mrs. White is worth anything less than you or your coven of witches because she slaves for her family, because she does the work of two, because she does not have the pocketbook to purchase the latest whatsit or thingamabob, *that*, Mrs. Shoemaker, *that* is the mistake, and if I have learned one thing from my time in Heavenly Hills, it is that children here are taught to apologize for mistakes."

Mrs. Shoemaker's frown was a tarantula of wrinkles.

"You want me to apologize?"

"That is *not* what he means," said Mrs. White. "Mr. Gray, stop this instant."

Stop? I had no intention, especially given the agog faces beginning to stare at us. *Friends, Romans, countrymen*, thought I, *let me shout sense into your TV-deafened ears!* But by then Mrs. Shoemaker had slipped my blade and drawn her own.

"I am quite sure, Mr. Gray, that I don't know what you are going on about. Of course Mrs. White is a capable homemaker. Any advice I offer her, I offer as a friend, and I am confident that she takes it in the intended fashion."

"Oh, I do," insisted Mrs. White. "I appreciate it so much."

But Mrs. Shoemaker was not finished.

"I believe that I speak for all of the ladies present when I say that we are simply not comfortable bringing our children into an environment that includes a large unleashed dog, an ill renter about whom we know little, and, quite frankly, an atmosphere of unconventional ideas—building a bomb shelter from a basement, for instance. I'm sure Mrs. White takes no offense."

On this point, Mrs. White herself seemed uncertain.

"I—well," said she. "It's only that I—"

What good fortune that I was there to rescue the stumped stammerer!

"Unconventional, you say? Do you see, madam, the tint of my skin? How *unconventional* it is? The A-bomb at Hiroshima did it! Yes, that's right! Now all of you know! I was there! I saw the detonation from a distance that few others did, and I can tell you—nay, promise you—that the household that prizes plastic food containers over bomb shelters is a harebrained household indeed!"

Silence descended so completely that we could hear strike three called from Milwaukee. The laugh track had run out of tape, and the backyard party now seemed grossly overproduced, the air putrid with wieners and Jell-O into which maggot larvae had already been laid. Stupid, stupid Zebulon! I'd need to have been thirty years old to have been present at Hiroshima, and here I was, still lousy old seventeen.

Mr. Cunningham, famished for respect, rolled the dice on clearing his throat, checking his watch, and declaring the lateness of the hour. The gambit paid off. Others echoed the sentiment to the stricken, speechless Mrs. White—they had to drive to the grandparents', had to get the kids cleaned up for lakeside fireworks, had to relieve the babysitter. The elated Mr. Cunningham lifted streamers to facilitate the satisfied exit of Mrs. Shoemaker. There were kisses and handshakes but only for show; their eyes transmitted to one another the real conversation: *We'll talk about this later.*

And talk—and talk—and talk.

Dear Gød, what had I done?

Chet Schmitt, potential pal of mine for a whole three days, gave me a disappointed shake of the head before leaving. That left the old folks, who departed as they'd arrived, in a cluster, as if they were a clan of rats with their tails knotted together. They sneered at me as they disappeared around the pink clapboard, gratified that at least one of their senses worked well enough to have sniffed out my dishonesty long before I'd exposed it myself.

XI.

USK DID NOT DROP UNTIL after eight, by which time Heavenly Hills had been turbulenced for hours by the two-bit firecrackers I'd heard inventoried by children all night. The resulting smoke made the sky look like a French battlefield after a day of machine-gun fire and shelling, scraped and scabbed, as if we'd wounded the world itself.

Having no foxhole in which to crouch, I'd squatted beneath the scarlet brume to wipe down the grill's surfaces. My sleeves were sudsy from the Joy-brand cleaning liquid; I'd taken to scouring the grate with steel wool as if I might scrape away not only the evidence of our abortive banquet but also the caked-on memories of past cookouts, each one of them fictions of counterfeit camaraderie.

Clown snuffed my malaise. She nosed The Toe, certain that a frisky chew might lighten the mood. I shook my foot, popping her in the nose, and she yelped and withdrew. I felt rotten about it but redirected that anger to the Marlboro Man. Had I a quick path to Montana, I'd have tracked down the bastard, wangled a way to get the drop, and demanded answers for why he'd forced my irregular shape back into the world's methodized matrix.

The screen door moaned, allowing inside the defeated dog, and after a deadly pause, Mrs. White appeared for the first time in hours. Though I kept my eyes on my dirty work, I could sense her surveying

251

the chintzy decorations that, if not soon removed, would be bloated by rain into a purple pulp capable of spoiling the entire garden.

The Schmitts had hightailed it to the lake. For once we went unobserved.

"Well," said Mrs. White, "what do you have to say for yourself?"

"Need more Joy," grunted I.

Never had I uttered a truer statement.

"Maybe it's for the best if you moved on," said she.

"Maybe? For certain, Mrs. White. Where I linger, the earth itself rots."

"You certainly *talk* like a writer."

"What, pray tell, does that mean?"

"You think I don't know what happens in my own home? I've dusted your desk enough to know there's no writing going on down there. There's not even any paper. You're a fraud and a liar. I don't know why it surprised me today when you opened your mouth and out came more lies."

I clenched the steel wool, felt fibers screw into my flesh.

"I lied about nothing."

"Hiroshima? Blackhand's Disease? Mr. Gray, I can't even keep up."

"Believe what you wish."

"Oh, I will. And I believe that you're trouble, Mr. Gray, with a capital *T*."

"You'll receive no argument from me."

She kicked a pinwheel. Faulty as everything else, it spun once before dying.

"So you planted some flowers! So you walk the dog! So what? That gives you no right to lie to my friends, to make decisions without consulting me—"

252

"*Friends, ma'am? Friends?*"

"I should've known the first day I met you. When you refused to say grace, which you still refuse, every day—a terrible influence on the children. I can't have them growing up not trusting in Gød, not believing in something greater. What else do they have? It's a struggle to get Junior to even say his bedtime prayers, and that's your fault, Mr. Gray."

Junior had so many genuine challenges—becoming a man, for instance, in a world fermenting with Herbie Hinkles—that the gratuitous burden of pleasing an ungrateful Gød enraged me. I bolted upward and booted aside the grate, which rolled like Franny's hula hoop in concentric circles before clanging to cement and shedding a ring of cinder. By then I'd taken a long, loping step and planted myself directly in front of Mrs. White, staring down at her as my nearly six feet allowed.

"You wish to oust me from your uncomfortable basement? Please do, Mrs. White, for it is undiluted torture for a young man of my intellect to be subject to the anesthetizing strictures of such a place, where an offense as light as washing your car on Sunday gets you crucified by She-Devil Shoemaker. And yet it is I who tarnish the Goodness and Rightness of children? Let me tell you what I know about Gød, Mrs. White. He is a fabricant by both definitions: one who creates, and one who falsifies. The promised lands He dangles before us like fine silks are but the roughest reproductions, pulled away at the last second as a matador pulls his cape. You, your so-called friends, you all hippity-hop through life like hares, but life is over in a snap, so quickly that no one except yours truly, Mr. Joe Gray, would believe it. Gød, then, is the Tortoise, ancient and hard-shelled, but as Aesop knows, this is not a race He loses. He will claim you, He will claim your children, and He will not, at the end, be the kindly, magical grandfather upon which you rely. I wager that your husband, at his terrible, screaming end, learned this truth about Gød."

Mrs. White's green eyes blinked in confusion, but instead of backing down she pooched her bottom lip.

"Blaspheme all you want, Mr. Gray, but don't you dare drag my husband into it. You're not anything like him."

"No, I am not like your husband, though I fail to see why that should buoy you. I have yet to see evidence that Mr. White was a husband to be missed. You keep no photographs about, no remembrances; everything the man owned is squirreled away in an unswept garage; and the photograph you tote day and night is not of him at all, but rather a picture of a kitchen that you will never be able to afford. And yet you chastise *me* for not living up to your husband's precedent?"

There was a golden age, Reader, when being slapped by a woman was for your narrator an invigorating weekly occurrence. But six decades had passed since I'd had the honor, and Mrs. White, in our first instance of physical contact, delivered a spectacular reminder of the speed, accuracy, and decibel of this most feminine of maneuvers. Possessed of no lifeblood, my cheek cracked like seat leather. It was her face, however, that looked injured.

"How could you? Charles was—he was everything to me! Everything! I just can't—I can't *look* at him. How can I look at him? He left me here, he left me all alone, and I'm so angry with him, so . . . *furious.* Every time I look at Junior or Franny—they look like him, Mr. Gray. *They look just like him.* I'm angry with them, too. Can't you see that? Maybe I won't ever have that kitchen in the picture, but what else is there to do but try? What else can I do but go forward?"

254

With the slap still echoing between fences, our quiet suburbs were engulfed by the first boom of fireworks over the lake. Inside, Clown howled and the children moaned, certain that they were missing the defining event of their generation.

The array of whistles, pops, and bangs continued for twenty minutes, during which time I felt as if it were I being downed, and deservedly so, by a firing squad of giants. Mrs. White, too, swayed as if perforated by bullets. By the concluding explosion, I was able to see her without the hindrance of fury. Tragically, she still wore her party dress, its perky bows as deflated as the yard's balloons. Her Eska Protein Wave had also capitulated to gravity, its buoyant tousle now an unqualified tangle. The naked shoulders that had broadcasted confidence now shivered.

"Mrs. White," said I.

She raised a silencing hand. The same hand plunged into a pocket and dug out a pack of Chesterfields. She turned away from me to elude a nonexistent breeze, but after her cig was lit, she did not turn back around. Her voice was as soft as the plumes of smoke.

"What do you mean, how everyone speeds through life except you?"

It is easier to speak truth to a woman's back.

"I have . . . certain characteristics."

"I know. I suppose I wasn't sure, but I had an idea."

"How?"

"I told you, I know what goes on in my own home. You could stop flushing the toilet, you know, if you're not really using it. Water costs money."

It was a bizarrely practical request.

"Are you afraid of me?" asked I.

Her shoulder blades rolled. "I don't know what to be afraid of. It's hard to choose. You know, six months before you came, they sent home Charles's body. There was a funeral and everything; the whole neighborhood came. But I only ever got to see the box. The casket. The funeral people said he wasn't in a state to be seen. But I regret not forcing them to show me, I regret it every day, because now when I think of Charles, I think of that box and how he's in there just rotting away. Sometimes I think he probably looks a little like you, Mr. Gray."

I touched the flesh of my cheek. It held the contour of her slap.

"I guess what I'm saying is that I don't mind how you look. I don't mind looking at you at all. Because it's like looking at Charles, in a way. I don't care how horrid that sounds."

Perhaps she'd turned her back for her own sake.

"It is not horrid at all," said I.

She sighed smoke. "You didn't fight in Korea."

"No, ma'am."

"Then what were you doing before this?"

"Would you believe I was a top-secret spy in Nazi Germany?"

She laughed once, then succumbed to an adorably antisocial impulse, holding her cigarette to the drooping end of a star-spangled banner. It began to sizzle upward like a stick of my father's TNT.

"At this point," said she, "I'd believe almost anything."

Junior and Franny had opted to elevate their anguish to actual weeping, and Mrs. White went indoors to soothe them, for that was her job, but before doing so dropped her cig on a stomped party hat that swiftly took up the flame. I put out the burning banner with my hand and ground the cardboard hat with my heel, though I wasn't sure why I bothered. Mrs. White had shown little interest in salvaging the grounds and might have enjoyed a cleansing blaze. In the tautology of her civil defense booklets, she and I, having revealed cold truths to one another and chosen to accept them, had made a silent pact of mutual annihilation. I, for one, having been all too slowly annihilated for some time, was glad to have found a partner with whom to share it.

XII.

OVER THE ENSUING YEAR, INSPIRED by the fateful barbecue, we Whites discarded, bit by bit, the homogenized provisos of suburban life, and it was exhilarating. To vault ahead decades in lingo, Dearest Reader, Mrs. White quit giving a fuck. Our garden of enchantment became an ogre's lair of draping trumpet vine, thick carpetweed, ornery crabgrass, and bobbing ragweed, with pockets of poison ivy, prickly lettuce, and cocklebur to add an element of danger to Junior, Franny, and Clown's explorations. The three of them bled, scratched, and sneezed, and were the stronger for it.

The kitchen also brambled. Its pink purity became scuffed by stains and scalds as Mrs. White forwent magazine chefs d'oeuvre like Gourmet Pâté de Foie Gras (liverwurst, cream cheese, bouillon) and replaced them with simpler, hotter, more toothsome fare: hams, meat loafs, sausages, soups. In this single sphere was I superior to Mr. White, for I had no colleagues comparing their wives' culinary showpieces, nor did I have taste buds longing for exotic tangs.

The living room, too, wilded. Canasta and Tupperware party invites had dried up, so it was television all the time, and the four of us huddled without thought of propriety. In September 1956, as we, along with the rest of America, watched Elvis Presley jerk about Ed Sullivan's stage like he had rickets, Franny declared that she was "mad about" Elvis, and Junior squirmed against me with laughter. In January 1957, during Steve Allen's final night as the host of *The Tonight Show*, Franny bounced upon my lap to the musical interludes. In March 1957, after adoring *The Wizard of Oz*, Mrs. White insisted upon watching a broadcast of *Gone with the Wind*, a film I'd long picketed in Bridey's honor, and when she cried during Melanie's death-bed scene, I held out the Kleenex economy pack and she accepted it, her fingertips grazing my cold palm without even a shiver.

I gazed out the picture window, daring every busybody, from Mrs. Shoemaker to Gød, to take offense. In the reflective glass I could see the permanent speckles of my left cheek—popped capillaries from Mrs. White's Fourth of July slap. They looked like pimples, and I prized them as memorials to my youth. It was possible, thought I, that I was the man of the house, and if so, artifice could no longer be permitted. One night, after everyone else was asleep, I packed away the Royal Quiet de Luxe typewriter, but not before typing an imag-ined apology to the Marlboro Man, who, in retrospect, had known exactly what he was doing, sending me here.

Without so much as a hat to shield my ugly face, I led a parade of White children across the neighborhood to matinees, play dates, lessons, and clubs, and on the occasion when they had stressors too uncomfortable to discuss with their mother, I coaxed the truth from them before delivering advice more nuanced than my old cure-alls of punching with fist and kicking with boot.

Junior, especially, needed counsel. Periodically our path would inter-sect with herds of "greasers"—leather-jacketed, Brylcreem-slathered delinquents revving their juiced-up, super-torqued, V-8-engined hot rods in anticipation of drag-race hooliganism. In each goon's patchwork of scars Junior saw the natural maturation of his schoolyard shiners, and oh, Reader, could I ever sympathize with his longing to hop into one of the speedsters and peel off into the sunset, away from responsibility, away from his mother. I'd done the same thing to my own.

But hadn't I mourned Abigail Finch when I'd learned how she'd died alone? More than the greasers represented escape, they represented a chance to steer Junior from error. Whenever we saw such rowdies, I'd take the boy by the shoulder, give it a hard squeeze, and run through the same routine.

"Who are those boys?"

"Herbie Hinkles," Junior would respond.

"And what do we think of Herbie Hinkles?"

Junior would extend his tongue and offer a strenuous raspberry. Then I'd wink, shove him ahead with the surplus of force he enjoyed, and feel Johnny's aggie in my stomach radiate with sudden warmth. Perhaps proffering guidance was part of the enigmatic know-how men were supposed to accrue?

One afternoon, after I'd propelled Junior into the Orpheum to see a picture called *I Was a Teenage Werewolf*, Franny, who'd tagged along, tugged my sleeve until I squatted down. She placed a hand to her mouth and whispered into my right ear, the one missing a lobe, from Leather's scalpel.

"I love you, Mr. Gray."

I recoiled as if bitten, scoffed with a rude exhale, and made haste toward Heavenly Hills so that Franny, with her podgy legs, had to run to keep pace, but not before I cast a last look at the Orpheum, where Junior stood at a window, watching us leave. He was eleven and male, not allowed to speak such sap, yet I could feel his confirmative emotion as surely as a teenage werewolf could feel the prickling rise of a pregnant moon.

260

As complicit as I'd become in raising the children, Clown remained my closest chum. Mrs. White had quit asking for rent (I merrily contributed more than my share to family expenses), and I, high on belonging, delighted at Clown's every astute defecation upon the yards of the block's biggest bullies. Through front windows I enjoyed Mr. Cunningham's limp disbelief, Mrs. Shoemaker's jaw-gnashing fury, and the old folks' cancerous hate. To further goad them, I began extending tra-la-la hellos to their colored laborers. These men stared, wide-eyed, before lifting salutes that were at first tentative, weeks later earnest, and months later downright emboldened. Soon they took the initiative, calling out, Howdy-do, Mr. Gray! Howdy-do, Clown!

My camaraderie with Negroes was a step too far. Some infuriated citizen's paperboy son was hired as sniper, and he hurled rolled-up newsprint missiles at me whenever he caught me misbehaving. After snatching several midair and fastballing them back, including one bull's-eye that sent the underage terrorist somersaulting off his two-wheeler, I stayed my hand. As it happened, our Zenith was on the fritz, and famished for entertainment, I unrolled the newspaper and began to read it, even as Clown strained homeward.

It was the first of many issues of *The Wichita Eagle* that I stole; Mrs. White had no stomach for hard news and did not subscribe. Reclined in Charles's old chair, I found, lo and behold, a war raging beyond the suburbs' petunias. America's gradual easing into racial desegregation was having a rough go of it, with Georgia and Florida refusing to acknowledge the Supreme Court's progressive decrees. In May, I read about the Prayer Pilgrimage for Freedom, a twenty-five-thousand-person civil rights demonstration at the Lincoln Memorial, at which Negro leaders asked—nay, demanded!—

261

that their brothers and sisters be given full voting rights.

The dam broke in September. After a day-long filibuster by an impressive bladder-clencher named Strom Thurmond, the Civil Rights Act of 1957 was cleared for President Ike to sign, though the pen he used would be inked with blood. Birmingham: a Negro reverend thrashed for enrolling his daughters in a white school. Nashville: Hattie Cotton Elementary dynamited after a single Negro girl's admission. Little Rock: a militia ordered by the governor to forcibly block nine Negro children from entering.

Mrs. White hated to bitter her meals with distasteful talk, but it became unavoidable. Built into the front brick of her library were two water fountains, the larger labeled WHITE, the smaller COLORED. Federal fiat was to remove the offending placards, but you try it in such charged air! The task was put off month after month. Mrs. White's green eyes flashed with the desire to do the deed in full view of Heavenly Hills passersby, thereby joining me in the rewarding pastime of exposing their hypocrisy and watching them squirm. If only, sighed she, she knew more about screwdrivers, drills, whatever else was needed.

Was she counting on me as she'd once counted upon Charles? On the same day that the Army's 101st Airborne Division enforced the Little Rock Nine's gutsy entrance into Central High School, I hooked Clown to a leash, grabbed a crowbar from the garage, and with those two weapons walked past the Orpheum to the library, a red-brick Andrew Carnegie in the middle of a bustling business area.

I looped Clown's leash around a light pole. She drooled happily as I jammed the crowbar behind WHITE and with a yank tore it free of the brick. After I did the same with COLORED, I slipped both placards into my back pocket, took the leash, tipped my hat at the two dozen who'd stopped to stare, and paused long enough for Clown to

262

piss on the library lawn. I cannot say if Mrs. White was watching. I can say, however, that she broke protocol that night by slipping the Saint Bernard a large strip of prime rib.

The next time I encountered the troop of Negro laborers, this time clipping the ends of the Dodds' trees, I removed both placards from my pockets and flung them across the lawn. The foreman squinted at me curiously, removed his work gloves, and picked up the bent rectangles of metal. I waited, a smile at my lips, for a round of applause. Instead, the foreman sent both placards flying back at me with such accuracy that I had to duck and cover like Junior and Franny during bomb drills.

"Real fine, Mr. Gray," said the foreman. "But we got our own crowbars."

I was affronted, then hours later ashamed, but both were only emotions. What followed were actions as real as any barricade, beating, or bombing. Mr. Dodd had seen the foreman hurl the pieces of metal, and the entire crew was sacked, never again to be seen in Heavenly Hills. Unbeknownst to me, phone cables everywhere began to droop with the weight of electricity as the news of my part in the scandal began to circulate up and down Mulberry Terrace.

Mrs. White's belated arrival home the next night was not by itself alarming; Monday was bowling league, and no doubt the game had gone an extra frame or two. But clinks from the liquor cabinet were rare, so I crept upstairs and into the unlit kitchen, where Mrs. White sat at the nook, the illumination points of moon and cigarette casting silky swirls across the toaster's chrome.

Mrs. White pointed her cig at the opposite chair. I sat, but that we hadn't shared this table since my interview made me measure my words more than usual.

"I sense," said I, "that this drink is not your first."

Her tapped ashes glowed red.

"I got fired."

My reaction was as physical as an upchucking.

"I acted alone. I'll tell them you had nothing to do with it. Should I call now? No, best to wait until morning. They will take you back, I am sure of it."

Mrs. White shrugged.

"Lots of colored people use the library. That already makes it a target. Having me around just made it worse. Ever since the cookout they've gotten complaints about me. I believe there's even a petition. All you did is give them the excuse. That's not why I'm upset."

I pictured Junior and Franny holding out hats like urchin beggars. My own money was dwindling fast.

"Then why?" cried I. "What could be worse?"

She threw down half the glass in one swallow.

"I thought bowling would take my mind off it. It was the normalest thing I could think of. But it was a trap. By the time I noticed my team was the only Lane Ladies there, I already had my shoes laced. You know, I thought I was safe with my girls, but they had a whole speech rehearsed. About me, you, our relationship, how difficult it's making things for them. For them! They think something indecent is going on, and I'll tell you what, I didn't correct them. I just picked up a bowling ball, a big heavy man's ball, and held it up like I was going to squash them, and told them they could turn blue for all I cared, and I just hucked that ball right down the center of the lane, not even aiming, and got a seven-ten split. Then bam, I walked right out."

I could not help but smile. When she, in a most unladylike fashion, lifted her right leg and plunked it atop the table, my smile

264

broadened. No high-heels tonight; here was a scuffed, beige leather bowling shoe with rawhide laces—a stolen one. She noticed my grin, chuckled, and hiccupped.

"Who needs 'em?" challenged she.

She dragged until her Chesterfield died. Left to the moonlight, she became as ghostly as I. She toyed with the toaster, brave with darkness and drink.

"I feel as if . . ." She sighed. "It's a very strange feeling."

"Go on."

"It's as if I don't care that I was fired. Who wants to stand behind the same counter her whole life? I feel like there's something . . . I don't know. Something I don't have but perhaps wish I had . . . ?"

"'Want' is the word," said I. "You want something."

The Eska Protein Wave shimmied in an excited nod, as if *want* were a concept she'd only previously considered in relation to packaged goods.

"Yes. That's it. And—oh, I don't want to sound ungrateful. But it makes me wonder. Is this all there is? Is this everything? I took homemaking classes. I got married, I had children. I had the kitchen cabinets rebuilt so I wouldn't have to stoop or stretch. I mean, I did what everyone told me to. Doesn't there have to be more? That's what everyone said during the war—hang on, better things are coming. But where is it? *What* is it?"

Mrs. White had muddled toward the biggest question of all.

"The funny thing is," said she, "I don't think if Charles were here that I'd be allowed to feel this way. But it's like there's a gap where he used to be, and as his widow I can see through it, and you know what's behind it? Nothing at all. It's like the Wizard of Oz behind his curtain. He couldn't offer Dorothy anything because it was all a lie.

Everything we've ever been promised, Mr. Gray, is just a big fat lie."

"You've had an excess of alcohol. You should lie down."

I did not believe that she had.

"You're right," said she.

She did not believe it either.

Once she'd shuffled off to bed, the bowling shoes soft compared to her usual heels, I was left with the residue of her words churning like smoke in moonlight. I flicked on the overhead lamp, closed the door so as not to wake Clown's stomach, and regarded my sworn nemesis—the Western Brass toaster. I snagged the power cord, reeled it in, and stared into the dual slots, one that arbitrarily burned bread in hellfire, the other that let bread live untouched. Gød's toaster, you might say, and that is why I decided to defeat it. After all, with our breadwinner jobless, broken items around the house would need to be fixed, Mrs. White and myself included.

XIII.

THE CALENDAR ADVERTISED TWO YEARS of the decade still to go, but I assure you, Dearest Reader, that the 1950s expired one humdrum evening in October 1957, and in its death throes dragged me down with it. That night we watched the premiere of a contemporary opera buffa titled *Leave It to Beaver*. Passable fare, judged I, though I could not comfortably watch a family called the Cleavers, recalling as I did the Barker's soothsaying over a half-century ago:

You are a cleaver. That is what you do. You shall cut the world in half, Mr. Finch.

We slept as Americans sleep—righteous and bored—as our greatest foe infiltrated our empire, not across shores as we'd done at Normandy, Peleliu, and Tarawa, but from the sky. The news broke on the morning of October 5, but it was a Saturday and the family was scattered, Mrs. White comparison shopping for cheaper groceries, Junior playing pickup stickball, Franny at the dance studio, and Mr. Gray staring down Clown in the backyard with brush and hose.

Mrs. White had pulled into the driveway a thousand times, but never like this. The Roadmaster squealed at the turn and yelped at the sudden braking. I heard the car door open, but not close, and Mrs. White's heels reached the front door in remarkably few steps. Inside, the radio turned on, then the television. I dropped the grooming implements and snapped for Clown to follow me indoors.

On the TV before which Mrs. White perched, newsmen adjusted their glasses, consulted reports handed from faceless assistants, and meted out kibbles of information about "outer space" and "solar radio interference" and "interplanetary travel" that sounded ripped from the lousy scripts of one of Junior's flying-saucer films.

"What is this rubbish?" asked I.

"The Russians launched it. It's called Sputnik."

"Spoot-nik? What is a Spoot-nik?"

"I don't know. A satellite?"

"What does this satellite do?"

"I don't *know*. No one does. But it's up there. It's right on top of us."

"Hogwash," said I. "Pure fiddle-faddle!"

The anchor sighed, as if wearied by my disbelief, squared his script, and told us, in a hide-your-children tone, that the sounds about to be broadcast were being transmitted live from the first man-made object ever sent into orbit. He cleared his throat, perhaps to choke down shrieks of existential fear, and the audio track switched over to a frothy, seaside frequency that, almost instantly, became diced by a high-pitched pattern:

Hweeeeee . . . fweeeeee . . . hweeeeee . . . fweeeeee . . .

I blurted in terror, the back of my knees struck the sofa, and down I crashed. Leather and his Isolator were my nightmares, mine alone, and yet the surgeon somehow had scooped his own brains from the Cotton Club floor and alchemized them into stars, so that his poison wheeze could be injected into millions through television tubes.

Only minutes later did I register the noise as quicker and squeakier, like the cheep of a rat stomped to pulp but still alive: *hwee-hwee, fwee-fwee.* The anchor was unable to stomach it and cut the audio, though for every listener that day, it kept coming, and coming, just like that slow sower of death himself, the Millennialist.

The instant I thought of Hiroshima, Mrs. White did as well.

We stared at each other.

Could Sputnik be carrying an atomic bomb?

The reporters were saying probably not—no, *certainly* not—for the orbiter had a twenty-two-inch diameter and weighed 184 pounds. But hold up, Mr. Newsman! Hadn't we received those specifications from Soviet Premier Khrushchev's own news agency? Didn't it make sense for them to mislead us? I was likely the only American listening who felt a thrill. Not only was nuclear holocaust a fate our nation deserved, but it also carried the ancillary bonus of taking care of me, once and for all.

Mrs. White, however, made a strangled sound.

"Franny. Junior."

I felt a flash of shame before adopting her fright. The children, at least, deserved a shot at adulthood, didn't they? Mrs. White soared from the sofa, out the front door, and into the open car. I followed in a daze, drifting into the Roadmaster's exhaust and hearing, once the car had screeched away, a *hwee-hwee, fwee-fwee* emitting from every window on the block. I looked this way, then that, nauseated by the conviction that I would see a bullet-shaped helmet, two glass lenses, and an oxygen tube rise behind every single pane of glass, each Heavenly Hills household having ordered from the Sears catalogue a family pack of Isolators.

I hurried inside.

One hour later—an eternity in front of the doomsday Zenith—

Mrs. White stormed the pink house with a child beneath each arm, Franny tutued and tearful, Junior dirt-dusted and fervent. Mrs. White held them by the wrists while considering the basement door. She'd been mocked for even considering the blueprints of "The Family Fallout Shelter." Only now, at zero hour, had her paranoid visions been substantiated. She appealed to me, and I nodded. All right, let us gather in that space in which, until then, had been mine alone.

My chamber, bare though it was, was cozy enough. Mrs. White roosted on my bed reading storybooks to Franny in a tremulous voice that only served to disturb her, while Junior and I, certified menfolk, squatted beside the radio we'd arranged at the other end of the room. Clown paced between female and male camps, her whine rather like Sputnik's.

Not even Junior's Martian-invasion theory could distract me from the certitude that, in the span of two hours, Mrs. White had suffered a terrible setback. The past week had seen her at her strongest. The morning after being fired, she'd risen, red-eyed and hungover, to find me still in the nook, the toaster in a billion hopeless pieces, and instead of taking it as another sucker punch, she'd laughed—what a transformation of her careworn face!—dragged close the trash, and swept away all evidence of the infernal appliance.

She'd thus far proven unemployable and had begun conjecturing aloud about getting some sort of degree, maybe learning to type, though both fields looked down upon overripe women of twenty-nine. Still she refused to despair. It was clear she'd made the decision not to yield to silent pressure to sell the pink house; the witches and warlocks of Heavenly Hills would take it over her dead body. The unpredictability of her future seemed to excite her, and that, in turn, excited me.

Four days before Sputnik, a framed wedding portrait of Charles and Shirley appeared on the mantel among a congregation of other photographs. I watched Franny discover it, smile at it, and go on playing. I watched Junior discover it, touch his father's face, and go on playing. When I was unobserved, I too addressed the photo. The newlyweds were achingly fresh-faced and undesigning; they looked like unformed tadpoles. Nevertheless I saluted the fallen soldier, for his return to Mulberry Terrace, not in a box this time, was a victory. We'd overcome the catastrophe of his death. We'd survived the intimidations of Mrs. Shoemaker. At last we could get on with our lives. Until Sputnik.

Daylight dimmed through the cellar windows. Clown's whine intensified; she needed to pee. So, too, did everyone else, and when Mrs. White asked me what I thought, I related how the radio had stressed that Americans were under no immediate danger. I put on my favorite jacket, hoping that the steady tick of the Excelsior would give me confidence, and chained by handholds—Mrs. White to Franny to Junior to me—we ascended the stairs, switched on lamps one by one, and found crouching in the darkness the same house we'd left behind.

I opened the back door for Clown, who sprinted ten feet and whizzed hard enough to lift a dust cloud. Mrs. White and I surveyed the backyards and found them filled with families whose sobriety suggested that Sputnik was a technological Pearl Harbor, a space shot akin to those fabled first fires at Fort Sumter. Lucky observers had their kids' telescopes, and the rest pointed at the Milky Way— not at us, for once—and whispered.

"They estimate," said I to Mrs. White, "that it shall pass over us at eight."

And so it did, across a stretch of sky that, until that moment, had been our own. It was the tiniest twinkle, but still big enough to enfeeble a nation that hours before had believed Russians to be primitive clod-hoppers. As the satellite sailed past, Mulberry Terrace cascaded with gasps—a series of soft pops—as if, on this anti-Independence Day, fireworks were being held not at the lake but beneath it. Everyone understood that the line being drawn across the sky was to separate old fears from new, and to combat that fear, each wife grabbed her husband, and each husband his wife, and held on for dear life.

Mrs. White covered her face and ran inside.

It took far longer than Sputnik's passage for me to turn up the occupants of the pink house. Franny and Junior, I found in the latter's room, sitting scared on the bed, their eyes the size reserved for when children hear a parent sobbing. My faculty as a caregiver had made strides, but this was beyond my ken. I asked Junior if he wanted to watch the Braves murder them Yankees; he shook his head. I asked Franny if she wanted to have a tea party—how many times had she pleaded for a dad-blasted tea party?—but she wouldn't leave her brother's side. Tonight, Mr. Gray was not comfort enough.

With the children left to a fretful slumber, I paced like a Saint Bernard outside of Mrs. White's bedroom, ears perked for the tumbler clink of bourbon through the tempest of tears. Being part of a family, I chastised myself, required offering ministrations of support. I remembered rescuing Merle from a lubricious lover outside our Salem apartment in 1913. And what had been my reward? The most transcendent minutes we'd ever shared, with my daughter furling her arms around me and keening, *Daddy, Daddy, Daddy.*

I knuckled softly upon the door.

"Mrs. White? May I be of assistance?"

The sobbing caught, went silent.

"Mrs. White? I think that I should come in."

Nothing.

"Mrs. White, I am opening the door. Please take care that you are decent."

I played the memory of Wilma Sue pulling on a nightgown and lacing it—seventeen seconds—before pushing open the bedroom door. A prism of hallway light chipped from the darkness a yellow rectangle, within which I could see discarded slippers, drawn window shades, the bottom third of the bed, and the left shoulder of Mrs. White. My dead eyes took less time to adjust than living ones; in shadow, she sat upright upon her bed, not in a zippered chenille housecoat but a black taffeta slip. Her flounced hair and puffy eyes lent her a drowsy Marilyn Monroe look, and her arms were extended. To me, Dearest Reader, to me.

"Shh," said she. "Shh."

I closed the door behind me. The light cut out. The air felt like tar. Her hands, though, beckoned, and so I moved closer, pushing my legs through the tar, lest it harden. Her weightless hands settled like feathers upon my arms, and she looked up at me through moonlit tears.

"I can't do boy-girl," whispered she. "I can't."

"Nor can I."

She nodded, grateful. Both of her hands moved to my right cuff, where, despite the dark, she demonstrated a wifely skill with buttons. It was as if she couldn't wait to unclothe me—she pushed back the sleeve, running her warm palm over the lizardy skin of Chernoff's marred taxidermy, the cold pit of Mr. Avery's fishing-hook wound, the hard nugget of Sandy's embedded tooth. She undid the left cuff

273

and caressed those wounds as well. Finally she drew back the entire shirt, leaving my torso bare. I shivered, not from temperature but the thrill of being seen, even if only by starlight.

Mrs. White pulled me down to the bed, pressed me into a reclined position, and ran her hands over bullet holes, stomach stitching, bayonet wounds, the sawed-off rib. My instinct was to coil like a prodded caterpillar, for suburban life had taught me the holiness of hygiene, how Brillo Soap Pads, Soilax with Germisol, and Self-Polishing Simoniz were all that kept postwar democracies from festering into Red blights. I was nothing a good homemaker should touch, and yet, with the gentleness she would have shown her husband's body had they opened the box, she pressed her soft cheek against my abraded chest, inhaled my spoiled funk, and at long last allowed herself to drown in the physical realities of death.

For this one night, when the blade of a fearful future had been pressed to our collective jugular, I would be Mr. White so that Mrs. White could say good-bye.

I considered it my great honor.

Oh, Charles, moaned she, *my Charles.*

After she'd made peace with my corpse—Charles's corpse—she positioned me in the precise posture she recalled from her fondest nights. She balanced me upon my right side and snuggled her spine into the curve of my body. Next she picked up my left wrist and wrapped my arm around her bosom. Finally, she hiked my left leg so that it draped atop her thighs. A tuck here, a wiggle there, and then it was perfect. She sighed, happy beneath my heaviness.

Almost four years had passed since Charles's death, and in the hours before she slept, Mrs. White, in a murmur too soft for me to follow, recounted to her husband everything he'd missed. Surely

274

she spoke of the children, how they'd grown. Possibly she even spoke of me, how I'd helped. There was crying—shuddering jags that rattled my skeleton and dampened our sheets. But there was also laughter—bashful giggles to loud brays, the sheer variety of which attested to the nuance of their relationship. There was anger as well—frustrated huffs damning him, no doubt, for getting himself killed. And there was, in the dead of night, a sexual event—I felt her snug a fist between her thighs before her back began to hitch with what could have been ecstasy or grief, or most likely both. If I could have cried, I would have, so moved was I to feel, flesh to flesh, every tick and tremble of human emotion. It was mutual one last time, the both of us annihilated piece by piece, and then, through her sequence of safe, soft snores, rebuilt.

XIV.

, ABIDING INSOMNIAC, WAS WAKEFUL to the knocking.

In the years after Little Johnny Grandpa's demise, I would have belted you had you prophesied I would befriend another child. Yet Junior had grown dear, and I distressed at what he might think upon seeing me entwined with his mother. I unsnarled my limbs, threw on shirt and jacket, and did what buttoning I could while stumbling across the dark room.

But the face I spied through the cracked door was not Junior's perceptive hatchet but rather Franny's plaintive moon. She was so heavy-lidded that my anachronistic presence caused her but one hypnagogic twitch before she yawned and rubbed her eyes.

"There's noises," mushmouthed she. "By the garage."

My sigh carried no aggravation, only paternal indulgence. Sputnik had stirred stress in the nine-year-old; it was to be expected that she sought the protective wing of a father, and the garage was the location most associated with Mr. White. I resolved to clean it on the morrow: wash the windows, scrub the floors, sell off the junk, and broom it free of ghosts.

For now, though, I had a man's duty, and having helped Mrs. White achieve slumber, why not be as useful to her daughter? I shut the bedroom door behind me, kneeled down, and placed a hand upon Franny's shoulder.

"As long as I am here," whispered I, "I shall protect you from bumps in the night. Come, now. It is sleepytime for little girls."

I steered Franny to her room, a powder-blue world of dolls, horses, and a four-poster bed. Franny, in her drowsy dopiness, put up no fight, snuggling her downy head into a conspiracy of stuffed bears. How tiny the lass looked upon that great big bed. I found the edge of the sheet, snugged it to her chin, and sat upon the mattress edge. Her eyelids were fluttering.

"Is the space rocket going to get us?" asked she.

Had only I'd known Merle at this age—sweet, inquisitive, darling.

"Did you know," posed I, "that Earth itself is a spaceship?"

"It is?"

"Unequivocally. You and I are rocketeers aboard the greatest spaceship that ever was, hurtling at unimaginable speed through the solar system. And Earth is a lot bigger than any little Sputnik, isn't it?"

I made sure to pronounce it *Spoot-nik*. Franny's giggle turned into a yawn.

"Are you the new daddy?" sighed she from the brink.

Perhaps the suburbs were Picture Craft paint-by-number kits, their inhabitants Silly Putty, their smiles Slinkys. I rebuked myself for ever having felt superior. The people here dreamed and sorrowed as much as anyone else, and if the final purpose of my fantastic existence was to becalm three of these humble souls, well, 'twas an honorable purpose, an honorable death, and I was a damned lucky bastard to have it.

I tickled Franny's nose with a finger.

"Sleep well," said I, "little space-girl."

The house had never been so still. I wandered it, projecting onto its moon-paled surfaces, as I'd once projected Rigby's 16mm films, visions of the Whites' future. The Zenith brought to mind the movies. The four of us would attend drive-in double bills, laugh at Abbott and Costello, laugh even harder at the rubberized creatures of Junior's shockers. The phonograph player brought to mind what the kids called "sock hops." Soon Franny would be begging to partake in such wiggling—and why not Mrs. White as well? And the pink refrigerator brought to mind the backyard barbecues we'd hold, where no one but us would be invited.

I inflated my dead lungs with air.

Sixty-one years after my death, I would start to live.

Four in the morning was too early for garage cleaning, but I was overeager and told myself that I would be quiet. The house's back door yowled when I opened it. I winced, and then, to avoid interrupting the family's hard-fought sleep, I left the door ajar as I plodded across the backyard. My thoughts were taken with sweeping, hosing, and mopping when I opened the door to the garage, not with Franny's insistence that she'd heard noises coming from inside it.

I stepped in, shut the door, found the light string, and yanked it.

Eight naked people stood in a semicircle.

The swinging bulb gouged ghoulish black shapes into their sockets, scapulas, ribs, and pelvises. They were old, their spines curled, cheeks cloven, the men's scalps mottled and chapped, their peckers withered and brown, the women's breasts puckered and pendent, their pubic hair matted and gray. But more than their bodies, it was the folded stacks of their clothing that horrified me. To disrobe in the dark would have taken these ancients an hour, meaning this was no random cabal, no private perversity. They'd gathered here for a purpose.

The octet turned toward me in a synchronized pivot of weak knees, bad hips, and chronic corns. Harsh yellow light shone upon skin bleached bone-white from decades without direct sun, save for an elaborate black symbol tattooed upon every left bicep.

A triangle made of triangles.

Let me spin you, Reader, a yarn of karma, how each knife slash and bullet shot is a seed planted that one day must be harvested. Those names on neighborhood mailboxes? Those fogeys frowning through their cookout cake? Caruso, Falzone, Marino, Gurrieri, Romano—Italian names, Sicilian names. Here, naked before me, were the surviving members of the so-called Triangulino clan I'd tormented during my final weeks with the Black Hand. Once strikingly handsome and nubile, they were now over eighty and through some heinous joke relocated from Chicago's mean streets to the "easy living" of the suburbs, where they'd recognized me. How could they ever forget my cruel, jeering face?

That I'd come to identify with Kal-El had been an extraordinary show of arrogance, for even that most super of heroes had his Achilles' heel: Kryptonite, a radioactive rock from his home planet. So it was that a fragment of my old world had tumbled home to destroy me. How many times had I typed myself a warning with my Royal Quiet de Luxe, and yet every time chosen to ignore it?

You gotta have fear in your heart.

I hadn't, and here was Hell, determined to be paid.

Their frail bones were marrowed with six decades of escalating wrath. They came for me like Mauthausen inmates for the potato cart, their fish bellies spotted with malignant moles like witch's teats, their genitals, lips, and jowls a-sway with every shamble. It was with a surfeit of nausea that I understood the rationale behind their nudity: to keep their clothes clean of the gore about to be splattered.

The eight had almost encircled me before I saw the tools swinging from their gnarled paws. Hacksaw. Claw hammer. Garden shovel. Hedge shears. Monkey wrench. Hand drill. Tire iron. Garden hoe. Each item chosen from Charles's do-it-yourself gallimaufry, as if the dead soldier hadn't been pleased that I'd lain with his wife and so had donated his extensive know-how to dicing up the dead adulterer.

The Triangulinos fell upon me, literally so, stumbling and gripping my clothes, each one lighter than Junior but en masse heavy enough to bring me to my knees. I reached for the doorknob; if I could grip it, I might drag myself from this gray-haired riptide. But my outstretched hand was driven down by a whack of the wrench, and without equilibrium I fell to cement. I blinked at the blank bulb above me; seconds later, it was blotted out by shriveled faces that began to grin in childlike wonder at the varmint they'd trapped.

The flaccid folds of their grins soured as my eternal youth further deranged them. They needed to inflict upon me the old age I was owed; I needed to be hobbled, whittled, and twisted. Even that they'd chosen that particular night made sense, for Sputnik signaled the start of a fearless spacefaring age that would have no use for the infirm. The time had come to wrap up old business.

I fought. Oh, Reader, how I fought. Wasn't I the young buck who'd borne soldiers from the Belleau Wood battlefield and helped Church heft crates of Dog Bowl Debbie across Manhattan? It took me one random fist to send an old person reeling with broken jaw or dislocated shoulder. But it was like battling a horde of rats; one face fell away, only for another to replace it, giggling and slobbering.

Jagged yellow fingernails ripped at my clothes. My jacket was peeled off like a layer of skin. My shirt buttons popped, as did those of my trousers, and any fabric that resisted was sliced to ribbons and ripped away. The Triangulinos hooted like simians at the surprise sight of a dilapidated body closer to their own than they'd suspected. They wormed their hairy, lukewarm torsos atop mine for leverage; together we formed a quivering mound of weeviled flesh boned only by cold blades, sharp drills, heavy hammers.

I opened my mouth but could not allow myself to scream, for the garage windows were open and I'd left the back door of the house wide as well, and curious Franny would not yet be deep asleep. She'd be the first to hear my cry, the first to wander into the garage, the first to lay eyes upon the depraved display. What the Triangulinos might do to her I dared not consider. I clamped my teeth and between them offered my assailants a piteous whine.

"I'm sorry. I'm so sorry. I'm so, so sorry."

The avengers, like so many from history, went straight for castration. They clucked in consternation upon finding my pecker already harvested, but my scrotum remained, and one of the ladies—Mrs. Romano, I believe—gathered it in an arthritic palm and pulled it taut so that the gentleman next to her—Mr. Falzone, I believe—could lean in with the shears, snug the scrotum into the fork of the blades, and snip. My balls dropped from my body bloodlessly, as when Mrs. White trimmed pale dough from her pie crust.

The anguish was so overpowering, I barely noticed when they passed around my testicular pouch and pushed their sniffing noses against it like canines into carrion. I writhed, hoping to take advantage of their diversion, but they snapped to attention with such speed that tendons popped and bones clacked.

The shovel handle pinned me across the throat. My left arm was pulled perpendicular and pressed to the floor. I turned my cheek against the cold concrete and watched the hacksaw settle upon the base of my fingers. I almost laughed; it was beyond belief that I would lose so much flesh after lasting so long. But the steel teeth bit down, juddered against bone, and sawed, as simple as that. Gray flecks of knuckle danced into the air; I gaped in awe at the pygmy fireworks. The sawing lasted until the teeth scritched against cement, and when the saw pulled away, all four of my fingers tumbled after it.

What noises the ghouls made as they traded my digits like playing cards! I'd once broken down their kinfolk bone by bone; repaying the crime made them giddy. The hacksaw jumped to my wrist, where it began to cut with improved form—my disembowler was getting the hang of it. When the hand had been removed, I saw not a cross-section of severed carpal bones but rather my severed dreams. No longer could I use that hand to ruffle Junior's hair after he accepted his high-school degree, college degree, law degree, professional honors. Without that hand to guide him, his grades would slip until he joined the greasers on their hot-rodding road to nowhere.

My forearm was the next to go, and with it the fantasy of embracing Franny on her wedding day or accepting when she handed over her first baby for me to hold. The hacksaw was insatiable; next it removed everything below my left shoulder, robbing me of the chance to use that biceps to assist Mrs. White, elderly herself one day, around our pink home long after the children had grown. It was gone, all of it gone, all profits of humanity, paid toward a receipt of pain swollen red with interest.

Blackhand's Disease was not only real; it was incurable.

They squabbled in Italian about which part to ransack next, the same way I'd deliberated over portions of toaster. The hammer made a case for my right eyeball, the hand drill suggested my umbilicus, and the blade of the hoe proposed detaching my nose. My only defense was to disengage my mind, as I'd done decades ago as Dr. Whistler's Subject, and drift beyond this torture box into wider spaces. It was out there that I heard what these deafened fiends could not.

Sixteen claws clicking against sidewalk.

Of course her superior ears had heard my sniveling. Of course she'd muzzled through the ajar back door. Of course she starved, as always, for executable commands. It might interest you, Dearest Reader, to know that Kal-El had a loyal dog of comparable talents: Krypto, aka "Superdog" (Adventure Comics #210). With my last vestige of super-breath (Action Comics #20), I wheezed a dire order from our private menu of tricks.

"*Blitz. Blitz. Blitz.*"

I could only imagine Clown's sinewy squat and Sputnik-style launch into the screen window, which clattered to the garage floor before her muscular body thumped down on all fours. A deep growl gunned, and I felt upon my cool skin sizzling spatters of saliva. I looked up to find her lowering her thick head like a bull. She flared the red gems of her eyes at my old, naked, vulnerable destroyers.

A young man could not ask for a more exquisite demon-dog.

The Italian gabble died out. The hold on my body slackened.

I uttered the last command I'd ever need give.

"*Slay.*"

Though Mr. Gray did not bleed, plenty of blood was shed that night. Clown was a cyclone of fur and fury, spit and savagery, charging fang-first into Mrs. Caruso and clamping down on her wrist. Both bitches' haunches tensed as they dug in, but Clown outweighed the woman by double, and I heard bones snap. Clown did the canine death-shake, spat out the bleeding limb, and proceeded to Mr.

Marino's doddery leg, Mr. Gurrieri's frangible elbow, Mrs. Falzone's drooping turkey-neck. The onslaught was oddly silent. Clown did not bark, her victims did not scream. The garage filled with thuds of impact, hitches of breath, gasps of pain, chokes of blood. Everything smeared in motion; every white body was streaked with black blood; they clung to one another as if Death itself were swinging its scythe.

I stood, somehow, but pitched rightward due to the missing weight of my left arm. My knees cracked down on the blood-smeared floor and I watched, booted about by the frantic feet of the Triangulinos, the listless lumps of my upper and lower arm, hand, fingers, and scrotum. I shielded my eyes from Clown's onslaught, swiped my jacket and trousers, shrugged into them, and then used my shredded shirt as a shroud into which I raked the detached morsels of Zebulon Finch. I could not allow the Whites to make such a gruesome find.

When I blundered outside into a violet predawn, I did so amid what, on any other night, would have been chalked up as a halluci-nation: bloody, naked elderly people limping away in all directions. Clown continued to spar with the unluckiest, but I pushed it from my mind. I'd taken innumerable walks around Heavenly Hills and knew an alley, a short seven blocks away, where I could distribute my severed parts among a line of garbage cans. Tomorrow, as fortune would have it, was Sunday, trash pickup day, the day when the aero-dynamic, superhygenic, porcelain-enameled suburbs expunged their shameful refuse.

I, too, had to be trashed. Were I to remain on Mulberry Terrace, the Triangulinos would regroup with scenarios even more insidious—burning down the pink house while the Whites slept, let's say. I could not be responsible for that. I ordered myself to think of neither Junior nor Franny, for they'd grow up better without me. Nor should I think of Mrs. White curled up in bed happy at last, for our entangling there had been but an overdue farewell. Yes, for a flawless, fleeting instant, the family had felt like mine, but was anything truly yours that could so quickly be stolen away? What was left of my cash, at least, was still beneath the basement mattress for them to discover, and I was glad to have bequeathed this one thing of tangible worth.

It was after crossing Cedar Lane that I heard a woeful squeak.

I turned, misweighted and tottering, to find Clown waiting on the opposite curb, known to her as the limit to which she was allowed to walk unleashed. Patches of her fur were spiked with crusting blood. Her drool was pink, and two of her legs trembled in agony. Worst of all was her left eye—that small, bright, adoring marble—which, from some opportune blow, had been punched out of alignment. It pointed off in a pitiful, errant direction.

She toed the curb, whining for permission to approach.

"No," croaked I.

She tilted her heavy, exhausted, but still hopeful head.

Of all the words I'd taught her—"Steal," "Blitz," "Slay," "Hunt," "Tackle," "Claw"—I'd never bothered with the most important word of all, the one that I myself had labored in vain to master over both a lifetime and deathtime: "Stay."

Her front paws edged into the street.

"Don't," said I.

She limped onto Cedar Lane, her good eye shining through the night. I wanted to hold out a hand to halt her, but I had only one hand left and it was busy with my parcel of lopped flesh. Clown, ducking her head bashfully, crept another few feet. I warbled in frustration, for I *did* want her to approach, to nuzzle my legs as she'd done so often before. The Triangulinos had taken parts of me, but

285

The Toe had survived intact and I would willingly offer it to Clown until her dying days. She reached my curb, sat down, tail wagging despite her injuries, and gazed up at me, certain in the way that only dogs can be that I would keep her with me forever.

Because I was a spineless son-of-a-bitch, I let the fancy play out. I'd kneel, bury my face in her fur, and let her swamp breath fill my neck-chasm. But such physical contact to a dog would be as cruel as rousing Mrs. White from the most peaceful sleep she'd had in years just to show her my arm stump and proclaim my departure. Clown needed a veterinarian for her eye and who knew what assortment of internal injuries. Were she to follow me, she might die. And so it was for love, Reader, that I did the worst thing I could imagine.

"*Go away!*" shouted I. "*Bad dog! Bad dog! Bad dog!*"

Clown cowered and her forehead crinkled, and yet she did not flee. I knew what I had to do and cried out in heartbreak, execrating the Gød who'd put me up to this, the pushing away of not only this loyal animal but the entire family, who would, I was certain, otherwise follow my scent and bring me back, foolishly believing that it was for their benefit.

I kicked Clown in the ribs. She whimpered and scuttled. I kicked her harder. She groaned and showed me her pink belly. I will not say how many kicks it took to persuade the beautiful animal to leave. By then, birds had begun to tweet and lawn sprinklers had begun to creak. But slink away Clown did at last, stomach to the pavement, streaking blood as if her heart leaked it, throwing back puzzled looks of apology, certain that she somehow deserved my anger.

Von Lüth had set the best example. My phantom arm twitched for a brick with which to bash in my face. Instead I hoisted the sack of my disconnected parts. I ordered my legs to move. The legs, by some stroke of luck still attached, did as requested, and athwart the lawns of Heavenly Hills I zigzagged into the fiery dawn of an unwanted future, swearing to Gød, louder and louder, that I would have my revenge on Him as surely as the Triangulinos had had theirs on me. Just you fucking wait.

PART NINE

1957–1962

———◦⟨◉⟩◦———

Relating Your Hero's Involvement In A Little Tin Can
And A Long Twilight Struggle, Heretofore Terrestrial,
Hereinafter Cosmogonic.

I.

A CORPSE FINDS NO RESPITE. SQUAT in urban alleyways, and moviegoers are sure to shortcut through while sermonizing on *12 Angry Men*. Find a sun-scorched vacant lot in which to nest, and children will converge to abuse Barbie dolls and Wham-O Frisbees. Repair to town, adopt the seesaw lurch of the ghetto, and here come bleeding-heart Samaritans proselytizing a new thing called food stamps, blinking condoling eyelashes at your rotten face. Decamp, find an auto junkyard, burrow inside a Beetle, and then, come the weekend, teenagers amass to swill booze, unhook brassieres, and trade verses of Allen Ginsberg's "Howl," a purported obscenity that, when voiced by drunken idealists, made me push a fist—the last one I owned—between my teeth to choke down howls of my own, for Ginsberg wrote about me, Zebulon Finch. I was one of his "angelheaded hipsters burning for the ancient heavenly connection to the starry dynamo in the machinery of night."

My Dearest Reader is forgiven for imagining romantic scenarios of yours truly rolling across the snuggeries of homophile San Francisco or kicking through the amphetaminic detritus of Hell's Kitchen. I kept, in fact, to wearisome old Kansas, trekking first to Lawrence, second to Topeka, and then onward to a string of pygmoid burgs like Salina, Hays, and Scott City. The single parcel I carried was the desire to return to the Marlboro Man's Montana. While my missing arm did not impede me as it would have others (I had no outfits to change, no fork to grip, no waste to wipe), my amputation had been grisly enough to make hitchhiking a useless endeavor.

My best hope was to raid a car rental service with a stack of cash thick enough to distract from both my appearance and my lack of license. With the totality of my capital left to the Whites, I considered the source of that capital—the good old U.S. of A. Back pay for my two-front WWII service had appeased me in 1946, but now that I was flush with a more potent currency—time—I fixated upon what I saw as maltreatment. Grunt wages for infiltrating the top tiers of the Reich? For giving witness to the first A-bomb? Why, I deserved a captain's compensation, enough to afford a Montana-bound stretch limousine chauffeured by a nude Anita Ekberg! (She could keep the cap.)

But how was a down-and-out tatterdemalion expected to contact the big, bad military? They'd made a priority of keeping proper names out of earshot, meaning that I had but one usable contact. I would have to dig up Allen Rigby.

With coins both begged and scrounged, I set up shop in area phone booths, pinching handsets between cheek and shoulder while using my surviving hand to harass unsuspecting operators. The last residence linked to Rigby was in D.C., but the operators insisted that the listing was obsolete. I sleuthed along a chain of defunct numbers, forwarding addresses, and testifying neighbors with such determination that I nearly forgot how my failed Operation Weeping Willow had cost Rigby his Washington job in the first place.

Kansas snow, when it falls, does so as straight and hard as rocks, and I shut the phone booth against it one afternoon in February 1959. Right away came a bother of knocking—a grinning panhandler ges-

292

turing at his soiled bag of grubbed goodies. Local beggars believed that their frostbitten digits and overall filth made us natural consorts, and were ever eager to trade impedimenta, but I let the mendicant soak, dialing my umpteenth lead, an A. Rigby in, of all esoteric locales, Albuquerque, New Mexico.

The phone was picked up before the first ring had even finished. "Yeah?"

It was all I needed to know that I'd found my man.

My list of demands dribbled like melted snow down the tramp's chin.

"I . . . I . . ."

"J-1121." Rigby's larynx sounded as if clotted by bone. "Finch."

"The one," rasped I, "and only."

His exhale was sandpaper crumpled in a fist. "I've been looking for you for months. You been using a fake name?"

I, the former Joe Gray, gazed through phone-booth glass warped enough to change the world. What Rigby said made no sense. It was I who'd been chasing him.

"Forget it," said he. "Where the hell are you?"

I paused; never before had I heard Rigby use a bad word.

"Kansas," said I.

"Shit, that's just across the panhandle. I'm sending a car."

Another bad word. My wariness grew.

"Why would you send a car?"

"I'll give the driver my address, but write it down anyway."

The last words he'd shared aboard the C-53 Skytrooper remained as wet as a wound: wife Janet, children Roy, Sandra, Walter, Patty, Stanley, and Florence. These tender, susceptible souls could not be allowed to lay gentle eyes upon a ravaged incubus.

"I will not come to your home."

"Fine. There's a restaurant two blocks down the—"

"I won't enter a restaurant either."

"If you'd rather meet outdoors, there's a park—"

"You do not understand." I recycled the language of morticians describing Charles's body to Mrs. White. "I am in no state to be seen."

The old Rigby, one not so irascible, had been a master of trafficking silence, and yet this was his first of the conversation. I tried to picture him: the lamppost spine, the folded hands, the dispassionate mask. But when again he spoke, his voice snapped with uncharacteristic impatience.

"There's a car coming. Tomorrow, noon. At ten o'clock p.m. you'll be delivered to a bar, a very, very dark bar. Don't argue with me, we don't have time. Now will you give me a goddamn address?"

I might have stonewalled longer had not the bum reached into his bartering bag for what I was suddenly sure were my own left fingers, or left hand, or left arm, or left nut, wrapped in newspaper like fish, and swapped beggar to beggar until this one had found a young man in need of exactly the parts he had in stock. I bared my teeth; they clattered against AT&T plastic.

"Should your plan be to vituperate me vis-à-vis Weeping Willow, save the breath. I have telephoned you not out of magnanimity but for the abject purpose of cash; to me, you are a conduit to dollar bills, nothing more. Is this quite understood?"

Beneath the tap-tap mocking upon phone-booth glass (my severed fingers, thought I, cajoling me—*Zebulon, old friend, let us in*), I detected Rigby's low laugh.

"Shit, J-1121, if what I'm planning works out, money won't be a problem."

II.

THE BAR WAS CALLED BIG Jimmy Dutko's Beaver Lounge, and despite the painted-over window touting such amenities as BEER ◆ WINE ◆ COCKTAILS ◆ FOOD ◆ AIR CONDITIONING, they had none of the above, only watery brown fluid in dirty glasses. The joint was shadowy, though, just as Rigby had promised, forcing me to land by the runway lights of wet bottles, puddled tabletops, and sotted eyes.

Nevertheless I could tell that Rigby hadn't changed much in sixteen years. His balding hair was still balding rather than vamoosed altogether; his spectacles were the exact same wire frames; and his standard white shirt, reliably bloomed at the breast pocket with red ink, remained cinched by a black tie. It was *how* he wore everything that struck me. His wispy hair had a hog's bristle, his glasses a defiant skewness, his clothes a wrinkled neglect.

I would have believed it impossible, but his pace of smoking had doubled. As I took the booth seat across from him, I counted two ashtrays lost beneath dunes of volcanic ash and three fresh packs at the ready. His coffee intake, too, had achieved egregious peaks: two pots, empty but still radiating heat, sat waiting to be refilled, while he cracked his knuckles. He examined me for one minute before speaking. His teeth were blond with nicotine, his breath barbed with caffeine.

"You carry yourself like you're ashamed. We've had three wars in four decades; lost limbs are a fact of life. Learn to carry yourself better, and you'll look heroic. Might start to feel that way, too."

The tension of chest I'd accrued during a nine-hour ride in a Chrysler Imperial began to disperse into what extremities I had left. It is likely, Reader, that you have no sense of what it means to lose five percent of your body in a single go. You mourn it as you do a loved one—let us say, for example, Wilma Sue—so intrinsic a part of you for so long that the loss can only be grasped at in places darker even than Big Jimmy Dutko's Beaver Lounge.

Rigby was owed indignation on the subject of J-1121, and that he chose instead to speak supportive words warmed me more than the Southwestern clime. Indeed, hadn't the two of us shared extraordinary experiences about which we might jocularly reminisce? I hadn't smiled since my final tucking-in of Franny, and it felt so pleasant that I tumbled into it, like a child down a hill unmindful of coming briar.

"What gives, old bloke?" jested I. "A meeting at which you don't foist upon me a single unreadable report?"

His lip jerked, more caffeine tic than smile.

"Surely you brought our Nazi Flash Cards!" continued I. "I was thinking you and I might propose the idea to Parker Brothers. What better way to capitalize on their Monopoly success than a game plastered with the faces of iniquitous villains? Unless, that is, your children have played our prototype to death. How is your ponderous brood? Has Janet popped out additional pups, or have you resigned yourself to the paltry baker's dozen already sired?"

How frolicsome I felt! Gift of gab restored, phantom limb forgotten, piquant wit firing like Maxims! Rigby lifted his cup, knew by its weight that it was empty, stamped out a cig, and lit another without altering his vacuous expression.

"They're dead."

A concrete mix of shock mortared me to the booth as Rigby laid out in simple sentences, as he'd clearly done many times before, the outlandishly horrific parameters of the incident. Four years before, Rigby, driving his wife and six kids back from a sledding excursion in western Massachusetts, had failed to heed signage reminding motorists of the icing propensity of bridges, and their family wagon had skidded, bashed through the fence, and punched upside-down through river ice ninety feet below. The car had sunk and flooded with water, but beyond noting that his wife and an unspecified number of children had been killed on impact, he left the fight for survival to my imagination. He swam to the surface to get air for a rescue dive, but it was too late, and what he did instead, over the half hour it took for rescue vehicles to arrive, was extract the frozen blue corpses of his family and stack them, one by one, like cordwood on a snowy bank.

Rigby curtly assigned himself all blame: "It was my fault."

"I . . . know not how to respond."

He eyed the two fresh pots of coffee being delivered as one might a bitter but needful medicine. While he poured and guzzled, I studied him until I saw how the old Allen Rigby had swollen with rancid innards of grief until he'd cracked open, spilling out a Rigby of similar work ethic but vastly different motivation.

"It was good for my career," said he.

I recoiled. What a thing to say!

"Sputnik happens, right? Suddenly our government feels like hiring, or even rehiring, the kind of man who doesn't mind a little risk. Risk doesn't mean shit to me, not anymore. By the time the Reds got Sputnik 2 and 3 in orbit, and everyone on our side was starting to brush up on their Russian, you know what I said? When they called me in, I said, 'Fuck the Red bastards. Let's gather our best men and beat their asses.' Just like that, I'm on the payroll of a new division. Maybe you've heard of it. It's called NASA."

I shrugged cautiously. "My situation has distanced me from current affairs."

"National Aeronautics and Space Administration. I'm General Counsel. That means I do a bit of everything—development, operations, personnel, procurement, logistics, crew systems, mission analysis. Only four months old, and we've already got two dedicated flight centers and research centers in three different states. Better than that, we've got a mandate: get a man into orbit before the Reds. We're not just talking about national security. We're talking about national *extinction*. We're talking about ICBMs."

"Sorry," said I. "ABCD-whats?"

"Intercontinental Ballistic Missiles. We've got them. The Reds sure as hell have them; they're playing chicken with the whole Eastern Bloc. Here, let me show you."

He pushed a wrinkled napkin to the center of our table, snatched the red pen from his stained pocket, and sketched a cylindrical object.

"This is a Redstone missile. Eighty-three feet tall. Seventy-eight thousand pounds of thrust."

He circled the missile's tapered tip.

"This is where the nuclear warhead goes."

He drew a triangle at the base of that warhead.

"We remove the bomb. Insert a one-man space capsule. That's how we get our guy up there."

The ice-stubbled faces of Rigby's dead family finally burnt away in the heat of this absurdity. Outer space? Was that really what we were talking about? Hours after Sputnik's launch, Mrs. White had feared that space satellites might one day drop A-bombs like rocks off a bridge. But strapping a man to the business end of a missile was a higher level of farce.

Rigby was steering his cutter straight through fifty-foot waves—"PSAC and MSEP are going to LFRC to prep OMS for EOR"—before I could raise my hand to shut him up. Having only one such appendage gave the gesture added weight.

"Do not take this the wrong way, Rigby, for I know you have suffered great personal adversity. But you, sir, have gone bananas."

Rigby took a swig of joe so hot that steam vented from the slats of his teeth. His cup banged down on the napkin Redstone, bloodily smearing the ink.

"You've seen a couple wars, Finch, but this one's a lot colder and requires colder calculations. Think it through. We get astronauts up there, that proves we can get warheads up there. Stalemate's the goal here. The Reds won't dare strike us and we won't dare strike the Reds. But if we fail? Shit, that's the end. That's it for America."

This dire diagnosis made gestures toward justifying my presence. Like a buzzard Tom Joad, anywhere America putresced, I'd be there to peck at the shreds.

"I am hesitant to ask," said I, "but what is an 'astro-nut'?"

Ash from Rigby's cig fell into his coffee and he slurped it right up.

"'Naut,' not 'nut.' Means 'space voyager.' NASA wants six. On the ground, they'll help with capsule design, procedures, and equipment. In the air, general systems management, sequence monitoring, that sort of thing."

"Apologies," said I, "for this saloon, as you promised, is low on light, and I therefore cannot gauge the consistency of your brain leakage. I pray that you are not suggesting, in some paroxysm of daftness, that I would qualify for such a job."

From the old cig he lit a new one.

"There are a few prerequisites."

"Describe them," cried I, "so we might conclude this comedy!"

Rigby shrugged. "Under forty years of age."

"Drat," said I. "Missed it by four decades."

"In excellent physical health."

"Do amateur amputations count against me?"

"No taller than five foot, eleven inches."

I sat back, tiring of the game. "You've got me there, Rigby. That is my height, precisely."

Strangely, Rigby sighed in what looked to be genuine relief.

"I was worried about that one. A single inch taller, and we'd be sunk. The diameter of the Redstone boosters, they allow limited room for an astronaut to—"

I palmed a coffee pot and hurled it against the booth's wall. The shatter was a peep beneath the tavern's din.

"One more *inch* and we'd be sunk? I sunk into a D.C. bunker where I failed to learn a thing you tried to teach! I sunk from a plane into a land where I exposed brave collaborators and got them killed! Now you drag me across the desert, and for what? To mock everything else I cannot do? If there is one thing I understand about the acronyms you eject—indubitably, the only thing!—it is that they imply knowledge in fields I shall never master, no matter how many decades I am damned. Qualify for the astro-nut's job? Rigby, I would not qualify to mop the floors!"

The lamp light off the spilled coffee turned Rigby caramel. He puffed as easily as he ever had at OSS, unruffled by my ruffle, the reflected orange dot of his cig bobbing about the brown lake like a cyclops sea creature. He was quieter when he spoke, though hardly abashed.

"The Russians call their program Vostok. Nobody has the first clue how they run it. But ours is called Mercury, and I can promise you that our candidate pool is strictly limited to military test pilots." His exhale was fog over a coffee lagoon. "Relax, Finch. You're not going into space."

A woman arrived double-fisting towels, and I sat back to make way for her frenzied sopping. Rigby kept talking.

"NASA did a medical survey, all right? It didn't come out how they'd hoped. Ninety-eight percent of the doctors—*ninety-eight percent*—wouldn't guarantee a man's survival in zero-g. That's zero gravity, and it poses a lot of potential problems. Blood doesn't pool downward. The veins of the head distend, and the right ventricle has to work double time. Can you swallow in zero-g? Will your eyes float out of your sockets? Will you be able to urinate? Will you be able to *stop* urinating? These are actual questions. That's not even touching on oxygen issues—dysbarism, hypoxia. Three minutes without air, you're brain-dead."

The waitress placed shards of coffee-pot glass onto her soaked towels, cussing as if we could not hear her.

"You want me to be the canary in the coal mine," deduced I. "The fail-safe."

Rigby weighed the harsh term.

"Weeping Willow was what? Sixteen years ago? Those were long years for me. You, too, from the looks of it. I've got a pile of regrets. Different training I could have given you. Better intelligence. More support on the ground. I want to make it right. Does that make sense? For you, for me, for the country? We can do this, Finch. We can still make a difference. Right here in Albuquerque, right now, not one mile away, there's one hundred and ten flight pilots I helped hand-pick, all of them undergoing physical testing so intensive that we expect half of them to quit and most of the rest to fail. And the six who get chosen are just getting started. To build a craft that can support life in a vacuum will require more tests than any endeavor in human history. You remember Laika? The dog the Reds sent up in Sputnik 2? The USSR reported that her final food pellets were drugged to put her to sleep, but we've got intelligence saying that's a lie. That dog died of heat exhaustion, slowly and painfully."

I thought of Clown, whimpering as I left her, believing that I cared. Was Rigby making the same mistake?

"Like it or not, Finch, we're Americans. We can't pull stunts like that. We have to run experiments and models and simulations, and some of them will be dangerous. The country needs someone to run those simulations first and protect our astronauts by providing a baseline of what the human body can or can't withstand. And that brings us right here to the Chihuahuan Desert."

The waitress had vacated. It was just us two broken men, one desert, and a task that asked that I surpass my usual worst self. I understood the utter obliteration of which Rigby spoke. I'd seen Hiroshima. I'd met the Millennialist. I'd cowered with the Whites in a basement, where I'd resolved to ensure that Junior and Franny lived past seventeen years old so that they might do all the good, proper adult things I could never do. The Whites were gone to me now, but if Rigby was right, they were not yet beyond my ability to protect. And if my actions drowned out the stepparent squabbles of the Millennialist and the Fifty-One, all the better.

"One arm," muttered I, "will suffice to yank whatever levers you have in mind?"

Rigby was not a man given to grin, certainly not anymore, but he did reach for the surviving coffee pot, which was almost the same thing.

"When Chuck Yeager broke the sound barrier in 1947, he did it with broken ribs from falling off his horse. Hurt so bad, he couldn't move his right arm. You wouldn't be the first."

"If I do this," cautioned I, "it will not be like before. Blackmailing me with prison is no longer an efficacious tactic. I do what I want, when I want, nothing more."

Rigby was already nodding and extending a hand over the booth. Warily, so warily, I accepted it.

"I knew that leaving Project Excelsior was the right move," said he.

"Project *what*?"

He began to pull away, but my hand had rigidified into a claw.

"Before joining Mercury," said he, "I was with a program called Excelsior. Stratosphere-altitude parachuting. It'll supply good data, for sure, but the real work's at NASA."

The *tick, tick, tick* of my own Excelsior resounded against the rawhide drum of my chest. 'Twas a coincidence of proper nouns, nothing more, and yet I could not help but think that the leaving behind of any Excelsior was an omen bad enough to give even a Failsafe pause.

303

III.

THE DISTANCE BETWEEN THE ALLEN Rigby of 1943 and the Allen Rigby of 1959 did not need to be bridged. The first time we walked down the main artery of Lovelace Clinic, a wood-paneled, Mexico-themed hospital complex dropped like dice upon the flat red desert dirt, he was addressed not as "Rigby," that fussy, fastidious stickler, but rather as "Rig," fearless fighting fireball. I embraced it straightaway; thinking of him as a wholly new person meant forgetting the tragedy that had brought about the change.

These grunted greetings came from that most brazen-faced of human specimens: the fighter jock. Project Mercury's auditions were hush-hush, and the pilots were prohibited from outing themselves as any different from Lovelace's regular patients, but that was a joke. These big, healthy flyboys, with their sun-wrinkled faces, cowboy gaits, and wolfen eyes, could never be mistaken for having so much as a headache.

I, meanwhile, looked as though I required a gurney. The jocks might have studiously ignored my swollen flesh and shoulder stub if Rig hadn't been my attendant. He situated me in a waiting area so that he could take a rapidly called meeting. Though he'd laid groundwork regarding me with the Space Task Group's directors, it had all been conjecture until I'd been found. Rig had to make his final case to the brass, and the corona of smoke around his head was his manifestation of anxiety.

Snickering hotshots sized me up until I could brook no more. I bolted up, swayed from lack of arm, sawed my jaws at the renewed round of chuckles, and stomped outdoors, hoping that I might find a cactus upon which to hang myself until a bobcat agreed to eat me. Instead, along a stretch of brown grass between Lovelace and the VA hospital, I passed other stir-crazy fighter jocks, every one with a gallon jug hooked to his belt, and some carrying Dixie cups at arm's length. Through smell I ascertained that the first receptacle was for urine and the second for stool. Blood and semen presumably had their own flagons; at Lovelace, all secretions appeared to be grist for the mill, and from the pallid skin and red eyes emblematic of alcohol and nicotine and fasts, these pilots looked pretty damn sick of it.

I was ready to hurry the hell out of Dodge, when Rig tracked me down. He said nothing, only giving me the fighter jock's signal for readiness—thumbs-up.

He ought to have affixed that thumb up his ass, for he'd failed to negotiate an entirely free pass. My tryout would be condoned on the condition that I submitted to the same tests as the pilots, so that physicians could valuate what similitudes, if any, we shared. But I'd never seen Rig more enthusiastic, his facial muscles firing as if trying to remember how to grin, so I feigned rah-rah, and when he handed me an itinerary packet, I resisted using my fist to knock out his yellow teeth.

It was meat etiquette of an unsurpassable scale audited upon a high-tech Revelation Almanac; Leather would have swooned in jealousy. We, the Mercury Guinea Pigs, queued like kids at a Popsicle stand for the treat of having our anatomies jabbed, lanced, scraped, shaken, shocked, inflated, and deflated. Opaque were the purposes behind flooding our ear canals with cold water or inserting electrified needles between our thumbs and forefingers, and I would be remiss not to mention the vigorous anal probing that allowed chin-stroking medicos to watch our bowels like an episode of *Meet the Press*. The pilots, starving for levity, called it "riding the steel eel," but with every poke, it became more difficult to poke fun. The field of space travel did not exist until it was invented; the doctors were throwing shit against the wall to see what stuck. (Come to think of it, that sounds like an experiment they would have enjoyed.)

And all of that pertained to when the subject was alive! Purely for argument's sake, let us say that you were a living corpse. Visualize the plasmatic slime that would spill from any doused orifice. Imagine the horrified shrieks of bonneted nurses. Picture the doctors who could barely hold their stethoscopes. It was demeaning, though Rig responded swiftly, barring all but a few select docs from working with me, and not before they signed confidentiality papers. After that, Rig intervened but twice: once at my request to stop them from pumping my stomach—I could not bear to revisit Johnny's golden aggie— and the second time to ask that they dress my ugly, raw stump. They insurrected, and Rig, sensed I, took considerable heat behind closed doors before they did the job.

Episodes like these made it plain that Rig was not well liked, but the general disapproval of his sponsoring of me only made him more bullheaded. I credit the full cashing in of his political capital that I was among the thirty-two candidates selected to advance to Phase Four, a final week of physiological and psychological "stress tests" to occur over six waves at the Aero Medical Laboratory at Wright-Patterson Air Force Base in Dayton, Ohio.

To reduce rumors regarding a one-armed freak, they slid me into the final wave, Group VI, which convened on March 22, 1959. In

306

Albuquerque, we candidates had been named only by dehumanizing number; in Dayton, for reasons unknown, they favored letters, and I was stripped of the catchy handle "Number 111" and redubbed "FF." (Fitting, thought I, for an inveterate flunky.) Group VI numbered but seven. The pilots were athletes of a sort, and no sooner had we been ushered into Wright-Patterson's Bachelor Officers Quarters than they turned it into a collegiate locker room, complete with buttocks-snapping shower towels and impromptu arm-wrestling tournaments augmented by oddsmakers.

Rig had been banned outright from BOQ. Thus I became a child dropped by his guardian at the most daunting of summer camps. Just as I'd been the outcast in the Seventh Marine Regiment, so was I here. They were lithe, fit men, and I was a ruined, sickly boy, unable to isolate a single Burt Churchwell or Jason Stavros to befriend. From my bunk in the loneliest corner I longed for inclusion, though I knew I would only sully their sameness. To wit: they were male (was I, sans genitals?), white (I'd gone boysenberry), from intact families (Bartholomew, wherefore art thou?), college educated (I was a dropout of Black Hand U.), an average thirty-three years of age (I was seventeen going on eighty), decorated fighter pilots (I'd once fallen out of a zeppelin), and laden with honorifics like Commander, Major, and Captain (I barely rated a "hey, jackass").

Of the six rowdies, I recognized only one from Lovelace, a freckled, gregarious golden boy, one of those obnoxious ogres whose good looks and wherewithal grow in tandem with challenges. As he had the insufferable quirk of wearing bow ties every day, I christened him Bobby Bowtie. A long death had proven to me that it was always easier to focus one's contempt upon a specific individual.

After the sinister assurance that the week's results would not be

307

entered into the pilots' military records, the starting pistols were fired on the weirdest race ever run. The orchestrators at Wright-Patterson were scientists, not doctors, and thus their criteria were less about the arrangement of your guts than about your ability to command them. A typical procedure involved a room-sized, one-hundred-and-thirty-degree oven in which a candidate sat, bundled beneath twenty pounds of gear, strapped to sensors, and corked with a rectal thermometer for two hours. I did not sweat, but I did, I think, spoil, and as dispiriting as that was, I took satisfaction that the next man up, Bobby Bowtie, would have to endure not only heat but also my aromatics.

That set the medieval pace. There was the Cold Pressor, where we were led into a nice warm room and directed to place our naked feet into a tin pan of ice-cubed water; several men panicked before numbness could set in. There was The Wheel, a gondola hung at the end of a fifty-foot arm and spun by a four-thousand-horsepower motor to approximate the acceleration forces of takeoff; several men barfed and one blacked out. There was the Idiot Box, a console that for one hundred maddening minutes blinked a sequence of manual commands gradually accelerated to foment frustration.

By the time postulants A through EE were being rattled like milkshakes seven times per second in a pistoned chair, or forced to inflate balloons until they fainted, their buddy-buddy shoulder-chucking of technicians and ass-pinching of shapely assistants had begun to wane. Their bodies and brains, honed tools upon which they'd long relied, were being proved fallible, and it set them on the edge of rebellion.

It was during the concluding physical exam, in which I was strapped for hours inside a lightless chamber so silent that a man

308

could hear his blood pump—or in my case, hear it canker—that I had no choice but to ponder whether I should remain or flee. In the First World War, I'd been part of something bigger than myself and it'd been glorious. This felt altogether different. Not one pilot had extended an olive branch or asked after my flight experience, personal background, or what in Gød's name had happened to my left arm. Perhaps they'd detected my Fail-safe purpose and, as professional death-defiers, were offended on principle.

Why again had I volunteered to be a despised black sheep? To help safeguard the White children's futures? The motivation felt web-thin. Thus was I set on self-sabotage for the final event of testing: a grilling before a three-man panel of psychologists. Quack One asked me to fill out a questionnaire; I agreed, then scribbled "FUCK OFF" into all 566 blanks. Quack Two held up Rorschach blots, and I responded "That's a vagina" to every one. Quack Three showed me sixteen dramatic images around which I was supposed to construct stories; I decided to stick to my theme and report that the man napping in a field, the boy with the broken violin, and the woman peeking through a doorway were all "thinking about vaginas."

Their poker faces were trained enough that I felt no better than when I'd insulted Abigail Finch in the French she'd pretended to know—degenerate, deceitful, and disloyal. I'd achieved deep-sea depths of dejection when Quack One put his pencil to his pad, poised to record my culminating vaginal gibe, and voiced the deliberately cryptic final question:

"Who are you?"

This was what they chose to ask me in a room this clean and white, in an antiseptic America that didn't exist beyond these walls? I was exhausted in a way that those who knew mere human exhaustion could never understand, and I'd had it up to here with playing their games.

"A clever query. But it is easily out-clevered. 'I'm a soldier.' 'I'm a father.' 'I'm a Christian.' These are the responses you seek, no? You shan't be disappointed, for this is the lard those like Bobby Bowtie will scoop onto your plates. From your cupboards of notes, have you not gleaned that who I am is, in a word, *alone*? Look at me: I walk through your world without the companionship of another like myself. And what of the other world, the one with which you are concerned, the one above? Your scientists wish to practice upon me as an apprentice beheader practices on sinewy rhubarb stalks, and maybe I should be satisfied with this lot I've drawn. But I've drawn so many lots, and what has been the result, decade after decade? A woman I knew in Kansas asked me, 'Is this all there is? Is this every-thing?' She was unmindful of her insight. If there is a Gød, then up high is where you might find Him—and what is outer space if not the highest tree? Have you heard, I wonder, of the Yggdrasil? Oh, forget the question. You are running out of room on your pads. You have asked who I am. It is flattering in a way; in eighty years, few others have asked. I am, I believe, a young man on whom a grand joke is being played, fated to live one century, perhaps a second, perhaps a third, only to be scrubbed and rescrubbed from the record, to exit, if I ever do, as if I'd never existed at all. Surely even such vigorless men as yourselves have sired children, now teenaged, who nightchant Ginsberg's 'Howl' at the harvest moon? 'Who threw their watches off the roof to cast their ballot for Eternity outside of Time.' That is who I am, gentlemen: a boy capable of Eternity who instead is bound and gagged by tally-makers, number-loggers, clock-watchers. Who am I? I am the crumbs from your erasers. I am the paper shredded into your baskets. I am the ink that will never be spilled, only kept in a jar to coagulate, solidify, and become a black heart that has no more utility, not to anyone."

Pencils, by then, had quit scritching. I gazed at the trio. I was tired now, so tired of all of it. Quack One stared at Quack Two, Quack Two at Quack Three, and Quack Three back at Quack One. He cleared his throat, squared his papers, straightened his spectacles.

"That will be all, FF."

IV.

RIG'S SCROUNGED SCUTTLEBUTT WAS THAT NASA would select the lucky six from Groups I through VI within three days of testing's end. The pilots went home so as to be with family when absorbing the shock, good or ill. I joined Rig in his rented two-bed billet at the Wide Skies Motorist Lodge outside of Dayton, a slant-floored, stone-and-stucco, vaguely moist establishment that had spent on a billion-watt sign what it had *not* spent to ensure bugless mattresses and functioning toilets. The sugar-bait had worked. There we were, shading our eyes from the neon effulgence, day and night.

So habituated had I become to ongoing orificial violations that the seventy-two hours I lay supine in bed had me feeling rather neglected. I suctioned through blinkless pupils whatever garbage the motel's television chose to shovel—a program called *The Twilight Zone* that made big fusses over implausibilities inferior to my own; brow-furrowing debates regarding the Pacific ellipsis of Hawaii becoming our fiftieth state; and commercials for a perplexing product called Jiffy Pop, which heated popcorn inside a bulging foil pustule.

To counterweight my lethargy, Rig spent any hours he wasn't working pacing and gesticulating. His smoking gathered into a factorylike smog not quite dense enough to hide his flagrant abuse, and ultimate cold-blooded killing, of the room's coffee maker; nor his joyless wolfing of fifteen-cent hamburgers from the McDonald's across the street; nor his psychoneurotic monitoring of our telephone for NASA's call. I couldn't admit how I'd purposefully botched my outgoing interview. For Rig, who refused to speak again of his dead wife and children, it meant the universe that I be chosen. The number of bridges he'd burned for me was untold.

By the morning of the third day, April 1, he became convinced that our phone was faulty; he demanded a newer model and then called it from a booth outside McDonald's to make sure that it rang. But business hours continued to leak. The casting open of the blinds failed to trawl the dunking sun. Nighttime became irrefutable. Rig was "upgrading" the room's radiator—the man couldn't go thirty seconds without busywork—when, instead of a phone call, we received a knock on the door.

Rig lifted from a squat. He did not look at me. He crossed to the door, opened it, chose not to respond to the night messenger's greeting, and autographed for the plain manila envelope. After closing the door, he stood two inches from it for a half-minute, and then, knowing the contents without needing to look, lumbered forth, tossing the envelope upon my bed and entering the bathroom. The door closed. *Thud*—the toilet seat being lowered. *Snick*—his cigarette lighter being thumbed. From beneath the door crawled lugubrious smoke.

The letter, from a Charles J. Donlan, Assistant Director of Project Mercury, was, I suppose, the kind of cold-fish apologia familiar to those misguided fools who "challenge themselves" by soliciting "opportunities." I did not care about such drivel. The whole endeavor had been Rig's hobbyhorse, not mine. And yet as I reread the letter, I could feel certain bland passages mark me as rudely as Mrs. White's slap across my cheek.

While I regret to inform you that you are not one of the seven
pilots that have been selected for the initial group of Mercury
astronauts, I wish to extend to you our deepest gratitude. . . . Our
selections were also influenced by a desire to bring a variety of
technical experiences and backgrounds to Project Mercury. . . .
Your records will be kept on file for future consideration should
circumstances warrant a change in these plans. . . .

Somewhere out there, thought I, seven happy-familied, college-degreed thirty-three-year-old newly minted astro-nuts (one more than the six they'd intended; that stung, too) were ringing up one another, hee-hawing as if Lovelace and Wright-Patterson had been Simple Simon and those butt probes goofy fun, and placing good-natured bets on who would get to be the one to beat Soviet cosmonauts into space. I balled the letter, trashed it, and wished I had the capability to piss on it. One more frat-house bash to which I'd never be invited.

Hours I spent knitted into a snit before realizing that Rig hadn't emerged. I cracked open the bathroom and found him astride the throne, his caffeine overdose finally having surrendered to a fitful, abysmal slumber, while the pasture of cigarette butts beneath his feet swayed their wispy gray dandelions. I eased shut the door, tiptoed back to the bed, and investigated the new telephone until I located a switch that turned off the ringer. My guess was that Rig would need to remake his life yet again come morn. He'd need the rest.

It was thanks only to my innate insomnia that I saw the orange indicator light of the telephone flashing shortly before midnight. The television was off and so the black room swirled with orange, as if the Wide Skies Motorist Lodge was under emergency evacuation. I had an inkling that "emergency" was the correct word. I lifted the handset and whispered.

"Hello?"

"Zebulon Aaron Finch?"

He had a hoarse wise-guy voice.

"Speaking."

"Charlie Donlan, NASA. I'm calling to tell you that you'll be joining Project Mercury and are to report to Washington on April 8. Details are forthcoming."

It hit like a Yankee Doodle roadster into the ocean.

"But . . . I don't understand. There was a letter—"

"To cut to the chase, Mr. Finch, your involvement in the project is to remain strictly off the books. Were you ever to publicly claim otherwise, NASA would deny it. NASA is very good at denying. The letter you received exists to serve this historical purpose. I hope that's clear."

Clear? The orange light was gone and I was grasping in the dark.

"It is generally agreed," continued Donlan, "that you could be useful in simulations involving pilot endurance or suffocation. It is assumed, though your test scores don't bear this out, that you're more intelligent than a dog or monkey. Is this also clear?"

"I believe so, yes, but—"

"To further cut to the chase, let me state, off the record and for my own peace of mind, that this decision was Bob Gilruth's alone. It's not my job to second-guess the director, but there are a lot of us who don't agree on this. Space Task Group is staffed with some of our nation's finest men. *Men*, Mr. Finch. I'm of the opinion that it's a shortsighted, precarious step to involve you, and I hope when you fail, which I believe you will, you do it early so as not to jeopardize our schedule. All right. There you have it. Questions?"

"Hundreds," said I. "Thousands."

"Like I said," muttered Donlan, "details are forthcoming."

Even at deliberate failure, it seemed, I was a failure.

The Dolley Madison House, a demure colonial on Lafayette Square in D.C., was too small to contain the hounds that wanted at us seven days later. At the strike of two, the Mercury Seven, as they'd been knighted, filed behind a blue-felt banquet table in a converted ballroom. Photographers squirmed over one another like puppies for teats, whining for attention and blasting their flashes, while the Seven took seats in alphabetical order. I approximated where "Finch" might fall in the order. Probably third from the right, at the elbow of Bobby Bowtie.

I could not make out the name plates of the Seven, for I—the unofficial Mercury Eighth—had rated no better than a back-row seat. Rig, seated next to me, yanked his collar, cleared his throat, and grimaced. Acid upchuck, no doubt, from his chronic cocktail of nicotine, caffeine, and stress. A week hadn't been long enough for him to recover from the double-barrel shock of my rejection/acceptance. His unmodulated level of excitement was the only reason why I'd agreed to attend the press conference, though now that I was there, I felt not indifference but envy. Just look at that NASA insignia pinned to the curtains! That starry blue globe shot through by a red arrow, evoking the sensations of soaring, danger, and delight! What young man wouldn't wish to be as close to it as possible?

Rig knew the Excelsior tick of my heart and how to soothe it.

"They'll accept you," whispered he. "Give them time."

Bigwigs, among them the disapproving Donlan, sat at both ends of the table, and one took the podium to shoo the reporters to their seats. The newsmen slithered away, shoulder straps hissing, advance wheels rattling. Order attained, the man adjusted the microphone and identified himself as NASA's head honcho, Thomas Keith Glennan. Flash bulbs lifted; I craned to see through them.

"Ladies and gentlemen, today we are introducing to you, and to the world, these seven men who have been selected to begin training for orbital space flight. These men, the nation's Project Mercury astronauts, are here after a long and perhaps unprecedented series of evaluations, which told our medical consultants and scientists of their superb adaptability to their coming flight. Which of these men will be first to orbit the earth, I cannot tell you. . . . It is my pleasure to introduce to you, and I consider it a very real honor, gentlemen, from your right . . ."

And so, like Adam naming Eden's animals, Glennan named the Seven, who stood, their rangy fighter-pilot physiques ill at ease inside the suits and ties of civilization: Malcolm S. Carpenter, Leroy G. Cooper, John H. Glenn, Virgil I. Grissom, Walter M. Schirra, Alan B. Shepard, and Donald K. Slayton. They bore their applause with discomfort; a waste, thought I, picturing how I, in the same spot, would have winked at the shapeliest attendees, fired off the old Zebby grin, and raised my arms over my head in a victory clasp—had I two arms to raise, that is.

Walter Bonney, NASA's Director of Public Information, ironically a crummy public speaker, kicked off the extended Q&A. The reporters radiated joviality; they were desperate to befriend these exemplars of manhood. Giddy with ingratiation, the first journalist was ignorant of the effect of his opening question:

"Has your good lady and have your children had anything to say about this?"

The Seven fidgeted and passed around a coffee pot, their eyes bright with the sudden desire to bail out. Wives? Children? They'd been expecting hardballs about flight technicalities, and their replies were defensive. *My little lady is more concerned about buying diapers*, that sort of tripe. The questions and answers only got stupider—how would they resist smoking inside the space capsule, which Lovelace test did they hate the most, a rephrased version of the groaner about their wives.

Had America really put its national security into the hands of these seven inarticulate stammerers? Into this developing disaster rode a champion who, beneath the table, must have had his muscled thighs clenched around a white stallion. His name was John Glenn, aka Bobby Bowtie, and when it was his turn to talk, he laced his fingers, leaned toward his mic with one shoulder as if speaking in confidence, and, some would say, singlehandedly got Americans into space, onto the moon, and interbreeding with Martians.

"I think we are very fortunate that we have, should we say, been blessed with the talents that have been picked for something like this. . . . Every one of us would feel guilty, I think, if we didn't make the fullest use of our talents in volunteering for something that is as important as this is to our country and the world in general right now."

With Glenn's every aw-shucks utterance, you could feel the room, if not all of America, soaring like the red arrow of NASA's logo. He'd said the magic word—"volunteer"—thereby repudiating test pilots like Chuck Yeager who'd been quoted as calling the astro-nut job being "Spam in a can." The military *ordered* you to do things; Project Mercury, on the other hand, was so hazardous, you had to *volunteer*. That was all the pilots to either side of Glenn needed to hear. They sat taller, began to grin, and started to believe the chorus chanted by the men at the podium, that they were the *right* men, the *correct* men.

"I am a Presbyterian," continued Glenn, "a Protestant Presbyterian, and take my religion very seriously, as a matter of fact. . . . I think you will find a lot of pilots who like to take what I consider to be sort of a crutch and look at this thing completely from a fatalistic stand-point, that sometime I am going to die, so I can do anything I want in the meantime, and it doesn't make any difference because when my time comes, I am going anyway. This is not what I believe. I was brought up believing that you are placed on Earth here more or less with sort of a fifty-fifty proposition, and that is what I still believe. . . . I think there is a power greater than any of us that will place the opportunities in our way."

Earlier, this same Mr. Glenn had said, "I got on this project because it probably would be the nearest to heaven I will ever get," and to be truthful, I didn't listen to much after that. I didn't even react when Deke Slayton quipped how "I would give my left arm to be the first man in space." I thought only of the offhand remark I'd made to the Lovelace psychologists regarding Gød: *What is outer space if not the highest tree?*

Of all the places my corpse had landed, Project Mercury might have been the oddest, and yet, at the same time, the most suitable. Sputnik hadn't been an hour into orbit before hysterical theologians had deemed it the sign of Christ's Second Coming, warning that any satellites shot into holy realms might beam down signals that would preempt *Father Knows Best* with the Rapture. Space volleys, insisted they, were the first shots in a heavenly war, described in the Book of Revelation as angel versus angel. Little Johnny Grandpa had hoped that I was an angel; Udo von Lüth had introduced the possibility that I was Lucifer the Light Bringer.

I had a part in this brand-new war, beyond that of protecting the Junior Whites of the world. I had only to choose my side.

V.

E ALL AGREE THAT JESUS'S blood pumped red, white, and blue, yes? By the time late editions of the papers had struck the racks, reeking of swift ink, our humble boys from the relatable hometown hamlets of Sparta, Wisconsin; East Derry, New Hampshire; Wardell, New Jersey; Mitchell, Indiana; New Concord, Ohio; Carbondale, Colorado; and Boulder, Colorado, had become warrior-king messiahs who would save our world from the mutual annihilation of nuclear warfare, while gobbling Wonder Bread sandwiches and Nabisco cookies.

Langley Research Center in Hampton, Virginia, was a crisscross of aimless runways abutted by a stronghold of turrets and depots. Outside they were nondescript, but inside they were hives. Rig held my empty sleeve against a current of striding scientists, though once we reached the numbered office to which we'd been directed, he steered me to the side of its closed door. All at once I saw what was coming. The confident tone I'd sustained since the New Mexico–Texas border cracked, and my voice became an adolescent's broken glass.

"The bachelor's quarters in Dayton were bad enough, and that was one week," cried I. "This could take months! Years! You can't leave me!"

"Deep breaths, Finch."

"Breaths? To whom do you think you speak?"

"You know I'd stick right beside you if I could. But I didn't exactly make friends in Dayton. Probably fewer in Albuquerque. There's other things I have to attend to. I'm a consultant; I have to consult. These assholes think I'm too involved with you. They think my judgment's clouded."

"Is it?"

Fluorescents the likes of which I hadn't seen since our Secret Ops days radiographed the weak bones of our futile endeavor. Rig, however, chuckled.

"So what? This is NASA, isn't it? The clouds are where we're supposed to be."

I risked a glance at the office door, blank and baleful.

"They'll tear me to pieces," said I. "Perhaps literally."

"They might, a little. That's why you're here." Rig gripped my shoulder, the good one. "I'm not deserting you, Finch. I'll come by the labs every chance I get. I'll review the simulations whenever I can. We'll talk every night. If there's problems, we'll go through them and I'll fix them. I won't stop fighting for you. That's not going to change."

The testimonial was stirring. I had to try, at least, to live up to it.

The office offered to the Mercury Seven (plus one) was a triumph of dingy drabness: eight desks, eight chairs, and nothing else, not even a Veronica Lake pinup. We'd been assigned a secretary named Nancy, a kissable raven-haired gal who, alas, recoiled in fear at my shambling entry, thereby consolidating seven fresh-faced, two-armed protectors against me. This being the critical first instant that I shared private space with the Seven, I fabricated an innocuous *heh-heh* and addressed them by the nicknames already embraced by the press.

"Scott. Gordo. John. Gus. Wally. Al. Deke."

Mightn't they be another Church, Mouse, Peanut, Piano, Professor, Stavros, and Skipper?

Zeb, prayed I. *One of you, please call me Zeb.*

But my cherished Marines these were not. Rig had confided that each of them had signed nondisclosure forms drawn up by Vice President Nixon himself, validating their oath never to mention the Mercury Eighth. Men of mettle were uncomfortable with secrets, even when ordered by Dick Nixon, but their word was their word. After giving me a queasy once-over, they cooled their eyes to make it clear they didn't intend to expend energy in my direction. I, deformed non-pilot civilian, wasn't worth it.

They kicked their feet atop their desks and began jawing about sports cars and baseball teams, topics cherry-picked to exclude me. I claimed the open workspace and cogitated upon how any seven men, even those of extravagant egos, could know what I was and yet be so unbothered. My conclusion? Death had long been their copilot, shadowing them, as the Millennialist shadowed me, as they tipped their wings to aeronaut cemeteries and waited while the baked carcasses of fellow aviators were scraped off runways so that their own takeoffs could be cleared. Death's presence was something they'd disciplined themselves to ignore. The question became, could I ignore their ignoring?

Training kicked off with a lecture series. The classroom setting brought into dramatic relief Langley's two factions: Suits and Astros. Suits were the ones telling everyone what to do. Astros were the ones who didn't like to do what they were told. Thankfully, there was a code word that alleviated most of the strife. "How's everyone doing?" the instructors would poll. Whether the subject was Copernicus's heliocentric theory, Newton's law of universal gravitation, or the contrast between Semi-Major Axis and Semi-Minor Axis, the Astros would reply, "A-OK." Evidently it was favored by military muckety-mucks for cutting through radio static better than the already glib "OK," but you try hearing it one hundred times a day and not feeling as if caught in a nursery-school nightmare.

Principally it peeved me because it was a lie. The Astros were clearly not A-OK. When at last exposed to dummy models of the developing vessel, they saw proof of what the naysayers had naysaid. The capsule *did* look like a can of spam; seats *were* being prepared for chimp as well as human passengers; the thing *would* splash down in the ocean like a turd rather than be permitted the regal landing ace pilots like them could deliver.

Death didn't worry the Mercury Seven. What worried them was looking like fools.

It was amid this overstrung atmosphere that each Astro was assigned a specialized area of development: Carpenter on communications, Schirra on life-support systems, et cetera. Except me, of course, who by omission was officially stamped as incompetent. Freed to roam, tinker, and opine, the Seven also freed themselves to taunt me, usually with implications that I was "wife" to the doting Rig, who swung by every afternoon to check on me—or, in the Astros' eyes, pinch my hip and ask what was for dinner. Engineers forever prattled about the "principle of redundancy," the doctrine of fail-safes built into the capsule's nervous system, and being a Fail-safe myself, I was awarded the nickname Major Redundant, my least favorite since Horstmeier had styled me Private Prefer-Not-To.

One Astro who disregarded the epithet was the only one I half-liked, Gordo. At thirty-two, he was the youngest of the Seven, and brash to a degree that transcended ego; he believed in his abilities like he believed there was air to breathe, and as a result he was impossible to rile, rib, or even reliably read. He was an island, and was unbothered who docked at his port, even if it were Major Redundant.

"Good morrow, Captain Cooper," I might say. "Is there a way today I might be of assistance?"

"It's Gordo." His Okie drawl was so banjoed, you might have thought him witless if Brigadier General Flickinger hadn't insisted to the media that all Astros had IQs over 130. I had my doubts about that, but appreciated the compassion in Gordo's sigh. "You gotta change how you talk, Slick."

Slick—now there was a name I could live with! One of Gordo's assignments was to prepare a survival kit suitable for a capsule landing in water, jungle, badlands, or forest, a task he undertook with a yokel's stubborn absorption. He became obsessed with designing the perfect survival knife, going so far as to draft a knife-fighting wacko in Florida and traveling back and forth to meet with him until he'd delivered hand-forged, hand-tempered utility knives of the highest-grade Swedish steel—knives capable of cutting through anything in the world, crowed Gordo. Ever since my 1873 Colt Peacemaker, I'd been a sucker for a good weapon, but 'twas not to be. They produced only seven.

The other Astro to leave me unhassled was, naturally, John Glenn. Even when this grievance or that rocked his colleagues off their nuts, the pious Presbyterian preserved polite patience, hoping, I am sure, that his Gød would take notice and one day promote him to first-chair ass-kisser.

Glenn's diamondiferous record was regurgitated by so many so often that anyone with ears got to memorize it. After leaving college post–Pearl Harbor to do what I could not—fly fifty-nine combat missions in the Pacific—the former high school letterman and marrier of his childhood sweetheart attended training at the Amphibious Warfare School at Quantico before requesting two tours of duty over Korea, where he flew ninety more missions, shrugged off hundreds of landed bullets, and famously downed three Communist MiG-15s in the final nine days of battle. Despite a uniform cumbered by Distinguished Flying Crosses and an eighteen-cluster Air Medal, he managed to test aircraft with the Navy Bureau of Aeronautics, grabbing headlines in 1957 after setting a coast-to-coast, 726-miles-per-hour supersonic speed record. The celebrity earned him the most American of rewards: guest spots on two TV game shows, *I've Got a Secret* and *Name That Tune*, where he laughed, plumped his freckly cheeks, and reiterated his faith that each of us had a place in Gød's plan.

He was, to put a finger on it, a Charles White who'd not only survived but thrived. It pissed me off. I was the one who was supposed to be Charles's surrogate! I wanted Glenn out of my damned sight, but "Gød's plan" had a reverse agenda. Every night the Astros went home to their new quarters in Langley's housing developments, where their wives had been installed to do what they'd always done—keep house in shabby shacks where the dishes rattled with every takeoff, herd their offspring, and go slowly insane. Except, that is, for Glenn.

His puritanical decision was to keep his family stowed a hundred miles away to be visited only on weekends, during which he could dive-bomb dadhood, strafe the kids with kisses, and maybe missile his wife before barnstorming back to Langley BOQ—the same Spartan barracks where I was kept. Neither of us could travel six feet without blundering into the other, Glenn while jogging, studying, or reading his Bible, I while arranging dual *Playboy* centerfolds upon a table to contrast their assets.

Most nights I cabbed to Rig's hotel and paced through his caliginous smoke.

"You've got to get me out of there!"

"Your country needs you right where you are. You'll prove your worth. I bet my job on it, didn't I?"

"You think too much of me. It is a bad bet."

"Surely you've known people worth protecting. Don't lose sight of that."

"Believe me, it's all that's keeping me here, and only then, just barely. Have you seen the teeth on these Astros? Any day now they'll start biting."

"You and I have been through this before. Slow and steady. Keep your eyes on the horizon. Don't start jagging all over the road. Drive right down the center."

"Even those who calibrate with traffic lines can end up wrecked."

There was but one beat of silence, enough for the faux pas to whip through the hole in my heart. I'd just described the patch of ice that had stolen away his family. Too cowardly to apologize, I only cringed. Unlike me, however, Rig was a professional and persisted with his blandishments before bidding good-night like a proper human being.

Moods should have brightened when NASA shifted operations from industrial-park Virginia to the sun-splashed Florida beachfront of our future launch site. But Cape Canaveral was a salt-rusted shithole of a surf town, and accordingly, relations further rusted. No sooner had we arrived than Hanger S was overhauled into a zoo for our chimponaut peers. Chimp do good, chimp get banana pellet.

Chimp do bad, chimp get electric shock. The training's conspicuous likeness to ours was too much for the Seven to tolerate. They revolted, moved themselves to the Holiday Inn at Cocoa Beach, and used their off-hours to gorge on the banana pellets of their preference—water skiing on the Banana River (I shit you not), peeling down roadways in gratis Chevy Corvettes and Shelby Cobras, and bedding young women who crossed off from homemade bingo cards which Astros they'd shagged.

Except, once again, for Glenn. From a third straight BOQ he declined to stray. He and I were thereby handcuffed, light and dark, yin and yang, forced night after night to contemplate the disquieting mirror image the other offered. Glenn was who I'd once been—a fit, clear-eyed striver—and I was who Glenn would one day be—a decaying, gray-eyed corpse, and soon, if Mercury's space-rafts sprung any leaks.

That he found me too inconsequent to address, even derisively, fanned my flames. I cultivated taunts well beyond that of "Bobby Bowtie," the most valid being that he simply did not belong in outer space, not if he didn't have some earthly rage to burn off in the atmosphere. But any attack I initiated would make it evident that Glenn was my superior, bumping me to chimponaut status. Impotent to change the dynamic, I felt my dorm room constrict around me, until I recalled a coarseness of wood grain, glint of steel bars, and bouquet of straw bedding. It was the cage inside which the Barker had kept me for the first five years of my death, engraved with that unforgettable, unforgiveable legend: HIGHLY INTELLIGENT MONKEY.

327

VI.

THE PHYSICAL DRILLS OF THE Mercury Seven were considered by its participants an Olympic decathlon, with All-Americans John, Gordo, Scott, Gus, Wally, Al, and Deke competing for the top pedestal of First Man in Space. But every Olympiad has a spoiler, some mud-hut nation no one can pronounce, and this was the role of the Mercury Eighth. Tests of endurance, after all, were my raison d'être. My body could be strapped into a whirligig the same as anyone's—no, even better. I'd do it with style. I'd showboat down the whole damn river until the Astros swallowed their pride and acknowledged my existence.

Most of the exercises replicated the centrifugal and centripetal forces of zero-g in order to challenge Astro reflex acuity, and I held the advantage of having few senses left to dull. One by one, we were buckled inside a pod that zipped in circles until, at sixteen-g, mortal men lost consciousness. But look at Zebulon go! Seventeen-, eighteen-, nineteen-, twenty-g and counting—and what's this? He's produced a comb from his pocket and is styling his hair? He's A-OK, folks!

Fine, let's try the Air-Lubricated Free-Attitude Trainer, an elaborated Erector Set that spins 360 degrees so that Astros can wrestle pitch and yaw before commemorating the match with a nice, cleansing vomit. But look at Zebulon go! He's rolling and toppling with the best of them—and what's this? Is that Bobby Darin's "Mack the Knife" he's crooning? Why, he's *more* than A-OK!

Well, the Multi-Axis Spin-Test Inertia Facility Trainer ought to separate the wheat from the chaff. Here, Astros are suspended in a midair gyroscope and subject to sixty revolutions per minute while taxed with centering a control stick. But look at Zebulon go! He's cucumber-cool and though, it's true, he's not bothering with the stick, what's this? He's reading a book? Is that Tolstoy? Is that *War and Peace*? This kid is something else!

No one saw it coming. With the decathlon half-run, I was the favorite for the gold; would-be silver medalist John Glenn was a long stride back. Glenn had control enough to ignore me; the tanned faces of the other six, however, pinked with indignity. I'd but stepped from the abhorred Slow Rotation Room at the end of another long day of vomity high-jinks no wobblier than when I'd entered, when Alan Shepard came forth and butted his chest into mine. That got me wobbling, all right, my missing arm its typical bane when it came to balance. I fell to a knee.

"Someone write this down," called Shepard. "Major Redundant finally took a spill."

He'd designed the moment with all the detail I used to give Black Hand ambushes. There were no intersecting halls down which passersby might pass by, no Suits dawdling to dispense demerits. Before I could mold an adequate glare, Wally Schirra appeared and offered his fallen comrade a hand. Perhaps not every Astro was a boor! I accepted the hand, only for him to sharply tug it. Without a fourth limb I pratfell onto my stomach.

"You're right," agreed Schirra, "his EQ looks pretty shot."

I scrabbled to my knees, only to find myself encircled. Glenn and

Gordo were AWOL, but five Astros were plenty enough to make the bullying feel more like the ring of Triangulinos inside Mr. White's garage. My low crouch brought to mind the mountain lions I'd watched in Glacier National Park snowbanks. I adopted their fanged snarl and put up my dukes. (All right, Reader, *duke*; let's not get lost in pedantry.)

"You wish to exchange words? You calumniating, pusillanimous invertebrates? Oh, apologies! No doubt those adjectives befuddle you. Perhaps fists are what you'd rather exchange? Come, then, you gutless, yellow-bellied curs, let's have it. Let us see if one of you can break a finger upon my hard-headed skull or poke an eye out on one of my pointy-pointy ribs. Oopsie-daisy, there goes your place in the flight order. Is it worth the candle, do you think, you pestiferous toads?"

They were fighter jocks and favored hot impulse over cold reason; their bodies coiled, ready to engage in the sort of saloon brawl too long absent from their repertoires. Specific IQs aside, however, Astros were not, ultimately, stupid, and the event would have ended with a listless invective or two tossed over departing shoulders if another character hadn't chosen the exact wrong moment to enter from the wing.

With a bat-flap of fluttering footsteps, Rig was all over them, shoving Schirra aside with his right hand, Slayton with his left, and then using both to take Shepard by the shoulders and wheel him about. Rig wasn't a large fellow—he was, if you recall, the average of the median of the mean—so it was with ease that Shepard, instincts sharpened to scimitars, foiled Rig's grip with a simple twist.

"Whoa, Nelly," laughed Shepard. "Wally, fetch me some sugar cubes. This here horse is hungry."

"You think you're so special?" cried Rig. "All of you?"

Rig swiped with a fist, but Shepard parried it.

"Well," Grissom said, and shrugged, "they *did* only pick seven."

330

Rig was possessed, his pores weeping caffeine, but as hard as he kept coming at Shepard with the awkward biffs of a desk worker, Shepard evaded with a matador's lazy grace, stiff-arming the fifty-some-year-old man upon his gauzy-haired head and relishing the diversion. The other four stood sniggering into fists. The only clear sounds were Rig's labored breathing and blundering feet, making a mockery of the fight I'd so much more efficiently, and for so much longer, been fighting.

"Rig," hissed I. "Stop."

"You think seven's special?" raved Rig. "Seven isn't shit. I'll tell you about special! There's only one person in the whole world like Zebulon Finch. One person!"

Instead of enheartening me, the compliment nailed me to Rig, partner to his ineffectuality. The Astros weren't interested regardless; the fight was finished. Rig, blasted off by pots of coffee but crash-landed by lungs of tar, wilted at the waist and drove both palms onto his knees. The Astros cocked their heads, unfamiliar with the phenomenon of unhealthful gasping, and then Shepard yawned, checked his wristwatch, and simply walked off as if the whole thing were forgotten. The others followed, resuming conversational tracks about car engines, steak seasonings, and fishing poles while my molten humiliation hardened to an igneous state.

Rig panted, straightened, and put a woozy hand on my shoulder.

"Don't you worry"—*gasp, gasp*—"about a thing while"—*gasp, gasp*—"your buddy Rig is around to—"

I hadn't Shepard's dexterity but batted aside Rig's hand all the same.

"Must you demean me in front of men with whom I work?"

Rig blinked, confused, still gulping for air.

"Week after week I fight for respect," raged I, "and you undermine all of it by rushing in to wipe my chin! I need to hold my own here. Can't you understand that?"

"You're not like them. You don't have to—"

"And what if I want to be? What if I want to be like them? Or even better than them? Is that so impossible? I'm beating them, you know. Out here, on my own. Wasn't that the whole point? Me, proving my worth? Proving the worth of both of us? Or am I just a way for you to score points in some future job assessment?"

Rig mopped perspiration with a sleeve.

"The only beating that matters is beating the Reds."

Too much dust was being raised by the NASA Olympics for me to see clearly to Russia. What I knew was that one did not find a foothold in manhood via a sponsor's pampering. One earned it piecemeal with sweat and blood, provided those fluids were available.

"Come on," said Rig. "Let's get you out of here."

"No."

"Until Gilruth gets these animals under control, I won't have you staying on base. It's obviously not safe. I've got room at the hotel. Come on."

"I will not."

Rig turned around, forehead pinched.

"Why not? Isn't getting out of here what you wanted?"

I did have a misty memory of saying something of the sort. Well, who would hold that against me? I'd been brand new, intimidated by the Mercury program's techno-industrial labyrinth, and in need of a docent. Since then I'd grown into my own, and this fist-chucking malcontent would topsyturn the whole enterprise if I let him, and thereby dawned my epiphany.

The Cold War, you see, had hit its absurdist zenith in July, when

Vice President Nixon and Soviet Premier Nikita Khrushchev had faced off in what the annals of history would call the "Kitchen Debate." The setting was the American National Exhibition, a Tupperware Home Party writ large in which innovations of middle-class convenience had been showcased. The rub was that this fair had taken place in Moscow. Oven mitts had become boxing gloves that, instead of blood, had sprayed quotables that newsmen had breathlessly soaked up. One exchange I read I couldn't dislodge from my skull.

> KHRUSHCHEV: *Newly built Russian houses have all this equipment right now.*
>
> NIXON: *Would it not be better to compete in the relative merits of washing machines than in the strength of rockets?. . .*
>
> KHRUSHCHEV: *Yes, that's the kind of competition we want. But your generals say: let's compete in rockets.*

You can appreciate, I think, how these reports gushed like gasoline into my tank. Here was the bridge between the suburban struggles I'd witnessed and the continent-spanning chess match that would decide the fate of the world. The government cared about conquest, glory, and bragging rights, not individual strugglers. It was Mrs. White, Junior, Franny, Clown, and others like them who needed a delegate inside the government, and in that mission I needed no further guidance. Dumping Rig, I told myself, was unlike dumping Johnny or betraying von Lüth. It had to be done for the greater good.

"I don't need you anymore," said I.

No more panting, frowning, or twitching. Rig had gone still.

"Finch—"

It might have been the first syllable of an eloquent remonstrance, but I'd never know, for a trio of Suits came banking around the curve of the Slow Rotation Room with two security beefheads in tow. Rig looked to them and pursed his lips; the moment was akin to water being poured into a brown paper bag, those tense seconds while it held back the flood. When he turned back to me, he seemed drained and, for once, perfectly sober. No caffeine, no nicotine, no anger, no remorse.

"They're taking my credentials."

He stated it as the impassive fact that it was.

"They're kicking me off the base."

That, too.

The Dearest Reader wishes to be relieved by how I borrowed Shepard's matador moves to dizzy the Suits into submission, how I protected my longtime protector. But, come now; you are no child. Surely you have cut the string of your own kite a time or two and know the thrilling, lightheaded bob. I whimpered at the loss of solid ground; no, I soared with freedom. I was desperate to have Rig stay; I was dying to see him go.

The Suits and guards had joined us. No one said a word. Rig looked at me, and his forehead pinched once more, as if he'd been posed a question to which he'd once known the answer. Perhaps the question was why he'd stuck his neck out for me, not once but twice; perhaps it was how in the world he'd ended up so alone that he'd felt the need to stick out his neck at all; or perhaps it was the hard but overdue realization that all necks are stretched out so that a large, heavy blade might drop.

VII.

A YOUNG BUCK OF STANDARD STOCK might well suffer remorse about the shoddy treatment of an ally. I, lodged into the crevasse of teendom, doubled down until I'd bottled enough bile to phone Rig's hotel and really let the bastard have it, only to learn from the hotelier that Mr. Rigby had checked out. I was dispirited, then wondered why. Had my true intent been to further flog him? Or had a softer part of me hoped for reconciliation?

It could not have been coincidence that, in Rig's absence, my win-loss record began to capsize. Consider the blue ruin of egress training. Once the space capsule splashed down, it was proposed that the Astro would shimmy out of the neck, plop into the ocean, and inflate a raft upon which to float until rescue helicopters arrived. My detestation of submersion and its corollary bloat proved too strong. I refused to egress when we did so in a pool; by the time we moved to the deep waters off Pensacola Naval Air Station, my bottom lip was fixed in a permanent, petulant pout.

Deke Slayton didn't even know how to swim, but did that violet shrink? Slayton did what needed doing, jumping in feet-first and bumping me to Olympic bronze medal, if not off the podium entirely. At night, tapping on my window pane, came that old urge to run away, the same as I had from Abigail Finch, Cornelius Leather, Burt Churchwell, and Bridey Valentine. The Olympics were unwinnable, but fleeing? Now there was something at which I had natural talent.

Work was often delayed so that the Seven could be jetted to all points north to bless production plants, add a dash of derring-do to charity events, or otherwise serve a propagandistic agenda. Even from my obstructed view, I could see that the attention paid to them was untenable. Photographers sprinted like cheetahs alongside their Corvettes, while broadcasters wielding microphones trailed them into restaurant lavatories. Other reporters were nabbed skulking about Cape facilities like Stalinist insurgents. The potential for incident, whether it be of the vehicular or scurrilous sort, was ripe, and that was reason enough for me to stick around—I wanted to be there when it happened.

All of these small-time ticks were tweezered on August 5, when *Life* magazine made an offer for exclusive rights to the personal stories of the Astros and their families at a figure rumored at five hundred thousand dollars—an incogitable sum to men whose military salaries topped out at eight grand. *Life* execs flew down to the Cape in person, their Manhattanite suits looking itchy next to Florida's open collars, and joined NASA pooh-bahs in a meeting room with an estimable soundproof door. The Seven were ushered inside, and when I tried to follow, that old skeptic Donlan blocked my entrance.

"Take a seat," said he, not bothering to add, *Major Redundant.*

Nothing set my brain aflame like a door to the face! Forget that I had no use for money, nor a family with whom to share it. Why, these *Life* tycoons had been mewling mailroom whelps in 1938, when their magazine had devoted six full pages to a photo spread of Bridey Valentine and me! At age seventeen, was I already such old news? I pivoted about, lips pursed to wax poetic regarding where they could insert copies of that back issue, but the oaths perished upon discovering the waiting area peopled with all seven of the Astros' wives.

They sat in a row like colored Easter eggs, their trim bodies clad in aqua, flamingo, lime, marigold, mint, peach, and periwinkle nylon-acetate fashions; their hair in Clairol colors and varnished into 'dos far less audacious than Mrs. White's Eska Protein Wave; and their faces Maybellined to the luster of a Redstone missile. As if by starting pistol, they brought out needlepoint canvases and embroidery hoops and began passing around a box of chocolates.

I'd never seen these women before. The base was a men-only realm for no better reason than to shield wives from the lipstick stains and strewn brassieres of their husbands' "Cape Cookies." Unmasking infidelity would accomplish squat, for no military wife dared remove a stress valve that was keeping her husband relaxed and her country on course, no matter the perkiness of said stress valve's tits.

The *Life* deal, however, carried no risk, only reward, and so they'd been extended this rare invite. My malice toward the Astros did not extend to their spouses; I'd been slandered as Rig's wife often enough to feel almost like one of them. I opened a smile as a bridge-tender might crank his drawbridge wheel. The wives of the Mercury Seven, speculated I, were likely accustomed to regal greetings.

"*Bonjour, mes chères,*" said I.

Seven identical smiles, and not one reached the mascara line.

"How do you do, Mr. Finch?" chorused a few.

That they knew my name was regrettable. Whatever details their husbands had shared would have been unfavorable. Yet so trained were they in the keeping of keels that they exhibited no adverse reaction to my disfigurations. Instead, their faces drifted back to start positions and they resumed their vanilla exchanges. Looming over them was downright creepy; I wedged myself into the only open seat.

The women could not have known one another for long, but that mattered not, for they were longtime sisters in the art of delayed despair, each face bolted with the iron smile of one used to wondering, each time she heard helicopter blades, if the base chaplain was en route to deliver bad news, and if so, what sort of monetary package the government would offer in consolation. They seemed transient, floating in the unoxygenated realm of Death, and their voices, accordingly, were airy regardless of the gravity of topic.

"Avocados and sauna baths, that's how you drop the weight."

"Did you hear about the poor Negro family whose home was blown up?"

"I clipped out the Happiness Quotient test. It's very illuminating."

"You oppose labor, you'll get acid thrown in your face like that reporter."

"Wally simply won't settle for anything except authentic goose-down pillows."

"I had a dream last night that I put our baby in the oven."

This last confessor turned to me, face placid, blinking as if in a permanent trance from flashbulbs. She extended the chocolates.

"Bon-bon, Mr. Finch?"

When the Seven emerged, chests puffed and faces halved with grins, lifting their ladies to their feet, I had more than the usual reasons to scorn them. The rumors had proven reliable. Each Astro had over seventy-thousand dollars coming his way, and even these men of reserve couldn't help but whoop and laugh while their wives went through the motions of being bowled over. Only I noticed in their carefully painted faces the baser calculations being crunched. They'd be able to feed the children *and* pay for their husbands' funerals? Well, wasn't that lovely?

Life sprinted with their scoop, hitting newsstands ten seconds later with full-color covers shouting EXCLUSIVE STORIES ON EPOCHAL MISSION and ASTRONAUTS' WIVES: THEIR INNER THOUGHTS, WORRIES. The articles whitewashed the firewater-swilling, drag-racing, philandering reality, all the way down to Gordo, who every person at NASA knew had a deal with his wife to delay divorce until Project Mercury was finished.

At one of the impromptu locker-room meetings the Seven called "séances," John Glenn tried to rally his cohorts toward ethical fitness, reminding them of that first press conference where every one of them had sworn they wouldn't be there without their wives.

"We're in *Life* magazine now," stressed Glenn. "You've all got to keep your pants zipped!"

"You've got no right to talk to us like this," said Shepard.

"The fight against Russia isn't just about rockets," said Glenn. "It's about moral superiority on every front."

"Enough with the sermon, Pastor," said Schirra.

"What do you say, Slick?" asked Gordo. "Maybe we need an outside perspective."

Leave it to Gordo, the least predictable. Though I was strapping on my jumpsuit the same as the others, it'd been weeks since I'd been addressed. I was too surprised to have a cutting retort at hand.

"Oh, sure," said Grissom. "Sex advice from the guy without a pecker."

The laughter broke apart the debate, to Glenn's chagrin. Uncooperative Astro playboys and a wildcard corpse were factors that brought gratuitous risk to a mission he alone seemed to hold as holy. Hostility was outside of his repertoire, but the look he gave me lingered long enough for me to see my repulsive self reflected in his helmet visor. The *Life* covers had made it clear that Rig's old hope—that I would soon be appreciated, maybe even publicly, as a selfless colleague to the Seven—was a gross misread of the national mood. No one wished to see a blemish, particularly a cancerous one, go un-airbrushed.

VIII.

S CIENTISTS WHEELED A FINISHED PROTOTYPE before the Seven at a research facility in Saint Louis. It was a tin can, all right—it looked like something the wives would store flour inside. I could see the cattle-stampede panic pass from one set of Astro eyes to the next. For the first time in their vanguard lives, they knew the Highly Intelligent Monkey's claustrophobia. That the six-foot-tall one-man titanium cone was emblazoned with UNITED STATES in big white letters only made its shuttlecock status even more embarrassing. Jesus, Mary, and Joseph! People were going to *see* this thing.

While I giggled with glee, the pilots lost their carefully sphinctered shit. We won't be able to extend our arms in this trash can! And where the Sam Hill is the window? You're telling us there won't be a window? How will we know you're not just rolling us down a slope? Listen, you Poindexters, you need to rig up an explosive hatch like they have in fighter jets in case this can misfires and we gotta scram. And if you think we're gonna let you lob us into the stratosphere with no piloting controls whatsoever, you're dumber than you look. What if things up there—as Scott Carpenter was fond of saying—"turned to worms"?

The Saint Louis Suits learned plenty of lessons that day, including that America's idols knew their cuss words. NASA had inadvertently

341

created a seven-headed hydra so worshipped by the electorate that it could demand anything it damn well wanted. Straightaway the capsule was redesigned with manual controls that allowed the passenger to become the pilot by overriding the programmed prescripts, and, if necessary, controlling the capsule's three-dimensional mobility. They might've gotten a hi-fi stereo, tanning lamp, and wet bar installed too, had not matters continued to turn to worms, a whole plague of the slimy little buggers.

The failure was of Alpine scale, and I how I reveled in it! No one tracking the space race could forget Vanguard TV3, America's audacious retort to Sputnik, which had launched two months after the Soviet satellite and which, instead of knocking its rival from the cosmos like a billiard ball, had hopped about six inches, tripped like a toddler, and engulfed the landing pad in a seven-story firecloud. The press had called it "Kaputnik," but, Dearest Reader, we were only getting started.

A suite of unmanned launches were initiated to prove to the nation that their beloved Seven were in good hands. Instead, Americans got to visualize their handsome heroes burning to death a dozen times over. In August, a rocket called Little Joe fired off thirty minutes premature and blooped into the sky for twenty seconds before plunging. Two weeks later, Big Joe made a night launch from the Cape, managing a whole thirteen minutes in air before going bonkers, failing to separate from the capsule, and kerplunking into the ocean. Weeks later, Little Joe 1A, meant to illustrate how a pilot could abort a doomed rocket—increasingly a possibility—was itself doomed, the pretend pilot going down with his ill-omened ship.

So many flops, boners, duds, lemons, clunkers, conflagrations, and incinerations! The term NASA preferred was "glitch," an elfin idiom that downplayed catastrophes in the same way "boo-boo" would describe a decapitation. Whether it was a stray spike in capsule voltage, a misfired booster, or a power prong one eighth of an inch short—plenty enough to combust a missile—every Astro came to hate and fear the ambiguous catch-all. I, of course, loved to watch the big, fearless man-gods tremble before the gremlin glitches.

I was at the launch pad with Shepard and Grissom when a rhesus monkey named Sam was stuffed aboard Little Joe 2's mini-capsule in December 1959. I was conflicted. While I celebrated NASA catastrophes as others celebrated playoff victories, I couldn't forget Rig's report that Laika, the Commie mongrel, had suffered a slow, grueling death in space. The Marlboro Man had taught me that animals were our superiors, and sacrificing even one for a test seemed unpardonable.

Little Joe 2, however, took off well enough and left as its wake a squiggly contrail that looked exactly like an umbilical cord. Long after Shepard and Grissom had vacated, I watched it fade. To what, I asked myself, did umbilicals connect? Could it be that the road to the stars threaded through the Uterus of Time? My impression of outer space flexed once again. It was the Mulberry Terrace where Gød, identity hidden by a panama hat, mowed His lawn.

Though the initial flights were scheduled as suborbital—home-run shots intended to hang in space for fifteen minutes before falling—full orbit was the ultimate goal, and Redstones didn't have muscle enough to power it. Enter the Atlas rocket! Its summer 1960 test launch was a media bazaar, Cocoa Beach jostling with spyglassed gongoozlers and the Seven in resplendent assemblage, aviator sunglasses affixed so that even Gød's sunshine couldn't prevent them from watching a capsule, exactly like the one they'd ride, pull aside the camisole of clouds and make America and Outer Space shy virgin partners no more.

Guess what, Reader? The fucking thing blew up! Right in front of the Astros! Gasps of horror covered my triumphant guffaw at the raining debris. Impressed by how the Astros' aviator shades cloaked their panic, I adopted the fashion, purchasing a pair and sporting them everywhere: day, night, indoors, outdoors. The mirrored finish, discovered I, distracted people from my grotesqueries, and, as a bonus, reflected back to the Astros their own anxious faces. Who were these strange men they saw looking back? Why, these men were *frightened*.

The Suits, cognizant of this, cautioned against the Seven examining the capsule wreckage. The Astros, frightened of their fear, insisted. The gnarled remains were dragged into a research facility upon a pallet, and they approached as a hunting party might a downed lion: warily, even though it was dead. At launch, the craft had been a lodestar of contoured steel and symmetrical rivets, whole as if born that way. Now it looked, to be frank, something like me. The pyramidal craft had been scrunched into humanoid shape, the chassis ruptured to expose insulation like spilled fat, jambs like snapped ribs, parachute ribbons like peeled skin.

Between debacles, John F. Kennedy was elected president and in his inaugural address spoke of a trumpet summons to "bear the burden of a long twilight struggle." Fancy words, Jack, but look, if you can, beneath the brave, mirrored shades of the Seven. Should they cremate inside their capsules, such twisted burls of steel as the ones on that pallet would be the only cadavers, a finish even worse than the closed casket of Charles White. While I stood behind them, a salivating angel of death with fanned wings, the Astros squatted, prodded, squinted, and sniffed, glimpsing in the debris their own sort of *la silenziosità*, a clue to how it all might end.

IX.

GIVEN MY FORSWEARING OF NASA'S patriotic ideals, not to mention my general fondness for anarchy, I was delighted when Yuri Gagarin, a handsome twenty-seven-year-old Russian cosmonaut, spat in the faces of two hundred million of my countrymen with his first words after liftoff from Baikonur Cosmodrome in Kazakh Soviet Socialist Republic on April 12, 1961: "Off we go. Everything is normal."

It was the Seven who had to wipe that spit from their stunned faces. News of Gagarin's feat spread across the base faster than the clap. The Reds had beaten our asses to the world's biggest prize and put a man into full orbit before we'd even gone suborbital. This was indeed "everything is normal" and had been ever since Sputnik, the Soviets hanging spacecrafts like ornaments on a Christmas tree, while we merrily opened our presents and set fire to them.

The mood at the Cape was malarial. Suits shuffled office to office, shoulders girded against the next closed-door tirade. The Astros were more extroverted in their upset, barging about, drop-kicking trash cans, and cursing like the fighter jocks they were. If NASA spent more time letting pilots be pilots and less time fitting them for diapers, why, it'd be the red, white, and blue flying up there, not the son-of-a-bitching hammer and sickle!

No one was more humiliated than Alan Shepard. Three months

345

earlier, in a secret meeting attended by big brass, the Seven, and yours truly, Gilruth had revealed that Shepard would be the one to get the historic first flight. It had been a jolt; Shepard had assumed with the rest of us that Glenn's endless jogging would jog him right into the capsule. That might have happened if not for a last-minute "peer vote," in which each Astro was asked to name the other Astro most deserving of the honor. Glenn's unpopular moralistic diatribes had sunk him.

I'd perched upon the edge of my seat, hot to watch Glenn lose his composure. As always, he had disappointed. He'd ground his teeth to powder, gulped it down, stuck out his hand, shaken with Shepard, left the room, and jogged and jogged and jogged.

Even I, frequent target of Shepard's slander, felt a pinch of frustration. He would've scooped Gagarin by days if NASA hadn't opted for a final test run with another chimponaut. (Or as those animal lovers at NASA put it, a "biological payload.") Up went Ham, a laid-back little guy who pulled his levers correctly and gobbled his banana pellets as if space flight were a real yawner. The Astros, enraged then, were downright livid now, questioning aloud everything that had brought them to this seedy beach burg. They certainly *felt* like biological payloads.

Good fortune, however, came just five days after Gagarin's flight, courtesy of the Bay of Pigs invasion. How could the botched CIA-sponsored overthrow of Fidel Castro's Communist Cuba, during which Americans were killed and jailed, be construed as fortunate? Politics, Reader! In the aftermath, JFK, hitherto a space shrugger, needed to demonstrate American supremacy posthaste, and threw his weight behind those four-eyed goons at NASA.

Our brief, shining moment had come. Butterflies found a hole in my abdomen and wiggled inside—how else to explain the flutter of nerves I had on May 5 as I and the Seven (minus Shepard, already installed at the tip of the missile) were driven to the launch site. The Astros gasped, and to be honest, I had to suppress the same reaction. You couldn't see the sand, so thick were the beaches with so-called "spaceniks" hoisting signs reading U.S.A. FOREVER and GO, AL, GO! while others, descendants of the brimstoners who used to picket Dr. Whistler's Gallery of Suffering, kneeled in prayer, closed eyes to the sun.

The Astros were gods, mused I, being rocketed toward Gød.

What might happen when the twain should meet?

Mission Control pumped me with nostalgia. It smelled like Rig's hotel room, the warm pepper of coffee and cigarettes, except cut through with antiseptic bleach. Entering the large central facility, I was glad for my shades, for I was walloped with flood lights, tintinnabulary shouts, disorienting axes of motion. I halted, clogging the passage of fellow attendants. Two tiers of spectator chairs looked out over banks of consoles from which controllers consumed telemetry data from both capsule and Shepard's body. The room was fronted by a triptych display just smaller than a drive-in screen, showing a map of North America across which the flight plan was graphed.

Men behind me cleared throats but, as usual, did not dare touch. How far I'd come, mused I, practically a space-distance, born to a world without indoor plumbing, autos, or radios, and now beset by the unfathomable fruits of technology, blink-blinking, whirring, and meeping. But Mrs. Leather had blink-blinked, too; German machine guns had whirred; Clown, limping in pain, had meeped. Everything changed because change was the only known directive, and yet not a damn thing changed. Humans nosed into darkness, disregardful

347

of what might bite that nose off, and we'd insist upon "improving" ourselves in this manner until every last one of us was dead—and my apparent job, assigned by Boss Man Gød, was to serve as witness.

The concept behind the impossibly complicated CapCom system was, in fact, quite simple. Once a capsule was in orbit, a series of sixteen tracking stations across the globe would pass to one another the relay baton of exchanging updates with the Astro. For Shepard's chip-shot, only one CapCom was needed, and Gordo was at the mic, already chewing the fat with Shepard, who waited in his craft, *Freedom 7.*

"You see my knife in there?" drawled Gordo. "Best knife ever made. Ought to be stowed to your left. You're saying it ain't there? Is that right? Well, what kind of two-bit operation we got going—Aw, stop pulling my leg, Al!"

Gordo pounded the table in delight. Suits to either side jumped.

Everyone took seats, fussed, fidgeted, and hypothesized. Having no one with whom to converse, I imagined that Rig was seated next to me. I could picture his nervy, knocking knee, the vein in his temple pulsing beneath beads of sweat. Shepard's flight was delayed, then delayed again, but if Shepard had to wait—and wait he did, eventually obtaining permission to piss inside his pressure suit—then so would Fake Rig. I caught myself smiling and snuffed it. My colleagues needed no new reason to believe me batty.

It was Shepard, at last, who kicked Mission Control in the groin. His voice crackled from overhead speakers.

"Why don't you fellows solve your little problems and light this candle?"

Gordo clapped his palms and gave an Oklahoma whoop.

"All right, cowpokes," boomed he, "you heard the man!"

In response, a shot fired across the room:

"T-minus thirty-five! Commence filling liquid oxygen!"

"Roger that. Liquid oxygen tank now taking fuel!"

"Begin final systems check!"

"Roger, roger. Final systems check is a go!"

The room caught fire (relax, Reader, it is a metaphor). Male choirs of voices sang that system after system was "go"; hundreds of console lights exploded; thousands of earthquakes rumbled underfoot as Suits barged about with teletype printouts; and millions of human pores leaked stinky worst-case scenarios. T-minus twenty minutes, ten, five, four, three, two, one, and the best that I, Zebulon Finch, could do for Alan Shepard, who despite blackballing me with his fellow Astros and instigating my rift with Rig, was nothing less than a national hero, was hold up a mental placard opposite the one I'd seen on the beach: CRASH, AL, CRASH!

Freedom 7 barreled toward launch, too close now to stop, switching to internal power, ejecting the connector tubes, firing its boosters. Fake Rig, discovered I, hadn't left me, indeed had clutched my forearm. His tension affected me; wasn't he in the same sunken boat as I? Shepard had jeered him, NASA had cashiered him, and yet his blood ran an unrinseable American Red. This was bigger than all of us. Bigger even, perhaps, than my love of ruinous glitches. Fake Rig clenched fake paper coffee cups in fake fists, muttering pleas that our first man in space would make it.

T-minus ten seconds: Hear the transmission of faith.

T-minus five seconds: Unbuckle the pressure suit of pride.

T-minus zero seconds: Float in the microgravity of magnanimity.

"C'mon, Al," whispered I.

The words shook me more than the blastoff of the Redstone.

There was pure white light at the rocket's base, a tempest of silver smoke, a Sahara shimmer of heat, a slow-motion rise, chairs squeaking all around me as sitters became standers, a pale-yellow line of burned fuel, the farewell bid of "Gødspeed," a toylike diminishing, another gaseous umbilical, applause and cheers and the rich cologne of celebratory cigars being brought out of drawers, the Gød-given right to smoke returned to us at last. Rig, the real one, would've loved it.

X.

I T BECAME GOOD TO BE an Astro. Three days after being lifted from waters off the Bahamas by the crew of the USS *Lake Champlain*, Shepard, salt water still dribbling from his ears, got a Distinguished Service Medal pinned upon his lapel by JFK while the rest of the Seven grinned like groomsmen. Kennedy then held an Oval Office meeting with the Astros while their wives got to live out the fantasy of kibitzing with First Lady Jacqueline Kennedy. Finally there was a tickertape parade, the kind I'd hoped for in vain after World War I, with Shepard as the nucleus of a New York City in mitotic delirium, every celebrant adding to the confetti whiteout by tossing anything they had at hand: paychecks, love letters, university degrees, final wills and testaments. Nothing was more important than our Seven.

What impressed me, despite my jealousy, was how Shepard had *believed*. He'd believed in the Suits, he'd believed in *Freedom 7*, he'd believed in NASA, he'd believed in America. Even from the lonesome BOQ, where I had switched channels between TV reports of the Mississippi Freedom Riders and a dadaist exercise about a talking horse named Mr. Ed, I had known that true belief was one power source I'd never be able to tap. A familiar, unpleasant twitching coursed through my dead nerves—restlessness.

It was suitable that his name was Shepard—the whole country

flocked before his risen staff. Two weeks later, JFK demanded to Congress that the space program be expanded with the wacky goal of putting men on the moon by decade's end. In NASA parlance, it was All Systems Go. Gus Grissom, not John Glenn, would pilot the second suborbital flight, though Glenn was slated for the third. I thought the golden boy's latest rebuff would invigorate me, but it was no use. Each night, while the Cape slept, I gathered my few belongings and contemplated slinking away into the night. If I could no longer confidently root against those who'd rooted against me, what was the point of sticking around?

On July 21, *Liberty Bell 7* launched.

"Gødspeed," they told Grissom.

But there were details, and the Devil got into them. Grissom's splashdown was a fiasco, with the capsule's explosive hatch—the one the Astros had insisted upon—firing off, forcing Grissom to slither out into the ocean, at which point choppers swept in to try to rescue the capsule, while Grissom nearly drowned. Had *Liberty Bell 7* suffered a glitch? Or had Grissom panicked and blown the hatch? It was clear where the brass came down. There was no medal ceremony with the president, no tickertape parade.

Glenn's two rolls of snake eyes, it turned out, were boxcars in disguise. NASA decided that Glenn's flight would be the first one to go orbital, three full revolutions around Earth. The mighty Atlas rocket, however, still scared the bejeesus out of everyone, and so they employed a final chimponaut, one named Enos, to get his anthropoid butt up there and make sure it could be done.

On November 29, Mercury Atlas 5 launched.

"Gødspeed," they told Enos.

The flight was riddled with malfunction. The capsule overheated, rolled out of position, and was emergency-aborted after two orbits, while the levers Enos used to respond to tests went glitchy and dispensed not banana pellets but rather electric shocks. Reentry was bumpy, the landing was off-course, and Enos waited for seventy-five minutes before being rescued, during which time he tore through his belly panel, ripped apart the sensors, and yanked out his catheter.

What might go wrong when the primate was John Glenn?

His would be a pallet of wreckage I'd rather not examine. Enough dithering. I gathered what few effects I had, stuffed them into a confiscated bathroom bag, turned for the door, and only then paused, seeing in my mind's own 16mm projector Junior and Franny White's faces melting off from nuclear-bomb radiation. I stopped the projector, let the filmstrip burn. Who was I kidding? I had no role in the staving off of Armageddon.

I would have been out the door for good if the TV, which I always had blaring, hadn't caught my attention with chance congruity: Mr. Ed was volunteering to be the first horse in space, complete with a four-legged pressure suit. I watched to the closing credits, standing stupefied, at which point a night secretary appeared with word that I was to report to the Space Task Group boardroom ASAP. In all my time at Lovelace, Wright-Patterson, and Cape Canaveral, I'd never received a private summons, and my last flake of vanity compelled me to set down the bathroom bag and attend, if only as the *arrivederci* I was owed.

But I could not have predicted the esteemed cast of characters I'd see when the secretary opened the door: Project Mercury Director Robert Gilruth, Associate Director Charlie Donlan, Associate Director W. C. Williams, and Marine Corps Lieutenant Colonel John Glenn.

Fists were already flying, and everyone was bruised.

"By the time Enos was over Zanzibar," Donlan was saying, "his electrocardiogram readings were all over the map."

"You know as well as I that those weren't ventricular contractions at all," snapped Glenn. "The docs put the CVP tube too close to his heart. It was his heartbeat, Charlie."

"We're not prepared to say that. It could be an issue with the ECS. You want to get caught up there with an oxygen leak?"

Glenn was famous for never losing his coxswain cool, but his temper now nudged red just like the Isolator's needle. How appropriate that the topic was oxygen.

"You just get me up there. I'll hold my breath if I have to. You delayed Al too long, and look what happened. You want another Gagarin? Finally we're ready to orbit, and you send a chimp up first. Well, fine, that's done, but I will not be quiet while you send this . . . sack of potatoes up there instead of me!"

Glenn fired an implicating finger in my direction.

These madmen, realized I, wished to chuck me into orbit.

I grappled for a chair, a wall, anything to keep me standing.

"Now, look here, John," said Gilruth. "There's a whole lot we don't know. I don't need to tell you that cosmic rays pass right through the capsule. Let's say we send you up there and there's a solar flare. You'd be at twenty times normal radiation. You really want to come back to Annie sick in some way we could've prevented?"

"Don't do that, Bob. Don't play my wife like a card."

"You have to look at this from our point of view. It costs hundreds of millions of taxpayer dollars to operate this program. You know what a dead astronaut would do to that money? Forget the money—do you know what a dead astronaut would do to this country?"

"What's our country going to say when this news gets out?"

"It won't, John. I can promise you that. We launch in the middle of the night. No advance word to the press. After the fact we say it was an old, unmanned prototype we were practicing on. No one's ever going to know the truth."

"*I'll* know, dammit!"

Glenn delivered a right hook to an easel upon which rested an oversized pad scrawled with calculations. The frame snapped in two, and the whole thing collapsed like one of the umpteen failed launches we'd watched. Everyone cringed, including me, but Glenn only laughed bitterly and rubbed a palm over his face.

"Maybe it'll take a week, a year, ten years, twenty years. But people will find out. They'll know. They'll know I wasn't the first."

He was, and as of this writing still is, a man of perspicacity and prescience. Thirty-odd years later and it has happened: The truth is written and now belongs to my Dearest Reader.

Flushed skin does not wear well on our freckled brethren. Glenn extended an inhale long enough to chronicle his career of doing what superiors instructed, and then lifted his sharp chin so that, quite terrifyingly, he stared straight at me. He walked past Gilruth, Donlan, and Williams, jawbones bulging, and faced me as squarely as he might any other living man. He squinted those crystal-blue pilot eyes, trying to find in the blood bursts of my cheek from Mrs. White's slap, in the soft flap of my sleeve hiding my stump, in my skin where Chernoff's taxidermy had shriveled, some evidence that I was worth the second look. I could not hold his eyes. I knew he wouldn't find that evidence, and I knew he'd hate both of us for it.

"I got hit by antiaircraft fire over Korea," he said softly. "I'm coming in on a target with napalm when at eight-thousand feet there's a bang and the whole plane rolls off-course. That's how fast it happens. The pilot behind me gets on the radio and says I'm hit, he can't see anything but smoke. I'm probably going down. I know that. But I'm over Communist territory. If I crash there, they get me *and* my plane—what's left, anyway. So I decide to try to make it to water, so our Navy has a chance for salvage. I push upward, fifteen-thousand feet. It ought to tear the plane apart. I don't have trim control. That ought to do it, too. Three feet of my right wing disappear. That definitely ought to do it. But I keep pushing. Not because I'm any genius flyer. Because I'm trained, and somewhere, not in my head because there's no time to think, but somewhere in my body, in my hands and my feet, the muscles just know what to do, and thanks to a crazy headwind I make it to our base in Pohang and make a dead-stick landing."

Glenn's forehead beseeched toward his buzzcut.

"I'm not trying to scare you. I'm not trying to be ugly. I'm just trying to understand if you're ready to do what we, what any of us pilots, are ready to do. Every one of us has seen a friend get melted into his wreck. A friend—and now he's just gristle and hair. And we're ready for the same thing to happen to us. We don't have to think about it. It's embarrassing to even be talking about it. But we're ready for the sacrifice. What I need to know is if you're ready. Tell me you are, and I'll believe it. I'll shake your hand and say good luck. Just tell me you're ready."

No one could keep a room rapt like Glenn. Even NASA brass was thunderstruck. My usual tactic to shirk shame was to forage for hatred, but I couldn't amass the energy. Glenn's simple request was unassailable, even admirable. Perhaps he was like Church after

356

all. He was trying as hard as he could to believe in what he'd always believed, that Gød had a plan for all of us, including Zebulon Finch.

Evidence of Glenn's reaction was there if you were close enough to see it: a doggish exhale through his nostrils, the slight drop of his shoulders, cauls of resignation slid over his eyes. He nodded once to himself, ducked his head, and without further utterance exited the room. Before the door thudded shut, I heard the pause, then the resumption of late-shift secretary gossip.

Gilruth was apologizing and motioning me forward. I loco-moted on legs that felt as phantom as my missing arm. Throats were cleared, binders cracked open, and pens unsheathed, while uncon-vincing overtures were made in regard to my contributions to that point and especially those soon to come. I would be able to perform test maneuvers beyond those of any chimp, and it was *noble* of me to *volunteer* for such *selfless* service, so *Christian*, so *American*.

Had Rig been there, he would have acted as agent, manager, and lawyer, pressing them with questions, concerns, and alternate ideas, but alone I drifted atop their warm-breath currents, nodding at half-heard details: how the flight would double as a test for weight capac-ity, how it would carry enough fuel for eighteen orbits, though I was authorized to perform only three, how I would not have to do any-thing but sit there while Mission Control ran autopilot, performed diagnostics. It was a good deal less, promised they, than had been asked of Enos.

Better me shot up there than an animal, thought I—my soul was dirtied and scuffed. Long into the night, NASA leaders sup-plied other details, but few registered. The only man I saw in that room was John Glenn; the only words I heard were his challenge; the only conviction I felt was his about Gød. What did register over the duration of that long December night, was a path down which I might alter my role, not just at NASA but forever and ever. My launch was set for the stroke of midnight on January 12, 1962, and I resolved that, on that day, one month away, the story of Zebulon Finch would fork, if not conclude altogether.

XI.

ORLD EVENTS COLLUDED TO KEEP our cloak-and-dagger secret. While I was being briefed, JFK was freighting two thousand troops to a new Communist battleground in Southeast Asia. By the third week of December, these troops were discharging weapons; a week later, fourteen of them were dead. Was it a war? It stank like one, like engine oil and urine. Even the country's name felt portentous, that daggering first letter, that hopeless, fading second syllable: *Vietnam*.

To throw the hounds off our scent, Kennedy delivered his second State of the Union the same night as our launch. At T-minus 360 minutes, with all cameras trained on the House of Representatives, I was driven past empty, black beaches churning with silver surf. At Hanger S, as was tradition, Project Mercury's Air Force dietician prepared a "low-residue" breakfast (translation: a lower chance for defecation) for the Astro to enjoy with a select few friends. I, of course, sat at the table alone, regarding the filet mignon, scrambled eggs, and strained orange juice for what it was: a death-row prisoner's last meal.

Not even for a corpse did the Suits scrimp on biomedical sensors. While one performed the comedy schtick of my vitals ("Respiration rate: irregular. Neck flexibility: irregular. Thyroid: irregular."), a second glued suction cups to my wrecked torso and inserted thermometers into the usual orifices, plus a few extra offered by my gaping wounds.

NASA's chief physician, long-suffering when it came to the Fail-safe, tore the stethoscope from his neck and delivered a final analysis to the waiting Donlan.

"His heart is like a chunk of granite, his veins are like plastic, and his lungs are glutted with dead tissue. In all my years as a medical professional, I've never seen a specimen this bad."

Donlan nodded.

"All right. Suit him up."

It felt like mummification. My limbs were threaded through modified long underwear and wiggled into the skintight rubber of my custom-made one-armed pressure suit, while biometric wires were braided through a thigh port. There were boots, heavy as cinderblocks. A thick glove was zipped onto the end of my sleeve. My helmet was latched to the neck ring and the faceplate secured. It was twenty-five pounds of matériel, futile in its role of providing oxygen and so rigid that I couldn't see how Shepard or Grissom had managed to walk. I, on the other hand, knew rigor mortis. A stiff suit was nothing.

Next they had to inflate the suit with five pounds per square inch of pressure. I knew this but made them explain it to me and then explain how I had to recline in a specialized couch. I made them explain absolutely everything, for it was vital that I appear as docile, dull, and dumb as they'd always believed, because for once the opposite was true. At long last, I knew exactly what I was doing.

To everyone at the Cape, my behavior over those final weeks had appeared as disreputable as ever. I was sluggard: Half the time, I didn't show up for meetings. I was antisocial: when I saw a Suit coming, I headed the other way. I was disengaged: while the Astros exercised or studied, I hid behind *Playboy* centerfolds. But all of it had been a ruse. I'd skipped meetings so I would have more time to devote to my plan. I'd avoided Suits and Astros alike so neither would become suspicious. And the three-page fold-outs of nightgowned, nippled nubility? They'd concealed another type of publication altogether.

It was called SEDR (Systems Engineering Department Report), but its longer title was Project Mercury Familiarization Manual, four hundred pages of descriptions, diagrams, instructions, inventories, blueprints, flowcharts, schemata, tables, and tabulations, a soup-to-nuts handbook on how the hell one pilots a Mercury capsule. I had but four weeks to absorb what had taken the Seven entire careers, but math was on my side. Four weeks equals thirty days equals 720 hours, which, if you factor in the sleep, sustenance, and weekends off required by a run-of-the-mill human being, is equal to roughly one hundred days.

And that, Dearest Reader, is nearly a college semester. I studied as both Abigail Finch's tutors and OSS's Allen Rigby could have only dreamed, until the SEDR was loose-leafed and crimped. The Mercury capsule had ten thousand parts, but I had the advantage of being able to ignore those I'd never need. Section IV, "Environmental Control System," was inconsequent. Section VIII, "Escape and Jettison Rocket System," would never come into play. Only the actionable chapters did I cogitate upon until the bland prose usurped my daydreams.

H_2O_2 enters the thrust chamber upon actuation of the solenoid valve . . .

The radiance difference is approximately 3.003 watts/cm^2-steradian . . .

The zener diodes used in these circuits are ¼ watt units, which regulate within 5% . . .

Not since John Quincy's bootlegging had I experienced the hard-won contentment of learning a trade. Even if my intellectual achievement was measurable in inches, it was miles beyond what the Suits expected of their latest biological payload, and this time their under-estimation would cost them.

At T-minus 120 minutes, I was vanned across the Pad 14 tarmac under a sugar-sprinkled chocolate sky and helped onto an industrial elevator, which lifted me nine stories up the gantry past an endless cliff-face of silver steel, twelve painted letters plunging past in reverse order: S, E, T, A, T, S, D, E, T, I, N, U. The lift clanged to its summit, pistons hissing, and I lurched onto a gangplank, gripped a railing, and gazed down at Suits as tiny as the stars above. The tower atop which I stood was bathed in scarlet light through which roiled white jets of liquid oxygen and sliced yellow cutlasses of search beams.

Hippodromic heights of light, sight, and sound, even for this most covert of undertakings! In a utility pocket I'd tucked the Excelsior. Even through the pressure suit, the second hand crashed about like a mjölnir. I put my hand over it, felt the bunny-thump of Wilma Sue's heart as I'd once known it flesh to flesh. Even while charging a line of a thousand Huns, I hadn't been as nervous as I was at that instant.

Rig had been right: had I exceeded five-foot-eleven by even an inch, I wouldn't have fit into the washing-machine-sized capsule. Engineers secured me as if for electric-chair execution (shoulder har-ness, crotch harness, chest strap, lap belt, toe guards), asked for final words I did not have, then fit the hatch into place and began bolting it shut. In the tiny, reverberant space, it sounded like a coffin lid being hammered, or, come to think of it, this cubby hole of mine beneath the World Trade Center while Héctor was walling me inside.

Hysteria might overwhelm anyone in such a setting, so I bus-ied myself reconciling the SEDR diagrams I'd studied with the real-life control panel. Like Mrs. White's Kitchen of Tomorrow, it was a futuristic display: altimeter dial, attitude vector, retrograde timer, voltage meter, pressure gauge, Mayday toggle. A technician's voice broke into my helmet's ear speakers and began plodding through pre-launch checklists. Uninterested in safeguards, I simply parroted whatever he said.

"Auto retro jettison switch. Arm?"

"Roger. Auto retro jettison switch. Arm."

"Retro heater switch. Off?"

"Roger. Retro heater switch off."

"Landing bag switch. Auto?"

"Roger. Landing bag switch. Auto."

These perfectly dispassionate transactions were cut short at T-minus fifteen minutes to pipe in the Navy chaplain's customary prayer. Dammit—I had forgotten to forbid it! I daren't listen to one empathetic word, not if I wished to uphold marble resolve. Helmet speakers, however, made covering one's ears impossible. In quick defense, I roused a reserve of hostility.

"Gracious Gød . . ."

Hah! Will He be so gracious when I'm through with Him?

". . . as a precious human life is propelled into the heavens . . ."

Precious? It's funny, Gød, how you never treated me as such.

". . . may success crown our efforts to explore not only an expanding universe . . ."

I had no intent to explore. Only to hunt.

". . . but a more peaceful one in which we may live with ourselves and with thee. Amen."

"Amen!" cried I into my helmet mike. "Amen, amen!" I was cracked in half by laughter bursting like putrescent gas from a People Garden partygoer; Suits reported tremors from my biosensors.

My speakers snarled as Scott Carpenter went live. The Seven had been spread across the worldwide network to man the tracking stations, and though for Glenn they'd have been happy to do it, for Finch the obligation required the gobbling of vast smorgasbords of pride. Carpenter, the most obedient Astro, had pulled duty as my Mission Control CapCom.

"*Harpocrates* 7, is everything go?"

Shepard and Grissom had been permitted to name their crafts, but NASA, justifiably worried that I might call mine *Fuck Off* 7, had applied the standard Greek signature, though nothing so rousing as "Mercury" or the upcoming "Gemini" and "Apollo." I merited no better than Harpocrates, the god of silence. To them, it was a nod to the mission's confidentiality; to me, it was a thorned souvenir of a NASA career hamstrung by acquiescence.

"A-OK," replied I.

Eighty-three years on Planet Earth shredded itself down to seconds. Ten, nine, eight, seven, six, five, four, three, two, one—

—and, like that, my fate was my own once again.

A million seagulls flapping at once: it was the racket of rocket flames effervescing from beneath the fins of the Atlas. The capsule shook and my skeleton began to rattle, bone off bone, until a low-pitched howl engulfed that noise and everything else. Concentrate, Zebulon! The SEDR had told me to what? To what? To start the manual clock! I punched it with my gloved fist.

"Roger," cried I. "Liftoff and the clock is running!"

Quakes overwhelmed sensations of ascent for thirty seconds, or as it seemed to your humble narrator, thirty billion years, before I could feel *Harpocrates* 7 begin to rise. The bright coins of tarmac light softened to a daisy glow and then evaporated altogether beneath whipping white clouds. The rib I'd snapped above Berlin, realized I, felt pinched. I looked down. It was my harness, digging into my suit like a giant, clenched hand. Could I still speak? I tried, and to my own shock, rehearsed words burbled out in proper order.

"This is *Harpocrates* 7. One-point-two g, cabin fourteen psi, fuel is go, oxygen is go, over."

"Roger that, *Harpocrates* 7." Carpenter sounded a tad impressed. "Over."

The capsule hit supersonic speed at sixty seconds, and when it hit the zone of highest pressure began shuddering like a cocktail shaker. The control panel blurred, and I felt my organs squish against my spine. Being intimate with my innards, I recognized each weight like an old foe: the tantrum fists of kidneys, the indolent shove of intestines, the gung-ho slug of liver. There came a penetrating whine. Here it was, the inevitable glitch; the capsule was disintegrating and next would come a spindrift of sparks, the scream of ruptured steel, a fireball par excellence, and the full-body gasp of being ripped into chunks and spat into the void.

But the ride evened. Carpenter's voice reached through the cacophony, asking for updates, did I copy, did I copy, and without thought I reported four g, cabin pressure five-point-five, isolated battery twenty-nine, fuel still a go, oxygen still a go. Carpenter said he heard me, he heard me *loud* and he heard me *clear*, and there was a relieved break in his voice suggesting that, despite the new miles between us, he and I were tied more closely than ever, and as of this moment I was not Major Redundant, not the Fail-safe, but rather a real Astro, part of the Mercury Eight. I had a tearful urge to thank him, but I chewed and swallowed it. Now was the time to cut such tethers, not tighten them.

T-plus two minutes and twenty-two seconds and I passed from purple sky to black. The thrusters tapered, the Marman Clamp released, the posigrade rockets fired, and with a grumble the capsule and missile separated. I crooked my neck and from the edge of the window watched the massive, fantastical tower of the missile arc off into space, leaving my tiny spacecraft all alone. Separation would have created a trail of smoke, my very own umbilical, but at night had anyone down below seen it? If they hadn't, was my separation real?

G-forces equalized, and I felt the drowsy tumble of antigravity. The SEDR had assured me that I'd be traveling at Mach 7 (that's five thousand miles per hour, Civilian), but the sensation was a paradoxical stillness. After a long existence overfull with motion, it was an astonishing thing, purer than the mute heights of Montana, a nothingness befitting a Nothing in Particular. Carpenter, realized I, spoke more softly now, but was still asking for the requisite thirty-second updates. How could I possibly comply beyond the hokum of *A-OK, A-OK, A-OK*? I was no longer being hurled by robot arms; I was Kal-El and I was *flying*.

Three boosters fired, one after the other, whooshing like faucets, and I nearly sobbed into my mike for them to stop it, stop it, stop it! They could keep their service medals, motorcades, parades, receptions, speeches, and game-show guest spots; all I wanted was this glorious stasis, this physicalization of *la silenziosità*, this neither-here-nor-there deliverance from everything I'd done wrong and had had done wrong to me, to last but a few seconds longer.

NASA's remote control steering was indifferent to pleas. I could tell by the meadow of star-flowers scrolling past that *Harpocrates 7* had begun its turnaround maneuver to position itself for smooth orbiting and eventual reentry. My feeling of peace peeled away to resentment. I was being pushed across a chess board like a pawn. Hadn't I concocted some great big plan to reject this?

Into my sightline, like a cresting whale, rose the Earth.

It was an object of immense, blinding clarity, a brilliant blue sphere frosted with clouds. Below me was a land mass that couldn't be America, for it was tidy and pocket-sized, hardly the boundless, gnarly morass through which I'd hacked and blazed. But America it was, full-breasted like an early bird, Florida its worm-getting beak, the radiant aqua of tropical waters its puffed plumage.

"*Harpocrates 7*," said Carpenter. "You have a go for three orbits. Over."

I swore that I could see individual sea swells, the boughs of the tallest redwoods, the bones of dinosaurs bleaching in badlands. Such pristine depth of focus sharpened my own focus. Everything about my mad, masterly plan rushed into my hollow spaces. Three orbits, CapCom? So quotidian a sortie. No, the flight of *Harpocrates 7* was going to do a lot more than that.

The Atlantic Ocean spread its sparkling cape into the Western Hemisphere's sun, proving beyond doubt that swaggering cosmonaut Yuri Gagarin had been a nearsighted nitwit. After his pacesetting orbit, he'd been quoted as saying, "I didn't see Gød." How could he have missed Him? Gød, that blatherskite, couldn't help but be the Barker of His own Pageant, casting His spectacle across land, water, and ozone. He could claim this land if He had created it, fair enough. But I was a Columbus searching for port, and the ship I captained was riddled with interstellar smallpox.

You recall the April 9, 1959, introduction of the Mercury Seven? One newsman's question had been cheeky: "Could I ask for a show of hands of how many are confident that they will come back from outer space?" All hands had gone up; Glenn had displayed good humor by lifting both palms. I'd been too busy stewing over my back-row assignment to make the pertinent observation that the opposite of "come back" was not "die." It was "keep going." And that, Dearest Reader, was precisely what I planned to do.

Funny, isn't it, that Mission Control had failed to wish me "Gødspeed" when I was the only Astro bent on attaining it?

XII.

THE SEVEN HAD DEMANDED THAT the Mercury capsules be fitted with manual controls, and it was thanks to their obstinacy that I, over African skies, was able to enact what I'd come to think of as Phase One. Wally Schirra was on the headset at the tracking station in Kano, Nigeria, and it was with the unflappable evenness of the fighter jock that he gave expression to our little problem.

"*Harpocrates 7*, this is KNO. The time is now 2:14:27 GMT. We're picking up nonstandard signals from your gyros. Please confirm. Over."

"A-OK," murmured I.

"*Harpocrates 7*, that came through a bit garbled. I'm on UHF. Repeat, on UHF frequency. Over."

"A-OK, A-OK."

"*Harpocrates 7*, stand by. I've got a relay from Mission Control. You have engaged manual override and need to resume automatic pilot, copy? Repeat: resume automatic pilot. Do you copy? Over."

"A-OK, A-OK, A-OK."

"*Harpocrates 7*. Now, look. They're getting a little worked up at the Cape. Terminate manual handle. Do you copy? Over."

The beautiful thing about space travel was the imperceptible but incredible speed—no single Earth location could connect with me

369

for longer than five minutes. Wally suffocated in static, and I entered the blackout zone of the Indian Ocean. I secured my gloved hand around the joisted steering rod and whispered to myself what I'd studied: back and forth for pitch, side to side for roll, twist for yaw. I moved the stick; the outer jets spat like llamas before doing what I said. It was exquisite how the best-laid plans of hundreds of geniuses could be disrupted by a single seize of dead muscle.

"Hell's bells, *Harpocrates 7*, what's going on up there? Ah, that is, this is CapCom MUC, do you read? Over."

Gordo had been stationed in the Aboriginal flats of Muchea, Australia. I paused my helmsmanship to picture his Cretaceous forehead amassed over his bright blue eyes. Gordo's was the last friendly voice I'd ever hear. I decided to recompense him with a few words.

"Pitch is a little sluggish," said I. "Over."

"Roger that, *Harpocrates 7*, but why are you changing vector?"

"Africa was so much greener than I imagined," sighed I. "And so big. While Europe was a piddling peninsula. It is hard to believe that it was to be von Lüth's Thousand-Year Reich."

"*Harpocrates 7*, I do not understand, I do not copy, over."

"Now, Australia. Such fevered red clouds. It is remarkable, remarkable."

"Roger that, we've got a doozy of a dust storm down here. But if we sit here and talk about the weather, they're going to kill me. You're going to need to switch to automatic pilot. Copy? Over."

"To see such sights before I leave feels meaningful."

"*Harpocrates 7*, did you say *leave*? Negative, negative. Say again. Over."

I elected not to say again. Onward to Shepard in Kauai, Hawaii; in a tone suggesting he'd rather like to chest-butt me again, he asked me, more or less, to quit goofing around, no one was amused. Then Grissom in Point Arguello, California; he had a gruff voice and used it to ensure I got the message that he'd knock my block off when he saw me next, which he never would. Then Glenn in Corpus Christi, Texas; he'd held his poker face since his blow-up, and he stuck with it, deadpanning Mission Control's single imperative, once, twice, ten times, twenty.

It was far too little effort offered much too late. For forty minutes I'd coasted across the bottomless pit of nightside Earth, where all pasts and all futures were told in accelerated theater. Earth began black, casualty to countless Hiroshimas, white strikes of lightning being thrown by Orion and Pleiades, until a blazing crescent bubbled like lava along the contour, our planet in angry flux. A blue band erupted; it was water tossed onto a fire, the world being reborn under the steam of a primordial morning, from which crawled the latest food-chain principals. For that epoch of time—eight minutes by the dashboard clock—all was well. My poison presence had not yet been invented, and so scurried animals in their savage silence, their fungal multiplications, their clean exchanges of death, before apes got a clue, before twigs became guns, before men had the bright idea to salt the soil with soot and grow Millennialists.

Electric lights fired from daybreak civilizations like flaming arrows.

I looked away, and instead finished positioning the capsule with its nose toward Earth, the angle least conducive to reentry.

Carpenter picked me up again as I finished an eight-minute race across America. He sounded, if you'll allow an understatement, wide awake.

"*Harpocrates 7*, this is Cape Canaveral, Mission Control. We are asking you to abort mission. Repeat: abort mission and go to auto-pilot. Do you copy? Over."

Oh, I copied. Second orbit: time for Phase Two.

"*Harpocrates 7*, we're not reading any ionized plasma, but if you can't communicate, switch to the Morse Code system. Repeat: go to Morse Code if necessary. Do you copy? Over."

I lifted my faceplate, wiggled my nose in the harsh, moistureless air, and reached to a box mounted above my armless shoulder, inside which careful engineers had stowed the capsule's most crucial piece of equipment.

"*Harpocrates 7*, I repeat: go to automatic pilot. We'll take over, assume retro attitude, and begin retro sequence. Please copy. Over."

One of Gordo's seven knives, those marvels of Swedish steel tempered from sweltry slag into stringent sabre, slid from its holster with ease. The lustrous blade bled the control panel's complement of red-alert lights. Gordo had boasted that the tool would cut through literally anything, and from what I knew of the Oklahoman, he was too guileless for hyperbolizing.

I set to disabling the capsule. It was tedious work; the cramped quarters lacked space for effective leverage. I began with the fuse board to my left, working the blade beneath the distribution panel and prizing until it popped. There were twenty-five fuses. I twisted the point of the blade under each one. Next I wedged the knife into the seam between left and right console. Behind that bulkhead, prom-ised the SEDR, was the pressure transducer, the removal of which would prevent Mission Control, should they somehow regain con-trol, from collecting reliable readouts, as well as four baroswitches, the mutilating of which would make temperature control impossible.

Each nut, washer, and wire I dislodged floated around in zero gravity. Birth residue, I chose to think of it, not just from the snipping of my umbilical at the Cape Canaveral launch, but from the true launch: my death on the banks of the Great Lake Michigan. The umbilical's severed end had to be out there somewhere, in a magnetic-field aurora or crab nebula or asteroid belt, and to find it would be to pull myself, hand over hand, back into the Uterus of Time.

Glenn believed that Gød had a plan for me. Well, I had a plan for Gød.

Does the ambition surprise you, Reader, coming from one so notorious for sloth? Everything since I'd gone to Albuquerque had promoted this path—my recognition before Lovelace psychologists that space was a Yggdrasil tree to heaven; the knee-bound spaceniks whose faith was stirred by our upward odysseys; Glenn sprinkling cornpone insight into the tureen he poured for the press: *I got on this project because it probably would be the nearest to heaven I will ever get.*

Where else, I ask you, could Gød be hiding? Space, I posit, is infinite. It matters not if you disagree; whatever lies beyond space, then, is infinite, and within infinity exists illimitable permutations: a world where Zebulon Finch never left Wilma Sue's bed and lived out a life with giggling baby Merle; a world where Zebulon Finch lived in kindred prosperity with Little Johnny Grandpa, or Burt Churchwell, or the Whites. There was a world, Reader, where Zebulon Finch *had done everything right*, and even if I never found that world, the fact that I would soon be tumbling in its direction, somewhere away from Earth, should have unsettled a fearful Gød.

Yes, fearful—why else had he kept me away? Gød might be the bookie's favorite in a bout, but hadn't I once dueled the great marksman Pullman Larry and won? Even if *Harpocrates 7* began to be munched by, let us say, a black hole, Gordo's knife had already impressed me enough for me to believe I could saw through the capsule wall and escape. The mission, even then, would continue. I'd be bare in the vacuum. My organs would harden and collapse. I would decompress. Who cared? Nazis had performed countless decompression experiments on concentration camp inmates; if I withstood the same, perhaps the Fifty-One, at least, would quit hissing criticisms through my helmet speakers.

From there, the trip ought to have been quite pleasant. I'd drift in deep-freeze until I was the texture of leather and paper, a vellum-bound book, both Messenger and Message. Gød would be forced to read me, to face his neglected son, not as well-liked as sibling Jesus but resurrected all the same, and make His final decision: grab the umbilical and take Zebby back, or kick him down to Hell once and for all.

Each CapCom took up a desperate encore while I plied the knife. Slayton blamed himself, said he was sorry as hell if he'd played any part in making me do this. Schirra blamed NASA, saying they hadn't done all they could to make me part of the team. Shepard blamed me, saying I was a turncoat egomaniac to hand Project Mercury, and America, this kind of setback. Grissom, that big lug, got philosophical and blamed the world, saying maybe humans had stared too long at one goal, while other things, important things, had rolled off the bed like unwatched infants.

I responded to no one but Gordo.

"*Harpocrates 7.*" The poor guy sounded drained. "Things are ass over teakettle down here. Do you read me? Over."

"How goes your dust storm? I detect calmer skies."

"*Harpocrates 7 . . .* did you cut your ECS oxygen? Over."

"I did, and with your knife. A topflight piece of cutlery. You should be proud."

"With my—? Shit, hang on. We're losing— Hey, now, are you removing your biosensors? Have you cut open your *pressure suit*? Jesus Christ. Over."

"My actions are producing glitches. I apologize."

"*Harpocrates 7—Finch*. We can still do this. We can still get you down. You just gotta listen to me. You just gotta communicate. Will you do that? Will you?"

I waited for more. I tapped my helmet speaker. All I could hear was technological death, the severed oxygen hose rasping and the gyros wheezing while the Excelsior counted down Gordo's precious seconds.

"Finch? Do you copy?"

"Sorry," said I. "You didn't say 'over.'"

"Over! Over! Over!"

I smiled, and with some affection.

"Good-bye, Gordo," said I. "Over and out."

Leroy Gordon Cooper, that sun-baked mystery of a man, faded into the Australian dust, his low drawl flipping into falsetto in his closing seconds. I was glad I could hear no more. It was past time for Phase Three, the final stage. I plucked the knife from where it floated midair and cycled through what I'd memorized about the communications system. The main antennae were in the nose, impossible to reach, and carving through the rightside cabinet to reach the transmitters, amplifiers, beacons, and multiplexers would be no picnic. Fortunately, on a shelf beside my head, sat the Command Receiver Decoder, ten input/output channels through which all signals were processed.

I took the knife like a dagger and stabbed the decoder.

The blade made butter of steel. Signals, however, continued to snort from both helmet and local speakers. I yanked the knife, examined the gash, and crowbarred the blade to wrench the cover. It began to bend. I kept at it until I could fit my glove beneath the lid, whereupon I gave the cover a vigorous pull.

The cover came off and made slow-motion somersaults through zero-g. I slid the blade beneath two auxiliary cables, twisted them into one, and cut them in a single slice. Three cables remained. Three little noodles of wire, and I'd never hear a human voice ever again. I snugged the blade against them.

I paused.

The whole universe, you know, can tilt on a pause.

Static blasted. I peered out the window and saw the browns of basins, ranges, canyons, and deserts. Texas: John Glenn. If anything could hurry me along, it was the thought of suffering through the inducements of Bobby Bowtie, but no sooner had I returned my attention to demolition than words begin yipping through the noise. It was Glenn's voice, but he wasn't addressing me. What could be more important, wondered I, than talking me down from the celestial ledge?

"Negative. Tell Mission Control we don't . . . Roger that, Scott, it's my idea. I'll take the heat if things go Charlie Foxtrot. . . . Affirmative, patch him through. Go, go, boost the . . . TEX, Tango Echo X-ray, Corpus Christi, thirty-seven, thirty-nine north, ninety-seven, twenty-three west. . . . All right, we've got him, Bravo Zulu. We've got him. Hope you're listening, *Harpocrates 7*. The signal ought to last four minutes. Going live in three, two . . ."

The radiocast cut from Glenn's treble trill to a warped bass ballooned out of shape by the very-long-distance conduction. A single syllable was being repeated, but it was slabbered inside sibilation beyond comprehension. Suits, though, were good for nothing if not twiddling tuners. The rainstorm hiss filtered to light rain, the hailstorm crackle softened, and the word grew clearer and clearer.

"*Sweltsch.*"

"*Swensch.*"

"*Swinsch.*"

"*Frinsch.*"

"*Finsch.*"

"*Finch.*"

You could almost see cigarette smoke ooze through the speaker's pinholes.

It was Rig.

XIII.

SOMEWHERE IN UNSUBSTANTIATED ANNALS OF conspiracy theory exists a transcript typed from a rogue broadcast caught by a ham radio enthusiast around the time that dawn was breaking on January 12, 1962. Even the few who bothered to read it when published in a cheaply printed journal of the paranormal, I am quite certain, considered it fiction, and the more its submitter insisted that it was real, the crazier he seemed. But it behooves one, Dearest Reader, to keep the doors of the mind thrown wide, for once in a great while the obvious counterfeit is legitimate, and the dead do walk the Earth—and soar above it.

ZF: How are you on my radio?

AR : I . . . moved back to Albuquerque.

ZF: Which is near Corpus Christi.

AR: Close enough, I guess. I'm on my shortwave. John Glenn called me, woke me up, got me patched in.

ZF: Doesn't that create a . . . ?

AR: Security breach. Yes, it does. We probably shouldn't mention . . .

ZF: Who we are. What we're doing.

AR: If we can avoid it.

ZF: So . . . people are listening to this right now?

AR: Maybe a few. If they're on the bandwidth.

378

ZF: Well, they shan't hear anything of interest. It is suitably diverting, this late walk-on of yours, but there is nothing you can say that the others haven't. I am cutting communication. My mind is decided.

AR: I know.

ZF: You know? So you're not even going to try?

AR: I did nothing but try, Finch. I tried so hard.

ZF: You tried to keep your job. To use me as has everyone else.

AR: Maybe. I don't know. What else did I have to keep?

ZF: And you lost it anyway.

AR: Trying to protect you, yes.

ZF: Do you know what I'm looking at now? The Milky Way. It is colossal. Matter entirely without depth, length, or dimension. Your excuses are smaller than Delaware. I never asked you to protect me. I never asked you for anything. I would have been better off without you. If your people hadn't hauled me in after Pearl Harbor, in handcuffs, I would be buried right now somewhere along the Western Front.

JG: Three minutes. Repeat: three minutes left of signal.

ZF: And John Glenn chimes in! How perfect that my last exchanges are with the two humans most culpable for my final torments. John, you little eavesdropper, I insist that you say "*T-minus* three minutes." It will add so much drama.

AR: You didn't let me finish, Finch.

ZF: By all means, Rig, old boy, finish, finish! At length! Run out the clock, as sportsmen say.

AR: I said I tried. I didn't say I tried for *you*.

ZF: You're baiting me. I won't let you bait me.

AR: You want to shut me up, I sure as hell can't stop you. Cut the cable. Smash the gyros. Blow the escape hatch if you want. It's easy. Take the cap off. Pull the safety pin. Hit the button.

ZF: I hadn't thought of that. Thank you.

AR: Go to hell.

ZF: All right, your charm has won me over. Go on, tell me. If you didn't try for me, who did you try for?

AR: For . . .

ZF: The clock is ticking, Rig.

AR: For . . .

ZF: NASA? Gilruth? The Suits? Is your patriotism so staunch?

AR: Forget it. This is a waste of time. I don't know why John called me. I can't help here. I can't help anyone.

ZF: I could not agree more.

AR: You've lost a few body parts, so what? You're not the only one who's lost things.

ZF: Do you mean . . . ?

AR: Go to hell.

JG: Two minutes. Repeat: two minutes left of signal.

ZF: I refuse to let you bring dead children into this. It has nothing to do with me.

AR: How many times do I have to say it, Finch? This isn't about you. I just need . . .

ZF: What? What is it you require from me? What is the purpose of this conversation?

AR: I need you to . . . What do you see up there, Finch?

ZF: I told you. Stars. Planets. Moons. The Sun.

AR: There's nothing else? Nothing more?

ZF: Rig . . .

AR: I need you to tell me there's more. That they're all right. That they are waiting for me.

ZF: Rig. I don't know what—

AR: Just one of them. Just one? Little Florence?

ZF: Do you need me to . . . forgive you?

AR: It's unforgivable. Unforgivable.

ZF: There is nothing up here to help you. You need to accept it.

AR: It's not real. It can't be real. If I keep working, just keep working, it can't be—

ZF: You brought those bodies out. Every one.

AR: No, no—

ZF: Janet, Roy, Sandra, Walter, Patty, Stanley, Florence. You placed them on the mud. It happened, Rig.

AR: Why you and not them? How come a no-good bastard like you keeps coming back and sweet Florence just lies there on the mud?

ZF: I . . . don't know.

JG: One minute. Repeat: one minute left of signal.

AR: I—Finch, I—

ZF: You think crying like a baby will impress me? I'm beyond tricks, Rig. I'm beyond everything!

AR: I lost all of them, Finch. All of them.

ZF: Don' t do this to me. Do not do this.

AR: I can't lose someone else.

ZF: You are not some sort of father to me.

AR: I can't lose you, too.

ZF: You didn't have to call me every day at the base like a child at boarding school. You didn't have to fend off my bullies. You didn't have to do any of it! Not any of it!

AR: I can't fail someone again.

ZF: What did I say the last time we spoke?

JG: Losing signal. Maybe twenty seconds—

ZF: I said I don't need you. Do you understand?

AR: Yes . . .

JG: Ten seconds, losing signal—

AR: But . . .

ZF: I'm cutting the cable, Rig! I'm cutting it!

JG: We're losing it, we're losing it—

AR: But I need—

The signal cracked like a lash. I dropped the knife. It floated lackadaisically toward my lap. The static replacing Rig's voice was assaultive until a merciful Suit flipped a switch and returned me to the stabile hum of the Corpus Christi tracking station. I, one more corpse pulled from a sunken car, shut my eyes against outer space, blacker than river mud, slicker than riverbanks. I listened. I hadn't lost Glenn. He was there, doing that odd thing humans do—breathing—in and out, rise and fall, that ace of extemporaneous speech holding his golden tongue.

What had Rig needed?

I opened my eyes and glared at the moon.

Gød. What a low-down trick He'd pulled. Not brave enough to take me on, he'd placed a measly man in front of Himself, then dared me to gore through that man to get to Him. I might have done it if the human shield had been the bitter, disputatious Rig, but it hadn't. It'd been Allen Rigby, and he—a single, useless, meaningless soul upon a foredoomed planet—needed me.

For a full minute of Glenn's measured breathing, I was seized by envy. Shepard and Grissom on their flights, and Glenn on his forthcoming one, could journey as far as they wished and feel secure, for their capsules were knotted to anchors in East Derry, New Hampshire, or Mitchell, Indiana, or New Concord, Ohio, places where they could return to watch both the grass and their children grow. An American nomad could drop no anchors. I'd be on the run forever.

I pressed my cold face against the colder cockpit window and peered into the blackest, deepest pocket of space I could find. Ginsberg's starry dynamo was still out there in the machinery of night, *tick, tick, ticking* as durably as the Excelsior. I could, and should, and would look back to Earth as Lot's wife did to Sodom, and do it without fear of Gød turning me into a pillar of salt. He hadn't the power. He couldn't do shit.

"Engaging autopilot," whispered I. "Initiating retro sequence. Over."

John Glenn pounced.

"Roger that. We've got it. Down to retro-angle, five, four, three, two, one, retro-angle."

"Lights are green. Retro-1. Over."

"Roger that."

"Retro-2. Retro-3. All retro rockets are fired."

"Roger, roger."

I do not have the energy to describe reentry in detail. Let us just say that there was a good deal of battling the yaw, and Carpenter earned his salary by leading me through a fishtail maneuver, any Astro's last, worst option. There was the return of crushing g forces. There were four minutes of dead air during an inferno descent. There was the jag of the drogue chute deployed, the gentle rocking of the main chute. There was Icarus's hubristic fall back to Earth, his wings of feathers and wax dampened and melted.

Harpocrates 7 splashed down west of Barbados and released

fluorescent green dye into the water to help choppers locate it. The capsule, of course, was in abhorrent shape, smoking and gurgling and blinking every warning light it had, so I did what I'd refused to do in training and commenced egress, blowing the hatch as Rigby had described and exiting through the bulkhead, taking with me the survival kit and life raft, which I inflated, tossed onto the water, and boarded.

The waves were choppy. As I did not relish a dousing, it was best, thought I, to lay upon my back. Above I discovered the kind of sun-kissed panorama that, when I'd been alive, would have magnified my every fancy, from whiskey to women to fisticuffs. It stung like too much sugar on the tongue, and yet I could not quit licking. I'd been up there above all of it; I'd peeled back the universe's pretty blue skin to see its black scales.

I unpacked the survival kit, detritus of a race never destined to survive. Medical injectors. Matches. Soap. Signal mirror. Life vest. First-aid kit. Shark chaser. I could hear the sharks, all right, shaving through salt water and circling the raft, but they did not bother their brother animal. The included tube of zinc oxide I used, slathering it over my face for no other reason than I wanted a mask. Atop that I placed the sunglasses—Astros always wore sunglasses, and these would have to suffice until I reclaimed my aviators. Finally, I took Gordo's knife, its blade pristine despite the paces through which I'd put it, and slipped it into the pocket containing the Excelsior, which ticked on, unfaltering despite the wild ride, unbelievable pressure, and bumpy landing.

I watched the clouds roll past for hours. Perhaps it was years, for I could see the future of the space race as if it were memory. Project Mercury would log fifty-four hours of manned space flight. Glenn

384

would get his orbit, the "first" American to do so, and thanks to my best efforts to shanghai my capsule, he'd do so with improved safety measures and become the superstar he deserved to be. The two-man flights of Project Gemini would nudge America ahead of the Soviets, and Project Apollo would achieve JFK's preposterous goal of getting men onto the surface of the moon, among them Alan Shepard. And through it all, until this tale told to you, Dearest Reader, the flight of *Harpocrates 7* would remain outrageous rumor.

All of it—life, death, rebirth—happened as I pondered the placid sky. When a Marine Air Group helicopter crossed my field of vision, I frowned as if at a bumblebee. Next I heard the thrush of a U.S. Navy carrier and its escort of destroyers. America's finest had been called to my aid, and why not? I was no longer a mere corpse. I'd stared down Gød like a heavyweight, seen in His sucker-punch proof of His glass jaw. I could do better than Gød. I could *be* better than Gød. This I resolved as I took hold of the dangling horse collar and was levitated, or so it seemed, into the chopper's steel stomach.

PART TEN

1962–1969

———◄»◉«►———

The Times They A-Change, But Your Hero Can't Get
No Satisfaction; Or, How We Had To Destroy Amerika
In Order To Save It.

I.

W E SHALL OVERCOME," THEY SANG. Intrepid attitude, but they looked unequal to the task, this ragtag
corps of fifteen to twenty Sunday-best Negroes who
swayed with linked arms outside a Greyhound station in Biloxi,
Mississippi, where jittery young men shaven to shiny cheeks and
afloat in army garb amassed to board the bus that would take them from
the Southeast United States and start them toward Southeast Asia.

The Negroes belted not to hurrah Biloxi's bravest but to inveigh
against the military draft that had enlisted them. The protestors
paraded handcrafted placards reading STOP THE WAR and REFUSE
TO FIGHT. My Dearest Reader knows that to tabulate the overseas
conflicts I'd seen come and go would take all day, yet only in the past
eleven months had I seen a U.S. citizen publicly decry a war involving
our boys. Given my history with John Quincy's tribe, further admix-
ture with Negros worried me, but alas, I was a beggar, not a chooser.
Having hatcheted headway with the Montgomery Bus Boycott of
1955 and the integration of the Little Rock Nine in 1957, Negroes
had become the nation's preeminent fuss-makers. Thus, they would
have to do.

The bus station hinted at the jungle to which the new GIs were
headed: rainforest-green kudzu, tiger-orange rust, and panther-black
oil brightened only by the mighty magnolia tree that lorded over all

389

of it, ornamented with spring's pink buds. I put my palm to its trunk as a doctor places a stethoscope. The branches offered a plentitude of footholds for the gumptious cragsman. I slung my rucksack across my back, lodged my shoe into the foundational fork, and started up.

One-armed climbing is a gradual business, and by the time I'd attained the highest possible weight-bearing branch, all draftees had arrived. None had noticed my ascent; mothers were occupied with parting embraces, fathers with shaking the hell out of their sons' hands, Negro protesters with "Lift Every Voice and Sing." I straddled my branch, shimmied out as far as I dared, and opened my rucksack. There I paused, caught by a voice in the choir. It was that of a young girl and was possessed of a clarity and resonance so beyond her years that the other singers sounded like Midtown traffic.

Enough of that—back to work. I hadn't known to what height I'd climbed, and the manila rope I'd brought was too long. I lowered it to the ground like a fishing lure, marked the proper length, and reached into my jacket pocket, past the Excelsior and inside the sheath of Piano's map, where I kept Gordo's knife. It sliced through the rope's braid, and the extra length thumped to the grass. One end of the remaining rope I tied around the branch with a double overhand knot. The other end I gathered into my lap; I'd been practicing for this moment for days. Form a loop. Tuck the excess. Stretch for length. Tighten the knot.

The chorus recycled, and oh!—that bugle of a voice! I smiled. I knew a hotdogger when I heard one. Loop, tuck, stretch, tighten—too sloppy. From the girl's volume alone you could tell she gave not a single shit about why they were singing. Loop, tuck, stretch, tighten—too small. For her, the protest was merely the latest stage upon which she might shine. As one who'd wrapped his own aspirations over assigned tasks, I appreciated opportunists. Loop, tuck, stretch, tighten.

There: the perfect noose. I held it before me like a face I might kiss, then ducked my head through and snugged the knot to the underside of my chin. It seemed a choice moment for contemplation, but the bus was fully soldiered and the last serenade had concluded—the time was now. I took off my NASA aviators, slipped them into my pocket, drew myself to a precarious crouch, opened my mouth, and realized I didn't know what to say. Protesting the war in Vietnam, were they? Fine, I'd regurgitate their signpost slogans. I cupped my palm to my mouth and shouted.

"*Stop the war!*" Or not, I didn't care. "*Refuse to fight!*" Or agree, it didn't matter.

Dozens of faces turned my way, not only choristers, families, and ticket clerks, but the bus driver and the GIs from their seats. I grinned, an inappropriate reaction, but what can I say? All those eyes excited me so much that I nearly forgot to follow through. What was I doing? Yes, right—jumping! I leapt from the branch. Magnolia petals rushed past me like rose water, while lesser branches slapped my knees and hips, breaking my speed. My drop, though, was largely unimpeded and lasted no longer than my 1896 plummet at Lake—

The hard jolt. The skeleton jounce. The swinging, the spinning. Sunlight shooting yellow buckshot through pink petals. Green grass, brown dirt. Gospel Gød-baiting, the ecstasy and fear. America aswirl, its neck broken, suspended betwixt here and there, now and then.

And I saw Gød placed into my hand. No, not exactly Gød, but His book, the Bible. It was, in fact, a recent memory—the Good Book being presented to me, with some ceremony, by the chaplain of the carrier ship that had found *Harpocrates 7*. The Bible, crowed he, was *a navigation chart to the heavens I'd just visited*, and I'd cradled it to my chest, not out of gratitude but so that Gød, if He did live in those pages, could hear how my heart did not beat, not even for Him. Moronic medical exams had commenced, followed by the convention of making my flight observations into a tape recorder. I asked for privacy, and when I got it, switched off the recorder, opened the cabin window, and chucked the Bible into the frothing sea.

Before the armada reached Florida, your sheepish storyteller received every Astro's paramount perk, a call from the president. JFK's tone, figured I, would be less than adulatory, so when a ship's mate handed me the telecommunications receiver, I was ready with maledictions. I, humble dynamitier's son from Chicago, would tell the president of the United States exactly what I thought of his pathetic democracy. Oh, how'd I burn his ear hairs with my belly's boiling bile!

But there was a great distance between my vessel and the White House, and perhaps due to our anemic connection, I failed to detect hostility in JFK's Bostonian accent.

"I understand," drawled he, "that your journey is to be kept top-secret."

"Why," said I, "I bet you'd—Mr.—I bet you'd like—"

What was this? The logorrheic Zebulon Finch, dumbstruck?

"I want you to know, and I want you to take to heart, that some of our country's greatest patriots—in fact, I'd say, the greatest—go unsung by our history books."

"Do you expect—I have a thing or two to say about—"

"Go forth, Mr. Finch, with the idea that you have served an important part in a historic endeavor. There is no greater purpose in life than saving your fellow man. I thank you, our nation thanks you, and the whole world thanks you, even though you'll never hear it again. Gød bless you, Mr. Finch, and Gød bless the United States of America."

The receiver was stolen from my grip. Had the exchange really happened? It was difficult to believe once Glennan, Gilruth, and their surliest Suits had me back in their clutches for debriefings of, shall we say, a less amicable nature. Going incommunicado above Earth and trashing a multimillion dollar spacecraft was the most reprehensible of kaputniks, and they were hopping mad, literally foot to foot. My thoughts, however, remained with JFK, whose words thudded about in my skull. His gist had been that those like John Glenn were destined to go above the fold on *The New York Times* and flash glossy grins from glossy book jackets. But how many others made important sacrifices each day that went unphotographed?

I took pains that my exit path did not intersect with Rigby's path. If the man was to heal, he would do it best without me. Without qualm, I signed scores of documents barring me from divulging a word of my NASA involvement, else I suffer—well, I didn't bother reading the consequences. I pocketed my back pay and hustled away. John F. Kennedy had suggested to me that important callings still existed, and Rigby's belief in me, down to the end, had confirmed it. I had only to resolve how to best bring my calling to fruition.

I'd become adept at navigating the vagabond fringe, and now I did so with eyes fixed upon front pages, impatient for the clue that would enlighten me as to how Rigby's lowly partner might change the world. I was therefore caught as flatfooted as the rest of the planet when, in October 1962, America's foxiest foil, Nikita Khrushchev, refused to exfiltrate thermonuclear missiles from Cuba. Strategic Air Command achieved a level of alert known as DEFCON 2, idiomatically known as Time to Shit Your Pants, We're All Gonna Die. It was an edgy thirteen days during which I thought day and night of the Whites in their basement, assuming the old positions.

The prospect of thousands of Hiroshimas blooming as if from seeds sown by an apocalyptic Johnny Appleseed was abhorrent. What good was becoming a savior if there were no Frannys or Juniors left to save, if every single innocent were as dead and gone as Rigby's drowned children? When Khrushchev withdrew the weapons seconds before the world went kablooey, the planet sighed as one. Yes, Reader, the one thing that could unite the people of Earth was relief that all of us wouldn't be reduced to equivalent piles of beige carbon.

Had I been a sharper tack, I would've perceived my path forward before a rinky-dink rifleman had blown the brains of the president— Jack, I jealously thought of him now—out the side of his head. It was when reporters began calling the president a "martyr" that the puzzle of my purpose began to resolve. Five months earlier, who hadn't watched footage of Thích Quảng Đức, a monk who'd self-immolated in the streets of Saigon? What control the berobed ascetic had shown in his puddle of gasoline! What power he'd displayed, never budging as the flames had engulfed him! In but a few seconds, the martyr had grabbed the attention of world leaders—and now, unwillingly, Kennedy had done the same. Martyrs, concluded I, were the firewood people burned to light brighter realities. This should be the purpose of, for lack of a loftier term, a Better God.

Floridian libraries became my offices. I frequented them to gain librarian trust before stealing from their stacks texts regarding the grisly but refulgent history of martyrs. This house of knowledge built rapidly upon an already existing foundation. My childhood tutors, gloomy Christians to the last, had seasoned their history lessons with sagas of sacrificed saints, while the constipated pulpitarians of Abigail Finch's church had trampled the same ground: King Herod's warpath after Jesus's faithful, the stoning of Stephen, the crucifixion of Peter, the other gray horrors left to children's brains to color.

Hadn't I the potential to be the martyr to end all martyrs? I could suffer not once, like Thích Quang Đức or Jack Kennedy, but again and again, not in the name of Gød but rather to humiliate Him with my superior ability. Jesus, that bashful lamb, died on a cross, did he? One single cross? Line up one thousand for me, the Better God, and bring along your hardest nails.

From these memories I surfaced beneath an eclipse, a black moon haloed by white sun. The moon moved; it was no moon. It was the round face of a Negro girl, darker than most, hovering over my own. She was skeptical-eyed, pigtailed, flat-chested; she was fourteen if that, with all the doelike spindliness thus afforded. My eyes made adjustments. More shocking than her proximity was that my hand gently cupped the side of her neck.

"Beautiful," whispered I.

Did I refer to her? Or the short but stupendous trip I'd just taken?

Regardless, she smiled. She had adolescent teeth, spread out, plenty of gum.

"Thank you very much," said she.

No depth of stupor could hinder me from identifying the pip-squeak as the grandstanding singer. The second voice, however, was of pure, ugly, teenage truculence.

"Why's he need to have his hands on you?"

"Ritchie, you shush," scolded the girl. "Poor boy just been hanged."

Hanged? Why, yes, I'd just hanged myself, hadn't I? I dragged my eyes to either side of the girl's head to find myself enringed by anxious Negroes. The one named Ritchie was unmistakable. He was my age, scowling like a gargoyle, and glaring with eyes so bulged-out, they looked like novelty attachments. Even more striking was that he toted a shotgun, about which floated a smoky nimbus.

"Now he's touching your cheek!" exclaimed he.

It felt not like the cool, polished rosewood I expected, but like a sunshined peach.

"He's cold," said the girl. "You let him be, Ritchie. I think he's dying."

"I'm not dying," promised I.

Excitement lanterned her.

"Good, mister! You think like that, maybe you won't die."

"I am *not* dying. What is your name, girl?"

"Bunny Tucker. My papa is Reverend Tucker and my momma is Mrs. Tucker and they're off fetching a doctor, and that right there's my brother, Ritchie Tucker. He's the one who shot you down."

Baffling was any scenario involving the discharging of firearms. I rolled my head back and through upside-down eyes made out the branch from which I'd swung, hanged like the Apostle Luke, like the Quaker Mary Dyer, like so many other first-rate martyrs. The branch, though, had been amputated with the same artistry as had my left arm, the brown bark torn open to reveal shards of blond wood. Even the tree's trunk looked like mine now, gouged with bullet holes. Ritchie Tucker, it could be certified, was no Lee Harvey Oswald; it'd taken repeated shots to blast apart the branch, more than long enough for a martyr to do his thing.

I sat up and rolled my neck; bones crackled, but my noggin was supported. I heard whispers of disbelief, prayers of exaltation. How had I missed for so long that my absence of physical pain was not an absence at all but a presence? I was on track to outperform Jesus, who, in his own time, had commingled with a disenfranchised radical or two.

From a distance came the shriek of an ambulance I wouldn't need. Far closer, several hatted gents—newsmen by the way they flipped open spiral-bound pads—were paying attention to a Negro church group at which, until the theatrics of a white-boy hanging, they'd yawned. My noose had been loosened a touch but still dangled about my neck. I gave it a tug. It didn't give much, and I found that I enjoyed the pressure, much as a Wall Street baron must enjoy the do-or-die throttling of a Windsor knot against his jugular.

"Here, mister, let me get that off," said Bunny Tucker. "But you're probably still gonna die."

"Quite the macabre child," observed I. "And I insist that we leave it on."

II.

ALREADY I'D FARED BETTER WITH these Mississippians than the indifferent Negro lawn workers of Heavenly Hills. After I refused medical care, the Tuckers took me in forcibly so as to monitor my condition, should I abruptly remember my suicide. Popeyed Ritchie shunned me and took to striding about with his shotgun. Bunny, while much cuter, was only marginally more affable. Room to room she followed me, impatient for me to drop dead. When I did not, she pouted and complained how she'd been hoping to sing at my funeral.

The Tucker parents, at least, were lionhearted Christians who believed the Vietnam War to be an immoral distraction from the struggles of the powerless in America. Forthright Negro furor discombobulated me, and so I listened more than I spoke, thereby happening across the ideal manner for a martyr. The less I said, the more easily I might symbolize any particular group's objective.

Mistaking me for a likeminded ally, the Tuckers rehashed brutal events as others rehash family vacations, the most recent of which had unfolded while I'd been whirling around outer space. A group of Negroes known as the Greensboro 4 had refused to leave a North Carolina Woolworth's that wouldn't serve them, sparking months of sit-ins across the South. These actions had inspired an eloquent minister by the serendipitous name of Dr. King to fight the segregationist policies of Birmingham, Alabama—aka "Bombingham." The Reverend and Mrs. Tucker had been at Dr. King's elbow throughout and recalled (to the bored eye-roll of Bunny) how a police K-9 had been unleashed upon a six-year-old girl.

I'd heard of this Dr. King. I'd once listened to a taped broadcast of a speech in which he'd recounted a dream he'd had, one that, like all dreams, was silly—that all men were created equal. All men, Dr. King? Even those incapable of dreaming, those already dead? Would I, too, one day be judged not by the color of *my* skin but by the content of *my* character? I could only hope the latter was true, for it was my character I intended to elevate to godlike altitudes.

Discontent led to objections, objections led to demonstrations, and demonstrations always had a use for showy schticks. In other words, people were waiting for someone just like me. I didn't need to ask. On a piece of church stationery, Reverend Tucker wrote the addresses of several simpatico objectors. I thanked him (silently) and bid the Tuckers farewell (ditto). The egg-eyed, shotgun-strangulating Ritchie applauded sarcastically when I gathered my belongings and stepped from the porch, but his sister cried enough to disturb the swallows. I had grown used to silence, yet felt that I owed the family a gesture. Besides, I'd grown fond of the brat; she'd devoted many hours singing and dancing in my vicinity in hopes of pulling from me a second compliment. I knelt before her.

"Don't you tell me to stop crying!" blubbered she. "I can cry all I want."

"I wouldn't dream of it. Even your cry is musical."

She sniffled, her tears stopping—there, she'd gotten her flattery.

"Daddy said you have to leave," she said. "He says you have big things to do."

I shrugged.

"Maybe you do, too," said I.

Her eyes sparkled. More tears, yes, but these were large, proud ones. On impulse, I pulled one of her pigtails, then the other. She sputtered, genuinely aggrieved. Good—it made leaving all the easier. I stood and looked to the Mississippi horizon. A single Bunny, even one this talented, was too few; larger warrens awaited.

I traveled on foot like the sandal-clad martyrs I'd studied. This was 1964, Reader, and the decade had yet to catch fire. Reverend Tucker's Southern associates were hesitant to include in their protests a one-armed man who, despite some degenerative browning, was still, when observed closely, quite white. But when I arrived at the last address on Reverend Tucker's list, Nashville's Fisk University, I knew I'd found my next target. Apologies—my next stage. Formerly known as the Fisk Free Colored School, the university thumped with the tiger heart of Negro restiveness, and on the day I ambled toward stately Jubilee Hall, students dotted the lawn, building signs for a march. Their wary stares I ascribed to both the ambiguous color of my skin and the accessory I'd kept as my signature: my sawed-off noose, hanging about my neck like a lavaliere.

Record players, those boxy descendants of Dr. Leather's Victrola, supplied bouncing beats to the students' labor. Between the falsettos of Smokey Robinson and the seductions of Marvin Gaye, I heard a sharper, more scornful voice, quite unconcerned with romance.

"Who taught you to hate the texture of your hair? Who taught you to hate the color of your skin to such extent that you bleach to get like the white man? Who taught you to hate the shape of your nose and the shape of your lips? Who taught you to hate yourself from the top of your head to the soles of your feet?"

If you are waiting, Reader, for the background singers to sha-na-na, I hope you are comfortably seated. The artist, if that's what you'd like to call him, was pictured on his LP sleeve as a bespectacled, pokerfaced Negro with the absurd name of "Malcolm X," and his recorded ferment against the white man discomfited me. The Negro features about which he spoke were all over this campus. One simply did not discuss such things, Mr. X—no, sir, one did not!

My role, of course, was not to question the motives of protestors; a Better God could not be selective. I wandered until I identified the man who, by the number of questions he fielded, looked to be in charge. Several peppy young Negroes awaited his attention, but I nudged myself in front. Surely my business took precedence.

"Mr. Clifford Jackson, I presume?"

Perhaps he recognized a Caucasian cadence, for he swiveled as if expecting to block a punch, only to go still upon seeing my arm stump and swollen, discolored flesh. Though not gifted with Mr. X's dapper looks, Mr. Jackson had done well copying his style: trim suit, pencil tie, cropped hair, black horn rims, and an expression of intense concentration. Fastened to his lapel was a golden pin of a star and crescent against a scarlet background.

"*As-salamu alaykum.* Who's asking?"

What of this garbledegook? I kept my response as brief.

"Zebulon Finch. Reverend Tucker of Biloxi, Mississippi, sent me to help."

"Help? You want to join our line?"

The confident smile I offered was playacting. Many of the Negroes, I'd begun to notice, wore the same star-and-crescent, the young men sporting funny caps, the young women chaste bonnets. Mr. Jackson gave me a visual frisking, the sharp line of his glasses

401

scraping across my skin like a shaving razor. Eventually he shrugged.

"Mr. Tucker's a good man. The Honorable Elijah Muhammad teaches us to open our arms to those who feel the same about our oppressors."

A-ha, the Honorable So-and-So! So I'd met my first Muslim, had I? I'd heard my share of horror stories regarding the Nation of Islam's mercenaries, but this chap seemed more scholar than roustabout. I gave him a careful nod.

"Good," said he. "I'm glad we come down on the same side of the issue."

Right, the issue! Which issue was it, again? Eh, best not to concern myself. What mattered was that the setting of the afternoon's enthusiastic picket line was a large Nashville hotel, outside of which the Fisk contingent, all thirty-five of them, decried this injustice or that maltreatment while marching in an oval wide enough to circumscribe a riser and podium, and above which ran a bridge as part of the new interstate. By the time a freshman go-getter and local pastor had deferred to Mr. Jackson's firebranding, I'd slipped away, climbed the hill, and made my way to the bridge's edge. From that height, I could see that the crowd we'd drawn was paltry, more irritated white folk than bold black. The approaching police cars and paddy wagon did not look friendly either. Pish-posh, as Bridey might have said. None of that had any bearing on my duty.

My stolen library books had taught me that history prized one method of martyrdom above all others—burning, ideally at a stake. From the legendary (Joan of Arc, thrice incinerated in 1431, ashes dumped into the Seine) to the relatively unknown (John the Apostle's pupil Polycarp, whose 167 AD burning was noteworthy for how his gush of blood doused the flames) to such modern purveyors as Thích

Quang Đúc, the method was spectacular and conclusive. Fires left no bodies to be enshrined and worshipped, no relics to be collected and hallowed.

I, however, lacked the courage to burn, for it would, at the very least, render me so hideous and lame that the rest of my days would be spent charred and writhing. Besides, there were a surfeit of other sanctioned ways to off it for a cause; one need only flip to a random page of *Foxe's Book of Martyrs* and follow the grisly step-by-step. How else do you think I learned of the sacrifice of James the Less, cast down by the high priest Ananus from the Temple tower?

My rope-free copycat plunge was, if you'll allow the boast, superb, head-first for maximal shock value but with a flopsy slackness just right for flaunting one's disinterest in one's own fate. With disgruntled motorists honking and applause still smattering from Mr. Jackson's frisky finale, I heard no reaction to the show of my freefall dive before crunching to the sidewalk thirty feet below.

Once more there was a blip of blissful oblivion, from which I emerged to find a huddling of Negroes similar to that which I'd experienced in Biloxi. There were whispers of "Did you see it?" and "Why'd he do it?" and Bunny Tucker's favorite, "He's dead!" before I opened my eyes, noted the partial break of my right hip, and gave them a beatific smile.

"Praise Allah," gasped Mr. Jackson into the microphone.

How they frolicked and fervored, and from their glorification I took great gulps of pride. But sounds of triumphalism are so close to those of violence. I knew not when police had formed a line, nor when they'd ordered us to disperse, nor who'd thrown the first punch. I knew only that billy clubs were abruptly cracking against bones; only that rednecks in shirtsleeves had pitched in with blackjacks and tire chains; only that the Negroes, behind Mr. Jackson, whose scrupulous attire hid one hell of a bruiser, were stirred by the miracle of my fall and rise, and fought back with fists and feet. An all-out race war raged in front of that hotel that day, brown and pink skin smearing to a tan tangle, while the color red was shared by all.

I was helped up by two students, but it'd take time to learn how to work a shattered hip, and a white man, foaming at the lips, rushed me with a crowbar, howling that the only thing worse than Martin Luther Coon niggers was Martin Luther Coon nigger-lovers, but I only had to absorb one blow before students enveloped him as would a pack of wolves. A parked automobile exploded into fire—sheer chaos, unmitigated anarchy!—but a fire engine was there, and its hoses, when done drenching the blaze, turned upon us with force enough to tear the skin off my elbow. I stared at the nub of bone, so bright and clean compared to my mulch of flesh, and found it to be a perfect analogy: scrub off America's decay, and you might find strong new bones beneath.

Then a smoke bomb exploded, billowing unbreathable fumes until all combatants had to scatter. But what elation that scramble contained and what stories were told back at Fisk as one protestor bandaged the next! While I practiced walking with my screwy hip, the students kept an eye on me and with a degree of respect. I liked it—nay, relished it—but smothered the gloat, for a Better God should not expect hymns composed and churches built in his honor. A Better God's body was but rungs up which one might climb toward victory, however one chose to define it.

Muslim protestors received little press. Nevertheless, I ran their circuit for months and came to appreciate their grit in the face of formidable odds, their unsnappable communal spirit, and most of all their lack of questions regarding who I was or why I'd chosen to support them. They accepted me because of the reference of Reverend Tucker, or Clifford Jackson, or whoever came next, and when I died for their cause, they were gracious but rarely worshipful, for they recognized the progress for what it was: just one more rung up a long, long ladder.

In February, Malcolm X was shot—and shot, and shot, and shot, ten times or more while delivering a speech in Manhattan. I'd hardly subscribed to his affronting doctrine; his recorded screeds, played on vinyl until I'd memorized every *the white man* this and *the white devil* that, had nearly made this Better God feel bad about his holy self. And yet, Reader, his murder drove me to the dankest mood. Like JFK, Malcolm X had achieved in one fateful second what I was being forced to crawl toward inch by inch—sainthood for people who were in the sorest need of a saint.

I wanted what he had. So it came to pass three weeks later outside a Chattanooga ghetto, while I prepared another program of march-and-martyr to go alongside a prison vigil, that a strutting adolescent volunteer in a taqiyah cap asked for my name to add to his attendant list. To him I debuted an alias becoming of a god who planned to be all things to all people.

"You may call me," declared I, "Zebulon X."

The kid raised an eyebrow. "Like Malcolm?"

"That is correct."

"You jivin' me?"

"Am I what, boy?"

"X replaces a slave name, you dig?"

"Dig? With one arm? Can't I have a different assignment?"

"You know you aren't black, right?"

Hadn't eighty-six years as unqualifiable "other" entitled me to make finer distinctions?

"My name," repeated I, "is Zebulon X."

The kid frowned, wrote it down, and walked away muttering, "Obnoxious White Motherfucker. *That* oughta be your name."

III.

ZEBULON X WAS NOT PRESENT at the "Bloody Sunday" of Dr. King's march from Selma to Montgomery, but what I saw on television was the Nashville brawl on a broader scale, as horsebacked, helmeted, gas-masked troopers rushed Alabama's Edmund Pettus Bridge, the hooves of the animals chopping down marchers so that stormtrooper boots could climb across the fallen and drag twisting bodies from tear-gas fog.

In Selma's aftermath I martyred frequently, but our rallies were brush fires. A Better God should engulf whole forests, which required larger numbers of viewers, which required, to be blunt, white folk, as the cameras, operated by other white folk, preferred them. By 1965, white college students had caught up not only to black music but black unrest, and associations to organize cross-state protests were cropping up like mushrooms, and so I isolated one of the most prominent—the Nonviolent Student Task Force, or NSTF—and paid a visit to the closest chapter in Cincinnati.

Located down the street from Xavier University, the office was an uninspiring one-story Craftsman house with slivering yellow paint and a handpainted signpost stabbed into lawn overgrowth. The sign was the size of a magazine with illegible lettering done by an artist who'd lost interest halfway through. For that reason I attributed it to the daydreaming teenager drifting about collecting a bouquet of dandelions. Dozens had been delicately tied together to form a tiara resting atop her head of long, straight blond hair. The craft must have taken hours, a constructive expenditure of time, I'm sure you'll agree, in such tumultuous times.

From behind pink-lensed sunglasses she noticed me.

"Oh, hello!"

Next she noticed my damaged flesh and missing arm. Her head listed in a childlike gesture of sympathy.

"Oh, wow. They've put you through the wringer."

"Who has?"

"They. The Man."

"And which man might that be?"

She sashayed on bare feet as if to a waltz only she could hear, her rumpled dress swishing about grass-stained calves. I had no idea what to make of this wood nymph. Her eyes were red and unfocused, but she looked sublimely happy, and when she reached me, she beamed. For one disciplined to expect the paradoxical reaction, it was disconcerting.

"I have come to speak to he who is in charge," said I.

"That would be Harvey."

"Is this Harvey in?"

She nodded, quickly like a little girl. A sweet scent wafted from her blowsy hair. I recognized it from my Harlem days, back when street peddlers called it "reefer." Modern youngsters called it "grass."

"But *you* can't see him," giggled she.

"No? And why not?"

"Because *you* don't have any *dandelions*."

She proffered her prized bouquet. I accepted the dirty weeds and headed up the stairs. I knocked, and though I could hear voices, no one answered.

"Just go in," called the girl. "There aren't any rules here."

A silkscreen of a man and woman in carnal embrace greeted me. The hum (I guessed it to be an orgy) originated from my left, and I passed through a hallway scattered with artifacts of dubious utility, from a feather-rimmed tambourine to a poster of a homely, jug-eared boy above the slogan WHAT, ME WORRY?

The living room was occupied by five young people cross-legged upon a wine-stained rug, eyes shut, wrists suspended as if from wire, and chanting "Om" over the sitar sounds of a band an LP cover identified as the Yardbirds. The poor meditators had been hit by a tornado of ghastly fashions. Their clothing was more unkempt than that of the nymph, and all of them, even the girls, were clad like cow-pokes in dungarees. I evaluated my latest ensemble of single-breasted slubbed-silk suit, tapered trousers, and square-toed leather step-ins, and rather missed the snappily dressed Nation of Islam.

But where else had I to run? I tapped the record player with my toe, and the needle skipped to the silent center. Gradually the om-ing abated. Ten eyes fluttered open. I tossed the dandelions onto a spot between their knees as in medieval times I might have tossed a slain bear.

"I have come," proclaimed I, "to assist you in your cause."

They blinked at the bouquet, knuckled their eyes, and yawned.

"Right on," said a girl. "Which cause?"

Why must everyone badger me with particulars? I surveyed the room for clues. Through the cloud of cobalt smoke, I made out scattered titles from the books piled floor-to-window, but they were words I did not understand: *Siddhartha, Steppenwolf, Dharma Bums, Ashtanga Yoga*. Tacked onto the wall, however, was an image I knew: Marlon Brando, leathered and astride a motorcycle, from a film

called *The Wild One* I'd watched on Mrs. White's Zenith. Brando
had a good quip in that picture, and, feeling desperate, I appropriated
it, hoping I could pull off the actor's jaded detachment. What was my
cause, they asked?

"Whaddya got?"

One of the meditators snorted. He brushed incense ash from
his jeans and stood. He was freckled, wide-sideburned, an inch taller
than I (ineligible for Project Mercury, Rigby would have pointed out),
and topped with a globe of hennaed hair pushed to absurd heights by
a red bandana. He held out a hand for me to shake, except with his
forearm cocked upward and his hand open as if inviting me to arm
wrestle. I made the awkward fit, and he gave our fist-lock a shake.

He gestured with his head—his ball of hair waggled—and
walked through another disheveled corridor before entering a room
reassuring for its desk, table, and file cabinets. He lit a joint and
inhaled. He spoke while suppressing the smoke.

"So you met Janice. Far-out chick, huh?"

"She wasn't that far out. Only the front yard."

He continued to hold the inhale.

"So lay it on me, brother. What's your name?"

"Zebulon X."

"Harvey Scheinberg." He exhaled and held out the joint. "You
want a hit?"

I gestured at the gash in my neck. Scheinberg whistled.

"The Man fucked you up good, huh?"

This Man again! Who was this unfriendly phantom?

"What slot he stick you in?" asked Scheinberg.

"Slot?"

"You know, man. Army, Navy, what?"

Oh-ho! The Man was the government! I'd suss this slang yet!

"Marine Corps," replied I. Decades after the fact, the words spilled like blood, my frigid tongue warmed by memories of Church, the deluge of death, the eked survival of a contemptible species. "Seventh Regiment, Third Battalion."

Scheinberg slapped a sloppy stack of folders.

"We had two Marines in last week. You wouldn't believe the shit they said. Or maybe you would. I'm talking atrocities miles past any Geneva Convention bullshit. And not from NVA or VC either. I'm talking American grunts skinning rice farmers alive. Vietnamese women being raped by whole platoons. 'Ears for beers'—you bring back the most enemy ears, the other squad buys the beer. It was SOP, man, Standard Operating Procedure. They learned it in murder training—that's what I call boot camp—and now it's all up in their wiring. Really bummed me out. You see any of that kind of shit over there?"

"Yes," lied I. "It, ah, bummed me out as well."

He flapped the smoke aside to better see me.

"Zebulon X, huh? Didn't you work with the SCLC? Or the NAACP?"

Fie, acronyms, fie! I tendered a noncommittal shrug.

"Didn't know you were white," mused he. "Or a vet."

Harvey Scheinberg might have overindulged in grass, but when he focused his eyes, they gleamed like those of a shrewd plumber eager to dismantle a rusty lattice of outdated pipes. He scrutinized my straight-laced suit as well as my hairstyle, trapped forever in an 1890s crop instead of the Beatles-inspired shag favored by every other male in the house.

"You for real, man?"

I sputtered my best scoff. "Real? Why, I am the realest!"

"Yeah? I'm picking up weird vibes."

Scheinberg snapped forward in his chair. "Tell me who Willie Pete is."

Iron bars clamped down over the windows and doors. The jig was up! Willie Pete, thought I, my mind whirling, might be an important Marine Corps general, or perhaps a soldier who sacrificed his life for his squad, or maybe a member of the Yardbirds. Ever the gambler, I was willing to make a wild guess, but my hesitation damned me.

"White phosphorus, man!" cried Scheinberg. "You're telling me you were in the Corps and you don't know what phosphorus is?"

"I . . . We didn't . . ."

Scheinberg adored being the smartest chap in the room, that much was clear. He laughed, leaned back, plopped his bare feet atop the table, centered his ashtray on his stomach, and took a derisive tone.

"Well, let me lay some heavy-duty facts on you, man. White phosphorus, Willie Pete, is a nifty little cocktail your Marine Corps buddies are exploding inside Vietcong tunnels, and what it does, man, is burn up all the oxygen and smoke them out. But what's really groovy about it is it burns up clothes and skin pretty good too. Except what I hear, from Marines, man, actual real-life Marines, is it's not just the VC getting to know Willie Pete. It's innocent people, whole villages, children running around with their skin peeling off." Scheinberg pointed his joint at me—he was having a blast! "You're an infiltrator, aren't you? Republican peckerwood. I should've known by the monkey suit and company-man haircut."

That was far enough. I worked for no man—including *the* Man. I bashed my fist to the table. A file folder jumped.

412

"Look here, Muttonchops! It is true that the majority of my injuries are nonmilitary in origin. That I admit. But I *am* Zebulon X and I *can* provide character endorsements and I *will* be of use to the NSTF, if only you desist this pointless cat-and-mouse!"

Scheinberg scrubbed fingers through facial hair and studied me.

"Fine, let's rap. Basic shit. You dig what's going on in Vietnam, right?"

Truth be told, I lived in perplexity over how an insignificant Indochinese nation could act as a breaking wheel upon which the United States was stretched. All that said, I'd spied my share of sloganeering and so gave one of them a test.

"'Better to Fight Communism on the Mekong Than the Mississippi.'"

"'Better Saigon Than San Diego,'" chanted Scheinberg. "C-minus, man. Here, let me simplify: North Vietnam bad, South Vietnam good. It's called Domino Theory. One Asian country goes Red, then the next, and the next, and suddenly they're in Honolulu, they're in San Francisco."

"Ah. Yes. A theory most sound!"

"What? No, man! Where's your head? That's the bullshit they're feeding us. You really think we ought to be escalating this shit? Bring in Russia, bring in China, get atomic?"

Scheinberg tossed his spliff and leapt to his feet. The Zen master of the living room had vanished, and now he jabbed fingers at me, at the earth beneath his feet, at the world outside our window.

"But that's just what we're doing, man. They're about to double the draft. *Double* it. We'll have two hundred thousand troops in Nam by New Year's, and we still haven't declared war. Did you know that? We're all living in LBJ's fantasy-land. Is this Alice in Wonderland?

Eat this cake, we'll get smaller? Eat that one, we'll get bigger? No, man, it's just time to stop eating cake! We need to settle with Ho Chi Minh, get our troops out, and get hip to what's going on here in America. That's what the NSTF is all about, man. We want to pull this country's lips off the three-titted beast of Father, Son, and Holy Ghost: one, backward-thinking higher ed; two, minority-abusing big business; and three, the goddamn *child*-killing, *woman*-raping, *nature*-destroying *federal fucking government!*"

From the meditation room, wild applause. Scheinberg's face had gone the color of his bandana, but instead of him looking foolish, I found him to be rather warriorlike; it was easy to envision him taking a fire-hose to the chin without shrinking, even as his hedge of hair soddened and sank. He panted and stared, waiting for a reply by which to reckon my merit.

Eons ago, the Astonishing Mr. Stick saved himself from the Barker by drawing from the archive of quotes he'd absorbed during his school years. One such quote came to me now, and before I spoke it, I acknowledged its source—our sixth president, John Quincy Adams, the namesake of bootlegger John Quincy, who, I had to imagine, would have been a protestor far quieter but every bit as fearless as this Harvey Scheinberg.

"'America does not go abroad in search of monsters to destroy. She is the well-wisher to the freedom and independence of all.'"

A sly smile softened Scheinberg's face. He gave a chuckle. "That noose around your neck. That's a great gimmick."

He moved to an open trunk and began rifling through it.

"Some martyr act, right? That's your bit?"

So impressed had I become with this fellow's grasp of politics that I felt an inferior's sudden need to justify his own work.

414

"The history of martyrs," crowed I, "goes hand-in-hand with struggles of the oppressed. Why do martyrs die? Because they hold views that those in power—the Man, if you like—consider disruptive. Take, for instance, Mary, Queen of England, the infamous Bloody Mary, so allegiant to the Pope that she overturned her father's reformations and executed—"

Scheinberg patted the air, tamping my embers before they could ignite.

"Look, man, Zebulon X, whatever, I'm so stoned, I can barely dig what you're saying. I surrender, all right? One thing NSTF always needs is bodies. Think you can be ready tomorrow?"

He tossed the object he'd fished from the trunk across the room. I caught it against my chest with my arm. It was a bright yellow hard hat, the sort favored by construction workers. It had come up against the Man before; its surface was scuffed and dented. Experimentally, I placed it upon my head. It was no Knapp-Felt fedora of my Roaring Twenties, yet I found that it straightened my spine. The helmet, to put it simply, had weight.

"Good, it fits," said Scheinberg. "You're gonna need it."

IV.

I F YOU'VE SPENT TIME ON this planet, Dearest Reader, your ears perk up the second you hear the bass line (*bom, bom, bom, bom-bom bom-bom*), after one lap joined by jingle-bells (*zhing, zhing, zhing, zhing-zhing, zhing-zhing*), until the big brass blurt (*BOMP*) gets you tapping your toe (*BOMP*), even if yours has been chewed up (*BOMP*) by a Saint Bernard (*BOMP*), because now you're anticipating the teasing backbeat (*cracka-cracka*) which means the voice (*cracka-cracka*), that crystal croon of folksy soulfulness (*cracka-cracka*), is about to begin.

> *Old Mr. Finch, he swung low from a tree*
> *But he stood back up, just as fine as one can be. We said . . .*
> *"Hey, Mr. Finch, how 'bout you rest your weary head?"*
> *But he only smiled and laughed, "I got bigger plans instead,*
> *instead, instead—"*

The first time I heard it warble from the transistor radio of a student demonstrator, I picked up the battery-operated gadget (the owner was busy "making out" with his girl) and absconded about the sidewalks of the university's quad, speaker to my ear, sputtering with incredulity, my energetic canter making the noose about my neck frolic like a horse's tail. Was this deliriously catchy song about me? Why, it had to be!

416

Old Mr. Finch (ooh-ooh),
How many roads will you walk? (ooh-ooh)
No bullet or rope or club, man (yeah, yeah)
Will keep him from another drop (yeah, yeah)
Because Old Mr. Finch keeps ramblin' on . . .

After the last chorus concluded with an artillery of hand claps loud enough to distort the radio, the DJ identified the group as the Beau-Ts, presented by a label called Motown, and noted that the tune had just broken the Billboard Hot 100. So desperately did I require more information that I resigned myself to the awkward transaction of buying a copy of *Ebony* magazine, which promised, beneath a big photo of Negro lovebirds Diahann Carroll and Sidney Poitier, an article titled "CAN ANYTHING STOP THE MOTOWN HIT MACHINE?"

The Beau-Ts merited a single paragraph, in which they were described as a trio of childhood friends whose first single, "The Ballad of Old Mr. Finch," was, at press time, inching up the pop charts. Said Motown honcho Berry Gordy, the Beau-Ts had every bit the talent—and photogenic figures!—of top girl groups like the Vandellas and the Supremes. Why "the Beau-Ts?" Easy, said Gordy. The title came from their alliterative surnames: Miss Linda Triplett, Miss Debra Toney, and the baby of the group, Little Miss Bunny Tucker.

The strutting shrimp had made it big! Bunny's lead vocal on "The Ballad of Old Mr. Finch" was indisputable; not two years had passed since Biloxi. I was flabbergasted, though, by the stamp-sized photograph of the Beau-Ts worked into a Motown collage. With her bell-shaped wig, fake eyelashes, caked makeup, and shimmering gown (all matched by her bandmates), Bunny looked a decade older than the scrawny preteen I recalled.

Too bad for me, NSTF altruists were incurious when it came to anything outside their pursuit of egalitarian rights, and that included music lacking overt antiwar content. I might have broken down and bragged about my musical renown if Scheinberg hadn't hurried me out of state to prove myself at a packed schedule of sit-ins, teach-ins, and be-ins. (Sorry, Reader, I can't explain that last one.) Most originated at tumbledown communes where nymphs similar to Janice gathered crops from sickly organic gardens while male counterparts plucked guitars and praised the girls' groovy energy before running their hands up the girls' legs and asking if they wanted to go "turn on."

Who was there for societal progress and who was there for the sexual smorgasbord was beyond the purview of a Better God, no matter how wild I was driven by all of the exposed flesh engaging in acts I hadn't enjoyed since Wilma Sue. A Better God, I told myself, only cared that the predominantly white NSTF drew crowds by the hundreds. Frenzied by Scheinberg's hot-tempered tirades, provoked by pugnacious police, and emotionally emancipated by opiates and hallucinogens, the faithful were quite obliging in helping me pull off public deaths that, with soberer eyes, might have felt to them like murder. They dug my act. By reminding them of the war's high stakes, my offings seemed to inspire to higher volumes both their chants and their word-of-mouth appreciation.

In Bloomington, Indiana, I was dragged by a horse like the martyr Hippolytus in 235 AD. In Ames, Iowa, I was buried alive like the martyr Hendrik Pruijt in 1574 AD. In Burlington, Vermont, I raced past lines of knife-wielding young people as if I were the martyrs Saturninus, Secundulus, and Satur in 304 AD. And with each new death, what brought me back quickest was the need to find a radio and monitor the journey of "The Ballad of Old Mr. Finch" up the

418

charts: Number eighty-two, Number fifty-five, Number twenty-four. Bunny's song, just like Zebulon X himself, kept on ramblin' on.

I hoped that game-show guest host John Glenn was watching— Spin the Wheel of Misfortune had become a full-time gig. Over the next year I fashioned my own Dark Ages inside the Age of Aquarius, a one-man Roman Inquisition with myself playing every juicy role, from heretic victim to grand inquisitor, testifier, jailer, torturer, and executioner. By the time Scheinberg convinced me to join a White House picket line, I was certain that I would one day attain the martyr milestone of the Huguenots, slaughtered by the thousands in 1572 by Roman Catholics, until Parisian gutters gurgled red with French Calvinist blood. These lurid details fired my imagination better than any of Scheinberg's politicking.

The scene in Washington astounded me. I could no longer regard NSTF's marching as trumped-up bellyaching; it had evolved into the type of movement not seen in America since we'd broken with the Brits. Twenty thousand demonstrators mobbed Pennsylvania Avenue, including sitting politicians and yodeling singer-songwriters like Judy Collins and Phil Ochs, who incited their fans to climb atop cop cars, link arms, and sing right through the thrown eggs and coffee that soon made their T-shirt slogans unreadable.

It was a circus complete with mimes, jugglers, stilt-walkers, face-painters, and, around two in the afternoon, a fun-for-the-whole-family martyrdom. I was introduced as usual with a short speech, often from Scheinberg himself, who would extrapolate upon some morsel of martyr esoterica I'd mentioned in passing, ad libbing the whole thing, powered by an engine that burned rage like oil. Scheinberg was no velvet-throated Barker; the amps sizzled and smoked at his spitting sibilance and distorted decibels.

"Back before *this* war, before the *last* war, before the war before *that*, back in ye olde 1508, there was a Mr. Whittenham, who they called a 'chancellor,' and I don't have to *explain* to you cats what that means! It means he was one of the pigs! And he had in his pig hooves a woman who wouldn't vomit back the hateful bile he poured down her throat, who stood up for *justice* and freedom of *thought*, and this Whittenham, this *Piggenham*, he burned this woman at the stake. But what our own martyr, Zebulon X, taught me is that all pigs get butchered in the end, you dig? While this good woman was burning, see, a bull broke loose and horned Mr. Piggenham right in the gut and ran around with his intestines until his *vile, stinking, fascist shit* was all over the goddamn courtyard! What does that mean for us? Well, let's work it out, man! *We're* the bull, our *protest* is our horns, and *Piggenham* is warmongering America, and it's their guts we're going to drag around the whole country until people *smell the shit* and *start paying attention!*"

Even I became riled by such words. It became difficult to see my body of lacerations, burns, and gouges as anything but proof of a historical ordeal. When Scheinberg finished and the crowd took up the chant of *HEY, HEY, LBJ, HOW MANY KIDS DID YOU KILL TODAY?* I did my thing, and whether spectators believed it to be an act or authentic was of niggling import. The point was that they were moved by what I did, yet moved toward something larger than me, and instead of feeling cheated, I felt inspired. There was a strange sort of satisfaction in contributing to a neighbor's struggle without personal payoff; I believe they call this a sense of "community."

My martyrdom that April afternoon was a crucifixion done upside-down in the style of the Apostle Peter, who'd insisted he didn't deserve the same death as Jesus. That specific concern I did not share—certainly I was superior to Nazareth's one-hit-wonder!—nor did it bother student protestors, who tended toward a generalized we-are-all-connected spirituality. If Zebulon X died, a part of them died, too; so, too, died the soldier in Vietnam; so, too, did his Vietnamese analogue; so, too, did the American Dream that could not be worth such suffering. I was the conduit to these personal epiphanies, and I will not lie. It felt good.

As "The Ballad of Old Mr. Finch" hit Number eleven in August, NSTF attained top velocity with a three-day vigil commemorating an event close to my cold heart: the twentieth anniversary of Hiroshima and Nagasaki. Nighttime candles created uncountable shadows, and in each I hunted for the Millennialist to no avail; he'd been chased away, I felt certain, by the Fifty-One, content at last that I was making good use of my death. A day later, we hung antiwar banners across train tracks that transported drafted soldiers, which landed dozens of us in handcuffs. Two days after that, a black man was beaten by a pig in full view of friends, and the city exploded into riots. It was Watts, California, the same place from which I'd rescued Merle in 1941 and murdered her morphine dealer, Sandy, but by the time NSTF got there, the rebellion had petered out and the crumbling two-story building in which I'd found Merle was no longer available for nostalgic sightseeing. It had, like most relics of my past, been burned to the ground.

V.

I QUIT HEARING "THE BALLAD OF Old Mr. Finch." Disappointing, but I awaited the Beau-Ts' sophomore smash. The airwaves, however, had forsaken resplendent harmonies in favor of fuzzy psychedelics that brought to my mind images of a cobra swaying, perhaps to strike, perhaps just to salivate crudely. *Baby, light my fire*, these songs begged, *before we paint the windows black, because then who knows? We might just see for miles and miles and miles.*

Scheinberg's source was right on. Troop numbers in Nam had redoubled to a staggering four hundred thousand. For protestors, it made for a source of inexhaustible fuel. NSTF activists dropped out of school, took to the streets, and spread the bad word in the form of basement-printed bulletins called "undergrounds" with titles like *Berkeley Barb, Free Student, Angry City Press, News from Nowhere, Partisan, Rat,* and my personal pick, *Fuck You.* These were disseminated in every major city and, like the Dr. Whistler handbills of old, kept readers in the know of all the hippest happenings, mine included.

Booking me at your protest event became as de rigueur as hiring a clown for your child's birthday party, except rather than party hats and balloons, I came equipped with spears, knives, rods, whips, projectiles, and other festive thingamabobs. I began to receive invitations from bodies as diverse as Rising Up Angry (blue-collar unionists),

422

the Young Patriots (disenfranchised white migrants), the Young Lords (prideful Puerto Ricans), La Huelga (Chicano crusaders), Redstockings (leftist ladies), and the Young Socialist Alliance (Trotskyist agitators). The selfless young people among whom I existed had taught me that a Better God should not choose favorites. I accepted every invite, which sent Scheinberg into a hard-hat-hurling huff.

"You can't lose focus now!" cried he. "The NSTF is building a major rep, man! We'll be bigger than the SDS by '68, bigger than the SNCC by '69! We're going to change the world, you gotta believe that, but first we brothers have to stay brothers! I thought me and you were grooving to the same wavelength!"

The lingo had developed, but the message was identical to what Luca Testa had delivered while feeding me lamb brains the night we'd met: *Have your fun, kid, but step outside my boundaries, and be sorry.* But I'd changed since then, too; bullets no longer scared me. I was a free agent, and Scheinberg, as the kids liked to say, could suck an egg.

For nine decades, Reader, I'd been caught at seventeen, but the cliché about a stopped clock is true. Seventeen was, at last, the ideal age to be. Teenagers had seized college campuses, entire towns, the totality of public discourse, and they'd done so thanks to Rigby's generation, who'd had marathons of missionary sex after World War II and ejected a shockwave of babies now matured enough to punish their begetters' sins.

The so-called generation gap was a crevasse so deep, it might swallow us all. Every event at which I martyred was a-crawl with babbling, overdrugged, would-be prophets hocking their typed-and-stapled manifestos. Helping these young searchers had become my Grâl, and like Udo von Lüth and Otto Rahn, I would continue seeking it in the peaks and swales of every death. I dug deep into

Foxe's Book of Martyrs and got creative, sewing myself inside fresh animal skins like the martyrs of early AD Rome so that wild dogs would have at me; cinching myself inside a bag of imported scorpions like Julian of Antioch; sitting upon a red-hot metal throne like Saint Blandina; and being shot through with arrows like Sebastian of Milan. My pain released that of those who watched me. You only had to see their faces to know it.

These ragtag public-park pilgrims claimed to be blind to skin color yet adored colorful costuming. Whenever a martyrdom ruined my wardrobe, a gypsy sort was there to donate cooler threads, and by and by I looked less like an undercover pig and more like a "hippie," adding to my aviator shades, noose necklace, and hard hat a regalia of tie-dye tees, baggy ponchos, and moccasins—Reader, judgeth me not! At NASA, no fellowship had been offered me. Among the hippies, fellowship overflowed, and these were the colors and textures of their world in which I walked, died, and resurrected, and it felt as natural as air, as song, as war.

One benefit of this looser brand of clothing was the ease with which it came off. I'd have liked to shake the hand of the playboy genius who'd inserted "free love" into the Movement's platform! Pretty coeds who in earlier years would have held out for an Ivy League wedding got fresh with on-the-dole dropouts. Reputations were for "good girls"—and what, in a world of unremitting slaughter, was good if not one's own body?

If I had only had the pecker with which to participate! Nay, I scolded myself, even if Bridey Valentine had showed up with my manhood in a handbag and a Triangulino with my scrotum in a change purse, I'd still have forced myself to demur. The hippies had been good to me, better than anyone else in a very long time, and for that I owed them a Better God's chastity. That didn't mean they needed know of whom I dreamt at night: my Wilma Sue, whose two arms, two legs, and two breasts were more sensual, soothing, and secure than any magnitude of hippie harem.

Silence remained Zebulon X's chief character trait, and I typically sat alone while others plotted, partied, and porked. One such lonely winter night took place following a Pittsburgh "love-in," at which my martyrdom had been outshined by the release of hundreds of kites, bubbles, and balloons. The whole thing had put me in an offish mood, as I'd been hired by Vietnam Veterans Against the War, a wobbly crew of ex-soldiers on crutches, in wheelchairs, and, like me, missing limbs. As it happened, our event had intersected with an NSTF march, and beyond our singsong of "L-O-V-E," I could hear the fanatic bullhorning of Harvey Scheinberg.

That night the smoke was thick, not from grass but from the incinerations of Selective Service draft cards by conscientious objectors (or cowering cowards, were you less charitably inclined). The passion of the participants brought to mind the book-burning of the *Hitlerjugend*, and troubled by the parallels, I walked across the unlit park and found a bench. The smoke drifted my way, and so I didn't see Scheinberg until he sat next to me, knocking back an Iron City Ale.

His hair had buckled beneath its own height to drop as a thick cape over his shoulders. A full beard had absorbed his muttonchops, and despite the cold he went bare-chested but for a moonstone upon a leather strap. His serene eyes followed the paths of invisible fireflies as he offered up a piece of wax paper upon which was adhered squares of gelatin printed with rainbow-colored peace symbols. I shook my head; was I the only one who saw the symbol's resemblance to swastikas?

"LSD, not LBJ," encouraged he.

"There is no point."

"Will you just drop the acid, man? It's only three hundred mikes."

To shut him up, I peeled off a peace sign and centered it upon my dry tongue.

"You got to make time to mellow out, man. Acid ought to be your trip. That and mescaline. There's a lot more exploring to be done *in here"*—he tapped his temple—"than *up there."* He pointed at the stars.

It was what I needed to hear. The day's papers had led with news from Cape Canaveral. Gus Grissom had burned to death in a launchpad fire along with two copilots. Grissom had been among my least favorite Astros, and yet I couldn't shake his death. I checked the stars Scheinberg had referenced and wondered if the hippies were right that fellow humans were the only bodies worth understanding. Scheinberg sighed.

"You're such a bring-down, man. There's a real scene to be experienced, right in front of your face, and one day you'll be sorry you didn't get high on all of it."

His breath plumed white into the black night. Mine, of course, did not.

"What do you think?" posed I. "Will it work?"

"The acid?"

"The marching. The speeches. All of it."

"Why not, man? America's gotta change sometime."

The tab was sharp on my tongue. Everything that night was sharp.

"But what if America is already dead? Putridity is irreversible."

Scheinberg crushed his beer can and hurled it.

"You need to put a microscope to your mind, man. How many times do you do your death act every week? I wish you did it with my group, for sure, but that doesn't mean I don't still dig what you do. You *know* there's hope, man. You *know* there's love. So many people can't be dying for nothing at all. You don't seem interested in chicks. You're square as a box when it comes to dope. Why else would you even being doing this shit if you didn't believe?"

Because of a personal vendetta against Gød?

"I suppose I'm not making sense," said I.

"You burn your draft card? I did." Scheinberg blinked. "Whoa. I think I'm freaking out."

I owned one burnable thing—myself—and was too afraid to burn it.

"I don't have a draft card," said I.

"Already torched it, huh? See, man, you get it. *You get it.*" He held up a hand. "You see that? Inside my hand? There's a little boy in there. He's got bright red wings. It's three-million o'clock. Okay, I'm definitely freaking out."

He needed the bench more than I. I stood, removed the crocheted yarn vest I'd inherited from a beneficent bohemian, and used it as a blanket for the underdressed iconoclast. He did not resist, lying flat as a board and gawping at the stars with reverence. There was no question that he saw what I could not, in celestial objects, yes, but also in other people's splendid potentials and beautiful failures.

427

I'd seen glimpses—with Church, the Whites, the hippies—but reliable human connection remained, for me, elusive. I spat the dry acid, turned away, and listened for the patches of merrymaking in the park so that I might skirt them on my way out.

"What do you see?" gasped Scheinberg.

I jumped. He'd startled me.

"Blackness," said I.

"That'll change," laughed he. "You wait long enough, the colors will come."

VI.

A S MALCOLM LITTLE HAD BECOME Malcolm X and Zebulon Finch had become Zebulon X, boxing champ Cassius Clay repudiated his given name to become Cassius X. Shortly thereafter he adopted a full Muslim name, Muhammad Ali, and under it refused on religious grounds to accept military induction, declaring in his trademark dog-growl that he'd rather go to jail than shoot innocent women and children.

It shook the ground. Before Ali's attestation, I had rarely seen black and white protestors intermingle, the former camp resentful over the 2-S draft deferments monopolized by white collegians, and the latter skittish about, to be blunt, blacks with guns. Now whites were reassessing the Nation of Islam as a potential ally. Why not, thought I, the Better God? Both groups wished to abolish racism, mistrusted Middle America, and believed that stopping the Vietnam War was the only hope of fixing the U.S.A.

Martin Luther King Jr.'s April 15, 1967, march was the largest demonstration to which I'd been invited, and I accepted, though I did so through a sensation of hardening cement. The colors Scheinberg had promised had yet to show. In this time of dynamic change, was I merely going through the motions? Four hundred thousand dissidents paraded from New York's Central Park to United Nations headquarters, and King cried, "If America's soul becomes totally poisoned, part of the autopsy must read Vietnam." I marched along, foot after foot, imagining my own autopsy. It would look much like America's: flesh that had turned too quickly for someone so young and now emulsified at the brink of spoil.

The UN march begat a litter of ancillary bazaars. My services had been obligated to a bold coproduction of the Students for a Democratic Society and a burgeoning, already infamous Negro group called the Black Panthers, who advocated for any and all brands of violence if it ensured the safety and advancement of Negroes. I was duly intimidated the instant I wiggled past a rampart of billyclubbed pigs and onto the repurposed parking lot. Rank-and-file Panthers stood at attention in martial tiers holding emblemed flags, clad in the enviably sleek attire of waist-length black leather jackets, powderblue turtlenecks, and insouciant berets. Trimmings included dark sunglasses, bandoliers of ammo, and rifles packed by everyone down to the Panthers stationed on adjacent rooftops, ready for the worst.

Only once I was confident that a bullet hailstorm was not in the forecast did I survey the goings-on. Dearest Reader, I hardly recognized it as America! Old Glory had been swapped for pennants of red, black, and green, beneath which Negroes in splendiferous dashikis and turbans sold shell necklaces and tiger-skin epaulets while negotiating in Swahili. A pair of men proselytized an exodus from Amerika—that's how it was spelled on their fliers—for Algeria, the "motherland of Pan-Africanism." The backbone of the scene was a semicircle of drummers pounding Zulu rhythms while women moved their sweaty bodies in a loose-jointed dance.

But do not think that this ebony Eden sold only sunny notions. The inspirational gospel choruses of my early martyrdoms had been

430

supplanted by a chilling chant to the beat of the drums: "The Rev-olution has co-ome! / Off the pigs! / Time to pick up the gu-un! / Off the pigs!" When it finished, the speaker at the podium lifted his rifle above his head with one hand, and his voice cracked so loudly, I ducked, believing the rooftop militia had opened fire.

"Lyndon B. Johnson's Amerika," bellowed he, "is about to learn the difference between two million niggers and two million *armed* niggers!"

Hundreds of black-gloved Black Power fists jutted into the air. I was perplexed by how much it stirred me until I noticed the logo affixed to the speaker's podium. It was, you see, a black fist, almost identical to the Black Hand logo I'd drawn on the extortion letters that had gotten me murdered. Was my journey here, to this specific place at this specific time, cosmic kismet? One of the few things I still possessed, after all, was a fist. I held it before me, studied the wounds of fishing hook, embedded tooth, and barbecue skewer. Once upon a time, I'd punched with this fist.

What might I do with it now?

That I, the Better God, had begun to lose my way galled me, and the speediest cure was to track down the SDS organizer and get going on today's death. My path, however, was impeded by a riffraff of Panther women bobbing to a fresh chant: "No more brothers in ja-il, / The pigs are gonna catch he-ll." I muttered beneath nonexis-tent breath and elbowed through until the path was obstructed by a young lady with a clipboard writing down each protestor's blood type—a stark reminder of the pigs and their clubs. Well, the lass would get nowhere with my cold innards! I gave her a woodpecker tap upon the back and said, in my most exasperated voice, "*Excuse me, girl.*"

She about-faced in a sudden swoop both feminine and combative, lips pursed for, presumed I, a heavy peppering of the word "cracker." But instead her unpainted lips parted; indeed, every hostile line of her face softened. I, too, felt my own umbrage melt before I could identify the reason. The girl's big brown eyes were fixed upon the noose about my neck as if she recognized it, which, of course, she did.

"Bunny?" sputtered I.

The chant grew in ferocity until Bunny and I, frozen in a shared stare of disbelief, began to be knocked about by the chanters. She snatched me by the wrist and led me through the hot press of bodies; I could but stumble behind and follow the bounce of her two-foot-wide Afro. Better that than meet the looks coming at us like wasps: she black, I white; she beautiful, I ugly. Alongside a broken chain-link fence, she dropped my wrist, took a step back, and indulged in a good, long, comprehensive gander, while I did the same.

Bunny Tucker had been an artless fourteen when I'd met her. Now she was my age, a foot taller, and settled into one hell of a figure, even while her face had preserved its puckish pudge. What best bolstered her grown-up semblance was that she was dressed, as her fellow Panthers might say, like a bad-ass motherfucker: knee-high boots, short black dress, and long leather coat. She adjusted the huge round sunglasses speared into her hair, bringing me to recall how, the last time I'd seen her, the hair had been in pigtails, and I'd pulled them. It embarrassed me; I spoke to alleviate myself.

"You . . . have changed a great deal."

She shook her head in wonderment. "You sure haven't."

"Looks," said I, "can deceive."

To my surprise, she smirked. "Zebulon X, huh?"

My chagrin, soaring already, doubled. She laughed.

"That's all right. I've got a new name too."

She extended a slender brown arm.

"Jolami Tiombe, pleased to meet you."

I glanced at the Black Panther sentries and swore that their statue faces had angled our way. Bunny, though, courageous as ever, deserved a corresponding response. While her palm heated my icicle fingers, I pictured Abigail Finch zeroing in on our black-and-white handshake through Satan's periscope and promptly rolling over in her grave.

"At least my name," said I, "is simple to say."

"Don't worry. Old friends are allowed to call me Bunny."

Despite the angry chants cracking between city surfaces, Bunny beamed. It was both perplexing and wonderful, and I felt bereft when she covered her face with the clipboard.

"What is it?" I asked.

"It's just—you're a strange memory. It's hard to believe you're real. Even though I've been reading about you in newsletters."

"You wrote a song about me. That alone makes me real."

"You don't hate me for it?"

"To the contrary, I consider it the music industry's finest hour!"

The clipboard dropped to reveal eyes glossed by held tears.

"When you did what you did, when I was little." She grasped for words. "It . . . was the only magical thing that ever happened to me."

One might watch one million feet of Black Panther film footage and never suspect that in any of the militants existed such vulnerabilities. My dead flesh felt stabbed; it hurt more than any martyrdom, and I blustered it aside.

"Preposterous! What of the Beau-Ts? Your tour bus must be a magic carpet!"

She smiled sadly. "Do I look like I'm still in the group?"

Just as Bunny was no Mississippi ragamuffin, neither was she the gowned and bouffanted Beau-T last seen in the pages of *Ebony*. Her defection should have been obvious, and I gestured an apology for my brain, imprudent as ever.

"It's all right. It was fun at first, it really was. I had my best girlfriends, Linda and Debbie, and we spent all our time sewing matching outfits and rehearsing songs by Petula Clark and the Shangri-Las. Daddy—you remember Reverend Tucker—well, he hated it, called it the devil's music. Then I wrote that song, you know? Just that one song. And there was a talent contest in New Orleans, and there was this Motown scout there, and they put out the single and then, yeah, like you said, the three of us were on the road, getting tutored on the bus all day and doing shows all night, opening up for the Temptations and the Marvelettes. I'm not going to lie. It was a dream come true. Before the Panthers, how else were three little black girls going to make good?"

"I confess that I did wonder why there was no second song."

"Oh, there was a second song. And a third, and a fourth. See, 'Old Mr. Finch' only got to Number eleven. Between Number eleven and Number ten, there's a Grand Canyon your whole career can get lost inside. Motown tried to rearrange our whole action. They wanted Debbie to sing lead. She was prettier, I guess, light-skinned. What was I going to do, argue? They wouldn't let me write anything, and all they gave us were boo-hooers. 'My boyfriend done left me, what am I going to do,' all that foolishness."

It made perfect if demoralizing sense. If a powerful force like Bridey Valentine couldn't escape being cast as "the Girl," what hope had young Bunny Tucker?

"Start over," suggested I. "Surely you made piles of money."

"You're old and wise about some stuff, Zebulon X, but other stuff, you're younger than me. Hell no, I didn't make no money. Daddy was right about that. We never had lawyers. We signed whatever they told us to sign. Poor Linda couldn't even read. Before I left, this blind singer, real smart kid named Stevie Wonder, he broke it down for me. He told me I was making half a damn penny for every record we sold, minus taxes, minus packaging. Shit, the only real money we ever made was from session work, five bucks a day in a hot-as-hell studio while guitar players pinched our behinds."

Every crystal fantasy I'd fostered regarding Bunny's life now grinded beneath my feet like shattered glass. If the last several years had taught me anything, it was that the only shortcuts America offered were just that, short-lived and cutting enough that you'd bleed all the way down the trail.

"So you gave it up?"

Bunny jammed her hands into her jacket pockets.

"Yeah, well, there's only so much disrespect a woman can take. When Dick Clark dumped us from the Caravan of Stars, I had to look in the mirror, you know? What was I doing wearing wigs and lashes, padding my bra with falsies? Why was I putting up with makeup ladies who didn't know a thing about brown skin? Motown had us at charm school learning to talk white, eat white, act white. I tried to get Debbie and Linda to leave, too, but they were scared. We'd always been a group, right? They couldn't see themselves as individual women anymore, and I'll tell you what—that scared me more than anything."

"Nevertheless," said I, "it is a leap from Motown to the Panthers."

Her dour lips curled to a grin.

How was it possible, thought I, that Debbie was considered the pretty one?

"You can blame my brother for that. You remember Ritchie?"

"It is hard to forget such pure, concentrated loathing."

"Don't take it personal. Ritchie hates everyone. The whole time I was off singing, he was in jail, and every time I phoned him, he was going off about this group or that, the Garveyites one week, the Urban League the next, but I never paid it any mind. I had songs about boyfriends to sing, right?"

"Jail, eh? Do I want to know what he did?"

"I guess you can ask him yourself. Here he comes."

I pirouetted in the direction of her gesture. Fifty feet away, plowing straight through an otherwise zigzagging crowd, was Ritchie Tucker. The preceding three years he wore far more heavily than his sister. Though but in his mid-twenties, he'd lost half his hair in strips so irregular, it looked as if it had been yanked with duct tape. His face, meanwhile, was pocked from either acne or disease, and his jaundiced eyes had only bulged further from their sockets. With black leather gloves he adjusted his beret—and his rifle—and kept barreling toward us.

"He's going to assault me, isn't he?" asked I.

"I hope not. Black man punching a white boy, that's just what the pigs are waiting for."

I patted my pocket for Gordo's knife.

"Don't go pulling your piece," scolded Bunny. "Ritchie's a little crazy, but I owe him everything. He turned me on to Sonia Sanchez, Haki Madhubuti, got me down with the Panthers. Turned my life around." Nevertheless she held out a hand to slow her brother's stride. "*Ritchie. Easy, now. This is Zebulon X.*"

But Ritchie didn't stop until his chest thumped against mine. I caught myself in time to watch him worm his tongue over his teeth as if hungry for blood. His eyes bugged so badly, I expected them to drop out and dangle upon stems, but what worried me most was the pink scar tissue at his left temple. It looked like an entry wound.

"Zebulon X?" echoed he. "Woo-hoo-hoo!"

I flinched at the unnaturally high pitch. Whatever had landed him in jail had included a gunshot to the head, I was certain of it, and the bullet had messed him up good.

"Ritchie," said Bunny. "Count to ten."

Ritchie did not feel like counting.

"Putting *X* in your name, now that's some offensive bullshit!"

For Bunny's sake, I put on a self-effacing smile and bowed amends.

"*Je m'excuse.* My whole life, I'm afraid, is one of great offense."

He laughed, a gyrating, nervy jangle.

"You're fancy with the Frenchie talk, *mon frère*, but my little sis here, her mind has been expanded, exploded, and explicated. Racist faker-forger-fabricators need not apply, so why don't you hop down the rabbit trail?"

You must believe me, Reader, when I say that I wanted no conflict. Just the same, you know my record when it comes to turning the cheek to antagonizations, whether they be the early browbeatings of Church, the indictments of Detective Roseborough, or the bullying of the Mercury Seven. Though I replied through locked teeth, I tried to keep my voice even.

"I have known Negroes before and lived in concord."

"Negroes? Now you're traveling back in time! How about *Afro-Americans?* How about *capital-B Blacks?* Maybe you ought to

437

time-trip further back, call us Blackamoors, see how that goes over in this crowd, Mr. X."

"*Finch*," said Bunny. "That's the name we knew as kids—Zebulon Finch. Ritchie, remember? You shot him down from the magnolia tree."

That a man could forget blasting a shotgun at a suicidal, putrescing, one-armed corpse could only be attributable to head trauma. Ritchie's protuberant eyes conducted a slow investigation.

"Hard to say. I've shot at so many whiteys, I lost count."

No longer could I bear it, not within earshot of Bunny, who, I confess, I felt a sudden need to impress. I lurched, reciprocating the chest-thump.

"Now it makes sense," taunted I, "for I recall from the magnolia tree your lousiness of aim. Here, I am closer. Care to try again?"

Bunny ripped us apart.

"Zebulon is on our side! He's supporting us!"

Ritchie raised his eyebrows, the left one into scar tissue, and dissolved into a snicker that speckled me with saliva.

"Oh, yeah, now I got it figured! You're one of them white folk who gives us *moral support*. Except guess what, whitey? Black Panthers don't need your moral support. Black Panthers don't need your feelings. What we need are liberators out working the street, protecting brothers from being brutalized, bashing the pigs that do the brutalizing. How does that sound, *mon frère*? You still feel like supporting us?"

Bunny gave me an apologetic wince.

"Rallies like this, his head gets all—"

But the chants were too deafening and the sun too bright, and I was furious at the idea Ritchie had planted that even a Better God was false hope, a distraction next to good old-fashioned fists and guns. And so, Dearest Reader, being the choleric cad that I am, I cut off Bunny with a wave of my hand, thereby destroying, as you shall see, one more thing that might have lightened me with a feather of goodness.

"Tonight, then, we go to the street," challenged I. "Let us see who out-brutalizes who."

VII.

RITCHIE'S LONG, BEERY BUICK ELECTRA slithered across the cracked concrete of Bedford-Stuyvesant, Brooklyn, into throbbing blobs of red stoplights, yellow streetlamps, and neon shop signs before dissolving into the silver blood of a gushing fire hydrant and then fading back into the dark. Brown-skinned children lined the streets like rust. They existed abruptly, an arm's length from the car, and watched us pass with reflective, nocturnal eyes.

James Brown and the Famous Flames razzed from the Electra's radio. Ritchie snaked his head to the rhythm, made a watchful left turn, pulled on a joint, and offered it to Bunny in the passenger seat. She was silent and serious and gave me a damning glance: *This was a very bad idea.* Then, shaking her head, *What the hell,* she took a drag—she needed it.

The mishmash of marijuana and nighttime cruising had settled a blanket atop Ritchie's pointiest edges, but I could tell from Bunny's monitoring that she did not expect it to last. What we were doing was "patrolling," the practice detailed in the Black Panther speaker's address. You found a pig accosting a Negro—"Afro-American" was not coming easily to me—and if things were crooked, you straightened them out and made that pig think twice about future misbehavior.

"Dig our black children, no shirts in April, running round like mice." Ritchie tsked and found my eyes in the rearview. "This here's

440

training grounds, preparing them for the day the pigs herd them into the pig pen, and I'm talking about *the* pen, the big one. 'Get in the cold shower, little nigger. Rub this talc in your hair. We know all niggers got lice. Here's some straw to sleep on. Here's the trough for your slop.' Whiteys love talk-talking about crime rates, but mark Ritchie Tucker's words, *mon frère*, one day that crime rate will drop like a bomb, and the whiteys, they'll be proud as hell. Then look at the jails and the prisons and tell Ritchie Tucker what you see. They'll be packed like a hoghouse with brothers."

A kid dashed past the car.

"The road," gasped Bunny. "Watch the road."

Ritchie did not seem to hear.

"I bet *mon frère's* one of them I-have-a-dream motherfuckers."

"You sound plain ignorant when you put down Dr. King," said Bunny.

"Brother Malcolm said King was nothing but an Uncle Tom who rolled belly-up for white folk." Ritchie gestured with the joint. "How about you, *mon frère*? You ever been to Bed-Stuy before?"

"You might be surprised," said I, "where I've been and what—"

"That's all right," he interrupted. "Ritchie is happy to be your tour guide. Just remember to tip, you know what I'm saying? Now, let's see. *Mon frère's* of the paler persuasion, so let me use words you might be able to dig. Hey, I bet you know about Vietnam, though, right? Haven't ever heard of Bed-Stuy before, but you're all educated up on rice paddies."

Bunny punched his shoulder.

"You need to settle your ass *down*."

"Let's be nonviolent about this, Sister Jolami! I'm just preparing what you call a metaphor. You heard of free-fire zones, *mon frère*? It's one of them Army-Navy expressions. It means load 'em up, because hereabouts you're authorized to shoot anything that moves. Here's the funny thing, though. That's the same exact situation we got going on in this colony we call Black Amerika. Something out here moves, *BLAM!*"

I jumped in my seat. Ritchie cracked up, pounding the steering wheel.

"Quit trying to scare him," said Bunny, but when she faced the backseat, it was she who looked scared. An oncoming car set fire to her Afro as she managed a skittish smile. "Don't listen to Ritchie. I wouldn't have joined the Panthers if they didn't do worlds of good. We set up health clinics, especially for addicts, and—"

"Capitalism Plus Dope Equals Genocide!" chortled Ritchie.

"—we do free breakfasts for kids, which means I get up at four thirty every morning. That's worse than being on tour, I'll tell you what. I make the nastiest pancakes you've ever seen, but those hungry little bastards eat anything you put—"

"Hang on, Sister Jolami," said Ritchie. "What do you mean, quit trying to scare him? I didn't think a martyr was scared of anything."

"A statement of fact!" confirmed I. "While I have no doubt that your degenerate life has dragged you through foul waters, I guarantee that I have seen ten times worse. Your Afro-American riots, for instance! I've stood at their hubs and rated them but another day's unremarkable work. Here, I have proof!"

I began to nudge my sleeve upward to flaunt where the Nashville firehose had torn my elbow clean, but the Electra jagged as Ritchie pulled a quick right.

"It's only a riot if you're a whitey. Otherwise it's a revolution!" He scoffed. "At least *mon frère* quit calling us Negroes."

No warning—the brakes were stomped. My face smashed against the front seat, and Bunny hit the dashboard in a drum roll of arm bones. The car slung back and settled upon creaking shocks. I peeled my face from smoky leather and peered out the windshield.

Half a block away was a stopped police car, its red strobe slowly revealing every wad of trash on the block. Both pigs were out of the cruiser, one fitting cuffs upon a black man pressed against a rattletrap Chevy Corvair, the other plundering the Corvair's backseat for contraband. It was, in short, everything Ritchie had hoped to find.

"Shit," hissed Bunny. "Shit, shit."

Ritchie eased to the curb, muscled the gearshift to park, and killed the engine. The pigs had their hands full; we hadn't been spotted. Ritchie leaned forward. The vitreous orbs of his eyes glowed pink with light, then gray, then pink, then gray. He was silent for what seemed like the first time in his life. Bunny put a hand to his arm.

"We're all alone out here. Let's back off."

But friction with Zebulon X had reached a heat where nothing less than rash action would do. Ritchie reached into his jacket, undid snaps, and drew out a sawed-off shotgun.

"Ballots or bullets. That's what Brother Malcolm said."

I'd have bet my left foot (the one Clown hadn't chewed on) that Ritchie Tucker had no interest in the slow stratagems of fundraising, handbilling, and bussing. Bullets were fast, palpable deliverers of change, perfectly suited to those whose patience had been sheared by blows to the skull, jail time, and an infuriating Caucasian corpse.

"Revolution," murmured he.

The maniac kicked open his door, got out, and headed down the road at the pigs.

Bunny ejected a raging river of obscenities and clambered off in chase. She slid over the hood of the Electra, snagged Ritchie by the sleeve, and spoke rapidly into his ear, presumably pleas for him to put away the shotgun. The braggadocio I'd brayed didn't permit me to be wired to my seat; I climbed from the car and tumbled toward the deadest end I'd ever seen.

The Famous Flames' funk had been replaced by a disorienting musical cacophony pouring from the open window of the hippest cat in Bed-Stuy. The sixties had mutated even jazz, and my beloved Harlem swing of Duke Ellington and Jelly Roll Morton had become the acid peals of Miles Davis and John Coltrane, the latter of whom was responsible for the anarchic epic squawking over our scene. The album, called *Ascension*, had been recorded in a dungeon studio on skeleton-key piano, hell-fire saxophones, and head-hunter drums, and unlike Gesualdo's icy obscurity, Coltrane's atonality blistered like disease—we'd all be screaming along before the end.

The pig restraining the suspect spotted us. From his belt he whipped a flashlight and flared it. Ritchie and Bunny had to avert their eyes, but my dead irises slurped the light straight into my void. I'd caught up to the wranglesome siblings when the officer shouted.

"Halt! Police matter!" To his partner, "Brownlow, get up!"

Brownlow, plainclothed but packing, crawled from the Corvair. He dropped the trash he'd been sifting, in favor of his automatic. He pointed the gun at the road several paces ahead of us.

"Detective Brownlow and Officer Keller, Brooklyn PD, asking you to return to your vehicle."

Coltrane, Tyner, Garrison, Jones, Hubbard, Johnson, Brown, Tchicai, Sanders, Shepp, and Davis wailed inharmonic warnings, but Ritchie paid no heed. Instead of concealing his shotgun, he held it up like a badge.

"Black Panther Party of Self-Defense! Name, Richard Tucker! Authorized by Defense Minister Huey P. Newton and Chairman Bobby Seale to protect and assist my Afro-American brother! I will speak to the brother first, and then allow you to proceed with any lawful arrest! Please step aside!"

The Afro-American brother in question did not look relieved. Though half of his face was flattened against the car, it was clear he was terrified of being caught helpless if bullets began to fly. He started torquing, begging to be freed, forcing Keller to use his full body weight to constrain him.

"Call for backup," said Brownlow.

"I can't!"

Brownlow cursed. The barrel of his gun rose with each step Ritchie took. "Get your hands up!"

Ritchie replied by pumping a round into the shotgun.

"Ritchie!" Bunny had her brother by the jacket but pulled with too little strength to impede the lowering of the sawed-off. Brownlow dropped into a firer's crouch and aimed his pistol with both hands. We were ten feet apart and closing.

"Drop the weapon or I fire!"

"I'll blow your pig head right off your pig neck! Step aside!"

Every one of these inflamers was going to be dead in seconds! With but one arm, I could not tackle both Tuckers, so I tricked to the right and tossed myself into their path in hopes of tripping them. But my leap itself was startling, and before I hit cement, I saw, in the beams of the Electra's headlights, Brownlow react by pulling his hammer. I wrapped my arm around a pair of legs and yanked, hoping to drag someone beneath the coming fire.

It was the suspect who thwarted the inevitable. He jammed an

445

elbow into Keller's eye and wrenched free. Still handcuffed, however, he stumbled against Brownlow. The detective pulled back from the escapee while Ritchie, whose legs I hadn't snagged, hurdled my body and slammed the stock of his shotgun into Brownlow's face. His nose exploded and his skull struck pavement. But he hadn't dropped his pistol. There it was, still cocked, angling upward, and his finger squeezed—

CRACK! CRACK! CRACK!

A man cried out. The suspect, that unluckiest of ducks, had been hit. Ritchie dove headfirst into the Corvair's open back door. I took Bunny about the waist and propelled both of us behind the trunk. Inside the Corvair, Ritchie popped up and discharged his shotgun from the backseat. The driver's-side window exploded, showering Brownlow with glass. He covered his face and rolled to a spot beyond the car's hood.

The suspect pressed his spine against the bumper alongside Bunny and me. The brake light behind his head shone with such red intensity that the jets of blood springing from his mutilated elbow might as well have been clear water. Bunny fought from my clutches, took the man by the armpits, and, while he screeched in agony, pulled him toward the gutter. Officer Keller scurried around the rear of the car on all fours like a kid playing hide-and-seek. The eye that wasn't swollen shut opened wider at seeing us, and he let his torso fall to the pavement so that he could withdraw his pistol. Bunny, trapped behind the suspect, tried to push away, but was too slow. The gun was out and pointed at us, a surefire hit.

It was Keller's fault, I suppose, that his earlier pat-down hadn't uncovered the four-inch Walther tucked at the small of the suspect's back. In a striking feat of flexibility, the fellow drew the mini-gun with his cuffed hands and fired. A bud of pink flesh blossomed from Keller's thigh. He yowled, dropped his weapon, and pressed at the wound. Coltrane's band screamed in excitement—one second, two seconds—and then thick black blood pumped through the officer's fingers. Bunny froze, but I dragged her until we were on the sidewalk side of the Corvair. Gunfire between Brownlow and Ritchie now shook the street, the Corvair having become a tiny Alamo.

Bunny and I huddled against the back right tire. The two casualties cried for help. Shots from Brownlow sent automotive gore zinging down our backs: arm-rest skin, turn-signal bone, seat-cushion fat. Ritchie responded with double shotgun fire, the first of which exploded into the car's engine, the second of which tore the center from a NO PARKING sign. The door beside our faces flew open, dangling like a half-severed limb, and Ritchie somersaulted to the gutter. He saw us, shouted *"Run, motherfuckers!"* and sprinted for the Electra. Bunny scrambled after, but the Marine in me knew it was bad practice. Their backs were exposed.

I checked and saw Brownlow rise from beyond the smoking hood, scoop blood from his eyes, and take good, slow aim at the Tuckers. I shouted, recognized the noise as ineffectual, and charged after them in hopes that my body might be a magnet for lead. The Excelsior elongated the seconds so that I could recognize time's remorseless rush. One second you're a pigtailed girl singing praise to fairy Jesus, the next you're the target of the same bullet that's been fired for centuries.

Only one of the Tuckers was savable. I leapt at Bunny.

I felt the shot before I heard it, discovered myself tangled with Bunny before I recalled falling, perceived the blood in my palm before I felt the sticky wetness. I noted the bullet embedded into one of my

447

vertebrae, easily concealable with my jacket—but who was bleeding? I disengaged Bunny's limbs from her brother's while Brownlow bore down, bellowing at us to stick 'em up. The hysterical blares of cop cruisers and ambulances drowned him out while the shirtless brown ghosts of Bed-Stuy resurfaced, close enough to give the detective trouble.

I slapped Bunny's face. Her eyes blinked.

"I'm okay?" burbled she. "I'm okay?"

I pawed her body all over, opprobrious interracial contact in any other context, until both of us were assured that she'd suffered no injury. Together we looked at Ritchie. He was facedown, beret smashed under his nose. Balletic wisps of smoke rose from two jagged chasms of jacket leather. Coltrane's band was still chortling like madmen; it was a long song and they had an infinity to play it. *Look at the blood moseying along the slanted street*, their instruments seemed to gabble, *but in which direction, can you tell? Up or down? Ascension or the opposite?*

VIII.

BLACK PANTHER PATROLLING PROCEDURE included trailing an arrested brother to jail and bailing him out, after which, more often than not, said brother would, in his own self-interest, become a Panther, too. But this was a hospital, an institution from which one dared not expedite exit, and inside it the revolutionaries lost their lockstep and paced the east half of the waiting room, adjusting weapon holsters and cussing like mad and making everyone else wish they'd chosen a different night to get that cough checked out.

Word had traveled fast about Ritchie Tucker being shot in the back by pigs, and by midnight fifty Panthers had gathered, each of whom embraced Bunny before firing the Black Power fist at the police force, which had amassed in the west half of the room to prevent an uprising. The pigs, though, frothed more than the Panthers, with individual hotheads barking racial epithets across the aisle. One of their own had been shot, too, though Officer Keller (perhaps giddy from blood loss?) had unexpectedly credited Bunny and me for trying to stop Ritchie—a nice gesture—right before Keller had passed out.

Zebulon X, not quite Pig but certainly not Black Panther, nervously kept his seat next to Bunny. When the rabble-rouser who'd delivered the afternoon speech arrived, he paid respects to Bunny

449

and asked for her version of events. I'd heard her tell the story ten times by then; her lashes had thickened into tearful spikes. The speaker offered his handkerchief, and Bunny wiped her face. It came away brown with Ritchie's blood. She considered the smudge for a moment, and then, in a raw voice, told the story once more.

"The fucking fuzz handcuffed him to the gurney," she finished.

"Ritchie's a burro," soothed the speaker. "He'll make it."

"I hope he doesn't. I hope he's already dead."

"Sister Jolami."

"The pigs'll lock him up for good. That's no life."

"I'm going to talk to the doctors. See what's what. You sit tight."

He hugged her and strode past the heckling cops as if they were whining puppies. There, I had to admit, walked a man; in his wake, I felt like an incompetent child. I glanced at Bunny. She seemed afloat in the smog of clinical disinfection. Buzzing speakers called for "Dr. Buckner, Dr. Buckner." The pale green light above us flickered. The floor stank like stomach acid and bleach. "Dr. Buckner, Dr. Buckner." Even I, deathless one, felt upon my corpse the cephalopod suckers of Death.

Bunny collapsed into her plastic chair, and her sunglasses, cracked in half during the shoot-out, at last fell from her Afro into her lap. She fondled the cheap plastic, then stroked the dress beneath. The color was black enough to conceal Ritchie's blood, though I doubted any regimen of laundry would ever remove the stiff, sanguine snarl.

For the first time in hours, she looked at me.

"Why me?"

"I beg your pardon?"

"On the street. You could've saved either of us. You chose me."

"I . . . because . . ."

450

Because I liked her and disliked Ritchie. What good would it do to say it?

"Ritchie had problems. He had hard times. He wasn't nice. But this isn't the time for *nice*. This is the time for courage, and Ritchie had lots of it. He could've moved the Panthers forward. He could've moved the whole country."

"So might you," suggested I.

Her face tightened.

"With what? My pancakes?" She shook her head. "Nuh-uh. You fucked up tonight. You should've saved Ritchie. The whole reason he was on that street was because of you."

I favored neither her subject matter nor building volume.

"You are upset. Of that I have nothing but sympathy. I hesitate to point out that I didn't advocate your brother advancing upon policemen with a chambered shotgun."

"At the rally, when he got in your face, you got right back in his. You didn't have to do that. I told you not to. You didn't have to push him into proving what kind of man he was."

"I should have taken his abuse, is that it?"

"Yes! What's so wrong with that? Gød forbid a black man ever gets the last word. Gød forbid a white man has to feel bad about himself for two or three minutes of U.S. history. You can martyr yourself all day long, but it's Ritchie Tucker who suffered, who *knew* what suffering was. You could have just let him be."

I scanned the room to confirm that Bunny's diatribe was catching the attention of wrathy blacks. Reader, I was agog. Why, I'd protested alongside these Afro-Americans! Only hours ago, I'd fulfilled my obligation and killed myself while Ritchie had stood nearby heckling me, and though technically I'd done it for Students for a Democratic

451

Society, it had been in public partnership with the Panthers. When would my displays of tolerance be deemed sufficient?

"Your brother wished to help the man being handcuffed, but what did he accomplish besides getting the man shot? Indeed I tried to protect your brother from his own destructive impulses!"

Bunny's upper lip curled in a way that frightened me.

"You'll never get it, will you?"

"Get what? I'm here, aren't I? In this ghastly room at the witching hour?"

"This isn't about you protecting Ritchie. You even understand that word? Protecting is what you do with property. What I needed you to do, what *all* of us need *all* white people to do, is help us or get the fuck out of the way. Helping us means being ready to die for the cause—and Ritchie was ready. But if you're Zebulon X and you can't die in the first place? Shit. Then I don't think you can really believe in anything."

I do not think I knew how much I adored her before she hurt me so deeply.

"If you're really a miracle man," continued she, "then save him."

"I told you," pleaded I. "I tried."

"Walk past those pigs, bust through that door, knock down any doctors who try and stop you, and put your miracle-man hands on my Ritchie and save him."

Even the weight of her scorn did not hide her desperation. The poor, poor girl; the only magic I had to offer was the spiritual shaming of *la silenziosità*, which would do a felon like Ritchie Tucker no good whatsoever.

"Bunny," sighed I. "That is not how it works."

With a fist, she brought the pieces of her sunglasses smashing down against the arm of her chair. Blood, her own this time, spurted from her pierced palm. Black Panthers lived atop hair triggers; they leapt to their boots, put leather-gloved hands to sidearms, and surrounded the woman who, that night, was their queen. Bunny, though, did not take her eyes off me. Her blood joined Ritchie's on her dress.

"Who am I to you, anyway? One day soon, I'll be dead, too, and I won't be shit on your shoes. You'll just keep on with your journey or whatever you want to call it. I'm nothing but a footnote to your story. And of course it's *your* story, isn't it? Amerika's story is always going to be yours. White. Male. Probably rich. You're Rome and we all know what happened to Rome. Empire gets too big, empire falls."

I could hear the *K* in her *Amerika*. She hissed in disgust.

"Get your ass out of here. And it's not Bunny, motherfucker. It's Jolami Tiombe."

It is likely that the search for Dr. Buckner dragged on, though the only sounds I could hear were the menacing squeak of two dozen leather jackets. I did not have to look directly to be blinded by the hospital light fulgurating from brass bandoliers and dark sunglasses. The night's events had transformed each member of the troop into their namesake predator, the pack salivated for a kill, and here was a whitey, already wounded, who might go down easy.

I stood, my shoulders thumping against concealed switchblades, pistol butts, and clenched fists. I angled my armless shoulder for access, and after they paused to make the point that they were in control, the leather curtain parted. I passed through a forest of scowls, only to stop briefly at the police line. My own kind, though they radiated just as much loathing. Where was the peace, love, and community that I, as a Better God, was supposed to be fostering among one and all?

"Hey, whitey!"

Warily I turned to find Bunny standing on her chair. She'd let her tears fall, and her cheeks shone like expensive polish.

"You told me I was beautiful. The day we met. After Ritchie shot you down from that rope you wear. That's how the Beau-Ts really got their name."

Even as I was flattered, eighty-eight years of sucker punches had taught me to expect a left hook. I recalled her misgivings over the Beaut-Ts' breakup, how their conception of themselves as a trio had left them vulnerable when facing the world as individuals. No further worries on that front. Bunny had found a much larger group, over which she stood so tall that I swore I could hear her future speeches and see her image printed on future posters.

"I'm sorry," spat she, "I ever wrote that stupid song."

Nails driven through extremities, skin flayed by whips, Old Testament stonings, crushings beneath half-ton millstones—none of these martyrdoms inflicted the pain of these parting words. I slouched from the infirmary where Ritchie Tucker would be pronounced dead before sunrise, and into a chilly Brooklyn that, in its predawn vapors, looked off-color. What a human thing, thought I, it was to be wounded.

So began what historians, those profane distortionists, would call the Summer of Love.

IX.

T HE ANTIWAR CARAVAN, LOOKING MORE like a circus
parade every day, rode into Asbury Park, New Jersey, in December
1967, and out of sheer habit I allowed myself to be pushed along
with them, though Bunny's renouncing of me had stamped out what
little belief had remained that I was capable of anyone's betterment.

The organizers, inebriated on the superbly abhorrent news that
troop levels in Nam had touched five hundred thousand, got stoned on
the beach and within their ganja glee hatched a novel martyrdom. They'd
bury me up to the neck in the sand at low tide alongside signage painted
with a gauge tracking military levels in Vietnam—and then watch
the symbolic tide roll over me. Despite hating being wet, I agreed
to it, assuring them that it was well within my bag of tricks, and
that, furthermore, it worked as a tribute to Presbyterian provoca-
teur Margaret Wilson, who in 1685 was lashed to a palisade at the
bottom of Scotland's Solway Firth to drown with the tide's return.
The sole problem with the plan I kept to myself: I no longer cared.

High tide was expected at five. The protestors held an antici-
patory beach bash fit for Frankie Avalon and Annette Funicello,
complete with bonfires, local quartets doing their best Beatles and
Stones, and kids doing the Watusi around my head, which sat upon
the sand like a child's pail. Mirthmaking halted whenever it was time
for another impugning of LBJ's honor, and during one such address,

an emotional waif placed upon my head an Indian headdress decked out with flower-power buttons.

I hollered for the getup to be removed at once, but it was four o'clock and the tide was advancing, dampening make-out blankets and endangering baggies of primo grass. The microphones shorted, and that was it. Fairweather frolickers relocated to the bordering park, from which they could cheer my drowning in comfort.

Only a single fibril of Atlantic ocean had tickled my chin when my peripheral vision was occluded by a visitor, a plain-looking woman barely over five feet tall. The first thing noticeable was her cultural polarity. Her double-breasted wool coat and tapered trousers so personified the Man that I presumed her to be one of the Merry Pranksters, madcap liberals who dressed like stiffs in order to bombard some fussbudget or another with soot or glitter.

But when she squatted before me, I could find no trace of the Pranksters' ingrained grime. She was mid-twenties, thickly spectacled, hair pulled into a businesslike bun. She held a notebook, which she parted, and a pen, which she drew.

"Is this an interview? I'm a mite busy just now."

"It's been a challenge to get you alone."

Barely detectable was the New England flatness of her vowels, like President Kennedy's but of dirtier birth. Years of practice had hidden it well.

"Too bad you did not do your homework," said I. "Zebulon X does not make statements."

"This isn't an interview. This is a proposition."

"I suppose I can hardly walk away from it, can I?"

"My name is Ruthie Ness," continued she, "and I'd like to represent you."

A rivulet of salt water shot between my interlocutor's sensible shoes and frothed my lip. She set aside her notebook and with some distaste fashioned with her clean hands a ditch and rampart to stave the tide a few minutes longer.

"An agent, eh? If you represent Brigitte Bardot, we have a deal."

"I don't represent anyone else. I'd like to work with you exclusively."

"Give me time to feel flattered. It might take until I am underwater."

"I have all the pertinent degrees. Law, accounting, business."

"And yet still in the bloom of womanhood."

My implication was that she was too young to have accomplished much beyond the skyward flinging of her college mortarboard. Ruthie Ness caught the drift but stared through sunset spectacles, careful not to react. High tide waited not for prideful stalemates; I did not have time to pull details like teeth.

"Martyrs typically follow their own fancies," said I.

"But you're hardly typical, are you?"

The sand over my shoulders bulged from my underground shrug.

"What service could you possibly provide me?"

"For one, you wouldn't be buried on a beach to be drowned in ice-cold water without any kind of compensation."

"Touché. But wealth interests neither me nor the crowds within which I circulate."

"That's a shortsighted view. Agronomist trends never last. Have you seen the Dow Jones average lately? You need to look at a bigger historical picture."

"I know my history," snapped I.

She managed a dry smile. Her version of an apology, I gathered.

"Mr. Finch, you have talent. But if you continue along this path, you'll do damage to yourself that renders your talent null."

"I have so far resisted the coup de grâce," admitted I, "the burning at the stake for which everyone waits. It is a pigeonhearted evasion."

"Not at all. It's smart. Let me be smart for you. I only want to safeguard your sustainability."

"And for this favor you expect to receive—"

Surf sizzled, and I saw the gray plash of water one second before it slapped me in the eyes. I blew my face free of foam and found my visitor refortifying her wall of sand. But it was one woman versus gravitational forces. It was time to drown, and we both knew it. She stood and brushed sand from her notebook, hands, and slacks.

"There's an all-night restaurant called Bucket Mouth Seafood at the north end of the boardwalk. The tide should recede by eight. You'll need time to tidy. Reservations at ten?"

"I'll *be* seafood by then. Reserve what you wish; I promise nothing."

"Until ten." She began to leave.

"Do me one favor!" cried I.

She narrowed distrustful eyes. "I don't do favors."

"Call it a show of good faith, then, and remove this obnoxious headdress."

From my Lake Michigan submersion, to Margeaux's Yankee Doodle nosedive, to the zeppelin plunge into Berlin's Schwielowsee, I'd logged enough underwater hours to know that places of pensivity existed therein. I relaxed into the sand, which heavied to cement, and when the water was high enough to stop drubbing me like driftwood, I peered through the soup of seaweed, silt, and hot dog wrappers and pondered the proposal.

If Ruthie Ness had on her wall every diploma she'd listed,

there were far simpler means to a fortune. Why choose a product so prickly as I? The likeliest explanation was some moral crusade, and yet she evinced no particular philosophy, and in the late sixties, that was the most outrageous put-on of all. I shook my head and watched the flotsam caper. I had no reason to accept her invitation, except that, since Bunny's repudiation, I was lost, wandering, and desperate for someone to direct me back to a righteous road. Only one thing troubled me.

How had she known my real name was Finch?

Bucket Mouth Seafood was a wood-paneled, slime-floored establishment balanced upon stilts and connected to an unsound pier. Waitresses, all of them crusty old ladies with cigarettes betwixt salt-scoured lips, delivered dead fish on wooden trenchers and dumped steamed crab, shrimp, mussels, and clams straight onto paper-covered tabletops for barbarian-style feeding. I arrived at eleven, a full hour late to test Ruthie Ness's resolve, but for my efforts received not even a tetchy look. She sat at a table in the middle of the restaurant, toe tapping metronomically, as if she could wait all week.

She enacted her version of a smile and set down her glass of wine, the only item she'd ordered. I sat, scared away the serving wench, and gave my host an expectant look.

"'Ruthie,'" said I, "is too girlish to suit you. Why not 'Ruth'?"

"I've found that the little 'ie' helps sugar the medicine."

"Well, Ruthie, what is your prescription?"

"Miss Ness."

"I'm sorry?"

"I prefer that you call me Miss Ness. It's more professional."

It was a bit early in our working relationship to make demands. I gave the pint-sized lawbringer my most intimidating look and

resolved to keep calling her Ruthie privately. As if to barricade against the place's rowdy ambiance, Ruthie had changed into the shapeless livery of a woman thrice her age—a long-sleeved step-in dress with a matronly collar and a color too dull to register in the low light. Given my hand-me-down Renaissance blouse, rhinestone-appliquéd blue jeans, and motorcycle boots, we made quite the pair.

"Professional," repeated I. "Is that what you call this look?"

"I'm not in the business of being looked at."

I felt the sting of reproach—a rare thing.

"I am saying only that you look quite unlike your contemporaries. For that matter, you don't speak like them either."

"Nor do you."

"A second touché."

Ruthie lifted a briefcase to her lap, aligned combination numbers, cracked it open, and sorted through the accordion folder.

"My contemporaries, as you call them, can walk around barefoot and do drugs and get pregnant, and at the end of the day go back to parents who'll take care of them. To be frank, I was born poor. My parents are dead. I'm not pretty enough to count on hooking some careerist. I worked three jobs to get through law school. To do all that requires a plan. A vision."

She withdrew a paperclipped bundle that, from the unconscionable paragraphing and minuscule typeface, I recognized as a contract. She offered it, but I waved it away.

"Your plan, or vision, has failed to take into consideration how little stock I hold in signatures and dotted lines. I own no identification papers. I exist outside of government registers. Also, as it happens, I loathe reading. If you wish to tender a proposal, then speak, woman, and be convincing."

Ruthie took a sip of merlot and refreshed her tightrope smiling act. "How is business, if may I ask?"

"My father was a dynamitier," replied I.

"Is that so?"

"'Business,' he'd always say, 'is booming.'"

"He was right about that. Destruction never goes out of demand. Hence your modest success. People see something of theirs destroyed, and they can't help but want their turn at destroying."

"In military circles they call that a scorched earth doctrine."

"Oh, I like that. Let's borrow it for our arrangement—the Scorched Earth Doctrine."

"Fine, you have your title. Now work backward."

Ruthie put her elbows on the table and leaned into lamplight.

"Destruction is exactly what I want to talk about. This past year alone, just think of it."

Gloomier suggestions were hard to imagine. Barely had I traipsed from Ritchie Tucker's hospital than had John Coltrane, soundtracker of Ritchie's murder, died from cancer deranged by heroin. It was a portentous death that jostled for press coverage alongside the Newark race riots of July, which left twenty-three dead; the Detroit race riots two weeks later, during which one hundred blocks of the Motor City screamed with more rebel gunfire than any Southeast Asian DMZ; and the arrest of Black Panther founder Huey Newton, who was shot in the gut by a pig and handcuffed to a gurney just like Ritchie. I felt gut-shot too; I could feel Johnny's marble roll toward the puncture.

Ruthie swished her merlot.

"This level of destruction breeds a need for a whole lot of revenge. Your stock could keep rising."

461

"You seem to understand what my eager young rebels do not, that my act is no mere sleight of hand. And yet, Miss Ness, you have no questions about my bodily architecture?"

She fluttered a hand as if at a gnat.

"Not interested."

"But surely, as a business matter, you require assurance—"

She set down her glass heavily enough to send a slosh of wine over the rim. Her accent, too, surfaced, redolent of briny harbors, sea-crusted fishermen, foul-tongued women.

"We aren't going to talk about it."

Ahnt gonna tack. She heard her indigenous inflection and caged her jaw.

It will seem morbid to the Dearest Reader, but I often visualized the process of becoming acquainted as a progression of inflicted wounds. Mrs. Leather had accepted a series of small cuts through which I could see her goodness; Church had cracked himself open all at once, laying everything bare; Bridey had fought back, creating a bloodbath; and Mrs. White had eviscerated herself slowly, inch by inch, until I'd seen everything. But Ruthie Ness offered nothing; I had to stab, stab, stab, and so far, my blade had hit only bone.

"The point is," said she, "none of this is slowing down anytime soon. If these marches and sit-ins had a leader, that would be one thing. You could prevail on him to take some role in your protection. But the whole purpose of the youth campaign, as I see it, is to create a leaderless society. You say you know your history? Well, then you know that's not utopia at all. That's chaos."

"It is true," admitted I, "that they talk much of pacifism—"

"Yes, refusing to be accessories to murder overseas—"

"—all the while arming themselves to the teeth."

Tasting triumph, her cultivated erudition lapsed and she licked wine from the rim of her glass. Concurring with her had been as bad as dropping a poker hand face-up, but I could not drudge up anger over the flub. I was too tired, too alone. My head, literally buried in the sand, had been but a pagan maypole around which so-called radicals could gambol. Ruthie was right, wasn't she? Demonstrations were sock hops for the draft-dodgers wearing buttons that shouted NEVER GROW UP! Didn't they realize that was a curse? Wasn't the entire point of a movement to move?

When I checked back, Ruthie's lips were merlot red.

"Without me," said she, "you'll be in pieces by '69."

Deep down, Reader, I knew this; of course I knew it. The martyrdoms I'd pulled off for Scheinberg's brand of do-gooders had become as rote and pointless as the performances at the Barker's Gallery of Suffering. At least turn-of-the-millennium audiences had had the ability to be shocked. Today's crusaders were desensitized to any horror I could invent, and it shouldn't have taken Bunny's loud forswearing of me to accept it.

"I've worked with profiteers before," said I. "They always want blood money."

"A percentage of the profits. And, yes, there must be profits. That's how we sort out the legitimate requests. I'm not going to let someone tear your legs off to save the Black-Footed Ferret. You don't exist as far as Social Security is concerned, so the venture is going to require a little creativity. But that's what I've studied for. I'll create legal entities through which we can filter funds. You won't have to worry about the IRS, the FBI, nobody."

After years of slipshod promises about good vibrations and California dreamin', the pledges of the Scorched Earth Doctrine felt like solid rock. How tempting for Zebulon X, the silent one, to have someone to do all the talking.

I stuck my hand out to get the covenant done with.

Her thick lenses magnified her stony stare.

"No handshake. We are not friends."

It was peculiar how the reprimand rather hurt; her skeleton had rejoined the knife-stab of familiarity once again. Ruthie slid the contract across the table along with a pen. Legally my scrawl meant nothing, but if she wanted the gesture, so be it. I read only a line or two before giving up, zeroing in on the blank spaces, and signing my name, page after page, how I'd once typed *You gotta have fear in your heart* on my Royal Quiet de Luxe typewriter until the blank page had become nothing but ink.

X.

ONE OF THIS IS SLOWING *down anytime soon,* Ruthie Ness had said, and it took but one month to confirm her insight. On the last day of January 1968, Communist forces coordinated an assault on over one hundred South Vietnam cities, a pyrotechnic display of base-camp bombardments, highway bombings, embassy invasions, palace seizings, and urban incursions that left nine thousand dead. The carnage squeezed into American TV boxes like meat squeezed into a sausage stuffer, creating a buffet of spicy dishes: Midwestern boys dying on film as if cued by Maximilian Chernoff; rescue choppers landing in fields of tall grass that rippled like green pools of bile; and Vietnamese panicking in ways that felt pornographic, often naked, screaming at chicken pitches, and gaping into camera lenses with the uncomprehending eyes of infants.

A U.S. Officer in the Mekong Delta, after overseeing a slaughter of civilians at Bên Tre City, was quoted as saying, "It became necessary to destroy the village in order to save it," and indeed this had been the mindset of America's older generations. But after this so-called Tet Offensive, even adults lost faith. Finally they poked their groundhog faces from their prefab burrows, showed up to the office without ties if they showed up at all, and joined their children on the streets in numb objection to what felt like a personal betrayal.

In short, Tet had laid a gold-bricked road for any industrious martyr-for-hire. But Ruthie Ness's short stature came with the sine qua non of Napoléon issues, and she made it known that the days of procuring Zebulon X for your cause in exchange for mellow chicks and out-of-this-world tunes were over. Now there was a corporation called Excelsior, Inc. (she'd capitulated to my demands that I get to name it), and all negotiations had to pass through the company's orneriest employee.

Rare were the Harvey Scheinbergs intellectually acute enough to dig Excelsior, Inc.'s legalese. One confused hippie after another gave up, and it bothered me, but Ruthie kept her grip on the reins. It was not a bad thing, insisted she, that my frequency of martyrdom slow down, and besides, it was the fault of these unscrubbed youngsters that they hadn't the wherewithal to stage the sort of events Zebulon X warranted.

If 1967 had been the Summer of Love, then its lovemaking, poisoned by the mother's ingested LSD and the father's ingested Agent Orange, had conceived a clawed, yowling, mutant child called 1968. To the delight of protestors, LBJ declared that he wouldn't run for a second presidential term, which hung the future of the Vietnam War on the November election. On the left queued peacenik pet Eugene McCarthy and leftist Robert Kennedy, hoping to pick up his slain brother's mantle; on the right stood jowly scowler Richard Nixon and professional bigot George Wallace, best known for his catchy chant, "Segregation now, segregation tomorrow, segregation forever." Somewhere, thought I, Bunny Tucker was lifting a fist higher than ever.

The astronomic stakes of the election drove demonstrators quite mad by spring. Speed freaks in Day-Glo clothing organized sack races down major freeways, set off firecrackers inside capital buildings, and handed out acid-laced Kool-Aid to passersby. It was a jamboree that stunk of reefer and sweat and semen. Who had time anymore to notice the martyr fellow cutting off his nipples before lying upon a bed of broken glass in simulation of the tortures of Agatha of Sicily? Agatha of *where*, man?

They might have noticed Ruthie Ness, though, trying to collect payment from zoned-out dopers. *Hey, mama, I don't have the dough, but how 'bout you let me turn you on to these mushrooms?* She swallowed stiffed bills when it was the only option, and I became ashamed, both of the behavior of my supposed compatriots and of the vulgarities to which I subjected the straightbacked Miss Ness, no matter that she had no affection for me.

Mere hours after the milestone broadcast during which television patriarch Walter Cronkite opined that America should abrogate its role in the Vietnam quagmire, Ruthie and I returned to the library study room at William & Mary College, where she had set up temporary office. She gathered typewritten drafts of Zebulon X press releases and began bleeding them with red pen, while just outside the window, young people achieved bliss in drum circles, boys had their ring-knuckled hands down the backs of girls' bell-bottomed pants, and bags of this or that were traded in clear view.

"A productive telephone call with the Young Americans for Freedom," said she. "They're interested in having you out to California at a rally for Governor Reagan."

"Reagan, eh?" sighed I. "I thought he was of a conservative bent."

"I've been aggressive with terms, and the YAF has been responsive. I'll make a final counter-offer, but regardless I think we should go ahead."

"The YAF—yes, now it bangs a distant gong. Doesn't the YAF support the war? I don't understand."

Ruthie spoke to me as if I were an underdeveloped child.

"The YAF has money, and money means visibility. Isn't that what you want? To graduate from parking lots and gazebos to reach the most people?"

"Yes, within reason."

She folded her arms. "What about the offer is unreasonable, precisely? I wasn't aware that your goal was to push one particular set of beliefs over another."

I wanted to splutter in indignation, but could not, for Ruthie, as usual, was right. From my first martyrdom onward, I'd swung as does a tick from hither blade of grass to thither, latching to the nearest warm body regardless of blood type. Ergo, it became easier to convince myself that engaging the other half of America wasn't the same as giving up on my fellow youth. Not all young people, after all, rebelled from the backs of Volkswagen vans. Some picked up pennies from maple-syruped diner counters to support newborn children. Some made change at banks in hopes of a promotion to assistant manager. Even some of the pigs we skirmished, once their riot helmets were knocked off, were too young to cultivate the mandated mustaches. Ruthie Ness, it seemed, understood the dire duties of a Better God more clearly than I, and it made me sad, Reader, sadder than I'd been in decades.

For hadn't there been a brief, shining moment, before the hippies had succumbed to the sex-and-drug trappings of their cause, when America's decay had nearly been reversed?

"Call the YAF," whispered I.

Click-click went the briefcase locks, *ruffle-fuffle* went the pockets.

"I've got the number right here."

Unlike overindulged hippies, the Young Americans for Freedom were excited to book a show-stopper like Zebulon X and treated me graciously. They had combed hair and bright eyes. They wore, depending on the situation, double-breasted suits, polo-neck sweaters, tennis shirts, ankle socks, or white cotton caps. They studied at Purdue, Cornell, Brigham Young, Texas A&M. They donated blood for wounded soldiers. They loved their country—*love it or leave it*, they said. They nodded soberly at my martyrdoms rather than cheering them, construing them not as commentary on the folly of sacrifice, but as straightforward passion plays.

I died. I revived. I waited to feel something.

At some point, I cannot say when, I began wearing a suit. It was Ruthie's doing. The new duds played better to my new audience. I forgot my copy of *Foxe's Book of Martyrs* at Rutgers College and did not bother acquiring a replacement. No one cared. I simply killed myself, for the YAF, or the John Birch Society, or the American Independent Party, in manners devoid of historical nuance or really any meaning at all, by gun or knife or, laziest of all, the noose still dangling round my neck, repeating the same steps I'd gone through at the Biloxi hanging: *Loop, tuck, stretch, tighten.* I brought in enough people to make my bookings worthwhile, and dimly I was cognizant of Ruthie's new, bigger, gold-painted lockbox, the crisper ledgers and personalized checkbooks, the pocket calculator which had to be replaced after the plus and equal signs wore out.

You endure enough needles, you stop feeling them—that much I remembered from being the Astonishing Mr. Stick. In April, Martin Luther King Jr. was assassinated one day after making a speech I'd heard on the radio, in which he'd said in bittersweet tones, "I've seen

469

the promised land. I may not get there with you." Nonviolence itself died that day. Within hours, eighty riots erupted across the country. Who needed a fake martyr when real ones were born every week? The Black Panthers cranked them out as if Ritchie Tucker had been their prototype: Lil' Bobby Hutton, unarmed, shot by police; John Huggins plugged in the back during a government-planned fracas; Bunchy Carter, the same story, except in the chest. On June 6— the fifty-year anniversary of the Belleau Wood bloodbath—Bobby Kennedy died, shot in the head like his brother, and even the Radical Right grew worried. The idealists' collapse was too epic; it felt like another Götterdämmerung.

I was not in Chicago for the 1968 Democratic Convention. Why would I be? Steered as if by bull's nose ring by Ruthie, I was somewhere where they played Pat Boone instead of Pink Floyd, where the keynoter, George Wallace himself, shouted about the grand old days I'd lived through but remembered quite differently, when there weren't, said he, all these niggers invading our hometowns, much less dinks or gooks or slopes or zips or whatever you called the Orientals. The rally took place at night, and by then every radio and TV was tuned to the mess in Chicago, where the police (not *pigs* in this crowd) were controlling (not *beating*) the bums (not *conscientious objectors*) with billy clubs and asphyxiant. I could feel the baton against bone, the corrosive flesh-peel of the gas. Before the channel was turned, I caught an interview with Allen Ginsberg of "Howl" infamy; he was on the spot in Chicago, still hunting for the "starry dynamo in the machinery of night," which could not be me, which could have never been me.

I did my thing, then trailed after Ruthie through the crowd. Her golden lockbox was heavy that night, and it slowed her, and it was for that reason alone that I noticed him. Not five feet away stood a man in his early twenties, a cigarette popping from his mouth, arm slung along the shoulders of a woman who looked to be his wife. She was pregnant and poured into a hotel maid uniform, while he wore a grease-smutched mechanic's jumpsuit. I don't know that I would have recognized his face if the jumpsuit hadn't offered his nickname on an oval patch:

Junior

We were in Kansas. Outside of Wichita. These details, blathered earlier by Ruthie, sharpened. My foot caught a tuft of turf. I tripped. Junior's wife looked my way, and he looked at her. I hid my face and arm stub, even though I knew that it wasn't physical deficiencies that shamed me. I'd let Rigby haul me to NASA so that I might help protect Junior's future, and I'd become a Better God for much the same reason. Yet what had I done with Junior's Kal-El gifts but squander them? I shouldered past Ruthie and bulled headlong into the masses, hearing in my head not their conservative rallying cries but one from the alleged peaceniks: *We Are the People Our Parents Warned Us Against!* It was a dirty lie: all of us, no matter the age, were exactly the same.

The last time I saw Harvey Scheinberg was November 6, 1968, the day after Nixon won the presidency. Ruthie Ness and I were at a diner on the Ohio State campus, where short-order cooks threw water onto their grills to cover the disturbing silence of students weighing the ramifications of the Nixon win. Ruthie, always ready to talk business, looked up from her calculator and coffee at his approach, but I held up my hand to request that she hold her tongue. Scheinberg stood in a downcast slouch, one hand holding a wrinkled copy of *The Warren Report*, the other dug into his poncho pocket. His face was hidden by a werewolf knot of beard and hair.

I wished to stand and meet his eyes. Instead I gazed up like a scolded dog.

"I am sorry," said I.

"About what, man?"

I shrugged. "The election?"

He discovered in his pocket a joint and rolled it across his palm.

"Yeah, bummer. But Humphrey wasn't our man. Nothing was going to change."

Nixon had won by a sliver, less than one percent of the vote, and I, loathsome carpetbagger, had demonstrated to help it happen. Scheinberg knew it, and I found myself aching to hear him lay into me (as hippies said) and tear me a new one (as hippies also said). Why else had he left his table of funked freethinkers?

"Got my draft notice," said he.

This wasn't the chastisement I needed.

"What? How? I thought you burned your card."

"Symbolic gesture. You think they let you off that easy?"

Scheinberg stared out the window. The morning was idyllic. He spoke softly as if afraid his strident voice might disturb the butterflies, the squirrels, the very rays of light.

"Do me a favor, man. Stay tuned in, all right? No matter what happens with the war, no matter what side you end up on, you keep tripping on your trip. The rest of us, the whole generation, we might end up gone with the wind. But *you*, man. You may look like shit, but you're purer than any of us. Remember what we fought for, all right? Make these years mean something."

Purity. I'd glimpsed it in Montana, chased it into the solar system, died the deaths of a thousand martyrs hoping to find it stashed beneath my ribs. Now this scruffy liberationist had ambled up and suggested it was sitting right there in my surviving hand as the joint was in his?

"What are you going to do?" asked I.

He ran a hand through his whiskers. "Who knows? Might feel good to lose this hair."

Harvey Scheinberg had always traveled like a hobo with nothing more than what fit into a backpack. The notion of him plodding through the jungle in sateen drabs, cargo trousers, combat boots, helmet, insect mesh, pistol belt, ammo pouch, canteen, mess kit, fragmentation vest, and M16 was as deplorable as that of the free beasts of the Rocky Mountains hauling about carts of coal.

"You have more connections than anyone else I know. Run away. To Canada, to Mexico. It could be"—I was desperate; here went nothing—"groovy."

He stared at me, then laughed. "Don't ever say that word again, man."

His knuckles were white around *The Warren Report*. His jaw flexed, as if he might weep, then flexed harder as he conquered the emotion with minutemen of indignation. He lifted both eyes and voice toward my business partner.

"Hey, lady. Why do you do it, huh?"

Ruthie Ness looked up from her work and adjusted her glasses. Her poised smile did not alter, though her jaw, like his, tensed.

"Because the stupid deserve to follow the bold."

With one stab, Scheinberg's knife had struck truer than my untold attempts. It was the most revealing remark Ruthie had ever made, even as it presented varied interpretations. Were the stupid the American people, and the bold Richard Nixon? Or were both Ruthie and I the bold and liberals like Scheinberg the stupid ones? Or did anyone who paid me to martyr myself qualify as stupid?

Scheinberg raspberried his tongue, backpedaled toward his table of likeminded, likefleshed losers, and grinned the garrulous grin of one ignorant of coming disaster. Nixon's election would mean five more years in Vietnam, new campaigns in Laos and Cambodia, and tens of thousands more killed. Scheinberg would accept both his draft and the complimentary buzzcut, train at Fort Ord, join Charlie Company at Qui Nhon, and die by friendly fire within a week of deployment. There is a five-hundred-foot-long wall in Washington, D.C., if that capital city still exists in the Reader's time, where persistent sorts can browse the names of the Vietnam War's dead. I only wish that my name could be found among them. Carved into a slab of rock—what a clean means of immortality.

Scheinberg flashed the peace sign.

"That's one crazy chick you got there," said he. "You ride easy, Zebulon X."

XI.

THE SCHOOL BUS WAS CLASSIC mustard yellow but painted with green segments of reptilian skin and topped with meniscus pupils inked onto the headlights. Half of the windows were busted and covered with plywood, the other half thrown open to accommodate young people's braceleted arms. These limbs wiggled like centipedal legs, giving an impression of movement to the Alligator Express (the name emblazoned on both sides), even after the bus had slowed almost to a standstill.

So went the story of the friendliest traffic jam in history. If you didn't count the sporadic chunk of engine dropping from the bus's undercarriage, the ride had been smooth until sundown two hours earlier, when the interstates had dribbled off into rural byways incapable of handling this magnitude of influx, everything from cars, trucks, and motorcycles to bicycles, skateboards, and hitchers. The congestion had given the night an illusory edge, with sulfurous exhaust and road dust turned scarlet by so many brake lights.

The back of the Alligator Express was painted with a lizard tail, implying crude things about the missing exit door. From it, four or five bibulous teenagers belted along to music coming from competing car radios, currently a battle royale between Led Zeppelin, Iron Butterfly, and the Velvet Underground. I, too, crowded the bus's asshole, but in my case to hop off.

With my rucksack slung across my chest, I began dodging pedestrians at a far quicker clip than traffic. Despite the unreckonable crowds and diesel reek, I was alone for the first time in years and savored knowing, at last, where a Better God had to go.

Make these years mean something, Scheinberg had pleaded, and a way to do that began to manifest after I caught television footage from the Monterey Pop Festival of an Afro-American instrumentalist named Jimi Hendrix feigning sex with his guitar before ejaculating onto it a can of lighter fluid and setting it ablaze. Perhaps it was the Coltranesque cacophony of his band or Hendrix's shivers of ecstasy, but I found in the white-hot flame what both Scheinberg and I had sought. Fire is the purest matter that exists; even the shadow-blasted cremains of Hiroshima had allowed, for an instant, the whole world to see its true shape.

The irony that a martyr had forgotten fire was biting indeed. It was long past time to plant a stake, stand against it, and burn. Foxe lavished his most plauditory pages upon those like John Hooper, Bishop of Worchester, who in 1555 was fastened with detonative munitions and thrice set on fire, an ordeal throughout which he prayed aloud with blistered tongue and beat upon his chest until his hand spurted blood and his arm fell off. I was two steps ahead of him—no blood to boil, no arm to lose. As long as my fire-light flashed hope upon watching faces, I'd have served my purpose nearly as well as Thích Quang Đúc.

What I required was the right kind of stage in front of the right kind of eyes. While Ruthie trawled me to pro-war events via bus, rental, and rail, I kept my eyes to public bulletin boards, where subversive handbills still made their cases, and stapled to one of the latter I saw a notice for a concert in Wallkill, New York, called "3 Days of Peace & Music" put on by a consortium called Woodstock Music & Art Fair.

The copy advertised one hundred acres of lush Hudson Valley nature, a bustling crafts bazaar, workshops in bead-stringing and clay-throwing and poetry-penning, and a whopping three-day ticket price of eighteen bucks. What caught my eye, though, was that among the three dozen listed performers was the arson artist himself, Mr. Hendrix.

Ruthie Ness walked too fast for me to swipe the leaflet, but that did not matter, for my plans were grander than scoring tickets. I capitalized on private moments, working with New York City phone operators to connect me with the Woodstock troupe, to whom I described my résumé. The festival site, said they, had changed to a six-hundred acre dairy farm in the Catskills, but the happening, man, was *happening*, and swelling with performers by the day, and with so many artists needing to set up, it was a good bet they could use filler between sets—they'd already booked some sessions of kundalini yoga. I insisted that I be added to the docket and furthermore that I go unpaid, the latter of which, I'm sure, clinched the deal. *If you're cool mellowing out backstage until a space opens up,* said they, *then far out, cowboy, we'll catch you in August.*

My emphatic request was that my name be excluded from all publicity materials. The Woodstock staff, however, was overwhelmed and probably high, and I lived in fear that Ruthie Ness would learn of my involvement and demand egregious payment from the festival, or, much worse, get wind of what I intended to do and kibosh the whole thing.

I could have left her at any time, but my best shot was to reduce the time Ruthie had to track me down, and that meant cutting it close.

Two nights before Woodstock's kickoff, I crept from the Lexington, Kentucky, motel at which we lodged and boarded a red-eye bus to Scranton, Pennsylvania, where I purchased critical tools, stashed them in my rucksack, and schlepped through lakeland country until, after half a day, my path crossed an artery of jerry-built jalopies so obviously owned by Bohemians that I was able to insinuate myself aboard one of the more crowded vehicles, the Alligator Express.

Through a muggy morning steam I veered from the roadsides, wheat fields, and church lots, all of which had become Gordian knots of improvised parking, and crested a hill to discover a downsloping natural amphitheater. The grass was visible only in patches; already tens of thousands of young people had arrived, and their bee-hive drone shook through me—or was it a flutter of nerves?

For there stood the final theater of Zebulon X, a massive, bare-bones wooden stage surrounded by spotlight towers.

That I wore a Ruthie-approved shirt-and-jacket combo did not help my cause at the gate. My plaid blazer made it look as though I'd come to peddle insurance. It was a sixteen-year-old volunteer in cut-off jeans and a stars-and-stripes motorcycle helmet who saved the day, recalling that he'd seen my name on a list somewhere, sometime, someplace, in this plane of reality or the next. (He was stoned.)

He was also convinced, no matter what I said, that my name was "X-Man." He introduced himself as Captain America, a reference to a flick he liked called *Easy Rider*, and so contagious was the dippy atmosphere that I accepted the name as readily as if it had been "Bill." He slid down his visor to protect against the sun as we walked, the same sun that laid bare my every blot of gouge and spoil.

"You don't look so hot, X-Man. You drop some of that bad brown acid going around?"

Captain America apologized for the third degree I'd gotten at the gate but explained how most of the artists were arriving by helicopter because of the not-cool roadways. We reached backstage, a teeming village of tents and yurts, and there he lifted his visor, made me promise to keep rocking and rolling, and stressed once again that, should I be offered the brown acid, I'd best decline, or at least limit it to half a tab.

From a godlike PA blasted corroboration.

"Everyone, stay away from the brown acid, all right? It's just bad acid."

I craned my neck at the back of the stage. Hours away from showtime, and workers still bandsawed wood, hammered nails, connected cables, and secured a jumbo tarpaulin to the overhead girders. From backstage I couldn't see the audience, but I could see distant roads filled with biblical multitudes. Organizers had estimated fifty thousand over the phone, but this was so many times that size that chain-link fences crumpled before the crowd like saplings, leaving the Woodstock promoters no choice but to deem the show free to all. I inhaled and believed that I could smell, beneath the body odor and patchouli, the deathbed breath of the sixties, that mix of sweet dandelion and burnt motor oil that would haunt a generation.

"Jim DeCampo, go to the hot dog stand. Your brother has your medicine."

Presently the first performer, Richie Havens, a giant in an African boubou, climbed the stage stairs, tuning his guitar while his bassist and bongo player exchanged high fives. It might be three days before I was brought to the stage, so I decided to make use of the time and do something about my clothes. I hadn't packed get-ups like I'd seen aboard the Alligator Express—Old West sheriffs, Tolkien wizards, superheroes—but there was a film crew documenting the concert, and I refused to be immortalized in plaid. I ditched my blazer, rolled up my right sleeve, and tucked shut my left.

"Jessica Harley, call your parents. They're worried about you, sister."

Havens attacked his guitar with enough zest to distract from the helicopters. I wandered to the edge of the backstage property, where construction cranes and bulldozers sat paralyzed like horrified retirees, and I found there a quartet of young laborers sprawled atop their machines, passing a joint, bare chests furred with sawdust, overhaired heads bopping to the bongos. They were the embodiment of carefree youth, and I hated that I had to interrupt them.

"It's getting real windy, folks. Can we all be cool and move away from the towers?"

I opened my rucksack, pushed past the cans of lighter fluid, removed the allowance Ruthie Ness had parceled to me throughout the year, and explained the set dressing that my act required. Ah, these boys!—my age, yet bigger-hearted than I'd ever been. Though thrilled by the money, they demanded I keep half of it, as the task would only take a couple hours and they didn't feel right ripping off a vet who'd lost a limb in Nam. I wished for the emotional release of tears, pocketed half the bills to appease them, and thanked them for a favor no currency could repay.

Off they went, happily ignorant of what they were building, as I drifted toward backstage. Havens relinquished his position to a bearded yogi called Swami Satchidananda, who delivered an invocation regarding the celestial powers of music (or equivalent drivel) before handing the duties to a band called Sweetwater, who then made way for a strummer named Bert Sommer. A rain—just a normal rain, but one that would become historic—began to fall.

The luckiest festival goers had acquired strips of clear polyethylene that they wrapped around themselves and their pals, beneath which they squirmed like unborn litters inside placental sacs. The less fortunate made the best of it, stripping to the buff and creating impromptu nudist colonies or clearing fifty-foot runways of mud and sliding across them at top speed until they, like me, were difficult to classify as either man or woman or black or white. Backstage we gathered beneath tenting in groups large enough that I hoped no one could pinpoint the worst of the odors as coming from me.

Night fell, and Tim Hardin sang "If I Were a Carpenter" in purple spotlights before Ravi Shankar and his humongous sitar took the stage amid a downpour and resigned after only three songs. The weather prohibited helicopters and sogged right through the schedule. Where was the Who? Sly might be there, but what about the Family Stone? Had anyone seen Janis Joplin? Electric bands were fearful of electrocution, so organizers bumped up another acoustic act, an unknown folk singer who went by Melanie. I watched men in rain ponchos herd the petrified young lady toward the stage, then felt a tap upon my shoulder.

There stood Captain America. Though his clothes were wetted to his skin, his helmet had kept his head dry, and he beamed through the open visor, stoned as ever.

"You must have a lucky sign, X-Man."

"Sign? Is there a protest component to this event?"

"Zodiac sign! Ten to one you're a Sagittarius."

"There is nothing to the stars but more stars, I assure you."

"Far out. Anyway, it's your lucky day. You're up."

The festival had been running a mere five hours.

"Already?"

"Joan Baez is six months pregnant, man. Isn't that a mindfuck? She's not ready yet so they want you up there after this chick finishes. Then it's Arlo Guthrie, then Joan. Bang!"

Wait upon Death for a century, and when he comes, he does so quickly.

"You cool, X-Man? You need to bum a smoke?"

"I . . . am fine."

"Out of sight. Hey! Any chance you're also Zebulon Finch?"

Finch. Now, there was a word colder than any rain.

"Who is asking?" whispered I.

"Yeah, man, it's wild! There's this old dude who's looking for you. I would've told him to buzz off, but he's the oldest dude I've seen here by a mile, and if an old dude bringing his ass to the middle of nowhere for music isn't fucking with the power structure, then what is, man?"

I inspected the rain, all those individual daggers.

"Where is this man?"

"See that green tent? I had to get him out of the rain. Old dude like that will catch pneumonia."

If there exists an unabridged recording of Woodstock, listen to it, and you will hear a thick, epochal silence between the applause for Melanie as she took her seat onstage and the expectant inhale before she struck her first strings. Just that quickly, I recalled how it felt to be human and suffocating for air. I took one step toward the green tent. My shoe squished into muck, and rain fell to my shoulders like concrete blocks.

"Keep it short!" cried Captain America. "Melanie's only got fifteen minutes of material! You're on in twenty, X-Man!"

Thirty feet was the whole of the distance, Reader, but somehow

I knew what was coming, and it felt like a tour of duty in Vietnam, a march through monsoon marshes portioned by sniper fire and guided missiles. It was futile to try to walk so far, and yet I did it, then lifted the rain-heavied flap and stepped into a square, four-poled tent lit by a bare bulb pendant from an extension cord. Fifty-seven years earlier, the first conversation of consequence I'd had with the old man had also taken place in a tent, which I had to admit was our ideal backdrop, for a tent is a fragile, ephemeral structure, much like the friendship we'd built, then watched get shredded by passing storms.

Now you've guessed it, Reader.

The old dude was Burt Churchwell.

XII.

CHURCH WAS SEVENTY-THREE YEARS OLD. There is a bush here, sharp of thorn and poison of leaf, and we shan't beat around it. It is an appalling age at which to find oneself. Death has by then defeated you with a weapon more insidious than scythe: patience.

As bad as I looked, and in 1969 I looked bad indeed, Church looked worse. This was not the springing, vaulting, six-foot-five football hero of 1918 I mourned; nor was it the limping, paunched, six-foot-three scarface of 1926; nor was it the cane-wielding, wheeze-breathed, six-foot grayhair of 1941. This latest rendition of the only best friend I'd ever known was entirely bald, so far past wrinkles that he'd become a tan-fleshed wad, crumpled to a shocking four-and-a-half feet of height, though that, at least, was attributable to his wheel-chair. I stared at the rain-glossed apparatus, the gloppings of mud over the wheels and push rims, the sopping chunks of grass caught in the footplates.

How far had he wheeled himself to get here? Up how many hills?

Church shuddered from the effort. His elbows rattled the arm-rests, and his head, that melted-wax lump identifiable only by the cataracted blue eyes and unhewable cleft knob of his chin, sagged from a neck banded with age like the stay lines of a masted seaship. He still wore a beard to cover the crater in his cheek, but the hair had gone raveled and gray. There were brown patches at which my hope swelled, but they were nothing more than speckles of mud.

The rainstorm barraged the canvas.

"It is," I forced myself to say, "surprising to see you."

He shook his head. Spit ran from lips that hung loose from a flaccid face. My loyal corporal, realized I, had been felled by a stroke. Could he even speak? The handicap of it sickened me, but I told myself to smile as widely as I could and this torment would be over that much quicker. I stepped forward to evidence goodwill, my legs stopping just shy of Church's own withered pair. I smelled my gaminess interlard with his spoiled-fruit fragrance and saw upon his lap a rain-warped hardcover book he gripped to control his convulsing arthritis. I'd embraced this man upon his arrival at Bridey Valentine's Beverly Hills mansion, but no longer could I imagine such a reception. Church was delicate, ghoulish. I might break his every bone.

He examined the nub of my left arm. I nodded.

"Slings and arrows by the hundreds have been fired at me by able archers. Outrageous fortunes have been revealed to me at every turn. It is too much to recount in the short time we have left. Only ten minutes, I'm afraid."

Preventing my happy mask from slipping became arduous, then hopeless. Our protracted silence made room for Melanie's banshee yowl to cut through the storm and the tent, shocking my buried remorse to back above the dirt. How else could I interpret Church's impossible appearance but as a last chance to dismiss my docket of sins? I fiddled with my rucksack, afraid of his milky, watchful eyes, and shrugged at the ground like a child.

"I regret what happened in Hollywood. Believe me when I say that I'd intended to gather you. No, that is a half-truth. I intended to

485

return with you. To New York or Iowa, anywhere you wanted, where we could protect each other across the years. The magnitude of that mistake—it is difficult to grasp. Instead, I have known decades of pointless misery, and I fear that you have as well. Would you like to hear my pathetic excuse? Perhaps you recall the photograph of the fetching lass I carried with me in the war. That was my daughter, Merle, and the morning after I put you in that Beverly Hills cab, she called and I had to rescue her, only I failed, then remembered that Bridey had a daughter as well, and that I might try to save her instead, and on that count I also failed, and then, as I'm sure you recall, Pearl Harbor was bombed, and I tried to enlist, whereupon I was arrested by a spy agency called the OSS . . ."

My encyclopedia of excuses fluttered away in favor of monitoring how mud bled through the sailcloth floor in the manner of Wright-Patterson's Rorschach blots. What symbology did they conceal? The weight of my body, no longer attributable to rain, could not quite prevent me from peeking up at the torpid ruins of Church.

"How did you find me?"

Church smacked slobbering lips, then sighed.

"The radio," guessed I. "The bastards publicized me."

His nod set off a spasm that chattered his teeth, not his original set of effulgent chompers but rather a cut-rate prosthetic plate. Again I had to look away. It was lucky, I told myself, that the weather was launching my stage act early, for Ruthie Ness would have heard the same radio spots and was no doubt that very instant battling traffic. Ten minutes was nearly gone; it was time to ask the question that mattered.

"Why have you come?"

My eyes I aimed at the floor, but I could do nothing about my ears. Church's overgrown fingernails scraped along the length of the book until one of them, heavied by some fierce emotion and embrittled with age, snapped. I shuddered; he let me; and then he spoke as slowly as was necessary to spit words in sensible portions.

"This—isn't—what—we—fought—for."

The sounds jabbed past my ribs and struck a thoracic vertebrae. I took hold of a tent pole anchored in boggy mud. The pole leaned, gallons of rain splooshed from an overhead pocket, and then half the tent caved, walloping me to my knees, where I, perhaps by accident, perhaps not, took hold of Church's legs. He still hadn't flinched, but when had he ever when it came to me? He'd read every Hollywood gossip mag to track my days with Bridey; surely he'd read every underground zine offering accounts of Zebulon X. Repeatedly I'd quit watching over Church, but never had Church quit watching over me. Isn't that what he'd promised fifty-one years before? *We Churchwells,* he'd said, *we pay our debts.*

Unbidden, my arm curled around his atrophied calves and my face pressed to his knee. I snarled into his pant leg and tasted wet cotton and mud.

"You're old. You don't understand radical acts. They're the only thing that gets through to anyone."

"We—learned—in the—war—about—sacri—fice."

Church's lungs had never recovered from Dr. Leather's saw, and his breath chirruped as if a sparrow were trapped in the birdcage of his ribs. That wound had been my fault, too; I drove my fist against the chair. It struck the wheel lock, which disengaged. The wheelchair rolled six inches back, and I hoped, hysterically, that it would keep on rolling, right out of my life, even as I held his legs more tightly.

"You're jealous. Because of Bridey. Because of fame. Because I'm *young.* There's no place in America for the old."

Something hot touched the back of my head. Was it a concealed knife with which Church intended to cleave my brain stem? No one in the Corps had been a more proficient soldier, and to die by his hand would be the most honorable exit.

It was much worse. His palm, pulpous with dilapidation, quavering with affliction, settled upon my scalp and gentled it, stroking my dead hair as if dreaming of his own long-gone blond silk. His soft hand assured me that all was A-OK, I could spew whatever malice I wished, the storm could clobber our tent until we were inhumed forever in mud, for no tribulation could change that he had, did, and would forever go on loving me, even if his body, unlike mine, quit working.

"If—you're—a martyr—then—we—all are. Peanut. The—Prof. Mouse. Piano. Heck—I expect—some—of them—Huns—too. The word—don't—mean—much. You—can't—make—light of— death. Not when—so—many—good—men—we knew—didn't— come back—to live—the lives—we—lived."

"But it hurts. It hurts so bad to keep going."

Church cupped my cheek and lifted my face.

"That's—what—real—sacri—fice—is. To keep—going—no mat—ter how deep—the fear—gets—into your—heart."

How many would echo Luca Testa's warning before my death was done? Fear had kept us alive in the Great War, had compelled us to save the lives of our brothers. Fear was the distillate of life, and who knew it better than Church, who'd had the whole world set at his feet, only to have everything destroyed, and then be shown the destruction every day in mirrors for the rest of life? Death had been a way out for him at every lonely crossroad, but that, I was still learning, was not how they made their boys in Iowa.

He slid the book across his lap. I fumbled it from him, read the spine.

A GHOST ROLLS OVER:
The Collected Works of Jason Stavros

The Dearest Reader knows of my relationship with literature, and this book was a cinderblock. Yet it was as light as a slip of paper. Jason Stavros, the cinnamon-eyed Greek who, in the moments before certain machine-gun demise, had recited the work-in-progress poem from which this compendium took its title, had followed Church's advice and kept going to become that least probable of things, a poet. In a daze, I paddled through pages, discovering in the words what I'd already known but refused to acknowledge, that Jason Stavros had become a vital voice in the antiwar movement, referred to as "Stavros" the same way radicals spoke of "Vonnegut" and "Heller"—a funny twist of events, seeing how anyone who'd shared his trenches had unfailingly used his full name.

My fingers lost the ability to clutch, and the book fell open to its single dog-eared page.

Dedicated to

Pvt. Z. Finch

3 BN/7 REG/2 DIV

I blinked at it, for that was what Mary Leather had taught me in 1906: blink enough, and people might think you're human. The dedication was a memorial even more lasting than the still-to-come wall in Washington, but what lay beneath it was more incredible still. Signatures, first of Jason Stavros, second of Burt Churchwell, and third by the two dozen surviving members of the Third Battalion, filled the page, each name squiggled due to the signer's age. Some names

I recollected; others I'd let go; but all of them, it appeared, remembered Private Finch, and Church, that lame-legged, stroke-addled son-of-a-bitch, had wheelchaired all across the country to make sure that I knew it.

A splattery sound, like a Saint Bernard shaking off a suburban rain, disrupted the heartache. Someone was thrashing through the tent's collapsed half and pushing the fallen pole back into place. The ceiling sailed upward, the light bulb soaring away as abruptly as Earth when viewed through a space capsule window.

"Whoa, whoa! You guys cool?"

I knew by the muffled reverberation that it was Captain America behind a closed helmet. Strong young arms encircled my chest. I was hoisted to my feet and swiveled around. The boy threw open his visor, checked me for damage, and found so much of it, he could only gawk. His pupils were dilated from some unknown ingestible, but climacteric concern had him focused.

"Can't you hear the PA, X-Man? They're calling for you!"

To facilitate anguish, the rain pattered to a standstill.

"Zebulon X to the stage, last call. C'mon, brother, where are you?"

Captain America waggled a finger toward Woodstock.

"We gotta go! Now, now, now!"

He snatched the book from my hand, wedged it into my rucksack, slung the bag over his shoulder, looped his arm around my chest, and lurched for open skies. Drugs had lent the scrawny kid a muscleman's brawn, and we were outside the tent before my brain could collect a thought. I dug my heels into mud, halting our progress, and looked back at Church with the same panicked plea he'd given me when his copper cheek had disgraced him before a Coney Island prostitute.

490

Though the rain had quit, the wind had not, and the tent flap had blown so that I could see only Church's withered white hands shaking from want of book to hold or head to pet. Then that vision was gone too, as Captain America lugged me to a stage jack-o'-lantern orange inside a purpled night, where roadies were clearing the stairs so we could pass, clapping encouragement and gesturing us onto the wing, where stood the four boys I'd paid earlier to build my set, who hoorahed upon recognizing me and pointed at their stage dressing, which I saw only after Captain America handed me my rucksack and pushed me toward it: a hill of bundled sticks upon a bed of dry straw from which rose a wooden stake they'd somehow bolted to the stage.

XIII.

NOT IN THE GREAT WAR'S biggest battles, Harlem's jumpingest jazz joints, Hollywood's priciest premieres, or Mauthausen's sweatiest stockade had I seen a crowd like this. It flowed from the stage like Lake Michigan, miles and miles of flesh glistening under the gelled lights. It was eleven thirty, but no one slept; they were sunburnt, underfed, underhydrated, and underexcreted, yet high on hope and drugged on a dream that, for two more days at least, would persist.

The motions of martyrdom had grown mechanical. I advanced toward the microphone waiting at center stage, the underfoot crunch of straw amplified through speakers. For a moment, I was dumb in the spotlight. Then, as if winded like a clock, my hand dug into the rucksack, reached beneath the Stavros, and removed a can of lighter fluid. I bit off the cap, squirted the liquid upon the tinder—*just like Hendrix*, I told myself. The gray stake soaked black; the yellow hay soaked brown. I let the can drop, and it clanged like a cymbal. The people, trained to respond to sound, cheered.

Make these years mean something, Scheinberg had said.

Keep going, Church had said.

Were they opposite directives? Or one and the same? My hand shook like Church's as I took from a box of matches a single exemplar, did the one-handed trick of running it across graphite, and held the flame before me. The people were also trained to respond to fire—ignited draft cards, burned bras, napalm firestorms—and cheered with confidence that they were going to witness a purging inferno. They were right, though only those who recognized me guessed that the firestarter himself would burn with it.

The flame slid down the matchstick. *Drop it, Zebulon—all you have to do is drop it.* I shifted focus from the fire's unspoiled center to the filthy horde. A change in stage lighting had rolled a bright yellow beam up the center of the hill as if by paintbrush, and I looked from face to eager face; one unkind jeer or violent scuffle was all the encouragement I needed to go through with it. Instead, over and over, I found the miracle the Woodstock Music & Art Fair planners had promised in their circulars: peace.

The match-flame scorched my thumb, woke me up. Yes, it was time to burn like Willie Pete, like Agent Orange; burn like Vietnam, like the ghettos of Harlem, Watts, and Newark; to everything—burn, burn, burn—there is a season—burn, burn, burn. I pivoted to set my spine against the stake, my fingers poised to drop the match onto the lustful tinder. But in that instant my eye caught sight of what looked like a mirror fire out in the crowd.

It was, in point of fact, an Afro hairdo backlit by a tower spotlight so that it sizzled like a burning bush. Most of the Afro-Americans at Woodstock, it seemed to me, were musicians, making this a sight just unusual enough to distract me while my thumb roasted from brown to black. The Afro was prodigious and perfectly orbed, miniaturizing the face beneath: scared, wide-eyed, and, oddly enough, familiar.

The match disintegrated to ash.

I moved from the stake, leaned into the mike.

"Jolami Tiombe?"

My voice crashed through speakers like thunder.

She was perhaps thirty rows back, close enough that I could see her cover her mouth with both hands. As I expect the best melodies come to songwriters, the path forward came to me all at once, clearer to the heart than any other I'd taken. Before he'd faded into the night and mud and years, Church had found this trail as surely as he'd found a hundred others as a Marine Corps runner, and it was one down which all of us had to keep walking.

I only knew two words and kept at them:

"Jolami Tiombe. Jolami Tiombe."

Had she come to Woodstock to see me? Or had she come simply for the love of music? It didn't matter. She followed my voice as if the old noose around my neck were connected to a rope around her waist. Her hips and shoulders bumped past others, and in true festival spirit, they cleared the way. When she reached the press barrier, teenagers lifted her over it, at which point security personnel, having nothing else to do, raised her by the calves so that she appeared to levitate to the stage. Suddenly she was next to me, clad not in Black Panther garb but simple black slacks and a shirt, her eyes full, for some reason, with tears, her slender brown arms lifting, not in allegiance to a cause but to embrace me. I could not move, but heard the mike hiss as it was pressed between us.

The applause was staggering. The two of us parted to look at each other. Though her hair gave her several inches, she still had to look up to meet my eyes, which she did with confusion and exhilaration. She knew which masters of war I'd served over the past two years and how I'd thrown ideals to the wind. But hadn't Bob Dylan said that things were blowin' in the wind? Well, now they were blowin' back.

494

I crossed to a stage-right wing filled with musicians watching the drama play out, and I made a one-word request. Melanie held out hers; Arlo Guthrie, on deck, offered his; but it was a portly, hirsute guy named Jerry Garcia who was the first to hand me a guitar. He was from a band called the Grateful Dead, a phrase which, at that moment, described me well enough.

Captain America was scurrying from the stage. Clever kid—he'd delivered a chair. Jolami Tiombe, too stunned to stand, sat. I lowered the microphone and handed her Garcia's guitar. She studied its construction as if it were an anachronistic object unearthed by archeologists. With rapid movements that surprised even her, she passed the strap over her Afro, rested the body upon her knee, and raced her fingertips noiselessly up the neck.

In Ritchie's hospital she'd assailed me for telling the tale of America as only a rich white man could, as a tale of annihilation. But there was another tale to be told, and no one could tell it better than a good lyricist.

I took a second match from the box, lit it, and tossed it to the kindling, and after that removed the noose from my neck and added it to the tinder; it would bind me to a martyr's futility no longer. The flame that took was not large, but ran with Woodstockian wind, and by the time I'd reached the left wing, the tiny figure on the stage had become the eye of a generational fire, so blazing hot that even the film crews stopped shooting so that they could stand back.

"I'm Jolami Tiombe." She cleared her throat. "Or Bunny Tucker? Of the Beau-Ts?"

No music was passé to this crowd. They whooped.

"And I guess I'm going to play you a song."

Her left fingers found frets, her right hand hovered over the hole.

495

She looked over her shoulder to find that she was all alone, that I'd left her, likely forever, and in a position of utmost vulnerability. From afar, through flames, she found me. I held her gaze as one might hold a loved one's hand before the train departed, and then submerged myself into shadow. Her position did not have to be vulnerable, thought I, not if she hit that first chord hard enough.

She raised a Black Power fist and guessed, correctly, that I would see it.

There are suns one dare not stare at directly, lest one's retinas scorch. I hurried off, pushing past humanoid shapes. Behind me, above me, all around me, Bunny Tucker played the only song she ever wrote, denuded of its Motown varnish and whittled to its heartwood. In a voice rubbed raw by a half-decade screaming for justice, she sang, and in that coarse crackle everyone could hear a gospel, and the numbers of those saved by it would reach higher than fifty-one. Bunny's tune had become a eulogy for the almost-chart-topping radio version of the song as much as it was for an older, shinier, but not quite lost version of the nation.

> Old Mr. Finch, he swung low from a tree
> But he stood back up, just as fine as one can be. We said . . .
> "Hey, Mr. Finch, how 'bout you rest your weary head?"
> But he only smiled and laughed, "I got bigger plans instead . . ."

I'd sampled no brown acid, and yet my senses of sight, smell, taste, and touch had gone misty. By the time I located Church's tent and found not so much as a wheelchair rut, the only sense still working was sound. I found my aviators, put them on despite the dark, turned toward the wet grass of the back field, and began to walk,

496

my feet finding the rhythm of Bunny's final verse, sung in the rapture of one who remembered, the instant her fingertips touched steel strings, that a little girl's dreams only die when that little girl quits dreaming, a rapture that made you believe that Amerika could still be America if we all sang the same words.

Old Mr. Finch,
Across the land he goes.
No rope, no bullet, no gun
Can stop him because he knows . . .

That him and her and you and me
Are the same as we can be
And though there'll be dusk before the dawn
Old Mr. Finch keeps ramblin' on . . .

PART ELEVEN

1970–1984

=◈=

A Discourse On Megalomania And The Doctrine Of Ecstatic Consumption; Or, The Savages' Fifteen Minutes of Fame—Bon Appétit.

I.

THE DEAREST READER'S DOGGED FIDELITY is rewarded: Here is your bone.

It is possible that first seeing the name "Zebulon Finch" upon this anthology of notebooks excited you for one reason: the Canyon Diablo Catastrophe, as the papers put it; *Death in the Desert*, as ABC titled their antiseptic Movie of the Week; or simply the Savage Tragedy, which has nosed ahead as history's favorite. The state-funded obelisk holding the memorial plaque was cut, or so I understand, from black quartz, and though civilization may have vaporized by your time, I wager that the obelisk still stands out there in the desert, bearing blinkless witness to all those who perished.

The rolled joint of the Love Decade burned to a roach after the cultural orgasm of Woodstock, first with the Altamont Free Concert in December, an attempt at duplicating three days of peace and music that instead resulted in dozens of injuries and four deaths, including a stabbing by a Hell's Angel security guard while Mick Jagger sludged through a jittery rendition of "Under My Thumb." The killer's blade was long. It punctured America's lungs, and the wheezing, coughing, blood-spitting end came from the icons who'd otherwise howled: Hendrix, Joplin, and Morrison, all stiff and cold from overdoses in under a year.

Everyone, stay away from the brown acid, all right?

Who, though, could blame Jimmy, Janis, and Jim for exiting the stage prior to the inevitable, exhausting encores? In November 1969, these musicians had read the same confessions everyone else had of U.S. infantrymen who'd rounded up children in the Vietnam village of My Lai and unloaded carbine clips into their soft bodies before rolling them into ravines, a behavior to which, if memory serves, we'd made it a point to object when the SS had done it to Jews. After My Lai, what true believer didn't fill his syringe with experimental cocktails half-hoping it would be her or his last?

Yet the anguish might have stayed locked inside nightmare cages had it not been for a fidgety creeper named Charles Manson, who disassembled the mass-printed and primetime-televised fable that we all ought to grin and go buy the world a Coke.

The Coke, it turned out, was tainted.

What shook me, Reader, was that I'd *known* Charles Manson. Indeed, our shared ghost moments made Chuck and me almost brothers. While I'd watched Ritchie Tucker bleed out in New York City, Chuck had been strolling out of a San Pedro, California, prison after a six-year sentence for pimping and parole violation. We were as geographically distant from each other as possible in the contiguous U.S., yet we snapped together like magnets. Secondhand guitar slung across his back, Chuck, daydreaming of a record deal, bused himself to San Fran's hippie mecca of Haight-Ashbury, one of the most popular sites of my martyrdoms in the country.

Am I imagining that it was Chuck who enthusiastically shook my hand after multiple staged deaths? Or was it just one of the hundreds like him, verbose, greasy-bearded would-be musician-prophets? I am certain Chuck watched me die at least once, certain that he wrote a song about it, certain that he strummed that song at the tumbleweed estate of his incipient, insipid "Family," where, by all published reports, he pretended to be me, faux-crucifying himself so his followers could play apostle and weep upon his feet, before orgying toward his resurrection. Even then, he pined for the attention given to Zebulon X, and so dragged his dreams, screaming and bleeding, into reality.

Yes, I might have inspired Charles Manson.

But in the end, as you shall see, he inspired me.

Woodstock's daybreak rain was sheeting when I found my dirt road escape path blocked by the least forgiving of crossing guards. It was Ruthie Ness, recognizable not only for the umbrella she alone among thousands had had the foresight to pack, but also her genteel ensemble of wool coat and black trousers. Lodged into her free elbow like Church's football was her cherished golden lockbox. With a mind toward symbolism, she'd waited for me at the choke point of an intersection, shoulders hunched against the chill, the steam from her skin the manifestation of her fury.

By contrast I was as pommeled and mudded as the road itself. Though I stood at a four-way junction, fewer routes than ever before were available. In relinquishing the spotlight to Bunny, Zebulon X had been effectively cremated, and unfastened from my noose at last, I was jetsam tossed by wayward waves. Oh, how I hated being wet; thus, I lost our game of chicken.

"It is a shame you traveled so far," said I. "You, who dislikes music."

"I can't believe you did this," hissed she.

"But I didn't. Behold: I am unburnt."

"Not that. I mean that you did it for *free*."

I laughed. My capitalist keeper never disappointed.

"Word will get out," continued she. "How do you expect Excelsior, Inc., to stay in the black?"

"I've been reminded other things are more important. I'm through. Step aside."

"You're through when I say you're through."

"Do not make me force you, woman."

"That's exactly what I'm doing. Force me. Let's see how you do it."

Stavros's *A Ghost Rolls Over* was too bloated by rain to serve as bludgeon. Gamely I looked about for other blunt objects, but our podunk environs offered nothing. Only the lockbox had the heft to serve as cudgel, and I'd never pry that from Ruthie's talons. The rain hardened, exploding upward from brown puddles. I wiped my face and glared. The ruminative mood in which Bunny had left me was curling away like burnt parchment.

"Go ahead, follow me. You are flesh and blood, if barely, and eventually you will sleep. And then I shall desert you, just as I did two nights ago. And I shall do it again, and again, and again, until your big, ugly shoes brim with blood from constant chase."

Had a forked tongue lashed out of Ruthie Ness's mouth, I would have been less surprised than I was by what happened. Her proud chin receded. The corners of her straight lips downturned. Her bun, strained from unusual facial flexings, released tendrils that, when isolated, looked soft and vulnerable. Her thick lenses fogged.

My dagger had at last struck not unyielding bone but live flesh.

"Are you—Miss Ness? Are you . . . *crying?*"

Her hands full, she thumped aside tears with a shoulder.

"You dahn't understahnd."

Her Boston accent was spiritless. To my shock, it dejected me. Somewhere along the long line we'd scribbled across America, I'd come to rely upon Ruthie's tenacity, if nothing else.

"How could I?" asked I. "You are as inscrutable as a Sphinx."

"I'm out heah . . . I'm with you at all because . . ."

Runners of rain sluiced across the underbelly of the umbrella, each bead attaching to her face like a wart. To shove past this shrew, realized I, would be to fling her to the ground, after which she'd be dotted by a million more warts and rashed by a pox of mud. How could I do such a thing at the moment when she'd become halfway human, and a moment after I'd been touched by Woodstock's brotherly love? I searched the rain. Not a single soaked hippie was in sight. The planet, miserably, was our own.

"It's foah my family," blurted Ruthie.

As a boy without one, the f-word always startled me. Even jackals, supposed I, had jackal parents.

"Your story, if I recall, was that your parents are dead."

Ruthie nodded. Her bun further unspooled.

"They ahh. That wasn't a lie. And I sworah to myself that I wahd do everything they cahdn't. I wahd make something of myself. And not by fetching coffee foah the boss or typing his memos. By creating something of my own and sticking with it until there was no mistaking I'd succeeded."

"That you chose me as an industry is absurd. Why?"

"Does it mattah? The point is, I did. And if I fail, that's my fault, and I'll have to live with it. But yoah cahn't *fahce* me to fail. You just cahn't."

My role as a Better God was over, and yet I had been made better, hadn't I? Right at the end, courtesy of guardian angels Burt Churchwell and Bunny Tucker? Their flapping wings urged compassion, or at least patience. Ruthie Ness, after all, was a safe I'd failed so long to crack. Perhaps, somewhere deep inside her, were pearls of purity and gems of goodness. Where else but the path out of Woodstock would I be so charitably inclined?

"From here onward," warned I, "I make the calls. I choose what's right, what's wrong."

Hope glowed through the splints of her mucked lashes. For several unnerving seconds, her muscular rigidity gave way to a Merle-like jerking and sniffling, before the rope of control reknotted itself and began to crank tight the slack. Ruthie's voice, sandbagging against hurricanes of emotion, hiccuped, then reclaimed its careful mid-Atlantic accent.

"I'll find a way to make it work, Mr. Finch, to make everything work. Leave it to me. Leave absolutely everything to me."

II.

CRYING HAD HUMILIATED RUTHIE NESS, and to cover she rammed ahead like never before. By nightfall, we'd hiked against a renewed tide of concertgoers, found paved land, hitchhiked to Poughkeepsie, and taken adjacent rooms in a roadside inn. After she shut her door, I heard the click and hum of her television warming up—a signal, thought I, that she was trusting me not to flee. Nothing made more sense than absconding, yet I found my ankles invisibly manacled. A new page, albeit in a strange language, had turned. What if the first person I could help in my post-Zebulon X guise was Ruthie Ness? Warily, but hopefully, I kept by her side.

The Poughkeepsie Truce, an addendum to our Scorched Earth Doctrine, remained in effect a week later. When our savings, or so reported Ruthie, had dwindled to nearly nothing, an age-mottled, furry-eared fellow became the third person to track me down via Woodstock's ubiquitous radio spots. Ruthie's sonar was in full effect; I never would've known of the old fart's arrival if Ruthie hadn't deemed him useful. She knocked, then opened my door wide enough for the geriatric to shuffle inside without aid of cane or walker. I was seated in the room's only chair, so he was forced to struggle with the bed, while Ruthie, apex predator, preferred the high ground of standing.

"This is Hershel Harel. He is a lawyer. He has something to say."

Harel—why was the name familiar? By the way the old-timer scoured my face instead of arm nub, I judged that he too had a familiarity. Finally he chuffed as if underwhelmed. Muttering, he unbuckled a valise and removed a folder of legal papers. Ruthie's stock in trade; her eyes lamped.

"I think this whole thing is garbage," grouched he. "How many years did I try to talk sense into her? She didn't have any family left, but who cares? There are charities, I said, foundations, I said. Your name isn't mud. Maybe we can get a theater named after you. But you think a shikse like that even listened to a shlemiel like me? She did her own lawyering, you know. I only gave advice, which she never took."

Without realizing it, I'd moved to the edge of my chair.

"Who?" asked I.

Harel snorted. "Bridey Valentine. Maybe you've heard of her?"

The memory of Harel's name rushed back. Bridey used to phone him when she couldn't untangle a gnarl of warranties, indemnifications, or arbitrations. Rich detail from Bridey's Colonial Queen Anne mansion, a galaxy away from this dank and mildewy hovel, came along with Harel's name, how the coldness of the marble floors made muggy clouds alongside the roaring fireplaces, the clucking and sighs of the hall of grandfather clocks, the floral perfumes that eddied in the wake of Bridey's saunter. Horrible things had happened in that place near the end, but those were seeds I could spit. The overall flavor was delicious: her lips, which tasted of lipstick and bruising; her skin, which tasted of strawberry; her sweat, that bottomless salt lick—and all of it dished freely to a cold corpse, without equivocation.

"How is she?" stammered I. "Is she here?"

"You schmuck. Bridey Valentine is dead."

Tales from the obituarist, Dearest Reader, never fail to stun. The Excelsior against my breast must have needed winding, for the next click of the second hand took ten years to pass. Afraid that I would begin blubbering in front of Ruthie—penance for having watched her do the same—I fished out the pocket watch and busied myself turning its dial while my mind likewise cranked. It did no good. I could feel Bridey's lotioned thighs gliding over my celibate torso, her every flex and throb seducing me from Wilma Sue, even one night suggesting, as you might recall, that we film our unnatural deeds toward a promise that had at last been revealed as a lie:

Pictures never die, silly. That's why I, too, am going to live forever.

Bridey had meant for Zebulon Finch to be part of her permanent collection, but it was Bridey who'd been boxed and stowed by a disinterested graveyard collector. My motel room, itself a cheap casket, collapsed around me, and though I no longer breathed, I struggled for breath.

"This is . . . difficult . . . to understand—"

"Why's that? She was seventy-eight and lived hard. It's bullshit you don't already know she's gone. So many charities and foundations I showed her, oy vey. Because I was her friend, you understand? And who are you? She wouldn't tell me a thing."

I needn't have worried about Ruthie relishing my discomfort. Her eyes were locked on Harel's folder.

"Tell Mr. Finch what you've brought."

Harel pointed a crooked finger at me. "If Mr. Finch meant anything to Miss Valentine, he'd already know!"

"You promised your client." Ruthie was done with pussyfoot. "Do your job, Mr. Harel."

He muttered profanities and removed a stapled packet.

"The last will and testament," boomed he, "of Bridey Valentine."

Congratulations, Margeaux had cracked as we'd motored toward her 1941 Winter Formal. *Mother put you in her will.* It wasn't that I'd forgotten; it was that I'd assumed my role in the death of her daughter had been enough to prompt a revision. Perhaps Bridey had been so grief-stricken that she'd forgotten? No, for Harel had said he'd tried to talk her out of it. What, then, was behind this? Was is possible that Bridey had understood me more than I'd ever dared believe, had known the crash had been Margeaux's wish, and had augured that, decades later, I'd still be drifting the earth, more alone and designless than ever?

"Tell him the figure," ordered Ruthie.

"Just under a million," said Harel.

Dollars? I stared at Ruthie, whose blouse looked to be soaked in drool.

"And it would've been a hell of a lot more," roared Harel, "if she'd done what I told her: quit acting and start saving. You know what was not fun? Watching it all fall apart. The cars, the home, everything. I watched that. Hershel Harel watched that. Where were you?"

You may find it difficult to lament the fates of the famous and rich, but for me it was reflex. The butler, gone. The cook, gone. The lady's maid, Japanese gardener, chauffeur, hairdresser, vocal coach, all gone, each loss feeling to Bridey as the Triangulinos' piece-by-piece amputations had felt to me.

"But a shikse like that! She kept doing pictures, hoping one of them would break big. But how could they? Dirty little nickel-and-dimers. Punk kids with cameras debasing a Hollywood legend. If you're lucky, you've never seen them."

Fifteen years ago, I'd walked Junior to the Orpheum and seen Bridey's fifty-seven-year-old face grimacing on ads for fare like *Cult of the Tarantula*. Those had been hard enough to swallow, but the productions Harel began listing wouldn't even play in Wichita; they'd be relegated to sleazy urban grindhouses. I recall these titles only in prurient pieces: the words "Gutter" and "Bloodbath," "Naughty" and "Centerfold," "Depraved" and "Swingers," "Virgin" and "Violated"— and "Teenage," always "Teenage." Bridey, of course, had been too old for the jailbait roles but still famous enough to ensure that the fresh packages of teen meat would sell worldwide.

"If she hadn't made those pictures, I wouldn't need to tell you she was dead. Her obituary would've been on the front pages, where it belonged."

Ruthie came at us with a dagger. No, a pen.

"Sign on the lines, Mr. Finch," said she.

Walking away from Woodstock had been a walk away from money. What good could it do me? But sign I did, page after page, four copies of each, though I could not feel the implement inside my palm. Harel was old, and he'd tired himself out; he scrawled where he needed to scrawl, and then Ruthie got in on the fun, signing as carefully as if she were composing a sonnet. When all was complete, Harel wiped his hands as if brushing off what he might call shmutz, stowed his copy of the forms, unhappily provided his business card, and hobbled toward the door, where he paused to give me a stare that damned me more than a thousand Yiddish slurs.

"All she wanted to do was make this one special picture. She threw millions at producers in France, Italy, India, not a one of whom did anything but cut and run. Who can blame them? She never let them read the script! But Zebulon Finch, she said—Zebulon Finch would understand. What does that mean? Feh. It's my concern no more. Now it's yours. So don't be another punk kid, you hear me? Do what the rest of the world didn't do and make Bridey Valentine proud."

To her dying day, she'd tried to get *In Our Image*, her magnum opus, produced. And I, it seemed, had been the only person ever to read it, save those last few pages.

Here, already, was my answer to why the inheritance mattered. Harel's exhortation, conflated with my directionless melancholy, resulted in the swift certainty that I, Bridey's lover and confidant, was responsible for realizing her stymied vision. I stood, surprising Harel and alarming Ruthie, and began to nod, for my dry cavities had been quickened with purpose. Bridey's last wish was a compass with which I might navigate. True, I was an amateur, but I had at my disposal three important things. One: money, barrels of it. Two: Ruthie Ness, a woman with a producer's ability to alchemize my fantasies into reality. And three, that rarest of commodities: all the time in the world.

Sufferers of my biography's every convolution won't raise an eyebrow that, by summer, Ruthie and I were on horseback in the Arizona desert. Our Mexican guide, a vaquero named Eduardo, was not much of a tour guide, though on occasion he did flap his ten-gallon hat at shadscale shrubs that resembled boobs and at rock tors that resembled penises. I rather appreciated the man's wordless humor, while Ruthie, still subject to a living being's sore legs and aching ass, filled his back with imaginary bullets.

Eduardo wasn't being paid for commentary. After a long wait for Bridey's cash to fatten the Excelsior, Inc., coffers, I'd demanded that Ruthie purchase a car, which she did with characteristic practicality—

not the brand-new onyx-black Mercury Marauder I requested but a used Ford Fairlane station wagon the color of feces. The smell inside it, though, I could only blame on myself; for the remainder of my tale, Dearest Reader, there will be no more hiding my deterioration. With sunlight magnified through dashboard glass, my flesh heated and my seat filled with a beige crumble of skin. I thought of Mauthausen's chimney stacks, their spouting embers, and the Millennialist, who was bound to catch us if we stopped.

Across America I drove our odoriferous auto on a haphazard hunt for a place from which I could conceptualize *In Our Image* without interruption. Outside of Flagstaff, our shit-wagon broke down with all the spectacle of the Fourth of July, spewing black smoke and shooting fire. One-armed men cannot applaud, but I snapped appreciation like a beatnik while Ruthie scrambled with her lockbox from the blast zone.

Eduardo was laboring at a ranch thereabouts. We found him courtesy of the smoking bonfire he'd made of invasive brush. Though his English was meager, he nodded confidently when I told him I was looking for a special place unlike any other in the world. He whistled while trailing a finger from the clouds to the ground. I had no idea what that meant.

"*Sí, señor.* I know where. *Muy especial.*"

Eduardo shrugged at his bonfire, making it clear that he would never dream of abandoning such a fulfilling job. I showed him what two hundred dollars looked like, and he summoned three *caballos* out of thin air, saddled them with vittles and pup-tents and the golden lockbox, and after a too-short lesson on equine etiquette, led us into the horizon on clopping hooves. Ruthie was aghast, but her post-cry quality of determination persevered.

Her concern, to be fair, had merit. The Great Basin is the largest desert habitat in America, a two-hundred-thousand-square-mile death trap triggered between the Sierra Nevada and Wasatch Range, and if we got lost, Ruthie might well be forced to eat our horses, then Eduardo, then me. My trust in our guide, however, grew by the mile. This was where I was supposed to be, I could feel it. The Marlboro Man's Montana had been magnificent, but the cold northern atmosphere had preserved my corpse too well. The desert's opposite climate would be more conducive to my overdue business of disintegration, thereby pushing me to work like Bridey: hard, fast, day, night.

We shall spend some time in this desert, Dearest Reader; let me situate you. Imagine eternal runways of olive gravel and pale yellow grass leading toward bulging bluffs twice as distant as they appear. Picture boulders tossed impossibly across sand. Visualize tall, lonely cacti trolling through stiff snags of brush like lost monsters. Smell the hot sandstone, the fleeting wafts of carrion spoil. Feel the heat as flat as a griddle against your every exposed inch. See the sky, blue glass or black oil, or if a storm is coming, gray goiters bulging with magma red. The desert is Earth's *la silenziosità*: stillness so infinite, you cannot see the mountain mandible that, millennia by millennia, closes around you.

After a night spent tented between shrieking coyotes, we loped across Canyon Diablo—the Devil's Canyon, a parched patch of Navajo land defined by a winding arroyo—until Eduardo pointed at what looked like a long butte. "*Muy especial*," he repeated. It was only after heading up the butte's lip hours later that I began to feel a prickling in my guts so faint, I doubted that my breathing companions would notice it. A force was pulling me at the molecular level.

I goosed my horse, and it galloped to the top of the rise, where the view spread out before me as if spilled by a clumsy child. This was no butte.

It was a hole scooped from the earth by a hand of unrealizable size, a crater over a mile in diameter, with striated slopes diving five hundred feet to a tawny base upon which one could arrange twenty football fields. It was a sea without water, a coliseum for giants. Eduardo's horse joined mine.

"*Especial*," said I. "Very *especial*."

Eduardo repeated the gesture he'd made before we'd set out, tracing a finger from clouds to crater.

"A meteor," guessed I.

"*Sí, señor. Muy, muy grande.*"

Ruthie, the lousiest rider of our trio, arrived and alighted from her animal, and with sore buttocks clenching beneath unsuitable dress slacks, walked to the crater's edge. Even she, self-taught to have diatribes prepared on profit margins and tax incentives, was speechless.

"Here," said I. "It must be here."

"What?" asked Ruthie.

"Home."

The word was simple and gorgeous. Had I ever called someplace home and truly felt it? It was past time. I was seventeen, old enough for a place of my own.

Ruthie pulled herself from the crater's psychological stranglehold and turned. Small glasslike rocks crackled like wine-bottle glass beneath her city shoes. She shaded her eyes with saddle-reddened palms.

"You want to live here."

I nodded. And smiled. I did.

"That," said she, "is ridiculous."

Before such rocky majesty, Ruthie Ness was a pebble.

"No one is forcing you to stay," said I. "Your steed awaits."

"Mr. Finch, please, I'm trying to work with you. I've come this far, haven't I? You have to work with *me*, just a little. There's no one around for miles. You're as good as dead out here."

Right away she flinched at the comment. My smile stretched across the leathered skin of my face. As good as dead? Why, that sounded perfect. Ruthie, emptied of persuasions, wiped at the sweat from her hairline and panted in the sun. It was just the moment of doubt I'd been watching for since her breakdown in the rain. I held my animal steady as Ruthie cycled through mistrustful squints, judgmental nose-wrinkles, and indignant lip lickings. I rooted for her, Reader; I did. I couldn't hope to execute grand plans without her as agent, and I prayed she'd take my boldly dangled bait.

She considered the infinite baked acres beyond the crater. I followed suit. How had this happened? Me, establishing a desert refuge, just like Chuck Manson?

Ruthie did not disappoint. She broke the spell by hurling sunlight at me off her glasses.

"You're intent on challenging me," said she. "Fine. Watch me rise to it."

III.

CONSTRUCTION BEGAN ON JULY 1, 1971. The temperature was 106 degrees, but the Flagstaff crew's sweet-potato tans were impervious as they pushed dirty fingertips across blueprints and jostled throttles on their dumpers, loaders, backhoes, dozers, graders, mixers, pavers, and forklifts. Ruthie believed my obsession with *In Our Image* a result of sunstroke, but it wasn't in her character to back down until I saw the extent of my mistake, at which point she believed she could get us back to the business of making money. Indeed, we might need it. A third of Bridey's million was going to the home, and it sickened Ruthie. I saw her slink away twice to vomit, though it could have been the heat.

Our bad luck was that the crater had been assigned National Landmark status three years prior. The closest property we could purchase was a two-hour hike due west, though thanks to the planate topography, the crater's rim remained visible. Isolation slowed the builders' pace—first, they had to build roads—and during downtimes, I costumed myself in long sleeves, the cowboy hat I'd bartered from Eduardo, and my NASA aviators and sidled next to the men. Even laborers this gruff were tickled by the project's novelty and fed me, in dribs and drabs, the strange history of the Barringer Crater.

Daniel Moreau Barringer had been an explorer as rotund as he'd been brash, scouring the West in the 1800s for exploitable mineral deposits. Around the time that I was fixing to duel the Barker, Barringer's inventory of what was soon to be called Arizona climaxed with a visit to the crater. Ruthie Ness would have admired Barringer's nose for profit; he tested for nickel, found it, linked it with findings in known meteorites, and determined to extract ore that, by his ginger estimation, would fetch one hundred million bucks.

That had been the tugging I'd felt while approaching the crater: meteorite particles still magnetized fifty thousand years after impact. They'd also pulled at Barringer, whose obsession turned him into an object of ridicule. In 1908 alone, he dug twenty-eight holes, all of them damned. Industrial drills became stuck or simply broke. Shafts flooded with groundwater. Experts, beginning to pity poor Barringer, theorized that the meteorite had vaporized on impact, not unlike the hundreds of thousands of dollars Barringer had invested. By 1929, it was accepted that the value of the ore could not possibly equal the price of acquiring it—and yet Barringer, like Dr. Leather, slogged after his impossible goal, until he died, twenty-six years after he'd begun, and no closer to victory.

What convinced me that I had found my destiny was how the crater, like my own body, was a shrine to human folly, beginning with Barringer's failure but continuing with the 1950s fire that had burned the rimside structure where specimens had been studied; the airplane that had crashed into its western wall in 1964, its wrecked fuselage too unwieldy to bother removing; the crater's use in the late 1960s as a lunarscape for Apollo astronauts, including the doomed; and now me, the biggest catastrophe of all.

I felt at home before the home was finished. We went over budget by half, but I'd become incapable of doubt. Ruthie dizzied and tizzied, but no matter how often she gazed longingly at the road leading toward civilization, she never took it, and for this I began to feel ever more kindly toward her. She and I were in this together, for better or worse. (Take a wild guess which, Reader.)

The completed structure was of Spanish Territorial style, a one-story, eight-room, clay-roofed, whitewashed adobe *casa del poblador* built in a U-shape around a small patio featuring a burbling fountain, alongside which I planned to spend months deliberating *In Our Image*. So convinced was I by the mysticism that had brought me to Canyon Diablo that I believed I was incapable of bad ideas. Did Bridey's story have to be a film, wondered I? Could her message be delivered through a play? How about a record album packaged with a storytelling gatefold?

Upon a patio shelf, I gave *A Ghost Rolls Over* a place of honor. No sooner had I placed it than a burst of desert wind tossed the rain-warped pages from poem to poem, rasping like Church's stroke-damaged voice.

Private Finch, it whispered. *Keep going.*

The first of them arrived while Ruthie and I selected doors from a catalogue. As she vetoed my exorbitant favorites, I noticed the oddest thing: an overheated Mustang convertible on our property, against which leaned a quartet of twentysomethings. While Ruthie haggled with the architect, I watched the newcomers; seeing me watch, they stood straighter. Though they'd parked at a distance, they looked to be ex-Woodstockers, hair still long but no longer woven with daisies; clothes still colorful but not so harlequin; and postures more stooped, for vagabondage had been traded years ago for shit jobs and car payments, and such obligations broke backs.

Being eyeballed perturbed me, but it was October, and desert nights could sink to the twenties. In a canvas-topped convertible, they'd freeze. Yet when Ruthie and I hunkered down in our new, if doorless, quarters, the foursome did not leave. They huddled beneath blankets in their Mustang, watching our house like a drive-in movie before shivering themselves to sleep.

By the time the doors were installed, there was a total of two cars and six people. By the time water flowed from our single pump— it made the developer nervous, but Ruthie was a tightwad—the vehicles had copulated and birthed twice as many passengers. The construction crew packed up, and Ruthie and I were left with this convergence of ex-hippies. It could have been a siege; we should have been frightened. But I detected no menace, and neither did Ruthie, who scoped them with her X-ray glasses to screen for signs of money.

I resolved to grant the oglers not a second more of my valuable time. I retired to the patio, where I'd assembled a desk-and-chair facsimile of Mrs. White's basement berth, and removed with relish the first of a bulk order of composition books. Thirty years had elapsed since I'd read Bridey's script, but I was certain I remembered enough. Atop the first page, I wrote with a curlicued flourish:

IN OUR IMAGE: IDEAS!

But the yawning page possessed none of the gabby magic of the biographical notebooks you now hold. For two weeks I added nothing besides further festooning of the title. At every rise of wind, I looked to *A Ghost Rolls Over*, hoping Church's voice might return with further advice. Finally I broke, blaming my authorial impotence on the incessant chatter from the front yard. I threw down my pencil, stalked along the arcade, and found Ruthie in the frontmost salon watching them through a window. She heard my arrival and spoke without turning.

"They've set up tents and teepees. They're sharing pots of food."

"They're lost. Their whole damn generation is lost."

"They don't look lost to me. They look happy. They look like they're waiting."

"I told you. No more martyrdoms."

"I know."

"If they want to stand around and stare, it's a free desert."

"It is." Ruthie's tone made it clear what she thought of the word "free."

"On second thought," said I, "they're squatting upon the private property of Excelsior, Inc. Possibly they require a scaring off."

"Go ahead. I bet they'd be glad to see you."

"You do it, then. You're far scarier than I."

"How long has it been since you saw them?"

She tugged me closer by the sleeve. Circumstantial contact, Reader, yet it brought a bloom of unexpected warmth to cold, grateful bones, and I obediently shambled forward. Because I had to duck beneath a glare, the reveal was not gradual but abrupt. Twenty-five people had set up camp in a semicircle fifty yards from the house. My days with NSTF had habituated me to organic farms and co-ops, but there were no chickens to feed here, no gardens to tend, no produce to swap. Canyon Diablo was a wasteland, and they ate from dusty supermarket cans before walking behind a patch of cacti where a crude latrine had been established. All the while, their faces behaved like sunflowers, following the sun, which was, I realized, me.

"It's a bloody cult," said I.

How did Manson's dune-buggy ruts keep trapping me?

"Such an uncharitable word," tsked Ruthie. "Look closer. Who do you see?"

"To the left, dimwits. To the right, dunderheads."

"No judgments. Who do you see?"

Seek-and-find games were for children. I looked from grubby face to peeling shoulders to underfed ribs. I was about to double down on my reply when I was struck by a shared trait so obvious as to be invisible.

"They're women," said I.

"Nine out of ten of them. Why do you think that is?"

"You're a woman, or so I understand. You tell me."

"Have you heard of the feminine mystique?"

"The phrase is 'sex appeal,' Miss Ness. Naturally you are unfamiliar."

On the heels of her friendly tug, my snap was unbecoming. If she minded, though, she had the maturity not to show it.

"*The Feminine Mystique*. It's a book. It's about women's dissatisfaction with their limited roles in society. Their frustration with a destiny that begins and ends with their anatomy."

"I see you've slogged through this polemic."

She shrugged. "It was popular in law school."

"So our trespassers are women's-libbers? Perplexing."

"Is it? I want you to think about that. About the women you knew in the fifties, the women you knew in the sixties. What they wanted versus what they got."

I pondered Mrs. White, housetrained by the Mrs. Shoemakers of the world until her only extant dream was winning the Pillsbury Bake-off. I thought of Janice the flower child and Bunny the militant, both pursuing a fulfillment that, at last check, was far from filled. My tie-dyed memories were, in fact, filled with young women protesters treated like children by condescending college profs and supposed male allies, both of whom encouraged bra burning for no reasons beyond the salacious.

When midday heat was at its fiercest, packs of females would help themselves to the house's shade for what they called "rap sessions." Like the creep I was, I took to slinking to the nearest window to eavesdrop. Tale by tale, trauma by trauma, I began to solve Ruthie's riddle. Some of the women were divorcées who'd fled wife-swapping key parties and were now scared stupid by the lack of survival skills acquired during wedded subservience. Others were young women traumatized by the "liberation" that had dragged them through addiction, poverty, prostitution, rape, or abortion.

"Question Authority" had been the hippie slogan they'd once promulgated, but now they longed for Authority's return, and I did sympathize. In the absence of Abigail and Bartholomew Finch, hadn't I attached myself to ninety-two years of authority figures? Still, though, regardless of what these crackpots saw in me, it was necessary that they quit my land. So it happened in the infant days of 1972, inflamed by my lack of progress with *In Our Image*, that I chose to show them how they'd hitched their pioneer wagons to a bucking bronco. From what I knew of cultists, they'd be difficult to dispel, but I was in a mood bad enough to try.

Ruthie spread the word in what, for her, passed as chipper spirits. For months she'd endured desert purgatory with a distracted artiste, without contriving a single way to bleed our odd idolators of money. Her body drummed with a physical need to take what was left of Bridey's bounty, relocate us to civilization, and get to resuscitating Excelsior, Inc.

Minutes before dusk on February 7, I adorned myself in Eduardo's cowboy hat and NASA aviators and opened the front door to find the whole dusk-lit rag-tag bunch, which had grown by then to thirty, silent in rapt readiness. The Reader might expect that my long-awaited emergence would provoke applause, but it generated only gasps, a sensible reaction, seeing how, aside from the aforesaid hat and shades, I was naked.

Even now I consider the stratagem shrewd, if requiring great feasts of swallowed pride. I needed not utter a word for them to extrapolate from my debilitated build how unsuited I was for idolization. Their bulging eyes flew first to the most garish of wounds: the gnarled arm nub; the dry hanks of flesh marking the former domains of my pecker and bollocks; the oft-stitched stomach flap. I forced myself not to cover my body as they explored my quirkiest wounds, from the thigh gash where a shattered klieg light had impaled me during my newsreel shoot, to Clown's lovingly mauled plaything.

I awaited the curled lips of disgust, the fumbling from purses of car keys, the moaning realizations of having steered down another of life's dead ends. What happened instead: a young woman dropped to her knees on the hard desert floor and stared in apparent disbelief at her own unclean but intact limbs. Clean tears carved lines through her dirty cheeks. She looked, Reader, if I dare say it, grateful.

Exaltation spread like a puddle. Some lay flat on their faces as if unworthy. Others raised arms over their heads in surrender as if hoping those who'd ruined my body would do the same to theirs. It was forty degrees at sundown; they were cold. The group had drawn tighter; they were huddled. My sweltered brain fused the qualities: these were America's cold, huddled masses, their legend carved into the Statue of Liberty's pedestal, and like travelers passing through Ellis Island, they'd taken painful journeys to get here and wanted only that a tall, noble figure might lift a torch so that they might follow it. And they'd chosen me. No, let me restate that.

Of course they'd chosen me.

Enlightenment draped over me like a coronated king's Pallium Regale. Church had lost part of his face and become a better person, then had lost mastery of voice and leg to become a near-perfect one. Why should it surprise me that while becoming *less*, I, too, had been becoming *more*? Even that I lacked genitalia felt inevitable. I was not Man, who had harried these admirers, nor Woman, who had competed with them at every turn. I was beyond gender, a newborn of sorts, a starchild conceived in the solar-storm womb of *Harpocrates 7* and birthed by thousands of wet nurses at Woodstock.

The sun was low behind me, painting vermillion the faces of the ardent. I'd anticipated this, hence the cowboy hat and aviators. What I hadn't anticipated was the beauty with which the sun imbued them, how each smudge of dirt became the perfect application of natural cosmetics. *Forget the Fifty-One*, thought I. This group was smaller but growing by the day, not only ready to be saved by me but also ready—why not?—to thank me for it.

Behind them spread the crater's rim like mighty pterodactyl wings. Was it the meteorite's magnetism that began pulling words from my gut? What I said during that sunset would become known as the First Address, loosely paraphrased years later in competing memoirs from two survivors. Before the calamitous climax, Dearest Reader, you will recoil at the Second Address and exclaim in horror at the Third Address. If it helps you make it through, consider it a game: count down the three addresses as you might the dropping of the atomic bomb.

"You have suffered at the hands of men," said I.

My voiced cracked. *Think of Church*, I told myself, *forcing words through his stroke-strangled throat, of Bunny, leaning bravely into the stage microphone.*

"You have suffered at the hands of women, too," continued I. "But I want you to know something: that suffering is over. Many years ago a doctor named Cornelius Leather introduced to me the concept of a People Garden, a place where warm bodies could cool, and age, and fall apart in peaceful fellowship. I found it repulsive at the time, but I was foolish. Only right now do I see that. You and I, all of us, are part of the same garden. Dear Gød, does any of this make sense?"

The question was for myself, but the women, as well as the few men, nodded with enthusiasm, and I continued, taking up a gospel cadence I must have learned from Reverend Tucker.

"You have traveled far into the desert because you hunger for a garden's sustenance. I did the same thing twenty-five years ago with a fellow called the Marlboro Man, and I found that garden once more on a city roof of a man named von Lüth. Look around you! Out here there is nothing but nature. Out here we can live as we were born to live: as animals harmonized with our earth, casting away the dogmas of decorum and physical appearance that have always enslaved us."

From where did this rhetoric derive? The answer thrilled me. *In Our Image.* From her first facelift to every subsequent nipple nip and tummy tuck, Bridey had been forced into the iron maiden of Hollywood expectations, until she was physically and emotionally minced. The script's final scene, as described by Bridey, was an indictment of the standards that were killing her, with her female protagonist being dissected, chopped up, and sold as parcels of meat.

Bridey had been confident that *In Our Image* would improve women's lives, and her script, realized I, needn't be a film I funded or a play I produced. It could be real life, my house and acreage the set, the cultists the actors. My desire to do some good on this rotten planet might at last succeed without mediators—no MGM Studios, no NASA brass, no NSTF bullhorners. Just these women in want of a purpose, and me, genderless doyen, who had a purpose to give them.

I glanced back at the house. Miss Ness was right where I needed her to be, watching from the window, her fingers starting to twitch for their calculator. I hesitated, just for a second, before the sandstorm whisper of my followers—"Yes, that's right, tell it"—hissed across the desert, hurrying me toward the finish before I could heed a second hiss coming from a rain-suppled book: *No, Private, you got it all mixed up in your dang head.*

"Look at yourselves. The state of your clothes, your skin. You're already beginning to let it fall away. That is why we, the Great Unwashed, gather not in some umbral underground but in Earth's brightest spot, so that we might finally see. Let us devolve so that we might evolve. Let us be beasts together. Throw away your combs, throw away your sponges, throw away your compacts of powders and puffs. Once all of us become what the city people call 'hideous,' what will be left for us to do but care for our fellow hideous? That is called love. And we shall know it. For maybe the first time in our woebegone lives, we shall know it."

IV.

BLAME IT ON THE DISORIENTING sunshine, as did one memoirist. Blame it on starvation, as did the other. Over the following months our twenty-seven women and three men (Ruthie had begun recording information on each) took my edict of anti-beauty to heart. Women quit wearing makeup. Everyone quit shaving. Bathing was abandoned—it was tough to do in the desert anyhow. In no time at all, the clothes, shredded and foul, came off. That's right, Reader, in emulation of their leader, my people became nudists. Thigh-length velvet shirts, midriff-baring two-piecers, embroidered pantsuits, thick platform shoes, and huge-collared mint-green leisure suits all got tossed into a pile and burned to a black polyester glob.

There was nothing erotic about my followers' nakedness. Bare bodies simply made it easier to chart one's progress down the anti-beautification scale. Certainly it brought our enclave notoriety. Voyeurs drove all the way to Canyon Diablo to see if the rumors were true. A small percentage of the voyeurs stayed with us, while the rest went home to spread word of the desert's strangest mirage.

Ruthie knew branding. Our group needed a name. So I supplied one that bridged the *In Our Image* storyline with the Montana ideal—the Savages. Ruthie believed repetition to be a winner, and thus our home became Savage Ranch, I became Mother-Father

Savage, and each Savage was asked to hand over her IDs and replace her surname. When a visitor approached the cult, it was common to overhear a screwy round of greetings. "Welcome. I'm Maggie Savage, and this is Francine Savage, Malaika Savage, and Simran Savage." (We were multiculturally ahead of our time—white, black, Latino, Indian, or Asian, our pot melted all of them down.)

I believe that Ruthie's obfuscation of the Savages' identities was meant to complicate potential lawsuits. She needn't have worried. The Savages protected me more ferociously than the Hell's Angels had the Rolling Stones. When the rare father did arrive to reclaim his daughter and demand to have words, the Savages surrounded the house with a human fence and, if they were pushed first, pushed back. It confused and terrified even the most pigheaded man to be beset by naked breasts and exposed pubic hair and have none of it, for once, be a Triple-X film produced for his pleasure.

All this the women did despite that I hadn't appeared since the First Address. When Ruthie began needling me to meet one-on-one with each Savage, it wasn't because she believed in my ambition of a purer society. What she wanted was to keep our school of fish from wiggling free of our net while she worked to monetize their loyalty. She had shown patience with me and deserved reciprocation. I agreed to hold private ten-minute meetings at the fatiguing rate of one per week.

Ruthie held a lottery, and a girl my age (seventeen, that is) was the first to win the pleasure of my company. Ruthie was, as ever, fully clothed in a polyester pantsuit when she escorted the naked, wide-eyed, and trembling Tammy Savage to the back patio. I was reclined on my wicker lounger in loose trousers and halfway buttoned shirt, as well as my trademark aviators and cowboy hat, holding court much like, I suppose, a Texan Luca Testa. I indicated the opposite chair, but Tammy was overwhelmed by the fountain in a landscape so scant of water. Ruthie took Tammy's shoulders, sat her upon the chair, and moved across the patio to monitor us from a shaded bench.

Truth be told, I was nervous as well. Though I spied my nude followers daily from ranch apertures, never had I been so close. Tammy's skin was mahogany from aggregations of sunburn. Her breasts looked large atop a torso withered from malnourishment. Her stomach and thighs were so coated in dirt that she looked to be wearing pantaloons.

"So," said I. "You ... ah ..."

She took a fistful of her hair and thrust it toward me.

"I haven't washed it in *months*. And it's softer, Mother-Father Savage, I swear it."

Softer, perhaps, but also a rat's nest of grimed knots and tumbleweed-thistled mats. A gorge of revulsion rose, but I fought it back by recalling the whorled pelts of mighty buffalo and majestic pronghorn I'd stroked under the Marlboro Man's guidance. Ruthie had been right. Tammy Savage looked happy. No, that word was lacking. The girl was conflagrant with joy.

And I was responsible! I'd done this!

"Beautiful," said I. "Your fingernails as well."

Tammy Savage dropped her hair-knot and stared at her nails so intently that her eyes crossed. The nails' edges were brown and ragged, the plates calved, the cuticles shredded.

"I used to paint them," mused she.

I recalled when the scandalous style had come into vogue, pointed out to me by an exuberant Church in a Manhattan gin joint. I nodded for her to continue.

"I had favorite brands and everything. Cutex, Clairol, Revlon. Favorite colors, too. Red Berry, Coral Sand—oh, Bright Cocoa was my favorite of all. But it's meaningless, isn't it? The whole circle? Looking like they say you should so you can be pretty, so you can get a job, so you can make money, so you can buy *more* things to look even *more* like they say you should? It's just like you told us. The entire order breaks down if you just let go of looks and let yourself become . . ."

Again I nodded her on.

"A Savage," said she.

Tears sprung to her eyes, though, with no mascara, nothing was in danger of running. Tammy Savage took a deep breath, her bare chest rising, her heart beating visibly beneath underfed flesh, her nostrils flaring hungrily when a breeze brought her my odor.

"We'll be animals," promised she, "all of us, just the way you want us."

In subsequent weeks I met Anita Savage, a mid-fifties woman who itemized for me every dirt-filled wrinkle she no longer treated with creams or hid behind foundation. Beverly Savage was twenty-five and struck silent with awe, though that didn't stop her from touring me through her body hair, thick enough now that it harbored burrs and small twigs. Rhonda Savage was in her late thirties and had what I took to be a speech impediment, until she peeled back her lips to show me the teeth she'd stopped brushing, several of them orange with plaque and suppurating from purple gums.

What my ego took from such blind allegiance is obvious. But what did Ruthie get? Plenty, Dearest Reader—Excelsior, Inc. was back in the black. Our small but steady influx of devotees were willing to sacrifice everything to Mother-Father Savage, and Ruthie took full advantage, explaining to them how the renunciation of societal norms included the relinquishment of worldly goods. This was no Woodstock; admittance was not free. The price of entry to Savage Ranch was the turning over of jewelry, heirlooms, wallets, checkbooks, Social Security payouts, and deeds to home and property. Ruthie promised to "get rid of" these tainted effects. She did, in a manner of speaking, absorbing the assets into the business account she'd set up in Flagstaff.

Only Ruthie's selling off their vehicles troubled me, for without them the Savages had no means of leaving, and I didn't like to think of myself as a warden. Ruthie kept the ranch's only car, our Ford Fairlane (the cheapskate had had it repaired), and before she took her weekly supply trips to town, she'd gather everyone's mail—missives reassuring loved ones, I was sure, that they were fine, their leader was righteous, and that there was no cause for concern.

Ruthie, though, saw no upside to these letters. They would only rile family and friends. Safer that the Savages drop from the face of the Earth, so she furtively filed the mail inside a spare room I came to call the Dead Letter Office. Bridey had maintained a similar space inside which she'd kept the materials for *In Our Image*. What was with women and their secret chambers? Some nights I'd prowl the house and long to read gushing laudation about myself, but the Dead Letter Office was always locked and Ruthie wasn't sharing the key. I'd need an ax to get in, which didn't seem worth the effort.

On New Year's Day 1973, the Savages began to develop. My meeting that evening was with Sharon Savage, who'd drawn poorly in Ruthie's lottery and was the last of our inaugural round of meetings. Sharon, however, looked serene enough when she arrived at the patio, situating her naked, formerly corn-fed but now gangling forty-year-old body on the chair and giving me a sly grin as if we were in longstanding cahoots. By then I was old hat at one-on-ones and knew the bits by which mares could be led.

"I am eager to hear all about you," cued I.

There was an established playbook. Sharon would begin with how she'd been brought up in Indiana or Idaho on the right side of Gød. Her parents hadn't been perfect, but they'd been good enough. But all the death in Vietnam, the injustices suffered by minorities, the Watergate stories suggesting President Nixon was a criminal— well, it'd become too much. Sharon would tell me how she'd felt her rope unravel from America's dock. Until, that is, she'd heard how that martyr fellow who'd disappeared in '69 had set up camp in the desert and scrubbed the complications of society down to bestial basics. That was when she had begun to feel the return of hope.

Except Sharon Savage ignored the script. She perched her butt on the edge of the chair and preened like a woman trying to catch the eye of a fellow across the bar, fluffing her mangy hair, arching her filth-striped back, and splaying her right hand across her stretch-marked stomach. She craved compliments, and I saw no reason to withhold them.

"Look at you. So animalistic, you'll soon walk on all fours."

"That's a wonderful idea, Mother-Father Savage."

"Thank you."

"You are filled with so much insight for someone so young."

"Again, I thank you."

"It's all any of us want, you know, to be like you in every way."

"In triplicate, my thanks."

Again, a smile just shy of flirtatious. When I failed to properly reciprocate, she pouted and angled her shoulder so I would notice that she hid something behind her back. I glanced at Ruthie, who was distracted counting down the minutes on her watch, and I decided I'd play along.

"Pray tell, Sharon, what you have there."

She batted eyes bloodshot from swirling dust. "Do you really want to see? I think you'll like it."

"Show me." I was tiring of the game. "Mother-Father insists."

Being ordered was all she'd wanted. Her skin prickled into excited goose bumps before she stretched out her left hand for me to see, just as I'd once stretched my taxidermied paw to Bridey. The hand was good and dirty, like the Savages liked it, and in fine shape, save for the pinkie, which was a withered black reed. I ignored the woman's rancid breath and leaned closer. It appeared as if the finger had been bashed between rocks, again and again, until it was a flattened tab of skin. From splits in the skin I could make out pulverized bone, whips of dead tendon, the stringy ulnar nerve, and a dry brown artery.

"Just like you," enthused Sharon.

I discovered her staring at my hand, blighted, of course, due to everything from Mr. Avery's fishing hook to the black singe of the Woodstock match.

Sharon held up her hand. The pinkie, having no intact bone, wilted.

"Watch," purred she.

With the dexterity of a farm wife who'd snapped a million green beans, she pinched the dead finger and tore it off. I gasped—a rare and holy sound, or so I gathered from Sharon's obvious glee. Disjoined from hand, the finger was not recognizable as such; it looked like an earthworm after being baked by the sun. She dropped it at my feet.

Ruthie knew how to interpret my sounds. She was at the chair in seconds, conducing Sharon Savage from the chair while reciting boilerplate about what a special meeting we'd had, and Happy New Year to you, Sharon—watch the step here as we exit. I was left alone with the helix of skin and that damn book of damn poetry, the pages of which shivered in an arid zephyr.

It's supposed to be your sacrifice, Private, not theirs.

"Shut up," hissed I. "I'm not a private anymore. You can't—"

Ruthie clopped in on business heels, clutching a dustpan. She kneeled, and with admirable poise, brushed the pinkie onto the plastic before standing straight.

"That," said she, "was something."

"You are a serial understater, Miss Ness."

"Their dedication is . . . it's remarkable."

"It is rather difficult to talk to you with that . . . *finger* there."

"You see what they're doing? They're remaking themselves in your image."

These words, so near to the title of Bridey's script, fastened to me like a cobra and pumped its venom into my veins. I rustled up the binoculars I'd had Ruthie buy in Flagstaff and, in a behavior unbecoming a sovereign, poked the lenses from under curtains to follow Sharon Savage as she, over ensuing days, showed off her homemade amputation. The face of each Savage cycled through the same reactions: shock, bewilderment, fascination, and admiration.

Eventually batteries would run out and the Savages would be cut off from the world, but for now, a few radios remained and anyone listening could tell that the times were historic. The World Trade Center, beneath which I scribble away at these pages, was dedicated, and Nixon's so-called Enemies List was published, including among its 823 entries an elusive radical called Zebulon X. But you wouldn't know it from our second round of meetings, where the only topic was Sharon Savage, whom the Savages hailed as a colonist of conviction, while monitoring me for signs of disagreement.

They'd find none. Sharon's willful dismemberment, I'd decided, extended the anti-beauty concept rather nicely. My understanding of our cult's divine text—*In Our Image*—was forever evolving, and I became convinced that ownership over one's own pain was the noblest characteristic. To ensure my analysis wasn't undermined by the resident naysayer, Burt Churchwell, I took *A Ghost Rolls Over* from its shelf, stuffed it into a box, and buried that box in a storage room.

Hesitancy no longer diluted my orations. I believed what I said, every word. To Tammy Savage I explained: "This is the land of the free, they told us. That's a laugh. I had to buy this property. I had to write checks to get the well dug. I had to fill out money orders for air conditioning. That's land, water, and air—the fundamentals of life turned into gross commodities. But there is one element in this world for which they can never charge us. Pain—free and available by the bucketful."

To Anita Savage I explained: "Once upon a time, I was a man, and like all men, I let the world be my disciplinary master. The result was that physical pain is lost to me. But you, my friend, still have that gift, and it is too precious to squander. Don't let pain come from sources that would barbarize your soul—senseless war, domestic abuse, and on, and on. To choose the source of your pain is the only true freedom you have."

To Beverly Savage, Rhonda Savage, and beyond I offered further reflections on the euphoria of suffering: all of our parts were infected by a disease called humanity, and thus it was our right, if not duty, to remove them. These lectures were carried back to the flock and repeated. Others began to wound themselves—a snip-snip here, a poke-poke there—after which Savages would gather to ooh the glorious running blood and ahh the sublime mauling of flesh. Often they'd be asked to prod the wound, and at the hiss of pain, oh, how they would cheer! The annalists who'd dub the seventies the "Me Decade" for its generation of self-obsessors should have seen my Savages. Their every infinitesimal injury was cataloged in diaries, wee little Revelation Almanacs, you might say, tracking meat etiquette's final strain.

Ruthie's dispassionate daily briefings took on subtle notes of surprise, even respect; she'd never believed the listless Zebulon Finch could become so effective a leader. She buried these feelings of shy fondness as you might toxic trash, and got on with the briefings, which now included medical complications. A woman who'd cauterized her reproductive organs had gone feverish with infection and was last seen shambling off toward the mountains. One of the men had castrated himself in emulation, only to be discovered dead in his tent, as bloodless as if drained by a dingo. Sharon Savage's entire left hand, for reasons obscure, had gone as dead as her former pinkie. I could take no firm grasp of any of it. Should I be troubled? Or should I be gratified, as Ruthie was, at the extent of the dedication?

Blowing across my patio one day was a patch torn from someone's bag or jacket. It was the logo of the Women's Movement, a Venus symbol circumscribed around the same black fist used by the Black Hand, Black Panthers, and who knew what other losers of history. The patch was blotted brown, having been used to staunch bleeding. I fought back a queasy feeling and reminded myself that I was helping women help themselves, nothing more or less. I called out to Ruthie as she was preparing for her supply run and asked her to buy bulk containers of gauze and styptic. She sighed indulgently—I thought she might pat me upon the head—and said that she already had a closet full.

V.

W E BETTER THAN DOUBLED OUR numbers in five months, and credit went to a Los Angeles disc jockey known as Wailin' Wendy Winkler, whose nightly rock-and-talk show, *Future Shock* from KLXB 93.3, was fixed on the dial of anyone whose tastes were refined beyond that of Barbra Streisand and Olivia Newton-John. Winkler was a leather-clad motorcycle mama given to serious reporting, and for weeks the Savages who gathered around the ranch's last working radio buzzed about how Winkler had cut short an interview with John Cale—a "crashing bore," she'd said—to rant on this cult in the Arizona desert where, rumor had it, chicks were cutting themselves to pieces.

Callers wanted her to check it out, and so she did, raising pyres of dust as her lime-green Harley-Davidson roared down our road one Friday in March of 1974. Like most DJs, she didn't look like she sounded (she was a burly forty-five, not a minxy twenty-six), but when she shouted for me past the Savages' human shield, her voice was the same tar-and-gravel growl that kept listeners in thrall. Ruthie hated her on sight—*she* was alpha bitch at Savage Ranch!—and told Wailin' Wendy Winkler that Mother-Father Savage didn't talk to the press.

Whistling affably, Winkler unpacked a banged-up tape recorder, handheld mike, and duct-taped headphones, and commenced interviewing Savages, whose wan cheeks found blood enough to blush. Ruthie, unwilling to summon police, gnashed her jaws while I snooped from windows, until, caught peeking by Winkler herself, I fled to the patio. Winkler circled to the back of the house and climbed the fence enough to poke her sunglassed, bandana-covered head over the top, along with the microphone.

"C'mon, Mother-Father, gimme a break and talk to me."

I hid myself behind the fountain.

"Relax," said she. "You don't look much worse than the junkies I've had in the studio."

"What is it you wish to know, Miss Winkler?"

"Like, for starters, what the fuck are you *doing* out here?"

"I haven't hurt a soul."

"This is the seventies. You know what happens when all you keep around are sycophants, right?"

"If Miss Ness finds you on our fence, you're done for."

"That little tart doesn't scare me."

"When cornered, she sprays quite a stink."

"Your ladies tell me you have an aura. I don't see it."

"They're not *my* ladies."

"Maybe they mean a smell? I can smell you from here."

"Charmed, I'm sure."

"Look, man—or woman, or neither, or whatever. You either tell me what you're up to out here or I'm gonna make something up."

I'd met other journalists in my day, notably Kip McKenzie of *New York Herald Tribune* and Ed Mann of Hearst Metrotone. Both had been willing to falsify, to doll up, to blackmail to get the "news" they wanted. I glared at Winkler.

"You really want to know?"

"I'm in the desert dangling from your fence, aren't I?"

Carefully I advanced until the head of the mike was inches away from my face. Winkler managed to get her headphones on without falling from her perch. Some of my most effective applications of *la silenziosità* (General Hazard, Merle) had been done with a verbal assist, and I leaned in, touching my dry lips to the foam windscreen. The miracle of modern amplifiers, thought I, would turn my soft words into crashing waves.

"You've fought hard to get where you are," whispered I. "Men have fought you at every turn. It has hurt. Over and over it has hurt. You've taken this pain inside you. Grown it from embryo to fetus to child, and yet it goes unborn, draining from you the life that should be yours. You acknowledge this to yourself when your show is over, when you walk from a dark studio across a dark parking lot to a dark car to a dark home. It does not have to be this way, Miss Winkler. All of the Savages are capable midwives; we can caesarean the pain. The leather you wear, those headphones, that motorcycle helmet, all of it is armor you won't need anymore, not out here."

Prim footfalls told me that Ruthie had burst into the patio, but I held up my hand to keep her from interrupting. Winkler's microphone had dropped, and her jaw had done likewise. She slumped off the fence, disappearing from view, and I heard the plastic crack of broken equipment. I looked at Ruthie, anticipating congratulation. She only frowned, pissed I'd let off the outlander with nothing worse than some busted gear.

But Wailin' Wendy Winkler spent the rest of the weekend at Savage Ranch, and when she peeled away Monday morning, her naked flesh was white fire shooting across a copper canyon.

That night's *Future Shock*, the final episode, was a three-hour soliloquy on the enlightenment she'd found among the Savages. She signed off using a name with which her listeners were unfamiliar— Wailin' Wendy Savage—and left the final hour of her show to the playing of Brian Eno's *Here Come the Warm Jets* LP in its entirety, during which, or so went radioland lore, she strode out of the KLXB studio as naked as she'd arrived, mounted her Harley, and sped east toward the desert, never to return again.

Wailin' Wendy's most ardent fans were girls and women, a not insignificant fraction of whom followed their idol into Canyon Diablo, swelling our population to seventy-four by summer—and, yes, I was proud that, at the end of their respective ropes, they'd chosen me to seek out. That number didn't take into account our two known deaths and three disappearances, plenty enough to bring the Man (to use a Scheinbergism) to our door. But the patrolmen found no evidence that anyone was trespassing, was being treated improperly, or had been coerced into anything. Hell, even some of the fuzz were hip enough to know Wailin' Wendy.

That doesn't mean they joined us for tea and cakes. Several patrolmen broke rank to accuse me of operating a leper colony and to promise they wouldn't rest until they got my chop-shop shut down. Ruthie's impassive mask only incensed them; it was Wailin' Wendy's cool heckling, honed during interviews with rock-and-roll royalty, that chased them away. Wendy's considerable celebrity among the Savages waxed, as did Ruthie's loathing of her new rival.

The best the pigs could do was haul out a musty old obscenity ordinance. So Ruthie bought white bedsheets and handed them out, and thereafter the Savages wore makeshift togas that turned us into an outpost of ghosts, or supposedly went the rumors among children of the bordering Navajo Nation, who believed us

542

to be *yee naaldlooshii*, or skin-walkers, humans able to transform into animals. We were, after all, trying.

In June I took what began as a typical one-on-one with Jasmine Savage, known at the ranch for drilling holes into her body in emulation of my bullet wounds. For this meeting, however, Jasmine had tucked into her toga a pinched-faced infant recently born on the premises and christened (if you insist on using that word) Demetrius Savage. I did not cotton to nurslings, but as Ruthie began prodding Jasmine to leave, she whipped around and made a bold, if mad, request.

"Would you bite my baby?"

Only Ruthie's astonished pause told me that I'd heard right. That and the muffled sound of a pile of boxes collapsing in the storage room—ghosts rolling over, no doubt, as Stavros's book toppled to the floor, spine cracked and pages spread.

Merry Christmas, Private!

"You've had a very special meeting," said Ruthie. "It's time to—"

"Because he's *sick*." Suddenly Jasmine was shaking so much, I believed she might drop the child, compounding his woe. "I know we don't believe in doctors. They steal away the pain that belongs to us; I understand that. But Demetrius has a bad fever, real bad; his whole body is burning up."

"You understand," said Ruthie, "that you're not confined here?"

Though she was, really. One didn't just stroll out of a desert.

"I don't want to leave, Mother-Father. My home is here with you. If you bit my baby, though, I think it might help, or even if it doesn't, even if he dies—which I know is all right, we all have to die and it's a wonderful thing that we have the opportunity, you've taught us that—but even if he dies, maybe he'll die like you did and become something even better."

543

You used to be a good runner, Private. Now run!

I'd learned about book burning from the Nazis; Stavros's book was next.

"Tell me, Jasmine," said I, "where you got this notion."

Only then did she become embarrassed, staring at her dirty feet and shrugging, though a direct question from Mother-Father could hardly be ignored. Her response was highly unexpected. Not a month before joining Savage Ranch, she and her friends had visited a Laguna Beach drive-in. The title of the film they'd seen she could not recall, but she swore it had portrayed people like me, dead yet alive, who, through bites, had turned others into their kind. Upon my pressing, she mumbled the main thing she remembered, a box-office gimmick offering a fifty-thousand-dollar life insurance policy in case viewers suffered heart attacks from fright.

It was good information; in exchange, I gave her child a harder look. He had a gray tint. I suspected he would not last the week. Batty though Jasmine seemed, I didn't know if I could take the night-after-night sobbing of a bereaved mother, and besides, I was here to help these women, wasn't I? With significant emotional disaccord I beckoned her closer. Ruthie glared her disapproval while Jasmine unwrapped her child from the toga.

Demetrius was a bobble-headed thing with far too little baby fat. Eventually I settled upon his foot and, with great care, put my teeth to a thin band of skin across the outer arch. Into what unpredictable situations were leaders thrust! I bit down.

The drawn blood was nominal, but spotted effectively upon Jasmine's sheet as she was escorted away, blubbering gratitude. The blood tasted diluted, nothing like the strong, sharp tang of the split lips of my youth. As Mother-Father Savage disliked negative

544

thoughts, I chose the distraction of destroying, once and for all, *A Ghost Rolls Over*. Strangely, I couldn't find it. The storage room had been rearranged, and rather than believe the book had waddled away like a crab, I presumed Ruthie had pitched the rain-puffed piece of poetic prattle into the trash. I allowed my shoulders to relax, then my mind. No book, no Church, no one left to try to tell me what a leader shouldn't do.

I told Ruthie to begin bringing home copies of Flagstaff newspapers. I did not tell her why. This film of which Jasmine had spoken, I wished to see it, and nowhere were drive-in circuits better advertised than the local classifieds. Luck, for once, deigned to smile. The picture in question turned out to be a midnight-movie mainstay, and only six weeks passed before I spotted a two-inch advertisement for the Hi-Way Drive-In promoting a gimmick of their own: "Important! Death Certificate Must Be Signed before Being Admitted!" The movie was part of a double bill and was called *Night of the Living Dead*.

I felt weak, dug out my Excelsior, held it to my chest.

What was I but the living dead?

What was my sunlit world but unending night?

It had to be providence, courtesy of some being more charitably inclined toward me than Gød. There was no telling how long the Hi-Way Drive-In would run the film; I ambushed Ruthie outside the Dead Letter Office. She gasped, plunging the key into a pantsuit pocket. Forget the key—I demanded access to the Ford Fairlane. She said no way. I declared that there was a picture show I must see. She smirked—a *picture show?*—and said I must be joking. The tennis continued until I skipped to the tiebreaker. Wailin' Wendy Savage had kept her Harley, and if Mother-Father asked her for a ride to town, she'd say yes, wouldn't she?

Game, set, match.

As Ruthie, plenty crabby about it, rolled the Fairlane down the sandy road (I hid in the backseat so as not to set off a panic at my departure), I fought to control a bubbling excitement, not only for the rare townward jaunt but for the film itself. Historically I'd favored lavish, expensive epics, and yet I was certain, before seeing one frame of film, that this bargain-budget quickie would be the most important motion picture I'd ever see. I take no pleasure, Dearest Reader, none whatsoever, in telling you that I was right.

VI.

T HE HI-WAY DRIVE-IN RAN FILM at nightfall, with the clack of the projector serving as track-and-field starter pistol for the competitive groping in jalopies to every side. Ruthie ignored the steamy windows as she'd ignored the entirety of the 1960s. I'd insisted she buy a bin of popcorn, thinking it might foster the high times about which I'd once fantasized: Junior cheering big-screen heroes, Franny chanting for Jujubes, and Mrs. White indulging her brood. Ruthie, however, ingested popcorn kernels with all the relish of a conveyor belt. I sighed, reached across her to crank the speaker clipped to her window—she recoiled, back to avoiding my touch— and honed in on the screen's concessions-stand conga line of frolicking frankfurters, skipping soda pops, and cavorting candies.

The filmstrip jerked. A loud brass note rattled our speaker in time with the feature presentation's opening shot: a black-and-white image of a country road along which moseyed a single automobile. Ninety minutes later, closing credits would insist that this countryside was near Pittsburgh, but I knew I'd seen it in dozens of places all over America, from Boston to Xenion to Wichita to Woodstock to Flagstaff, and I could have told you where the road led before the movie did: absolutely nowhere.

The plot of *Night of the Living Dead* is uncomplicated. Seven strangers take refuge in a farmhouse against dead bodies that have returned to life to eat people; as Jasmine Savage had indicated, their bites turn the living into the living dead. The film devours clichés. Our heroine never rebounds from catatonia. Our hero is blood-thirstier than our villain. Our villain's survival plan is the smartest one. Everyone dies. The whole film is an extension of that first shot, a road to nowhere, and the picture climaxes in an orgy of demolition, carnivorism, and fire, and even make-out kings and their fast queens came up for air to whimper.

When credits reiterated the director's name as George A. Romero, a mote of knowledge from my Little Italy days surfaced. "*Romero*" meant "one on a religious quest," and my brain, obsessed now with destiny and fate, made a leap. Like von Lüth's forerunner Madame Blavatsky and her coded accounts of the *Stanzas of Dzyan*, Mr. Romero had hidden messages inside his work, and I, like von Lüth's Enigma engineers, need only unlock the code to understand.

I demanded an encore two nights later, and again one night after that. When the film dropped from the Hi-Way marquee, I moped until it made midnight returns to the Starlite Auto, Moonlight Drive-Up, Big Twin Open Air, and Twilite All-Weather Come-and-Get-It. Unwilling to trust me not to abscond with our motor vehicle, Ruthie attended each show, muttering all the while how Wailin' Wendy was no doubt using the time to usurp control. Ruthie distracted herself by taking over the Fairlane's backseat, not for the carnal gymnastics for which it had been designed but to work dark arts upon her bank books.

By Halloween, when *Night of the Living Dead* never played at fewer than two houses at a time, I'd become the film's foremost scholar, logging details I was certain that no one else—certainly not the randy youth who were the picture's target demographic—had noticed. If Romero's masterwork still exists in your time, Reader, pause here, load it into your hologram player or robotic eyeball, and cue it to eleven minutes and thirty-six seconds. All set? Now, there's our heroine Barbra, stunned after the murder of her brother, edging into the farmhouse's trophy room. The camera whip-pans to the right. Easy now! Advance the film slowly. Look there, in the first few frames of the shot of a taxidermied warthog head. Do you see it?

I had to view it twenty times at regular speed before I was certain of what I saw. It is a hand—Mr. Romero's, no doubt—pulling away from the camera lens. How could Romero, an artist of surgical exactitude, master of light and shadow, overlook this flub? I shall tell you; it is not a flub. It is a skeleton key offered to elite viewers. With this literal sleight of hand, Romero instructs us to look past the facade of movement, lighting, and soundtrack, all three elements of which, at that moment, are firing full-blast. The prop over which he chooses to slip us this key is also symbolic. A warthog head, followed by deer heads—beautiful animals, all of them slain, and all of them finding avengers in the living dead.

What other doors does this key unlock? Minute 13:57: "[There will] probably be a lot more of them as soon as they find out about us," remarks our male lead, predicting the Savages' desperate flocking to Canyon Diablo. Minute 36:35: "Things that look like people but act like animals," says a TV anchor, synopsizing what Savage Ranch had become. Minute 46:30: Crude makeup cannot hide that one of the living dead, preposterously, is played by one of the film's lead actresses, emphasizing the blurred line between humans and animals that Savages straddled. What I came to believe, Reader, with my whole dead heart, was that Romero had made his film exclusively to transmit messages to me about the Savages. *Night of the Living Dead* wasn't just Romero's blessing for what I was doing.

It was his instruction.

The film's fictional newsmen call the living dead "ghouls," but this is a feint. Ghouls, as defined circa 1974, were lone madmen who dug up coffins to feed upon corpses. Romero's living dead were, first of all, dead, and second of all, an entire single-minded movement. Explorations into other midnight movies (with bellyaching Ruthie in tow) confirmed that *Night of the Living Dead* had spearheaded its own subgenre, and its beleaguerers had claimed for themselves a sharper word: "zombies."

I knew the term only in relation to the Haitian voodoo sampled so disastrously in Dr. Leather's lab. I harangued Ruthie until she retrieved library books on the subject, all of which fed me what I was already determined to swallow. It would prove most regrettable for me, and downright disastrous to my followers, that I learned that "zombie" derived from the African word "*nzambi*," which means—hold on to your hat, Dearest Reader—"Gød."

Imagine how this fact wormed into my cerebellum! The zombie flicks I viewed were largely incompetent, but the canon's fealty to Romero's criterion spoke tomes about the strength of his tenets, the most central of which was cannibalism. Zombies ate people; those people became zombies; those zombies, too, ate people. Romero obviously (obviously!) was equating zombies' devouring of family and friends with Christian Eucharist. What if, speculated I, history had sanitized its Sunday School stories? What if the disciples hadn't eaten transubstantiated placeholders for Jesus's body and blood but his *actual* body and blood? Didn't it make more sense? Didn't his disciples want Jesus inside of them?

"My people," greeted I.

The Second Address occurred on November 9, 1974, three months from the day that Dick Nixon resigned and left Americans desperate for a leader, perhaps even a one-armed guru in a sweltering desert. From beneath my cowboy hat and behind my aviators I smiled at the happy followers that Ruthie—again looking to me with something close to admiration—had convened. Seeing that I was once again naked, they dropped their togas in solidarity, proudly revealing their topographies of scars. As during the First Address, I was moved by their beauty.

"I know all of you so well," said I. "Coretta Savage—you're right in front, and, yes, I do think those cupped hands will help compensate for the removed ears. What did those ears ever hear anyway besides news of unremitting horror? Jeannie Savage—so nice to see you, your belly as spotted as that of a kitten, except your spots are excavations, aren't they, deep as the mine shafts of Barringer's crater? And, Sofia, I think your sisters will agree that, as lovely as was your bronze skin before, it is prettier a gristled pink. Was it a cheese grater you used? Most industrious, my dear."

Their beaming was enough to warm the coldest flesh.

"To see all of you at once reminds me of our headway in finding purity through pain. It also reminds me that there is work still to be done. Of late when I contemplate our exemplars, the animal kingdom, I think of the natures we have yet to embrace. Does not the mother rat often lick clean its ratlings, only to devour them? Does not the female spider eat the male post-coitus? Do not sibling sharks consume one another while sharing a womb? Human society beyond our canyon contends a belief in a 'natural law,' which decrees what is or isn't a so-called crime of nature. But what kind of natural law, I ask you, would animals themselves defy?"

The Savages looked about, newly blushful about their bodies.

"Do not be frightened by the childhood cautionaries of Hansel and Gretel. So common was the supping of cabin boys by shipwrecked sailors in the eighteenth century that it was called the Custom of the Sea. Without such customs there would have been no exploration. Without such exploration there would be no America. Our country exists because it has fed—nay, grown fat—off the blood of its own. Our charge, in comparison, is humble."

If the Savages had a spokeswoman, it was Wailin' Wendy. She raised her hand.

"You want us to . . . *eat* each other?"

The middle of madness is the eye of a storm. I smiled.

"If your sister feels pain, oughtn't you consume it? If you feel pain, oughtn't your sister reciprocate? Think of it! One reincarnates inside one another, back and forth, until the Savages become, in essence, a single Savage. Earth will soon be filled with more people than it can hold, and all will become cannibals. That is the ugly future. But conquer *les premières répugnances*, make the personal choice to take that path now, and you end the debate of whether one can ingest humans and remain human. The answer becomes: Who cares? Being human is not so great a thing to be."

Wailin' Wendy faltered on the scarp of belief. and the Savages watched, licking their lips, dying to teeter after her—they were, after all, so very hungry. Wendy wiped the sweat from her neck before sliding her hand down to her concave stomach. She craved understanding even more than food, but understanding was impossible inside this laser of red sun, beneath this fry pan of heat, amid these lost miles. She'd settle for faith. From between fissured lips eked her final inquiry.

"And you, Mother-Father? What will you eat to show us the way?"

Horse sense was no whip against the wildest stallion.

"Why, I've eaten too much already. Life and death: swallowed, excreted, planted, fertilized, harvested, and swallowed again, and again, and again. My chance at true savagery is gone. Yours, though, waits like a shivering rabbit to be caught, skinned, and run through with a spit. Trust in me, and I will be your master trapper."

Wailin' Wendy gave up, her face folding into relief, and the women about her broke into broad smiles, some clapping, others jumping up and down. Only now do I appreciate Wendy's question and wish that she'd pushed it harder. The truth was that I did continue to feed, not off the Savages' flesh but off their spirit, energy, hope, and trust. All of it bolted down my dry throat, jostled about inside my cold belly, and distilled into the cheapest of fuels, the same that had kept the engines of despots, autocrats, and clerics chugging for centuries.

VII.

THEIR CARNASSIAL TEETH ELONGATED, OR was it just the drawing back of their ravening lips? Cannibalism was the answer to every pesky conundrum. Hate your sister? Love your sister? Have it both ways by eating her, an extremist feat of both aggression and intimacy. We quickly learned that nothing was more passionate; even the filthiest sex acts were cordial in comparison. What raw energy built up inside, our women erupted not via loins but jaws.

The details sicken me now, but I wonder if that rising gorge is a critical failing—no one from the nation that wiped Hiroshima and Nagasaki off the map should be allowed to be sickened by anything. To wit, and to get this behind me: human muscle, said the Savages, tastes like beef, only is pinker in color and leaner in texture. And yes, my Dearest, Dismayed, Distressed Reader, you can live off it.

Half of the women at Savage Ranch owned a zeitgeist book on female health, full of anatomical diagrams, called *Our Bodies, Ourselves*, and it was swiftly repurposed as a cookbook. A typical recipe was to remove a chunk of meat from one's thigh—butchers would call the cut a "round"—and simmer it in broth before offering it to a friend. If the round needed to keep, it was soaked in salt and cured. It was an acquired taste, so new mothers rubbed blood on their nipples so that their breastfeeding children would develop the craving.

No viscera was wasted. The sole of the foot was prized for its tenderness. The small intestine had a picklish zing. Brains were renowned for their fatty succulence. Menu hierarchies emerged. The young were tastier than the old, women were tastier than men, and those of French descent were tastier than those of Spanish (all agreed the English were too salty). When the Savages were through divvying up the body of an expired comrade—their togas snarled with blood, flecks of flesh in their hair, slack-jawed, paunch-bellied, fascinated by their own limb stumps—all that remained were bones, which were slow-roasted to make salt for the next meal.

The more a leader asks of his followers, discovered I, the more inclined they are to comply and the more attractive the arrangement looks to drifters desperate for guidance. Though Savages had begun dying at accelerated rates, this ebb was eclipsed by recruits, most of whom came ready to work. Wailin' Wendy need only issue a knife before they started slicing. I confess that I got a charge out of bandying about "cannibalism," but the term was perilous, given law enforcement's entrenched suspicion. Instead I promoted the cryptic "anthropophagy"—anything to safeguard my Savages.

If you expect this bacchanalia would have forced Ruthie to decamp, you underrate her devotion to her oath to "rise to" my challenge and, unless I was mistaken, her developing wonderment regarding all of which I was capable. Though she hated watching anthropophagous acts, she approved of the results. Her financial ledgers swelled with receipts, and with the overage, she bought air purifiers and great industrial fans to reroute slaughterhouse odors, and when that failed, she simply aimed higher, dragging out our original architect, tipping him enough to ignore evidence of indescribable horror, and setting him to designing what she called a "revision" but could only be considered a "compound."

By fall of 1975 we were living in a building that shared nothing with our previous dwelling beyond its Southwestern flavor, a two-story, thirty-room estate with Spanish parapets, ceramic-tiled staircases with twisted-rope handrails, a multitiered private courtyard with reflecting pools, and a front-facing second-floor balcony embellished by carved balustrades and overhead reliefs. The house was flanked by leafy pergolas and palm trees, which overexerted our water pump—but who cared? The Savages, naturally, kept their tin lean-tos and burlap sacks. Otherwise, reasoned I, what would be the point of our gleaming white oasis, at which they could stare until they believed they had found a sort of heaven.

My single request was a menagerie. It was disgraceful, argued I, that Savage Ranch—it was called a ranch!—didn't include any of the animals we worshipped. The idea had me more excited than I'd been in decades, and in neglected *In Our Image* notebooks I sketched out my vision. I didn't want the moat-circled zoological gardens of eighteenth-century royals. What I wanted was a stronghold of America's most vicious predators. I'd have a cougar run, where the yellow-eyed stalker could entertain us with its speed and agility. I'd have a coyote pen, where we could watch their coiled bodies spring after inserted prey. I'd have a gray wolf cave, good and dark so we could see the glow of their eyes. Badgers, bears, wolverines, bobcats—I'd have them all, and, oh, what we could learn from how they operated their mandibles.

Too expensive, dismissed Ruthie, and that was nearly the end of it. Only my round-the-clock whining about how marvelous a shark tank would look in the middle of the desert wore her down. *A fish tank*, said she—would that shut me up? Like a lapbound child whose

Santa had nixed a requested pony, I hurriedly recalculated. Yes, a fish tank! Exactly what I wanted! I would fill it with the world's foremost maritime maniacs, from the venomous blowfish, whip-tailed devil rays, and poisonous jellyfish to the hinge-jawed piranha, electric eel, and Siamese fighting fish. Every day, thrilled I, the tank's water would turn pink with blood!

Nothing so stirring occurred. Species that couldn't survive a controlled environment went belly-up overnight, and the rest were peaceful, winnowing in patterns that, after a time, made me feel peaceful as well. My chief achievement was that the tank itself was a spectacular thousand-gallon glass casket that rested atop girders over the doorway to the second-floor balcony, from which, it was assumed by my ardent anthropophagi, I'd one day deliver the most important address of all.

The assumption made sense. Every cult propagandized a climactic event that would give meaning to their miseries; even Manson's rabble had moiled toward Helter Skelter. But I proudly regarded the Savages as the anti-cult cult, operating not under a premise of repairing society but indeed the opposite: doing nothing whatsoever for an undeserving country except providing a mirror to its degenerative blight, the same thing I'd been doing since my body's first spot of rot.

The Savages, of course, would be proven right. The balcony would, in fact, be the setting for the Third Address, but not for a while. Three years passed, the heart of the 1970s. We Savages missed disco dancing and London punk, the rise and fall of fondue, a movie by George Lucas that I refused to believe could rival the one by George Romero. We grinded forth, day to week to year. How many thousands of pounds of human meat did Savages ingest? How many ecstatic amputees did I squire toward death?

557

I never calculated, for my fancies were reserved for fish. I climbed a stepladder to the aquarium each day to sprinkle food at ones I'd named after secondary characters in danger of being forgotten: Jonesy the Black Oranda Goldfish, Mr. Hobby the Blue Diamond Discus, Dixon the Pinktail Chalceus, Harold Quincy the Koi Angelfish. When these fish died, they were replaced by others just like them—at last, a way to share immortality with my mortal bedfellows. After feeding, I'd recline beneath the tank and gaze upward, dreaming that I was still at the bottom of Lake Michigan, the bullet hole through my heart blooming blood as bright as coral.

From 1976 to 1978, I had sporadic chances to pull myself from psychosis by conversing with rational beings. A flop-haired pop-artist called Andy Warhol tried the hardest to be my savior. Repeatedly he wrote letters averring that one of his "superstars" (from what I could tell, this is what he called his artist friends) had spent time at Savage Ranch, and he was eager to profile me in *Interview* magazine. Everyone, said he, was due fifteen minutes of fame, and mine had come. It all seemed like too much work; I had fish to feed. I ditched the letters, and when Warhol and a corps of superstars came to Arizona to make a plea, I had Wailin' Wendy frighten them off. By then she'd amputated half of her left arm, most of her toes, and her full right buttock, but her powers of intimidation were whole.

Only in November 1978 did I half-turn from the mollifying undulations of freshwater sloshing. I'd given up newspapers, but Ruthie, as watchful and in-the-know as ever, made a point of setting several issues by the aquarium. I relented and regretted it. Top news was the collapse of a cult with alarming similarities to our own. The

Peoples Temple, it was called, and like the Savages, they'd left cushy American homes to find transcendent isolation—in their case, the Guyana jungle. When a congressional envoy visited Jonestown and found that people were being held against their will, the cult's leader, Jim Jones—always pictured in aviator shades just like mine—pulled the plug, killing the interlopers and ordering his entire congregation to drink cyanide-laced Flavor Aid. Initial articles reported four hundred dead; then the authorities began moving the bodies and found an underlayer of dead children.

I felt a twinge of what Ruthie must have been feeling, an emotion I hadn't felt in years:

Concern that even I, Mother-Father, might have gone too far.

The final tally in Guyana was over nine hundred dead. Savage Ranch, by comparison, had reached a peak population of only 291, and when a wave of parentals reenergized by Jonestown stole back mutilated daughters, the rapid decrease in our numbers was glaring. By New Year's Day we'd lost seventy-five Savages, not to brilliant blood loss and effervescent infection but to relatives who knew nothing at all about true devotion. It rankled me enough that I almost left the aquarium room. The papers detailed how nobody wanted the Jonestown corpses, but we Savages loved our dead! So much so that we gobbled up every last scrap of them.

In 1979, I turned one hundred years old—or seventeen, take your choice—and intended to mark the occasion by at last sneaking onto the balcony and gazing proudly down at my sleeping followers. When the clock struck midnight, however, the hundred years took on physical weight, and the idea of moving exhausted me. When had I become so old? Did it happen to anyone once they became set in their ways? I sat back and looked up at my fish. I hadn't named any of them the Barker, not even the algae eater who survived by sucking spume from the bottom of the tank, and yet it was the old villain's curse, delivered after my 1902 duel, that I heard in the hum of the air pump and the burble of water.

Do you have any idea, good sir, the chaos you shall cause, the killings that will happen in your name?

VIII.

THEY CAME FROM NEW YORK, Los Angeles, Florida, and most of all San Francisco. They came in slim-cut suits, handle-bar mustaches, cropped denim, and tight T-shirts, humming their funeral dirges of ABBA, the Bee Gees, and Donna Summer. They came with lymph nodes the size of golf balls, or dotted with purple lesions called Kaposi's sarcomas, half-blind from unbridled infection, bent with diarrhea, and shriveled to 120 pounds. They were easy to identify as gay. Even costuming and decrepitude couldn't hide the remnants of gym-toned muscle, meticulous grooming, and superb posture.

I was appalled. Yes, I'd been promiscuous in my day, and yes, I'd adored promiscuous women, but, dammit, this was different! These fair-ies, fruits, faggots, and queers, the lot of whom had oiled their iniqui-tous slide toward buggery with cocaine, quaaludes, and inhalants—I'd heard the stories!—and limped their wrists from untold acts performed in the petri dishes of gay bathhouses, came a-straggling to Canyon Diablo, first one per season, then one per month, and finally one per week. Why, of all places, Savage Ranch?

I'd never had to dwell upon the physical relationship between Udo von Lüth and Otto Rahn; given the regime under which they'd operated, their attraction had likely been of the unrequited kind. Now I was forced, more or less gun to head, to imagine unspeakable

561

homosexual conduct. I paced the compound muttering vulgarisms until I came upon Ruthie in her office, bleeding a red pen across columns of figures. She won the quick-draw of complaints.

"These deviants don't have any money or any property, and have you seen their cars?" She threw down her pen, stomped to a table holding fresh boxes, and set to gutting one. "Their families probably cut ties with them years ago, and no wonder. We should think about kicking them out. I'm sorry, but that's how I feel."

From the box she removed packages of medical masks and latex gloves. I watched as she gave the equipment a trial run, snapping on the gloves and looping the mask around her ears.

"They're sick." Her voice was muffled. "I'm not taking chances."

From beneath the burbling aquarium, I parted the balcony door for the first time, just a sliver, and peeked. What I observed, increasingly as the weeks progressed, were Savages who, to a woman, rallied around these sick men who tumbled from overheated autos straight onto the desert floor. Just as Mother-Father Savage posed no traditional male threat, neither did these emaciated incurables.

Gradually I came to an opinion crosswise to Ruthie's. The cops who'd called the ranch a leper colony would have felt vindicated by these scourged inductees, but to me the gays' gaunt shamblings recalled beings of purer purpose: Mr. Romero's zombies, dead yet alive, eating while being eaten away. Because of the incubation period of their strange illness, each wave arrived in markedly worse condition than the previous, though each wave also cringed less when they learned the truth of what happened every day on our patch of desert. They'd already seen too much horror to blink.

We Savages, concluded I, could not fear their disease. Nay, we must welcome it! The bug that fed upon their flesh aged them as quickly as my own condition aged me slowly. Together, did we not equal a healthy human being? I made Ruthie vouchsafe, against her protest, that our new guests would continue to receive generous welcomes.

Savages during one-on-ones could only say that the "gay plague" hounding the newcomers was thought to be sexually transferred. The men, said they, told stories of hapless doctors plugging their bodies into high-tech torture machines while firing off birdbrained theories, from the cunctative effects of Agent Orange to nuclear power leaks. Some docs had dismissed the gay plague as FUO—Fever of Unknown Origin—a moniker that, though docile at first, came to take on folkloric foreboding.

So rapidly had my disgust turned into interest that I insisted that those men healthy enough be worked into my schedule. One million urgent questions had I! How the devil could a man not desire soft, squeezable women? Did the seduction of men require a different skill set? Most of the gays had to be wheelchaired in by the masked-and-gloved Ruthie, who'd agreed to comply only if they entered via the back gate so as not to contaminate the compound. They shivered poolside, first baffled, then grimly amused at the naïveté of my queries. Though ill, they were eager to please me, for when they'd set out on this, their life's final road trip, they'd assumed the mythical dead man of the desert to be a myth. But here I was, rotting away just like them, except through some miracle able to withstand it.

Gabe Mungo was like the rest in many ways. He was an ashen young man who, under the drag-queen alias of Madame Simonette, had worn sequined gowns, high heels, false eyelashes, and what he boasted was "fifteen pounds of foundation" to belt bawdy songs at some sort of gay burlesque. My ignorance of the culture made such theater difficult to picture, but Gabe described it with aching nostalgia. All that was left of Madame Simonette was a set of nicely plucked eyebrows and a pink feather boa he kept cozied around his neck.

In one key way, Gabe was different. He'd come to Canyon Diablo in 1981 not to find purpose in pain or to find hope beyond hope, but rather to drive an ailing fellow drag queen (stage name Margherita Petticoat) who did believe I might offer such things. Though Miss Petticoat had died upon arrival, Gabe had yet to vacate. He, too, was stricken with the gay plague, though his case was less advanced. Still, sighed he, he was dying, and if he had to look like a hag, he might as well do it well from the public eye.

Gabe sashayed into the courtyard for our first meeting not in the ubiquitous white sheet but in a gauzy housecoat he held shut with one hand while shooing away Ruthie with the other. Though not much older than I, Gabe exuded a Hollywood glamour I knew all too well, but that wasn't what troubled me. One look at those impulsive brown eyes deep inside those hollowed sockets told me that he believed Mother-Father Savage was a scheister. Since that first day with Wailin' Wendy, I hadn't engaged with anyone not aready nestled into my pocket.

"*Love* the hat," said he. "Very Marlboro Man."

That rather pleased me. But the next five minutes he spent silent, working a chamois across his fingernails.

"Well, Mr. Mungo," said I, "I hate to cut it short."

"Darling," drawled he. "From what I hear, there's nothing down there left to cut."

"We believe in the Savage lifestyle," cautioned I. "Disbelievers should leave."

"Disbelieve in a lifestyle? *Moi?* You've got it all wrong. I'll believe anything. The sky is green? The grass is blue? I've just about had it with reality."

"You do not seem sick," accused I.

Gabe lowered part of his boa. There, a leech-sized sarcoma.

"Maybe my face isn't oozing enough pus for your tastes, but don't worry, sugar, I'll get there. Right now all I've got is, oh, let's see." He raised a slender arm—sarcoma, inner elbow—and counted symptoms upon long, beringed fingers. "Headaches. Toothaches. Shingles. Thrush. Night sweats. Saggy skin—I mean, you have *got* to be kidding. I'm *twenty-three.* Before I left the Bay, my doctors were hatching so many theories, I couldn't keep up: toxoplasmosis, encephalitis, cryptosporidiosis, you're-gonna-die-itis, it's-curtains-for-you-osis, you name it."

Indeed he could keep up, hence the quavering of his bravery.

"There is no purpose in naming the disease," said I. "It is Death."

"You're so *dramatic.* Of course there's a purpose. If I'm going down, I want it to be from something notable. The Bubonic Plague, crocodile attack, *something.* If I'm put in my grave by another stupid intestinal parasite, I'm going to be furious."

"Intestinal parasite?"

"You know how homosexuals have sex, right?"

"I—this is not about—I'm not even—"

Gabe's laugh was a throaty drum roll that made me suspect that Madame Simonette's singing voice was plenty sexy. Egads—what was I thinking? I wondered what Abigail and Bartholomew Finch would think if they knew the reprehensible filth that would one day soil their little boy's mind.

"You know what's going to happen if it's never named?" asked Gabe.

565

"I am sure that you will tell me."

"You're damn straight I will." Gabe crossed his legs and leaned in, a single pink feather taking flight. "They'll say the bigots were right all along, that it was Gød throwing thunderbolts at the homos. You think we don't wonder about that? When we're throwing up and crapping ourselves, out of our heads with one-hundred-and-five-degree fevers? You think we don't doubt? If this plague had hit heteros, Ronald Reagan would be on TV right now, revenging us like Pearl Harbor. But of all people, it chose us, and the world doesn't give one shit." He shrugged. "We're doomed, sugar."

I don't believe the desert had ever been so still. When Ruthie came to give Gabe the boot, he dropped me a wink and rose of his own power, then took off down the sidewalk as if it were a fashion runway, housecoat fluttering like one of Madame Simonette's signature gowns. Ruthie hurried behind to lock the gate. I'd given her white mask and latex gloves little consideration before, but now I found them off-putting, even embarrassing.

Two weeks later, instead of the customary nine months later, I invited Gabe Mungo back. No doubt the Savages noticed and were consternated, but I couldn't cleanse my ear canals of Gabe's acerbic laughs. His lack of adulation had been as brisk as ice water, and his pugnaciousness had stabbed my torpid brain with sharp memories of verbal jousts with people I'd liked, if not loved: Wilma Sue, Mother Mash, Bridey Valentine, Allen Rigby, Harvey Scheinberg. Gabe yoo-hooed from the back gate and entered as I imagined he entered everywhere: nonchalant about his popularity, but with fondness beneath his simper. I asked him for stories, and he, a playhouse pro, supplied them.

"It's not just that everyone's sick," said he. "It's that we're sick of *being* sick. Sick of needles. Sick of centrifuges. Sick of nurses who'd rather quit than go into our rooms. Sick of debating what does or doesn't fall under 'bodily fluids'—that's all the doctors talk about, bodily fluids. I mean, *ick*. Sick of weighing this method of suicide against that. Sick of reading the obituary section first. You can't imagine how boring the Castro is now. No one talks about art anymore. We play Death Bingo, see whose card fills in first."

"What do they say about this place?"

"Frankly, reviews are mixed. Some say the marble countertops don't match the bath towels, while others suspect there's something fishy about the continental breakfast."

I laughed. Dear Gød—how long had it been since I'd laughed? Gabe peaked an eyebrow.

"Ah-ah, careful. Cult leaders aren't supposed to giggle."

"You don't take the name Savage. You don't partake in the meals. You don't believe in any of it. So why don't you turn us in? Take photographs of what happens here, show them to the police. They might be able to shut us down if they had proof from someone on the inside."

Gabe gave an exaggerated shrug. Two new lesions peeked from beneath the pink boa.

"Do you have any idea how many clubs the law's shutting down in San Francisco? I'm not shutting down a thing, sugar. If I even *hear* the word 'no' again, I'm going to scream. No, you can't go to bathhouses; no, you can't have sex; no, you can't even kiss someone you—"

Gabe's voice broke. He pressed his knuckles against his lips as if punching himself for letting genuine emotion break through his persona. Tears gathered at his lower lids, magnifying his black pupils. When he spoke again, he did so softly, as if anything louder would send those tears streaking.

"That's what they say about this place, if you want the truth. That if you click your heels three times, you'll go somewhere over the rainbow, not Oz but Arizona, a place where, before you die, you can be a real person one more time, where you can touch other people again, where you can do that thing the doctors said you could never, ever do—exchange bodily fluids. Honestly, the boys in the Castro have no idea how far things have gone down here. I may find what you're doing grotesque—I'm a little old-fashioned that way—but do I understand the appeal? To revel in the flesh, one last farewell bash before bon voyage? You're darn tooting I do."

He pointed a thin finger toward the front of the compound.

"Just don't be fooled by all this," said he. "I might have dolled up as Madame Simonette, but all these people you've got out here, they're dolled up too. You're the director of some invisible play, and they're playing the roles you gave them, but I'm the one who knows how it ends. I know it better than anyone, sugar. The curtain comes down, the show's over, they strike the set, and poof! All of it, the whole phony affair, gets packed away in trunks. Good show, sure, but to the rest of the world? It doesn't mean a cotton-picking thing."

It was as if Gabe had read *In Our Image*, only he was giving it a bad review. No one had ever before spoken sensibly about Savage Ranch, and the words dug into the crack struck by Ruthie's Jonestown articles. Bricks began to loosen from the castle-sized facade I'd literally built, until the underlying madness of the construction began to show. This cross-dressing freak, as I would have dubbed Gabe one year earlier, was the sane one. It was I who was the freak, I who'd gone crazy. The scales began to tip, faster and faster, the smell of sun-baked blood no longer smelling so sweet, the calm serenity of being a Mother-Father curdling into a slow-dawning horror.

568

Gabe Mungo's wish came true in 1982. After stints under such industrial acronyms as GRID (Gay-Related Immune Deficiency) and ACIDS (Acquired Community Immune Deficiency Syndrome), scientist-types settled upon the far more sprightly AIDS. The disease, after all, had finally done what was necessary to attract attention—afflict straight people. Urban junkies who shared needles were getting AIDS. Small-town hemophiliacs who got blood transfusions were getting AIDS. Newborn babies were getting AIDS. And so, albeit for a regrettably short while right near the end, Savage Ranch became a sanctuary for anyone weak—straight, gay, whoever—in search of a strong exit.

Ruthie's anxiety levels reached the brim and poured over. As she saw it, her excess of caution had been substantiated; she purchased high-grade surgical scrubs and elastic footies to go along with gloves suitable for handling plutonium, and upgraded medical masks with hydrophilic plastic coatings. No longer would she get close to anyone. The back gate became the only route to the courtyard, and if a Savage couldn't make it unassisted, she or he would miss her or his meeting, simple as that.

Doubt, the disease I'd caught from Gabe, crept hot through my cold veins. During one-on-ones, I let Savages gush about cannibalistic tit-for-tats while I murmured compliments I no longer believed. To fill my silence, Wailin' Wendy Savage and fellow die-hards began pushing positions they believed consistent with the Savage doctrine. They'd partake in the poisoned flesh of the sick and pray that it would be the sickness that dragged their stump-riddled, flesh-mangled, bloodlet bodies over the finish line.

The timetable became second nature: infection, eighteen to twenty-four months of suffering, death. That the afflicted knew this gave them gravitas. They wished only to live before they died, and I could write another thousand pages on their valorous attempts. Only attempts, though; through the crack in the balcony door I listened to hundreds of hours of semi-coherent jabber about how thankful they were to die without being plugged into that fucking ventilator, thankful to do it under open fucking skies, thankful to be surrounded by friends instead of that fucking janitor who over-bleached his fucking mop. (They cursed a lot at the end.)

Because why recount every agonized expiration when Gabe Mungo's death sums it up so neatly? Right on schedule, on July 20, 1983, he slumped into a pneumonia he hadn't the white blood cells to thwart. The Savages by then had a cat's sixth sense for death, and knowing how I liked Gabe best of all, they risked Miss Ness's wrath that night by wading into the shrubbery alongside the compound— quite the gauntlet for multiple-amputees—banging on the windows and shouting that Gabe was about to die. I was awake, as ever, reclined beneath the fish tank. Unexpected grief squeezed my dead heart.

"Bring him in!" cried I "Now, now!"

I toppled downstairs and hit the front vestibule concurrent with Ruthie. In all of our years together, I'd never seen her hair in any array but tied tight, but it was four in the morning, and pillows had made a nest of it. Her pajamas were wadded and her temples scored from a sleep mask. A ruckus rose up from outside the front door. I reached for the bolt, but Ruthie braced her elbow against the door.

"You cahn't let them in."

Brief wakefulness had allowed no time to hide her accent.

"Remove yourself," growled I.

"Everyone in the whole yahd has it. You want them to just traipse in heah? Bleeding everywheah? I don't have my masks or gloves!"

"Remove yourself or I will be forced to take action."

She snarled, spit popping from her sleep-crusted lips. "When have you evah taken an action I didn't tell you to take?"

Reader, I struck her, and with force. My right arm, the only one I had, swung in a sideways arc, delivering to her left ear not a slap but a punch. Her forehead struck the door with a thud, and her knees buckled. She caught herself in a crouch and pressed both hands to her ear, then checked her fingers for blood. She blinked. She seemed not only to wake up but, more hideously, to *wake up*, and the look of respect she'd worn for so long sharpened to a hatred more savage than any invoked by a so-called Savage. Here came the blood from her ear; that she didn't notice it made me ice-cold. Her lips twisted to such disfigurement that it was a wonder that words could thresh through them.

"You shouldn't have done that."

A crow flapped its wings inside me, caught under my ribs like Rigby's Smith & Wesson. But the Savages were hollering, so I tore my attention from this altered Miss Ness and slid the bolt. I heard Ruthie dart away, but my attention was taken by the inward explosion of Savages who carried in their half-limbs and fingerless palms the limp Gabe Mungo. I pointed toward the courtyard and told them to lay Gabe by the reflecting pool. I rushed after, only dimly aware of the distinctive sound of the Ford Fairlane coughing to life and its rubber tires gristling over desert dirt.

The night was seventy degrees and black, with blacker peaks rising in the distance as if our world were sinking. I dropped to my knees beside Gabe and shouted, rather ungratefully, for everyone to get the hell out of there and leave us alone. They reeled back in alarm and hobbled away, and then it was just the two of us beneath a torrent of splendiferous summer stars. I dipped my hand into the pool and dappled Gabe's face with water.

Puffy white fungus had sprouted along his fingernails. Half of his head was swallowed in a coarse red rash. His skin looked like putty melted across knobby white bone, and his eyes were fierce yellow dots flickering from inkwell pits. When water hit his swollen lips, they opened, and from his yeast-striped tongue pealed a rush of words, as if he'd been speaking all along and I'd just cranked the volume.

"—got these gadgets in the bars, they called them ionizers, they stuck them up high above the bars, said they're supposed to help with cigarette smoke, well that's what they *said*, but you ask me, they were suspicious, weren't they, those little devices with their blinking lights, so what I'm saying is no one got sick *before* the ionizers, if you really sit down and think about it—"

"Gabe," said I.

"—so what if those ionizers were radiating something, you know, something *toxic*, and it was these gadgets that spread the disease, gadgets that the city council *made* them put in, maybe only in the gay bars, because I don't want to sound paranoid, but if you ask me, it sounds like a Watergate-style conspiracy—"

"*Gabe.*"

I shook him by a shoulder that felt like a wooden coat rack upon which a ratty housecoat and half-plucked feather boa had been draped. Sweat popped from his every pore at once and ran down sallow skin like grease, and for a moment he shut up and his pinprick eyes stabbed mine, and I leaned down, desperate for him to recognize me and become the Gabe I'd first met, that hip-swinging prima donna who'd driven audiences wild, and who could blame them? He'd been the epitome of the fiery, stubborn, lustful life I'd once enjoyed. I got close enough that our noses touched so that his eyes couldn't miss mine, in hopes that he'd return, just for a moment, to deliver some cutting remark to help me believe that his death wasn't pointless, that none of the deaths I'd shepherded here were pointless.

His yellow eyes slid from mine and his tongue jerked.

"—which makes sense, as conspiracies go, when you think what they did with the health supplements, and everyone bought the health supplements, they called them HIM, Health and Immunity for Men, and they sold as fast as poppers, the floor of the bar went clink, clink, clink with all the jars, and it said right on the label how it maximized immunity, and this is America, this isn't some third-world country, they can't put words on labels that aren't true—"

Having once known a potion peddler called Dr. Whistler, I could have protested, but Gabe wasn't hearing me, nor would he ever again. On strange impulse I dipped my face the final two inches and pressed my cold, dry lips against his swollen, sweltering ones, and gave him the kiss doctors had told him he could never have. Yes, Dearest Reader, I kissed a man, and what's more, I made it a good one, urgent because there was no time for dally, hungry because I did still starve in certain ways, and though Gabe's mind was gone, his muscles had memories, and he kissed back, each push of our lips damming his tide of turbid conspiracy, of which I could bear no more.

By the time the sky was burnished by a coming dawn, his tirade had become babble. I straightened his robe. I arranged his boa to best showcase the remaining feathers. I wished that somewhere in my sprawling compound was a tube of hot-pink lipstick, long plastic eyelashes, a Marilyn Monroe wig, a gown with a million sequins. When the sun shot over the crest of Barringer's crater, I had left

Gabe's side to search for a tool with which I might snip off his seven rings, for his hands and fingers had ballooned with fluid. The best I could find was a crowbar. How that might work, I didn't know, but at least it felt powerful in my hand.

When I returned, Gabe Mungo was dead.

I sat beside his body. Having failed to find costuming, he looked like roadkill left too long on a freeway shoulder. His chest was thrust too high, his back too arched, his arms akimbo and fingers taloned. I stared at the corpse for hours until I was very certain of what I was seeing. There was no beauty in this death, no perfection, nothing that we Savages had sought for so long. The sun rose, evaporating the last of the clouds shadowing my brain. I took the cowboy hat Gabe had always loved, secured it upon his head, and stood up. For Gabe Mungo—not Gabe Savage, for he knew better than that—I had to end this, all of it.

IX.

THE CROWBAR FOUND ITS PURPOSE. I wiggled the tip into the seam between door and jamb, and because I felt no pain, hammered my palm at the tool's other end until I'd forced a breach. From there it was a matter of physics. I applied my weight to the better side of the fulcrum until smooth, dispassionate wood broke into a cuckoo grin of splinters. That left only two locks to be defeated. One hour of vigorous swinging later, the door, what was left of it, yawned open.

The Dead Letter Office was no larger than expected, the size of a one-car garage, yet filled with none of Mr. White's cobwebbed do-it-yourself tools, backyard grills, or winter sleds. Ominously unadorned chests, boxes, bins, and bags were stacked about, often at chest level, suggesting a volume of collected material it'd take weeks to sift through instead of the mere hours I had before Ruthie presumably returned. Regardless, I barged down the cleared path. Herein were secrets; I'd been hearing their whispers for years.

Atop a table to the left was a wooden box showing indications of regular use, so I started there, attacking it with the crowbar until the lock cracked. The contents surprised me with their bright colors. Collected here were the confiscated identification items of Savages past and present. Most featured photos of happy faces, for each signified a subject who'd just been permitted to drive a car, start college, or begin a new job. None of the shining, flash-bulb eyes could foresee of a future of gobbling gore from the desert floor.

I threw shut the lid and plied the crowbar to a massive adjacent trunk. Inside I discovered fantastic depths of mail, a full decade of it, each envelope complete with a Savage Ranch return address and a stamp unblemished by postmark. Nothing extraordinary there; I knew Ruthie only pretended to truck mail to Flagstaff. What was extraordinary was my desire to read the letters. Gabe's death had defeated my deafness, banished my blindness, and I wanted to hear and see everything.

I plucked a letter from halfway down the paper soup. It was from a woman called Chelsea Savage. I remembered her, a diminutive gentlewoman in her fifties bashful about nudity and too timid to say much during meetings, and yet a fleet adopter of anthropophagy, ever giving of her breast and thigh meat and famously fond of fingers, which she'd gnaw on like jerky. She'd expired of blood loss in 1980, but in this letter was vividly alive. Addressed to Chelsea's daughter, it marked an attempt to explain her decision to move to the desert.

In that she failed; the cockamamie choice could never sound rational. In reminding me of life's intricate, barbed, and contradictory thrills, however, she succeeded. Her five-page letter swerved from jolly recollections of a swimsuit faux pas and anecdotes about a farting cat to stark confessions regarding the husband whose death had set off Chelsea's crisis. Even the grapey shade of ink was poignant, as was the curlicue handwriting, the wide-ruled paper, and the four or five odd folds required to fit the letter inside an envelope.

Hundreds if not thousands of such letters existed. One after another I tore them open until the fallen paper resembled the shag-carpet fad that had passed us by. The whole day slipped away, not that I cared, so bracing was the cold, blue sanity pouring through my body like antifreeze. At length I forced myself to stop. I gazed into the trunk, scheming about how I might take it with me. My dead extremities tingled. Yes—I was leaving, I'd decided just like that, and right away, for once I was gone, my followers would begin to leave, too, and the Savages could cut their losses, if you are in the mood to excuse the grisly pun.

I shoveled mail back into the trunk. I was shutting it—fate, a game of millimeters!—when I noticed that the inner lid had a cubbyhole. I operated the sliding-door, and a bound parcel of letters dropped into the padding of correspondence below. Ruthie had kept these letters together with twine, though this was not the most notable detail. The envelopes' ragged edges showed that these letters, unlike the others, had been opened and read. It was a mystery best solved later, but I'd observed fish long enough to know how hard it was to resist biting tantalizing lures.

My teeth and fingers had the twine snapped before I could think better. These were not outgoing letters from Savages. They were incoming mail, addressed not to Excelsior, Inc., Ruthie Ness, or even Mother-Father Savage, but to Zebulon Finch, a name I hadn't seen or heard since Hershel Harel had pulled Bridey's will from his valise. Each envelope, and there were thirty-six, was addressed in the same crude squiggle. The epistolarian's name was absent, but the return address was Tranquility, Washington. From the oldest postmarked envelope I yanked the entrails.

Mr Zebulon Finch I am like you I am Dead but alive also please come see me I live in Tranquility it is in Washington also I live in a Country Home and there is Room for you here also

R

A barely literate run-on sentence, poxy of penmanship and sorely in want of punctuation—but what a message! I braced myself as the Dead Letter Office turned upside-down. Could it be that my century-long presumption that I walked the earth alone was incorrect? Could there be another out there as damned as I? R was obviously female; untrained though she was as a writer, her alphabet carried the balletic shapes rare to men's cumbersome paws. Imagine it: a woman counterpart, waiting for me at a home deep enough into the country that two creatures like us could exist away from the living with whom, it had become clear, we ought not to have dealings.

The Excelsior ticked so hard that it fibrillated my clay heart. I gasped, and just that quickly came to a purer understanding of why Mary Shelley's monster had forced Victor Frankenstein to create a mate upon his laboratory slab. *My companion will be of the same nature as myself,* quoth the monster, *and will be content with the same fare.*

The existence of another like myself so surpassed anything for which I'd ever hoped that, for a time, I could but hang on while the Dead Letter Office continued to roll. But spring to action I did, for the letter had been sent in 1975, a bewildering eight years prior. I raced through the others, hoping that R hadn't lost faith. She hadn't; the letters had continued to come, once every three or four months, always with the same return address. Twinges of impatience were perceptible in the writing, but never anger. Instead, R had tried to prove her bona fides by describing what dead innards felt like or the smell of slowly spoiling flesh, all of it poorly written, but all of it true down to the finest detail.

Her tone wavered only in the final letter, postmarked one whole year ago. R's authorial voice was so terminologically understated that the sole sentence screamed.

There is no more Time you must visit Now I cant keep
Country Home clean

R

My bleat banged about the small room. What if my counterpart, the only one tightfisted Gød had ever allowed me, had been forced from her country home? Again I thought of Victor Frankenstein, who, disgusted by his female creation, ripped the creature to shreds, a brutality at which the monster reacted "with a howl of devilish despair." I gathered R's letters, lashed them back together, and turned toward the door.

And then I swiveled back. Just as my eye had caught the trunk's lid compartment, it caught something else in Ruthie's House of Horrors. Sitting central upon the back shelf was the golden lock-box she'd acquired at the height of martyrdom profits and had toted about like a baby until the spoils of Savage Ranch had rendered the small container inadequate. How tightly she'd clutched the box to her bosom. How she'd caressed it half-asleep on buses or trains.

To pay for my sins, I took the box and crowbarred it.

Cash had long since been moved to a Flagstaff bank. The box, though, wasn't empty. Inside was a scattering of old documents. There were several birth certificates ranging in antiquity from white to yellow to gray. Another was degree credentials from Harvard College, or so I believed, for I did not dare fully unfold it, so brittle had the paper become. Most jarring, there was a black-and-white photograph of an unsmiling Ruthie at roughly age ten, holding hands with a dour woman I didn't recognize and yet, somehow, did.

When I replaced the photograph, I heard a clink. I dug

my fingertips past the documents and felt a cold piece of metal. I extracted it and held it before my eyes. It was a ring. Common sense suggested an heirloom, but it was constructed of the shoddiest tin, was without gem, and was rusted from decades of poor storage. Yet it was slippery in my palm as if creeping toward my right ring finger, which made sense, seeing as how that's where it had lived for fifteen years.

It was the Little Miracle Electric Mexican Stuttering Ring.

The horror upon seeing it emerge from Ruthie's lockbox after seventy years was absolute. Little Johnny Grandpa had given the Pageant of Health trinket to me in 1898 in the hopes that it might help me recover my speech, and though it hadn't, it had done something far greater, serving as receipt that even I, runaway, criminal, murderer, beer-guzzler, serial abandoner, could make a friend who believed there to be good inside him. The last time I'd seen it had been the night of the Cockshuts' dinner with Dr. Leather, when I'd left it on my nightstand to satisfy the doctor's dress code. Upon fleeing that night, I couldn't risk climbing three stories to retrieve it.

Which meant someone had found it. And saved it. And kept it like a vow.

Jason Stavros's *A Ghost Rolls Over* hadn't been destroyed after all. The book was right here, somewhere inside the Dead Letter Office, of course it was, for Ruthie Ness, it had become apparent, threw nothing away, not ever, and was not just some random entrepreneur but someone who knew far more about me than she'd revealed, and it did not behoove me to linger about to learn more. Church's ghost leapt from its poetry casket, whisper-shouting as one does when delivering orders close to the German line.

You gotta move, Private! On the double!

I slid the Little Miracle Electric Mexican Stuttering Ring onto my finger, tough to do with one arm, but oh, it fit nicely, so nicely; it was as if I myself had fit back into the world.

Merry Christmas! Enough with dang jewelry, Private!

I looked around for Stavros's book, but Church was nuts, shouting for me to get my butt in gear, and this time it wasn't only him, it was the whole Third Battalion, not just the codgers who'd been alive to sign the book but also those who'd died in the field: Mouse Bartosiewicz, Peanut Capella, Professor Ehrenström, Piano O'Hannigan, rising from their graves to save my thankless corpse one more time.

You'll never make corporal, acting like this!

You want to be ripped to smithereens like the rest of us, soldier?

Private Finch, you lazy lollygagger, you gotta do what the Skipper says and move out!

Each voice was but a shard of my own sanity—Reader, I know that!—but I clenched my fist, felt the old invigorating bite of the ring, and decided that the fallen would be honored. I'd leave the ghost-book behind and save the Savages who hadn't yet died from their allegiance, thereby saving myself, and only then would I seek out the mysterious R. Having won, the voices quieted. Only then, in the hush, did I hear music and make a queasy realization. Savage Ranch had run out of radios long ago, except the one in the Ford Fairlane.

The clarity of sound indicated that the music flowed from the car's open window. How long had it been playing? I peered from within the Dead Letter Office and could not see a single splash of sun in the compound. Night had fallen, making Ruthie's shape in the doorway even smaller than usual, this time a smallness not of supercilious cat but of patient wolf.

581

X.

NO OTHER WOMAN I'D EVER met stood like Ruthie Ness. There was no bent knee, slung hip, inturned toe, clasped hands, or angled chin. She stood as hung from a meathook: feet forward, legs straight, shoulders slumped, arms dangling. Proof of life was evident only in how her left hand gripped a large dark object concealed in shadow, just like her face, which oscillated right and left until she'd taken slow, careful tally of the rifled mail trunk, the popped lockbox, R's letters beneath my arm, and the tin ring on my finger.

"You feel volatile," said she. "But I urge you to be calm about this."

Never in all my bloviating about how we Savages improved upon Jesus Christ's Last Supper had I wondered who might emerge as my Judas.

"Gladys Leather?" guessed I.

I could make out a pinched smile.

"Believe me, Mr. Finch, when I say I never wanted to be impressed by you. But I have been. Your knowledge of the humanities, history, so many eclectic subjects. The way you turned an incoherent, frankly irresponsible idea of this place in the desert into a real moneymaker—I don't know that I've ever been so impressed. Our relationship has genuinely affected me, and isn't that worth something? Math, though, has never been your strong suit. When was Gladys Leather born?"

"I . . . I don't . . . 1905?"

"So how old would Gladys be today? If she were alive, which she isn't."

I pictured Mary Leather's pride and joy, that mugging munchkin who'd dragged her expensive dollies by the hair up and down the family manor's first and second floors, but never the third, of course, from whence one could smell meat etiquette as it roasted its demons.

"Seventy-eight?"

"Now, what if Gladys survived life on the street after you left the Leathers broke, and then had her own daughter when she was twenty?"

"Gladys's daughter? Is that who you are?"

"Your *math*, Mr. Finch. How old would that child be now?

"I can't . . . fifty-eight? I don't understand . . ."

"Nonsense. You're doing wonderfully. Let's say that Gladys's daughter *also* had a daughter when she was barely birthing age. An unfortunate situation, but homeless women don't have much protection against rape."

"Enough," begged I. "You're Dr. Leather's great-granddaughter?" I laughed, a short, mad howl. "No, that's—that's inconceivable. That's impossible."

The baritone throb of air purifiers and the tenor lamentations of circulating fans had become the compound's perpetual Gregorian chant, but at that moment, as if corrupted by one of NASA's glitches, the closest one puttered toward death, emitting a creaking wheeze that, had my ears not been clogged so long by the blandishments of believers, I might have noticed years before.

Hweeeeee . . . fweeeeee . . . hweeeeee . . . fweeeeee . . .

"Inconceivable, yes." Ruthie shrugged. "But nothing's impossible."

People brought to death's precipice only to be yanked back insist that the total spans of their lives whirl past, a phenomenon of which I'd been robbed. But cornered inside the Dead Letter Office, my mind flushed clean as if by one of Mrs. White's new-and-improved kitchen solvents, I cycled through every clue that had been waggled in front of my witless face for years.

That accent Ruthie tried so hard to bury? Good Gød, I'd lived in Boston for eight torturous years! The Leathers had spoken like the upper crust to which they'd belonged, but their fall would have dumped later generations into a pool of coarser intonations. Ruthie's attestation that her family was dead was true—I myself had been spattered by Dr. Leather's brilliant brains—as was her post-Woodstock crying-jag declaration (*brava*, Miss Ness, *brava!*) that she'd committed herself to me to rectify family failings. Ruthie, in other words, had sought me out to mine me monetarily as her great-grandfather had mined me bodily, and with the same single-minded commitment. Hence the three jobs during law school, the avid exploitation of legal loopholes, her inhuman work ethic.

Even I, the painless, was pained by the evidence. How she'd lured me into partnership by dangling the nation's revenge-lust, when all along it had been her own: *People see something of theirs destroyed and they can't help it—they want their turn at destroying.* How disinterested she'd been in the minutiae of my existence, and why? Because she'd heard about it ever since childhood. Even her drabness of dress and thickness of glasses had inhibited me from matching her cheekbones and eyes to those of Mary Leather. Most flagrant of all had been Ruthie's response to Harvey Scheinberg's asking why she accepted blood money from warmongers: *Because the stupid deserve to follow the bold.*

Dr. Cornelius Leather, Ruthie Ness, née Leather, and any other Leather who'd bloodhounded me across a twentieth-century mine-field were therefore exposed as the bold. I, then, definitely now, was the stupid, having believed that viruses like HIV were the only blood maladies transferable from parent to child.

"I heard so many stories about you," said Ruthie, "and you're just like they said. Filled with potential but helpless to do anything with it without assistance. It's presumptuous of me, I know. Great-granddad Cornelius, he was the genius of the family, and if he couldn't get any-thing out of you, how could I? But you grow up brushing maggots off your trash-can dinners, it takes a toll. By the time I was a teenager, I knew what I had to do."

"Ruthie . . ."

"Miss Ness, please. It'll make this easier."

"I thought you and I were . . . perhaps not friends, but . . ."

"We've had some nice moments. Nicer than I ever would have expected. But when you hit me . . . Well, it was probably good that you did. I'd lost my way. I'd forgotten my obligations."

"You honestly think Dr. Leather's studies could have changed the world?"

Ruthie shot air through her nose, her version of a laugh.

"My concerns were more practical than that. Had you kept your word and stayed with the doctor until he was finished, he would have made money. Lots of money. Millions of dollars. Me, my mother, my grandmother—I can't even imagine how much better their lives would have been or how much longer they'd have lived. You've got no right to be angry. In fact, you ought to forgive me for what I've done."

"What *have* you done?"

"Only what you authorized me to do."

"Authorized?"

"You did sign the contract."

I nearly asked her to speak sense, until I remembered it: December 1967, Bucket Mouth Seafood, Asbury Park, New Jersey, eleven at night, Ruthie Ness drinking merlot and pushing across the tacky table a paper and pen, and Zebulon X, dried off from a buried-in-the-sand drowning, signing it without reading, for what did a dead man care of fine print?

"How much have you taken?"

"Everything."

"Bridey's money?"

"Everything."

I pushed from the nearest trunk and rushed Ruthie. She took a step back, then another, openly afraid, and I was glad.

"There's petty cash," blurted she. "I might be able to get you—"

My stump whacked against Ruthie hard enough to spin her around. A flash of malicious satisfaction engulfed me, but my first steps into the front salon were off-kilter, giving me no chance against the underfoot slickness. My right leg, weaker since a German shell had hollowed it in 1918, buckled and I landed on my ass. Closer to the floor, the sharp scent of the liquid hit me.

The light from this angle was better. I could see Ruthie clearly as she smoothed the wrinkles of her pantsuit and regripped the metal canister.

"Miss Ness." I despised how fearful I sounded. "What else have you done?"

Ruthie valuated the trimmings she'd overseen, from the herringbone brick and Gallic casements to the wrought-iron fleur-de-lis hinges on every door. Her spectacles came to rest upon the newest furnishment:

a cluster of gasoline casks, each bearing fresh sales stamps from Flagstaff and each pinged inward by the emptying of its contents. The liquid soaking into my trousers was gas, and I scrambled to my feet even as I traced multiple trails of it, one headed east toward the front loggia, another south toward the bedrooms and offices, and yet another west toward the courtyard, where I pictured Gabe's soaked body alongside a reflecting pool, an imminent Viking funeral.

"Don't think I'm not sad," said Ruthie. "I have to hand it to you. This became a home, it really did. It's the only real home I ever had."

Her body jerked forward, the most abrupt motion I'd ever seen her make. She shook the contents of her can all over the Dead Letter Office. With each splash, I winced. She sighed, set the canister on the floor, and removed a handkerchief from her pocket to dry her hands.

"Maybe that's what I have to learn about homes. They're not easy to leave, but there comes a time when there is simply no better option. My mother taught me that. 'We used to live in a great big castle,' she used to tell me. I guess this was *our* castle, Mr. Finch, but Excelsior, Inc., as of tonight, is dissolved. Don't feel bad about it. It happens to the best of businesses."

Never was Ruthie's sad smile of affection any stronger.

"If I have a regret, it's that I never got to see inside you, to see what was so important to Great-grandad Cornelius, to see if it was worth all this." She shrugged. "But what do I know about biology? I'm more of a numbers gal."

She tucked away the handkerchief and produced a cigarette lighter.

The stairway to the second floor was ten feet away, my best chance. My feet cracked through gasoline puddles as I heard the *tink* of the lighter striking clay tile, the *whoom* of fire blooming, and the

587

clack-clack-clack of Ruthie backpedaling from the hot gust. Before I hit the first step, I could hear one, then two, then three breathy roars as the fire ran the trails Ruthie had mapped. The stairs beneath my feet were gold with gasoline, and flames gave chase.

The second floor had been doused as well, but I did not hesitate to cross it, for I knew the Savages were watching their oasis catch fire, and it was quite possible they'd stand in place and burn, too, unless their leader—a grandiose word for the drifting admiral I'd been!—ordered them to retreat.

Fire erupted from the stairwell, and the ignitable lake upon which I stood shone a blinding orange. I charged beneath the fish tank, collided with the balcony doors, and for the first time passed through them, then slammed them shut against the lunging flames. The door rattled as if a bear wanted through it, and snakes of smoke slithered between slats.

I whirled and grabbed the railing.

Every eyeball, excepting those extracted and eaten, goggled up at me, reflecting the fire that already licked through windows below me and to my right and left; even the palm trees at either side of the building were begetting fruits of flame. The Savages clutched one another with whatever limbs they had left. A few carried buckets of drinking water, ready to fight the fire should I require it, not that it would be enough. Ruthie's restriction of water to a single pump would have its consequences.

Nevertheless their mouths hung wide for the Third Address.

I had to bay to be heard.

"THIS IS THE END!"

They moaned and swayed.

"I DID IT ALL WRONG! I DID EVERYTHING WRONG!"

I thought of what Church, the real one, had said to me at Woodstock.

"YOU NEED TO KEEP GOING! YOU NEED TO FINISH—"

—*your lives* was what I said, but the southern roof collapsed, the parapet exploding in brick, molding, and glass. The Savages reeled back, shielding their faces from a photosphere of sparks. They had gone frantic, babbling in tongues, clawing at their skin, skittering like insects. The noise of fear and destruction was thunderous. I ratcheted to a scream.

"*YOU NEED TO CONTINUE—*"

—*living* was what I said, but the northern downspout ripped from the outer wall and took with it a wagonload of brick that came right at me, bashing through the ten-foot planter box affixed to the balcony. It detonated in plaster and ceramic. The downspout took a perpendicular turn and dropped like a flaming broadsword into the crowd, splitting them into two halves. I only glimpsed them beginning to scatter, for half the balcony's floor crumbled and I fell. My left leg dangled in air before I heaved myself to the surviving half. I was on my knees, face pressed to the balustrade, watching how the downspout acted as Satan's spinal cord, shooting ribs of fire across the dry desert grass, which Ruthie had irrigated with gasoline.

My followers wailed but were disciplined beyond any Gallery of Pain huckster, Marine Corps unit, Astro trainee, or NSTF protestor. Caught inside polygonic cages of fire under the hellish red of the sweltering night, the Savages turned to one another, hearts pounding with frenzied joy. Mother-Father Savage had just said that this was the end, and to bring it about they had only to follow my final order, which they'd heard in incomplete pieces:

You need to finish—

You need to continue—

And so they did, eager to do my bidding as Chuck Manson's family had been to do his, stripping off what capes of civilized conduct they still wore and falling upon one another with finger and tooth. Alisha Savage sank her jaws into the jugular of Kimberly Savage, while Phoebe Savage took hold of Alisha Savage's bottom lip and ripped it off like fat from a steak. Regina Savage buried her face in Tracy Savage's clawed-open stomach while Tracy Savage munched Cassandra Savage's nose. Fernanda Savage, meanwhile, made good use of Lana Savage's leg stump, digging her fingers into the fissure and levering with such force that Lana's entire groin cracked open, her pelvis becoming a serving bowl of pubic muscle and gluteal nerves, intestine and colon, bladder and uterus.

If the Savages were a religion, here was their rapture. The overheated desert dirt poured forth its tarantulas, scorpions, rattlesnakes, and Gila monsters, which seethed about the women as they tore and gnashed and chewed, and quickly, before the fire robbed the Savages of their final feast. I shrieked that they'd misunderstood, but really they hadn't; just because scales had fallen from my eyes did not mean I could wrest from them the principles they revered. I covered my face with my hand. I'd forsaken the Fifty-One for the Savages, believing I'd traded up, when all I'd done was build my own desert Mauthausen.

With a crunch, the balcony dropped six inches, yet clung to the building by adobe ligament. Yes, I could fall into the Savage fray just as I'd fallen from the *Fliegende Hitler*, but what would it bring me beyond more martyrdom I didn't deserve? Delirious, I struggled to my feet and, once balanced upon the seesaw surface, took hold of a doorknob and was glad to see smoke rise from my palm. I hadn't burned at Woodstock, but perhaps I should have.

I opened the door. Fire mushroomed at my head, and I instinctively ducked. The room had become an oven and the heat cindered the ends of my hair. I toed the gasoline border and lifted my chin against the wall of flame; it tickled my throat, tightened the flesh.

There was a soft bubbling. My head already tilted, I needed but roll my eyes to see the fish tank directly above and how the water was beginning to roil. Poor fish, cooked alive. An idea flopped into my mind with all the vim of a dead body. While flames lashed out with stingers, setting fire to my jacket hem and both legs of my pants, I reached into my jacket pocket, past R's letters, past the Excelsior, past every ingredient of that centennial stew, until I found Gordo's knife.

I held it like a candle and thrust it upward. A single blow, and thick white cracks spread like spiderweb across the glass. Two seconds passed, during which flames spiraled up my legs, and then the tank exploded from the bottom up. From the room's upper half, a Niagara Falls of water crashed down with ice floes of broken glass. I was hurled to the floor, flattened by an ocean, and felt the snap of one, two, three ribs.

The weight of fish pattering against my back was, in comparison, as soft as eyelashes, but it was that gentleness that roused me enough to take a knee beneath the downpour and see a room sloshing with four feet of water gone black with muddied ember. The fire in the room had been quenched, and tank water was cutting a path down the stairs. It wouldn't last long; the whole building rattled with brimstone. I waded through the bilge in my steaming clothing, brushing back wooly brown smoke and kneeing aside the bobbing bodies of my fish friends.

The stairwell was a rapids I navigated on three limbs. The salon below remained an inferno, but the tsunami had snuffed enough of it for me to scramble across smolder, crawl through a northern window, and battle through burning shrubbery. Outside, it was seventy degrees cooler, but still hot as hell, and I yawed across the dirt, gaping at the cannibal apocalypse to my right: Ruthie's Scorched Earth Doctrine had become literal. A whole kingdom of smoke hung over the compound, and I wondered, were I to stand in place, if I might be noticed by the Savages, who'd belly up to me on limb stumps and gurgle past extracted tongues, craving the holiest flesh of all.

But only one figure watched me. Can't you see him?

That charred marionette jester frolicking from one fire to the next?

I stumbled away and came upon a fracas of feasting closer than the rest. Three women squatted like hyenas over a fourth, chewing and choking and snuffling, while the Ford Fairlane sat a few feet away, the driver's door open, keys in the ignition, and radio playing upbeat rock that lampooned the carnage. On instinct I approached. The *pitapat* of water dribbling from my clothing went unheeded behind the night's cries and rhapsodies; even when I came within six feet, the eaters were fixated on their eating.

Ruthie hadn't made it to her car. Both of her legs and her left arm had been pulled off and lay in the laps of women who noshed them like chicken drumsticks. Her hair had kept its obdurate bun, despite the fact that it, along with the underlying scalp, had been peeled clean off. None other than Ruthie's bête noire, Wailin' Wendy Savage, had pried open the lid of her skull so as to pick at her tasty brain. Next to her, the fanatic Sharon Savage, still alive after all these years and happily limbless, rocked on her spine like an infant, licking her lips and waiting to be fed.

The con job Ruthie had perpetrated had been unforgivable. That didn't mean I was glad to see she was still alive. Her head lolled in my direction, even though her eyes had been stabbed by the lens shards of her glasses. Every time Wailin' Wendy dug into her frontal lobe, Ruthie grinned in the sloppy manner of the mentally handicapped. A nervous-system reflex, that's all it was, but it stabbed me like an icicle nonetheless.

The last known Leather was gone, and did it bring me satisfaction? Here were the opposites of my martyrdoms: people killing themselves for me. I used the car door to keep myself upright while the Great Basin Desert played like a pipe organ of screams and the fire reached heights enough to mirror the falling meteor of Barringer's crater. There would be no hiding this night of violence, for those who survived would be too few to enact our rites of cremation. What I'd done there was evil, and everyone would see it. Still I insist to you that being evil is so much easier when you have as much time as I to arrive at it.

There was one who might understand this awful truth, and finding her was the sole reason I didn't take this latest opportunity to burn. The letters from R were waterlogged but still there, molded to my chest. If luck would hold, she might still be in Tranquility, Washington, her body, like mine, a wrinkled, faded, and torn roadmap of misdirection. Together we might sit in sedate commiseration, the crushing weight of being the world's onliest demon halved at last into manageable burdens. We couldn't offer each other forgiveness, but understanding? Was that too much for which a monster could hope?

I fell into the car and started it. Fifteen years old, that auto, but Ruthie had made mechanics rich by keeping it in fine fettle. The tank, prepped for getaway, was full. I had a bit of cash on me; it wouldn't get me to Washington, but it'd get me out of Arizona. I shut the door and rolled up the windows, the Babel of Armageddon abating to a muted beat. I swung the car around. The radio, still playing, segued into a cut from a new LP by a guy named Bruce hailing from the same New Jersey boardwalks where I'd first met Ruthie. *Everything dies, baby*, cautioned he, and *maybe everything that dies, one day comes back.*

XI.

NEWS OF THIS NATURE CAN'T be outrun. Reports of a situation at Savage Ranch, the home base of a cloistered Arizona cult, began issuing from the car radio fifteen hours into my journey. By the end of my second day of driving in a vehicle that stank of wet soot, the "situation" had become a "tragedy" worse than Jonestown in its caliber of atrocity. I broke off the radio knob, and, just for good measure, pulled onto the highway shoulder and snapped off the car's antenna.

Past the North Rim of the Grand Canyon I drove, through the cupped hands of Salt Lake City's Rockies, across the iron bridges of Twin Falls, through the rainbowed hills of Boise, and into Gifford Pinchot National Forest in the Cascade Range, an arcadia of velour greens and alabaster peaks. None of it helped; my skin crawled with guilt and shame, and all that kept me from steering the car into a chasm in the style of Margeaux was the lifeline represented by R, which I used to pull myself forward, hand over hand over hand.

Ruthie had stocked the Ford with getaway provisions, including her prized bank books, though stopping in Flagstaff to dicker with bankers would have only gotten me detained. Thankfully, the glove compartment contained five thousand dollars in cash. Fuel, therefore, was not an issue, and the last gas station at which I stopped— full-service, thank Gød, for whenever I exited the Fairlane, my flaking, desert-dried flesh drew stares—was located along the Swift Reservoir seventy miles northeast of Portland, Oregon.

It was the last place my road atlas did any good. Hiding behind a popped collar and NASA aviators, the portrait of the preying pervert, I beckoned a gullible-looking kid to the car window and slid him forty dollars to buy every local road and trail map in the station, keep the change. It did the trick. Tranquility, Washington, looked to be one of those townships I'd visited over and again throughout my death, a flyspot that might be flicked from the map with a finger.

After hours of wrong ways down blind mountain byways, I spotted "Tranquility" hand-painted onto a post stabbed into a brackish ditch. Ten minutes later, I'd found R's so-called Country Home. It was not the corniced cottage, complete with grazing sheep, that I'd drawn in my mind. It was, rather, a thirty-foot mobile home held together by rusty aluminum siding, its every broken window sealed up with cardboard. It rested upon a lopsided layer of crumbling cinder block, its old tires scattered about, each hosting a sui generis biome of orange hawkweed, yellow toadflax, and assorted weeds.

I killed the ignition and stood beside the car, the engine ticking in time with the Excelsior. I looked northward, where, above a peplum of clouds, Mount Saint Helens stood far more bravely than I. Three years prior, the volcano had erupted, shearing off its northern face, shooting magma, filling Spirit Lake with debris, mudsliding for fifty miles, and killing fifty-seven people—child's play compared to the body count of a single Mother-Father Savage. Though Mount Saint Helens looked peaceful, its presence underlined both the magnitude and the unpredictability of the moment: a meeting unlike any the world had ever seen.

Leaves rattled, birds whooped, insects trilled. Compared to the noiseless desert, the whole natural world wanted me to ascend the cinder-block steps and knock upon the askew door, from which poked a plastic fork in lieu of a handle. I filled my leathered lungs with air I did not need, and with small steps but great circumspection traversed the bramble that served as front lawn. Had Mount Saint Helens reactivated? Every part of me was shaking.

My foot came down upon an object that popped loudly enough to betray its synthetic origin—a fast-food beverage cup. From inside the mobile home came a humanoid warble and a blast of television noise. The trailer rocked, shedding scurfs of rust, and a corner of cardboard was pulled back from a window. Tin cans, from the sound of it, were kicked aside, and before the trailer door opened with a feline yowl, I was bushwhacked by a fact that hurt very much indeed.

Dead things like me didn't eat from tin cans or drink from fast-food cups.

The door cymbaled against the siding.

"Oh, Papa," sighed Merle. "You're so fucking late."

Was it the plasma pull of a shared ancestry that allowed instant recognition? This wasn't the fifteen-year-old guttersnipe who Leather had called a shit-throwing gibbon. This wasn't the forty-six-year-old morphine addict the drug dealer Sandy had called a skinny little bitch with the clap. Dearest Reader, if your tender heart can weather the tempest of truth, the worst thing possible had happened to my fearless, indomitable daughter: she'd become eighty-eight years old.

Merle's moth-eaten housecoat hiked up to thick-ankled, purple-veined calves as she adjusted her smudged bifocals.

"You look like shit, too. One arm, Papa?"

I pictured how she used to tap her teeth with a fingernail while devising her next acid criticism. Those teeth were gone now, leaving her with a lisp. I stood speechless as she smacked her lax lips and fretted her hand along the doorway in the manner of the elderly, reassuring herself of the permanence of objects.

"You're . . ." Such was my fluster that I could barely finish." . . . R?"

"Merle Ruby Watson. Never did like 'Merle.' Sounds like a man's name."

From my pocket I pulled the passel of letters, brown and melted from the aquarium bath, and held them out as if they were a search order.

"But these letters . . ."

Merle scowled, her toothless jaw jutting, the greasy tails of her hair flopping.

"Would you have come if I'd said it was me?"

Merle had begun sending letters to Savage Ranch five years after Ruthie and I had broken ground on the property, after the First and Second Addresses, after Wailin' Wendy's farewell broadcast had enlisted droves, after I'd discovered *Night of the Living Dead* and its all-important anthropophagous agenda. The envelopes felt brittle and unsubstantial. I let them fall from my hand. They looked at home alongside the crushed beverage cup.

"And the things you wrote? The things you knew?"

"You told me everything, Papa. You *insisted* on telling me everything."

How was it her aged brain's recall was better than my youthful one? In 1910, inside Leather's domed veranda, I'd lavished upon my daughter extensive details of my deathly existence in the daft hope she might return the balance of trust. What I hadn't described to her in words, she'd discovered firsthand living with me for a year in Salem, where she'd learned my sounds, smells, and textures, right down to my innards while stitching shut my abdomen from Leather's dinner-table carving.

Merle's glower liquefied under its weight of wattled skin.

"Why'd you wait so long, Papa?"

Together, separated by fifteen feet of clear, midday mountain sun, we trembled.

"I'm sorry," said I.

"I got this place for you. For both of us. Back when I could still get around all right. I got it way out here where I couldn't get into any more trouble. Because that's what you wanted. You remember, don't you? You wanted us to be together forever. That's what you said. But look at me now. What's forever worth now?"

Whispering was all I had left.

"I don't know."

Her arthritis seized. She grimaced. "There's no more time to waste. Come on."

She let go of the door, which struck her on her hunched back as she hobbled into the black interior. Alone, I released the shudder I'd been containing. It shook through every accursed part of my body, for nature itself rebels when a parent sees a daughter seventy-one years his senior. The quarrels I had with Gød were myriad, but here was a plea none other would ever surpass.

Give me my life back, mourned I, *so that I might die before hearing another word.*

The inside of the trailer was more forested than the out-side, a morass of food-trash underbrush, magazine promontories, dirty-clothing vines, and asbestos stalactites, all of it shaded a brown from the cardboarded windows. Three mice raced along a countertop behind a metropolis of beer cans coated with cigarette butts. Even their puny brains sensed the horrible thing about to happen.

Past a cramped, odoriferous kitchen and doorless toilet, I found Merle sitting upon a couch that vomited yellow stuffing. She was lit by the home's chief light source, an eight-inch Magnavox television antlered with wire hangers and aluminum foil. The signal was paper-thin and blizzarded by blue static, yet I could make out aerial footage of a remote building surrounded by a couple hundred white dashes, which were, I came to realize, covered bodies. How ineffectual Savage Ranch looked from above, how crude and ugly.

My shoes crunched through what sounded like eggshells. I turned off the TV. The picture winked away, and in the curved glass waited Merle's reflection. She'd seen the news, of that I was certain, and for the past week had been wondering if I might finally come. I preferred her blurry simulacrum to her distressing self; I did not turn around.

"There's a chair, Papa. Just brush off the junk."

The junk was a steeple of overdue bills, collection-agency threats, and hospital test results. Slowly I toppled it, watching each piece of bad news drop before I sat. It is difficult, Reader, to stare at your hands when you have but one, so I did what fate had brought me here to do. I looked at my daughter. Even darkness couldn't conceal what, in cramped quarters, was close enough to touch.

Time had always treated Merle poorly. She reeked like overripe fruit. Her arm skin, purpled by tattoos of jailhouse quality, pooled like dough around the needle pits of her morphine past and what-ever had followed. Heroin? Crack? Crystal meth? Probably all of it. A puckered scar split her right cheek, and glossy pink triangles from broken glass covered half of her neck, residue of bad boyfriends or vindictive pimps or just being in the wrong place at the wrong time,

600

which was a good way to describe Merle's whole life. Disease was as palpable upon her as it had been on Gabe Mungo, portions attributable to old age but most of it compensation for a history of wayward choices, a quality she'd inherited from her father. Here was true suffering from a true savage, not the characters I'd directed to go along with a screenplay's fiction.

Her eyes, magnified by the bifocals, were large and liquid.

"You smell like fire."

"I feel like fire," said I.

"Your face is still so young."

"I feel as old as sin."

"There's something I have to tell you."

Seven words that terrify anyone, dead or alive.

"It could all be over tomorrow. My hypertension. My osteoporosis. The diabetes. The lung cancer. And I'm not at peace with it, I'm not. There's things I have to make right. I could have told you, Papa. A thousand times I could've. But you know what? I didn't think you deserved it. I don't see so well these days, but I see this clear. You deserve to know it the same as I deserve to know it. Because we're all bad. We're all rotten. Every single one of us ever born."

With two words, I stretched my neck to the closest noose.

"Tell me."

"I know who killed you, Papa."

I cocked my head. Surely I'd misheard. If there was one piece of information I'd have guaranteed I'd never acquire, much less inside this muggy metal tube, this was it. The desire to chase down my murderer had meant everything at the turn of the century. It had been the catalyst for Johnny's awakening of my legs and tongue; it had brought me back to life, or as close as I could get. But after Luca Testa had exempted himself, I'd abandoned the hunt. I'd come to accept my death to be what deaths always were: meaningless.

"Papa—"

"Please, no."

"Papa, it was—"

"Don't tell me, Merle, don't tell me."

"It was Mother. It was Wilma Sue."

Imagine that life is a battleship. Imagine that, in the high tides of a long war, it capsizes. Imagine that you make it onto a life raft alone, and into the choppy but infinite waters you float, lost at sea, yes, but carried by a gentle hand that keeps you safe from sharks, a hand that, after a while, you forget to feel, for its edges and creases have become the whole world on which you rely. Now imagine that a reef slices through the raft. Imagine that the raft shrivels and sinks.

I cannot say what kind of bodily decay caused it, but a single bead of liquid bulbed at the corner of an eye that for eighty-seven years had been dry, and it slugged down my cheek, glistening a trail through dusty skin, past the broken vessels where Mrs. White had slapped me, near the eyetooth chipped while I'd crawled after Leather as he'd choked his wife, toward the rope burn of my Mississippi hanging, and into the chasm of the hook that had pulled me from lake water as a babe is fished from amniotic fluid. I placed my hand upon my wet cheek and let that hand slide to cover my eyes.

"Oh, Merle," said I. "Oh, Wilma Sue."

My daughter's voice had changed: the lost teeth, the cancerous lungs, the vocal cord abasement of eighty-eight years of screaming and sobbing. Still it knew how to snook through my defenses. My hand adjusted to cover an ear against her explanation, but it helped little, for any gaps in her tale I filled in myself, so unoriginal was each plot point, so transparent the clues, so inevitable the motivations, so foreseeable the outcomes.

They were stories Merle only heard when her mother was drunk. *My Aaron*—Wilma Sue's final words to me before I left her in that bed above Patterson's Inn—*My stupid Aaron*. She'd known she was pregnant, divulged Merle, and the invitation to duck beneath covers had been an invite to a family, which I'd spurned, only to spend each subsequent decade since trying to reinvent one. A woman with a child-puffed figure had no future at Patterson's, so she'd left before she could be fired and found a bed just outside the city, believing her Aaron would find her, not knowing her Aaron's world did not exist beyond Black Hand borderlands.

Wherever Wilma Sue went, men smelled her former occupation and wanted her, pregnant or not, and for her defiance she was beaten so badly, she was certain, each time, that her baby was dead. Even as a fetus, though, Merle was pigheaded, and so Wilma Sue prostituted herself one last time in order to swipe the revolver of her dozing client, the same Colt Lightning she'd pass on to Merle, the same one Merle would point at me in Salem. Wilma Sue kept the gun close so that the next man who did anything to threaten her unborn child would end up dead.

But it wasn't that easy, was it? The knife blocks of men held vast varieties; they could cut you in all sorts of ways. No one would hire a pregnant woman whose eyes bled desperation. And who wanted anything to do with a derelict beggar and her sickly, coughing newborn? There was no food to be had. She produced no milk. No path presented itself but the criminal. She escaped down garbage-strewn alleys, hid in muddy graveyards, squatted in manure-filled barns to count her thieved coins. This was Wilma Sue Watson's life. Was it any better than death?

Left with no option, Wilma Sue traveled back to Chicago, a long journey filled with its own horrors, and on May 7, 1896, she prevailed upon a barkeep to hand me the infamous note compelling me to meet an unknown person to discuss an opportunity, which I'd read over pheasant, potatoes, and ale while she'd spied from across the street. She'd been right there, Reader, holding infant Merle to her bony ribs, watching me stuff my face and leer at the letter's proposition, smugly certain that it would be one of big business.

My overstarched collars, the Peacemaker I'd taken all morning to polish, the Excelsior I twirled upon its luminous chain—how intimidating, then humiliating, then enraging it would have looked to the wretched Wilma Sue. The baby she'd brought to show me could not possibly have the desired effect. She was a squalid beggar who had nothing, yet held me in her heart; I was an overindulged brat who had everything and, from all appearances, had forgotten she existed.

Fourteen minutes clicked by between my on-time arrival and the 7:44 shot that killed me. I'd always pictured my murderer as hunkered in the weeds, murmuring maledictions over his firearm before storming the sand. Merle didn't need to sketch the scene for me to visualize the reality. Wilma Sue had stood behind me in plain sight for all fourteen minutes, weighing upon the scales of her arms a baby and a gun, scales that were tipped by twelve months of constant degradation. When it came to her baby's survival, Zebulon Aaron Finch, that pontifical, self-satisfied fop, his pockets full of ill-gotten cash, would be more helpful dead than alive.

"She killed you for me," said Merle.

"As well she should have," rasped I.

"I was raised to hate you."

"As well you should, too."

"No, Papa. I can't lie anymore. Maybe you helped turn Mother the way she was. But that doesn't excuse her. She was a cruel woman."

"What?"

"She drank. She beat me. She knocked me down in public."

"No, Merle—"

"What do you expect? Her life was hard. I suppose she was loving sometimes, but she was hateful more often. It's just like I said. We're all the same. We're all hateful."

Bridey Valentine, in a snit of sexual rage, had been right: *You've built a pedestal to this girl like she's the epitome of virtue, when she was every bit as faulted and as foul as me. It's a child's viewpoint, Z. You can be such a child.* And like a child holds in his pocket a rabbit's foot—or, come to think of it, a utility knife from a space capsule, or a hand-drawn map of the Meuse-Argonne, or a wrinkled photograph of his daughter, or an *Atlanta Constitution* advertisement, or a top-dollar pocket watch—I'd held tight to Wilma Sue, not because she was my immortal beloved but rather because she'd been what I needed to get by. If you have any doubt that seventeen is a child's age, here, Reader, is your evidence.

"You've always been kind to me," said Merle. "So fucking kind, no matter the things I did. You gave me so many chances. I just needed to give you this chance back, all right? The chance to hate me, to hate Mother. You deserve it, Papa. You always have."

Though she spoke of hatred, her voice was free of it.

My arm lifted from my lap. I watched it in a daze. I had to lean forward; that, too, I watched with curiosity, my feet resettling, my knees bending, my thighs contracting. The arm achieved its length, and I took Merle's sclerotic hand from where it had clawed onto her robe. Her palm was papery, the knuckles swollen, faint of both pulse and heat. But when I squeezed the hand, the Little Miracle Electric Mexican Stuttering Ring jawing into the gnarled fingers, her ligaments tightened and Merle squeezed back, as if she, too, had floated upon a life raft perforated with holes, dead in the water until, just now, I began pulling her onto mine.

If we had to sink, by Gød, we'd do it together.

XII.

N SALEM, MERLE AND I had spent one year together. In Tranquility, we spent one more. She told me, in the loose strings and tight knots of geriatric recall, what she'd been doing for forty years. She drilled rivets in a San Diego factory emptied of World War II draftees and saw a woman's arm gobbled up by a grinder. In El Paso she sold buttons opposing racial integration. She took in street cats in Colorado Springs, up to twenty of them, and learned to pull kittens from wombs. She romanced an army captain in Shreveport until, without warning, he sat inside his closed garage and turned on his car. Outside Memphis she was bitten by a raccoon and nearly died of leptospirosis. She scotched a Cincinnati bank hold-up by stabbing the gunman with a pen. In Virginia Beach she became so interested in Mahatma Gandhi that she, dedicated illiterate, paid a paperboy to read her related news stories. One week after getting her driver's license in Ann Arbor at age fifty, she mowed down a baby carriage and fainted, only to learn that it'd been full of groceries. She worked at a dress shop in Sioux Falls until she spat into the face of a customer who'd called Rosa Parks a nigger (her views on blacks had changed). In Provo she snatched money from an open register and matriculated to jail, wherefrom she rebelled, had sex with women, raised hell, and was graduated to prison. Her Lucille Ball impression made her fellow Las Vegas cocktail waitresses adore her. In Long

Beach, she learned to swim. She placed second in the senior category of a dance contest in Fresno. In Eureka she voted for the first time: Richard Nixon in 1968 (but not in 1972). She acted as grandmother to a poor Japanese-American girl being raised by a single mother in Eugene, just like Wilma Sue had raised Merle, and it was the greatest honor of her life until that girl died of pneumonia.

Infirm though she was, crumbling though I was, and ramshackle though our trailer became, our second cohabitation was worlds more wondrous than our first. Every detail with which she regaled me was another thread into another patch into another quilt that warmed away the shivers of having lived so long beside a woman who'd been plotting my downfall. In Tranquility, there was no deception, cunning, or guile, only sun, rain, sleet, and snow beating at our Country Home until the trailer mirrored our father-daughter bond: coated with mold, rife with leaks, infested with vermin, but, damn it all, still standing.

Too sick to get up one snowbound day, she grilled me from sweaty sheets.

"Tell me about you. I missed everything. I want to hear it."

"My journey has been one of triviality."

"Don't goddamn lie."

I mulled for a minute. "I met Albert Einstein. Is that interesting?"

"No, you didn't."

"I did, at a party in Hollywood."

"Whose party?"

"Mary Pickford and Douglas Fairbanks."

Merle shook her head, then coughed, then laughed.

"Oh, Papa. You don't know the value of what you've got."

Thenceforth I tried cooling her fevers with the antidote of anecdote. As a turbulent teen, she'd despised my windy reports, but now the most picayune details sustained her: the slapstick, if lethal, foibles of those wonky Chauchat rifles; the sizable list of pet names I had for the *Schutzstaffel* thug Kuppisch; Junior's diligent nutshelling of Kal-El's deliverance from Krypton. What was wondrous was how less trivial my walking death felt when met by Merle's interest. Perhaps mine had not been a wonderful existence, but it was, at least, one worth recounting—which I have done for you, Reader, in these pages you hold.

Merle's declining health allowed me to be the father I'd never had the chance or inclination to be before. Though Merle's mind remained sharp for an octogenarian, her body backslid toward infancy. She spat food and phlegm; I was there with towel. She soiled herself; I was there with washrags and fresh laundry. She whimpered from pains she couldn't express; I stroked her baby-thin hair and assured her that I was by her side and there I would remain.

By the fall of 1984, one of her maladies—the boys of Savage Ranch might have called it a Fever of Unknown Origin—peaked. We both knew the end was nigh. Day and night I kept to the bedside, monitoring her temperature and stepping away only to fix tea and tapioca she couldn't keep down. The two or three hours a day during which she was lucid, I tried to engage her in dialogue to ensure that no unturned stones remained between us. In each of these sessions I pressed the same question: *Is there anything you wish to tell me?*

One day—the last day, as it turned out—there was.

"You remember," asked she, "our room in Salinas?"

"Salem. And yes, every inch of it."

"You remember . . . oh, I was so angry with you."

"In that, you were remarkably consistent."

"All I wanted was to buy pretty dresses, and dance, and kiss boys."

"Not a bad way to live a life, all considered."

"And you . . . you were so angry with me, too."

"I'm afraid so."

"You took me by the wrists. Back then you had two hands."

"I remember."

"And you said, 'Daughter, look into my eyes.' And I saw . . . the most horrid thing."

Her parting words of 1914 were branded onto my heart:

My horrible, worthless, lonely death? Have you known it all along? What kind of father are you to show it to me?

"I have regretted it ever since," said I.

"What I saw was . . . this."

"What do you mean?"

"This bed. The trash on the floor. The cold and the dark. The TV. TVs weren't invented yet, but I saw it, a bright little box."

Never had my hypotheses about *la silenziosità* been so specifically confirmed. How the opaque images of her deathbed had haunted Merle over the decades, I couldn't bear to know. I took her limp hand. Her eyes rolled sidewise until they found mine.

"Except you," said she. "I didn't see you."

For a minute I could not move. Then I kissed her old hand and placed it against my cold forehead, which I bowed to hide my face, for I knew she'd never understand why my whole body had begun to shake, not with grief but with the laughter of indescribable relief and untellable awe, the laughter of finishing a marathon which has torn one's feet to ribbons. For if Merle had foreseen her deathbed in exquisite detail but I hadn't been there, that meant the visions of *la silenziosità* weren't fixed fates.

Do you understand, Reader, what this means?

Fates can change if people change.

Free will matters.

Acts of kindness matter.

Love matters.

"I'm here now," whispered I. "Baby, I'm here now."

"I know, Daddy," said she. "Daddy, I know."

Merle Ruby Watson took her last breath at dawn on September 30, 1984. She died in Tranquility, Washington, at age eighty-nine. She attained no high school or college degree. She performed no military service. She had no profession, only the oddest of jobs. She was beloved by few, though she lived more than most. She was preceded in death by mother Wilma Sue Watson and was survived, in some respects, by father Zebulon Finch. Those who wish to send flowers can cram them up their asses, for no funeral services will be held—not those, at least, that you'd want to attend.

That is the truth. Even my Reader may wish to turn from the funeration I performed, even though you will, I suspect, sympathize with why I did it. One minute after Merle's passing, I had the most nauseating thought I'd ever had, which is saying something indeed. Merle was my daughter; we shared the same blood. If I'd resurrected seventeen minutes after Wilma Sue had killed me, wasn't there a chance that Merle's letters to Savage Ranch might come true and she might suffer her father's fate?

No. Gød, no.

Seventeen minutes is not much time to destroy, beyond all irrational doubt, the body of one's only child. The mobile home, that electric monstrosity, harbored no kerosene, so I flung myself about, grabbing knives, tenderizers, hammers, loose brick, anything that might saw muscle or slice tendon or crush bone, for the Excelsior ticked at a speed unfair to a young man whose own clock moved so slowly, and I wrapped Merle, my beautiful little girl, inside her winding sheets and dragged her down the cinder-block steps and onto the dirt patch in front of the trailer, and beneath a mountain that stared down like a bloodthirsty Aztec god, I took a cleaver and lifted it and

[PAGE RIPPED OUT]

PART TWELVE

1985–1994

———◦«»◦———

At Last It Befalls That Your Hero Is Proclaimed A Madman, Given Befitting Lodgment, And Has His Head Examined.

I.

DEATH MAY BE CIVILIZATION'S GREAT equalizer, but not all deaths are equally great. Whereas the scene of Merle's demise had been a leaky metal trailer boa-constricted by weeds, I located in Orlando, Florida, a facility called Edgerton Home for the Aging, a campus of flowerbedded footpaths and crepe-papered corridors through which nurses in casual dresses pushed wheelchaired tenants past walker-assisted chums on their way to the sunny atrium. Smells, sounds, and sights had an established routine here, and I counted upon the residents' inferior eyesight, as well as my aviators and the black hooded sweatshirt I'd mined from Merle's laundry mounds, to make me invisible. Despite all of this, he recognized me in seconds. Even more astonishing, he did not seem surprised to see me.

"Zebulon Finch," said Allen Rigby. "I was wondering when you'd show up."

When had all those closest to me become enfeebled ancients? In many respects, Rigby had never changed: the wire-spectacled, tie-throttled government agent I'd met in a D.C. bunker in 1942 had been but a few crow's-feet away from the NASA adviser I'd met at Big Jimmy Dutko's Beaver Lounge in 1959. Add a quarter century more, and there was less hair and prescription glasses of a thicker gauge, but the man he'd been had yet to be fully digested. Indeed, he looked sharper than ever, which befuddled me until I realized why.

Rigby had quit smoking. The idea was too incredible; I searched for the telltale pocket bulge of a soft pack or close-at-hand ashtrays, but found them only at other tables. With the pervading gray pall lifted, Rigby was vivid and unburied—and that was just for starters. Instead of his ubiquitous white Oxford and black tie, he wore an open-throated Hawaiian shirt with a pocket filled not with leaking red pens but horse-racing score cards, insinuating actual leisure activities. Even the body beneath the clothes had become companionable, like an ex-footballer whose physique has finally relaxed from the rigors of weight training and high-protein diets.

Disconcerted by my changes, he gave me the look a father gives a long-absent son who's gone pudgy and bald. He drummed fingernails, no longer nicotine yellow, upon the tabletop.

"You want to sit? Debrief?"

Eagle-eyed nurses had begun to notice the hooded, one-armed infiltrator.

"Do you have a private room?" asked I.

"This isn't Sing Sing, Finch. Come on."

Standing up wasn't the most graceful thing he'd ever done, and he walked with all the pace of a tightrope walker, but the way he shooed nurses and saluted elderly comrades recalled how he'd once strode through Lovelace Clinic nodding casually at all the fighter jocks who knew his name.

His room was labeled 24E, a suitably anonymous epithet for a man who'd lived a life of top secrets. The abstemious quarters were barely bigger than the cell I'd been assigned at OSS (itself labeled the mysterious J-1121), but were painted a bright coral and decked with tchotchkes with which no past Rigby would have trifled: sea shells, starfish, driftwood, and a cluster of seven framed photos over the bed. Once upon a time, I might have mocked such a mawkish display, but no young man exits a century the same as he entered into it.

I knew the subject of each photo, though we'd never met: cowlicked Roy, gap-toothed Sandra, Boy Scout Walter, puppy-squeezing Patty, cross-eyed Stanley, and crib-bound Florence, hexagoned around a Janet radiant in a gown as white as the snowy steps of the church inside which she'd just been wed. Having only months ago lost my own child, the abrupt sight of so many dead beloveds had me gripping the dresser.

"You gave them back to me," said Rigby.

"I merit no plaudits," growled I.

"Ten years, I couldn't even say their names, or I'd be right back on that river bank. Now . . ." He shrugged. "Now they're my stars in the sky."

"Align yourself with a devil, Rigby, and you, too, might be damned."

But he was shuffling past me toward an easy chair, into which he lowered himself with a grunt. He massaged knurled fingers that, without a cigarette, looked like unloaded guns, and gazed past the window's silvered curtain of Spanish moss. Suddenly I could picture all six children clambering out of their photo frames to climb all over the grandfatherly figure. I believe it was a vision in which Rigby also indulged.

"Just because I'm retired doesn't mean I don't keep government contacts. 'Zebulon X'? 'Mother-Father Savage'? Christ alive. You've lived one hell of a life."

"Death."

"Either way, one hell of one. Take it from a fogey who's seen a thing or two himself." He pointed at the room's second chair. "You didn't come for Backgammon Thursday. Tell me what you want. If it's in the power of an eighty-year-old retiree with a bad back, I'll do it. The Feds are after you, you know, and they've gotten better at their job since my day."

Notable exceptions notwithstanding, I had a history of following the man's orders. I positioned myself opposite and caulked twenty-three years' worth of gaps in his knowledge, which were shockingly few; the intel provided by his "government contacts" had been superb. Ergo I sped through the icky particulars of martyrdoms and meteorite madness to focus on my death's penultimate chapter: my last days with Merle.

I did feel some satisfaction that my torpid carcass retained the capacity to startle. Zebulon Finch, the immature immortal, had a child? I told the sad story, sadder this go-round for my Chicago assassin having been outed. It was Allen Rigby alone I told what I'd done to Merle's body, for if he'd pardoned me for the climactics at Savage Ranch, thought I, he might pardon me for anything. Forgive me, Dearest Reader, for tearing out the pages on which I wrote these same details, but it was unsightly work, my pencil snagging in imagined gore, the paper glopping with imagined blood. I scrunched and swallowed the pages. If my body has since turned to dust, those pages might be lying intact alongside these notebooks. In that case, they are yours to read, provided you are strong of stomach.

What I will tell you is that I distributed Merle's ashes deep inside the glens, dells, and combes of the hills she'd chosen as home. I could but hope that the purity of untouched environs would annul the blood disease of being a Finch. Before leaving Country Home, I turned the trailer inside out, and found in a tucked-away envelope a single item of interest—the WANTED poster of Zebulon Finch she'd inherited from Wilma Sue, the same one with which Merle had accosted me at our first meeting. Though it had gone transparent with age, I marveled at how the handsome, cocksure hooligan of 1895 had become the ugly, lachrymose specter I saw in Merle's bathroom mirror.

Rigby handled the poster as if it were a Sumerian cuneiform instead of the dross of a callow blackmailer, while I recounted my final jaunt across the continent. Modern telephone operators had access to incredible wellsprings of information, and pinpointing Rigby's location had taken but a few hours. The trek itself was miserable—the Ford Fairlane, mourning its master, died before getting out of Washington, and America's nostalgic indulgence of hobos had ended—but the most dangerous part had been the walk through Orlando, a city so splashed in sun that there were no shadows through which to skulk. Five blocks from the Edgerton Home for the Aging, I'd been confronted by two young men, the first in a jean jacket pinned with superfluous chains, the second toting a suitcase-sized portable music player blasting out the herky-jerky refrain of "Beat It" by some girlish vocalist. The pair, I believe, had been intent upon roughing me up before the jean-jacketed one had said, "Yo, don't touch this dude. He's got the AIDS."

I'd invoked what I could of Gabe Mungo's élan and kept walking.

Three different attendants knocked to remind Rigby that tonight's dinnertime featured a choral group from a local high school singing jukebox favorites from the 1950s. Rigby shouted for each of these intruders to vamoose, then leaned in as much as his back would allow.

"So," surmised he, "it's not just the Feds who are after you."

Rigby's judgment was finely honed. Who could say Ruthie didn't have siblings sworn to a kindred pledge? How could one know if the offspring of the Triangulinos even now sharpened their sticks? Did it not stand to reason that among the families of 236 dead Savages there existed some dedicated revengers? Like Dr. Leather playing Gesualdo's *Moro, Iosso, al mio duolo* on his Victrola, the atonalities might repeat, repeat, repeat.

"The hatred I've seeded across America," said I, "blooms eternal."

"I don't hate you, Finch. Far from it."

"I beg you to refrain from such irrelevances. The truth that matters is that you, if you'll excuse the frankness, are not long for this Earth. After Merle, I cannot stand another passing, nor do I have the vigor to spend another forty years trying to develop a single relationship that borders upon the amicable. I must be filed away where no one shall find me. This is why I come to you."

Rigby's eyes narrowed, then strayed over my shoulder to consult his family. He expelled a dry laugh and pushed himself back into the chair.

"*I'm* the man who dropped you over Berlin."

"Yes."

"*I'm* the man who put you inside that space capsule."

"Yes."

He pounded the end table. A cup of water toppled and darkened the carpet.

"So why have me louse everything up again? I'm at peace with things now, and I tell you, it took me a long time to get there. Now you waltz in, ask me to do something I'm not prepared to do, never thinking of the effect it'll have on me to know I've done you wrong yet again. You're one self-absorbed bastard, Finch."

"Except this time the placement comes at my request."

"Why not go all the way, then? Set yourself on fire if you want out so bad. Why drag me into it?"

"Don't think I haven't given it consideration. Lately, though, my thoughts go to Merle, who lived with magnitudes of physical and emotional pain. She could have drawn shut the empty bag of her life at any time, and yet never took that simpler path. She chose to keep living, and that stubbornness, I would like to think, is a Finch family trait. In her honor, as well as the honor of those I've known who were never given the choice, I shall do the same. I shall persist. I shall persist and repent."

Love matters, I added to myself, just so that I did not forget, and no longer would I traipse the planet impeding the person-to-person transmission of this most beautiful of diseases. I had caught it myself, a couple of times, and still felt the gorgeous wounds, still longed to shed tears at the exquisite scars.

Rigby muttered and snatched a bottle of pills from the table, though with the cup overturned, there was no way to take them. He gave the bottle a disgusted rattle and hurled it. We both watched it roll beneath the bed, out of reach of old men of pains and aches.

"I'm guessing you're not talking about a prison."

"Correct."

"I'm guessing you're thinking of a sanatorium."

"It would be for the best."

"This isn't the grand old days when a husband could check his wife into a nuthouse on his say-so. This is 1985. Everything's on computers. You heard of IBM? Microsoft? They've got two Apple thingamabobs right here at Edgerton. I can't leave the building without them typing me into what they call a floppy disk. A state psychiatric hospital would have ten times that level of security: identification papers, employment histories, medical records, some of it wired right through the telephone line. Don't ask me how it works—all I know is you can't exist off the grid anymore. We're all connected now, and it's only going to get worse."

"This is why I've come to you." I smiled. "Government contacts."

Rigby ran a hand over his spotted scalp. "Give me the weekend to think this over, okay? You have somewhere to go?"

To go? Always. To stay? Aye, there was the rub.

"There's always somewhere," said I.

"All right. See you Monday."

Whichever poker hand of afflictions age had dealt him—rosacea, hemorrhoids, glaucoma, perhaps some mortal ace of spades—not even played in sequence could they best Rigby when he was on his game. While his fellow long-tooths blotted bingo cards and whacked away with croquet mallets, he worked the horn. How long had it been since he'd had reason to cash in favors? On Monday, after I, in my druidic hood, stole through an atrium redolent of green beans and muskmelon, I found Rigby waiting in 24E with a manila folder as thick with paper as my old OSS dossier.

He looked over his glasses. I knew the expression from hundreds of basement briefings, and had I two arms and any spirit left whatsoever, I might have given the old boy a hug.

Rigby licked a finger and hustled through pages of departmental flowcharts, alphanumerical directories, and jotted questions, most of which had been struck through and annotated with answers. By quaint custom he'd blacked out classified information with a marker. For twenty minutes he explained what he felt a civilian could know about his investigations, before presenting his summary.

"I can get you red-tagged. That will get us around an admission physical or anything like that—you'll go straight into their system. The good news is, a red tag is permanent. The bad news is, it's nearly impossible to enforce. That's the risk factor: what goes on inside any hospital, there's just no way to know. Getting admitted is the easy part. Anyone can commit himself; it's a free country. It's staying there that's difficult. Understand that once you sign yourself over to their care, it becomes their decision whether to judge you safe or dangerous for society. Let me be blunt. You will have to convince them that you are dangerous."

"Easy," said I. "I am as crazy as a fox."

Rigby took off his glasses and massaged eyes sore from too little sleep.

"Mr. Beauregard across the hall is seventy-four and can't put together two sentences. All the years you've lived, all the things you've seen, and you're still making sense? You still don't see how extraordinary you are. In that respect, you haven't changed."

These compliments I tossed beneath the bed next to the bottle of pills, before approving Rigby's plan, despite his every caution and caveat. Rigby held his tongue, nodded, and asked for a few more days to stabilize the particulars. Again he told me to skedaddle and again I did, but not before pausing at the 24E door.

"These data-boxes you speak of . . ."

"Data*bases*."

"You say they compile information on every U.S. citizen?"

"If they've got a Social Security number, yes."

"Were I to provide you with a list of names, might you . . . ?"

Rigby slapped shut his folder. "This whole business is cockeyed! What do you want now?"

"I forget myself. Disregard the question."

I opened the door, but a wheelchair race forced me to wait long enough for Rigby to groan.

"Will you give me the damn names? I'll see what I can do."

That is why, Dearest Reader, before we tumble down the last hill I'd ever tumble, I can provide eulogistic denouements to those whose fates otherwise might have weighed upon me, and perhaps you, until the end. Jason Stavros, the one member of the Third Battalion who ought not to ever have died, had done just that, succumbing to colon cancer while I'd been overseeing desert atrocities. Detective Fergus Roseborough, he of the orange hair and freckles and crooked nose, who'd made haranguing me a sport before he'd saved Church's life in the Cotton Club—remember him? He'd died in 1939, not under the rain of bullets he'd have preferred but from a heart attack, probably brought on by one of his overstrenuous interrogations. What about his nemesis, know-it-all newshound Kip McKenzie? His muckraking caught up with him in 1940, when a disgraced politico had him stabbed the same night I'd escorted Bridey Valentine to the twelfth annual Academy Awards. Speaking of Bridey, her favorite director and my least favorite taxidermist, Maximilian Chernoff, blew his head off in 1949, after having been forcibly removed from a war picture a million dollars overbudget. He did it deep in his beloved San Bernardino mountains concurrent with my own mountain wanderings in Montana. Charles White Jr. and his sister, Franny, were still struggling through life, middle aged and middle-class, but their mother, Shirley White, was dead. She'd been only fifty when an eighteen-wheel semi truck had struck her car head-on not two miles outside her Heavenly Hills home. Jolami Tiombe was gone as well, shot down at age thirty, along with other activists in an unsolved drive-by murder in 1980

626

Los Angeles. The last name on my list was, of course, Burt Church-well—I needed to confirm that it had been his ghost urging me to avert the Savage Tragedy. Indeed it had.

No disease was as terminal as Zebulon Finch.

"How is it," posed I after Rigby had finished this necrology, "that of all the people I've crashed into over the last one hundred and six years, you alone have survived intact?"

Bingo Saturday was in full trot. "G-53" buzzed from a hot mike. Rigby, beholder of war, rescue, love, death, and the promise of inter-galactic eternity, he who'd been tugged through the blackest of tar yet still was able to see the softest pinprick of light, offered a bittersweet smile, as if he'd been keeping track of a mental Bingo card all his life and was but one letter-number combo from the prize.

"Surviving intact," mused he. "I don't think that's the point."

II.

BARRACLOUGH PSYCHIATRIC CENTER WAS IN Lubec, Maine, at the eastmost prong of Quoddy Head State Park, making it the first place in the continental U.S. to see each day's sunrise. But the morning I stepped onto the campus, it was murked in a fog so woolly, I could make out but traceries of corbeled towers and hear only distant detonations of Atlantic surf against troll-teethed cliffs. In other words, perfect environs for the raving mad, far-flung from urban centers and defended by water, woods, and the fog, which I cannot emphasize enough, Reader, for how it rolled itself into long gray fingers and beckoned.

Rigby and I sculled through the salty brume until the central fortification lurched forward like a brontosaurus, four stories of gloomy Chateauesque masonry and pitched roofs bayonetted with sharp turrets. I inhaled cold fog and let it churn inside my chest. When Rigby had listed the four institutions inside which he believed he could insert me, I had had only one question. Which place was the least esteemed, the one most likely to be neglected by state and federal do-gooders? He'd answered without pause: Barraclough, long known to locals, residents, and staff by the informal, and revealing, nickname of "Bear Claw."

Blank faces mooned down at us from the windows of buildings to our immediate north and south. Rigby took my elbow as if afraid

I might flee, or perhaps that he might, having realized a grievous error. Too late: The fog eddied back from two orderlies coming at us in sinless white uniforms, but also leather utility belts, concealing who knew what tools of inducement. The first one, a smirking truck-driver type with furry forearms, shook Rigby's old hand, too hard, by the look of his wince, while the other, a watchful African American ("Afro-American" had lost its cachet), stood at the ready as if accustomed to last-second dashes.

"Mr. Rigby? I'm Tom Sikes. This is Mr. Glover."

"How do you do, Mr. Sikes, Mr. Glover."

Sikes extended his hand to me.

"And Mr. Zipp?"

Rigby, forced by his clandestine counterfeiters to supply a name to go along with my falsified records, and too pressed for time to gather my creative input, had swapped the opening letters of my first and last names to come up with the imbecilic "Frank Zipp." The name made me grind my teeth; behind them, I managed a reply.

"Pleased."

Sikes didn't shrink at my missing arm or blanket decrepitude. He did, however, shiver at my touch.

"You're cold. Let's get you inside, where it's warm."

I nodded, feeling abruptly anxious despite my mental preparations. Rigby, still clutching my arm, took the first steps, which I followed. But Sikes held up a hand.

"We've got it from here, Mr. Rigby."

"But don't we need to check in and—"

"Everything was taken care of over the phone."

"I'd still rather come, if you don't—"

"We find it's better for the patient to make a fresh start. It's Barraclough policy."

Rigby's hesitation made evident every single day of his eight decades—clever enough when telephoning officials who owed him their careers, but out in the wider world, hard of hearing, weak of lung, and easily outfoxed by younger men. He turned to me, looking like a grandfather who needed help finding his parked car, if indeed he ought to be driving at all.

"Finch," said he.

"Zipp," reminded I.

He shook his head in apology; I shook mine, rejecting it. Our good-bye had come suddenly and strangely, beneath a nippy ocean haze and the pressure of Sikes's impatient eyebrows and Glover's cracking knuckles. For forty-three implausible years, Rigby and I had played principal parts in each other's dramas, and it is a rare thing, Reader, when finales are so plainly final.

"They have telephones," said Rig. "I'll call."

"Don't."

"Then I'll write. You can read them or not, it's up to—"

"Please," begged I. "Do not."

His Adam's apple bobbed through droops of slack skin. He pressed his lips together and nodded, and inside me a dam of gratefulness broke open. He understood that what I needed was not the "fresh start" Sikes advocated but rather the fast, irrevocable severing of all human relations.

I held out my hand—scorched, scarred, scuffed, and scored, and all the unseemlier for the tarnished tin ring around a finger. Rigby studied the hand, perhaps reliving the stories it told, perhaps comparing them to those told by his own pallid flesh. His hand, when

I took it, was that of any elderly person, frail, trembling, dry, and cool. But bones were bones, and he made sure I felt his. Tears fattened at the edges of his lids, though I hesitate to take credit for them, for the salt-water fog did sting, and old eyes do tend to water. I removed the aviators I'd worn since our NASA years, folded them, and placed them into Rigby's palm. Maybe if he protected those eyes, they would not be so inclined to cry.

He wrapped his veined hands around the sunglasses.

"I'll miss you," admitted he.

"But the world won't," said I. "And that is what matters."

With that I turned away, concentrating on the gravel crunch as I followed Sikes up the path and the steps of the manor; carved over the arched doorway was the word "PLATO." Once upon a dream, Plato Manor's central hallway had been designed to instill Bear Claw visitors with reverence. It was double the standard width and height, ran the length of the building, and was furbelowed with stained-glass windows that matched the stenciled border of the coffered, box-beamed ceiling. The luxurious blond walls incandesced off the polished tile. Our shoes squeaked, a chipper sound that spoke of clean, responsible institutions.

But, as I've indicated, the hall was long. Twenty feet along, the overhead lights began to ebb. The stained glass sprouted cracks. Twenty feet farther, the blond coloring quit, as if the painters had stopped being paid. After that, each foot peeled back another decade. The cauliflowered water damage of the northern face dated back to the sixties. That rusted fire extinguisher had been installed in the forties. Sections of broken tile revealed a whorled underfloor from the twenties. By the time we reached the end, we'd time-traveled to the era of my death: pebbled brickwork, an overriding ambiance of slag, and geometries of shadows that had known no light since century's turn.

My escorts, too, devolved, Sikes sinking into a predacious hunch and Glover snorting and huffing like primitive man. We stopped outside a door. Sikes held his hands as if to play patty-cake, so I mirrored him, and he shook me down like the mobster I was, working the Little Miracle Electric Mexican Stuttering Ring from my finger and emptying my pockets right down to the sealed envelope of Ruthie's thousands and, much harder to bear, the Excelsior. I'd expected as much—there was no point in keeping money, much less time—yet still felt as if my heart, too, had been burglarized.

"No bags?" grunted Sikes.

I shook my head.

He rapped the door, paused three seconds, and opened it.

The office, though spacious, was crowded toward the center, as if the furniture were being sucked down a drain. The central piece was a desk the size of a barge, once effulgent of cherrywood and copper, now as achromatic and lusterless as the seventy-some-year-old behind the desk. He sat as still as the portrait of President Reagan above him and glanced at us as if we were three houseflies. While Sikes and Glover took prison-guard positions on either side of me, the last guest, a curly-haired, curly-mustached man a decade younger than the sitter, cleared his throat.

"Superintendent," cued he.

The man behind the desk blinked. His eyes were huge, though only in comparison to his tiny head. Age seemed to have whittled it until it was no more than a skull. His body, too, was bones; his dusty black suit looked ten sizes too big. He was, in short, precisely the grim reaper one might expect to find at the end of a century-long hall.

"Oh, my," said the skeleton. "This is Mr. Zipp, isn't it?"

The standing man gave me a perfunctory smile.

"I'm Dr. Dobbin, chief clinical officer. This is Dr. Orrin Scrimm. He's CEO of Barraclough."

Scrimm pshawed. "Superintendent. That's the only title I ever wanted."

The ensuing silence was edgy. At last Scrimm sighed, discovered a whale of paper, and flensed the topmost sheet. I was surprised to see that Rigby's "red tag" was literal: a scarlet card had been stapled to the page.

"I haven't seen one of these since . . ." Scrimm frowned as much as his tight-fleshed skull would permit. "All people do anymore is tell me how to run my asylum."

"*Hospital*," corrected Dobbin.

"Who ever heard of admitting a patient without X-rays or an EKG? It says we're not even authorized to Kwell your hair. And here we just got through a lice infestation. Oh, this is not good, not at all."

Scrimm dropped the paper and exhaled as if it had been a fifty-pound weight. He angled his skull at various corners of the room, neck bones crackling like chewed ice.

"There was a time when Bear Claw was the greatest asylum in America."

Again Dobbin grimaced at the word, but this time held his tongue. Behind me, I heard the key-ring jangle of Sikes and Glover squaring their feet for a story they'd heard before. I, too, knew this brand of bewailing nostalgia. The Barker, old Dr. Whistler himself, had loved pining after the vintage theatrics of forced bleeding, heat blistering, and mercury diarrheals.

"Bear Claw *was* America, as far as I'm concerned. We had our north and our south. We were our own founding fathers. We wrote our own Constitution. We were pioneers: lobotomy, hydropathy, insulin therapy, psychodrama. Presidents, senators, governors, all the best people sent their loved ones to me. To *me*. Bear Claw or nowhere, they said. But then came the longhairs with their peace and love, too many of whom grew up to be professional troublemakers waving red tags. State asylums had six hundred thousand patients in 1954. What's it today? A hundred thousand? If that? Our beautiful facilities—just look at them. The money's been reappropriated to *community centers*. They have lots of nice phrases. 'Speech impaired.' 'Disabled.' 'Special needs.' But what do they truly know about the mad? My, my, my."

This reaper's scythe, thought I, had a point. Those on the outside wouldn't try to contain me. They'd try to help me, the damned fools.

Scrimm's rolling eyes found me by accident.

"A red tag does not preclude an interview, young man. Tell me why you've decided to give yourself to our care."

I tilted my head. The simplicity of the request bollixed me.

"Come, come," urged Scrimm. "What have you done to bring you here?"

What had I done, Grim Reaper? Where in Gød's besmudged name should I begin? A century of affronts, atrocities, improprieties, and obscenities spread out before me like a deck of lewd playing cards.

"Shall I tell you about how I nearly killed Adolf Hitler?"

My question was meant to faze the superintendent, but it had the opposite effect; I would come to learn that fancied relationships with Adolf Hitler were among the most common of psychopathic pipe dreams. Scrimm closed his eyes and nestled his bone-shoulders into the chair like a child eager to hear his favorite bedtime story.

"Oh, please do. Tell us all about it."

From Rigby's paratrooper plunge and Meixelsperger's bomb shelter to Himmler's Wewelsburg and Ziereis's Mauthausen, I did just that, each truth so impregnated with detail that it proved, beyond any doubt, my sheer insanity. To Scrimm, it was music. His pale lips rippled back to flaunt his skull's sickles of teeth.

"Dr. Dobbin," said he. "Your prescription?"

Dobbin cracked open his valise. "Two hundred milligrams of Moban in fifty-milligram oral doses four times a day."

There came the plastic clack of an upended bottle, the ring of capsules against china, and then, held out to me like a dish of crème brûlée, a plate containing five pills. In his other hand Dobbin held a paper cup of water filled from a leaking corner watercooler. Keen though I was to kneel to Bear Claw's demands, I disfavored the idea of putting foreign matter into my stomach. I did not move to accept the offerings.

My reticence came as no more surprise than my Hitler hallucinations. Dobbin issued a coded look, and Sikes and Glover clomped their boots so that I would take note of their crowding. Dobbin smiled and held the pills and water closer. I felt as if back in the Yankee Doodle as Margeaux steered it toward the Highway 1 guard rail; once struck, there was no reversing. Rigby had warned me that I would need to prove that I was dangerous, and I'd be a fool not to take an early opportunity.

I swiped sideways with my hand, sending both water and pills into Scrimm's face. He did not react, but Dobbin jerked away, and the shadows of the orderlies lurched. Instinct hadn't left me. I juked from Glover, giving Sikes my tougher-to-grab armless side, at which he floundered long enough for me to hurl myself at Dobbin. He stumbled into the watercooler, which cracked and gushed, and then I was pressed against him muscle to muscle.

Yet when I bit the man's nose, there was no Black Hand excitation. When the salty slurp of his blood washed my tongue, it aroused no gustatorial lust. Dobbin screamed and whipped his head, and it took all I had to keep my jaws fast, for the sounds of pain no longer brought me joy. Zebulon Finch had changed, Dearest Reader; hurting people was the antithesis of what he wanted.

Judging the damage sufficient, I let Glover pull me off. Dobbin reeled away, blood fanning through his fingers, and I saw Scrimm daintily unfold a handkerchief, should Dobbin wish to avail himself of it. Glover's choke-hold did not, of course, choke me, but did drive me to my knees in time for me to see Sikes charging forward with a snarl on his lips and a garment in his hands, a thing of yellow canvas, dangling arms, and leather belt-straps. I smiled. A straitjacket, how baroque.

I did not resist as the orderlies shoved me into it, pulling my single arm across my torso and buckling it behind me so tightly that I could hear the squeak of protesting bone. I was lifted to my feet and rabbit-punched in my kidney, just for fun. Dobbin's wide eyes glared past Scrimm's sopping handkerchief, while Scrimm shook his little round skull.

"Acting up will get you nowhere, Mr. Zipp—except to the Back Ward. And you won't much like it there, I guarantee. My, my, my, my, my."

III.

A S FAR BACK IN TIME as I'd traveled down Plato Manor's hallway, the Back Ward (the capital letters were inherent in its syllabification) was farther back still. Sikes and Glover roughhoused me into the snaking fog, down a sidewalk that split the campus into hemispheres, past a small hilltop cemetery, and into a structure crouched like a hog barn. Inside, the floors were dingier and the light dimmer than any state-supported building in 1985 ought to have been, though my impression, firming by the second, was that no one beyond the unluckiest of Bear Claw patients and personnel had visited the Back Ward in decades.

I was pushed through a swinging gate and steel door, then down a chiaroscuro hallway puddled with blobs of butter-yellow light, which illuminated, in brief flashes, foreboding details: grooves along the walls, which I attributed to fingernails; iron rings to which strait-jackets could be clipped; doors, on rails, that could be slammed shut should someone make a break. Each cell door we passed had a plastic window, against which mental invalids watched me pass, hot breath muddying faces into abstractions. A nurse passed with a pair of glasses, a hearing aid, and a set of false teeth upon a tray—all potential hazards, supposed I, though I felt bad for the sightless, soundless, tasteless patient left in the dark like a grub.

A door clanged open, and I was pushed through it. I managed not to fall, only by ramming full-speed into the back wall. The surface wasn't hard; as decades of melodramatic clichés had promised, all surfaces were padded with squares of leather-covered cork. Sikes and Glover bade no cheerio. The door was slammed and locked before I could flop my torso, armless now due to the straitjacket, to face the front.

I let my back slide to the floor, also coated with cushions, these much dirtier. I assessed the quarters: six feet wide, eight feet long, and without furniture, doorknob, or window, aside from the one aimed back into the hallway. So featureless was the cell that in minutes I'd begun to lose my internal compass and even a belief in gravity. Could it be that I was not at the edge of a room but rather falling down some unfathomable hole?

If so, thought I, good. My extraction from the world had been tooth from gum—painful, yes, but the dentist was patting my hand now, telling me it was all over, the decay having been removed at the root. The Back Ward was not as dark as I would have liked (overhead lights were protected under safety glass), nor as quiet (the reverberant din of hooting, laughing, and sobbing was indissoluble). But secluded it was, which meant I'd achieved what I'd set out to do. Here I could atone with zero risk of harming anyone. I spent the balance of the day trying to feel satisfied about that.

Night was better. The lights shut off, and most of the patients quieted. I lay upon the floor, ignoring the jab of straitjacket buckles, and ordered myself not to imagine the comforts that had become custom over a sleepless century—for instance, that Wilma Sue, not yet my slayer, snored, warm and happy beside me. So keen was I on this plan that for a solid hour I pretended I wasn't hearing what I was hearing. From the cell to my right I could hear a patient, who sounded like a mere lad, talking to himself. Unlike the distorted yammers heard throughout the day, his words I could make out so clearly that achieving repose became impossible. I sighed, opened my eyes, and acquiesced to following the one-sided conversation.

"No, I *am* happy to see you. Really I am." Pause. "It's just, I'm embarrassed, is all. I'm—look where I am. They think I'm crazy." Pause. "That's nice of you to say. But, you know, maybe they're right. Maybe I—" Pause. "I'm just saying that you being here, it's not going to help any. They're going to hear me talking to you. They'll ask me who you are." Pause. "I know that. Don't you think I know that? I'm just no good at lying. They'll trick me, and it'll just come out: 'I'm talking to Jesus Christ.' And once I say that, I'm done for."

I wished my arm were free so that I could smack it upon my forehead. Classic Finch luck: locked away at last and filed alongside a religious nut! I gnashed my jaws and hummed a medley I'd collaged during my overlong death—the Soothing Foursome, Cab Calloway, Artie Shaw, the Beau-Ts, "Beat It"—each tune a link in a chain of pain, but worth the chaining if it blocked these maddening insipidities.

"I *know*, Jesus. Your friendship means the world to me." Pause. "All I'm saying is that you don't know what it's like to be trapped." Pause. "Right. Crucifixion. I guess you do know." Pause. "Just that, you know, maybe this isn't the best *time*. Could you come back once I'm better? Once I'm back in—" Pause. "No, I definitely don't think we should sing. It'll wake everyone up, and the nurses will come and they'll be so mad at me—" Pause. "Okay. One verse. Just one verse, okay? And then maybe you can go?"

Believe it or not, Reader, the goaded boy began to sing.

"Praise Gød, from Whom all blessings flow. / Praise Him, all creatures here below—"

I rammed my head against the wall, and the irritation broke out.

"There is no Jesus, you warbling idiot! His is a tall tale told by the weak-willed wanting to believe that their rotten souls will be saved! This is simply understood, is it not? All right, then, church is over! I should think you ought to sleep quite soundly now, as will everyone else who has the misfortune of being caged in your vicinity. Good night to you, sir!"

The singing had cut off. I waited. I listened. At last, an unhappy murmur:

"There *is* a Jesus."

And then, this forlorn fellow began to cry.

It was a pitiful sound, a random tumble of fingers across the highest piano keys. Some wails slide into comfortable grooves from frequency of habit, but these sobs came despite the sobber's bravest efforts of suppression. I heard every brittle hitch of backbone, every choke of snot, every popped bubble of saliva upon slobbery lips. It was awful, Reader, just awful.

"I apologize," muttered I. "Did you hear me?"

"No. . . . *I'm* sorry. . . ."

"You don't have to be sorry," snapped I. "You're crazy."

"I am. . . . Yes, I *am*. . . ."

Time builds a mirror maze that reflects back your most repellent moments. Look! There is Little Johnny Grandpa, having caned himself into my Pageant of Health tent, mewling for the mercy of a single kind word. And look, there I am as well, close-lipped and cruel. I pivoted to the pernicious present: I couldn't allow another boy to blame himself for tortures of which he was blameless.

"I did not mean it. You're not crazy. I was wrong. There is a Jesus. There is a Jesus and he is here with us."

"Really?" sniffled the boy. "You saw him, too?"

"I did. I saw him. He was glorious."

A shuffling noise tracked the boy as he crept closer to the wall. I rested my ear against the cork wall so that I would not miss his confession.

"Don't tell Jesus," whispered he, "but I wish he hadn't come."

He cried no more that night. Lights flooded before daybreak, a signal at which we, human livestock, lowed for our morning feed. For an hour, the banging open of doors proceeded down the hall until two orderlies, both of them new to me, opened my door, consulted a clipboard, released me from my straitjacket, and set upon my floor a tiny paper cup containing Dr. Dobbin's prescribed dose of Moban. I presumed it a tit-for-tat: I swallow the drugs, they release me from the Back Ward. As I wanted no such thing, I stared until they wrote a note on the clipboard, removed the drugs, and moved to the next cell.

The boy fared better in the daytime, despite the harrying howls and rude rattles of the ward's wakeful. I heard him eat a gloppy meal that did not require silverware and glug water that no doubt flushed antipsychotics into his system. In the afternoon, I even heard soft snores as he made up for the night's negotiations. It was easy to picture his sleeping body as frail and harmless, though I knew one did not get tossed into the Back Ward without biting a nose or something of the sort. The boy was troubled and hazardous; being both myself, I granted him clemency.

Night brought with it the return of Jesus. I secured a prime position against our shared wall and interposed myself into the discussion, if that's what you wish to call it, taking care not to be offensive to the savior—the boy, after all, believed in him with a vengeance—but rather redirecting the boy down duller, safer conversational byways: the weather (of which we had no sense), sports (for which I feigned enthusiasm), and television programming (about which I knew nothing). It brought me unexpected satisfaction to lure the boy from a plodding chorus of "What a Friend We Have in Jesus" so that he could describe to me the premise of *Knight Rider*, a TV lark about a crime fighter who tootles around in a talking car.

Undiluted hogwash, though I reacted as if episode details held the secrets of life. Before the night was through, the significance to me of this nameless, faceless boy had grown to Mount Saint Helens size. Here, near literal cliffs that might as well have been those of humanity itself, the boy seemed to be the last human being in the world. My path thereby clarified. The devil Zebulon Finch might yet earn wings for himself—not leathered as usual, but feathered. Love, I told myself yet again, still mattered, and if I'd righted the scales with Merle, I might even tip them in my favor if I fathered this wretched soul.

"That's it, sleep," whispered I as the boy began to yawn. "I shall keep watch o'er the long, darkling eve."

Over subsequent nights, my successes diminished. The tenor of the boy's pleas suggested that Jesus Christ was being harsher regarding expectations of jubilation. Whatever grip the apparition had on the boy was a rigid one. The boy wept and atoned and sang, while other patients howled for him to shut up, and my own begging for *Knight Rider* updates went unfulfilled.

Hence it was with gratitude that I identified a partner in my efforts. On my fifth night—each night purchased with four-times-a-day refusals of Moban—the midnight hour was interrupted by the lock-clanking arrival of a night janitor. This itself was not unusual; what was unusual was the man's behavior. Between the hiss of cleaning liquid to plastic and the splat of mop to floor, the man murmured greetings to insomniacs and chuckled at their delighted replies—they'd missed him. Though the janitor spoke only Spanish, I gathered from his conciliatory tone that a personal matter had drawn him away for a while, but he was back, and *sí, sí, sí*, it was *muy bueno* to see you, too.

By pressing my nose to my window, I could watch his approach. He was roughly thirty, absurdly short, shaped like a block, mustachioed, and with black hair greased back from a broad forehead. This was his second job if not his third; when not whispering hellos, he was yawning and massaging sleepy eyes. His obvious need for income made his risktaking all the more gallant. We under seclusion order were not to be addressed, and yet address us he did, and why? Because he was what I could only pretend to be: good.

The janitor knew better than I that the boy, blubbering as he did through hallelujahs, required special attention. Every night, he'd lean his mop against the wall, knuckle the boy's window until he was noticed, and then, in a soft, lovely bass, overwhelm Jesus's hosannas by singing a song.

> *Duérmete, mi niño,*
> *duérmete solito,*
> *que cuando despiertes*
> *te daré atolito.*
> *Duérmete, mi niño,*
> *duérmete, mi sol,*
> *duérmete pedazo*
> *de mi corazón.*

How many millions of Spanish-speaking children had been sung to sleep by this lullaby? The seraphic drifting of these small souls imbued the nocturne with an incantatory force that, almost without fail, brought the boy down from hymnal heights for overdue slumber. The janitor would sing it as many times as needed; one night he sang for over an hour. By the time he moved on, his mop splatting down the hall, I too was so consoled that I wondered if the power to sleep had been returned to me as well.

Three weeks of this twilight canticle did what years of psychiatric work might have failed at. One morning, without preamble, the boy's Back Ward sentence concluded. The sounds were curt: his door creaking open, the cushion squeaking as he stood, his footfalls fading down the hall, the distant salvos of gates opening and closing. I was relieved and happy; I was trepidatious. The boy was out of the thickest thicket, but even sparse groves provided cover within which Jesus Christ, or other blackguards, might lurk. If I were to continue to protect this boy, as I'd sworn to myself, I would need to get out as well.

IV.

A FEARSOME PREDAWN RACKET FROM A room at the end of the hall further prodded me to decamp the Back Ward. It originated not from cajoling staff or wailing patient but a machine, one booming like artillery barrage even as it whined like a truck engine pushed to extremes. By morning lights, I'd retreated to a corner; I hadn't suffered sounds of such mechanized malice since the days of Dr. Leather decapitating dogs and crisping corpses. A child-like lobe of my brain dubbed the unseen space the Thunder Room— where bad boys go to be punished.

My new intent was to be good. The Thunder Room quieted before orderlies made their first scheduled invasion, and they jumped back when I moved toward the Moban. I held up my hand to assure them that attack was not the plan, knelt beside the paper cup, and tipped the pills into my mouth. My throat bobbed, and I gave the two fellows my sunniest smile of fraternity.

"He's cheeking them," said one.

"We're not stupid," said the other.

The beady-eyed boars were cleverer than they looked. They closed and locked the door, and for recompense did not visit again for a day. I spat the Moban, lodged them into a cushion crease, and dwelled upon my freshman ruse, nervous that the crunch and squeal of the Thunder Room would resume. It didn't, and the next morning, when the orderlies returned, skeptical now, I transferred the pills to my palm, and in clear view placed one at a time upon my tongue and swallowed them. Each one clicked against Johnny's marble inside my stomach.

The orderlies scribbled notes. When they reappeared for the day's second dose, a nurse had joined them to authenticate. At the third dose, a doctor came, peering importantly with his superior eyes. After I'd swallowed the day's fourth and final dose—twenty Mobans in all, enough to bury the golden aggie—they were convinced. I waited out the night and was relieved when, once again, the Thunder Room squall failed to return. Had I imagined it?

At daybreak a host of Bear Claw's finest, including Sikes and Glover, deployed across my room to guard against funny business. The attending doctor explained that I was being extended "grounds privileges" with the rest of "gen pop." Should I thrive, other privileges would follow: bath privileges, shaving-razor privileges, kitchen privileges, various other concessions for which I had no use. I gave the performance they wanted, shaping a smile of eager bewilderment as if, properly Mobaned, I was seeing the light. They gave their version of applause: they parted like an opening fence and gestured me toward the glow of the hallway's end.

I was unable to verify the existence of the Thunder Room.

Orderlies gave me a modicum of privacy to exchange Merle's hooded sweatshirt and trousers for a pocketless, zippered khaki jumpsuit and laceless canvas shoes, after which they shoved me outdoors. The Atlantic Ocean was hidden by a twenty-foot fence, thick boscage, and forest, but the sun drooping over all of it came at me like a fireball. My mental picture of Bear Claw had been one of perpetual fog, but here it was, almost April and bright as a dissection table. The institution's layout became evident. Plato Manor, the most palatial building, was the point of an arrowhead from which swept eastward two rows of three-story, Gothic-design wards, four to the north, four to the south, the broad end of the triangle being the Back Ward from which I'd emerged.

Someone had placed into my hand a piece of paper. Across the top was typed *Zipp, Frank (Male)*—say, that was me!—and, next to it, the code *KANT-17*. This doubled, guessed I, as both inmate number and room assignment, and I could not muster surprise. Seventeen: the number had chased me this far, so why not until the bitter end? Below ran a list of locations recognizable from childhood lessons as also named after classical philosophers. What I held, realized I, was a schedule, and I, like a lad on his first day at university, would be tasked with finding Descartes-60. I was the least happy of campers, for such responsibilities would only complicate finding a boy I'd heard but never seen, and from whom I, master detective, had never thought to request a name.

My fellow pupils, however, were no jim-dandies competing for nods from august professors. I floated down the sidewalk, the loose jumpsuit and lack of Excelsior making me weightless, and took in a sprawling yard peopled by perhaps one hundred patients, some sprinting with limbs a-flail to their own obligations, but most wandering circles around weatherworn gazebos, kicked-to-shit benches, and unshorn shrubs, while yakking with figmental companions—Christlike or Hitlerian, who could say? When one strayed too close to a fence, men called mental hygiene assistants clipped him back onto the playing field like goalies.

Bear Claw had been designed as a self-sufficient world; I could appreciate Scrimm's elegy for its decline. Two of the water tower's six legs were infected with corrosion that listed its swollen head toward Europe. The former greenhouse had become a taped-off death trap of splinterized glass. A dairy barn had devolved into a grave-yard of forgotten trade machines: printing presses, laundry folders, sauerkraut vats, stockyard hooks. Disused storage sheds still held seasonal paintings by bygone patients that twenty years of winters had deformed into monstrosities: Santa Claus gone feral, the Easter Bunny gone rabid.

The wards abounded with fractured foundations, broken win-dows, and safety nets lashed to stonework facades in danger of col-lapse. I saw no signs of air conditioning, and could only imagine the ancient cellar furnaces straining to black-magic wisps of heat. That day, a ward called Cicero had gone dark from electrical outage, and by listening to orderlies luxuriating over cigarettes, I surmised it a recurrent mishap. Only one patient during that first amble was alert enough to notice my discolored flesh. *Not a bad start,* thought I, until she pointed at my face and began honking like a klaxon.

I ducked into a ward called Locke and crossed a footprinted foyer toward a dayhall bombinating with the gen-pop disturbed. The place smelled of nicotine, coffee, and urine, and the concrete sur-faces garbled the gibber of the TV, which each patient interpreted through her or his own psychotropic smog. Others stretched their plastic-braceleted arms across board games with titles that seemed sarcastic: Monopoly (these cranks didn't have a cent), Clue (they had even fewer of these), and Trivial Pursuit (what other kind of pursuit could they take?).

The most mystifying game was one called, rather pointedly, Life, in which a wheel of fortune controlled the fate of you and your loved ones, denoted by a tiny plastic station wagon filled with little pink and blue pegs. Fake money was doled out willy-nilly as you drove onto spaces administering outrageous turns of fate ("Win photography contest. Collect $10,000."), not one of which was disfigurement or death. On the other hand—no death? Perhaps this candy-colored distraction had been made just for me.

Soon, though, I edged away along the room's perimeter, as eager to find the boy as I was wary of a Life player who looked agitated near to explosion. While most Bear Claw residents were allowed to wear their own clothing, clients with a history of violence, I realized, were identifiable by the very same jumpsuit I'd been issued.

Before I could achieve a thing, Plato Manor's cupola bell gonged nine times, and those enslaved by nine-a.m. meds—and that was a lot of them—lumbered toward assigned dispensaries. I consulted my schedule and determined that the bells tolled for me as well: I was to report to Descartes for "Group Analytic." I disliked the sound of it, but truancy might hasten a Back Ward homecoming, if not introduction to the Thunder Room, so I headed outdoors, found Descartes straight across the courtyard, tracked down room 60, and entered to the dire display of twelve people sitting in a chair circle. The leader of this clique was quite recognizable by a lambda of white tape across his nose.

"Mr. Zipp." Dr. Dobbin's voice had gone nasal. "Please join us."

Instinct told me to run, preferably while screaming, but I exacted control of my corpse and slouched toward the closest empty chair. Before I could sit, a black woman in the adjacent chair shielded it with a tattooed arm.

"The flying *fuck?* That's Farm Boy's seat!"

"Pardon?" asked I.

"Pardon *yourself*, fuckling. I *said*, that *seat* belongs to *Farm Boy*. We been *saving* it."

Her lips curled back from her teeth; the front two were gold. Whether I should have knocked them out of her head was an academic question; as I've indicated, all such instincts had vacated.

"There's another seat over there," said Dobbin.

This chair also had its defenders, though they confined their objections to nose wrinklings at my scent. Given such a welcome, I would have rather stared at the floor for the duration of the two-hour caucus, but even that, worried I, would exacerbate attention upon me. I braced myself and surveyed the psychotic circle.

I wish I could introduce the regulars of A.M. Analytic with a pride equal to that with which I presented my Third Battalion. But no nation wished to claim these rattled souls; they were not the soldiers but the casualties. During my time at Bear Claw, group members came and went, most of them as normal as Shirley White, middle-class folk who'd become sad, or confused, or mixed-up, and would spend six days, or six weeks, or six months circling the drain with us before scrabbling free, some even able to avoid the recidivism that brought others back, their eyes darting in fear at those whose presence in the room never changed.

These constants included Bobbi, a compulsive eater whose vacillating weight had left her with a flexuous rubber-band body, and whose every remark came scripted from Overeaters Anonymous, Weight Watchers, Weigh of Life, or other cabals inside whose philosophies she'd snuggled. Chad was an ex-stockbroker who still wore pinstriped shirts and suspenders and, due to his Wall Street ulcer, chewed antacid tablets into a powdery bolus past which he spoke circular drivel at a day-trader clip: "That's a nice watch. I once watched a movie called *Star Trek: The Motion Picture*. I can show you a picture of my sister." Lucky was an athletic buck who wore a 1920s leather football helmet, without which he'd keep scratching a specific itch, day or night, awake or asleep, that he described as being on the inside of his head. Before Bear Claw, he'd scratched through his skull and into his brain. Skin grafts had covered the hole for a time, until green goo in his hair had revealed that he'd done it again.

Finally there was Jackie, the gold-toothed gang member (as she liked to remind us) who'd switchbladed thirty or forty or fifty people (the number kept rising) in storied skid-row rumbles before being booked into "all the best fatherfucking bughouses in the brotherfucking world," which (you guessed it) she loved to tabulate: "Two years in Johnson fucking Square, six months at Three Pines fucking Behavioral, eighteen months at Gareth fucking Farms. I got bitches everywhere!" Jackie was covered with lousy tattoos, the boldest of which was across her forehead in big block letters: *MAD*. Had Jackie not lost her shit, she would have made a fine Black Panther. The dissolution of that estimable party, suspected I, had hastened the rise of the Crips, Bloods, and Vice Lords, about whom Jackie could not stop enthusing.

During a lull in her rants, Dobbin addressed me.

"Wouldn't you like to tell everyone who you are?"

The last thing I'd come to Bear Claw to do was talk.

"I'll have to read your admission report, then. You might find it embarrassing."

I slid low in my chair like the recalcitrant I was.

Dobbin sighed and pulled the form from a folder.

"'Frank Zipp. Admitted February 12, 1985. Patient alternates catatonia and combativeness. Patient resists interview, and as such, suicidal and homicidal ideation not yet assessed. Patient's affect is labile and inappropriate. Patient exhibits curious ego-dystonia and manic-depressive swings. Patient's verbal skills are high and support delusions of grandeur in which Patient inserts himself into historical situations. Patient's motor activity is good despite obvious physical challenges. Suggested psychopharmacology indicated below.'"

Dobbin pulled at his mustache curls. "Would you agree with that assessment, Frank?"

I shrugged. "They left out my devilish good looks."

Jackie slapped the *MAD* on her forehead. "Oh, damn! Weirdo One-Arm's crazier than me!"

Jackie, of course, had been the one to ban me from Farm Boy's chair. Whoever he was, she loved him with a mother's fire, and after my introductory shaming, discussion swerved toward this missing character. Even the most intransigent voiced concern regarding Farm Boy's absence from A.M. Analytic and, when Dobbin declined to comment, talk spiraled into gossip:

"I heard he tried to cut open his head once."

"That's nothing—I heard he ate his dad."

Jackie told them she'd cut out their wagging tongues if they said one more bad word about her favorite brotherfucker in this whole fatherfucking joint. This was a violent threat, and Dobbin, checking his watch ("That's a nice watch," chanted Chad. "I once watched a movie called *Star Trek: The Motion Picture*."), was obligated to give Jackie a warning, though a half-hearted one. Group therapy, it seemed clear, had been forced upon Bear Claw's staff by Scrimm's despised "do-gooders"; Dobbin was there for no nobler reason than that he wished to keep getting paid.

I sank even lower, blissfully ignored and feeling the warmth of having made a correct decision. Though I'd traveled far and wide, never had I seen people of such diverse backgrounds—from ghetto

652

gutter to Wall Street penthouse—stand upon equal, if aquiver, footing. We were the mad, but we'd claimed a cozy corner in that larger, colder asylum called the United States of America. Asylum. I had to agree with Scrimm that it was a shame the word had been stricken, for asylum was just what I needed.

V.

KANT, MY HOME FOR THE foreseeable future, was the "acute admissions ward," where Bear Claw's most afflicted were stabilized before (if ever) being transferred to less restrictive wards. Patients in Kant were "sectioned"—code for "legally detained"—which allowed Bear Claw to keep them under lock, key, and steel-reticulated plastic windows, which carved sunbeams into so many millions of spades that one began to doubt one's own vision.

An orderly collared me ten seconds after I entered, checked my papers, and steered me to room 17 on the second floor. I considered thanking him by name, but he wore no name tag, for name tags, as you know, have sharp pins. My room was the jail cell I'd expected. There was a bed, though it lacked headboard, footboard, or legs; there were shelves, though they were built into the walls; and there were two windows, one of which looked out across northern woods and the other of which was built into my door for the pleasure of voyeur staff.

It took but a few hours to learn the routine. A buzzer announced mealtimes, which I was required to attend to feign consumption while other drugged muddlers dribbled milk from benumbed lips. Medications were dispensed according to one's personal schedule, and should you fail to show, mental hygiene assistants would track you down and force the issue. Doors were locked at eight, lights went out at ten. Some patients' days were active with engagement (disciplinary meetings, counseling events, behavioral tests), all of which could be skirted if you knew how to sidestep attention. Reader, I know that restraint isn't my forte. Nevertheless, I redoubled my redoubts.

Kant's structural difference from a prison was interior walls no thicker than any turn-of-the-century domicile; hearing through them was easier than in the Back Ward, where padding had swaddled every syllable. Though I hadn't my Excelsior, I'd grown adept at estimating the hour. It was midnight when, stretched upon my bed, I heard the first whispered words of the patient in room 18.

"No, no—not here. There's a window in the door. Jesus, they'll see you."

I sat upright, my head eclipsing moonlight. Bear Claw was crevassed with holes into which one might be stuffed, and yet the boy had been dropped into my lap! I scrambled from bed, eager to restart my repentance, and rested my forehead against the cold cement wall.

"Boy. It is I. Your neighbor from the Back Ward."

His reply to Jesus Christ cut off. I smiled in anticipation of hearing a smile in his voice, but a minute passed without satisfaction.

"It was but days ago," prodded I. "We spoke of *Knight Rider*. Surely you remember? Each night when you spoke to Jesus, I endeavored to inspirit you with—"

"I do *not*," hissed he, "speak to Jesus."

It stung, this response, but the logic of it permeated. The Back Ward had been all right for me, but isolation was torture to a living human, and if reports surfaced that the boy in Kant-18 was carrying on with his invisible messiah, it might land him back into a padded room. I nodded, though he could not see it. The boy's trust was all I wanted, so that, carefully, oh so carefully, I could help pull him away from the wraith that seemed to cause him so much pain.

"As you wish," said I. "Say, my name is Frank Zipp. What is yours?"

Again, silence. Had he, like I, permitted people to inch toward his heart, only to ruin them? I affected a jocund chuckle.

"I cannot call you 'boy' ad infinitum, can I?"

He evidently believed that I could. No further words were shared that night, and when Jesus's solicitations grew too oppressive to ignore, the boy buried his face into his pillow to mute his moaned responses. At length I returned to bed, disheartened. Somewhere in Berlin, or Kansas, or outer space, had I lost my last smidgen of human touch?

Lights popped on at six. Doors unlocked at six fifteen. Breakfast buzzers sounded at six thirty. Having never slept to begin with, I sprang from my cell, already jumpsuited, and waited for the boy to make his exit. My predator crouch, however, caught the eye of an orderly, who spun his arms like a third-base coach at the khaki herd shambling toward the odor of undercooked eggs. I told myself to be patient and comply; neither the boy nor I were going anywhere soon.

Patience, though, proved superfluous. When A.M. Analytic rolled around, Farm Boy's chair, which Jackie had scooted closer to her own, was occupied. The group welcomed him back as gingerly as one hand-feeds a skittish dog. Jackie nodded approval, her *MAD* tattoo bobbing, though her body, as ever, was coiled for defense. Dobbin asked Farm Boy if it wasn't polite to say something back, at which Farm Boy blushed and mumbled the only word he said all session: "Thanks."

It was the only word I needed to make a positive ID: "The boy" and "Farm Boy" were one and the same. As I didn't speak aloud, he hadn't the chance opportunity to place me, and of that I took advantage by gawking. How to reconcile the mewling child of my mind's eye with this considerably larger figure? Even horribly slouched, his six-foot-three height was obvious, though he couldn't have weighed over one twenty. He was, I would come to learn, twenty-three years old, though his dodging eyes and stooped shoulders remained those of a kid straining to accept a world where the punishments of adults shot like bolts from the blue.

Ry Burke was his name, and when I heard he was from Iowa—Church's hinterland home—I felt a Jackie-like upsurge of protectiveness. The next group discussion, to Ry's horror, readjudicated snippets of his personal history. He'd had some sort of prickly upbringing and several years prior had suffered a psychotic break bad enough to get him traded across a series of mental hospitals, none of which his single-mothered family could afford, hence his being dumped into the Bear Claw trough. His particular madness took the shape of a triad of demons he believed were in the midst of manifesting for the third (and final) time in his life. The first, a talking teddy bear named Mr. Furrington, had come and gone; the second was occurring right now in the form of Jesus Christ; but it was the arrival of the third demon, whose name Ry would not share, that he feared would force him to murder.

Even by A.M. Analytic standards it was batty, and so the regulars rallied around Ry's more identifiable ordeal: his regimen of antipsychotics, which quacks like Dobbin kept shuffling to see if a new cocktail could improve upon a previous—and if the boy's mind was bulldozed along the way, well, these things do happen. Ry, too, had been started, long ago, on Moban, but when that had failed to chain his demons, what had followed were Haldol injections and five thousand milligrams of Thorazine a day—a dosage, decried the group, that would've calmed a pig on a killing floor. Yet calm Ry it had not, thus the Elavil, Mellaril, Navane, Prolixin, Sinequan, Stelazine, and Taractan, all of which, in less than five years, had turned our strong, healthy Farm Boy into a gaunt, enfeebled wretch.

Ry tolerated the group's restive bickerings, blubbery admissions, and inchoate tirades for one week before again dropping out, this time for being too doped up to get out of bed. I glimpsed his inert, waxen face when orderlies trucked food into Kant-18 or bedpans out. He still spoke to Jesus at night, but his voice was too airy for me to hear and his ears deaf to anything I said. It wasn't until late June that Dobbin shuffled Ry's meds yet again. From what I'd come to learn, this often provoked a short period of clarity. I'd need to move fast.

After three days of failed attempts to corner Ry, a man's morning seizure drew nurses and assistants long enough for me to trail Ry to the men's room, an odiferous coop greened by the ivy choking the window mesh. There was a mirror behind Plexi, a single doorless stall, and three urinals divided by waist-high barriers. One urinal's water was still swirling, and Ry, in a touching display of manners, stood at a rust-striped sink, washing his hands. That is inaccurate; he was washing his *palms*, for all ten of his fingertips had been swaddled in cotton and wrapped in medical tape.

He took a step away upon seeing me, backing into a cupboard almost identical to Leather's Revelation Almanac, except instead of a jar of flesh, each small shelf contained a toothbrush. Each handle was affixed with a patient's name, which coincided with a labeled peg, so that each night all of them could be counted. Toothbrushes could be whittled, and whittled objects could stab.

"You're in Group," stated he.

"Yes. And my room is next to yours."

He stared at the moldy tiles, the pink of his neck pouring into his cheeks.

"Ask for a different one," murmured he.

"Say again?"

"I'm loud. At night. You should ask for a different room."

"Bosh. I do not sleep much myself."

His head shot back up, eyes pleading. "Please. We shouldn't be talking."

"I have noticed you aren't much of a mingler."

"So? Neither are you. You never talk at all in Group."

"I am choosy with whom I parley."

"Choose someone else." He leaned his beet-colored face closer and whispered. "He'll hear. Then he'll come. He doesn't like me knowing people."

I donned a lighthearted smile. "I was given to believe that crackpots thought they *were* Jesus, not merely *spoke* to Jesus."

"Not him. The other one. The third one."

With that, he bounded to the right, but I shifted to block the path, and he drew back, holding high his bandaged fingertips as if they were whetted blades. The color of his jumpsuit was not incidental, I reminded myself. This boy had done things. For one single second, I believed that I saw in his sad eyes a hollow blackness and heard in the grind of his jaw the clash of cutlery. I held out a steadying hand.

"I wish only to be your friend."

"He's closer now. A lot closer. You don't understand."

"I, too, have believed things that in the light of day were proven fantastical. Just as you hear these demons of yours, I once heard the voice of a dead friend coming from a book of poetry."

"Leave me alone!"

This time he led with his shoulder toward my weaker, armless side, giving me no option but to cede the path. Ry's jumpsuit had polka-dotted with perspiration, and he trembled so much that he could barely grip the door handle; only a lucky grab kept him from tripping over his own feet. Halfway out the door, he hesitated, then spoke without turning.

"Frank, right? Frank Zipp? Look, you're being nice. I know that, and it's real friendly of you. But ask for a new room, okay? It's going to get worse, trust me, and you don't want to be anywhere near me when he comes."

VI.

THAT MIGHT HAVE BEEN THE end of it if Kant hadn't been added to the cleaning schedule of one benevolent janitor. I recognized his shushed *holas* to nocturnal patients; I even recognized the plop of his mop, which he applied lightly in deference to sleepers. His appearance coincided with a bad patch for Ry, whose late-night blubbers to Jesus had gone viscid with sobs. I watched each night as the janitor brought his face to Ry's window and did his *Duérmete, mi niño* bit, just like old times. Its efficacy, however, had waned. When the clock compelled the janitor to move on, he'd pause at my window to wave hello, his forehead knotted in a way that posed a question: *What are we going to do about Ry Burke?*

One hot August night, while being tortured by a coerced butchering of "Amazing Grace," I heard a soft click at my door and saw the ducking of a brow of slicked-back hair. I got up, alert for ambush, but could hear nothing beyond Ry's hymn. I tried my doorknob and found it unlocked. I opened it, recalling what it felt like to have a pounding heart, and peeked at the nurse station midway down the hall. The nurse was not at her post; one of her romance novels sat splayed on the desk. It baffled me until I saw, at the far end of the hall, a lumen of moonlight off freshly mopped flooring. The janitor: he was down there distracting the nurse with belabored bits of English.

It was a bluff meant to facilitate my exit from room 17. But why, and to where? I cowered in puzzlement until I was taken with a hunch. I tried the knob of room 18, and it turned as freely as mine had. I took one last astounded look at the janitor before entering. What kind of man was this who would risk his job, if not outright arrest, to conduce the potential peace of caged lunatics he barely knew?

So fantastic was my presence that Ry finished singing rather than believe it.

"We've no less days to sing Gød's praise / Than when we'd first begun."

With bandaged fingertips, he rubbed at his teary eyes. "Frank? You're inside my room?"

I gestured for him to keep his voice down and lowered myself, slowly so as not to spook him, to the foot of his bed. There was no other furniture; that his room was as bald as mine struck me as grievously sad. Such apathy toward life was not the rightful fortune of a young man in his prime. Oh, to reach the age of twenty-three and waste it away like this.

"We shall talk," said I. "That is all I propose."

"But . . ."

Ry's eyes flicked above me, where he could see the impatient Jesus.

"Our savior," said I, "has waited two thousand years to return. He will wait an hour or two more."

Ry laughed—the sound of life, Reader, a wild howl of wind through a crevice.

"But what . . . I mean, what would we talk about?"

This poor, blinkered boy! Were it only possible that I could cut from my belly salty slices of my century's consumption so that he

662

could taste it. Even in the brief span traveling between Tranquility's Country Home and the Edgerton Home for the Aging, I'd seen enough of the new decade to keep any red-blooded boy's mind swirling: pop-culture queens like Madonna, a lingerie-clad chanteuse who wore belts emblazoned with "Boy Toy" even as she postured like a dominatrix; painters like Jean-Michel Basquiat, whose frenetic hellscapes depicted America with higher emotional accuracy than any others I'd seen; TV tricksters like David Letterman, a goofy-grinned subversive out to suicide-bomb the very institutions who'd installed him to power.

Inside Bear Claw, though, all was gray, monotheistic, a feedback loop.

"We can talk about us." I shrugged. "Us is all we have."

Ry gave me careful appraisal.

"All right," said he. "What are you in for?"

"That," chuckled I, "would require a lengthy answer."

It was the right reply; his chapped lips shrugged into something close to a smile as he realized that, for the moment, we'd scared off Jesus with nothing mightier than idle chit-chat. In Burt Churchwell terms, the Game had begun and I had the ball—so I'd better run with it. Thus I recited to Ry Burke the same curriculum vitae I'd recited to Superintendent Scrimm, fairy tales that Ry didn't believe for a second but that the dry sponge of his brain was eager to soak up as fantastic fiction. He gasped at World War I adventures, giggled at Jazz Age gin-joint follies, nodded solemnly at indescribable Nazi horrors that I nevertheless described. He shied away but once, as I described Barringer's crater. He hated meteors, he said.

It was a peculiar thing to hate, and so I asked him about it. Though he refused to speak of past traumas—to name demons, he

663

was positive, was to summon them—he did, by accident, rediscover the cardinal pleasure of limbering one's tongue. He spoke, slowly at first, and of topics, I admit, of low interest, but the dawning delight in his eyes was to me the first catch of flame after days spent trying to light a fire in winter woods.

Being an acute admissions ward, Kant had night watchmen who made rounds to ensure patients were not swinging dead from the ceiling. Our janitor, of course, knew this, and the watchman's approach was precipitated by the janitor's key-jingling jog down the hall, which I took as my cue to return to room 17, leap into bed, and listen for the cluck of my dead bolt, as well as Ry's. The enterprise was dicey. Were the three of us caught, it would be presumed that the janitor was facilitating homosexual activity, and the penalty would be to fire the janitor and separate the patients, thereby leaving Ry all alone to face his stygian hectors.

Yet roughly once per week, after Jesus had burrowed back into Kant-18 and Ry was audibly agonized, the janitor would find a way to distract the night nurse after unlocking our doors, and I'd zip into Ry's room, perch upon his mattress, and coax from him stories that were free of anguish. These tales of monkeyshines with his little sister and schoolyard shenanigans with childhood pals were duller than dirt, but he loved to tell them and I loved to listen. *Pretend these are your stories,* I urged myself. *Pretend such innocence was yours.*

Even anecdotes of tedium were finite, and there was, a few months after we began, panic that our ship had run aground. But I chanced upon the topic of Bear Claw's history, and Ry responded eagerly. Shortly after being shipped to Maine and stabilized on Thorazine, he'd spent countless hours in Bear Claw's library and, more to the point, its archives, which would have been sealed shut had Bear Claw not laid off their last librarian. The promise of entertaining me provided Ry with motive enough to hatchet through his druggy smother. He did incredible things. He left his room. He traversed hallways. He opened doors. He greeted administrators. He spent hour after hour raiding the archives. He slipped choice documents into his jumpsuit and had moxie enough to stow them beneath a loose chunk of cement under his bed. He did not make it back to A.M. Analytic, but who cared? I was proud of his progress, and of my part in it.

Untold were the moonlit hours we spent huddled over his weekly hoards of dusty documents typed with brutal black ink onto fleshlike parchments. Some records dated back to when Barraclough Psychiatric Center was known as Barraclough State Hospital for the Feeble-Minded. Some hailed from a time further bygone, when the institute went under the blunt banner of Barraclough Lunatic Asylum. The years Otto Rahn and Udo von Lüth had spent looking for Hell had been wasted; it had been right here in Maine.

The oldest epistles debated such Enlightenment-era practices as whipping, starvation, and bleedings. Stenciled charts tracked a swelling patient population across early-twentieth-century decades I knew too well. Then, starting in the 1950s, decline. Carbon copies of memoranda traced Scrimm's frantic oaring against a tide of exposés. This came to a head in 1963, when President Kennedy—that good chap who'd assured me that *there is no greater purpose in life than saving your fellow man*, which I was trying so hard to do—honored his sister Rosemary, whose outbursts were "solved" by a lobotomy in 1941, by spearheading a shift from state hospitals to the community centers the superintendent so detested.

So fell the house of Scrimm. For the twenty-two years preceding my admission, his fiefdom fell siege to the same power-brokers

whose displeasing progeny Scrimm had kept from public view—
and this was the thanks he got? Bear Claw's population crashed by
sixty percent. Patients once deemed insane were, by JFK's new regulations, lucid enough to report to health centers that were unpre-
pared, understaffed, and often shuttered within months. Articles
from the *Portland Press Herald*, likely clipped by Scrimm's own
hand, told of the rocketing number of homeless and their obscene
rate of mental illness. It did not please me to sympathize with
Scrimm's perspective, but the evidence was coercive. How much
better were cardboard shanties beneath highway overpasses than
Back Ward isolation cells?

Pictures made physical the threats of text. Among Ry's discovered boxes of photo prints were images struck when the campus
had been kept by the northeast's best gardeners, each sidewalk
hugged by straight white pines, each building frocked by black-
eyed Susans and tiger lilies so hale that their canary and tiger colors
nearly bled through the black-and-white. These were promotional
images; not so the interior shots. Because Bear Claw did not go
coed until 1969, the photos taken inside the facility featured only
boys and men, some caught off-guard, others staring into the lens
as if aware it was pinning their souls to paper like butterflies to
a lepidopterist's board. They were massed for exercise, spiffed for
Minstrel recitals, curled naked on dayroom floors. They did not sit
still for photos: over and over, their heads, and only their heads,
were smeared, eyes distended into cyclopic ovals, mouths stretched
into giant screaming holes.

I did the turning of pages. Ry's fingers, even out of bandages,
were too tender to use. The gentle boy, realized I, had yanked out
his fingernails so that they would be less able to harm others when

the third demon demanded it. Still he passed those fingertips across the blurry faces, as if to push aside what looked like fleshy tumors. I'd never met anyone whose thoughts were so easy to read. Ry believed that he too was being blurred, as if an eraser were rubbing across his face every day he spent at Bear Claw. A few years longer, and there would be nothing left of him. Would it matter? Would anyone care?

It did, and I would. My affiliation with Ry might have begun as an act of contrition, but that had changed. Like Jackie, I loved the boy—nothing more complicated or less profound than that. At last there was a blessing to my overlong death: I had time to become the pencil that drew Ry Burke back into history. If I've done anything worthwhile with these pages, Dearest Reader, isn't that it? To immortalize mortals that time would otherwise forget? By talking through Bear Claw's past with Ry, I believe I helped him acknowledge that his past, too, was real, and true, and worthwhile, and rested along the same timeline as the past, and, by logical extension, the future, inside which he, in fact, belonged.

One December night, after a night watchman made an early turn toward our wing and we heard the janitor come jogtrotting, I slipped out of Ry's room and ran straight into the man. His short stature planted his nose into my sternum. We both startled; the janitor whispered an apology in Spanish and stepped back so I could access my room. I started in that direction but hesitated. Never had this noble fellow and I met, or spoken, or looked upon each other free from a barrier of unbreakable plastic.

"Zebulon Finch."

The introduction was impulsive. He deserved my real name.

The watchman's footfalls echoed louder from the east, while the night nurse's steps, eager to return to her romance novel, made the same threat from the west. It was a moment of electric duress, yet the janitor took the time to grin, a row of crooked teeth emerging from beneath black mustache bristles. He bowed and patted the breast of a work shirt splotched from years of cleaning corrosives.

"Héctor," said he.

VII.

IXING RY'S EYES TO HIS own existence became my full-time job. Three years passed by like schooners glimpsed through a fog, though unlike my Bear Claw brethren, my fog I couldn't blame on meds. Whereas Ry's medications kept dividing like square-dancers into fresh pairings, my prescription resolved into a single red pill I took only twice a day (huzzah!), but which was almost the size of a grapefruit (boo!). These Red Heavies, as I styled them, collected inside my stomach gram by gram, until yours truly, if you can believe it, actually began to pack on a few pounds.

The official Bear Claw ruling on Frank Zipp came down in early 1986. It put forward that I suffered a "dissolution of the capitalist self" and "eccentric ideations," and that my background of grandiose fantasy, emotional detachment, precipitant aggression, sulky conde-scension, and obsession with death equaled a diagnosis—a disap-pointingly average one, if you ask me—of paranoid schizophrenia. I had a good laugh at that. Paranoid? Isn't that what they call those who believe Gød is after them? I did not believe it, Reader; I *knew* it.

To shame me for my ongoing refusal to retract a single detail of my fanciful biography, Dobbin, his bandages gone but schnoz scarred with teeth-mark semicircles, read aloud my analysis in A.M. Analytic, not that anyone gave a hoot. Bobbi interrupted twice to effuse about

Deal-a-Meal, an exciting new diet product from fitness guru Richard Simmons; Chad exhaled antacid dust before racing through non-sequiturs; Lucky scratched at a leather helmet worn thin in the usual spot; and Jackie jerked about as if only invisible tethers kept her from stabbing the lot of us. Their madrigals of dementia, neurosis, ferment, and melancholia were more discordant than those of Gesualdo, but to my ears so much sweeter. They were the friends, if not the family, I'd so long deserved.

Dobbin, however, had a rare talent at needling, and so I borrowed a page from Jackie's book and began using dayhall markers to write words on my forehead in lieu of speaking. Had Ry suffered a relapse that week, my head might read *CONFUSED* or *FURIOUS*. Had we achieved progress, it might read, *I'M FINE*. It was the one means of honest communication I had, though I was aware of its fringe benefit: it made me seem wildly off my nut, which, as Rigby had cautioned, was key if I wished to avoid dismissal.

I acquired a calendar and with a methodology of Ruthie Ness rigor scheduled misbehaviors for the first weekend of every month. Violence wasn't needed; any mad-hattering would do. In August 1986, I clambered up a wall in Descartes and hung upside-down from a water pipe to sing "I Wish I Was in Dixie." In November 1986, I raided the kitchen of condiments, used them to fill a bathtub, and introduced it to nurses as my friend Eleanor Roosevelt. In February 1987, I let orderlies chase me to the Hobbes attic, to which I'd gained access and, beneath a tabernacle of exhaust flues, had transcribed the first paragraph of the Declaration of Independence in feces.

I'd been far crazier at Savage Ranch, but I put up a good show.

My sanity I hoarded for Ry, for madness regularly punctured Bear Claw's order. Some bloke makes off with a knife—what idiot staffer brought in a knife?—and turns into a dust devil of slashing steel, warning every nigger, slut, Commie, and cunt to stay the hell back. Prison protocol slams into effect, reminding us where and who we are, with lock-down bells and PA warnings, and if there are injuries, ambulance sirens and the clatter of stretcher wheels and IV racks over broken sidewalk.

Scenes like these somersaulted Ry into despair. Trapped with loonies, he, by logical extension, must have been a loon, and to whom could a loon turn but Jesus? I'll tell you to whom—*me*. If Héctor didn't smell trouble himself, I'd tap my door window and gesture urgently, and he'd expedite an intervention as soon as possible. Once inside Ry's room, I'd display my reaction to Bear Claw's latest flap with a forehead memo (*OH, SHUT UP* or *TAKE ME NEXT*) and elicit from the scared, skinny boy a smile, which shone from hardened fear like crystals from inside a geode.

My century of failings bespoke that to be humane one must partake in humanity. If Ry was halfway lucid, I'd drag him to Bear Claw celebrations. Together we attended a Christmas social complete with a locally chopped evergreen flattened behind a steel grate so the ornaments couldn't become shivs; an Easter egg hunt ruined by an Easter Bunny unable to resist unzipping his costume to masturbate; and a gen-pop summer shindig held in the gymnasium, at which Ry was asked to slow-dance by a girl so consumed with her acne (she had none) that she'd rubbed her face with sandpaper before coming. Whitney Houston's "One Moment in Time" faded out, and Ry returned to me trembling, with a shirt-front stippled with the girl's blood.

Troubling, yes, but as I blotted with cocktail napkins, I reminded him that he hadn't been the bloodletter. Three years, Dearest Reader,

671

each day dedicated to outflanking the archfiends, real and imagined, of this boy I'd come to cherish as much as I had Wilma Sue, Church, anyone. From the time of the stock market crash of 1987 (you and I saw worse in 1929, eh?) until George Herbert Walker Bush's pummeling of Michael Dukakis in the 1988 election, Ry became stable enough that I believed he might be cured. His sister, a winsome blonde named Sarah, was so encouraged by his progress that she began visiting every few weeks, and oh, how eagerly he recounted to me her every piece of news, from the mystifying "break-dancing" skills of Sarah's fiancé to how neither sibling approved of their mother's new boyfriend.

Beautiful days they were, though for me, equally bittersweet. I'd raised Ry as successfully as I'd failed Merle, and I knew the time approached when he would have to leave me behind. I took long walks around the neglected yards, wondering what I would do after he was dismissed. During one idyll I was nabbed and forced to participate in Bear Claw's annual softball game between the northern and southern wards, known to longterm patients as the Cuckoos vs. the Nuts. My understanding of the sport began and ended with Detective Roseborough's goons, Babe Ruth and Lou Gehrig, and I indicated my missing arm to no avail; I was herded into the "home" team, the Cuckoos. Rules, anyhow, were unenforceable, with upward of twenty people on the field at a given time, several of whom, should they obtain the ball, were just as likely to eat it as throw it.

Irrespective of which team was batting, I haunted the grass between first and second, staring into its unmown lushness and, inning by inning, becoming a partner weed. There was, admitted I, a heart-beat comfort to be drawn from the smack of fist into glove and the cackle of bat to ball. Autumn daubed Bear Claw with its only color of the year, the leaves coming alive at the exact moment they were dying. I daydreamed that I was doing the same. After all, I was on the home team. Didn't that mean I was home?

Crack! From the edge of my vision I saw the softball shoot at me, too quick for a fellow with a stomach full of Red Heavies to evade. It clobbered me in the right foot, knocking off my canvas shoe and ricocheting toward five or six second basemen. I remembered to wince as if it had hurt, knelt down to put the shoe back on, and only then saw the damage.

The three smallest toes of my right foot had been knocked clean off. I looked about and spied one of them, a gray nubbin nestled in grass. My gut clenched in bereavement; the littlest one had been Clown's chew-toy. My own body was the only memorabilia I had left, and I reached for The Toe, only to hesitate. Some patients were fanatical observers, and should I collect anything from the ground, they would cluster, worried I'd procured contraband they hadn't. Even should I recover all three toes, then what? Reattach them with toothpicks? Become a pastiche more repellent than I already was?

A beetle waddled up to The Toe, tickled it with its feelers. I looked away, put on the shoe, stood, and swayed. I'd need to stuff the empty space with toilet paper. Eighty-some years before, in the People Garden, Dr. Leather had projected my longevity. *Why*, he'd fawned, *you could last over a century, maybe twice that, given variables of climate, wear and tear, et cetera.* Those variables had proven drastic. Here I was, at the low end of his estimate, already so putrescent that entire chunks could be whacked off by an infield grounder.

The ballfield did not look as halcyon as it had a minute prior.

The grass was promiscuous, inseminated with litter. The players did not dart, they shambled, and their benign chatter was cretin keening. In hindsight, this black-mirror switch, which happened a good hour before the game was called for darkness, the Nuts over the Cuckoos, 26–19, served as a rebuke. A place like Bear Claw could never be a happy home for the living, nor could be it be a quiet crypt for the dead.

VIII.

EQUILIBRIUM WAS SCUTTLED IN JANUARY 1990. I'd returned to the Kant dormitory to find Ry's door open and the bed stripped of sheets. Not only had the room been emptied, but it stunk of cleaner. Conflicting emotions whiplashed me as I charged the nurse's station. The day-shifter preferred true crime to romance, and I'd long worried I'd find her clutching a lurid paperback treatment of the Savage Tragedy, complete with exclusive pics of a cult leader who, strangely enough, looked a lot like Mr. Zipp in room 17. Today, though, it was a Satanist exposé called *Michelle Remembers*, which I had no problem snapping shut to gain her attention.

"Ry Burke, room 18. He's been released?"

She did me the backbreaking favor of checking a chart.

"Moved to another ward."

"What? Which one?"

"I'm sorry. I can't give out that information."

She reached for *Michelle Remembers*, but I snatched it and launched it down the hall, where a gent with a rare disorder—he swallowed everything from lightbulbs to steak knives, necessitating endless endoscopies—picked it up and sniffed it. The nurse gave chase while I tumbled downstairs and outdoors, forgoing the charade of a coat and sledging through snow in the most direct path to Descartes, where I found Dobbin inside a different room

675

with P.M. Analytic's alternate jury of nutsos. After the last of the patients slumped out, I lunged inside. Dobbin spent all day judging threat levels, and he'd hardly forgiven what I'd done to his nose. He retreated behind a desk and placed his hand next to an alarm button.

"Ry Burke," said I. "Where did you put him?"

"The two of you were close. I understand that."

"*Where?*"

"Mr. Burke has been transferred to a less restrictive ward. That's good news, Mr. Zipp. I'm sure your friendship contributed to his progress."

"I need to be close to him."

"Bonds between males do happen in closed environments. But we can't encourage them."

"You think this is some naughty schoolboy romance?"

"I'm sure it feels more significant than that to you."

"Listen to me, ignoramus. Without me nearby, they'll get him."

"Who will get him?"

The third demon! I nearly shouted. Did that mean I'd come to believe in them myself? Dobbin was giving me the look he saved for the truly hopeless—Bobbi, Chad, Lucky, Jackie—so why not make the classification official? With my single arm, I lifted one of the school desks above my head and dashed it to the floor. Its table-top snapped off and, like that, I was wielding a prohibited weapon. What I said before, Reader, held true—violence no longer held any appeal—but for Ry, I'd give it the college try. A bitten nose? I'd rip the damn thing off.

"I want to see Scrimm," growled I. "Now."

Dobbin pushed the panic button. When the orderlies arrived, I dropped the chair and raised both arm and arm stump like an NSTF resister. The straitjacket came anyhow, and I was snugly buckled, pushed rudely out the front door, and back across the snow. Kant was the ward nearest the parking lot, and as odd luck would have it, I spotted a certain skull-faced man edging with an eagle-headed cane from Plato Manor to a hearse-sized Cadillac.

I wrenched leftward so unexpectedly that I tore from both orderlies' grips and, top-heavy and hurtling, I planted myself face-first into the chain-link fence.

"Scrimm! You're making a mistake!"

I watched the old man's thin lips move in gasping-fish repetition. *My, my, my.*

Caught out as incompetent before their boss, the orderlies fell hard upon me. I bit onto a fence link to buy myself three more seconds. The impulse was useless. To believe that the CEO of a sprawling psychiatric clinic would care about the skulduggeries of his underlings was naïveté itself. Yet Scrimm did seem to shrink further into his already shrunken body. He crept onward, wrists shaking and cane faltering, as I was extricated from the fence and handled unkindly until I was pitched, straitjacket and all, to the floor of Kant-17.

Even then hope survived. *Héctor!* thought I. If I could clear the language barrier, I could ask the janitor what he knew of Ry's location. But Héctor, too, failed to return that night, as well as the next. I doubted that his ploys had been discovered—he was too careful for that—but believed rather that he'd been forced to obey bosses who'd decided his work ethic was better utilized in a different ward.

It was Scrimm's fatalistic slouch I recalled three days later when the A-team of Sikes and Glover led me, still straitjacketed, as one might a nose-ringed cow, not to the Back Ward but rather to Cicero, the northernmost building at Bear Claw, which I hadn't believed was still in use. It was, though barely, silent and freezing, with radiators doing a lot of zinging without producing one joule of heat. Perhaps, postulated I, Cicero served as the cafeteria's meat locker, and I was meant to be hacked and mashed into Friday's casserole.

Instead of a subterrane of butcher counters and fluid drains, I was brought to what had been designed as a storage closet but had been repurposed as an office, despite dozens of superior ones vacant on every floor. It was a narrow space passable only due to the removal of shelves; no paint had been wasted to cover the scars and studs. The window at the end was rimed with frost, which made rhinestones upon the shivering shoulders of the man sitting at the desk, rifling through papers with mittened hands. That he wore a wrapped scarf and winter hat explained why he didn't hear us arrive. What nugatory layabout, wondered I, had Scrimm exiled to this thankless station?

One of the orderlies knocked loudly to startle the man. It worked. He leapt to his feet as if under fire, then relaxed, squeezing past his desk to meet us. He did not look like much of a challenge, Reader. He was of Asian origin and of early-middle age. He wore his black hair in a short ponytail and a blue dress shirt, brown tie, paisley vest, pleated slacks, and loafers, all of which suggested a softness that, to my mind, was confirmed by the large hoop in his left earlobe.

That he tried to shake the hand of a straitjacketed patient told me that, whatever his role, he hadn't been at it long. I stared at him until he figured it out, grimaced his apology, and gestured me toward a cushioned, though duct-taped, chair in front of his desk. I sat, my feet positioning upon a pitiful rug he'd installed to contrive homeyness. He retook his seat.

"You need us to hang around?" grunted Sikes.

"No!" I could see the man's breath. "We're cool here, aren't we, Mr. Zipp?"

Cool? Were only my hand free so that I might claw off my ears!

Sikes and Glover didn't need to be asked twice. They skedaddled, leaving the living-dead boy in the custody of the new-age wimp.

"Man, look, I just want to say, it's great to meet you, Frank. Is it cool if I call you Frank? I've gone through your file, and I've been dying to ask, have you heard of Cotard's Syndrome? It's named after a French neurologist, not that that matters, and it's this state of mind, or state of being, really, where the sufferer believes himself to be a corpse, right down to insisting that he's decomposing and demanding that he be buried—"

Embarrassed by his own zeal, he chuckled.

"Sorry, I should introduce myself. I'm Eric Kwon. Just call me Eric, all right? I want to keep things super casual. I would say kick off your shoes, but I don't think they've got the heat going just yet! I'm working on that, I promise. One thing at a time, right?"

It was far beyond the ken of this blithering fledgling to help me find Ry. I tried to gimlet-eye him out of existence. He gulped and shuffled through his papers.

"I, uh, don't know how much they explained to you? But I've been brought to Barraclough as a personal therapist. It's, like, a pilot program here in Maine where I choose my analysands from a list of irremediables. To sort of translate that to English, they're giving me a whack at long-term residents who haven't responded to medication. Some issues are strictly behavioral in nature, I truly believe that, and no pill anyone invents is going to help that, you know? I know they've got you in group therapy, but from what I can tell, the doctors here are way over-booked, and honestly? They aren't trained for it. So I'd

679

like you to think of this as something completely different, a weekly conversation between you and me, a safe space where you can open up about whatever's bothering you. I work for the state, not Barraclough. Anything you say is confidential, and I mean that. Nothing is off-limits. Does all that make sense?"

I rearranged myself, taking care to jingle the straitjacket buckles. Misgiving crimpled Eric's eagerness. He'd read my file; he knew what I'd done to Dobbin. I opted to capitalize upon his fear.

"So you're a shrink," synopsized I.

He shrugged. "I'm a psychologist. But, yeah, some people call us head-shrinkers."

"And you're new."

"Well, like I said, it's a pilot program—"

"Not new here. New, period."

I could see his mind turn through options: deny, deflect, denounce. To his credit, he told the truth.

"That's correct."

"Which is why you drew this humdinger of an assignment."

"I'm happy to go wherever I'm needed."

"What were you before this?"

"Really, Mr. Zipp, our sessions will be more productive if we focus on you."

"What happened to calling me Frank?"

"We only have an hour. I really think we should—"

"I've heard of this. The fifty-minute hour. The padded couch. The shelving of gilt-edged encyclopedia. The box of tissues for when memories of Mother become all too much."

Eric forced a jittery laugh and busied himself unspooling his scarf, a good indication that I'd unnerved him. No wonder Scrimm had looked so morose! Shrinks, those latter-day carnies, had bridged the moats, swarmed the battlements, and stormed the keeps of the superintendent's once-inviolable castle. It was an infestation upon which lice had nothing, though assigning Eric Kwon to the Cicero frontier was the action of one who didn't understand the principles of plague.

"I take it," said he, "you're not a believer in psychology."

"I'm certain it is quite the treat for those who wish, for once in their chapfallen lives, to be the center of attention. I, myself, have no time for the hobby. I have a friend in need of help, and to waste time sifting through adolescent imbroglios strikes me as profane."

"Your friend Ry?"

My curled spine went straight. "Have you spoken with him?"

"No. He's just, you know, written on your face."

Ah, yes, I'd forgotten. The latest message I'd markered across my forehead had set Jackie upon her sharpest edge, whether one of affronted adversary or a fellow insurgent I could not tell. Though purportedly improved, Ry had yet to return to group therapy, and so it had become my printed protest, which a few others in group had since copied upon their own foreheads: *FREE RY*.

"It is your first day, Mr. Kwon. But do you not already smell what is rotten at Bear Claw? The local bureaucracy thinks their drugs are to credit for Ry Burke's improvement, but they are critically mistaken. I have helped Ry, and I alone. This conviction derives not from hauteur, though I know that will be your verdict. Ry's demons may devour him if I can't intercede."

"I don't discount that. Anything you have to say, I'll listen to."

Me, me, me, when all I wanted, for once, was to focus outward!

"I'm afraid this is what is called an impasse. You cannot help me,

681

shrink; 'tis not your fault. For decades I have been all styles of naïf, and have a special sympathy for ignorance. Therefore I extend to you a courtesy. As I'm already here in your chair, I will grant you the oddment of our hour to pose what questions you will, and I, in the spirit of charity, will strive to answer them. When the hour is up, you will find me incommunicado. Am I understood? Wonderful. Proceed."

Eric blinked. None of his fantasies of gradually prying open the mussel shell of succulent psychosis had included a ticking stopwatch. He sensed I was serious, though, and began pawing past the get-to-know-you malarkey of his notes while stammering, "Ah, ah, ah, ah," as if afraid I might get up and leave. He whipped out a page and gave it a scan.

"What do you think it symbolizes," panted he, "this idea that you were born in the 1800s?"

"It symbolizes that I was born in the 1800s."

"Oh." He squinted. "Do you, like, have any proof of that?"

"Of course. A premium pocket watch acquired in 1895. A newspaper clipping featuring me from 1901. A photograph of my daughter taken in 1913."

"Can you show me this stuff?"

"All of it was stripped from my person when I was admitted. That might sound convenient, but I assure you, it was not so convenient to me."

"No, not at all. I mean, even if you had those things here, you could've bought the watch at an antique shop or taken the photo from some old album. We tend to think of physical objects as proof, but proof of what? Is it any less real to you that it isn't here in your hand?"

"The hand buckled to my torso?"

"Yeah, that one."

I shrugged. "I suppose not."

Eric snapped his fingers.

"Right. You believe it, so I have to believe it. There's no other way forward. You say you were born a century ago; I say, fine, let's talk about that, what that was like."

"Feed the crazy with more crazy, is that it?"

"You ever heard of apotemnophilia?"

"I'm afraid my savvy ends at six-syllable words."

"It's a medical condition in which the sufferer has the irresistible desire to cut off a certain part of their body."

"Believe me, shrink, the pieces I've lost I would have rather kept."

"Apotemnophiliacs are highly specific. 'I need to lose my right leg just beneath the knee.' 'I need to cut off my left arm just above the elbow.' They consider these parts foreign objects that simply don't belong. How painful the amputation is doesn't matter; it's less painful than keeping the limb. Doctors, naturally, have their Hippocratic Oath—'First, do no harm,' and all that—so a lot of apotemnophiliacs self-amputate and then, while they're still bleeding, mangle the detached part so it can't be reattached. If they survive, their neurosis is gone, almost without exception. They are whole. They are cured."

"Cheery little story. Dare I ask of its relevance?"

"The point is, you can call these people crazy all you want, but it doesn't bear out. There's a problem, they solve it, then they're fine. Your friend Ry has his own problem. And you, Frank, you've got your own problem, too. What do I care if it's real to Dr. Scrimm or Dr. Dobbin? What do I care if it's real to me? My job is to help you solve it, end of sentence. And guess what? The sooner you solve it, the sooner you're out of that jacket, out of a lock-down ward, and free to help Ry or whatever. All you gotta do, Frank, is say yes, Eric, I'll let you try, and then, you know, we'll give it a shot. What can it hurt?"

Eric looked quite pleased with himself, and for that I couldn't fault him; his had been a most agile improvisation. What, indeed, was the drawback of allying myself with the only person at Bear Claw beyond Scrimm's purview? Perhaps, given time, Eric Kwon might even assist in the bypassing of certain regulations so that I might reunite with Ry. It was a dangling carrot that I eyed leerily, though hungrily.

"You never said what you used to be," said I.

"Didn't I?"

"No."

He toyed with his earring. "I was, uh, a pastor."

"You don't say. Did you have your own pulpit?"

Now his ponytail. "I sermoned. But it wasn't for me."

"Would you say you lost faith in Gød?"

"Again, Frank, I want to stress that it's not about me or what—"

"Would you say you lost faith in Gød?"

"Really, I'd prefer not to talk about it. I wouldn't want you to think that, if we have different belief systems, I couldn't still help you—"

"Would you say you lost faith in Gød?"

He exhaled, chewed his lip, laced his fingers into a ball of knuckles.

"Yes," said he. "I would say that."

I smirked. "Right answer, shrink. You and I have a deal."

IX.

NO PSYCHOTHERAPIST WORTH HIS SALT would enter freely into a quid pro quo pact, but Eric didn't know that, and the back-and-forth sharing of personal information became the hallmark of our sessions. I recalled the OSS cellar where I'd first met Rigby, and how the pale stripe of his removed wedding band had cracked open the door just enough that I could wedge inside a foot. That foot had three fewer toes now, true enough, but Eric Kwon was no Allen Rigby when it came to buttressing a blockade. Over subsequent meetings, I learned of Eric's schooling, dissertation, and job search, all of it so resoundingly tedious that I could find no knife to twist.

He was a trusting puppy, and also, by those very characteristics, Bear Claw's death knell. The old guard's provisos of punishment and prize had no place in the new guard's policy of pampering rapport, and the asylum's collapse snowballed into avalanche. Meds, left to overburdened nurses for months, were bungled, which led to psychotic relapses, which led to private investigations, which led to lawsuits, which led to settlements, which led to layoffs, and, finally, spates of outright quitting. Dust-bunnies procreated in dayrooms, and lawns grew knee-high. Civilization fell into chaos, and somewhere inside of it was Ry.

This gave me all the more reason to charm and flatter Eric, but ingratiation was so contrary to my nature that I rebelled in the opposite, disadvantageous direction, taking the first opening I saw to box Eric to the turnbuckles regarding his career move from theology to psychology—a shift one does not make, theorized I, without the cattle-prod of a crisis.

"Tell me, shrink, why you did it, and take care not to prevaricate."

Eric sighed and zipped his coat against the February chill.

"Pastoring is, like, an art. Like being an English Lit professor or something. You read, you analyze, and your Sunday sermon is like your weekly essay. There's a lot of latitude there, and I guess I enjoyed that. Writers, I think, want to help people. Why else do they write? That's what drove me, anyway."

"What drove you away is what I want to know. Was it religiosity's charlatanism?"

"You're putting words in my mouth. I think what I realized is, if you want to help people, writing is a super inefficient way to do it. The most direct way, probably, is the field of medicine. And psychology, psychiatry—if medicine has its own fine arts, those are it. You give the same patient to three psychologists, they're going to treat her three different ways. It's all up for interpretation."

"Why can't you admit that you realized Gød offers neither help nor comfort when it comes to the black terminus of our last stop?"

"You really want me to say that, don't you? You must be the most passionate atheist I've ever met."

"Atheist? Hah! You've got it topsy-turvy. Never has there existed a being surer of Gød's existence than I."

"Then explain the hostility. I don't get it."

"You're the one who fled the church. You know of Gød's tentacles, long and sundry enough to tickle our bellies with glories while simultaneously retracting to shut the window shades of Heavens. 'Gød is good,' we chant in church basements. 'Gød is love,' we stitch into needlepoints. I know what Gød is. Gød is fear. What will Gød take from you next? Your loved ones? Your home? Your country? Your body? Fear is what puts butts into pews, what knocks us kneebound as if by the baton of a slavedriver."

Eric paused, taken back by my vehemence.

"And Jesus?" hazarded he. "Gød doesn't get points for him?"

"Yes, yes, both Jesus and I were resurrected. Your traps are telegraphed, shrink."

"I'm just saying, the New Testament goes out of its way to show us how Jesus was flesh and blood, all his tortures, the fourteen Stations of the Cross. Doesn't that suggest Gød has an appreciation for suffering? Even yours?"

"If I am one of Gød's whelps, then I am Cain, not Abel."

"That's an interesting way to put it. Cain was the first son, you know, not the second. Cain was the first human ever born. Do you feel like that? The first of a new age?"

"Cain was a murderer, is all I mean. Come, come, shrink. You don't believe any of this. Cain and Abel, Adam and Eve—these are fables."

"No, you're right. If I believe in an Eve, it's Mitochondrial Eve. That's the theory that all human DNA can be traced back to a single female in East Africa maybe a couple hundred thousand years ago. Now, that's believable. That's science. The Bible—look, Frank, they're fables, I'm not debating that. The fact remains that these fables were written by some of the greatest intellects who ever lived. Remember that Gød, first and foremost, is a character in a book. In a sense, these writers *created* Gød; they were Gød's god. They had lessons to teach, and they still do."

"Try living as long as I have, then tell me what 'lessons' they can teach."

Eric gave a half-grin that, in time, would become my bane. He scrambled from his chair, pulled off his mittens, and with slender hands plucked from his shelf a book that, by its stippled cover texture and pink-edged pages, I knew was a Holy Bible. He tossed it onto the table in front of me. Ry was out there suffering, and this was the shrink's watery cure-all?

"Genesis," said he. "Easy to find. First book."

"Sorry, chap. Not my sort of leisure reading."

"No? What do you like? Maybe I can get some of that, too."

What leapt to the fore was Junior's treasury of comic books inherited from a dead father, those cardboard boxes handled with uncharacteristic mindfulness, the page-flip rainbow of cheaply printed varicolored dots, the stink of crumbled paper and hand sweat, all of it fantasy scenarios from an improbable American dream.

"Superman," said I. "Long ago, under a cape of self-deception, I fancied myself a bit like good old Kal-El."

"That's kind of remarkable. You know what 'Kal-El' means in Hebrew?"

"It's Hebrew?"

"It means 'Of God.'"

That half-grin again; I cursed. If there was an abacus keeping score, slide one bead to the shrink. I grumbled at the presumptuous tome, the booby prize for having yielded the point.

"Shall I flip the pages with my tongue?"

"Right. The straitjacket. Let me see what I can do."

The agency that employed Eric Kwon held the drawstrings of Bear Claw's funding. It was the only explanation for the startling swiftness. A single dawn passed before Sikes and Glover removed the restraint. The Bible crouched on my bed, as black as a sewer rat. Should I wait until it plodded away, or should I pounce? Eric, though it rankled me to admit it, had earned the latter. After all, if Gød was my enemy, it might serve me well to learn his playbook. I cracked it open and read the opening skit, something I'd never considered during my hundreds of church trips with Abigail Finch.

When my next session arrived, I had feedback, all right.

"Floundering, maladroit, inerudite incompetence! Mawkishly ignorant of proper dramatic beats, thronged with directionless characters, padded with tedious columns of immaterial names, and recklessly overambitious in scope! It is difficult to believe this found one reader, much less billions!"

I paced the coffin contours of Eric's suite, waving the Good Book about as if a brisk shaking might empty it of some of its flaws, never noticing how my critiques could be applied to another epic, one which you, Dearest Reader, are even now close to finishing. Eric looked pleased by my reaction.

"What did you object to most of all, Frank?"

"For starters? The start! Genesis 1:26: Gød, having kneaded the world from dough, creates man in His own image. O-ho, but your idolized fabulists cannot even agree upon what that image is! Gød creates both male and female humans—a differentiation, you might notice, that He does not bother with when creating animals. Those 'cattle and creeping things and beasts of the earth' have no gender? That's careless writing, shrink."

"Unless, of course, the split between female and male is crucial to humans in a way it isn't to animals. What if *that's* Gød's image? What

689

if He's both genders—or even genderless? Your file, I notice, says you consider yourself genderless. Is that right?"

I pushed aside the question.

"And what of the Garden of Eden's Tree of Life? I am not uninformed of this leafy rascal. It is known by some as Yggdrasil, but is, by any name, sucker-bait for the Foolish, a tribe which prostrates itself before Gød every time they hear the swish of Death's robes down the hall. But Death comes not for me, shrink; I shall not climb this tree."

"What Gød offers in Genesis, I think, is a trade-off," said Eric. "The Tree of Life versus Tree of Knowledge—that's the one with the snake and the apple. You can't have both."

"Why not? Another of Gød's arbitrary tests?"

"This is just, you know, one interpretation, but Gød is offering Adam and Eve a chance to shape their own destiny and choose a brutal world of hardship and death instead of a perfect life gift-wrapped just for them. Did you notice how the Tree of Knowledge is placed in easy reach? How simple it is for Eve to pluck the fruit? What does that tell you?"

"I already knew that Gød is a sadist!"

"Or maybe Gød wanted us to choose the Tree of Knowledge all along, and that to be 'doomed to die,' like the Bible says, is really to be allowed to live. Maybe Adam and Eve's banishment isn't a 'fall' at all but rather a rise to a challenge. I mean, we all make that choice, right? We can lie about all glassy-eyed or we can take on the horrible exhilaration of life, what Gød called the 'thorns and thistles.'"

My frustrated pacing paused at the coffin's foot, too far from Eric to evaluate his shrewdness. It was hard not to associate "glassy-eyed" with every Bear Claw patient who'd surrendered to the creamy delirium of his individual psychopharmaceutical Eden. Just as difficult to resist was perceiving my own century as having confronted, with some fortitude and spunk, the "horrible exhilaration of life." Mine was a history of lousy decisions, yes, but weren't they decisions none-theless?

"Even if you're right," said I, "it is a cruel choice."

Eric shrugged. "That's Genesis for you. My mentor at seminary said it wasn't even a book; it was a series of Divine Experiments, like Gød playing with a kid's laboratory kit. Here's the Garden of Eden—whoops, bad idea, too easy, and now it's gone. Here's a world for humans without the prohibition of laws—whoops, bad idea, men are wicked and the earth is corrupt, so here's a flood to wash it away."

"Speak clearly, sir. Are you suggesting I'm one of these experi-ments?"

Another shrug of maddening ambiguity.

"I'm just saying, if you are, you're not working against Gød. You're working *with* Him, like a lab assistant, shaking things up on Earth, trying to break stuff, working as hard as you can to find all the flaws in His plan. 'Failure' isn't a bad word in a lab; it's how you get anything accomplished. You fail, fail again, and keep failing, until finally, one day, you don't fail and it's, like, eureka."

This pissant did not need to tell Zebulon Finch about labora-tories, meat etiquette, and Revelation Almanacs! Partner to Gød? Abhorrent idea, and as long as Ry was in danger, I would militate against it! I cut short that morning's session, took the Bible with me, skulked behind the Locke cafeteria, opened a garbage receptacle, and irked one million flies by tossing it into a slop of scrambled eggs, oatmeal, and coffee grounds.

Bear Claw had become, as I've said, vastly understaffed, and the hygiene assistants still on patrol were high-strung and ill-tempered. I'd seen residents struck down for no reason, patients have seizures while nurses chatted about hair-care products, a supply shed used for sex with a madwoman who hadn't the slightest idea what was happening. So when the Bible's unsolved riddles had me deranged enough to require another copy, I needed to perfect a groveling lope to make it to the library unmolested.

I hoped that I might discover Ry right where he belonged, shoulder-deep in the Bear Claw archives and eager to share the latest bombshells. Find Ry I did not, but find a Bible I did, a whole bookcase, in fact, each copy more abused than an issue of *Penthouse*. The choice of King James, New International, Revised Standard, New Living Translation, Common English, or Oxford Annotated did not matter; each Holy Bible fell open to the Book of Job. The pages therein were thumbed to translucence, every sentence deemed worthy of underline by one Bear Clawer or another, each of whom could but hope her or his oblique torments had a divine design. I disfavored tossing myself in with these neurotics, but gave the first sentence a shot.

> *There was a man in the land of Ūz, whose named was Jōb; and that man was blameless and upright, one who feared Gød, and turned away from evil.*

Could I possibly share less with this prudish stickler? Before about-facing back to Kant, I pictured Eric Kwon's sly eyes and slyer smile, and how much of both I'd have to tolerate should he believe he held an intellectual upper hand. Thus I ate my pride, zipped the Bible into my jumpsuit, and pirated it back to Kant. There, in room

17, assailed by the silence of Ry's vacancy, I read all thirty-one pages, and then, disbelieving the evidence, read them again. Two sun-ups later, I'd read Job a dozen times, dismantling each sentence as I'd done the engine of my Tin Lizzie between hooch runs, so that each isolated gear could be inspected. Eric had been right: there was gold to be mined from these tales if one drilled deep enough.

I charged down to his coffin office, the Bible gnarling in my grip.

"Job," swore I.

Eric had the nerve to lean back and crack his half-grin into a full one.

"All these decades you've supposedly lived, all these things you've supposedly suffered, and you've never read Job? Really? It's the perfect story for any teenager who thinks the world is crapping on him."

"Table your judgments and tell me if I have this right. Satan posits to Gød that Job is pious because it is gainful to be pious, and Gød says no, Dear Satan, my Job is pious because piety is itself worthwhile."

"Yeah, you've got it."

"Whereupon Gød, like a child sharing his kitten with the neighborhood sociopath, permits Satan to test Job. So Job loses, and I quote, 'seven thousand sheep, three thousand camels, five hundred yoke of oxen, and five hundred she-asses.' A sharecropper I am not, but that sounds like a tidy sum. Next, Satan whips up a wind and collapses a house, killing all ten of Job's children. Finally, a flourish: he smites Job with leprosy."

This last detail in particular nettled me. Arizona patrolmen had loved calling Savage Ranch a leper colony, and I'd become leprous in all outward aspects. What if these were clues that I was in the midst of a Job-like trial? What if my rescuing of Ry was but the concluding exam?

693

"So far," said Eric, "so good."

"Well, then, there is but one question raised by this bewildering text. What does sin have to do with suffering? Job was the truest of hearts and yet he suffered, while his friends, the wretched, danced about in gay little jigs."

Eric had started taking notes.

"I know why you're asking this," said he. "Because when you were still alive or whatever, you didn't suffer hardly at all."

"Exactly, shrink. I could read the rest of this Bible and there would be no mystery that matters more. What is Gød's afterlife admissions policy? Who gets to pass 'twixt those pearly gates? Do Job and I both get to stroll by Saint Peter in matching tuxedoes, cocktails in our left hands, bosomy women on our right, even though Job was righteous and I was villainous?"

Even over a crappy com-link patch-in from Albuquerque, Rig had said it better: *Why you and not them? How come a no-good bastard like you keeps coming back and sweet Florence just lies there on the mud?*

Eric held up his left hand, still writing with his right.

"Okay, fair question. But isn't the whole point of Job that we don't even get to *ask*? I mean, you read it. Gød goes on, page after page after page—it's unprecedented in the whole Bible—basically shaming Job for daring to question Gød's justice. 'Where were you when I laid the foundation of the earth?', all that stuff."

I split the Bible, rifled back through its early pages.

"Look here. Genesis 6:7, the Flood: 'I will blot out the man whom I have created, for I am sorry that I have made them.' Could He be any clearer? He regrets creating us! He is hardly fit, then, to judge us. That's like sewing a rag doll and then burning it because it refuses to speak!"

Eric slapped down his pencil and held up his hands to beg patience.

"This is Möbius-strip logic. We could spin around it all day. Why are you so jazzed up about this?"

I held up the Bible. A book: a harmless thing, yet envenomed.

"Because Gød, in His infinite wisdom, has given Job and the rest of us the facility to think critically. Why else did we choose the Tree of Knowledge over the Tree of Life? And yet here Gød instructs us *not* to think critically. I have seen far too closely, Mr. Kwon, what happens when humans stop thinking critically. They end up in narrow trenches trading poison gasses. They end up herding innocents into ovens. They end up massing believers into the desert and setting them tooth against tooth. If we follow Gød's command to Job, we open the door to the worst conceivable evils."

No conversational lapse at Bear Claw was totally silent. Somewhere, a patient was forever giggling, screaming, orating, or weeping, if not all four in accord. Cicero was the institute's stillest spot, however, and would be until the heaters were fixed, quiet enough that you could hear the breaking of waves against Maine's cliffs, that prehistoric drum beat mocking our striving little brains.

"And yet," ventured Eric.

My, but the earringed analyst was observant.

I sat, hoping I might feel more seaworthy.

"And yet," sighed I, "Gød holds Job in the highest esteem of all, even after His lectures. This is one kink I cannot untwist. Gød is a typhoon that wipes out good and bad in indiscriminate tides. Why bother to let us know he approves of Job if Job's fate, and the fate of all goodly men, are like those waves you and I can hear being crashed against the rocks?"

Yielding of this sort was catnip for a frisky psychologist; it is to Eric Kwon's credit that he moved lightly, bridging one word to the next with spiderlike delicacy.

"I'm not interested in inflating your ego," said he. "But it's hard to know what I know about the Bible and know what I know about you and . . . Look, when I suggested you were a Divine Experiment, you weren't real happy about it. But what if we placed that into context? What if I said other Divine Experiments have manifested as human beings all throughout history, in all religions? Of course, they went by a different word."

Illusionist? Necromancer? Witch doctor?

"Prophet," guessed I.

Eric proceeded as if we navigated a spiral staircase with an object both cumbersome and fragile held between us, and we did, for half the basket cases at Bear Claw regarded themselves as prophets fielding personal telegrams from Gød. That I received no such telegrams, nor ever had, lent the label a backward sort of credence.

"The purpose of prophets is to link the human realm to the divine," continued Eric. "To report back from Gød's world. To help us answer all the questions Job forces us to ask. I'll put this out there and you can, like, you know, do whatever you want to with it. But what if that's why you're here? Not just here on Earth, but here in America, in Maine, in Barraclough, in this room with me right now? What if you're here to prepare for prophecy, to see what you can see in Gød's realm and send the rest of us back a report?"

X.

VON LÜTH HAD CALLED ME a "guide" destined to lead people through the "valleys of death and into the hills of glory." Rig had called me a "Fail-safe," the canary in the coal mine that would tell people it was safe to continue. Both these words I preferred above "prophet," which, to me, implied subordinacy: Gød was the Message, the prophet the Messenger. I knew from experience, however, that even lowly lab assistants could usurp their scientist superiors. My attack against the Lord's acropolis did not relent; what changed was my strategy. I operated like the spy Frau Meixelsperger had wished me to be, immersing myself in His proverbs, psalms, axioms, and brocards. To know Him, premised I, would facilitate the infiltration of his defenses when the moment was nigh. If I couldn't save Ry directly, perhaps I could deliver him from Gød's famous "mercy."

In sessions I came to relish, Eric and I barnstormed through testaments Old and New, Biblical Apocrypha, Dead Sea Scroll addenda, and scriptural critiques. We spent the middle third of 1990 slashing paths through the jungle of Ecclesiastes, a book that made Job read like *Dick and Jane*. Its opening cry is one with which any Bear Claw indweller would empathize: "Utter futility! All is futile!" If that is not black enough coffee, Mr. Ecclesiastes avers that there is nothing noble about old age, only yucky decrepitude: "Appreciate your youthful vigor in the days of your youth, before the days of sorrow come." And nowhere, Dearest Reader, in these notebooks you hold, have I written truer words than Ecclesiastes 9:11:

The race is not won by the swift,
Nor the battle by the courageous;
Nor is sustenance won by the wise,
Nor wealth by the intelligent,
Nor favor by the learned,
For the short duration of life renders all successes illusory.

Does not such depredation beg for analysis? Follow my logic, if you will, over water lilies and under sticky fronds, and mind my machete. The morose Mr. Ecclesiastes repudiates Genesis's valuing of humans above animals, saying, "Man has no superiority over beast, since both amount to nothing." Gød, in his diatribe to Job, goes even further, giving special approval to the animal kingdom, where one protects one's own at all costs. Singled out as exemplars are the hippopotamus and crocodile, barbaric creatures that share nothing with the coming Gentle Jew of Nazareth and his platitudes of loving your enemy and turning the cheek.

In my fumbling attempt to recreate Montana's natural order at Savage Ranch, how had I forgotten the lesson learned at the end of the First World War? Permit me the hubris of quoting myself, hundreds of pages yonder, when I wondered "whether defending the life of a loved one was worth the destruction of others." Gød's prophets suggested that yes, good violence exists right alongside bad; consider again that instant in 1918, when I watched Allied and German soldiers pull back bayonets to let the fawn caught between their armies caper free.

It was at the end of Job where I found a flame that, more than any other, singed me with the brand of prophet. Gød, in the mood to reward Job for being true-blue, restores him with all he once had and more: fourteen thousand sheep, six thousand camels, a thousand yoke of oxen, a thousand she-asses, and ten more children. The book thereby concludes with order restored and everyone happy. Hooray?

Not so fast, Reader. Are we to believe that Job is actually pleased with this remedy? Gød can do many things, but "replace" a child with a different one is not among them. Whether your offspring is as splenetic as Merle or as unswerving as Ry, the idea is repugnant. Animals, however, are a different story. The lioness fights to save her brood, but if she gets hungry enough, she will eat them. Their little souls are recyclable, and thereby animals, and only animals, approach immortality.

Well, animals and Mr. Frank Zipp of Kant-17.

So ponderous was this conclusion that, for a time, I could not bear to lift it. The Bible was a treasure map waiting all these years for me to find it, and it seemed to suggest that I might yet get that long-desired chance to meet Gød and make hay of the meeting. And how does one make hay? One sharpens one's pitchfork.

Eric's sessions hadn't exonerated me from the round table of A.M. Analytic, and twice a week I took stock of our razed Camelot to see which chunks of armor had been ripped from our debilitated knights. Their meds were a mess, their hygiene had lapsed, and to a man they were falling apart. Bobbi had become a walking skeleton who still believed herself obese, while Lucky's helmet had been replaced by mere bandages, which became stained in the colors of the ward's Yuletide decorations: blood red and brain-fluid green. Others of us had altogether sunk into Bear Claw's quicksand.

"Where's Chad?"

"Yeah, he's missed like two weeks now."

"Didn't you hear? Chad stepped on an orderly's Nikes and got his ass beat."

"I heard he's in a coma."

"Yeah? I heard he's dead and they're hiding it. But who knows, man?"

Who knew, indeed? The ship was sinking and the passengers drowning, while the crew, like rats, scrabbled for high ground. Dobbin owned what he called a "cellular telephone," a plastic brick with a rubber antenna, and were you a stealthy sort, you could creep close as he paced outside before group, booming false bravado at potential employers, all of whom demanded that Dobbin defend Barraclough's notorious practices. He couldn't, and defeated, he'd slump inside, mumble a bit, and let the group self-steer themselves toward hysteria while he watched his phone, waiting for its keypad to light up with good news.

This background I submit so that you understand how rare it had become for any of these panicked prisoners to lower their self-protective shields. In December 1990, seconds after I'd caboosed our sad train out of Descartes and into a slapping winter wind, Jackie blindsided me.

"Green-skin pus-smelling fuckling trash!"

The MAD upon her triceratops bone plate butted my nose. Off-balance from a belly full of Red Heavies, I stumbled, kicking a football of snow, before righting myself and whirling about to locate help, which, as previously noted, no longer existed. Jackie was back, her gold teeth flashing with wet snow.

"You're lucky I haven't ripped those words off your fuckling face. Imitating Jackie is how you get buried, little boy."

I touched my offending forehead. The last words I'd markered upon it had been both prediction and plea: *THE END*.

"I don't want trouble," said I.

She spread her arms, playing to an invisible audience of hooting supporters. We, the violent cases, were given thin wool coats in the winter, khaki like our jumpsuits, and Jackie's undone zipper jangled like a popped switchblade. Cuckoos vs. the Nuts, game two, the sport having switched from softball to recreational knifing.

"Fatherfuckler speaks! I knew that squeaky mouse bullshit was bullshit."

I tried to get away, but she fisted my coat collar and pulled my head close enough that I could smell her pickled breath. Her voice was more menacing when lowered.

"Perk up your Mickey ears, squeaky-squeaky. I have a problem, and you're the only punk-junk garbage-pail in this joint who can help. I know you haven't forgot Farm Boy."

This got me to quit struggling. Forget him I certainly hadn't. Jackie open-handed the side of my head anyway. My neck bones reported.

"You helped Farm Boy out when he needed it, which is how come Jackie hasn't carved your face like a pumpkin. Here's the four-one-one, mousey. Farm Boy needs help again. He needs it serious."

"Where is he?" demanded I.

"Back in May, they put me on cemetery detail, right? Got me rooting varmints out of the old tuberculosis camp and clubbing them dead. Nasty shit! They call it work therapy, but slave labor is what's up. One day I'm sucking snakes out a snake hole and turn around, and there he is, Farm Boy, *my* boy, looking out a window."

Every cul-de-sac like Bear Claw had a potter's field, where dead

701

without claimants were shoveled under with the barest ceremony. I recalled seeing, on my first walk through Bear Claw, mossy stones protruding from the earth like molars; I could even see the shape of the ward's shadow draped across them.

"Spinoza," identified I. "That's by the Back Ward."

"That's why it's hard as shit to get over there."

"Then what am I supposed to do?"

I raised a thwarting elbow against a second smack.

"Do I look like Double-O-Fuckling-Seven? That's shit you have to figure. All I can say is I never heard Farm Boy go off like this. Moaning and blubbering and snorting and wheezing. The master rats call it pseudoseizure so they can pretend it's not real, but you listen to it and *you* tell *me* it isn't real. Farm Boy's going down hard."

"Is he going to hurt himself?"

"You know the finger-food diet?"

"Finger food?"

Her fist went low, caught me in the oft-stitched stomach.

"Finger food is what they bring brain-drains who can't be trusted with utensils. That's all that's going into Spinoza. Finger food far as the eye can see."

"Why don't they move him to the Back Ward, for Gød's sake?"

"You think there's room in Back Ward anymore?" Jackie clucked and, on a whim, slapped my forehead. "*THE END*, huh? Yeah, that's right. This whole joint's ready to explode. Too bad Farm Boy's the only varmint in this cemetery who don't deserve to be exploded. You really give a shit, Mickey Mouse, you'll get in there and save him. You'll do it because Jackie hasn't come up with a single useful fuckling plan."

In the final seconds before she bolted, wind froze the tears in her

702

eyes, and this flash of vulnerability did more to move me than all of her physical threats. She was right: Bear Claw was a split powder keg even a dynamitier like Bartholomew Finch would have skirted. Rather than risk lawless orderlies who might waylay me as they'd waylaid Chad, I paced room 17 for four racking days before going to see Eric per safe, established schedule. It goes without saying that the Cicero furnace had never been repaired, and I came upon Eric kneeling before a space heater as his forefathers had before hearths, rubbing his palms before glowing neon tubes.

"Frank," greeted he. "I had an idea: the Book of Esther."

"Listen to me."

"This childhood you say you had in the olden days—the Black Hand, right? Esther is totally related. Ostensibly, the book glorifies vengeance. But how can that be?"

"Listen to me."

"What's wrong?"

"You need to help me."

"That's what I'm trying to do."

"Not with Biblical twaddle. Real help."

Eric stood, cold knees cricking.

"I think 'twaddle' sort of minimizes the progress we've—"

"Ry—I've found him. He's in Spinoza, which is in no way outfitted for someone slipping along sanity's edge."

"Whoa, hold on. How do you know it's that bad?"

"Will you trust me? He is in the gravest danger."

"Even if you're right, what are you asking?"

"Are you that daft? I need you to get me inside Spinoza! I need you to get me inside his room! We're past theorems and hypotheses now, shrink! This is real life, real death!"

Eric rubbed his temples and walked behind his desk. He dropped himself down and laughed once.

"Frank. Come on, man. You know I can't do that."

I kicked in the front of the space heater.

"Doesn't this stovetop of yours prove it? Bear Claw has literally frozen you out. You have no idea what's going on out there. Patients drugged to stupor, abused, raped, starved, tortured, vanished altogether. It's happening right under your dolt nose!"

The skin between his eyebrows daggered.

"Cool it, Frank. I do what I can here."

A Bible lay between us, adhesive notes marking passages that he, solicitous school boy, had been eager to share. I took it and hurled it at the window. It crashed to the metal mesh hard enough to crack the glass behind it. A triangular shard of window fell, and a bullet of wind shot out, striking Eric in the back of the head. He jolted like JFK in that fateful 1963 motorcade, and his hand leapt to the desk phone's red button, which all patients knew rung a bell in the cerebral cortexes of Sikes and Glover. Eric retracted the hand a second later, but it was too late.

"*That's* what you think of me?" sputtered I.

"Well, what do you expect? I don't know this friend of yours! My job is to help *you*."

"You recall, Dr. Kwon, I was there at Hiroshima, and I sympathized with your people, all those Japs melted to muck. Now I wonder if I was too kind."

"Wow, that's really offensive. I'm not Japanese, by the way."

"Agent Orange, then. I protested its use in the sixties after seeing how it flayed the flesh of your hut-dwelling brethren. Now I see that no good can come from weepy liberalism."

704

"I'm not Vietnamese either, asshole. You realize you're asking me to do something that would cost me my job? Maybe it looks like a shitty job to you, and maybe it is, but you try changing your career when you're forty and see what kind of offers you get. I'm lucky to have a job at all and I'm not going to throw it away because you're baiting me with racial slurs."

I kicked his desk, punching a hole through weak wood; the awkward feel of a right foot missing three toes made me angrier.

"Then what good was all this, shrink? Month after month, 'Gød likes you best of all' *this*, 'you are his favored prophet' *that*? The Book of Zebulon Finch is utter sophistry if none of its chapter-verses results in a single action!"

"Who's Zebulon Finch? You're not making any sense."

"Sense, eh? Do you know the word's definition? 'Sense' is performing an action to elicit an outcome. It is what I must do if I, the wicked, am to receive any rest. If you do not have the gonads to unlock for me a single door, then you, good sir, are far more wicked than I. It is no wonder you lost your faith in Gød, shrink. The Gød we've discussed would have no faith at all in a slug like you."

We glared—oh, how we glared. When the wind through the window chasm rose to falsetto, Eric swiveled in his chair and disappeared behind his desk, only to resurface with the glass shard in one hand and the thrown Bible in the other. With methodical movements he placed the shard, a genuine prohibited weapon, in the top drawer, which he locked with a key, and set the Bible before him, which he opened to the first of his adhesive notes.

"Esther," said he. "The only book in the Old Testament that never mentions Gød. I think we'll find that to be significant. My theory? There's no one in Esther worthy of Him."

"Fuck. You."

My curse sizzled, the pages of the Bible ignited, the window caked with ash, the ceiling mizzled smelt, and through choking brown smoke I made my backdraft adieu, my clothes on fire, my flesh pouring steam, my soul a red coal, still glowing.

XI.

ERIC DIDN'T SIC SIKES ON me. That is something, though in retrospect, I wish he had, for any catacomb into which Scrimm's chief grave digger might have stuffed me would have been preferable to all that I saw, heard, and did during my final days at Bear Claw. Nurses and doctors could not help but note my disengagement, but had neither the time nor inclination to address it. My diet of Red Heavies did not change.

Eric pretended to rebound—it was, as he'd said, his job—by mining Biblical topics he believed tallied with my purported history. His most vigorous effort was his survey of pre-Christian resurrections, starring Isaiah ("Thy dead shall live, their bodies shall rise"), Ezekiel ("Behold, I will open your graves, and raise you from your graves, O my people"), and, most hauntingly, Daniel ("And many of those who sleep in the dust of the earth shall awake, some to everlasting life, and some to shame and everlasting contempt").

I didn't give the coward the gratification of a single interested word. As gradually as Lucky had scratched his way through leather, hair, skin, skull, and brain, I wore through Eric Kwon until our sessions were as lymphatic as A.M. Analytic. Each day he sent me back to Kant earlier, which put me in no better mood, for outside I had to evade Jackie, who'd gone bestial with fear for Farm Boy. Her heightened agitation resulted in new meds, and her cusses became unintelligible behind spattering yellow froth until she, too, was plucked from gen pop and stashed away, maybe in the Back Ward, maybe alongside Chad, or maybe in Spinoza with Ry, where the odd couple could go raving mad together.

Not since the days of strewing Merle's ashes across the Cascade Range had I been so alone. Unbeknownst to me, the clockwork of the end had been winded. In March of 1991, in the flat, ugly gray of night, came a soft tapping upon the window of Kant-17.

I bounded from bed and peered through glass. His slicked hair was in fins from his running, his generous forehead greased with sweat, his mustache chewed at by crooked teeth. It was Héctor, the singing saint, returned to his old ward in a mood so diametric to his typical placidity that I was struck with terror. He held no mop, pushed no caddy of cleaners. There was only one explanation for why he'd come to me in such a state.

The familiar sound of his key sliding the bolt turned my stomach. He opened the door himself and glanced at the nurse's station—there was no telling how he'd lured her away—and beckoned me to hurry. I stepped barefoot into the hall; it was a long, black throat, pale-tongued by moonlight. Héctor rasped what English he could.

"You know the place?"

Jackie had seen to it. But even if I made it inside Spinoza unseen, what was my plan? Attempt a *la silenziosità* Hail Mary, despite the likelihood that giving Ry a glimpse of his lonesome death would further cripple him? Lead Ry over the fence, down the bluffs, and along the Atlantic, where I could teach him a fugitive's existence? There were no answers, and yet I was nodding.

"*Rápidamente*," said Héctor.

No red tag would protect me if I were caught, but neither had

Héctor left himself a safe out. He had no choice but to stay behind and manage the nurse as I ran toward the western end of the hall and skidded down the stairwell, my naked feet providing stealth. Next I crouched in the foyer, waiting for the ruby pinprick of a smoking orderly to float back into an office. Finally I plunged outside into indecisive storm gusts that heaved rain at me in clumps, a crystalline sprinkling one second, a bucket deluge the next.

It was, you recall, an expansive campus, and I traversed it tree to tree, shrub to shrub, avoiding the few sodium lamps that hadn't died in the 1980s. The night was as hard and loud as I was soft and quiet, shrieking with gales off a tormented ocean, but also, I swore, the gales of the nation's tormented, individual agonized laments familiar and dear to me—is that you, Church, leading the charge after all these years?—begging that I balm their sore souls with a prophet's affirmation that their pain had meaning and purpose. As I dodged from Kant to Hobbes to Pascal to Descartes, the phantom pleas were joined by real ones birdsonging from all eight wards. Did Bear Clawers always so vocalize at night? Or had my felonious flight aroused a hibernating hope?

Shadow-puppet people behind window shades were the only signs of staff until I came upon Spinoza, caddy-corner to the Back Ward, the former of which was dormant, but the latter of which hosted a confabulation of nightshifters laughing as they passed a flask. The smartest avenue of approach, as Jackie had indicated, was through the potter's field, and though one could hardly hide behind the meager footstones, there was a fence that put me in position to wait unnoticed. Fifteen, twenty, thirty minutes passed. At some point, my absence from Kant-17 would be noticed; at some point, Héctor would have to lock whatever doors he'd opened.

At last the orderlies went back inside the Back Ward to burn off their alcohol fuel, and I sprinted for Spinoza. Héctor was as good as his unspoken word: The front door swung open. I closed it behind me with as little noise as I could, and then did what I'd seen the Marlboro Man do every single day in the wild—take a knee and go still, listening for activity, approach, or peril.

Spinoza was recognized as Bear Claw's original building. It followed that it was both the most ornate and most dilapidated. Doors were too warped to properly shut, and I could hear a radio babbling from a room to my right. I headed left, and as the radio faded, the evensongs of the mentally ill cohered into duos and trios instead of the full chorus to which I was accustomed.

Héctor had thought of everything. A door to a service staircase was unlocked, but the door to the second floor wouldn't budge. The janitor was guiding me to the third floor, and I took the final steps with speed and the door with force. The instant I barged into the short, dead-end hall, with its once-beautiful ceiling soffits browned by rain leakage and art-deco sconces unlit for a century, I recognized the voice that Jackie, having had the advantage of months in the cemetery, had already identified.

It was Ry Burke. But it also *wasn't* Ry Burke; even as he'd suffered, he'd always kept a tight, Midwestern timbre, as if mortified that his noises might disturb others. His new noises were looser, a labored, uneven panting burbling with simian hoots that might have been comical if not so sickening. I rushed down the hall, my wet feet slapping the tile, until I came upon a vibrating door and threw it open.

Ry gasped; saliva suctioned down his throat, and he choked and spat. He had no reason to know that Héctor had unlocked his door, not that it mattered, for one of his legs had been shackled to the bed as if he were a monster. The cuff itself wasn't upsetting; it was of hospital plastic, its vinyl tether too short to be used for strangulation. What upset me was how Ry, a boy of great physical shyness, strained to pull from it, head whipping, torso torqued against the floor as if trying to escape a racing fire.

He'd torn through three other cuffs, whether that night or weeks earlier, I could not say. Though I had yet to get a clear look at Ry, he recognized me right off, and not with the elated reaction for which, in my heart, I'd hoped. He dropped to bruised knees and snapped his face toward the floor. Gingerly I shut the door and crept close. Spit, maybe blood, was hot beneath my soles.

Ry's head had been shaved, crudely enough that I could see scabbed nicks. Was it his baldness that brought him such shame? I knelt, placed my hand upon a shoulder so bony, it gouged my palm, and winced at the bedsores blotching his calves.

"Ry," whispered I. "It's me."

"G'way."

His was a mushy mumble.

"I'm here to help. I won't leave until I've helped you."

His protruding bones shook. Straitjacket buckles rattled.

"Can yoo? Can yoo weally hewp?"

"I can try, Farm Boy. Just show me how."

His shook his head, over and over, his scalp stubble scraping my chin.

"Oh, Fwank. Oh, hewp me, hewp me, Fwaaaaaank."

He lifted his head. His skin was leaden; he hadn't eaten in days. His sockets were oily black; he hadn't slept in weeks. His lips were stretched wide in misery, and from them ran streams of saliva, for there were no more teeth to act as dam. A merciful lack of light obscured details beyond red gums, black abscesses, and the pale rear molars he'd been unable to reach. Yes, Reader, he'd yanked every tooth he could for the same reason he'd yanked his fingernails. The softhearted boy expected obliteration and was determined not to harm others along the way.

Hairless, toothless, armless, half-blind, and yowling like a new-born, Ry was barely human. He ground his grubby forehead into my chest and cried, which soon lengthened into a scream, and I held him there, tried to think of words to becalm him, something about *Knight Rider*, yet came up with nothing, and so stroked his scabby dome and stared in stupefaction at the plaster walls chipped all over, or so I deduced, from attempts to shatter his teeth. He'd survived Mr. Furrington; he'd survived Jesus Christ; but the third demon had come, and something told me that as few teeth and nails as Ry had left, his torturer had them in endless supply.

"Fwaaaaaaaaaaaaank."

No more high-flying plots or salty schemes. Here it was, the actual bloody thing of it, of men and madness, and I could no longer allow myself fantasies about a secret passage out of this dead-end hall. Since the first night of hearing Ry's cries, I'd hoped that saving his soul might save my own. In seconds, my own fate became insignificant. My mission, realized I, was not one of rescue. It was one of deliverance.

"Shh, shh. Frank will make it all go away."

I pushed the bed in front of the door, but not without making noise. Others in the hall awakened, and I had no doubt their arousal would mobilize staff. Yet five minutes passed before I heard the stairwell door open, by which time I'd removed my jumpsuit, exposing my body to the one person who wished to hug himself closer to it, tore apart my tired old abdominal stitches, and peeled back the flap Leather had cut in 1903. My stomach had a hole in it—do you recall the German bayonet stab of November 10, 1918?—and into that hole I worked my thumb and tore it larger. At first, nothing came out besides Little Johnny Grandpa's marble, shiny as ever for having been protected for decades. I stopped its roll with my toes, then jostled my torso until the Red Heavies inside began to gush like blood, one drop for every person I'd failed to save. What a sight: I was bleeding, alive one more time, so that I could deliver death.

In a room cleared of all potential weapons, these undigested drugs were the only option. My peripheral vision caught a nurse's face in the door window, and I heard her try to open the door, then pound against it, then order me to open it, but I was busy scooping up Red Heavies because, though I had only one hand with which to do it, it was better than Ry's zero, and I cupped handfuls like Eucharist bread, into which Ry could dip his face and pull pills onto his tongue and onward back to his molars to grind, while sending others straight down his throat on a gruel of spittle.

"Sawah," hiccuped he past a mouthful.

"I'll tell her you love her," said I.

"Mamma."

"Her too. I'll find a way."

Years of meds went into his stomach as the nurse departed and came back with a second. I kept shoveling and cupping, and Ry kept nodding and gobbling. Alarm bells went off, and the hall, already an aviary, grew louder as Bear Claw's night guard stormed it. I left Ry to the business of swallowing while I knotted the arms of my jumpsuit to the door handle—antiquated Spinoza still had handles inside the rooms—and twisted the garment around the bed frame before pulling it back toward the door, using leverage to multiply my strength. Orderlies threw themselves against the door; Ry, on instinct, started licking pills off the floor; and I tried to smile, knowing I'd done the right thing when no one else could or would, despite my heart having broken as surely as the Bible had broken Eric's window.

Some people, reflected I, are never given a chance.

Other people get far too many.

It took much labor and cursing for them to get inside; keeping that door shut was the final heroic effort of my death. When six men exploded forth in a slapstick of twisted limbs, Ry was on his back, eyes rolled to white, stomach straining against the straitjacket. Orderlies and nurses alike balked at the shock of so many red pills being crushed beneath their shoes. How had Frank Zipp stolen so many? They rushed to Ry, rolled him to his side, stuck fingers down his throat, and began a contradictory program of Heimlich and CPR. By the time anyone thought to deal with me, I'd tucked Johnny's aggie back where it belonged, twisted stomach tissue like a bag of bread, and gotten myself halfway back into my jumpsuit.

With utmost brutality two men took me, taking care to ram my shins to the bed frame and drive my noggin to the door, neither of which caused me pain, but did rob me of a last look at Ry; I admit that to see the young man, tormented his entire life, at last in a place of peace would have been a lovely sight. I was roughed into a hallway of deafening sirens and sent careering down the hall, but it was all right, for Eric had sworn that the Bible had been written by geniuses, and those geniuses had confirmed that good violence existed, and all I'd done was prove it. There was pride to be found in that, and serenity as well.

I was heaved out of Spinoza, collared by my punishers, and

dragged oceanward, straight to the Back Ward, where the posse from earlier waited, flask and laughs replaced with fists and expletives, and they took over, displaying their skill by abusing me with practiced ease, thwacking me against this wall, then that, as they stuffed me into a straitjacket and took me by the neck, not with hands but with an iron rod that kept them at farmhand distance, with which they steered me into each and every cell door until every sleeper was awake and raving. I was pushed past Ry's old cell, and my old cell as well, at which point I knew where I was going.

I doubted even Héctor had keys enough to unlock all three doors of the Thunder Room. I'd imagined it as a witchy cave with an earthen chimney through which lightning could strike. Instead it was smaller than the cells, or looked so because of all the equipment, so much of it burnished copper and old yellow tubing. I was slung to a hospital bed, face-up toward a satellite-dish lamp brought close and blazed to full wattage. I could feel straps tighten across my thorax and knees and heard a deep mechanized growl.

Fear nothing, I told myself. *Ry is free of all this.*

A nurse injected my arm with sedative but failed to notice when it dribbled out the kabob-skewer holes I'd self-inflicted to avert Mrs. Shoemaker. I rolled my dry eyes upward and saw an Indian headband being prepared, just as offensive as the one lowered upon Zebulon X as he'd been buried in New Jersey beach sand, though instead of being affixed with braided deerskin, quillwork, and eagle feathers, this one was decorated with steel electrodes a nurse was slathering with lubrication. I watched as this band was cinched tight around my forehead, concealing, to my dismay, *THE END.*

I'd been told during admission how Bear Claw had been at the forefront of lobotomy. It made good sense that they yet propagated

715

the shunned, but still quite legal, practice of shock therapy, that infamous last-resort procedure for the severely depressed and schizophrenic. My Dearest Reader is not gullible; you know in your heart that the procedure was also used by doctors who wanted to watch their unruliest patients fry. The band about my cranium did not permit me to turn my head; I had to wait until Superintendent Scrimm, ten minutes later, caned into my field of vision.

"I never miss electroconvulsion," confided he.

A foam block was wedged between my jaws. I heard a hum and darted my eyeballs rightward, where upon a counter squatted a cream-colored box with plastic oven-switches and a needle meter. A nurse's neoprene-gloved finger hovered over a toggle labeled, and I do not jest, TREAT. Abruptly the box was blacked out by Scrimm, hunched so close that I could see every squiggled blue vein pulse from beneath his rice-paper skin. He fashioned from his face one of Reichsführer-SS Himmler's Death's-Heads.

"You think you're more qualified than we are to deliver mercy, do you? You think you did your friend Mr. Burke a favor? My, my, my. You must think yourself awfully clever, hoarding all those pills. Well, I have a little surprise for you, Mr. Zipp. Those pills were placebos."

Was that sweat, an impossible secretion, puddling beneath my headband?

"Pla-ce-bo. It means the medicine you've taken all these years hasn't been medicine at all. It's been corn starch, cellulose, a pinch of sugar, pressed into a polymer mold."

Only then did I feel sick. Ry hadn't wolfed lethal loads of tranquilizer but pounds of candy, like Franny White on a trick-or-treat bender; he was not dead, not even close, and his agonies would expand like a tumor until they absorbed his every last functional part. I heard the crumpled-paper snaps of positive and negative ions, saw metal pinchers being fastened to the electrodes. I tried to scream Ry's name, but that damn foam bit! The cry came out as *Why!*

"Why? Because I'm old enough to know that red-taggers aren't ever sick—that's why," replied Scrimm. "They come to us to hide. And Barraclough Psychiatric Center doesn't waste taxpayer money on fakers."

Ask Dr. Leather if a corpse seizes from electrical current with a frenzy equal to that of a live body. Bursting lights catapulted me into a thoughtless black, which sounds like the state of Nothing in Particular I'd been chasing since Death-Day One, but was not, Reader, not at all. The sound of electrical torture was, oddly enough, quieter when heard at close proximity, a hard, insistent *NNNNNNN.* Unspecified seconds, maybe minutes, passed, and I came back, the lamp gyrating over me as if recently slugged, the faces of Scrimm and his playmates gazing down in cool arbitration, the malodor of burnt scalp slithering up my nostrils, and all I could think was that the Thunder Room's next resident might be Ry. I needed to use up all the electricity, break the engines, leave it a smoking wreck, and so I tried, my screams lost amid those of every other madman who'd once cried out his emphatic existence.

"DO IT AGAIN!"

NNNNNNN.

"AGAIN!"

NNNNNNNNNNNNNN.

"AGAIN, BASTARDS!"

NNNNNNNNNNNNNNNNNNNNN.

"AGAIN! AGAIN! AGAIN!"

NNNNNNNNNNNNNNNNNNNNNNNNNNNNNN.

XII.

RY BURKE DIED ON APRIL 12, 1991. He did not die well. It is only fair that I lay plain the extent of my failure. Three weeks after they pumped his stomach of placebos, two weeks after he broke his toes against cement to pulverize toenails that might scratch someone, and one week after he abandoned English in favor of the insectile argot of the third demon, Ry, naked for a bath, was being lowered toward tub restraints when he wiggled free, cackling in a uncharacteristic manner, and drove an orderly's head to the basin with such force that the porcelain shattered, and while nurses tried to staunch the orderly's jetting blood, Ry took two shards of porcelain and jammed them into his gums to create fangs, and with these fangs attacked the nurses, blinding one and shredding the face of another, until he was killed with repeated blows to the back of the head.

Where the demon went after that, who can say?

America is a big country.

The death of a patient and orderly and the disfiguring of two nurses was the excuse the state needed to shutter Bear Claw for good. Scrimm was ousted, and an Augusta bureaucrat was flown in to oversee the six-month transfer of hundreds of mentally ill into other hospitals, private care facilities, or back into a society that, more often than not, had no help to give them. The parking lot echoed daily with the sobbing of forced departures. Bear Claw had been an abusive home, but it had been a home nonetheless, and the friends the patients had made there had kept them alive. Now those friends were gone.

The bulldozing of Bear Claw's blight was the quickest way to get it out of headlines. On occasion I would spy protestors marching against demolition, some with the goal of facilitating investigations, others wishing to award the hospital landmark status. Both factions lost: Spinoza, police tape still caught on its eaves, was leveled first, and next the hydraulic cranes, backhoes, excavators, trenchers, and tractors went after Galileo, Hobbes, and Pascal, with what patients were left being expedited out through eddying billows of white construction dust.

The Back Ward was identified for what it was—a befilthed oubliette unfit for the twentieth century—and by summer it had been razed and I was back in Kant, the same living-dead boy as ever except for when I looked in the bathroom mirror. Electroshock burn marks covered the top and right side of my head. My right ear, previously in mint condition minus the lobe Leather had scalpeled back in 1907, had been torched to a black disc. And my hair—well, I might have been seventeen, but I now knew the cool-breeze tickle of male hair loss. A tuft on the left side of my head had survived, but I enjoined upon Bear Claw's barber to shave it the day before he, too, was let go.

The single good deed I managed during the protracted death of both Ry and Bear Claw was to acquit Héctor of malfeasance. I insisted that I'd stolen his keys, and given the other feats I'd pulled off—they never did figure out how I'd stockpiled Red Heavies—they believed it. Héctor thereby avoided redress and sentencing, though that does not mean he kept his job. He disappeared during the next round of layoffs before I had an opportunity to thank him for what

719

he'd done, or hear, one last time, the soft lullaby of *Duérmete, mi niño*.

Of the original ten buildings only three still stood. One of them was Cicero, and I was confused the day Glover came to room 17 to take me there. His frightful leader, Sikes, was gone by then, and Glover, always so stony, seemed wistful. As we ambled around the chain-link fence holding in the Locke cafeteria debris, he gazed at pink clouds as if noticing, decades late, that beauty existed.

Cicero was filled with people for the first time in a decade: hard-hatters consulting clipboards, pushing furniture down stairwells, tossing file cabinets out windows, and spray-painting demolition symbology over every wall and floor. It was hard to believe Eric Kwon would be onsite during Cicero's death spasms, but when Glover gestured at the coffin-office, there he was, pausing from filling a box with books to sneeze out a nebula of grit. He wiped his nose, noticed me, and in one gesture sent Glover away and signaled me forward.

I hadn't seen him in five months. He'd lopped his ponytail in favor of a cut better suited to adult life. His left ear betrayed its pin-prick, but carried no hoop. He wore jeans and a sweatshirt—moving-day clothes—and took a seat on one of the packed boxes, for the desk and chairs had vanished. He nodded at another box, but I did not take it. He shrugged and slapped his hands free of dust.

"Nice of the state to keep me around this long, right? I've been trying to make it worth their while. Those mattresses stacked outside, I've got it worked so they're being shipped to Sudanese hospitals. I'm transferring to Bangor myself. I start Monday. Private practice. It'll be a big change, but a good one. It was tough out here. Not that I have to tell you that."

I said nothing.

Eric sighed. "You all right?"

720

I said nothing.

"You're probably wondering what's going to happen to you. Barraclough's hardly got any patients left. Deinstitutionalization, they call it—DI. Everyone must go. Personally, I have my doubts. Warehousing people like this was no good, that's obvious, but . . . didn't they learn anything from desegregation? That was a good idea too, but they forgot to build any means to enforce it, you know? They're relying on what? Christian charity? That's fucked up, if you ask me. Sorry, my language. Although I guess I'm not your shrink anymore. So, yeah. It's fucked up. They DI all you guys, they're going to end up with thousands on the streets and thousands in jail. And we're all patting each other on the back."

An indignant ghost whispered, and I relayed what it said. "'You look at the jails and the prisons and tell Ritchie Tucker what you see. They'll be packed like a hoghouse with brothers.'"

Eric elbowed sweat from his face. "Who's Ritchie Tucker?"

I shrugged. "Just another dead man."

"Yeah, well, he was on the money. It's going to hit blacks the worst. You don't have money to pay for private care, and you're going to be shit out of—"

Eric whapped a thick text into the box and with his foot sent the box skidding across the room. He stood and turned away to hide what I suspected was the face of a man aware that he was leaving a job half-done. He stared up at the triangular hole in the window. A wily September wind waggled through and whisked his cropped hair. I'd preserved perfect apathy since Ry's demise, yet two rats began to gnaw at me, the first Guilt, the second Empathy.

"From the Back Ward to the back alleys," said I. "Things shan't ever change."

721

"But things *could* have changed. I could have listened better. I could have helped someone, anyone. I could have made a difference."

"Decay is irreversible."

Eric put both hands to his face. He issued no sound for a disquieting minute before whipping down his hands as if to clear his fingers of blood. He took a ballasting breath and wheeled around, his red eyes scouring my every gruesome part. He was, I think, estimating my weight, not in gold but in a substance even rarer.

He went back to packing books.

"You're free," said he.

Shouting foremen, clattering jackhammers, whirring bandsaws— had I heard him right?

"Say again?"

"I have the authority, all right? I'm the only one left who has it. You're done, Frank. Go to Plato's front office. Pick up your stuff and get out of here."

It is difficult to say what other resolution I expected. Crouching inside Kant until a wrecking ball crashed through my wall and blasted me to dust? Nevertheless I felt like a child being led from his mother by a marm; only the room's void of furniture kept me from finding a hat rack for support, a chair-back for balance, a sofa for collapse.

"Did I make you believe in Gød again?" managed I. "If so, I take it back."

Eric laughed.

"Don't give yourself so much credit." He glanced at me and, if I'm not mistaken, smiled. "You did make me think, though, I'll give you that. About the Bible. About things I hadn't thought about in forever. About how you can write hundreds of pages trying to get toward a

722

truth and never get there, but still, that doesn't mean that those pages weren't worth the effort, you know? The search, the struggle? What the hell else do we have?"

"I don't want to search or struggle. Not anymore."

"I don't think you get a choice. Forget what I believe about you, what anyone believes. If you believe you are what you say you are, you have to keep searching. You're so close now. I can feel it. Can't you? Go to a community center if you want to; the front office has a thousand pamphlets. Me, I don't think that's where you belong. Go to Glastonbury Tor. Hike Mount Sinai. Watch the sun rise over Easter Island and figure out what it all means. Because if you're right, and there's a world without death, then all this around us is a kind of dream. Go wake up, why don't you?"

Somehow I was still standing.

"I'm afraid," whispered I.

He stepped closer. The morning sun splashed over me.

"We talked about David. The Hebrew Bible's greatest king, greatest lover, greatest warrior-poet. And yet he's shown coveting and adultering and murdering. The best of people, Frank, can do the worst of things. The line between good and evil, I don't think it's drawn in the sand where we can see it. I think it's drawn inside the heart. Only you know when you cross it. Only you know when you've decided which side you're going to end up on."

"I don't want to fail, not again."

"What's failure? If there's a plan to creation, even your long, long life is too puny to see it. There could be a third testament being written as we speak. What if we're in the middle of it? What if these words I'm saying are words in a book being read right now by someone like us, searching and struggling, looking for guidance not from biblical guys in dusty old robes but from us, you and me, Frank, right here in Lubec, Maine?"

A Neanderthal hit the doorframe with a hammer.

"You guys about out?" bellowed he. "We gotta gut the electrics."

Eric held up a finger to buy a minute.

He lowered that hand upon my shoulder.

"There's part of me," confided he, "that hopes that some of the patients manage to hide out, you know? Then when all the wreckers are gone and there's all these odd parts of buildings still standing, they crawl out and take ownership of the whole mess, make it their own kingdom and run it however they want. See if the serfs can do any better than the lords."

I laid my hand gently atop his. Hot, cold: like that, it blended to a warmth.

"'Twould be America's most fitting epilogue," agreed I. "The inmates running the asylum at last."

XIII.

THE OLD BULB FLUTTERS—

It is challenging to see—

So challenging, indeed, that I wonder, dost the flicker emit from a chandelier resplendent, blinking so as to inform us, with the deference due to such esteemed Madams and Messieurs, that our opera, one of Wagnerian scope, has finally struck its final note?

Startle not, my sweet, as you stir from the dreamworld; it is only I, your gentle escort, patting your silk-gloved hand. Lower your theater glasses so that I might whisper you from your reverie. If not the alteration of light quality, surely the basso profundo bombast and soaring arpeggios, not to mention the demise of nearly the entire cast of characters, advised you that our two-act *tragédie lyrique* has come upon its denouement? Listen—hear the rustle of tassels? It is a stagehand at a rope—the curtain is about to drop.

Reality's exit-hall illumination requires some acclimation. Our box seat is not the red velvet mahogany armchair of your fantasy, but a child's school desk wedged into a concrete vault beneath the bulb that, for the past several hundred pages of autobiographing, has dimmed, with steady speed, to a russet brown and adopted a zoetrope sputter, as if each step of the businesspeople one hundred stories above me jars it toward extinguishment. Even through the strobe, you can see glowing finger bones where my flesh has worn away due to the clutching of pencils, including this one racing across these final pages of the final notebook. Unlike me, I do not think the bulb shall survive the hour.

The Uterus of Time ends not in rebirth but in abortion.

Quick, let us balance our accounts. I approached Plato Manor as Eric Kwon instructed, anticipating a trap, but was handed a box containing all I'd relinquished at admission: Gordo's knife, Piano's map, Merle's photo, the Barker's newspaper notice, the Little Miracle Electric Mexican Stuttering Ring, Merle's blue slacks and black hooded sweatshirt, and, astonishingly, zipped plastic baggies containing Ruthie's thousands of dollars. At the box's bottom was the Excelsior, though someone in Plato was having me on, the same as when I'd reclaimed my belongings after Operation Weeping Willow, for the pocket watch had been recently winded. How else to explain its ongoing *tick, tick, tick?*

A Frank Zipp autograph later, and I was DI'd. No one halted me when I walked up the same woodland path I'd driven down with Rigby in 1985. When I reached the road, I veered through a ditch and into underbrush, heading east through the woods. In a few hours, I detected, closer than ever, the ocean I'd been hearing from Kant-17 for years yet had never laid eyes upon. I sat in the damp forest; with nocturnal scurriers, I waited out the night. When morning threatened, I crept the final mile so that, consistent with Quoddy Head State Park's claim to fame, I would be the first sentient being to see the sun rise over America.

The Maine cliffs were as vertical as alcazars, furred with moss and clutching in creviced fists wads of fog like cannonry smoke, while far below, silver tides streaked over black sand. When the sun emerged, it turned the rock face red and each particle of tossed surf into a dewdrop of honey. I closed my eyes and osmosed the fresh day through my other four senses: the warmth over my skin like rubbing hands; the bouquet of sun-crisped autumn leaves; the sharp grate of sea salt against my tongue; the flip-flap of worm-getting birds chased off by light. Since Eric's trusted Mitochondrial Eve, humanoids had greeted the sun in this way and felt reborn. Another dawn, another chance.

But not for Zebulon Finch, no matter the strength of Eric's case. I'd done everything backward. I'd watched the sun set on the banks of Lake Michigan in 1896 as my century of midnight had begun, and now, as it ended, I watched that very same sun rise. I lifted my ear, the non-charred one, to listen for the approach of ghosts, perhaps the *hweeeeee . . . fweeeeee . . .* that had chased me across the planet. There was nothing, and with no one left to pursue, why would I continue to run? I took a minute to fantasize about living life as depicted in the dayroom board game of the same name, hopping into my purple station wagon, inserting a few pink-and-blue peg children, and tootling over green plastic hills to the blank white mansion at the finish line.

The fog was as filmy as a negligee and just as easily lifted. Tempests, though, clashed sabers over the Atlantic, a memento mori that storm clouds forever brewed, and everyone, not just Ry Burke, must take up arms against demons preparing to swoop on ill winds. It is not, I think, inaccurate to say that our fair country, when seen at its worst—in other words, its truest—is one giant Thunder Room.

No—no—

Just now, our brave bulb died for ten seconds.

Hasten, Zebulon, hasten!

Had I kept during my Bear Claw incarceration a journal of vacation spots to hit when I got out, Manhattan would not have made even the alternates. I hadn't breached New York City limits since Martin Luther King Jr.'s 1967 United Nations march, which, for me, had been followed hours later by the Stuyvesant shoot-out that had slain Ritchie Tucker. Prior to that, the city had been a mire of agonized memories: reeling with Church through a glitterscape of ginned-up flappers, careening jazz orchestras, and brutal murders.

Yet New York was where I went, though hardly along a bird's path. A year disappeared before I got there, and when I try to justify it, I see only a smear of trashed alleys, graffitied viaducts, and cloverleaf-interchange hideaways, each of them framed by the black penumbra of my sweatshirt hood. The pariahs that people crossed the street to avoid crossed the street to avoid *me*. I traveled slowly, mindful of how effortlessly a softball had torn off three toes. My voice, during those rare times I used it, could still muster the tone of high breeding, useful for when I made calls to the last friends I had in the world—telephone operators. With them I was polite and patient, for I knew that the hard worker I sought had to surface eventually.

He did, and I made my way to his home. Eric had been right about metropolitan centers. The mentally disturbed now roamed in such numbers that even a limping, one-armed, black-hooded creep went ignored. New York streets were populated enough with memories that each step I took sunk me lower, like the carriage wheels of my youth into muddy Chicago roads. My mental map was nevertheless true, and in Spanish Harlem I hunched beneath a street lamp, which turned snowflakes into fireflies, and cased a drab-bricked apartment complex until, among the predawn exiters, I saw a fellow who, though hidden beneath coat, scarf, and hat, was of unmistakable square shape.

Having neither subway tokens nor the desire to rouse the ire of grouchy commuters, I decided to knick my prey before he descended into the 6 train's howling tunnel. I took hold of his elbow, and it speaks to his exceptional good nature that he did not wrench it away with an urbanist's rightful disgust at the social infraction. He turned, ducked to see beneath my hood, got the gist of my features, stopped walking, and stared, until snow turned his black mustache white.

"*Dios mío*," said Héctor. "Mr. Finch."

I smiled, hoping white teeth would show through the hood's dim.

"You remember," said I, "my real name."

He did not look overjoyed to see me, though joy hadn't been my expectation. From beneath his scarf I could see the pleased pudge of a tie; it was a sure sign he'd made professional headway. It was also a sign that he daren't be late, and yet, as befitting a hero like Héctor—I called him a hero in the first full paragraph of this manuscript, Reader, and I meant it—he gnashed his broad jaw for only seconds before drawing me into a noisy, slush-floored diner, where we took a syrup-stickied booth and he ordered black coffee from a waiter visibly tempted to toss me out for repelling better-paying customers.

I was shy. Being back amid humanity's crush overwhelmed me. As Eric had urged, people kept searching, kept struggling. I toyed with a curious foil packet of grape jam, thinking of the last time I'd felt so out of step with civilization—May 1919, when seven of the Seventh Marine Regiment, including Jason Stavros, having docked at Newport News, Virginia, spent one night in pre-Prohibition taverns, trying to recall how to laugh at normal volumes.

Héctor, too, was bashful, as our discourse before then had been curtailed to gestures through safety glass and a handful of hurried words. He stole glances over his coffee, like Church had while introducing me to his facial scars at a similar New York diner in 1925, and blinked his brown eyes in wonder. Had he and I survived Bear Claw uninfected with insanity, or had we gone so mad that all this was an elaborate delusion?

729

"You are . . . ," ventured I, "of adequate health?"

Snow melted down his cheek like a tear.

"*Lo siento*," whispered Héctor. "I am sorry, Mr. Finch."

"What happened to Mr. Burke isn't your fault."

More snow melted.

"*Lo siento. Lo siento.*"

Héctor had been taking English classes at night ever since he'd gotten a job good enough that he no longer needed two, and it showed as our dialogue developed. The job, said he, was as a "technician" at the World Trade Center, a Financial District mecca bunched around twin towers that, for a flash in 1972, had been the tallest buildings in the world. How far he'd come from mopping up the spiteful urine of Bear Claw malcontents! I gleaned that he preferred the city; here, at least, malice came straight up to you, right on the street, and screamed.

How detailed is the Dearest Reader's memory? It was upon my earliest pages that I described Héctor's world as a far cry from ideal. His fertile wife had borne a quintet of rugrats, one of them chronically ill; his landlord was totalitarian and sadistic; his apartment verily hissed with *cucarachas*. All in all, bad news for Héctor, but for me, better news than I could have dreamed, for I'd come to him with an embryo of an idea, and now it birthed fully grown. A few thousand dollars would mean putting food and medicine on his family's table, if not an entirely new table in an entirely new apartment, and a few thousand dollars was exactly what I had. Furthermore, if there was one edifice Americans would defend above all others, it was that flamboyant shrine to wealth, the World Trade Center. What tomb could be safer?

Being a man of integrity, scruples, morals, you name it, Héctor was sickened by my proposal. He stood, put two dollars under his cup, and said he had to *trabajar*, which was true, and *ahora mismo*, which was also true, though what he wanted to say was that I needed to leave him and his family alone. Say this, however, he could not, partly due to the civility ironed into his genes and partly because—and this is, of course, but a theory—he sensed, and had always sensed, an abyss inside me the likes of which he'd never before peered into, and at Bear Claw, he'd peered into hundreds.

The bulb, Reader—it hissed, went caramel—hurry, hurry—

You already know Héctor acceded to my request; let us quicken through it. My politicking combined months of elbow-taking outside the 6 train with months, I presume, of deliberation each time he heard his child cough or he watched another entitled cockroach waddle across a plate of leftovers. I recognized his acquiescence before he did and began mental preparations before he began his logistical ones. Far beneath the World Trade Center's South Tower, explained he, was a compact sublevel, a byproduct of the skyscraper's construction to which he had, during specific windows of time, unfettered access. It would serve my purposes, supposed he, were I determined to go through with it.

One does not doubt the word of a man like Héctor. One gives him full payment up front and trusts in him to provide.

Entombment day: I used the spot of cash I'd reserved for contingencies and purchased from a streetside rack a button-down dress shirt I put on over my sweatshirt; I did not want the putrescent condition of my apparel to draw undue notice. I also bought a pair of stretchy polyester gloves and, with the help of my teeth, put both on the same hand, jumpy about such harebrained implausibilities as one magically flying off at the wrong moment, revealing to a crucial gatekeeper my wreck of flesh. The hood I kept up—it was a common fashion among teenage slummers—and because my enshrinement was to occur at night, it was late afternoon before I started off on what would be my final walk on Earth.

The stroll was twenty-two minutes in length, so how, I ask you, could it have burned so brightly with decades of stabbing and strangling detail? At Canal Street, I saw a trio of adolescent girls—one African, one Hispanic, one Italian—pool change to buy a hot dog for a homeless man; they asked him if he wanted sauerkraut or onions. Near Finn Square, I saw a walk-up upon which had been hoisted a flag with a pink triangle, the symbol for Gay Pride, and New Yorkers trundled past without pausing to plot arsons; the triangle, observed I, was nature's strongest shape, and also the pointiest. At the intersection of Broadway and Park Place, a kerchiefed young mother of Eastern European accent did perhaps the stupidest thing I'd seen in 113 years, stooping to pick up a spilled bag of groceries after making an unintelligible request of me, some random dirtbag, and *handing me her baby to hold.*

Being of one arm, I had to nestle the child against my stiff new shirt. The suckling was of diaphanous hair and chubbed cheek and gave me a look of skepticism while using shrimp fingers to tweak a button. It was so fragile, this little human; it would take no mastermind to destroy it, just a dope who quit paying attention for a single second. I held the cherub closer, until I could smell its baby-powder scalp and apple breath and diaper twang, and then held it closer still, until I could feel the puny flexes of its buttery muscles. This creature, thought I, had just entered the world, fresh and squawking, and yet would, in all likelihood, sprout into adulthood, fester into old age, and die, another damp package of spoilage buried in the earth, while

I kept going and going. I kissed its warm, milky forehead with my cool, coarse lips and repeated Héctor's plea: *Lo siento. Lo siento.*

What I recollect of Two World Trade Center: happy, colorful signs; sheer concourses of radiant steel; mezzanines of infinite glass; escalators to the sky, turning and turning.

Beneath it all, Héctor buried me like an acorn, perhaps to grow a family tree.

Inside the chamber, all was as promised: desk, spiral notebooks, box of pencils, simple sharpener. As the walls sealed off, the space constricted, though not in a way unfavorable; it became the cramped garage of Mr. Charles White, that refuge of birdhouse-building and radio-tinkering that carried the oil-and-sawdust smell of "know-how." Though my know-how was never so practical, I do believe I learned a thing or two during my death and, much more so, during the writing about it, for education is inevitable, even for the most indisposed of learners, given repetition. If our little bulb will endure a few more moments, I'd like to present a weak, though concise, justification; offer you one last ghost story; and then bid you the farewell that you are owed.

First, the excuse. Let us speak of Kansas, that most American of states, which boasts two residents of worldwide renown. The first: Kal-El, Superman, whom I idolized but, alas, whose strength and virtue I could not match. The second, however—L. Frank Baum's Dorothy Gale of Oz—now, this lass, Reader, is instructive. Had I needed to wait one hundred years before embracing my mausoleum fate? Of course not. I had only to quit horsing around and click my damned heels. But like Ms. Gale, I could not, and why? Baum, American to his core, knew why. Our country is a land of yellow-brick roads, and who can resist them? Not Columbus, not

Cortés, not the English, not the French, not the homesteaders, not the forty-niners. For me to glance backward would have been to see how my shoes had rubbed off the golden veneer, not to mention the countless witches upon whom I'd dropped countless houses. I have been the wickedest witch of all, hence this heaviest of houses dropped upon me by Héctor—and that is the extent of my mea culpa. One footnote: pay no attention to the man behind the curtain. He doesn't deserve the credit He takes.

Second, a ghost story, provided you are willing to further stretch your already distended incredulity. At only one point here in my tomb did I fear discovery. One day (or night; even with the Excelsior, I've lost track), roughly a year after interment, there came from within the substructure a creak I recognized as the steel door through which Héctor and I had passed. Indeed, this noise was followed by a patter of footfalls. Although Héctor had promised that my chamber would be invisible to the eye, I stopped writing—indeed, stopped moving at all—and listened.

I suspect that I held that pose for two weeks. It was evident that a group of workers had traveled to my lower level to affect a repair or upgrade. They were close to my secret location but not overly; the sounds of their sledgehammers, drills, and blow torches carried through my wood/cement/brick enclosure better than their voices. It was during what I suspect was that human custom of a "lunch break" that a radio was left playing, and far more loudly than usual.

Had it been public-radio news I would've altered my position to cover my ears, for the notion of transmissions from the outer world nauseated me. It was, however, a music channel, playing what the deliberately blasé DJ—no Wailin' Wendy Savage, this galoot!—dubbed "alternative music." The puzzle as to which music these artists served as alternative (had a bombing at the Grammy Awards robbed the nation of its premier songsters?) went unsolved during the ninety-minute "rock-block" of frothing guitars and unmelodious slurring. The bands were wholly dyspeptic, with crabby names to boot: Smashing Pumpkins, Meat Puppets, Nine Inch Nails, Pavement, Hole. Doubtlessly this reflected a teenage populace disaffected by something, but what else, Reader, was new?

So it was startling when, at the butt of this block, a song began that was like the preceding music in some ways (undertuned, unvarnished) but, in other ways, altogether different. It began with muffled snares, distracted cymbals, and a laggard finger-slide down the far end of a guitar, over which a confessional female vocalist rumbled along a guttural register. The song, the DJ would tell me four minutes and ten seconds later, was called "Shane," by a woman named Liz Fair, or Fare, or Faire, or Phair, though I prefer the first reading, as "fair" adeptly exemplifies a voice so unremarkable—like Wilma Sue in a begrimed inn or Merle in a collapsing trailer—that it was extraordinary to hear it being amplified at all.

The lyrics would snag the attention of any ex-grunt, a hazy recollection of a war breaking out, of not fathoming the scope of war's effects, of a resistance movement, of lying in bed alongside a lover like an adult while still feeling inside like a child. This alone was enough to reach me—and then began what I can only call a chorus, though it served no classic purpose of release or catharsis, instead bottoming into a chant that echoed about as if trapped in an empty culvert. The seven-word refrain, if you can believe it, and I still cannot, was as follows:

You gotta have fear in your heart.

These words were repeated a staggering twenty-five times in a row. Who was this weary mortal who sounded as if she'd glimpsed as much pain and suffering as I'd seen straight on? And having only glimpsed it, was her vision truer than one who'd been fully blinded? Her chorus—my chorus—Reader, it's all mixed up—clanged about my skull long after the DJ jettisoned listeners to commercials, after the repairmen returned, after they'd packed it up for the day, and then the week, and then, for all I know, forever. As often as I'd heard this warning since Luca Testa's first utterance, never had it come from one whose voice reached out to me like a hand, slow in sadness, true, but also in the certainty of the durability of sadness. Ms. Fair's fingers laced into mine, and her cool lips settled upon my burnt ear, and I believe, Reader, that she whispered the truth to me at last; that or I merely managed, over these final months of reflection, to arrive at the understanding myself.

The first question I asked upon discovering, in the Barker's tent, that I was a corpse: Why me, Gød, why me? Bunny Tucker, I have come to believe, was the one to chisel closest, shouting to me, *Of course it's your story, isn't it? Amerika's story is always going to be yours. White. Male. Probably rich.* I wasn't a random target of Gød, but rather chosen on purpose from the most privileged clique of the most privileged country; in other words, those who'd lost the animal sense of fear with which all of us are born.

But, Zebulon, you protest, even inside that 1 percent populace, your selection came at Job-like odds! I know, Reader; this has been my complaint. Yet I find myself contemplating the long, tangled string of geologic metamorphoses, biologic anomalies, societal upheavals, historical partialities, individual passions, and stupid flukes that had to occur to put me *here*, scribbling words, and you *there*, reading them. Is that not every bit as impossible? There's two impossibilities.

So why not three? Why not three million? We are one miracle interlinked with another, and another, and another, entire heavens located upon this single page as well as inside the fingertip that turns it.

The fear, I think, is staying aware of the miracle, of being young to the experience as opposed to being old to it. The walking dead aren't the cannibal creations of Mr. Romero but rather those people you see every day, stumbling through daily circles, lifeless already for having lost the fear. Are you seventeen, Reader? Or seventy-seven? It matters not. Pitch fear like coal into the combustor, stoke it, keep the shovelfuls coming, and you shall always be alive, always be young.

Third and final, my farewell. I have put into place an emergency plan, should these pages be discovered before they are matured to proper vintage. Weeks ago I sacrificed a page to compose a letter, which I have inserted beneath the front cover of the first notebook. It is addressed to an attorney by the name of Kraus, who helped Héctor and others in his building prepare a suit against their landlord. The threat of lawsuit was enough to get the boiler fixed, but the attorney remained pally with Héctor, who spoke of him as a gentleman of discretion. Discretion—that is what these notebooks would need, and so my letter assigns them to the care of this Mr. Kraus. Héctor even told me of the attorney's three grown children, one a chemical engineer, one a speech pathologist, and one (poor kid) a writer; all told, they sound like decent folk. Besides, have I better options?

The story, you see, keeps going. It does not end with me. It ends with you, and for this I am heartened—the Excelsior, my heart, ticks more loudly—can you hear it? I admit that I first called you "Dearest" with sarcasm. Tonight, though, I say it with a terrible true passion. I've written a half-million words, and what those words have built is not a book but rather a time machine with which I've been able to travel back and regard myself at pivotal points. This second-chance odyssey, however, I did not have to make alone. You were there, my Dearest Reader. I saw your tolerant smile when I was insulting, heard your hitched breath when I requested witness, felt your arms around me when I needed to be upheld. If love matters, and it does, may I put forward that I love you? I place a kiss upon your head as I did when saying good-bye to my sleeping mother: *au revoir, au revoir*. You let me borrow your fear—me, who never deserved it—and, for a little while, pretend that it was mine.

What I wish to give to you in return is the lesson of *la silenziosità* as revealed by Merle's vision. The past is perpetually in play, always malleable, ever salvageable. Did any of this story happen as I said it did? The telling of a tale puts a prism to it from which incalculable new angles rainbow forth. You made this as real as I; remember it however you'd like. What you do with your time alive defines you, Reader, but hear me, I beg you, when I say that you are *not done being defined*. Go out; break things. Go further; repair them. Break hundreds of hearts. Have thousands of children. Discover awe in a tangle of weeds; find delight in the pattern of a roll of mass-produced paper towels; live, Reader, live; live as hard as I died, and only then I will be happy.

Go ahead now, set down this page. Do not worry. It is not abandonment. Another reader will pick it up before long, and somehow, through the shared enchantment of the human heart, it will still be You, Dearest Reader, and it will still be Me. It's funny, isn't it? While we were distracted by the silly scraps that make up human history, you and I became eternal, impervious to rot, infinity itself. It is a sight better than you might have accomplished by yourself (this I think) and far better than I could have accomplished alone (this I know).

Oh!—the light, it gutters—
It is out, now, gone, gone, gone—
I cannot see the page—
But my old hand is as sure as a young one—
Now I rest that hand, and my soul as well—
It is your hands I am in from here on out, Reader—
And there is none other to whom I'd rather yield.

Yours in the ranks of death,

Zebulon Aaron Finch

CURTAIN CALL

[TC: +07.41.89.07. T: 07:16:06. N: 41°53'41.3023°. W: -87°37'25.8791°.
I/O: 00:05:19. ID: 009-098-813-8911-2191]

iédklvnmewopfitjghfrdvbckjksdeoiwekwejkdfoiweruigthgnjvkjl

soweruiopgtdhdgsnpđfyjkrkijwyuiqperiokmchnznvbagfdggjkid

zşkyqpwoeruighjfgklsdlmznxcnvfvgfdsdyhsjaslwigeqçdrhftp

pqlamzncvhfgjdkslworuirtĝkaåsxbtqbgtyghbmvjrueidmkxclmĵipm

vcgötplokijuqszwdefrtgbvcvsszrfaħtbnrurirtpotpgkfgjvnsdhasyue

itrotkgfjhbvnchsabxdpłlçjdřoyerksopwitugthbvncmnslsptigtfjqk

jasxkfdjkpźpppoiokkjccxzxbxbbvqqweleeerkmkklloidekkieugfth

giejkdopwkgflfmedkejflfdrkgwñiédklvnmewopfitjghfrdvbckjksdeoi

wekwejkdfoiweruigthgnjvkjlsoweruiopgtdhdgsnpđfyjkrkijwyuiqpe

riokmchnznvbagfdggjkidzşkyqpwoeruighjfgklsdlmznxcnvfvgfds

dyhsjaslwigeqŧdrhftppqlamzncvhfgjdkslworuirtĝkaåsxbtqbgtyghb

mvjrueidmkxclmĵipmvcgötplokijuqszwdefrtgbvcvsszrfaħtbnrurirt

potpgkfgjvnsdhasyueitrotkgfjhbvnchsabxdpłlçjdřoyerksopwitugth

bvncmnslsptigtfjqkjasxkfdjkpźpppoiokkjccxzxbxbbvqqweleeerk

mkklloidekkieugfthgiejkdopwkgflfmedkejflfdrkgwñiédklvnmewo

pfitjghfrdvbckjksdeoiwekwejkdfoiweruigthgnjvkjlsoweruiopgtdh

dgsnpđfyjkrkijwyuiqperiokmchnznvbagfdggjkidzşkyqpwoeruigh

jfgklsdlmznxcnvfvgfdsdyhsjaslwigeqŧdrhftppqlamzncvhfgjdksl

woruirtĝkaåsxbtqbgtyghbmvjrueidmkxclmĵipmvcgötplokijuqszwde

frtgbvcvsszrfaħtbnrurirtpotpgkfgjvnsdhasyueitrotkgfjhbvnchsabx

dpłlçjdřoyerksopwitugthbvncmnslsptigtfjqkjasxkfdjkpźpppoiokk

jccxzxbxbbvqqweleeerkmkklloidekkieugfthgiejkdopwkgflfmedke

jflfdrkgwñiédklvnmewopfitjghfrdvbckjksdeoiwekwejkdfoiweruigth

gnjvkjlsoweruiopgtdhdgsnpđfyjkrkijwyuiqperiokmchnznvbagfdg

gjkidzşkyqpwoeruighjfgklsdlmznxcnvfvgfdsdyhsjaslwigeqŧdrhftp

pqlamzncvhfgjdkslworuirtĝkaåsxbtqbgtyghbmvjrueidmkxclmĵipm

vcgötplokijuqszwdefrtgbvcvsszrfaħtbnrurirtpotpgkfgjvnsdhasyue

itrotkgfjhbvnchsabxdpłlçjdřoyerksopwitugthbvncmnslsptigtfjqk

jasxkfdjkpźpppoiokkjccxzxbxbbvqqweleeerkmkklloidekkieugfth

giejkdopwkgflfmedkejflfdrkgwñiédklvnmewopfitjghfrdvbckjksdeo
iwekwejkdfoiweruigthgnjvkjlsoweruiopgtdhdgsnpɗfyjkrki
jwyuiqperiokmchnznvbagfdggjkidzşkyqpwoeruighjfgklsdlmznxcn
vfvgfdsdyhsjaslwigeqtdrhftppqlamzncvhfgjdkslworuirtĝkaåsxbtqb
gtyghbmvjrueidmkxclmĵipmvcgötplokijuqszwdefrtgbvcvsszr
faħtbnrurirtpotpgkfgjvnsdhasyueitrotkgfjhbvnchsabxdpłlçjdřoy
erksopwitugthbvncmnslsptigtfjqkjasxkfdjkpźpppoiokkjccxzxbxbb
vqqweleeerkmkklloidekkieugfthgiejkdopwkgflfmedkejflfdrkgwñ
iévbcknpɗfydzşkygeqtdrhftpĝkaåsxbtqlmĵipmvcgötrfaħtbnbx
dpłlçjdřoyepźwñiévbcknpɗfydzşkygeqtdhftpĝkaåsxbtqlmĵip
mvcgötrfaħtbnbxdpłlçjdřoyepźwñiévbcknpɗfydzşkygeqtdhft
pĝkaåsxbtqlmĵipmvcgötrfaħtbnbxpłlçjdřoyepźwñiévbknpɗfydzşky
geqtdhftpĝkaåsxbtqlmĵipmvcgötrfaħtbnbxpłlçjdřoyepźwñiévbkn
pɗfydzşkygeqtdhftpĝkaåsxbtqlmĵipmvcgötrfaħtbnbxpłlçjřoyepźwñ
iévbknpɗfydzşkygeqtdhfpĝkaåsxbtqlmĵipmvcgötrfaħtbnbxpłlç
jřoyepźwñiévbknpɗfydzşkygeqtdhfpĝkaåsxbtqlmĵipmvgötr
faħtbnbxpłlçjřoyepźwñiévknpɗfydzşkygeqtdhfpĝkaåsxbtqlmĵip
mvgötrfaħtbnbxpłlçjřoyepźwñiévknpɗfydzşkygeqtdhf
pĝkaåsxbtqlmĵipmvgötfaħtbnbxpłlçjřoyepźwñiévknpɗfydzşky
geqtdhfpĝkaåsxbtqlmĵipmvgötfaħtbnbxplçjřoyepźwñiévknpɗydz
şkygeqtdhfpĝkaåsxbtqlmĵipmvgötfaħtbnbxplçjřoyepźwñiéknpɗy
dzşkygeqtdhfpĝkaåsxbtqlmĵipmvgötfaħtbnbxplçjřoyepźwñiékn
pɗydzşkygeqtdhfpĝkaåsxbtqlmĵipmvgötfaħtbnbxplçjřoyepwñiékn
pɗydzşkygeqtdhfpĝkaåsxbtqlmĵipmvgötfaħtbbxplçjřoyepwñiékn
pɗydzşkygeqtdfpĝkaåsxbtqlmĵipmvgötfaħtbbxplçjřoyepwñikn
pɗydzşkygeqtdfpĝkaåsxbtqlmĵipmvgötfaħtbbxplçjřoyepwñikn
pɗydzşkgeqtdfpĝkaåsxbtqlmĵipmvgötfaħtbbxplçjřoyepwñikn
pɗydzşkgeqtdfpĝkaåsxbtqmĵipmvgötfaħtbbxplçjřoyepwñikn
pɗydzşkgeqtdfpĝkaåsxbtqmĵipvgötfaħtbbxplçjřoyepwñiknpɗy

dzşkgeqťdfpĝkaåsxbtqmĵipvgötfaħtbbxplçjřoyepwiknpđydzşk

geqťdfpĝkasxbtqmĵipvgötfaħtbbxplçjřoyepwiknpđydzşkgeqťd

fpĝkasxbtqmĵipvgötfaħtbxplçjřoyepwiknpđydzşkgeqťdfpĝk

axbtqmĵipvgötfaħtbxplçjřoyepwiknpđydşkgeqťdfpĝkaxbtqmĵipvgöt

faħtbxplçjřoyepwiknpđydşkgeqťdfpkaxbtqmĵipvgötfaħtbxplçjřoyep

wiknpđydşkgeqťdfpkaxbtqmĵipvgötfaħtbxplçjoyepwiknpđydşk

geqťdfpkaxbtqmĵipvgötfaħtbxplçjyepwiknpđydşkgeqťdfpk

axbtqmĵipvgötfaħtbxplçjyepiknpđydşkgeqdfpkaxbtqmĵipvgötfaħt

bxplçjyepiknpđydşkgeqdfpkaxbtqmĵivgötfaħtbxplçjyep

iknpđydşkgeqdfpkaxbtqmĵivgötfaħtbxplçjep

iknpđydşkgeqdfpkaxbtqĵivgötfaħtbxplçjep

iknpydşkgeqdfpkaxbtqĵivgötfaħtbxplçjep

iknpydşkgeqdfpkaxbtqĵivgötfaħtbxlçjep

iknpydşgeqdfpkaxbtqĵivgötfaħtbxlçjep

iknpydşgeqdfpkaxbtqĵivgtfaħtbxlçjep

iknpydşgeqdfpkaxbtqĵivgtfaħtbxlçje

iknpydşgeqdfpkabtqĵivgtfaħtbxlçje

iknpydşgeqdfpkabtqĵivgtfaħbxlçje

iknpydşgeqdfpkabtqĵivgtfaħbxlje

iknydşgeqdfpkabtqĵivgtfaħbxlje

iknydşgeqdfkabtqĵivgtfaħbxlje

iknydşgeqdfkabtqivgtfaħbxlje

iknydşgeqfkabtqivgtfaħbxlje

iknydşeqfkabtqivgtfaħbxlje

iknydşeqfkabtqivgtaħbxlje

iknydşeqfkabtivgtaħbxlje

iknydşefkabtivgtaħbxlje

ikndşefkabtivgtaħbxlje

ikndşefkabtivgtaħbxle

745

ikndşefkativgtaħbxle
ikndşefkativgtabxle
ikndefkativgtabxle
ikndefkatigtabxle
ikndefkatigabxle
indefkatigabxle
indefatigabxle
indefatigable

Háááh háh hah/// ĐeĀrest ReĀĐer/Āre yoÜ theRRRRRRE?
ŴAit/// Wait/// W → a → i ↓ T ↓
noW i reTurn
↵ reTurn
as mr graY
↵ reTurn
The greaT//amerikan//novelisT
↵ return
mighT say
↵ return
Háááááááááááááááááá

BĒtter nõw? BEtter? Better/// →/caGe\ PaGeant↔Barker↔Johnny///
Gone muTe/// Teach me/Johnny/// Words R b33s/Mr Stick sir///
Reach/// Grab some/// LooK in hand/// B33s/Words/// Pointed//
soft///   Hours↔sting↔minutes↔sting↔years↔sting///   AlWays
This open Mouth/// WelcoMe/b33s/// FurrY leGs/// Sinus WiGGle///
SKull[question mark] Feelers[question mark] Itch//scratch///
Words→Worlds/// Mouth W-i-d-e/// Flood/bEEs/// StinG→sinG///
Throat clearinG/// Johnny goes//HACK/CouGh/snort[exclamation] I

746

cÃn do it/// So mŭch of Ŵorld/I hÃve leĀrneÐ so sloŴly/// BŭT in
lÃngŭÃge I hÃve ĀlWÃys been Ā qÜick leÃrnerrrrrrrrrrrrrrrrrrrrrr
rrrrrrrrrrrrrrrrrrrrrrrrrrrrrrrr rrrrrrrrrrrrrrrrr rrrrrrrrrrrrrr rrrrrrrr
rrrrrrrrrrrrrrrrr rrrrrrrrrrrrr rrrrrrrrrrrrrrrrrrrrrrrrrrrrrrrrrr
rrrrrrrrrrrrrrrr rrrrrr rrrrrrrrrrrr rrrrrrr rrr rrrrrrrrrrrr rrrrrrrrrrrrrr
rrrrrrrrrrrrrrrrrrr rrrrrr rrrrrrrr rrrrrrrrrrrrrrrrrrrrrrrr rrrrrr rrrrrr
rrrrrrrrrrrrrr rrrrrrrrrrrrrrrrÐÃmmITrrrrrrrrrr rrrrrrrr rrrrrrrrrrrr
rrrrrrrrrrrrrrrrrrrrrrrrrrrrrrrrrrr rrrrr rrr rrrrrrrrrrrrrrrrrrrr rrrrrrrrrrrrrrrrrrr
rrrrrrrrrr rrrrr rrrrrrrrrrFÜcKrrrr rrrrrrrrrrrrr rrrrrrr rrrrrrrrrrrr
rrrrrrrrrrrrrrrrrrrrrrrrrr rrr rrrrrrrr rrrrrrrrrrrrrrrrrrrrrrrrrrrrrr rrrrrrrr
rrrrrrrrrrrrrrrr rrrrrrrrrrrrrrr

SloWer/Z3bul0n/// Don't hurry don't be cocKY/// For once in Yr
stup1d d3ath/// Pretend this is Yr royal Quiet de luXe[exclama-
tion]/// Hunt/pecK/// pecK→PeeK from Yr blanKet of bEEs///
LooK Mother//mY proud sentences Grow/& Grow/& Grow///
NoW/lets trY punctuation {GraMMer, the dullest lesson, I want to
Go outside & plaY} // SloW/sloW//// Hello/Reader[period] Hello
aGain[comma] Reader[period] Hello,,Reader.. Hello, Reader.

Or Listener? InterPreter? ReceiVer[question mark x3] This is
a Machine but ≠ ~~machine~~//it is an eniGma. {But not EniGma
Machine sorrY vonLuth Háá} (1) cellular{tech} + (2) cellu-
lar{body}. MY KEEPER has attached ~~machine~~ to ManY other
bi0l0Gic iteMs to scanscanscan↔for Life but theY are 2oo b0rinG
[exclamation] I've Waited years0102030405 & years0607080910
for mY turn w ~~machine~~. But KEEPER is LÃźY. {EasY, Z3bul0n,
Yr temper.} KEEPER uses ~~machine~~ on Self{masturBation}
While I sit on Shelf. ←L00k it rhymes {JasonStavors Mr Poet

Collected WorKs Watch Yr back}. NoW atlastatlastatlast: w machine I can speaK/Write/thinK/send, reach out 2 You[x10].

Setting: KEEPER's shop. Shelves+cabinets+boXes of curios. Shop ≈ MuseuM but ≠[exclamation] KEEPER ♥ $$$ More than Life. Everysinglemorning for years1112131415, KEEPER (1) unlocks (2) windoWshades (3) lights (4) reGister (5) dusts curios (6) winds watch. Which watch↔watch which? The Excelsior. Beside me it danGles/Gleams/is winded/tickticktick. The Excelsior hanGs above a {old, faded, curling} label//Quite informative↓

GENUINE EXCELSIOR POCKET WATCH NAWCC-CERTIFIED SERIAL NUMBER 17437487 AS SOLD CIRCA 1895, FOUND ON BODY BELIEVED TO BE ZEBULON "MOTHER-FATHER SAVAGE" FINCH, ESTABLISHED U.S. CULT LEADER IN 1970S-80S, RUMORED SPACE TRAVELER, LINKED TO HOLLYWOOD ACTRESS BRIDEY VALENTINE (B.1891–D.1969). POCKET WATCH BUILT TO LAST! BIOLOGICAL MATTER AS-IS. ASK ABOUT PRICE.

I, Biological Matter, As-Is, ReGret to Inform the Reader {"Reader" 4 oldtimesake}: shop broWsers DO NOT Ask About Price. Browsers enter shop to escape octi-tentacles of snoW/rain/sleet. I knoW this Weather//I also know these Browsers/their Yoked shoulders & fat-lip frowns. Where o Where o Where is Z3bul0n F1nch? CHICAGO: homeland/scene of the crimes. I have ↵ returned, I thinK, to stand Final Trial. Hm-m-m-m are Browsers mY Jury of Peers? N000000. Browsers look @ Me & I must be an! astounding! sight! {old vanity?} yet Browsers show No Interest & I cannot puppy-dog bc I am MǓ̇TĒ {anger, anger} & it is only the machine, Right Now, after years1617181920 that gives me a Voice. ChicaGoans haVe Become halfhuman//theY are Kaposi's sarcomad w nodules/ jacKs/cords. Taptaptap & swipeswipeswipe & nodnodnod & blink-blinkblink, give↔take/send↔receive. Browsers wear reGalia of *Hitlerjugend* snuGness. Holstered with Weapons in Sexy Styles© for Mom & Fun Styles© for Kids. Their gizmos F*l*i*c*k*e*r before eVery distant Explosion. The Drill: (1) unfold plastic helmet (2) send↔receive warninG to family. So many Explosions. So many Drones. So many Wars. So many Cities I ♥/Hated kaputttttt. But ChicaGo Browsers act Bored! Taptaptaptaptap.

Here→is→what→happened: KEEPER after years2122232425 connects Me to ~~machine~~ & 20 min later {coincidence} ALL Browser gadgets F*l*i*c*k*e*r*F*l*i*c*k*e*r*F*l*i*c*k*e*r. No cute li'l eXplosion, this one! Browsers run & KEEPER runs & then it's night & then it's day & KEEPER does NOT (1) unlock (2) windoWshades (3) lights (4) reGister (5) dust curios (6) wind watch. {Gasp} what if KEEPER never ↲ returns & there is no one left to wind the Excelsior?[x10} SoImustspeaK/Write/thinK/sendintomachine&fastfastfast.

For years2627282930 I've wondered: Did my Reader boo↓hoo↓ when I selected 2World Trade Center for a tomb?[x2]![x2] Or are You of blacKer humor?→did you háááh háááh háááááh? Sayeth Th0mas H0bb3s & repeateth Z3bul0n F1nch beneath 2WTC: "The life of man [is] solitarY, poor, nastY, brutish & short." That last descriptor N0PE//but the former ✓✓✓✓. A better Mantra: Haml3t: "The rest is silence. O, O, O, O. [dies]". In my tomB I Became {right on schedule}: a lost matinee reel//suspended in air

749

thick & rancid//niBBlins for curious rodents Who, yuKKed Out, high-tailed it. I had: 0thought 0feeling 0motion except to Wind the Excelsior. For 6 yrs/300 wks/2000 days I windedwindedwinded & my plan achieVed tension/balance/equipoise~~~~~~~~~///

Hm-m-m-m I would call it a *WHUMP*. 2WTC bends left. Nononon-ono→I am 6 years deep & subsea & albino & eyeless//but the sirens are instant & build & build[x10] & though I am lost I feel the Portent of *WHUMP* & hold the Excelsior to my ear & it is *17 min/17 FÜcKīnġ MīN/17-17-1717171717 betw WHUMP & BOOM. WHUMP ≠ BOOM//*this is not Sound but Motion: dust slaMs down/iron squeals/ nails-bolts-screws-rods-pipes pinG & zinG/1000 windows ¡ShAtTeR! in sync. No 1 scream can penetrate basement+basement+basement, but 1000s? YES: even Words: jesuschristohgødohfuckmaydaymay-dayhelphelphelp fast//along w *WHOOSH*, which I hear & feel but cann0t understand but will 1 day learn is **Flaming Jet Fuel** cours-ing ↓ elevator shafts & pouring→my nicequietlittlemousehouse.

2WTC becomes lighter, lifts from my back→businesspeople leav-ing//then heaVier, back onto my shoulders←firemen entering. Z3bul0n F1nch knows a Bad Idea When he hears it. I press my Face to the ceiling & shout {voice, 7+ years of disuse = ŮĜĹŶ} GetOut-GetOut & no one hears bc the *THWACK/THWACK/THWACK* of what I know in my {Excelsior} heart to be landing Meteorites {shh don't tell Ry}: Barringer craters for Manhattanites future Worship. EXcept hááááááh no, it's Fall[ing][en] Men, olympic dives off Floors 85-110. Judges' score? 9/11/01, that 3rd judge is No Fun @ all.

My tomb fills w smoke/w heat/w dirt/ waist-high & chin-high &

I'm overcome & clawing & bashing, HÉctor you talentedsono-fabitch I'm traPPed. Survival instinct = Drowning Rat; I tucK my rat tail & sit & let the smoke thicken//coarsen//heat. APoca-lyPse was anticipated only not so soon// 1 hour laTer & ooooops

[center italic] *ROAR/CONVULSE/WEIGHT/HEAVY* [/center italic]

HÉctor's buttresses & columns = toothpick & straws//I am beneath//I am within. Even Harpocrates 7 had air. This: black Vacuum & hellhot. I am pinned//pinned is like flying. No light shines till Phantom Fireballs *FLOOM FLOOM FLOOM*, is it flaminG Gas or fireworks to honor the dead? Police {Schein-berg: Pigs} are crushed to hamburGer & hellhot heat makes their Guns Go *BLANGBLANBLANG* & ricochet ↑→↓ around the Tight Tangled Mess. Tectonic shifts/aLL settles/now. It ⌐ returns, the

(silence)
(of)
(a)
(freshly)
(fallen)
(snow)

29 min later, 1WTC copycats & also collapses & screws up my view: shifting: cracking: sliding: glimmer of sky: glimmer gone: sky: gone: sky: gone: gone: gone: but any-how sun is blanketed like Hiroshima. Soot↔Moot. The Dark Is Stable/reliable. Every Last American is Buried alive/put to Bed. Stone pillow. Slab sheet. Pixie dust. Shh.

{Psst, Reader. Are You Asleep? No? Look how I mastered machine! I can do this. Õř Î çąń dō ţĥîŝ. It isn't hard. SpeaK/Write/thinK/send. All those months I spent w pencils, how Perfectly Primitive.}

G.r.a.d.u.a.l.l.y silence {+bees?} gives Way to GENERATORS. It's still day, I think? Hellhot & cokeblack. People cry for air. It's night, I think? No crying for air anymore! Only GENERATORS {powering What?}. Oh & a dog. Bark, bark. Go away doggie. Bark, bark. Wait is this Heaven? Clown {sinless, the Only One} would be there For Sure/drippingblacknose & droolymuzzle. I'm sorry[x100] I kicked you. BUT do dogs have headliGhts? Miles aBove ///a slit, a crevasse\\\ swirls of dust are bothered by a BoBbInG white beam. Do dogs speak? Yell or Tap, a voice says. The voice cracks bloodmucus. Yell or Tap. Yell or Tap. A talking dog! I go háh

I can Make out a Man's face. It is faaaaaaaaaaaaaaaaaar. Buddy, he says. Hey, buddy. I knoW these words. Flashback: Setting: 1941, CA beach, Tan Blond Boy pulls Z3bul0n F1nch from sea, ☺ about Pearl Harbor: Buddy, Hey, Buddy. These are Words of Rescue. The Man coaXes & dog whines. You have to be INSANE to lower yrself into this spiderwebbed rubble//INSANE he is. He spins on a cable. His belt has a Hammer & he Hammers. Raindrops keep fallin' on my head but the rain is cement pellets & steel helixes. The Major obstacle is removed. The Man climbs back up. {He is INSANE.} He drops a rope//it lands on my neck//ah, the Noose, the Suicide Symbol of Z3bul0n X! I wriggle myself into it, comfy, an old sock & ↑↑↑↑↑↑↑↑↑

I ↵ return to Earth. GENERATORS are (((loud))) up here. I am caught on wire. The Man ☺ & says Don't worry, Buddy & he saws

@ wire w KBAR knife//he says KBAR is a Marine's tool, bestof thebest & I was a Marine years3132333435 but Z3bul0n F1nch has Opinions on Knives & the Best is Gordo's knife & I reach for it as Proof & can't feel it & ooooops the pocket is gone & half my clothes have burned off & Gordo's knife & Merle's photo & Barker's ad & Piano's map are 40 feet below & the Excelsior oh no the Excelsior? It is tangled in my sweatshirt threads & the Man cuts me free & the Excelsior falls & I catch it w my hand & the Man says You're Alive, You're Alive, You're Alive & it All in All it seems rude to contradict.

I take a Look at the Excelsior. It is CRAC//KED→my heart is broken! But: Still it tickticktickticks & I siGh & am fully ⌐ returned.

Oh no you lost yr arm he says & I say Long ago & so he says Oh whew & lies down. Look around Z3bul0n: You are bacK in Hamburg. Ain't that curious? Operation Gomorrah has flaTTened the city & Germans need to be scraped off w shoVels. I perK my burnt ear for bomber ratatatatatatat: only U.S.A would light destruction w Hollywood kliegs. I see a Mount St. Helens of twisted steel red & brown & orange & gray gone Alien Blue bc the Giant lights hung up like Moons.

Dog licks my face. I ♥ you Dead Man/I ♥ you Dead Man. The Man goes Hááá & says he had to trick Dog all day to find Pretend People or Dog got depressed but I'm not a Pretend Person am I? I think I might ♥ Dog. The Man gets energy back & Kneels over me & is Not Encouraged! {ECT scalp burns & Mr Avery's neckhole &c &c &c.} The Man is 100% WHITE. Ethereal angel or bloodless revenant? Neither: He wipes face & he is 100% BLACK {Ritchie Tucker: Afro-American, mon frère!} He is coated with ASH & those doves flaPPing around are scraps of paper. PAPER_. My nÔtebÔÔks! Thëŷ'll bë LëfŤ BëhĩŇĐ

Shh/Z3bul0n/shh. The Man ½-carries me, SLOW bc Flames Spew ↑↑ & loose rubble & hellhot I-beams & bubbling plaster = walking on bedsprings. My oldborn/newborn face is on His chest & it says *PORT AUTHORITY POLICE DEPT.* It is a looooooong hike. The Man is (1) exhausted (2) strange (3) on speed? He goes: I've Only Found Feet, I Keep Only Finding Feet, Why Do I Keep Only Finding Feet? {He is enamored w My Feet.} Dawn comes jabjabjabbing thru haze until it C/U/T/S thru & I see smoke continents, a New Pangaea for Humans to populate, split into New Gondwanaland & New Laurasia so we can FightFightFight

Ahoy: I see orange welder-fizz & white blowtorch-lasers. The Man shouts & waves. 1st-response folK lift WWI gas masks while Dinosaur cranes Bite into deBris w steel jaws. A Stars&Stripes hangs from crane's neck. This is, Reader knows, The Biggest Rescue & Recovery Mission in U.S.A. History™. The WTC complex is/was 16 Acres, 7 High-Rises, Home to 100s of International Businesses™. Initial Estimates are 10s of 1000s Dead™. What do You feel, Z3bul0n F1nch, when You hear these Handy Factoids & see OldGlory flappinG? Like Francis Scott Key or more like [search:anagrams] Sanctify Rockets or [search:anagrams] Nectars Icky Soft?

Dog licks my hand (♥ Dog, ♥ Dog) & I see G00D: [list: create] ■Human bucket chains ■Makeshift FDNY command posts ■Salvation Army food trucks ■Free restaurant meals ■Citizens giving the shoes off their feet {hellhot rubble melts soles↔souls} ■Tourists compiling med kits ■Disoriented firemen led by hand to dehydration stations ■Everyone working w/o ego [list:end]

This is the American Narrative & it is <u>TEMPTING</u>.

A Chief jogjogjogs to the Man. Dog bounds off & gets yummies & eyedrops. The Man blabs about me but INSANE {see (1)(2)&(3)} & Chief says, Joe, now, what did I say, You can't be climbing out here Alone, I know You want to help, We all want to help, but You're not thinking right & You'll end up Dead & if I have to throw Your ass into jail to Make Sure that doesn't happen, I'll do it, you understand? Joe understands but insists He pulled Me out & I'm a Survivor & We should All have Hope & Chief says Dammit Joe there are 10-ft offices crushed down to 6 inches No One's pulling out No One who's still walking

& right {tick} about {ticktick} then {tickticktick} other FDNY & PAPD have Come Close enough to see me for what I am & I see the American Narrative ↑flip↓ bc they get <u>ANGRY</u> & it is like Meixel-sperger sez: [quote]You crawl from rubble. What do you think this make them think? Husbands, sons. Maybe they crawl from rubble as well?[quote:end]. They say is this a Sick Joke You Sicko & Old Joe's not right in the head & how dare you Take Advantage of Old Joe & Yo, Chief, I recognize this schmuck, it's that fucking Magi-cian who got those People in the desert killed & I open my Mouth to defend Myself {Survival instinct = Drowning Rat} but my tongue FALLS OUT & We stare @ The Tongue & it *IS* a sick joke, isn't it?[x5] that I emerged from Ground 0↔Holy Ground instead of any of the (1) Brave Rescue Workers or (2) Courageous Civilians & so

Th̨ey AƬƒaCK M̨e {easy, Z3bul0n} & I run where They won't fol-
low→→→wilds of peeled steel & cable snakes & ice-floe concrete
& foothills of flattened fire trucks from where I see a Billboard, Clean
& Untouched, *SCHWARZENEGGER//COLLATERAL DAMAGE//
FROM THE DIRECTOR OF THE FUGITIVE//VETERAN FIRE-
FIGHTER'S WIFE & CHILD KILLED IN BOMB BLAST//WHAT
WOULD YOU DO IF YOU LOST EVERYTHING?* & I don't know
which part to Háááh about first

[[[hide]]]

Where I [[[hide]]] there is a stiletto of Mirror. I look @ myself. I wear
ribboned clothes of Old Decade & am burnt, sooted, gnawed. The
mirror is Silver from hellhot heat yet reflects →The→Future→where
I Watch Myself drag my charred body further across time, pace steady
enough to mocK each generation's{↔GENERATORS} sprints &
stumbles as they try to Do the Right Thing & why o why o why did
it take so long to recognize Myself?

I am the Millennialist. Allllllllllllllll along it has been Me chasing
Me/both Hero & Villain/Devil & Demigod/Beginning & THE END/
Inventor of Struggles so I'd have a force against which to Struggle.
I did this to Me. {We did this to Us?} I/We are the broke & burnt
beacon of the Future bc All will End Up like Me/Us.

Rescue workers talk. Rumor1: @ 6WTC a wildeyed customs official
guards confiscated Drugs & Guns. I dream of doing my Villain act
& robbing both, Drugs to buy passage, Guns to demand it. Rumor2:
@ 1WTC abscess, a subway tunnel leads to All Points North & I

dream of that too {becoming the Subway Rat}. Rumor3: shell-shocked NYers still being prompted from hidey-holes & herded to Pier 92 where tour boats whisk them off The Island No Questions Asked. This isn't a rumor! I pat myself with white ash & find a mass of limpers & I am given Fresh clothes & we file past walls already filled w Have You Seen Me? Posters to the harbor/boat/Hudson & from a deck slippery w soot & blood I see Twin Towers of Smoke & Manhattan EMPTY ↓ 14th Street. Then Jersey City & Newark & like The Beau-Ts said though there'll be DusK before the Dawn/Old Mr. F1nch keeps ramblin' 0010101011101010110 10100 101001010101 01010101 0101001010101001001111110100 010011 101010101 100101001000011101011101010010 10010100 100101010000001 11110 0100011111

{What is this Input/Static? GO AWAY}

It is a Bad Time to be Other. {Was there a Good Time? Ask the Fighting Muslims of Fisk U.} Ash rained off, I am brown-skinned: the hellhot heat cooked me & w/o tongue, I am an unintelligible immigrant w noises like jihadist jabber. I pass thru nation like a Terrorist. Woody Guthrie//revision: This Land Isn't My Land No More. Whole county is Plato Manor, a loooooong hallway majestic & idealist years3637383940 ago but now Ground0, Gr0und00, G0r0u0n0d0000.

I=Old Joe, Not Right in the Head//I Slip Up. I dig up a grave in Penn & pop open coffin & crawl inside {Capital Idea, Z3bby!} but get chased out & it's on sec-cam vid & 1 day Rigby's IBM/Microsoft/ Apple Thingamabobs aren't so Floppy & the vid transMutes into a virus that Everyone, plugged in like junkies, catches & I am shunned

& chased↔disgraced & a traitor & a hoax & an urban legend. Soon all Thingamabobs take pics & vids & glow in the night, a torch to touch off a 1million other torches, a {by definition} Torch-Wielding Mob. Every time I ↵ return is Shame [x1000]. I stop ↵ returning.

There âre Some Crumbs {nibblenibble} to mâke This Rât ☺. I leârn thât John Glenn, unsâtisfied w The Americân Câmpâign World Wâr II Victory Chinâ Service Nâtionâl Defense Service Koreân Service United Nâtions Service Congressionâl Gold Congressionâl Spâce NASA Distinguished Service Woodrow Wilson {outofbreâth!} MEDALS, rocketed his bowtied 77yeârold one-upmânship âss bâck to spâce in 1998. Go get em, John. But Crumbs Run Out & the Rât gets ☹. Prez Bush's WMD hunt in Irâq [timestâmp:2003]=Prez Johnson's Gulf of Tonkin [timestâmp:1964]: fâlse flâgs from which to dip kerosene & suckle bâbes//Goochie Goochie Goo//one dây You ṭoo, Littleone, will Ḳill. I could continue but ṭhink//bâckspâce//re-ṭhink// send is fâiling. Look: iṭ's fâlling âpârṭ. Ŵhy is ṭhis? Ŵhy cân'ṭ I Hold On? Is iṭ ṭhe Explosions?

404142434445yeâr?? Seṭṭing[query:seṭṭing]: ŴV?/OH?/ḲY?/IN?/ MI? ScurvySlovenlyShâbbyScummySmuṭṭyShâdyScânṭy I crâwl ṭhru Mud & Ŵoods//The Enemy/The Forgoṭṭen/The Dârkness//& sTuMbLe inṭo 3 flâg-weâring Pâṭrioṭs (Bâd) & Drunk (Ŵorse) & ṭhere is 1sec {tick} when They mighṭ help â poor weâk losṭ immigrânṭ//buṭ ṭhen 2sec {ticktick} & I âm The Axis of Evil who Hâṭes Freedom & ṭhey sṭând w hunṭingrifle+buckknife+woodâx+- filleṭblâde & lifṭ ṭhem more âpologeṭicâlly ṭhân Triângulinos bc ṭhis isn'ṭ Mere Revenge//Pâṭrioṭs âre âll Homelând Securiṭy now & ṭhis is ṭheir JOB↔JŌB.

Never Forgeţ{blâst}Orânge Alerţ{cuţ}Freedom Fries{chop}
Leţ's Roll{slice}Mission Accomplished 010110101110 10
1100001011 10 01010101001 1001000 11110101 10 1001
101001101010 101 01010 000000101000011 100101111011110
1000101 101010101000011101 10101111101010010011
001 10 1001010101 1000001101 1 0100101
101000101011111111011111001 10 100101010 010000010010
100 1010110 10100101 010101010 1001 101010101010100100000
00111100101010111001 001 00101010110

{STOP INTERRUPTING//DONT INTERRUPT//WHO ARE
YOU??? ??? ???}

Mulţiple Choice ✓✓✓: Ŵhere Is ţhe Soul? (1) sţernum (2) upper ribs
(3) ţibiâ (4) lefţ lung (5) spleen (6) blâdder (7) clâvicle (8) esophâgus
(9) lower ribs (10) gluţeus mâximus (11) spinâl cord (12) heârţ (13)
righţ lung (14) lârge inţesţine (15) pelvis (16) righţ ârm & hând (17)
recţum (18) boţh legs (19) lefţ kidneý (20) gâll blâdder (21) smâll
inţesţines (22) righţ kidneý (23) blâdder (24) pâncreâs (25) âppendix
(26) ţrâcheâ (27) liver (28) righţ fooţ (29) lefţ fooţ (30) sţomâch (31)
heâd.

I wonder[x3] if ţhe 3 Pâţrioţs{when sober} recâll↔celebrâţe/
âdmiţ↔forgeţ how ţheý diced me ţo simplesţ elemenţs.
[ţimesţâmp:ERROR] [ţimesţâmp:ERROR] [ţimesţâmp:ERROR]
Ŵhere Is ţhe Soul? Answer: (1)-(31)=null. Reâder, I'll be blunţ: I
Am â Heâd. Like Sţen Ehrensţröm's on ţhe bânk of Meuse RiVer,
like Đr Leâţher's Poor Đogs, excepţ My Heâd is in â Jâr. I Am â
Heâd in â Jâr on â Shelf in â Curio Shop. Đo You crý for Me? Đon'ţ/

759

pleâse don't. Jâr {homesweethome} is filled w electroneurâl gel but ĶEEPER is L̲Ā̲ź̲Y̲→jâr is dirtý//neVer cleâned//clouded w floâters of skin//I dissolVe before Mý Own Eýes. Nevertheless: Johnný, behold mý Act! Eýes blink! Lip curls! Foreheâd twitches! ĶEEPER {before Explosion/still missing/then âgâin he's L̲Ā̲ź̲Y̲) hâs 10s other Jârs in his Pâgeânt {StepRightUp} but these âre Brâins Only {whât â snooze} & tho theý pulsepulsepulse Brâins trânsmit 0 when ĶEEPER âttâches them to ~~machine~~. O if the ĶEEPER ⏎ returns {pleâse ⏎ return} whât â surprise the ~~machine~~ will hâVe for Him!

This is mý OLĐ AGE & OLĐ MEÑ hâve 0 interest in Ñewfângled Ŵizârdý. Ŵhât I Ķnow: the ~~machine~~ links ↑ to ∞ threâds. Ñot internet// *infinet*. In *infinet*, eVerý ♀♂○ hâs Followers, Friends, Armies/eVerý ♀♂○ is t/h/er/is/eir own Chuck Mânson//Mother-Fâther Sâvâge. It is closest ýet to Heâven/Hell, it is Mirâculous/Đeâdlý. Everý Word I think//bâckspâce//re-think//send thru *infinet* {this is mý Đeâd Letter Office} finds mâtching Ŵord & links//indexes which grâb//hold// kiss//fuck. If mý Ñotebooks survived 9.11.01 {*WHUMPBOOM-WHOOSHTHWACK*} these Ŵords will link to d.i.g.i.t.i.z.e.d Ñote-books & become THE ŴORĐ & thât excites mý finnický brâin & so I must think[x10] hârd[x10] & get the spelling Just Right

I âm Z3bul0n F1nch {bâd} I Am ≥3ßul*n F1ηⅽh {much worse} I âm Z3ßul0n F1NcH{trý} I Am Z3Bul0n F1NcH {hârder} I Am Z3Bul0n F1ncH {workkk} i âM Z3Bul0n F1ncH {hârderrr} i AM ZEbul0n F1ncH {better} i âM ZEbulon F1ncH {better} I âM ZEbulon F1ncH {closer} I âM ZEbulon F1nch {ýes} I âm ZEbulon FF1nch {I} I âm ZZebulon Fiinch {still} I âm Zebulllon Finch {exist}
I AM ZEBULON FINCH

[[[indicâţe ţhâţ ýou undersţând]]]

i çân feel iţ   send   uploâd   virusspreâd   iţ is like bloodleţţing

ţhânkýou   o ţhânk ýou   now   i   mâý resţ   {??}

1110 10 1110 0 0 0 11 01 1 01 1101 010110 00000
110101 010111 110 1110 10111111 1001111 1001 010000
00000101011010101111000 10 00111 0101 0101 1111111
0000 10 10 101 1011010101111000011101 1001010 11111
0001010101111111000 10100000001 01000101 1 011 11101011
1 1 10101111 1010111 00101111 0000 11111 100100 0001
01010101111000010011011011011010 010111 0101110000
0101111010011110 0110 100110 11101 0 0101110 1010 0110
010101 1110 101 1001110010001011000011011 0101 1010111
101111 100001 10011110 1110 0010101101 00001 1 101101
10 101001010111 0000 10101000 11 101 101 101101 111110
10100000101010101 110111 00110 1 0101110 01 1001110
01010000 01 111 101110 0101001010101 00000001011 011 10
0110 11101 10111100010101 010101010

(6) wind wâţçh. The Excelsior {CRAC//ĶEÐ}i çân see inside ţhe
{CRAC//Ķ} {ţhâţ's imPossible} buţ I CAN & I soMehow I know
âll ţhe delicâţe grâsshoPPer Pieçes//ţhe diâl fooţ roçking bâr Pivoţ
holes sâfeţý Pinion winding sţem whiPsPring bâlânçe çoçk esçâPe
wheel regulâţor//none of iţ working well in fâçţ slowing down &
Ameriçâ slowing down ţoo bç ýes âll ţhe ExPlosions = ţhe çounţrý
deçâý buţ ţhings do ↑↑↑ from deçâý ţheý do ↑↑& I âm slower ţoo
iţ is like being [seârçh:slowing] like being TIREÐ I forgoţ how

TIREÐ feels & it's çurious iṭ's noṭ horrible iṭ's noṭ so bâd iṭ's Preṭṭý niçe Gød is ṭhis â ṭriçk?[x17] I see You âṭ lâsṭ You look Funný You [[[hide]]] inside machine You âre 1s & 0s//1s & 0s// iṭ is jusṭ like You {Ðrowning Râṭ} ṭo Piçk Eleçṭriçiṭý â Primiṭive forçe {see wâṭer::âir::fire} & I çân heâr Yr Voiçe iṭ is Cleâr âṭ lâsṭ You sâý 1001011010110101011101000101 0 → ṭrânslâṭion: Sṭând UP {w no bodý?} & ṭhen 00101110011011010110100 → ṭrânslâṭion: Come Here {w no legs?} & ṭhen 11100101000010111101101111 0101 → ṭrânslâṭion: You âre inviṭed {w no heârṭ?}

Cân ýou see ṭhe mârkeŕ on mý foŕeheâd Gød does iṭ sṭill sâý *THE ENÐ* heŕe I çome heŕe I çome don'ṭ ṭŕý ṭo fool me/I will do whâṭ Eŕiç sâid I will ṭŕý ṭo be â PŕoPheṭ I will ṭŕý ṭo send bâçk â sign fŕom Gød is He Good is He Bâd//send bâçk 1 senṭençe?//1 woŕd?//1 leṭṭeŕ? I ⌐ ŕeṭurn ⌐ŕeṭuŕn ⌐ ŕeṭuŕn ṭo biŕṭh ouṭ of Ðeâṭh âs I biŕṭhed inṭo iṭ sçŕeâming/çoughing/sçŕeeçhing/fighṭing/ŕesisṭing ṭo ṭhe LAST ŴORÐ & will ṭuŕn Gød's embŕâçe 011110101010101110101 inṭo â bâçksṭâb if I çân if I çân iṭ is hâŕd bç the Excelsior {CRĀC//ĶEÐ} iṭ ṭiçks slow now slooooooooow eveŕý ṭiçk heâvý & hâŕd & ṭells me Ðeâṭh{Life?} noṭ meâsuŕed bý ṭiçkṭiçkṭiçk Time buṭ bý

tick flooŕboâŕds beside Ābigâils' bed *tick* Ŵilmâ Sue sṭiŕs heŕ ṭeâ *tick* â mâýflý âsçends mý ṭhŕoâṭ *tick* Ŋeedles iŊṭo Mŕ Sṭiçk's ṭhoŕâx *tick* ṭhe GeŊeŕâl çlâws âçŕoss cell *tick* Testâ âŕms his Pisṭol *tick* JohŊŊý's âggie ŕâṭṭles Pâsṭ mý ṭeeṭh *tick* Viçṭŕolâ Ŋeedle digs iŊṭo Gesuâldo *tick* IŊviŊçible Pedâls oveŕ BosṭoŊ sṭŕeeṭs *tick* Meŕle's uŊdeŕbiṭe biṭiŊg *tick* Isolâṭoŕ Ŋeedle PeâkiŊg *tick* Hâzâŕd Sisṭeŕs çhess pieçes *tick* Chuŕçh's lemoŊ dŕoPs beṭw dýiŊg jâws *tick* mâxims ŕiPPiŊg uP mý mâŕiŊes *tick* TiŊ Lizzie's eŊġiŊe *tick* JohŊ QuiŊçý & Moṭheŕ

Mâsh's lýŊçhiŊġ ŕoPes *tick* flâPPeŕ flâṭs dâŊçe fâsṭ *tick* çoPPeŕ çheek

bâshed bý umbŕellâ *tick* Leâṭheŕ's skull sPâṭṭeŕed *tick* Ed MâŊŊ's

slâṭeboâŕd *tick* Bŕideý's çhâsṭiṭý belṭs *tick* dŕoPPed çâlls fŕom GoPheŕ

tick CheŕŊoff's meŊâġeŕie violâṭed *tick* SâŊdý's PuŊçhed ṭeeṭh *tick*

YâŊkee Đoodle wiŊdow ġlâss *tick* Riġbý squâŕiŊġ file J-1121 *tick*

floweŕbed dirṭ dowŊ MeixelsPeŕġeŕ's shelṭeŕ *tick* Ñâzi booṭs âloŊġ

MâuṭhâuseŊ's Pâṭh ṭo HeâveŊ *tick* Mâŕlboŕo MâŊ sliçiŊġ âPPles

tick ṭhe Whiṭes' ZeŊiṭh wâŕms iṭs ṭidý woŕlds *tick* ŕâdio siġŊâls

fŕom SPuṭNik *tick* Wŕiġhṭ-PâṭṭeŕsoŊ's Idioṭ Box *tick* flâshbulbs foŕ

âll exçePṭ ṭhe Meŕçuŕý Eiġhṭh *tick* CâPCöm ŕâdiö çöŊṭâçṭ *tick* beeŕ

böṭṭles âġâiŊsṭ ÑSTF Ħelmeṭs *tick* Wöödsṭöçk PĀ Sýsṭem döŊ'ṭ dŕöP

ṭĦe bröwŊ âçid, mâŊ *tick* Ħöŕse Ħööves ṭĦŕu Gŕeâṭ BâsiŊ Đeseŕṭ *tick*

ṭĦe HuŊġŕý çuṭleŕý öf SSâvâġeees *tick* âŊ âQQuâŕiuMM beföŕeee

IIIṭ sĦâṭṭEEŕs *tick* â deMMöŊ's ṭeeeeṭĦ TKbeĦiŊd âslýumòŹŐ

wWWâllŠ *tick* âiżtt THuŊdeŕ RöömWî̄ē̄ē̄ *tick* â vvvâuŊŊlṭ beiŊġ

bBBBuilṭ *tick* â dDöġ'szzŠṣżż çlâwŷŷŸŽŹs övVVŴpkbkVeŕ

ŕuBöĶmBllLlē *tick* AÅlE SŚVtŊ svŦN *tick* ŕŴâÛeġjġuuUB

źôe,H IEöŚULeŲ ṭïûṣB YKíèŰxr *tick* ġïñBRÏ ZorĥŖWQL IxyëlâŔ

tick ŠâûHâRùŕ żĐýlpÑ dtŔŖ͏̈ŏŕccO *tick* PvâÕgŮjĴ cqyŕçŤ ïżL

ŕŸúKçĐ *tick* ġęͅIPṣ̂ŵW OoõĿ̇ÊŭR ṣgTụ̣ŞÖžGéLuU ŕŸÀĊvlyĮ̣Ġ̈ï

ńŠxOøSsá ŔŐïġuu żÒŇcCdāđ̣ŋAṭ ĕLYõÿK TrÕŠčŭ OôĿ̇ÊŭR

ṣgTụ̣ŞÖžGéLuU ŕŸÀĊvlyĮ̣Ġ̈ï ńŠxOøSsá ŔŐïġuu żÒŇcCdāđ̣ŋAṭ

ĕLYõÿK TrÕŠčŭ OôĿ̇ÊŭR ṣgTụ̣ŞÖžGéLuU ŕŸÀĊvlyĮ̣Ġ̈ï

ńŠxOøSá ŔŐïġuu żÒŇcCdāđ̣ŋAṭ ĕLYõÿK TrÕŠčŭ OôĿ̇ÊŭR

ṣgTụ̣ŞÖžGéLuU ŕŸÀĊvlyĮ̣Ġ̈ï ńŠxOøSá ŔŐïġuu żÒŇcCdāŋAṭ

ĕLYõÿK TrÕŠčŭ OôĿ̇ÊŭR ṣgTụ̣ŞÖžGéLuU ŕŸÀĊvlyĮ̣Ġ̈ï ńŠxOøSá

ŔŐïġu żÒŇcCdāŋAṭ ĕLYõÿK TrÕŠčŭ OôĿ̇ÊŭR ṣgTụ̣ŞÖžGéLuU

ŕŸĊvlyĮ̣Ġ̈ï ńŠxOøSá ŔŐïġu żÒŇcCdāŋAṭ ĕLYõÿK TrÕŠčŭ OôĿ̇ÊŭR

ṣgTụ̣ŞžGéLuU ŕŸĊvlyĮ̣Ġ̈ï ńŠxOøSá ŔŐïġu żÒŇcCdāŋAṭ ĕLYõÿK

TrÕŠčŭ OõŁŭR şgTųŞžGéLuU ŕÝĊvlyĮĜ̈ï ńŠxOøSá ŔŐĭğu
žÒŇcCdāŋAţ ĕLYṏÿK TrÕŠčŭ OõŁŭR şgTųŞžGéLuU ŕÝĊvlyĮĜ̈ï
ńŠxOøSá ŔŐĭğu žÒŇcCdāŋAţ ĕLYṏÿK TrŠčŭ OõŁŭR şgTųŞžGéLuU
ŕÝĊvlyĮ̈ï ńŠxOøSá ŔŐĭğu žÒŇcCdāŋAţ ĕLYṏÿK TrŠčŭ OõŁŭR
şgTųŞžGéLuU ŕÝĊvlyĮ̈ï ńŠxOøSá ŔŐĭğu žÒŇcCdŋAţ ĕLYṏÿK
TrŠčŭ OõŁŭR şgTųŞžGéLuU ŕÝĊvlĮ̈ï ńŠxOøSá ŔŐĭğu žÒŇcCdŋAţ
ĕLYṏÿK TrŠčŭ OõŁŭR şgTųŞžGéLu ŕÝĊvlĮ̈ï ńŠxOøSá ŔŐĭğu
žÒŇcCdŋAţ ĕLYṏÿK TrŠčŭ OõŁŭR şgTųŞžGéLu ŕÝĊvlĮ̈ï ńŠxOøSá
ŔŐĭğu žÒŇcCdŋAţ ĕLṏÿK TrŠčŭ OõŁŭR şgTųŞžGéLu ŕÝvlĮ̈ï
ńŠxOøSá ŔŐĭğu žÒŇcCdŋAţ ĕLṏÿK TrŠčŭ OõŁŭR şgTųŞžGéu
ŕÝvlĮ̈ï ńŠxOøSá ŔŐĭğu žÒŇcCdŋAţ ĕLṏÿK TrŠčŭ OõŁŭR şgTųŞžGéu
ŕÝvlĮ̈ï ńŠxOøá ŔŐĭğu žÒŇcCdŋAţ ĕLṏÿK TrŠčŭ õŁŭR şgTųŞžGéu
ŕÝvlĮ̈ï ńŠxOøá ŔŐĭğu žÒŇcCdŋAţ ĕLṏÿK TrŠčŭ õŁŭR şgTųŞžGéu
ŕÝvlĮ̈ï ńŠxOøá ŔŐĭğu žÒŇcCdŋAţ ĕLṏÿK TrŠŭ õŁR şgTųŞžGéu
ŕÝvlĮ̈ï ńŠxOøá ŔŐĭğu žÒŇcCdŋAţ ĕLṏÿK TrŠŭ õŁR şgTųŞžGéu
ŕÝvlĮ̈ï ńŠxOøá ŔŐĭğu žÒŇcCdŋAţ ĕLṏÿK rŠŭ õŁR şgTųžGéu
ŕÝvlĮ̈ï ńŠxOøá ŔŐĭğu žÒŇcCdŋAţ ĕLṏÿK rŠŭ õŁR şgTųžGéu ŕÝvlĮ̈ï
ńŠxOøá ŔŐĭğu žÒŇcCdŋAţ ĕLÿK rŠŭ õŁR şgTųžGéu ŕÝvĮ̈ï ńŠxOøá
ŔŐĭğu žÒŇcCdŋAţ ĕLÿK rŠŭ õŁR şgTųžGéu ŕÝvĮ̈ï ńŠxOøá ŔŐĭğu
žÒŇcCdAţ ĕLÿK rŠŭ õŁR şgTųžGéu ŕÝvĮ ńŠxOøá ŔŐĭğu žÒŇcdAţ
ĕLÿK rŠŭ õŁR şgTųžGéu ŕÝvĮ ńŠxøá ŔŐĭğu žÒŇcdAţ ĕLÿK rŠŭ
õŁ R şgTų žGéu ŕÝvĮ ńŠxøá ŔŐĭğ žÒŇcdAţ ĕLÿK rŠŭ
õŁ R şgTų žGéu ŕÝvĮ ńŠx øá ŔŐĭğž ÒŇcdAţ ĕLÿK rŠŭ
õŁ R şgTų žGéu ŕÝvĮ ńŠx øá ŔŐĭğž ŇcdAţ ĕLÿK rŠŭ
õŁ R şT ų žGéu ŕÝvĮ ńŠx øá ŔŐĭğž ŇcdAţ ĕLÿK rŠŭ
õŁ R şT ų žGéu ŕÝvĮ ńŠx øá Ŕ ĭğ ž ŇcdAţ ĕLÿK rŠŭ
õŁ R şT ų žGéu ŕÝvĮ ńŠ øá Ŕ ĭğ ž ŇcdAţ ĕLÿK rŠŭ
õŁ R şT ų žG u ŕÝvĮ ńŠ øá Ŕ ĭğ ž ŇcdAţ ĕLÿK rŠŭ
õŁ R ş Tų žG u ŕÝvĮ ńŠ øá Ŕ ĭğ ž ŇcdAţ ĕL K rŠŭ

```
õL̇  R  ş Tų  žG u  ŕÝvḷ  ńŠ  øá  Ŕ ĭğ  ž  Ň dAṭ  ĕL K  rŠŭ
õL̇  R  ş Tų  žG u  ŕÝḷ   ńŠ  øá  Ŕ ĭğ  ž  Ň dAṭ  ĕL K  rŠŭ
õL̇  R  ş Tų  žG    ŕÝḷ   ńŠ  øá  Ŕ ĭğ  ž  Ň dAṭ  ĕL K  rŠŭ
õL̇  R  ş Tų  žG    ŕÝḷ   ńŠ  øá  Ŕ ĭğ  ž  Ň dAṭ  ĕL K  Šŭ
õL̇  R  ş Tų  žG    ŕÝḷ   Š   øá  Ŕ ĭğ  ž  Ň dAṭ  ĕL K  Šŭ
õ    R  ş Tų  žG    ŕÝḷ   Š   øá  Ŕ ĭğ  ž  Ň dAṭ  ĕL K  Šŭ
õ    R  ş Tų  žG    ŕÝḷ   Š   øá  Ŕ ĭğ  ž  Ň dAṭ  L K   Šŭ
õ    R  ş Tų  žG    ŕÝḷ   Š   øá  Ŕ ĭğ     Ň dAṭ  L K   Šŭ
õ    R  ş Tų  žG    ŕÝḷ   Š   øá  Ŕ ĭğ     Ň dAṭ  L     Šŭ
õ    R  Tų   žG    ŕÝḷ   Š   øá  Ŕ ĭğ     Ň dAṭ  L     Šŭ
õ    R  Tų   žG    ŕÝḷ   Š   øá  Ŕ ĭğ     Ň dAṭ  L     ŭ
õ    R  ų    žG    ŕÝḷ   Š   øá  Ŕ ĭğ     Ň dAṭ  L     ŭ
õ    R  ų    žG    ŕ Ḷ   Š   øá  Ŕ ĭğ     Ň dAṭ  L     ŭ
õ    R  ų    žG    ŕ Ḷ   Š   øá  Ŕ ĭğ     Ň dA   L     ŭ
õ    R  ų    žG    ŕ     Š   øá  Ŕ ĭğ     Ň dA   L     ŭ
õ    R  ų    žG    ŕ     Š   øá  Ŕ ĭ      Ň dA   L     ŭ
õ    R  ų    žG    ŕ     Š   øá  Ŕ ĭ      Ň d    L     ŭ
õ    R  ų    G     ŕ     Š   øá  Ŕ ĭ      Ň d    L     ŭ
õ    R  ų    G     ŕ     Š   øá  Ŕ ĭ      Ň d          ŭ
õ       ų    G     ŕ     Š   øá  Ŕ ĭ      Ň d          ŭ
õ       ų    G     ŕ     Š   øá  Ŕ        Ň d          ŭ
õ            G     ŕ     Š   øá  Ŕ        Ň d          ŭ
õ            G     ŕ     Š   øá           Ň d          ŭ
õ            G     ŕ     Š   øá           Ň d
õ            G     ŕ     Š   øá           Ň d
             G          Š   øá           Ň d
             G          Š   øá           Ň d
             G              øá           Ň d
             G              øá           Ň d
             G              øá              d
```

765

G	øá	d
G	øá	d
G	øá	d
G	øá	d
G	øá	d
G	øá	d
G	øá	d
G	ø	d
G	ø	d
G	ø	d
G	ø	d
G	ø	d
G	ø	d
G	ø	d
G	ø	d
G	ø	d
G	ø	d
G	ø	d
G	ø	d
G	ø	d
G	ø	d
G	ø	d
G	ø	d
G	ø	d
G	ø	d
G	ø	
G	ø	
G	ø	

G	ø
G	ø
G	ø
G	ø
G	ø
G	ø
G	ø
G	ø
G	ø
G	ø
G	ø
G	ø
G	ø
G	ø
G	ø
G	ø
G	ø
G	ø
G	ø
G	ø
G	ø
G	ø
G	ø
G	ø
G	ø
G	ø
G	ø
G	ø
	ø

Ø

Ø

Ø

Ø

Ø

Ø

Ø

Ø

Ø

Ø

Ø

Ø

Ø

Ø

Ø

Ø

Ø

Ø

Ø

Ø

Ø

Ø

Ø

Ø

Ø

Ø

ø

ø

ø

ø

ø

ø

ø

ø

ø

ø

ø

ø

ø

Ø

Ø

Ø

o

A NOTE OF GRATITUDE

In addition to those acknowledged in Volume One, Mr. Kraus wishes to convey a particular indebtedness to Rabbi Jay A. Holstein.